ıι .

Kronos

By the same author

NILE
SAUDI
CRESCENT

Kronos

Laurie Devine

ANDRE DEUTSCH

First published in Great Britain in 1991
by André Deutsch Limited
105–106 Great Russell Street, London WC1B 3LJ

British Library Cataloguing in Publication Data
Devine, Laurie
  Kronos.
  I. Title
  813.54

ISBN 0 233 98673 1

Printed by WSOY Finland

For Mitsos

Time, as he grows older,
teaches everything.

— Aeschylus

Prologue

'Tell me a story, mama!'

Old Anna tucked the little girl into her bed drawn up near the blazing hearth to ward off the chill on this stormy winter's night. 'What shall it be tonight, Marika? Eleni and Paris and Troy again, or your favourite about the brave Amazon women charging on their horses, or a new one about how the king of the gods killed the meanest man in the world with a thunderbolt?'

'A thunderbolt?' Wide-eyed, Marika listened to the storm which shook their whitewashed cottage. 'Why did he do that?'

'For vengeance. You see, *paidi mou*, my child, Kronos – Father Time – had a fight with Mother Earth. And Kronos was so afraid that their children would grow up and punish him for hurting their mother that he swallowed Hestia, Demeter, Hera, Hades, and Poseidon whole when they were little babies.'

Marika looked at her little brother Vangelis, asleep in his crib. 'Oh, no! He ate his babies?'

'All but one, Zeus. Mother Earth tricked Kronos, and he swallowed a stone instead of his son. And when Zeus grew up, his mother brewed him a special drink that made Kronos spit up all her children. They jumped out of his mouth, and Zeus led them in a war against Kronos. Finally he threw his great thunderbolt, and that was the end of the greatest tyrant in the world. Zeus became the king of the gods, and he and his brothers and sisters ruled forever from atop Mount Olympus.'

Listening to the rolling thunder outside, Marika was suddenly not so afraid of the storm. She was glad Zeus had done that to bad old Kronos who

1

had swallowed his sons and daughters. 'But what's it mean, mama?' All her mother's stories had a message. 'What's it really about?'

Old Anna blinked like a wise owl. 'Kronos is about Greece, Marika. About how Greece eats its children.'

Carnival
February, 1949

One

Marika's black eyes smouldered like embers in the flickering Carnival bonfire light as she gave Christos a sidelong glance. *Him*! Tonight, body and soul, she was going to have him!

She was resolved to do what she had to do to win him forever. He was her man – *hers* – not the revolution's, not the party's, not the comrades'. She must come first with him, even before Mother Greece. After tonight, the closest he would ever come to politics again would be heated arguments with the other men in the village *kafeneion*. Let him play at *tavli* rather than revolution.

Her eyes narrowed as they locked onto her rival, the rifle, cradled in his arms like a baby. Once she had her way with him in the cave tonight, he would not pick up that gun and head for the hills in the morning with his band of leftist *andartes* partisans. She couldn't singlehandedly end this Civil War, but she was determined to impose her own woman's solution to finish her man's part in it. If this fighting didn't soon stop, the light of Greek civilization would once again darken and die. A people – and a country – could be as fragile as a love. Not – hastily she reassured herself – that she doubted the depth of their mutual passion. She was as certain of their love as she was of the rising of the sun, the pull of the tides, the waxing of the moon.

Marika's gaze softened as she feasted her eyes on the dearest face in the world. Now that the leftists were on the run and his *andartes* band had retreated to the mountains, every moment near him was precious. Christos was thinner than a fortnight ago. His cheeks were hollow, and his light eyes were ringed with dark circles of fatigue. Once she had him to herself, she would erase the careworn marks from his ravaged face. Except for those extraordinary green eyes of his, she supposed his rugged features – arched nose, slashing cheekbones, wide lips – were etched too deeply and moulded too boldly for him to be called merely handsome. But the intensity of his emotions transcended mere skin and bone so that he – like the brooding mountains, the volatile sea, and the white-hot summer sun – seemed an elemental work of nature. Just now, on this black winter's night, his face was astorm.

Marika followed his gaze and studied the haggard faces of her dispirited villagers who sat slumped around the bonfire on this cold February night. Before these last wars had shattered – perhaps forever – the traditional rhythm of village life, her neighbours had always thrown off their dark winter cares in the pre-Lenten revels of Carnival. For a few heady nights, even though this celebration was hallowed with the trappings of Christianity, the rollicking pagan spirit of Bacchus had once again caught and held the Greek soul. Here in Panagia as a child, Marika remembered dressing up – once as a gypsy, another wondrous time as a fairy princess – and staying up later than late to watch the fish being roasted over a charcoal fire. With her elders she danced and sang until finally she fell asleep on her mother's lap and dawn ushered in the austere season of penitential Lent. But these last terrible years of war and famine had shattered not only innocence but also belief. Now no one had the heart to masquerade as anything but what they were, a frightened people reduced to the primitive rite of huddling around a winter fire for not only warmth but the illusion of protection from the encircling hostile world.

She pulled her shawl closer to her, as though the homespun wool were a mantle of security. Through the starvation and bloodshed of the German Occupation during the Second World War and now the even more horrific brother-against-brother betrayals of this Civil War, she had bided her time and waited and prayed with the other women for a resurrecting spring of peace to transcend these blighted winters of war. But now she was tired of squandering her youth on her knees praying chastely before a melancholy icon of the Mother and the Child. Collective suffering was the woman-to-woman message of those mournful Virgin eyes. Endure, they pleaded. Hope a little or a lot, as you like, for hope – like other illusions – comes cheap for the poor. So light your candles. Kneel until your knees are calloused. And most of all, above all, you must wait for salvation, if not in this world then in the next. Marika had kept the faith for as long as she could. Finally, in the dark of this chill winter's night, other older and far more human gods had more passionate answers for an impatient woman. Here and now, the cave beckoned.

She looked down at the ringless fingers of her rough and reddened peasant hands. She was nineteen years old. At her age, her mother had already given birth to one son, a daughter, and two other babies who had died soon out of the womb. Just this morning in the church on the village square, four couples

– including one man from Christos' own partisan band – had sworn their marriage vows before Lent put all such joyous occasions in abeyance. Witnessing the service, Marika had rejoiced for those girls who had won the marriage crowns – even if it were only temporarily, for in wartime the jaws of death snapped shut even on the young and the brave. At that thought, she had wished she could clasp Christos to her and never let go. She was so afraid he wouldn't survive the last grim battles. Yet when she had pleaded with him to marry her on this final Carnival Sunday, Christos had answered that duty must come before love. In these perilous times, he had said, personal happiness must be sacrificed for the greater good of society. When tears had welled up in her eyes, tenderly he had taken her into his arms. Of course I love you, he had assured her. Still keeping up a brave political front, again he had promised that 'as soon as our campaigns are over and the comrades are in power in Athens, we will marry and be happy forever.' But he had said their love was different – stronger, brighter, truer – than those desperate village couples who thought the chanted words of a priest could cast a cloak of security on a world too fraught with danger. Surely, he had said, she understood that it would cheapen their love to marry out of fear. What he and she had would transcend war and revolution. And, as he had held her tight in his snug embrace, again she had been reassured by the inevitability of their love. But later, curled up alone by her mother's hearth, the vicissitudes of fate and the vulnerability of flesh against bullets had made her doubt again. Why, she had raged to herself, for once couldn't Christos be just like everyone else in their village? She didn't want to be brave, she wanted to be married.

Again Marika studied the anxious eyes around the campfire. Even in the best of times these villagers, like most peasants, dreamed no greater dreams than giving birth to a tribe of healthy sons and somehow, through not only hard work but *poniria* – 'slyness', a provincial Greek trait – accumulating more orange trees or a finer donkey than their brothers and cousins. But the wars had wrecked even those *mikro* dreams. All the old securities were gone now, and survival was a game of chance like *xeri*, the cards the men played all winter long. What Marika read in the frightened dark eyes of the women was fear that there wouldn't be enough to feed their hungry families tomorrow and after tomorrow. What she saw in the dreadful dark eyes of the men was worry that what had happened in other doomed villages could happen in Panagia. For, as the men whispered into their tiny cups of *metrios* late in the night in the *kafeneions*, it was possible that sometime soon, maybe even this month or the month after, one of the warring factions in this brutal Civil War would march in and massacre every man, woman, and child in the village. As Marika's mother had said to her only the day before yesterday as

7

the two of them were scrubbing the kitchen floor, truly, in these black times, only a fool – or a hero – could doubt that Greece was cursed by God and man. In her shapeless black housedress and flapping black scarf, the old woman had looked like an ancient crone delivering a Delphic oracle. 'Doomed, Marika, Greece is doomed. And we are, too.'

Marika shivered and crept a little closer to the firelight. She hated her mother's dark talk of curses. No matter what her mother said, all *that* was most definitely neither in her blood nor her future. She was born under the bright modern star of enlightened reason, not the howling full moon of superstition. She herself would always choose light over darkness, joy over despair, and Christos over everyone else in the world. To her, his eyes were beacons of a more radiant world where men ate ideas and got drunk on truths. When Christos talked, the inspiring words that most often tripped off his tongue were all about honour, and justice, and freedom. Yet sometimes she wondered if she never tired of listening to him because she believed the complicated concepts he espoused or simply because she was mesmerized by his shining eyes. Marika liked to think that she was a cut above the silly village girls of her generation. When she was just a child, before war closed the schools, she had always been the quickest wit in her class, quicker even than any of the boys. And yet now, exactly like every other lovesick village maiden, she was content to while away many a homely morning, as she chopped vegetables or washed clothes, simply dreaming of Christos. When he looked at her with those mesmerizing eyes – boom! – she forgot everything except the essential fact that she was mad for him. She wondered about that sometimes, how it was that this obsessive passion had grown and consumed her, far beyond reason and what her mother warned was her own good. But did she, or anyone else, ultimately have any choice in this matter of devouring love?

Her own eyes were radiant as she watched Christos charming the comrades around the bonfire. Of course she was proud of what used to be said about him when the leftists had been winning the war. She was his woman, after all, and she was capable of taking delight in all things concerning Christos. She always had heard the rumours about him secondhand from her brother or one of her cousins, for a good woman would never dream of sitting with the men in the coffeehouse. But every time the *andartes* had come in from the hills and settled down in the *kafeneion* for *tsipouro* and gossip, they had hinted to anyone who would listen that their very own young commandant – twenty-seven, he was, only twenty-seven! – had been marked out by the party leadership for big things in the socialist government that would surely someday be Greece's. As they drank, and their voices had risen to roars, fancifully their boasts about this village boy who was destined for greatness had swelled beyond all reasonable proportions. He would be the mayor of Nauplion, no, the national minister of trade and industry! He would be the general of the people's armies, maybe even the right hand to the prime minister! Before it was time to call it a night and head for their rocky lairs in the mountains, they had even drunkenly implied that someday, when Christos' hair was as white as the snow atop the Peloponnesian peaks, he would be prime minister himself.

And will I, Marika wondered, as again she tried and failed to catch Christos' eye, someday be the prime minister's wife? Fear smote her. She could never doubt him or their love, but who knew what cards life would deal in the next hand? Maybe even Christos couldn't control destiny. *Moira* could be cruel.

But maybe Christos was right. For so many years, she had believed that Christos was always right. As long as Marika could remember, his farsighted green eyes had been focused beyond what the insular villagers could see. To almost everyone else in their remote fishing village along the Peloponnesian coast, the hazy blue-grey mountains that hugged the Panagia horizon marked the boundaries of the only world that mattered. Here, history consisted of who had married whom last year, a decade ago, perhaps as far back as the memory of a greybeard coffeehouse sage. Here, philosophy was based on old wives' tales and a grandfather's platitudes. Here, mathematics soared no higher than the price of this year's oranges and a man's life savings buried in a pottery crock in the garden. But Christos would always dream and scheme of a wider world. Those bewitching dreams were what she admired about him the most and yet what she feared might sunder her from him. Christos might not admit it yet, but the leftists were losing the war and retreating over the borders to Yugoslavia and Albania. If he had to flee with the rest, Marika had to make sure he would take her with him. Duty before love? Oh, no! His world was about to shrink to what lay between her legs.

Yet she worried, as jealously she watched him playing his comrades as skilfully as the flute he kept in his back pocket, she wouldn't win this gamble after all. It might be easier to seduce him away from another woman than his politics. Even tonight, when everyone else was lazing around the fire, still he worked the crowd like the consummate politician he had evidently been born to be. He would flatter this one, respectfully listen to that one, and draw out that shy one to confide his hesitant opinions. Even back in the whitewashed shed that had served as their village school, Marika remembered Christos doing all he could to make the other children adore him. She had been one of the first to fall under his spell. Before she could even read or write, she had learned to love that green-eyed boy who knew everything, who charmed everyone, and who, wonder of wonders, had taken her under

9

his wing and protected her. She had loved him since the morning he had surprised a pack of village lads taunting her for her fatherless family's being the poorest of Panagia's poor. She still remembered how his eyes had studied her patched dress and bare feet before he had shooed away her tormentors and guided her under the shade of a fig tree. 'If only my *baba* were here!' she had sobbed, telling this kind big boy what he had already known, that her father had gone away to Australia years ago and never once sent a word or drachma to his destitute wife and children. Christos had smoothed back her hair and confided that he understood how she felt. His own father had been away in America for many years, and even though he sent dollars to his waiting family, no one and nothing could fill the void. 'You, too?' Marika had asked in wonder. 'Me, too!' Christos had answered. And then when he had taken her small hand in his, her world had felt almost as safe as if miraculously her father had been restored to her. The next week, when Christos' stepmother had begun paying Marika's mother to help with the heavy work in the Kronos household, the little girl had seen her protector's hand in this turning point in her family's fortune. And as the years had passed, the bond forged between them that morning had grown and flowered. Christos had been her hero then, and he was still her hero.

But the problem, Marika reminded herself, was that he wanted to be Greece's hero, too.

Yet here and now, once again, Marika swallowed her misgivings. He loved her and he would marry her. For even as he had turned down Marika's heart's desire, he had done so with such intoxicating words and gestures, covering her face with kisses and stirring her heart with noble sentiments, that he had succeeded in making her love him all the more. His *nom de guerre* in the partisans was 'Captain Prometheus', and his words and actions flamed with the gift of fire. She burned for her Prometheus . . .

Marika's eyes danced like her friend, the fire. In desperation one lonely midnight hour last week, she had hatched her reckless plan. Tonight she would meet fire with fire. She had always been the bravest of the shy village girls who hardly dared look a young man in the eye. Yet now that she had to muster her courage and go through with what she had resolved, even she was afraid to violate the taboos. What if it didn't work, and his politics took him away from her? Or what if – would this be a worse humiliation or a saving grace – he refused to take what she was determined to give?

She recalled her alternatives and bit her lip with resolve. Maybe it didn't matter that she was afraid. Everyone was afraid. But what made a mythic hero – or heroine – was that the fear was transcended and the deed done. She was fed up sitting patiently by the hearth, keeping the home fires eternally burning. She would rather risk doing the wrong thing than do nothing at all. She believed that what made a man, and a woman, different from the animals was this capacity to reason and act. Tonight she would take fate in her own hands and try to bend it to her will. If this was not courage but something more dangerous – *hubris*, the 'overweening pride' that always came before a fall in the Greek tragedies of old – then so be it. If she had a choice – and she did! Even though she was only a woman, she was a human being, and she had a choice! – she would choose the whooshing consuming fire of a pagan bonfire rather than the sputtering uncertainties of a Christian candle. Better on her back than her knees.

So it was that she tossed her blueblack hair toward the dark shadows of the pregnant night and crooked her finger at Christos.

The object of her calculating affections didn't appear to notice.

When he had come in early this afternoon to pick up supplies, Christos had expected to be back at his camp before the moon rose. But when he read the longing on the drawn faces of his spent comrades, he had curbed his impatience and tarried in the village for the final night of Carnival. His men were exhausted and depressed, and could use a bit of fun before they took to the hills to try to stem the tide that had been turning against them in these last anguished seasons.

In the shadows Christos spotted a young woman swathed in black from head to toe, so that all that could be seen of Evangelitsa's girlish face was a pinched triangle of sallow flesh and her dark grieving eyes. If he had followed his heart and married Marika this morning, in a few weeks she might have become another pathetic teenage widow like this poor girl. He rose, went to Evangelitsa's side, and solicitously enquired after her and the young son his fallen comrade had left behind. Renos, like so many of the *andartes*, had died fighting not the Germans or the Italians but his fellow countrymen. A Greek will always fight bravely. But since ancient times fratricide has tainted their blood, and only when he is battling his brother – and finally facing what he considered an equal and worthy opponent – will a Greek fight like a demon. The Civil War had been a dirty business, with bloodguilt on both sides. It was a modern Greek tragedy, Christos thought, that far more of his countrymen had died in this Civil War than in the local engagements of the World War. He dug in his pocket, came up with the handful of coins he had saved to buy bread and beans in the morning, and insisted that the young widow take it for herself and the child. When shyly she refused, he told her that her Renos had been a brave man and that he had loved him like a brother. So you are my sister now, he said with his green eyes all aflash, and must do as I say. He did not pull his hand away when quickly she bent and kissed it. And she did not protest when he filled her lap with his coins.

All eyes were upon him as he walked a little taller, back to his place amidst the comrades. Yes, out of the corner of his eyes, he saw that Marika had not missed his gesture. Her gaze, as always, was a benediction. But he tore his thoughts away from his love. They would have a lifetime together, but just now there were other claims upon him. By noontime tomorrow this story of how the *andartes* took care of their own would be repeated to every villager who had missed this gathering around the bonfire. In the unfinished struggle for the hearts and minds of the Greek people, parables like the one he had just taken care to enact could weigh as heavy as a military victory. Even though Panagia was under partisan control, most of the villagers – here, in his very home! – cared only about their own personal survival. Centuries of foreign occupation – by the Romans, the Slavs, the Franks, and most cruelly by the Turks – had taught the Greeks not only the chameleon wiles of all subject peoples but also that it paid to be cynical about any interests other than self-interest. Christos had no illusions about his friends and neighbours. Mostly they tolerated what they regarded as his eccentric espousal of the leftist cause merely because he was a son of one of the leading families of Panagia. The treasure in dollars his father had prudently sent from America before the World War broke out assured that his family was relatively rich in this village of the comparatively poor. Few could comprehend why someone who had more, like Christos, could embrace an ideology whose application would assure that he would end up with less. The villagers believed that it was only the very poor, who had nothing to lose and everything to gain, who would be mad enough to throw in with the Reds. Yet it hadn't hurt his cause to make a little propaganda with that widow around this campfire. And he had not lied; he had indeed loved brave Renos like a brother. He loved so many so much, as though each and every one were his true brother. Sometimes when he was alone, or after too much raki, the very thought of the era of peace and justice that would follow a socialist victory would bring tears to his eyes.

Yet as he resumed his comradely chatting and joking, Christos ached at the festering pain his own words had made him conscious of once again. To himself he admitted he wanted to weep just now not because he was moved by the ideal of international brotherhood but because of the personal failure of his own blood fraternity. True, it had been easier to love Renos than his own real brother. But it was easier to love almost anyone than Yorgos. Even though they had different mothers, they had sprung from the same loins and carried the same family name and so should be, in their way, closer than a husband and wife. Yet even as a stubby little boy, Yorgos had always

12

stubbornly gone against his big brother. The other children had all but erected pagan altars to their dearly beloved Christos, but Yorgos had doomed himself to unpopularity by setting himself up as his competitor and rival. Back in the classroom, only the hectoring schoolmaster had taken the side of the younger Kronos brother. Even then, Yorgos had always been adept at currying favour with whoever was in charge.

Christos searched the shadows for that wan, owlish face with the thick spectacles. By the radiance of his stepmother's face this evening, he had guessed that Yorgos must have slunk home from his rightwing policeman's post in a village far to the south near Kalamata. He supposed duty required him to report his suspicions to the people's committee, but he couldn't shake off his old habit of protecting his brother. He had tried so hard, for as long as he could remember, to make things the way they should be between the two of them. When he was very young and still believed in such things, time and again he had turned the other cheek like the priest said a good Christian should. Later, as he matured and progressed in his lessons at school and elsewhere, he had tried reason and he had applied charm. When still Yorgos had doggedly treated him like the despised enemy, he had once even resorted to beating the living daylights out of him in the hopes of exorcising whatever devil he carried inside.

One of his men insistently plucked at the sleeve of his cloak and another slapped him drunkenly on his back. Christos resolutely put aside his worries about his renegade brother. His comrades were bent on having a good time tonight, and so obligingly he tried to enter into the spirit of the occasion. In these last morose months he had begun to doubt the Marxist catechism, but he still cared little for Lent or any of the other religious observances which had enslaved the gullible peasants of the world for too long. Yet he supposed it didn't do any harm to let his men snatch what pleasure they could from this Carnival.

A young fellow named Aris, one of the comrades who had joined up just last week from a village along the Gulf of Korinthos, broke into Christos' reverie by whistling and nudging him in the ribs. He looked where Aris pointed just in time to see Marika tossing her head and making a pretty gesture with her hand. Almost he forgot about war, his men, and the intently watching villagers. But he fought the impulse to course to her side. He had warned her tonight that he wouldn't be able to sit with her all night like some stay-at-home grandfather. Yet she looked lonely. The years of waiting out these wars had taken their toll on her, as on all the women. He supposed it was easier to fight than to wait, alone and afraid. But it was for her, and all the others like her, that he had picked up his rifle and begun the great struggle. *She* was Greece.

13

His eyes met hers in a silent pledge that he would try to make up for his neglect later tonight, when they could steal away for a few hours together, and afterwards in the lifetime they would spend together if only he and his men could secure the future. He had to believe, and he did believe, that dream was still within their grasp.

But Aris cut into his thoughts. 'Look at that!' Obviously he thought Marika's invitation was for him. He took a swig from the raki bottle, spat half of it out on the ground, and made as if to get up and join her.

'No.' Christos' scowl stopped him dead. 'That one's mine.'

Hastily Aris apologised, passed him the raki, and averted his eyes from what belonged to the boss. For the life of him, however, he could not understand how any redblooded man would choose to sit here drinking and telling stories with the boys when he could be off in the night with a willing beauty like that hot one. The commandant was either a saint or a fool. The recruit once again doubted if he belonged with men like this. But then he shrugged and took another swig from the bottle. He liked to fight, and the 'progressive' cause might assure him a better future. In his village he had been born a poor man, and unless things turned upside down in that narrow little world he would die a poor man there, too. But if the Reds won the war, he might become a policeman, a postman, maybe even his village's mayor.

Christos' eyes were veiled as he smiled magnanimously at Aris. Once again he seemed lost in thought as he reached for the raki and took a long draught. Enough brooding about war and politics. He was a Greek and a man, and as he leaned back, he dreamed of quiet domestic pleasures: Marika, their children, a snug house, an honest day's work. He wished things were different, and that he and she were just a man and woman with nothing more on their minds than love and marriage. When the fighting finally stopped he would spend the rest of his life making everything up to her. But first he and his men had to win the war.

Across the bonfire he smiled at her, and when once more he saw her crook her finger he almost scrambled to his feet to follow wherever she beckoned. But just then one of his men started a vivid story about their last campaign in the high mountain passes. Christos passed around the raki bottle and once again became absorbed in the camaraderie of his comrades.

Marika's come-hither gesture had been observed by another pair of hungrier eyes.

Yorgos skulked like a lone wolf in the shadows outside the charmed circle of the Communist guerrillas. As he watched the glamour boys drinking, laughing, and telling one another outrageous lies, he wondered for a moment what it would be like to be part of such a tightly-woven group. Yet he was ashamed to crave the unattainable, and so he reminded himself that Christos and his gang were godless Communists and rotten to the core. An upright, Christian young man like himself must never associate with the likes of them. Besides, he was accustomed to the village louts turning their backs on him. He had jumped at the chance to join the gendarmerie, just to get out of Panagia. Yet still the old hurts rankled. Even in school, the others had unfairly taunted him for being smart, and volunteering for extra work, and not letting them copy his examination papers. He remembered once, when Christos hadn't been around to defend him, a gang of the bullies had tormented him and even beat him up on a deserted stretch of beach beyond Kyria Despina's lemon grove.

Not, Yorgos added to himself as he clenched and unclenched his fists, that he had ever asked Christos to shield him from boyish blows and insults. The only thing he had ever wanted to ask of his brother was that he would go away – but not to America, not to their father. Knowing that he was *there*, with the only one who had ever mattered, would be worse than having him here.

Yorgos spat on the ground and wished he could blow out the bonfire, order everyone home, and walk alone in the moonlight with the woman that he, too, loved. If there were any justice in this world, a second ago Marika would have made at least some of that possible by beckoning to him instead of his brother.

Yearningly Yorgos gazed at Marika of the blueblack hair and golden skin. She was so achingly beautiful. A poet, he thought, or even someone who was merely criminally glib like Christos could summon up the muses for the most extravagant of words to extol those smouldering eyes of hers, that voluptuous figure, that fiery nature which would inflame even a man of stone. But Yorgos, who was neither a poet nor articulate about his feelings, could never do much more than dumbly stare at her with his naked need. For years he had been baffled as to how to make her love him. He had little experience in this matter of love, for until now no one except his depressed mother, who didn't truly count, had ever loved him. When first he had fancied Marika, he had tried smiling every time she looked his way; but she seldom had even acknowledged his presence. Once – this was years ago, too – he had picked her a fistful of spring wildflowers, but he had felt like weeping when he had seen her throw them away in a ditch as soon as she thought his back was turned. Then finally one sultry night two Augusts ago when he had evaded the *andartes* to come home on leave, he had lost his senses. It had been so hot that summer – 'rutting weather', he had always thought of maddening nights like that, when all a man could think of was having a woman, any

15

woman, and shooting himself dry inside her. So when he had come upon Marika in a dark village lane, he had pushed her up against a whitewashed wall and tried to take by manly force what he had not been able to win with smiles and flowers. But she had fought him off, run away, and snubbed him every time she had seen him after that.

Yorgos' eyes roved over what he could see of that matchless body he had so fleetingly touched that stolen night. Even covered by that clumsy hand-loomed cotton, her full breasts had been so soft to his groping hands. If only he had succeeded in pinning back her arms and making her stand still, in another delicious instant he would have ripped the rough fabric of her bodice and had what he imagined were those golden velvet breasts in his mouth. He would have kissed them, and licked them, and then – if she angered him by still pretending to resist – he would have bitten into them and drawn blood. He wanted to hurt her so, sometimes, because he loved her so much, and yet she spurned him. Still, he was resolved that one day she would love him, too, and want him like he wanted her. Those hips that had writhed against him in fury would one day clutch him to her in passion. Her thighs would encircle him, and she would envelop him. And her almond eyes would plead to him for more . . .

Yorgos sank deeper into the shadows so that none would see how that wanton witch had excited him again. Even though she had probably cast him under some she-devilish spell, Marika was, for him, the only woman in the world. He had even decided, after that sordid encounter in the village lane, to make her his wife. And yet she and her wretched family had turned down his marriage proposal. What rankled even more was the coffeehouse gossip that she and Christos would be married as soon as the war was over.

Yorgos adjusted his glasses and shifted his gaze back to Christos. Not for the first time, he wondered if his passion for Marika had begun before or after he had discovered that she was the girl his brother loved. After all, Christos and Marika had been childhood sweethearts. Is that, Yorgos mused, what made me want her so? He and Christos had always been rivals for their father's long-distance affection. Was Marika just a pawn in their ancient chessgame to checkmate the king?

He put the tips of his fingers to his temples where his head was throbbing again. But, try as he might, he couldn't sort this all out. His memory was such a confusion of slurs and hurts and rejections, all of it mixed together, all of it riven with pain. He had always known their father loved Christos more. In the loves and hates of his family – and maybe here, too, with her own missing father – intense emotions consumed reason like a brutally hot July day obliterates a cake of ice. Everything – love and hate, bliss and

16

jealousy – was melted together and indistinguishable, except that for him they all stung. And still his obsession with Marika ate at him like a cancer that grew and grew.

As Yorgos continued to stare at his brother, in his troubled nearsighted eyes there was something akin to longing. How had it all gone so wrong with his brother? Sometimes in a recurrent dream he saw the glitter of green eyes; but when he reached out toward his father, he found it was Christos he was trying to touch instead. Maybe he had it all wrong. Perhaps it was his father he hated and Christos he loved, and Marika didn't matter at all. But no, that couldn't be. That didn't make sense. As he remembered too many unshriven pains and resentments, his gaze hardened. He hated his brother for being handsome, and popular, and loved by the only two people who mattered. It was devilish of God – or was this truly Satan's work – to give Christos both their father and Marika.

Yorgos held his hands up to his own face as though he had been suddenly struck blind and was trying to feel what he must look like. He and Christos had the same nose, the same lips, a face with the same shape. His own eyes were dark and melancholy like his mother's, instead of light like those Christos and their father shared. But aside from that, taken feature by feature, the two of them were so much alike that strangers would pick them out in a crowd as brothers. Yet Yorgos didn't need a mirror for confirmation that he himself was fleshier and cut to less graceful proportions. Marika had delivered the greatest insult of his life when, a few days after he had tried to rape her, she had hissed at him that he was a corruption of all that was good and noble in his brother.

Yorgos couldn't tear his eyes off that other face, so alike and yet so different from his own. Yet still he could not solve the old mystery. *Why him and not me*? Why did everyone love Christos so? How could they fail to see him for the dangerous opportunist he was? He had been a bad little boy – wilful, naughty, diabolical in his deliberate charm – and since he had joined those wicked Communists he had metamorphosed into an evil man. Yet everyone, especially their sainted father sending home remittances from Boston, thought the sun rose and set in Christos.

Yorgos' lips curled up in something akin to a smile. The sun did not shine forever. Night followed day, and darkness descended after light. Soon, when he led that rightwing assassination squad up to the mountains, he would even the score with his brother.

Yet apparently, Yorgos thought, even though his brother's days were numbered, these last nights of his were destined to be far more glorious than he deserved. He knew what was about to happen as soon as he saw Christos reach inside his back pocket and pull out the hand-carved

17

shepherd's flute their father had bought him when he was a child. The old anguish burned in Yorgos. He never bought *me* a flute. He bought me books and paper and a rubber ball, but never anything to make magic on, like Christos' flute. Yorgos gritted his teeth and stalked away from the bonfire so he wouldn't have to witness yet another of his brother's marvellous triumphs.

For at once, at first sight of Christos with his flute in his hand, the villagers fell silent and leaned forward in anticipation. Christos played his pipe like Pan. His mother, who had died giving birth to him, had also been blessed with the gift of music. When Sofia had delicately strummed her mandolin, that melancholy which is so intertwined with Greek *joie de vivre* had come to the fore, even the old grandfathers had crept off to be alone and cry for life's losses. Even now, when someone who had known her heard a lilting song on the wind, they would recall how her voice had been sweeter than baklava.

Sofia's son bent his curly head and touched his lips to the six-stopped flute so akin to the pipes shepherds have been cutting from hollowed cane forever. As he coaxed from it a tender melody, the villagers drew in their breath and waited for what they knew was about to come. The enchantment began, then, as it always did when Christos played. The cares of the world fell away as the Panagians listened to the sweet music dancing on the winter wind. The notes pirouetted here, and tiptoed there, soft as a stolen kiss under an olive tree. The hearts of the villagers leaped with joy, as the melody took a great graceful spring almost up to the full moon. As it trembled up there by the stars, for a lyrical moment the years of war and suffering were transcended, so that even the worn faces of the old ones glowed with the innocence and hope of the youth they had long ago lost. When the last notes died down, the village let out its collective breath in a sigh.

But then other hands began to play other music. Perikles the fisherman set his big *daoúli* drum in his lap and began slapping it rhythmically with a stick. Manolis the barrel-chested butcher put the mouthpiece of his home-made bagpipe to his lips and blew it to life. Yangos the grocer dusted off his delicate clarinet and tentatively ran up the scales he had learned from his uncle the musician in Argos. The drum sounded, the bagpipe whined, the clarinet skittered as the village band undulated with the high-register quarter-tone oriental rhythms brought to Greece during the centuries of Turkish Occupation. It began as a stately dirge and swelled into a breast-beating lamentation, the melody redolent with the swaying date-palms of the Tigris, the Euphrates, and even the Nile. But then the music subtly changed as it harkened back to Byzantine glories and further back still, to a time when the Hellenes ruled the world. Once again Christos picked up his pipe. Millennia fell away, and a simple shepherd's tune as old as the hills, maybe older than the Olympian gods, once again was sounded round the winter bonfire. In counterpoint, then, to Christos' flute, the drummer, the piper, and the clarinettist began again their oriental medley. East and west blended for a dulcet moment and then clashed in an army of cacophonous notes. But in music, as in all else, Greece conquers the conquerors. Finally, majestically, the essence of what was Greek began to grow and swell. Christos' flute triumphed, the others sounded their last notes, and West not only drowned out East but merged into something greater than either, something quintessentially *Greek*.

For an aching moment the silence hung in the night. But then the village band once again began to play. As if in a trance, or possessed by the gods, Christos, his partisans, and most of the other young men began leaping up to dance the defiant steps of free men who can never be altogether enslaved by despots or devils. They linked hands in a snaky line, their arms held high, and weaved magic around the bonfire. Christos held a handkerchief in his right hand like a fluttering cotton spear as he led his men in a mime of life and death. He leaped, kicked, gyrated, and all but flew while his *andartes* nimbly kept the primal beat. The music possessed them in the ancient Dionysian *geranos* steps which Theseus danced after slaying the Minotaur, which Agamemnon danced after burning Troy, which every hero in the Greek firmament danced after conquering every mythological monster in the underworld. Always and everywhere, dance is the most joyous of the arts, but nowhere in the world does a man so dance out his heart and his soul as in Greece.

When finally the music ended and the comrades sank back in their places, Marika was staring yearningly at Christos, Yorgos was back by the bonfire staring even more yearningly at Marika, and Christos was staring most yearningly of all into the red revolutionary flames. For a long moment, the souls of these three were aflame with conflicting loves.

But then, as the villagers at last began to make their way back home for a few hours' sleep before waking to the rigours of the Lenten fast, Yorgos saw Marika approach Christos and whisper in his ear. He saw his brother rear up his head in that Greek gesture that meant 'no', but then urgently she touched his thigh. Yorgos chewed his lip in despair. There was nothing in this world, he thought, that I wouldn't do to make her touch me like that, of her own free will. Why *him*, and not me? Why Christos, yet again?

As the two of them slipped away into the darkness, Yorgos impotently smouldered by the fire. Instead of killing his brother in that raid he planned on Christos' mountain camp, he wished he could murder him here and now.

What was happening in the moonlight between his brother and the woman he himself loved? After long moments of jealous indecision, he stalked off on a midnight prowl to find out.

Another pair of yellowed eyes blinked like the owl that was the symbol not only of the guardian goddess Athena but of wisdom itself. Marika's mother sighed, shook her head, and wished she believed she could change what was fated to happen by running after her daughter and stopping this affair before it went too far. Instead she stayed staring into the flames and wishing she had given birth only to her son who was leading his charmed man's life instead of this daughter who was apparently cursed with a woman's destiny.

The one they always called 'Old Anna' even though she had lived only forty-four winters clutched her black shawl closer round her thin shoulders. She had been married at twelve, her husband had abandoned her at twenty, and the harshness of her life had aged her far beyond her chronological years. Because of crippling arthritis, she could hardly walk on these damp winter nights. She would never be able to catch up with her daughter who by now must be well on her way toward the cave.

Old Anna shivered and held her hands to the fire. Had she done right today, when Marika had come to her for help? After the girl had blurted out her reckless plan to seduce Christos, she had cautioned her once, twice, and the blessed trinity of a third time on how tragic it could be to play out this dangerous game and maybe lose everything that mattered. If he took her and then didn't marry her, perhaps no other decent man would want her. She would have to endure the pitiful shadow life of a village spinster. But then, when Marika had vowed that she had to have Christos and that she would do everything and anything to get him, Old Anna had sighed and done her best for her daughter. She had been young once herself, and hot like all the women of her race. It had been her own bad luck to lose her man, but perhaps she could help Marika grasp a happier destiny. A mother had to do all she could to even up the odds stacked against a daughter. For as she had grown older, and more bitter at her lot, Old Anna had begun to believe that it was *us* against *them* in the great game of life between the sexes. Her husband Yannis had gotten away, but perhaps she could even the score by delivering Christos to her daughter. And so, hesitantly at first, she had confided the secrets that some mothers had passed down to a few daughters from the oldest of the old times, to keep the spirit of the Great Mother alive. Wistfully she had told Marika that mostly all *that* was gone now, like so much that had been full of wonder in the women's world that once was. But even now, in a few places – here in Mykenae in Greece, and in Delphi, always in magic Delphi, in some of the ancient shrines in the Levant, and even, she had heard tell once from a well-travelled gypsy, in the sacred Celtic circles in faraway Ireland and Britain – a woman could still summon some of the ancient mystic powers which once made men worship *Her* and *us*.

In her black shawl and black dress, Old Anna had looked like one of the mythological witchy crones once said to measure time and fate and man's destiny. Her voice had trembled with emotion as she initiated this latest generation into the old secrets.

'On the sacred island in our very bay, there is a cave, my child, an enchanted place that women have used since the ancient times to celebrate their mysteries and work their women's wonders. For long before a church of the Christians was on that island, a cavern of the pagans was there first. Maybe it's been there forever. We call it the Cave of the Great Goddess.'

She had paused to look deeply into Marika's eyes to make sure the girl was listening, and believing, before she went on. Had her daughter thought this was an old woman's mad mutterings, she would have stopped there and never mentioned any of this again. It would have been left to other mothers and daughters to carry on the tradition. But Old Anna had seen, reflected in Marika's trusting eyes, the perfect need of the suckling infant searching for her mother's milk, and the secrets of life. Satisfied, then, that Marika was truly her heir, she had lowered her voice like the gifted storyteller she was and continued.

'I have heard tell – my mother told me, and you must promise that someday you will tell your own girls – Yes? You promise? Good, then I'll go on . . .'

Old Anna had bared her toothless gums in a wide smile and settled back on her haunches to draw out this bewitching moment of female communion. Marika's life had to be different, and better, than her own. If she wanted Christos and what she fancied was the ecstasy of love, her mother was determined she would do her best to give it to her.

Again Old Anna had smiled that toothless smile, and began.

'In the light of a full moon, my daughter – on a night just like tonight! – this special cave is blessed with certain powers. A woman who dares to go inside this cave with the man she has chosen for her lover, and who lies with him there, will earn his eternal love.'

'Eternal love!' Marika's eyes had glittered like jewels. 'Tell me, mother, where is this cave!'

And so Old Anna had taken her out to the bare earth of their dead winter's garden and drawn her a map in the dirt: the beach, the bay, finally the island with its old church and older cave. Then she had leaned over and clawed up

21

a handful of the tired dust and held it up to her daughter. 'Inside the cave,' she had said, 'you must lie naked on the Earth Mother's skin. Naked, Marika. Naked on the belly of the Mother. In her cave, where all life begins. In the first womb.'

Old Anna's voice had quavered like a seer's as she said that, and, as Marika had shrunk away from her, strangely then, without being conscious of what she was about to say, a premonition had made her caution her daughter to make certain that no one was in the cave except herself and Christos. 'For whoever is there at the crucial moment,' she had warned, 'will forever be locked together.'

Marika had let out a nervous peal of laughter at the absurdity of her mother's words. Tonight in the cave, of course it would be only her and Christos. She didn't even want God as her witness. She had laughed again as she had said that.

'Careful, daughter.' Old Anna was cautious enough to fear other gods than the Mother. Life had taught her to be wary of almost everything. And so, just to be on the safe side, she had crossed herself three times like a good Christian. Again she had reminded her daughter that whatever was begun tonight would have no ending. 'Once you seal it in the cave, Marika, this passion will go on forever. Remember that.'

'Forever?' Marika had licked her lips and uttered that one word as though wandering through eternity in love would be a perpetual garden of delights.

'Forever.' But Old Anna had repeated that same word as though endless love were a curse. She had sighed, then, and given another warning. 'Be sure that Christos is the one you want forever. Once soldered in this cave, the bond between the two of you can never be broken by man or woman, god or goddess.'

Old Anna shuddered by the fire as she recalled how, then, her voice had swelled with an authority and a wisdom that came from somewhere outside herself. 'And remember, Marika! Mark this well! Love can shackle even more than it can liberate.'

Back at the sputtering Carnival bonfire, the old woman shook her head. Where had that final grim warning come from? Its essential truth, which her own life's sorrows confirmed, had never consciously occurred to her before. Perhaps she should have taken this as a bad omen and steered Marika away from what might be tragic folly. Or maybe not. Everything, after all, would happen as it was meant to happen. The fates would not be cheated.

Marika's mother was struck, as the bonfire began to hiss from ember to ash, by another unsettling thought. Of all the old powers that once were woman's, how could it be that this one which survived merely gave a woman the power of unending love over a particular man? Wouldn't it have been a greater gift of the Great Mother to give her suffering daughters eternal independence from the shackles of love? Or had it all been different in the good old days of matriarchy? Had love, then, made a woman strong instead of weak? Had men, once, been more worthy of a woman's love than they were now? And could it be possible that once there were no greater glory in life than the serenities and passions of an eternal love between a man and a woman? Was that still the best life had to offer?

Old Anna stared wearily into the dying fire. She felt so old now. For her, the best had passed her by. She would never experience a great love like the one she had just imagined. But maybe Marika would find such a love with Christos. Perhaps she was wrong to worry that she had done her daughter more harm than good today.

Old Anna shrugged her shoulders. Come what may, whether the result was a blessing or a curse, she had shared her dearest treasure with the daughter of her heart. And she had, after all, given the girl an added measure of insurance after she had begun to fear that Marika had tempted the fates with that careless laughing boast of hers. She had half-expected, when she had offered to make the girl a love charm, that her daughter would have called her an old fool and disregarded all that had transpired between them that afternoon. Instead Marika, who had always denied being superstitious, had eagerly accepted the offer. Ever since she could remember, the village women had been coming to her mother for simple charms and dark herbs said to cure certain illnesses. Until now Marika had been embarrassed by her mother's witchy predilections. But with her honour and her future hingeing on whatever happened in the cave tonight, she was not about to be choosy about anything that helped her achieve her ends. And so, on a small piece of cheap paper, Old Anna had drawn a circle pierced with a sharp line. Then she had waved that charm in the air above Marika's head as she muttered the old words in the old tongue. Finally she had instructed her daughter to keep that paper next to her skin – 'Between your breasts or your legs,' she had sagely suggested, 'for either are a woman's centres of power.' And it won't hurt, she had added, to spend as much time as you can by the sea this afternoon, for this charm's power increases when it's close to the currents of moving water. Marika had thrown her arms around her mother's neck and promised to do all of that for Christos. And she had thanked her mother again and again before she had tucked the love charm into her bodice and run off toward the sea, laughing.

Old Anna marshalled her strength to get to her feet and begin the sorry shuffle home to her cold, manless hearth. Just for good measure, tonight she would light a candle before the sad icon of the Virgin she kept by her

23

bedside. For, to her, a goddess was a goddess, even though the name and the theology had changed over the millennia. She would pray to that more modern Great Mother to help her daughter in the eternal cave.

Not so very far away, Marika was meanwhile leading Christos on to what she fervently hoped were the sweet chains of their linked destiny. With honeyed words, quick teasing steps, and astute questions about Christos' political opinions, she had deftly enticed him down the path that snaked away from the bonfire.

It was late now, and it seemed only they were abroad. The dogs were ahowl as they passed through the centre of the darkened village. Bats circled the dome of the church and the clock tower. The wind knocked over a rickety wooden chair which a café owner had forgotten to bring in for the night. Like an evil jinn, that chair all but pursued them through the *plateia*, thumping against the door, cobblestones, the bakery window. The spirits were walking on Carnival night. But resolutely, as she took his hand and continued onward, Marika disregarded these portents. All that mattered was to seduce her man inside that cave. Every time she turned a corner, she prayed that no one would waylay him with distracting questions about war and peace. But in this, at least, her luck held. They didn't encounter another soul as she all but dragged him past the shuttered shops and the locked iron gates, alongside the cemetery with its swaying cypress trees, toward the stony trail that led to the sea and, eventually, the cave.

But just when they were almost out of the village and she thought she had him safely to herself, Christos glimpsed a kerosene light still glowing in the house of one of his comrades. He let go of her hand when he suddenly decided that Andreas, instead of returning with them to the mountains in the morning, should be sent to Nauplion with urgent messages to be forwarded to their commanding officers. His men needed ammunition and boots, and he had to have money to buy food for them all. He fingered the rifle that was still slung over his shoulder. 'Sorry, *glika mou*, my darling. I have to talk to Andreas.'

She felt like groaning and grinding her teeth. To come this close and to lose! If he set foot inside that house, she might forfeit him forever. Next he would tell her to wait for him at home. Even if she insisted on lurking outside in the shadows, she doubted if he would remember she was there. For she knew how the men were. Once inside, Andreas would insist on getting out the raki. The two of them would sit and talk until the night and the bottle were finished. Desperately she touched the love charm she had tucked in the cleft between her breasts. Work now, she told it. She was far

24

beyond caring that until today she had been a modern woman who didn't believe in love charms and ancient cave goddesses. She had vowed she would do anything to snare Christos, and so she would. She had felt silly sitting on the cold beach for hours this afternoon with her mother's charm nestled in her bodice. But anything for Christos. Again she silently beseeched the love charm, 'work!'

She could hardly believe her eyes when, just at that instant, the kerosene lantern in Andreas' kitchen dimmed and died.

'It's too late to talk to Andreas.' Christos yawned as he turned back to her. He glanced back through the village where all the other lights, too, were dark. 'Maybe we should postpone this *volta* of yours. I leave for the hills before dawn.'

'All the more reason to talk now.' She managed to tuck her arm in his without touching that rifle. As they continued to walk, she smiled up at him as though the calculation in her eyes were true belief in what she was about to say. 'There are a few more things I have to understand before I join the Party.'

'Join us? Now?' He reared up his head in the Greek gesture of negation. He could not bear for her, too, to be at risk.

She hadn't been serious about her offer, only saying what she thought he wanted to hear as she led him on to the cave. But not so long ago, when the leftists were riding high, he had suggested she join one of the female guerrilla units who fought beside the comrades in the mountains. She had not been so desperate then, but now she would consider anything to keep him. If the rumours were true and the *andartes* were about to flee the country, she could marry him wherever they were both exiled. Maybe the cave wasn't the last ace in her hand after all. 'Why not? They might even let me fight beside you.'

'*You?*' Christos was moodily staring up at the mad full moon. 'No. Absolutely not.'

'But why?' She had never seen that look in his eye.

'It's too late, *glika*.'

Her stomach turned over as she caught the undertone of despair in his voice. Always before Christos had been so confident of the triumph of his cause. What she'd heard must be true. The leftists would be on the run, and soon. She had to save him, and what they had together, in this last-ditch gamble in the cave. Once she had given him everything, he would never be able to leave her. She had to keep Christos from heading for the hills in the morning. 'What do you mean, it's too late?'

In anguish he looked down into her eyes. With everyone else he could pretend the cause was not lost, but not with her. 'I think you know.'

'So it's as bad as that?'

25

'We may lose . . . everything.' He reached down and took handfuls of her hair in his hands, and then he sighed and let the strands fall away until his hands were empty. 'I've been meaning to talk to you. I hoped it wouldn't come to this, but now . . .' If, as he suspected, his unit was about to pull out for the border, he wanted her to wait in safety here in the village until somehow, someday she could join him. But he hated to admit that all — almost — was lost. If he lost her, too . . .

They were so close that she could read his mind. He was about to prepare her for a long and terrible separation. But now that she had him almost where she wanted him, on the beach facing Panagia Island, she wasn't going to let him speak those chilling words on the tip of his tongue. She put her finger to his lips. 'Hush,' she breathed. She smiled into her love's eyes. 'Listen to the night. And the sea. It's calling us.'

For once he did as she asked. In the luminous golden light of the full moon, the calm sea was as wine-dark as Homer has immortalized it. Pine-covered islands glittered black in the water. Nearby, silhouetted on the slope of a rocky mountain, a precocious almond tree bloomed fragrant, as though already touched by spring. On such a night, at such a place, it seemed that Aphrodite herself might emerge any naked instant from the foamy surf.

Marika scented victory as silently he continued to gaze out at the Aegean. Even though Christos was a dedicated partisan, other passions must beat within him. Here and now romance, not revolution, was in the air. The moonlight was on her side.

'*Ela*,' she said when she was sure a certain mood had built between them. He reached for her, but she eluded him and began dragging her uncle's small weather-beaten rowboat toward the sea. 'Come.'

A moment ago he would have promised her anything, but now he was bewildered. 'The sea? *Now*?' But when she didn't even look up from her persistent struggle with the boat, he helped her get it in the water.

When it was in the shallows, she leaped inside. 'Now, a push.'

'But — '

A smile of seduction lit her face. '*Ela*, Christo. You won't be sorry.'

Still he hesitated. They had to talk about his fears for the future. But when she tossed her blueblack hair and crooked her finger just as she had back at the bonfire, he tucked his rifle into some nearby bushes and threw his caution to the wind. The future could wait. *Now* was all that mattered. The cares of the war fell away, and suddenly the night seemed young. He gave the boat a heave and jumped aboard. 'Happy now?'

Her silvery laughter echoed to the moon. 'Not quite yet.' She gave him a smile that promised everything, and then she passed him the oars. 'But we will be soon.' Again the Jezebel smile. She had him now. The tricky part had been getting him in the boat. 'I'm sure of it. So sure . . .'

The wild wind was in her hair, the black water rustled like taffeta, the moonlight made it all seem an exquisite dream. They faced one another as he worked the oars, back and forth, straining as he fought first the tide and then the current. She couldn't tear her eyes off his arms, his shoulders, his thighs. The erotic rhythm of his movements hypnotized her. Every time he lunged toward her, she reached out to touch his hair, his cheek, his knee. Then languorously she leaned back and revelled in the sensation of being swept away in the night by this man with whom she was about to break all the taboos. She was Cleopatra on her barge, and he was her galley slave. Then he was a Turkish pirate and she a captured maiden about to be carried off to a sultan's harem. But no, she thought, enough girlish fantasies. Tonight it was magical enough that he was Christos and she Marika. For a moment she forgot that the reason for this seduction was to trap this man into marriage, and she merely wanted what she had long denied him. Her eyes told him what her lips did not yet dare.

But he understood. 'Tonight?' he breathed.

'Tonight,' she promised.

He rowed faster into the unknown. 'But where?'

Again her moonbeam laughter. 'It's a surprise.' Regally she gestured toward Panagia Island.

As the boat shot across the mile-wide channel, Christos' curiosity quickened. He, like everyone in the village, knew the story of this island and the miraculous intervention that had given their hamlet its name and their ancestors their salvation. Nearly a century ago, after another failed insurrection against the Turks in Crete, their forefathers had fled from Chania in their fishing *caiques* for asylum on the mainland. They had rowed a night and a day and another night when a storm had blown up and all had been sure they would perish. At that moment of peril, when the seas loomed as high as Mount Ada on their dear Crete, the terrified villagers had made a vow to the *Panagia*, the Saint of All Saints, the Holy Virgin. If she guided them to a safe harbour, they would name the village they hoped to found in her honour. As the tale was always told, no sooner was that promise made than the storm abated. As the sun rose, the refugees had seen before them a rocky pinnacle of an island and then behind it, the snuggest bay this side of Crete. In gratitude they not only called the village Panagia but also erected a small whitewashed chapel atop that island which had appeared to them as a lighthouse straight from the Mother of God. Every August fifteenth on the Virgin's Day, the Panagians rowed en masse to the island for an early morning service in the old church to give thanks for the miracle that had saved their families and blessed them all forever. Odd, Christos thought, that it was to this sacred island that Marika insisted they go in the dead of this winter Carnival night. Odder still that she was suddenly acting so seductive.

She was first to leap out of the boat, and together they waded through the icy water and beached the craft.

'Now what?' He was not about to make a fool of himself by taking her in his arms on this supposedly sacred island. Or at least not yet.

She beamed him a mysterious smile and silently began to climb the familiar stone path up to the chapel. For in these last few moments she, too, had been remembering all the pilgrimages she had made to this island on the Virgin's Day. And she had begun to worry that it might be sacrilege, and an offence to the all-powerful Panagia, if she took Christos as her lover in the lair of a pagan goddess. Just to be on the safe side, first they would make a ritual curtsey to the Mother of God. In a way, going together to the chapel would be blessing their carnal union. They would stand before the altar and exchange a private sort of wedding vows.

Doggedly Christos followed her up the steep moonlit trail, sure now that he had been mistaken back there in the boat. Marika was interested in the spirit, not the flesh. This bizarre excursion was the fulfilment of some preposterous vow she'd made. The women were always trying to barter with heaven. Nonetheless he would humour her. These last lonely years had been hard on her, and he suspected that, with the way the war was going, times were about to get even harder. It wouldn't hurt to light a candle against the darkness.

Marika unlatched the gate and waited for Christos to catch up with her. Hand-in-hand they ducked in the door of the small simple chapel. He lit a match, she held a beeswax candle to it, and together they caught their breath as the holy place came aglow. The candlelight caught the glint of silver and gold from icons, hanging lamps, and votive offerings left by the faithful. The musty air still carried the heavy scent of incense. As Christos set one candle afire in memory of his mother and then lit another nest of tapers, the faded images of the saints leapt to life on the walls. Marika crossed herself a devout three times and bent to a sacred icon to kiss the hem of the Panagia's robe. She expected Christos to follow her example, but when she turned around instead he was holding a candle up to paintings of the warrior Saint George and the fighting Archangel Michael. To Marika this was a sign that his heart was already back in the mountains.

Christos stared at the warrior icons. Even here, in this church, he couldn't escape the images of duty. He turned, then, and caught her questioning look. He would share his fears with her here. 'Marika.' He held out his hands and led her to the altar. 'We have to talk. The war – '

28

'No!' She couldn't let him say what she most feared to hear. To stop those words, she covered his lips with hers in a kiss of desperation.

She felt so fragile in his arms as he held her before the altar. Maybe it was better not to worry her with his doubts tonight. He would be back in the village in another fortnight. If the wartime situation continued to deteriorate, he would still have time to warn her that they faced a temporary separation.

Marika looked up into his eyes. 'You love me?'

'I do.'

'Swear it. Here! Before the altar!'

'But I've told you a thousand times.'

'Tell me a thousand and one.'

He held her more tightly. He hadn't realized the state she was in tonight. The war had taken more of a toll on her than he had thought. No, this was not the time to feed her fears with his own. 'I love you, Marika.'

'And we'll get married?'

Her voice, he thought, was as small and afraid as it had been that morning in the schoolyard long ago when first she had poured out her heart to him. 'I swear, Marika, that I'd marry you here and now if we only had a priest.' Now that he saw how vulnerable she was, he wished he had done as she asked and married her that morning in the village church.

'Ah!' She looked up at the fresco of Christ the Redeemer. 'As God is my witness, I believe you.' For tonight, she would be content with these words, Hastily she gave the icon of the Virgin a final beseeching look, crossed herself another trinity of times, and steeled herself to get on with what she was determined would happen tonight. Again she looked up into those green eyes.

'You know,' Christos said, 'you have icon eyes.' He gestured toward the silver-encrusted picture of the Virgin.

'Yes?' Throatily she laughed. 'But I'm no saint, Christo.' She let that sink in a moment, and then again she touched his cheek. 'It's time.'

'Time?' Wearily his eyebrows arched. It must be two or three in the morning. '*Pame*? We're going?'

Her diabolical smile that promised so much was back. 'Follow me.'

At first he thought, when she led him down the hill by another path, that she knew a shortcut back to the boat. But instead, halfway down, she waited on the edge of a precipice overlooking the bay and the sea.

He joined her, and arm-in-arm they stood on the windswept cliff looking across the channel at Panagia set so snugly in the cove this island sheltered from the open sea. The luminous moonlight cloaked the shabby poverty of this village, where they had been born and would die, in a beauty that transcended all other places and times. Spreading over it, almost to the clear bright stars, the mountain with its silvery trees cast a verdant benediction. The wind changed, and she moved closer in his embrace. Civilization lay over the water, but here they were alone. They listened to the night, and to one another's quickening breath. The blood was calling.

He was the first to answer it.

'Marika,' he whispered as tenderly he brushed her hair back from her temples. His arms crept around her slender waist and caressed her until shivers ran down her spine.

Now, she thought, *now* . . .

Marika turned in his arms, looked long into his eyes, and then, her black eyes still staring into his green ones, she slowly and deliberately kissed him on the lips. Last week, when she had plotted her erotic strategy, she had worried she might be too nervous to go through with it after all. She, like the other girls of her age who modestly held their hands over their mouths as they giggled about what awaited them in their marriage beds, was as innocent as the strict village moral codes could make her. And yet she, too, was a hot-blooded Greek. She concentrated all her love and need in an utterly abandoned kiss of desire. Her parted lips burned upon his, and she was greedy for more. She insinuated her body close to his, and then closer still. Her lips, her breasts, her thighs scorched his. She was startled by her own awakened passion and doubted, with an intoxicated mixture of pride and shame, if Christos would be able to return it in kind.

But as finally she drew away, his eyes still met hers, stare for stare. His hands were on her shoulders, and she nearly swooned as he swept her tight against him. He returned her kiss of fire, and then he surpassed it. She was dizzy in his embrace as his kiss burned on and on. The heat spread down through her body, and his devouring lips smothered hers. For her and for him, the rest of the world dropped away, and there was only his lips on her neck and his body pressed the length of hers.

'*Nai*,' she moaned, 'yes.'

His lips were everywhere, and so were hers. Locked in frenzy, she lost her balance and might have fallen off the rim of the precipice if Christos hadn't caught her and ground her even more tightly to him, away from the abyss. They staggered on the cliff, and this time she fell back against the rocks with him on top of her. His hands groped her thighs, and higher. She let out a primal cry of pleasure as his fingers probed between her legs. She had never felt anything like that before, and she jerked and shuddered as he pleasured her. When again his lips branded hers, there was surrender in her kiss. She would not have resisted if he had taken her then and there. But at that heightened instant, his weight pressed her back into the sharp stones hard enough to draw blood. That pain brought her almost to her senses. Not here, she thought frantically. The cave. Get him inside the cave first.

He leaned back and took his arms from around her as he unbuttoned his trousers. Quick to seize the opportunity, she wriggled away and crept to her feet. 'Not here,' she begged. Her voice, hoarse with desire, was an octave lower than usual. '*Parakalo*, please, I know a better place.' She held out her hand. '*Ela*, Christo. Come . . .'

Marika drew him into the Cave of the Great Goddess.

Inside the darkness that was as wet and tight as a woman's secret recesses, their kisses grew still more fevered. She – and he – knew there would be no stopping now. He tore open the bodice of her dress, filled his hands with her breasts, and again she moaned as his mouth found hers. He reached for the hem of her dress and pulled it over her head. As he threw off his own clothes, she slipped out of the rest of hers.

The cave was as warm as a womb. Faint moonlight shone in from the night sky as he gazed at her body and she looked at his. With a sense of wonder, he reached out and touched her, from her lips to her nipples and then her belly. They were in each other's arms again, and a thrilling moment later they were prone on the rocks. Their caresses left them panting. They writhed like snakes on the ancient rocks, and finally he broke inside her.

For a long while they were lost in love in the erotic cave.

In the after-bliss, then, they lay silent and spent. He was on his back, his arm was tenderly around her shoulders, and her head lolled on his chest.

Suddenly, in what they had supposed was the intimate sanctuary of their cave, they heard the hiss of a familiar voice.

'Devils! Sinners! God curse you both!'

A match was struck, the butt of a candle lit, and Yorgos stood above them. 'Marika! It *was* you, then, I saw with him . . .' His strangled voice was a rasp. 'You whore!' In the semi-darkness, his eyes glittered like an animal's about to pounce and kill. Yet as he saw Marika's naked white flesh spread out so invitingly before him, his eyes changed and what was in them now was not so much hate as need. 'Marika,' he whispered, 'oh, my Marika . . . so beautiful and so damned.'

Marika shivered as she remembered her mother's warning. So the other Kronos brother had been here, too. She had wanted Christos forever, but not Yorgos, too. If what her mother had said was true, the three of them would be locked together like this for an infinity. Again she shivered, chilled to her bones. She had gambled everything for a love that was an eternal blessing, not a curse.

For a moment none of them would ever forget, they remained frozen like the figures on an ancient Greek vase.

But then the candle sputtered out, and Yorgos lurched away into the night.

Christos tensed to lunge up and follow his brother. But before he could escape, Marika threw herself on top of him. She wasn't about to accept a curse, not her, never. With her body she would turn defeat into victory, with her love she would triumph over hate. She had come here tonight to win Christos forever, and by all the gods she would get her way.

Afterwards – because of the way everything turned out – she was always convinced that her son must have been conceived when Christos made love to her that second guilty time, after the curse.

Two

The cold woke Marika before dawn the next morning.

She was still mostly asleep as drowsily she groped for the thick wool blanket that her grandmother had spun as part of her mother's dowry a generation ago. If she could just get warm, she would snuggle into her narrow virgin's bed and settle into that heavy midwinter sleep akin to an animal's hibernation. She would dream, most probably of Christos, and maybe for once her mother would let her sleep long after the cocks crowed. But instead of her blanket, her fingers closed around the rough winter shawl someone had tenderly draped over her naked body. When she tried to pull it up to her chin, her feet and then her legs were exposed to the damp chill that was not her bedroom.

Marika's eyes shot open. *Where am I?*

In the dim light that filtered down through the narrow aperture onto the outside world, at first all she could see was that she was lying on the dank ground of a shadowy place that was most certainly not a house. The jagged walls of this cavernous underground chamber were pitted with indentations deep enough to hide the darkest secrets. A path seemed to lead down toward the bowels of the earth. Faintly she heard the gentle slap of waves breaking on the rocks. Then she felt a whoosh of air, saw a sweep of black wings, and heard a chorus of mousy squeaks. Instinctively she burrowed her head under the shawl and protected her hair with her hands. When she cringed still lower to try to flatten herself out of harm's way, her body met unyielding rock.

She remembered where she was when the bats were gone and she once again dared to open her eyes in the Cave of the Great Goddess. She smiled, stretched, and reached out. But Christos wasn't where she had gambled he would surely be. Where was he? She shouted for Christos, but the only answer was the echoing sound of her own need. Oh, dear God, was he gone? She shut her eyes in terror, but they shot open again as, in a rush of anxious remembrance, she recalled Yorgos and the curse.

She huddled in a fetal ball and clutched her hands at her naked shoulders to comfort herself in the same way she might take an hysterical friend in her arms. As she rocked back and forth trying to master her rising panic, waves of fear and anger swept over her like mad winter surf after a storm. He knew what she had risked to be with him, and yet he had abandoned her to face the consequences alone. But no, she thought, Christos wouldn't fail her. He had simply gone back to his men, as he had told her he would. He would return as soon as he could. And yet she had been living with fear for so long – what if he died in the fighting! What if he had to flee to exile! – that her strained nerves snapped. This is what she got for giving everything to her man before marriage! She knew what she'd done was wrong, and now she would have to pay for it.

In the cold cave, Marika broke out in a sweat. Her mind raced. If he really was gone, soon – this morning – she would have to face her family and maybe even the censure of the village. If Christos didn't want her, she doubted if any other decent man would condescend to make her an honest woman. She was ruined and disgraced. She considered the possibility, as Yorgos' bitter words came back to her, that she might even be cursed.

As she held herself so tightly that her arms ached, she succeeded, at least for a moment, in getting a grip on her emotions. She had been first in her class at school, and until yesterday she hadn't believed in nonsense like curses. Ignorant village women might be faint with fear that Yorgos' words would blight their lives, but she would never allow superstition to override her reason.

Marika's eye was caught by a scrap of tattered paper blown along the ground by a current of air. Thoughtfully she watched the love charm dance out of her sight, to be lost forever deep in the recesses of the erotic cave. Perhaps she, who had sat by the sea yesterday afternoon with that wretched totem pressed to her body, was neither different nor superior to the most superstitious old crone in the village. She was not only ashamed of yesterday's desperate trust in love charms and women's magic but also more than a little frightened that she had dabbled in a world she did not understand. Why had she tried to conjure up forces beyond her control?

She took a deep breath and thought hard. Even here and now, she was investing too much power in the supernatural. Instead of lying here worrying

33

about the supposed power of love charms and curses, she should be deciding on a course of action for this morning. She was strong enough to cope with anything, even this. It was even more than possible, she told herself with a burst of her customary optimisim, that she was jumping to the wrong conclusions. She cupped her hands around her eyes and stared at the entrance to the cave. Maybe Christos had just gone outside for a moment or two and would return. Together they might still make their way back to the village and tell her family that they would marry as soon as the priest allowed it. Yesterday, as she had nursed her love charm by the sea, she had rehearsed a triumphant speech and even imagined her mother making a whispered aside about the wonders of the cave. She had been so certain that Christos would be so adoring, this morning after their first night.

'Christo? Are you here, Christo?' Again only the echo.

A pair of solitary tears trickled down her cheeks. It was no use deluding herself that Christos had crept away on some pressing errand and would return in this hour of her need. She didn't need a gypsy's second sight to know that, at this very moment, he was off with his comrades scaling some forbidding mountain on the way to his camp. When she had first debated whether to seduce him, she had always been aware he might choose duty over love. Yet last night, here in this cave, she had been certain nothing in the world could matter more to him than her flesh and their love. But now she wondered if she had known Christos as well as she had thought she had. Perhaps she didn't know him at all.

From the uncertain light shunting in from the sky, she guessed that dawn was just breaking. He must have left her as soon as she had fallen asleep curled up next to him. After the way they had been together here in this cave, how could he have gone away without so much as a word to her? True, she had neither asked for nor been given any promises. But now, everything – love, marriage, honour, the future, and perhaps even her own life – could be in jeopardy.

Again Marika shut her eyes. She could not yet bear to deal with the terrifying possibility that she might have lost everything most dear to her.

Her head began to throb as though someone were thumping it with a stick. Like it or not, in a few minutes she would have to pull herself together and slink home alone to her family. Of course her mother was on her side, and her brother Vangelis would never harm a hair on her head. But her missing father had three brothers who might do anything in the name of family honour. It was possible, although, she hastily assured herself, unlikely, that they would even butcher her like a Pascal sheep for shaming the family if they ever found out what she had done. She had heard that just last year, in one of the backward villages in the mountains between Tripolis and

Olympia, a brother had slit his sister's throat after she had been seen emerging from an olive grove with a young man's arm around her waist. In some parts of Greece, still, a family's reputation rested on the virtue of its women. Yet she supposed she shouldn't let her fears run away with her. Panagia was hardly a primitive mountain village which time and progress had forgotten. Never in living memory had a woman here been murdered in a crime of honour. Beaten and ostracized, yes, but never killed. Panagia was civilized. Even if her uncles found out, the worst she would end up with was bruised skin and a shattered reputation.

Marika paled in the dim light as she faced a far more dire possibility. She had heard that a woman was most fertile a fortnight after her period, especially when the moon also happened to be full, like last night. What if she was pregnant?

She let out a deep intake of breath, and with not dread but wonder she touched her belly. *His child*! For years she had been dreaming of giving him what everyone always said was the greatest gift a woman could bestow upon her man. Sometimes she had even stood in front of a mirror assessing the width of her hips and imagining how she would look when she was pregnant with Christos' baby. She did love him so. Over and over again as he had pounded inside her last night, he had hoarsely kept crying out that he loved her. His feelings for her had to be as all-consuming, as faithful, and as deep as hers were for him. Or did they? She frowned at the possibility that love for a man might mean something altogether different than it did for a woman. Then, in a joyous moment of breathless surety she assured herself that of course he would marry her if she were carrying his child.

But, a sadder second later, as she looked around the gloom of the cave where he had left her, she admitted that she was no longer altogether certain that even then he would forfeit his revolution and commit to her forever. She might even end up madly trekking from one remote military encampment to another in search of the man who had run out on her and, once she'd found him, begging him to do what was honourable. The image was so real she could almost see her footsteps in the snow of the mountaintops.

Marika gnawed her lower lip and promised herself that – come what may, pregnant or not – she would never be so pathetic as to beg for love and marriage from someone who didn't want her. But what, in the name of the Holy Virgin, would she do if she was pregnant and still Christos wouldn't rescue her with a wedding ring? If she was very lucky and no one except her mother and brother had noticed her being gone all night, she might get away with her assignation. In this village of too many eyes and mouths, often what mattered was not what you did but what others observed that you had done. She would most certainly not be the first girl seduced before her wedding night or the first to give birth six or seven months after the holy sacrament of marriage. But if circumstances kept Christos away, and her womb began swelling with her shame, her uncles might be capable of anything. The sudden realization of how vulnerable she was made her shiver.

She felt something brush against her bare upper arm and looked down in horror as a grotesquely large orange spider scuttled across her breast and encircled her nipple with its long twitching legs as though it expected to be suckled. The hairs on the back of her neck prickled, and she shrieked as she leapt to her feet and brushed the repulsive creature away. Oblivious to the cold and her nakedness, she shrank against the dank wall of the cave and burst into tears. It was no use reminding herself that the old wives said it was good luck when a spider walked on your flesh. She could still feel those hairy legs creeping toward her heart. Marika shuddered. What was she doing in this place that bred bats and bugs and betrayals? She felt not only dirty and powerless but also so very afraid of so many things that were beyond her control. She gave way to despair and wept like the abandoned child she had been for most of her life. 'Patera,' she cried out, 'Oh, father!' She had been only three when the man she didn't even remember had gone away and never come back. As she sobbed harder, she realized Christos would leave her too. First her father, and now her lover. She cried for the loss of the two most important men in any young woman's life.

After a while, she wiped her eyes with her fingers and reached down and threw her heavy shawl around her shoulders. She could do nothing about her father and maybe about Christos, too. But instead of wailing in this forlorn cave, she should be doing what she could to save her own skin. If she moved quickly, maybe she could get home while most of the village was still in bed. Today – *Kathara Deftera*, 'Clean Monday', the first day of Lent – was a holiday.

Yet still, as though something begun in this subterranean cavern was left unfinished, she could not help lingering.

Like a blind woman reading by touch instead of sight, she faintly traced her fingers against the glimmering wall of the Goddess's cave. If these old stones could speak, what stories would they tell? There was a message hidden in these rocks, yes, she could feel it in her womb. Her mother had told her this was a sacred place where the magic earthy power that women had once wielded still endured as more than a mythic memory. The mothers and the daughters had come here, long ago, to celebrate not their individual weaknesses but their collective strength. She wondered how many women, over the ages, had stood here like this, trying to marshal their resources to keep a hostile world at bay. Yet once, when everything was different, this grotto must have rung with triumphant laughter. Sharply she wished it had

36

been her fate to live in those brave women's times instead of now, in this man's world, when she herself had just watered these rocks with her despairing girl-child's tears. Yet perhaps, she thought, something of what had once been still remained, for she could feel budding in herself hope, and courage, and resolve. Inside she, too, would have to be as strong and hard as a rock. For she, like this women's cave, was made to endure.

Marika assured herself, as she began to look for her clothes passionately scattered where she and Christos had thrown them, that she was not without power and resources. She had manoeuvred herself into this situation, and now she was responsible for getting herself out.

Dressed, she felt cloaked in confidence. Of course Christos would return. She had been such a fool to doubt him a moment ago.

As she was just about to go down to the boat, however, she paused and looked wistfully around the cavern. Hard as she stared at the place where he had taken her that first frenzied time, she couldn't see any traces of her virgin's blood which must have seeped there. Blood and tears, she thought, are what remains of me in this cave. I came expecting ecstasy, yet I leave remembering pain. She had not thought this consummation of love would hurt so. But her mother had warned her that love could shackle more than liberate.

She touched the swell of her breasts and the stretch of her thighs, sore from the ardour of his embraces. Ever since she had opened her eyes this morning, she had been so overwhelmed by her fear and anger at Christos' abandonment that she hadn't let herself remember the passion they had shared on the belly of this cave. She had imagined making love would be like a tender poem punctuated with romantic sighs and bliss. And, yes, it had begun like that. But there had been sweat and panting, too, as wildly they had writhed. At the memory of how he had touched her, she could feel a throb between her legs. She wanted him here, now, again. For a moment it no longer mattered that he had left her when she most needed him. She wanted him back here in her arms and then inside her in an animal heat on the ground. Christos had marked her with his scent, not just for now but forever.

With a sigh, then, she tucked away her thoughts. On another day, on many other days, she would relive every moment she had spent awash here in passion. But now she marched unblinking into the uncertain light and sprang down the stony path toward the beach. 'Christo?' Without much hope, she called for him again and again.

Before she slid the rowboat into the water, she examined a single set of indentations on the wet sand which must have been made by Yorgos' boat. Other than that, however, apparently no other craft had been beached here

37

in the night. She had been worried that Christos might have hitched a ride back to the village with a passing fisherman. If word got round that she had spent the night on this island, it would never do to have another witness – other than Yorgos, tartly she reminded herself – that Christos had been out here as well.

Marika managed to shove the boat in the water, jumped aboard, and rowed with what she fancied was the strength of an Amazon away from the Goddess's cave. The moon was still up and shining more brightly on the dark water than the dawning sun. But it was cold, so cold. All around her in the misty light worn mounds of ancient mountains guarded the entrance to Panagia harbour. Rhythmically she rowed to the shore, bowing with her whole body toward the moon, stretching her straining arms toward the sun. As Christos had rowed to the island last night in a fever of impatience, the journey had seemed only the length of a burning kiss. But now her arms ached with the effort. Panagia Island was more than a mile from the coast. Even a strong swimmer like Christos must have had a hard time making for shore in the icy water. How eager he must have been, she thought sadly, to get away from me. As she approached the beach, she fastened the oars in their fittings and waded through the biting surf. She took bitter satisfaction in how frigid the water was. If it was her fate to suffer with this love, then it was only fair that Christos, too, had experienced his measure of pain.

'Kali mera, Marika!' Against the odds, one of her uncles' fisherman friends waved as he shouted good morning from where he sat on the shore patiently mending his nets.

'Kali mera, Vasili,' she responded, furiously adding to herself that there was nothing good about this particular stroke of chance this morning. She had hoped to sneak home without anyone seeing her, but of course she had been spotted even before she stepped foot on the beach. She wasn't surprised when Vasilis began gathering up his nets so he could come over and inquire what intriguing errand had found her on such a morning at sea before the sun rose. If she didn't act quickly, in a moment he would be upon her with a multitude of questions about where she had been, and why.

She hauled the boat through the shallows and hastily moored it safely ashore. Then she waved in finality to Vasilis and all but raced up the beach with the winter wind behind her like a blessing. As she hurried up the deserted path toward the centre of the village, she clutched her shawl close around her face. Everyone could identify everyone else at a glance, and so she stooped over in the hope that spied from a distance her silhouette might be mistaken for an old woman. To give herself at least the illusion of an alibi for being up and about so early, every time she saw a branch lying on the ground she picked it up as though she were gathering twigs for kindling

38

wood. Frantically she gathered the sticks and tried not to worry about the story Vasilis would spread about seeing her row in from the sea at dawn.

Now that she was out of the cave and approaching the village, the enormity of what had transpired with Christos was overshadowed by the possible consequences. Was fear, then, she asked herself, stronger than love? She prayed to the Virgin that no one would suspect where she had been and what she had done. If the truth came out, she might even have to leave this village that had been her womb of a world. But where could she go and what could she do without her family and her friends? She, like most everyone else in the provinces, had distant cousins in Athens. But once they, too, heard of her shame, they might shun her as well. She promised the Virgin that, if only she could creep home with no one else seeing her, she would go to the church in the *plateia* and light a tall brown taper every day until Christos came back. But she had been lighting hopeful candles, just so, for many months. On this morning after, perhaps a greater vow was required. She looked up in the sky and, distant in the silvery light, she glimpsed the white chapel to the Prophet Elijah crowning the highest mountain which towered between Panagia and Nauplion. If Christos came back and married her, she would go down on her knees and crawl up every stony metre of that mountain in thanksgiving. At that thought, an inspiration came to her. Now that Vasilis had witnessed her rowing ashore at dawn, there was no use denying she'd been at sea in the night. When she was questioned about this, she would say she had spent this holy vigil before the beginning of Lent praying in the Virgin Chapel on Panagia Island in fulfilment of a sacred vow. Come what may, she would stick to her story. So long as Yorgos didn't give her away and no one had spied Christos swimming ashore, she might even increase her reputation for piety.

As she approached the quiet square, some of her prayers were answered. At this dawning of austere Lent, no smoke fires curled in the grey sky. The Carnival bonfire had burned until the small hours of the morning, and so for once even the children were lying abed. Even the watchdogs sprawled dreaming in the dim stillness. As she passed the first house, she craned her neck to see if Christos was sitting with Andreas in the kitchen. But like most every dwelling, this one remained shuttered and locked. Swiftly, keeping her head down and her eyes on the ground, Marika crossed the *plateia*. The wooden cane-seated chairs inside the *kafeneions* where the old men sat were empty. None of the sleepless old widows paced the lanes, hungry for gossip and company. Even the church bells were silent. It must be half past six, and by now on any other winter morning, at least the women would already be about their dawn chores. Yet once she saw the flutter of a curtain at an unshuttered window, and another time she felt dark eyes following her. Of course her progress through the heart of the village had been noticed, and she would have to answer for it later.

But her moment of lying truth was to come earlier than that. As she headed up the final steep hill to her mother's house overlooking the village, she saw her brother framed in the open doorway to the lane. She shifted her load of firewood in her arms and prepared for the confrontation.

Before she was inside the gate, Vangelis fired the first of many questions. 'Where were you?'

'*Kali mera.*' She brushed past him into the courtyard and stacked the kindling by the door.

'I asked you, sister, where you've been all night.' Vangelis was only sixteen, and always before he had been her adoring little brother. But now he had been transformed into the outraged man of the family demanding an accounting from one of his women.

'Getting wood.' With an outward calmness, Marika slipped out of her muddy shoes and entered the house. An anxious glance round the single room where the three of them lived like Spartans reassured her that at least her uncles weren't lying in wait. Her eyes met her mother's. The old one raised her eyebrows, and Marika shrugged her shoulders in eloquent despair.

Vangelis was at her heels. 'You weren't gathering wood all night.' He gestured toward their mother hunched on a stool drawn up to the hearth which blazed with a fire that obviously had been burning for many hours. 'We were waiting for you, sister. All night we waited. And now all you say is that you were getting wood?'

Marika sank into the other stool drawn up to the fire and held her cold hands close to the flames. Still, as she began making coffee in the *briki* beaker, she remained silent even with this brother who was so dear to her heart.

'We were worried, *paidi mou.*' Old Anna reached out, and as she stroked her daughter's tangled hair back from her face, she shot her son a look that commanded him to stay out of this.

But Vangelis ran his hands through his thick black hair as he began pacing back and forth like a prosecuting attorney in a court of law. Instead of addressing his women, however, he raised his angry eyes to the icon of the Virgin that rested in its place of honour high up on the blessed eastern corner of the room. 'All night she's gone! The last I see her is at the bonfire! We sit up all night waiting for her! And then she comes in the next morning with a handful of twigs and not a word of explanation! What am I to do with such a sister!'

Marika poured him the first foaming coffee.

He glowered at the proffered cup but then sighed and pulled up the third stool between them. 'I have a right to know where you were, that's all.' His brown eyes were darkened with concern. 'It's not decent, a girl out all night. What will people say?' He sipped his coffee and waited. When still Marika didn't answer, his bravado altogether collapsed and once again he seemed only a boy.

Yet still, like all Greeks, he couldn't quell his curiosity. He took note of the wet hem of her dress, the dirty smears on her shawl, and most of all the furtive way his sister still refused to look him in the eye. He had watched her approach Christos last night and then observed the two of them slipping off into the darkness. He had assumed they would return after a stolen kiss or two, for everyone knew Marika and Captain Prometheus would marry once the war was over. But Vangelis had waited in vain by the bonfire, until finally he had given up and resumed his vigil here by the hearth. From time to time in the night, however, he had prowled outside to watch and listen in case his sister was in trouble. He reckoned it must have been well after four o'clock when he had spied that familiar figure with the rifle leading the *andartes* out of the village toward Nauplion. Closely he watched his sister's face as he tried cunning instead of bluster. 'One thing for sure, you couldn't have been with Christos all night. I saw him myself, leaving the village.'

Marika dropped her coffee cup on the stone hearth and let out a cry that gave herself away. 'No, oh no!' She looked down at the porcelain, broken in pieces like her dreams. So, just as she had feared, he had left her. Her stricken eyes met her brother's. 'Where did he go and when, exactly?'

'Suppose first you tell me where you went and what you did with him last night, exactly.'

Her eyes fell in shame. The game was surely up, at least with her brother. Her head sank in her hands, and she cried because now she would lose him, too. Even Vangelis could not support a sister who had fallen as she had.

But her brother put his arms around her and held her tight. 'Don't be afraid. Never be afraid of me. *Poteh*, Marika, never!'

She clung to him. The other two had left, but this brother had not failed her. 'Oh, Vangeli!' For a while she wept in his arms, remembering how close they had always been to one another, growing up fatherless and poor in this village which was often unkind even to its own. Yet she had always been the strong one who comforted her little brother and shielded him from life's blows. But around her now his manly arms made her feel so secure. Christos was gone, but she was not alone. So long as she had her brother, her mother, and *herself*, she would be all right.

Finally Marika drew away, wiped her eyes on the sleeve of her dress, and smiled tentatively at her brother.

'That's better.' He gave her shoulders a final squeeze and then tried to look stern. 'But no more secrets, eh? Not from me. Whatever happened,

41

we're in this together.' He inclined his head toward their mother. 'All three of us.'

Old Anna leaned forward, unable to contain her impatience any longer. 'So tell us what happened.'

Over another bittersweet little cup of *kafe*, haltingly Marika told her tale of seduction and abandonment, leaving out only the erotic details, the womanly significance of the cave, and Yorgos' interruption. She concluded with the fisherman witnessing her return and her brainstorm that she would claim she spent the night on Panagia Island in fulfilment of a holy vow to the Virgin.

When she had finished, Vangelis shook his head. He supposed he should be incensed at his sister's breaking of the oldest taboo, but his loyalty to her was stronger than what others thought was right or wrong. 'And so he left? But everyone knew the *andartes* were going back before dawn.' He himself had always been one of Captain Prometheus' great admirers, and – young as he was – he would have joined the guerrillas in the mountains if he hadn't been needed here to support his mother and sister. Loyalty to that cause and the leftist leader he fancied as his brother-in-law made him wonder if his sister wasn't jumping to the wrong conclusions. 'There's no reason to believe he won't be back. He's always coming and going.'

Marika's ember eyes blazed. 'You think so?'

'Of course!' Vangelis warmed not only to the idea of Christos coming to the rescue but also to the flattering way his big sister was hanging onto his every word. 'Christos had to go. He had a duty to his men.'

'And to Marika.' Old Anna was not about to mince words or pump up her daughter with false hopes. 'But after all that happened, off he went without even a goodbye.' She gave her son a withering look. 'Try, my little boy, to look at this realistically, as a woman would.' She handed Vangelis a coin. 'Now, be a good lad and run down to the bakery for the *lagana*.' This flattish unleavened bread, sprinkled with sesame seeds, was traditionally eaten only on this one day of the year. 'With all that's happened, no wonder we've forgotten it's Clean Monday.' She wagged her finger at her son. 'And if anyone starts asking questions about your sister's whereabouts last night, you tell them she was praying for a husband on Panagia Island. But say nothing else. Not one word! Maybe we can nip the gossip in the bud.'

So charged, Vangelis meekly put on his coat to do his mother's bidding. But before he left, he indulged himself in another Greek manly practice and had what he considered the last word on the subject. 'He'll be back, Marika. Captain Prometheus never lets anyone down.'

When her son left, Old Anna's eyes slid around the bare dark room of the whitewashed stone hut where she had endured so many monotonous years.

42

Day after weary day, in the infernal heat of summer and the bone-chilling damp of winter, she had bent over that iron cauldron bubbling with the thick soup that would be their dinner. But now that Marika and Vangelis were old enough to work beside her in the Kronos taverna, at least there was always something to simmer in the pot. She remembered crying herself to sleep when they were just hungry babies, and there had never been enough to eat. Even before her husband had abandoned them, he had always preferred sitting with the men in the square talking about work rather than providing for the family he had fathered. Old Anna glared at the conjugal bed in the corner. Atop that lumpy mattress, she had conceived in loathing and given birth in agony to her four children. Two of the poor things already lay dead in the village cemetery that looked out on the sea. It was for those lost wee ones that she had put on her mourning black two decades ago. In the long bereavement that was her life, she would never wear anything else.

'*Lipon*.' The old woman smoothed down the skirt of her mourning dress. Please, dear God, it would be different for Marika! 'So . . .'

Again Marika felt the welling tears. 'How could he have left me, mama? I was so sure he wouldn't.' She broke down and sobbed.

Old Anna took Marika in her arms and held her as she cried. 'Just like a man,' she muttered. 'Just like his father. And yours.' The bitter lines of her face deepened as they always did when anything made her remember her husband's desertion. She sighed as she stroked her daughter's hair. She suspected more had gone wrong last night than Marika had said so far, but she judged it would be a while before the girl could pull herself together and talk sense. In the meantime it couldn't hurt to tell her a few secrets of the family she still hoped would be her in-laws.

When Marika's sobs finally subsided, Old Anna stirred the embers of the fire with a poker. 'Perhaps Christos couldn't help it, *paidi mou*. His father was like that, too.'

'His father?' Marika wiped her eyes. Always before Old Anna had remained curiously silent about Christos' father. Why was she resurrecting that old ghost now?

'There's bad blood in that family.'

Marika met her mother's eyes. What was she trying to warn her about Christos? She could tell by the way her mother had planted her feet on the earthen floor that she was about to find out.

'Nikolas Kronos was another one who was always too good for the village. No one and nothing in Panagia was ever enough for that one, either.' Old Anna shook her head as she said she hadn't been surprised when he left poor Eleni and went off to America to make his fortune. 'That's how the men always are, off and away, while the women wait. Sometimes we wait forever. Forever, Marika, and for nothing. *Tipoteh*, nothing.'

Watching her mother stare off into space as obviously she brooded about her own husband who had sailed to Australia more than fifteen years ago and hadn't been heard from since, Marika thought that would be her mother's final words on the Kronos *pater familias*.

But Old Anna continued. 'At least he came back. I'll say that for him, at least Eleni's Nikolas came back. Not so often maybe. Not so much as Eleni would have liked. But *ti na kanoume*, what can we do, what can any woman do, with men the way they are? At least Nikolas came back for a visit every five or ten years and sent her and the boys money enough to make them the richest in Panagia.'

At the mention of her lifelong friend Eleni's good fortune in which she had shared in these last years of war and famine, Marika's mother shook off her melancholy and warmed to the very nearly sacred task of recounting a bit of village historical gossip. Old Anna loved to tell a good story. 'Oh, but Nikolas Kronos wasn't all bad. In the beginning he was *leventis*, a fine man – always he walked tall, so generous he was, and so full of the big ideas.' She could still recall how everyone had taken to him when she was a girl, back in the twenties, when he had come to the house of his long-lost cousins as a penniless refugee from a village near Constantinople, after Greece had lost another round in their wars with the Turks and more than a million Greeks had been forced to leave their ancient Asia Minor communities. Contrary to the usual practice in the village, where anyone whose grandfather hadn't been born and bred there would never be anything other than *xenos*, foreign, Panagia had welcomed Nikolas as one of their own.

'We all loved him,' Old Anna confided, and as she talked of her friend's husband, for a moment her face lost its accustomed folds and weary lines and Marika could see that once her crone of a mother had been as she herself was now, fresh and fiery and unscarred. But it was as hard to imagine that her mother had ever been young as it was to accept that she herself would ever be old. No, Marika told herself, I'm wrong, my mother never could have been a little in love with Christos' father.

Yet it seemed Old Anna's face burned with evergreen jealousy as she recounted how Nikolas Kronos – who could have had any of us, *any*! – had courted and won the reigning village beauty, 'that Sofia', in what some had apparently come to regard as the tragically doomed love story of the decade. 'Neither of them had a drachma,' Marika's mother said. 'He got by doing odd jobs and she didn't have any dowry to speak of. I don't have to tell *you*, of all people, *paidi mou*, what that meant for Sofia's marriage prospects. Things were the same then as they are now. A man might say he wants a pretty face and a ripe figure, but he'll jump at the chance of marrying a plain girl if she has orange groves and a fine stone house. You don't marry for love, you marry for the family. Still, Sofia would have found *someone*. As I said, as everyone had always said since she was a very little girl, Sofia was very beautiful. And even though the likes of *me* never knew her so well – always had her pretty nose up in the air – no one had ever been able to say anything bad about her character. Although they wondered. She was too beautiful, Sofia. There was talk for a while of that old fool doctor from Nauplion – you wouldn't remember him, you're too young – asking Sofia's father for her hand. But instead, out of the blue, one fine day there were Nikolas and Sofia walking hand-in-hand in the square to announce their engagement to the world.'

At that recollection, Marika's mother looked as grim as though she were describing the sudden death of a loved one. 'How Eleni cried that afternoon! She had been so sure Nikolas would marry *her*. She had that land down on the beach by the harbour, where her house and the taverna stand now. Not to mention ten *stremmata* of olive groves on the other side of the mountain. But that match was not to be, at least not then. Poor Eleni, so many tears for so many years over Nikolas. And she's still crying . . .'

'Men!' Old Anna shook her head again and then went back to her artful storytelling. 'So they got married, Nikolas and Sofia, and for a while they seemed as moonstruck happy as stars in a movie, not like a real husband and wife at all. But there were some who said – and I was one of them – that something like that couldn't last. Life – real life, not movie pictures – isn't about love. It's about making a living and keeping the family strong and together for another generation.' Sagely she nodded. 'Sofia was dead within a year. Died giving birth to Christos. And *that* was the end of *that* love story.'

Old Anna folded her hands on her lap and smiled meaningfully at her romantic daughter who seemed bent on making the same headstrong mistakes as Sofia. 'Still, it was sad for her to die so young. And Nikolas was heartbroken. Everyone felt so sorry for him. At her funeral an overflow crowd – just like at the Easter Eve service – poured out into the *plateia* outside the church. It was a wonderful funeral. No one could figure out how Nikolas paid for it.'

Remembering what had come next, Marika's mother broke out in a smile. 'He married Eleni three months later. It wasn't a love match like with Sofia. But he needed a mother for his newborn son, and everyone hoped this new marriage would be longer-lived and as happy as Nikolas' first one had been.'

Old Anna shrugged. 'You know the rest.' Eleni had been a pale spectre of her technicolour cousin, and two years later, shortly after the birth of the son they called Yorgos, Nikolas had sold Eleni's olive groves and used the money to run off to America to seek his fortune. 'Maybe Christos is just like his father. He has those same strange green eyes as Nikolas, that same ambition, too, and the wanderlust. Don't stake everything on a man you can't count on, *paidi mou*. Don't make the same mistake Eleni and I did.'

Marika stared into the dying hearthfire. Just because her father had left and Nikolas had left, it didn't follow that Christos' leaving this morning meant that she had lost him forever. He loved her. She was sure of it. Last night, on the belly of that cave –

But Old Anna cut into her reverie. 'Now suppose you tell me what you didn't dare tell your brother.'

Her mother's intuition no longer surprised her. Marika blurted out the truth. 'Yorgos was there. In the cave. You know, when I was with Christos.'

The old one made a clucking sound with her tongue. 'I warned you. I told you. How could you let that happen?'

Helplessly Marika shrugged. 'I suppose he followed us. You know how he's always sniffing around me.' Hesitantly she confided the rest. 'He cursed me, mama. He damned me forever.' She shivered. 'I can still see him standing there like the devil himself.'

Old Anna raised three fingers of her right hand to her forehead, then to her chest, her right breast, her left breast, and finally rested them open on her chest. 'God help you, *paidi mou*. God help all of us.'

'I was afraid, mama. I'm still afraid.'

'It was very bad luck that Yorgos was there. He saw . . . everything?'

'It was dark in the cave. But I think, yes, he saw.'

Heavily the old woman sighed. 'He's nasty, that one. As I said, there's bad blood there. Even if he keeps his mouth shut about what he saw, still he can make trouble for us. For you especially.'

Marika defiantly tossed her head. 'I can handle Yorgos.'

'Careful, daughter.' Old Anna brought her index finger to her lips and looked around as though suddenly afraid. 'Do not tempt the fates any more than you already have.'

Marika wet her dry lips with her tongue. 'You mean what you said yesterday, about the cave and being linked for – '

'Hush now! No more of this!' Now Old Anna did look afraid, as again she crossed herself. 'I wish I had never spoken to you of those things.' Her tone was sharp. 'Forget all of it.'

'I will never forget.' Fiercely Marika gripped her mother's hands.

'You must. I never should have said such things to you. I should have told you to be a good girl, to pray in the church, and to wait until Christos came here and asked us to let him marry you.' Penitentially, she beat her breast. 'I am to blame for this.'

'No, no!' Marika's voice fell to a whisper. 'You were right about the cave. I could feel something wonderful in there.' She flushed. 'Not just last night, with *him*. But this morning, when I was alone. The cave gave me strength, mama.'

'Enough, I said! If you were strong this morning, that came from inside you. Not from some old rocks.'

'That's not what you said yesterday.'

'Yet again I tell you, for your own good, forget the foolish words of an old woman who talks too much.'

'Look me in the eye then, mama, and tell me that everything you said yesterday was a lie.'

The old one's eyes met the young one's, and the mother's wrinkled face cracked into a reluctant smile. 'I have never lied to you. But I hoped . . . prayed . . . that what I told you about the cave would help you. Not hurt you, as I fear it will.' And yet a ghost of a smile remained on her lips. 'Still, maybe it will turn out right in the end. Perhaps what my mother told me is true, and the women's power in the Cave of the Great Goddess is stronger than any man's curse. Especially from the likes of Yorgos.'

'You think so, truly?'

'I hope so!' Now Old Anna was broadly smiling. 'Just as I hope everyone accepts that story of yours about praying all night in the Panagia chapel.' Admiringly she slapped her thigh. 'I wish I'd thought of that myself. I can't wait to tell everyone all about it. I'll start with Eleni this afternoon down at the taverna.' For a moment she was silent as she prepared to embroider the fabric of lies Marika had woven. 'I'll say it was my idea for you to make that vow to keep vigil on the island. Then I'll say we couldn't think of any other way to get you a husband. That we were desperate, with you nineteen years old and still a spinster with no dowry except a couple of sheets and blankets. I'll go on a bit like I always do about how none of this would have been necessary if that husband of mine had done right by us. By the time I'm done, everyone will be calling you Saint Marika.'

'Don't overdo it, mama. I'm not *so* old. And I'm certainly not a saint.'

Old Anna laughed. But Marika's next words sobered her.

'There's something else. I should have maybe asked you about this before.' The girl touched her belly. 'What if I . . . you know . . . in the early winter, when nine months have passed . . . ?'

Again the old woman crossed herself. 'I pray it is not so. That would be a *katastrofe*!' Her eyes were hooded and she took her daughter firmly by the shoulders. 'We must not take any chances. If you were married and didn't want . . . *that* . . . we could go to the doctor and be done with it. But if we did that now, someone might find out. Here in Panagia, if you tell even one soul outside the family, someone always finds out. So we must take care of this ourselves, the old way. Come with me now to the mountain. There are certain plants that grow in a dark place in the high pastures behind the big rocks. I will use them to make you some special tea. And I promise, when you drink it, it will make you only a little bit sick, now, if you take it at the beginning. I know just where it is. I have to gather it up often enough.'

Marika wetted her lips. She had heard whispers about her mother's special tea, but she had never spoken of it to her before. 'You've done this for others in the village?'

'Of course. The men are all goats.' Old Anna spat contemptuously in the air. 'A woman can't have a bellyful all the time. Who could feed them?' Her voice was bitter. '*Pame*? So we go now to the mountain, eh?'

'No, not *that*.' Marika's jaw squared off as it always had, even when she was little, and intent on having her own way. 'If I am pregnant . . .' Dreamily she stroked her flat belly. 'Christos' baby.' She tossed her hair. 'Whatever will be, will be.'

Old Anna shut her eyes and shook her head. She would have thought the girl had had enough of her misplaced romanticism last night. Yet she decided to tread lightly on this just now. There would still be enough time to gather her deadly herbs later.

Restlessly Marika got to her feet. 'Enough of all this.' She eyed the dust coated on her dress and the mud splattered on her legs. 'Look at me, and on Clean Monday!' By now, all over the village, the women would be scrubbing the pots, beating the rugs, and even whitewashing the walls as part of the purification mandated by the beginning of Lent. 'I must wash myself. I feel so dirty this morning. So dirty . . .' Despite her intention not to give in to despair, her voice broke. With an effort she steadied it. 'And then, when I am clean, I will go to the church before vespers and light all the candles, so it is beautiful inside. Like Easter Eve.'

'But it is not yet Easter, my dear. First we have to get through the forty days of Lent. No meat, eggs, cheese or milk.'

'And maybe no Christos.' Marika sank back down on her stool and looked into the fire. Yet once again her optimism came to the fore. 'But don't forget, after Lent comes Easter.'

'You are so very young, my daughter. And I think you do not yet understand that everything does not always turn out as you want it to.'

'You forget. This morning I awoke alone in the cave.'

'I didn't forget.' Old Anna leaned closer. 'And Christos . . . what do you think about Christos?'

48

'You tell me.' Marika's eyes looked as old and knowing as her mother's.

'I wasn't in the cave,' tartly she reminded her. 'But it seems to me, from the way you're acting, that you think you've . . . lost him.'

Marika flinched. She dreaded even thinking, much less talking, about the heart of this matter. She wrung her hands together. 'At first it was wonderful. *Everything* was right. But then, when Yorgos appeared, it all changed.' Remembering that second time they had made love, after the curse, Marika crossed herself. 'Then, this morning, when I woke up and he wasn't there, I had the most awful feeling that he was gone for good.'

'You felt that, there in the cave?' Of course the girl's intuition would be sharpened inside that womb of womanly mysteries, but Old Anna kept that depressing bit of lore to herself.

'I did. And I still do.'

'Daughter, daughter, I feared this.' She now thought the situation desperate enough that she had to sugarcoat reality. '*Then pirazi*, never mind. Maybe he will come back, after all. You heard Vangelis. "Captain Prometheus never lets anyone down." Christos is a good boy, and he loves you, I think.'

But Marika had learned a few hard truths. 'He loves me, yes. But he loves his country, too. If he had to choose between me and her, now, I'm not so sure I'd be the winner.'

'Aiee, what can you expect? He is a man. You know how they are.'

'If I were a man, I wouldn't act like that.'

For once, the old one's wisdom outweighed her bitterness. 'If our situations were reversed, maybe we would be no better than they.' The mother reached out and stroked the daughter's hair. 'But I do know this, my child. We can never change them. They are one way, and we are another. It was always like this between the men and the women. And I suspect it will always be.'

'But I don't like it.'

'Women don't.' Again the old woman hopelessly shrugged. '*Ti na kanoume*? But what can we do?'

'Anything! Everything!' For an instant the life leaped back into Marika's eyes, but then that spark died. 'We can pray, anyway.'

'Ah, yes, they can't stop us doing that.' She jumped at the opportunity to ask Marika about what was worrying her the most. 'But tell me one thing more. At the church, when you pray, will it be that you have already started a baby inside? Or not?'

Marika shrugged and her eyes flew up to the icon of the Virgin on the wall. 'Mostly I'll just pray that Christos comes back to me.'

'So be it. I, too, will pray for this.'

'The Panagia and the saints will be sick of us, I think.' Marika managed to laugh. 'They will look down and say, what is this, those two in that village never shut their mouths, asking, always asking. Do they never sleep? We must give them what they want so they will leave us alone.'

'Always the laughter, *paidi mou*. Even now.'

'*Especially* now.'

By the time Vangelis burst into the house with the news that the village was abuzz with the story he had spread about Marika's vigil on the island, the women were down on their hands and knees – not praying, as he first thought – but scrubbing the floor as though their lives depended on it.

Hours later, at dusk, Marika was sedately clad in a clean wool dress and wrapped snugly in a heavy winter cloak as she set out for the church, calling out '*Kali Sarakosti*', 'Happy Lent' to everyone she passed. Serenely she kissed babies, patted the rosy cheeks of little girls, and clucked sympathetically when this old woman complained about backaches and that one fretted that she would never be able to amass a large enough dowry to marry off her skinny daughter. No one, she noted with relief, asked where she had been the night before. Either they hadn't heard the latest gossip, or they believed Vangelis' explanation and pitied her for having to pray all night for a husband. When from afar she saw the priest in his long black robe, however, she ducked her head and avoided his eyes. For the first time since she had lured Christos to the cave, she was ashamed of what she had done there with him. If the *pappas* knew, would he welcome her inside the church? If all the women she had greeted on her progress through the village knew, would they shun her as a dirty girl?

Vespers wouldn't begin for a while, and the empty church was dark but for a few flickering candles. Yet even in the wavering light, this place of worship sparkled as all Greek Orthodox churches do. The candlelight reflected on the highly polished brass oil lamps and the silver-coated icons. On the altar a gold cross gleamed, and tiny metal votive offerings – a crudely hammered ship, a replica of a woman's arm, a dented heart – shimmered hopefully near the holy pictures.

Marika crossed herself three times, picked up a handful of tall brown tapers, and carried them to her favourite dolorous icon of the Virgin. Reverently she kissed the hem of the Panagia's jewel-studded robe. Even when she had been a very little girl, she had loved to come to this church, kneel in the incense-laden shadows, and visit with this beautiful Lady who always looked so sad. Sometimes, as she had gazed into those suffering almond eyes, her own eyes had filled with empathetic tears. But until now she had not understood why the Virgin made her weep. 'So much pain,' Marika whispered. 'Always the women have so much pain.' She gazed into those tender eyes. 'You understand, don't you?' She set her candles in the burnished bronze holders, and her hand trembled as she lit them. Woman-to-woman, then, in the fiery light she poured out her hopes and her fears. Please make him come back to me. Please let him marry me. Please let us be happy together forever. Her eyes fell on the face of the Baby in the arms of the Mother. While she was at it, should she ask for one like this? Or was it better that only hope lived in her womb? Back there in the house, she had kept one thing back from her mother. She knew she was pregnant. She knew it as surely as she loved Christos.

Finally, as her candles burned low and she could hear the other women coming in for the service, she came to a conclusion. Considering the war and Christos' commitment to the guerrillas, perhaps last night she had gambled too rashly on love. If he came back to her and did what was honourable, she would be supremely happy as his wife. But her patience was wearing thin. The baby inside her couldn't wait forever. She would give Christos until Easter, and no longer. Surely by then he would be back. They would stand together before this very altar and become man and wife.

She felt better after she settled on the deadline, even though she had no one to deliver it to but herself. She looked up into the sad, knowing eyes of the Virgin.

Forty days, and no more.

Three

Long past sundown the men in black with the scarlet Greek crosses cunningly embroidered on the hidden collars of their shirts sat waiting in the *kafeneion* in Nauplion's venerable Venetian square, drinking raki not so much for warmth as for courage for what was to come later tonight, when they did what had to be done.

It was a balmy early March night in this picturesque port sheltered from the turbulent sea, and yet these men with the surreptitious crosses wore their heaviest sweaters and thickest boots. Their chairs were strewn with hats and scarves and even – strangely – shaggy sheepskin blankets. For tonight their secret mission would take them up to where the snow still lay deep on the rocks. Concealed under their clothes were the cold metal of pistols, knives and even primitive axes.

At nearby green felt-covered tables old men hunched over their inevitable cards and idly wondered why these dozen or so lads – strangers, most of them, from villages all over the Argolid – had come so far and dressed so warmly. They shuffled and dealt and threw their drachmas into the pot, all the while eavesdropping on the mysterious foreigners.

Yorgos reached for the raki, spilled a measure in the glasses of each of his mates sitting in a sprawl of pushed-together tables, and as one they lifted the drinks in a toast.

'*Sti zoi*,' they chorused as they clinked glasses. 'To life.'

'*Ke sto thanato*.' As he whispered, Yorgos looked his conspirators, one by one, in their eyes. 'And to death.'

They tilted back their heads and drank in great thirsty gulps to fortify themselves on this night of blood and vengeance.

As the others went back to their eternal gossip and laughter, Yorgos rolled a cigarette and savoured the certainty that tonight he would finally even all the old scores against his half-brother. His loaded rifle waited outside in the wagon, and his dagger lay in the leather sheath attached to his belt. He had gone to the meat market this afternoon to sharpen it. When he hunted down his brother like the animal he was, he would be ready to strike the final blow.

He blew fierce smoke rings in the air and contemplated how exactly he would make his brother's black heart stop beating. The gun would be sure and quick, but maybe too merciful for one such as Christos. The knife was better. He could take his time with the dagger. He might make his brother squirm and beg for mercy, before finally he would stab him in the heart. Christos would die in his arms. Brother to brother, they would be united in death as they had seldom been in life. Yes, the knife would make for a more intimate death.

Yorgos' hand stole under his sweater to caress the hilt of the antique dagger his father had given him on his last visit before the World War made travel from America impossible. Nikolas had arrived, as usual, with a suitcase of gifts. For Eleni, incongruously enough, there had been great sweeping lengths of turquoise silk, wobbly high-heeled shoes, a nightdress of fine Sea Isle cotton, a pair of delicate gold earrings. Most wondrous of all, however, had been a gleaming black machine that sewed the most perfect stitches when she sat up next to it and tapped it with her foot, like she was dancing.

Even now, on the night he meant to kill his brother, Yorgos could not help smiling as he remembered how he and Christos had insisted on sitting down at the machine, working the treadle, and sewing a seam as if they were women. How they had laughed, together, that night.

52

Yorgos contemptuously threw his cigarette on the worn cement *kafeneion* floor and ground it to ash with his polished boot. This was neither the time nor the place for foolish sentiment.

Methodically he shook another clot of tobacco onto his yellowy papers, rolled it neatly into a cigarette, and bonded it together with a practised lick just as his father – clinging to the ritual of his Anatolian youth – had always done. More misplaced sentiment, Yorgos thought; will I never be free of my family?

He clamped the cigarette between his lips and let one of his flunkies light it. He wouldn't have minded if his men had licked his boots. He did the same, after all, to those ranked above him. A little dust on the tongue whetted the thirst for the nectar of power. Finally, just last night he had been made a lieutenant in the Greek Cross, a local secret society that was part of a national grassroots movement of rightwing zealots dedicated to exterminating the Communists. After living for so many years under the shadow of Christos' glories in the *andartes*, Yorgos was intoxicated by the perquisites of command. He had thought, when he joined the police gendarmerie, that at last he would be able to match his brother's swashbuckling expoits. But instead he had been posted to a remote village in the southern Peloponnese where he shuffled papers, swatted flies, and gnashed his teeth reading his mother's letters about the latest adventures of Captain Prometheus.

Again his hand stole down to his dagger. That night when his father had presented Christos and him with their packages wrapped in shiny paper and pretty red ribbons, he had been the first to tear his eagerly open. He had gasped at the sight of the old Ottoman knife with its engraved silver hilt, its glittering inlaid blood-red rubies, and its fine Damascene steel blade.

'Take care of it, my son. It was your great-grandfather's. It was one of the only things I managed to bring from my village when we had to flee. But you must promise me that you will use it only for good. *Katalaves*? You understand?'

'*Katalava*. And I will, *patera*.' For the space of that one precious instant, Yorgos had felt certain that his father truly did love him.

But a moment later, when his brother began to open his package, Yorgos' sweet triumph had soured.

'What is inside, Christo,' his father had said, 'belonged to your grandfather. He used it to fight for a free Greece against our oppressors the Turks. My mother told me he had it in his hand when they found his body on the battlefield. He was a hero, my father. And I think that you not only carry his name, but that you are very like him.'

Then Christos had pulled out an even bigger and more splendid dagger than the one that had been given to Yorgos. Its hilt had shone with not only

53

silver but gold. It had been studded with sparkling gems as blue as the sea and as green as the earth in spring. And its glistening blade had caught the light and flamed as though still it dripped with Turkish blood. Of course Yorgos had once again felt cheated. His father had reserved the biggest, the best, and the most sentimental of the knives for the son of his heart.

Tonight maybe I will cut out that heart with my second-best dagger.

Yorgos inhaled, exhaled, and inhaled again until his breathing once again slowed to a regular rhythm. He was certain no one at the headquarters of his militia in Argos understood why he had volunteered to lead the death squad to the mountains to exterminate Christos' band of guerrillas. Now, thanks both to a massive influx of American aid and a new mood of Soviet indifference to their Greek comrades, the tide had turned against the Communists. While the national army was fighting the leftists in the mountains near the borders of Albania and Yugoslavia, Yorgos' rightwing Greek Cross militia had taken it upon itself to mop up the last pockets of leftist opposition in their corner of the country. Here in the eastern Peloponnese, his superiors took it as a personal affront that a leftist commando unit was still operating in their mountains. Yet when Yorgos had pleaded to lead tonight's mission, at first his commanding officers had demurred. Considering the circumstances and the family ties, they had said with some delicacy, perhaps this particular mission should be undertaken by one of the other more seasoned volunteers. But Yorgos had fervently insisted that the honour of the cause meant more to him than a mere accident of birth. He would sacrifice everything – even his brother, he had vowed, with his hand on his heart – to free beloved Greece from the threat of the godless Communists. When he had finished his emotional speech, he had been surprised to see his officers looking at him with a mixture of awe and something akin to contempt.

Crossing the far end of the *plateia* he glimpsed a slim, full-breasted woman in a familiar mantle of deep blue wool. At once he forgot war and politics.

He polished his glasses and craned his neck to be sure it was *her* in that homespun blue cloak. Ever since that cursed night in the cave a fortnight ago, he had imagined he saw her everywhere: striding along the cold silver beach in Panagia, emerging from the scented darkness of the church here in Nauplion, huddled round the warmth of the village bakery oven where the women gathered for their morning gossip. This time, exactly as on all those other wistful occasions, when the woman turned her head he saw that she was not the one he looked for everywhere. Since that night in the cave, he had not spied Marika once, for even a moment.

Though his eyes were apparently focused on the crumbling dome of the faded old Turkish mosque that had been converted into a cinema on the far side of the square, his mind's eye was seeing something else: *her* in *his* arms, her legs splayed open, his one hand stroking her breasts and the fingers of his other hand buried inside her. Longingly Yorgos remembered that hand lost in love. What must it be like to be inside her like that, and – even more! far more! – to plunge inside and have her beg for more. Seeing her for that one voyeuristic moment, he had been certain that what he had always believed was true. Marika was *poli thermi*, very hot, and she burned a man like fire. In Christos' arms her skin had looked so white and soft. Her breasts had swelled so full and rosy, like the buds of spring flowers. Her legs had coiled like serpents around his brother's thighs. Her tangle of satiny blueblack hair had been mingled with the short coarse hair on Christos' chest. Even to Yorgos' jealous eyes, the two of them had looked like a sculptor's vision of love in the flesh.

Again he ground his cigarette with his heel, rolled another, and let one of his underlings leap to light it as, for the thousandth time since he had surprised them in that cave, he asked himself how she could have done that with his brother. He had believed her a good girl. He had wanted to make her his wife. And yet there she had lain, shameless as a prostitute. Marika was beautiful, but nevertheless she was a dirty woman. He wished he could make a clean sweep and kill her tonight, too. First he wanted to rape her and then he wanted to break every bone in her throbbing body.

Yorgos looked at his watch and nodded to his men. Another time he would settle the score with Marika, but tonight belonged to her partner in the cave. '*Ela*, come. It is time. The others will be at Argos.' He stood to settle the bill from his own pocket and turned on his heel to stride out to his destiny.

The horse-drawn wagon was waiting down at the empty port, for the wars had paralysed local shipping. In more peaceful times, freighters had lined up here for succulent Peloponnese citrus; now the oranges lay rotting in the groves.

'You first, sir!' The guard they had left at the wagon leaped to help him up to the seat beside the driver, but Yorgos swung up unassisted. As the rest of them piled into the back where the guns lay covered with blankets, Yorgos wished they were in grand command cars rather than this rickety agricultural wagon which, because of the petrol shortage and limited militia funds, was the only mode of transportation they had been able to commandeer. Yesterday in Argos he had enviously watched his rakish major climb into the sidecar of a glamorous BMW motorcycle the officer had bought at cut rate or maybe stolen from a Nazi in the last days of the German Occupation. If he could have whooshed back to the village on one like it, Marika surely

55

would have admired the dashing figure he would have cut and the village urchins would have run beside him as though he were a conquering hero.

'*Deh*!' Thanos whipped the tired ploughing horses, and they were off in the moonless night to seek their prey.

With the black sea pounding at the shore, they rumbled along the muddy road past the coastal orange groves toward the snow-topped mountain that loomed before Tripolis. Then they turned inland in the direction of Mykenae and the haunted ruins of the citadel where the cursed House of Atreus once enacted an orgy of familial bloodlust: father killing daughter, mother killing father, son killing mother. They snaked through the lanes of shabby Argos under the brooding remains of the abandoned Venetian fortress atop the hill. Here, there and everywhere were reminders of not only ancient but modern strife. Near the archaeological excavations of an old temple and theatre, houses lay in a similar rubble of stones and raw earth. On one street pock-marked walls testified to a recent *andartes* raid, and on another fire-gutted shops attested to the swift rightwing reprisal.

At the first fork out of town, another wagon of militiamen who had driven south from Korinthos were waiting.

'Pull over.' Yorgos jumped out, and gravely listened to the Argos recruits relay the latest intelligence reports the regular Greek army had turned over to the militia. Christos and his band were believed to be still camped up there in the heights between Argos and Tripolis.

Yorgos punched the fist of his right hand into the open palm of his left. 'Then we've got them!' He had been afraid the rats would get away before the trap snapped shut, for there had been rumours that Christos' band was about to break camp and make for the Albanian border. '*Pame*, men, let's go.'

But before they were off and away, Yorgos showed that flair for the dramatic that was so to distinguish his later career. He reached under the neck of his sweater, pulled out his shirt collar, and struck a match and held it up to the scarlet cross his mother had embroidered there. 'For God and for Greece!' Yorgos shouted as he raised his fist to the heavens.

His men uncovered their own crosses. 'For God and for Greece!'

And for Christos, Yorgos silently added as his two dozen militiamen crowded back in their carts to begin the long shaky ascent up Mount Varson. An Argos man who knew the perilously rutted road climbed up beside the driver, and Yorgos joined his men on the rough plank seats in the back.

Thanos whipped the horses up the serpentine way as the path doubled round and round upon itself to tame the steep grade. The winter rains had washed away what barely passed for a road in the dusty dryness of summer, and in the back the men held on for dear life as the cart joggled and jounced up and up. The guns under their feet banged on the sides of the wagon, *rat-tat, rat-tat*, like machine-gun fire. The carts shuddered unsteadily as the horses picked their way along the edge of the precipice.

Halfway to the summit they had slowed to a crawl when behind them the second cart bogged down in the mud.

'Everyone out,' Yorgos ordered. 'We'll have to push.' He stood on a dry rock and barked orders while his militiamen struggled knee-deep in the muck to heave the wheels free. When finally they succeeded, they all lit cigarettes and gazed down at the panorama of the Bay of Argos spread before them. In defiance of the wartime blackout, they could see the winking lights of Argos, Nauplion, and even tiny Panagia glowing like a single candle.

Before they climbed back aboard, everyone bundled up. Here in the high country, the temperature was fifteen degrees colder than down on the plain and lashed by the winds as well.

They were inching along again when Panayiotis, a seventeen-year-old farmer's son, nervously cleared his throat. 'How many Communist bandits do you think are up there?'

'What does it matter?' A grizzled shepherd laughed. 'Five, ten, a hundred.'

Thanos, a butcher by trade, loosened his hold on the reins and brandished the carving knife he had brought from the market. 'We will kill them all.'

For a while, as the cart jostled along, the men smoked their cigarettes as best they could in the jarring silence.

'I have never killed anyone,' Panayiotis finally confessed. 'Only birds with my rifle.'

His comrades silently fixed their gaze upon him as they were flung first one way and then another in the back of the cart. Thanos, who had fought against the Germans and then served time with the government forces fighting the leftists in the mountains near Yugoslavia, was the only one who had seen combat so far. The others had a variety of reasons for having avoided serving not only against the Germans but in this campaign against the leftists as well. Some had been too young for the World War. Others had been excused from the fighting to plant and harvest the crops needed to keep the armies on the march. And all had been more than a little afraid of dying in combat. It was one thing to join a death squad that meant to murder the sleeping enemy. It was quite another for a man to take his chances in the front lines where any stray bullet might maim or kill. But even though all but the driver was a virgin in this bloodsport, none was about to make that admission to this boy.

Just as doggedly as the straining horses, however, Panayiotis continued his line of questioning. 'Tell me, please. How does it feel, to kill?'

'*Orea*,' Yorgos answered. 'It feels good.' He filled the silence by lighting another cigarette, all the while hoping that one of the others would elaborate on what to him, too, remained one of the mysteries of violence. But when no one helped him out, and he still felt those expectant eyes upon him, he exercised his *macho* imagination. 'It is a little like having a woman. Hot, like that.' He had never bedded a girl, and he did not want to betray his own lack of experience by saying the wrong thing to these knowing others, some of whom were married. He thought of Christos and Marika in the cave. 'The blood is up. And a man gets in a fever. *Katalaves?*'

'*Then katalava.*' Panayiotis sighed. 'I never had a woman, either.'

As his men laughed, Yorgos leaned over and slapped the lad on the back. 'Tonight you will kill your first man. And I promise you tomorrow I will buy you your first woman, even if I have to go all the way to Korinthos to find one who will do it for money.'

'You can always find a whore in Argos.' The shepherd laughed. 'They're all whores in Argos.'

The guide in the front swivelled round. 'My wife is from Argos.'

'And so are my sisters.' A second voice had sharply risen. 'And my mother.'

'Boys, boys . . .' Yorgos spread his hands in a gesture of peace. 'Save it for the bandits.' Finally they were nearing the crest of the mountain. He consulted with the guide, and the driver turned the wagon off on a path to the right, just beyond a tiny roadside shrine that had been erected to thank God for a safe ascent.

Everyone lit fresh cigarettes and expectantly bent forward as though ahead a line of Communists with red banners were marching in parade formation. But there were only the inevitable rocks, an abandoned shepherd's hut, and an occasional olive tree. In silence they looked into the black night as the cart rumbled along until finally a figure stepped out of the darkness.

'Elias?' Yorgos called.

'*Nai,*' a voice answered.

'Stop,' Yorgos ordered. 'We're here.' When they were all huddling in the dark, hugging their guns in the midnight cold, he rocked back on his heels and barked out a series of orders exactly like those they had all heard in American war movies. 'From now on, men, shut your mouths. And no smoking! This is *andartes* country now. Their camp should be about five kilometres away, and there will be sentries. Now . . . ?' He nodded to the militiaman from a nearby village who was to lead them to the Reds.

Elias' weathered old face cracked into a grin, he seized the hands of those fellows he already knew, and then he squatted down and used an olive branch to draw a map of the Communist encampment he had reconnoitred the night before. Forty years senior to most of the men in this squad, Elias had fought not only in the Greek army against the Italians and the Germans in the World War but also in a string of wars during his flaming youth. He was sitting out the final siege against the Communists only because, at sixty-five, with three of his sons in the Greek army, the high command had told him to keep the home fires burning.

The others gathered round and squinted in the faint light as Elias shone a torch on his makeshift map. 'We go along this ridge, down a ravine, and then begin to climb up a steep grade toward where they are.' He made two crosses in the dust. 'Last night the sentries were here and here.' He shrugged. 'But tonight, who knows? The danger is getting up this final hill. There are only a few trees and boulders.' He looked up at the moonless sky. 'Soon it will snow. But at least the heavens are with us.'

Yorgos didn't fancy a final charge with no cover, even if the Archangel Michael and his namesake St George were leading them on. 'There's no way,' he ventured, 'of getting into the camp from the other side?'

Elias brought his head up in a sharp negative. 'Sheer rock on all sides but this one. What they have up there, except for this one approach, is a natural fortress.' He looked back at his sketchy map. 'But at least there are no mines. That we know of, anyway. It's only a temporary camp. The word is that they're planning to move on very – '

'Yes,' Yorgos snapped, 'we know all that. So let's get moving. *Pame!*'

With Elias in the lead, Yorgos next, and the others trailing in single file with their guns at the ready, they trudged along the faint trail where stubborn patches of icy snow still lay from the last storm a fortnight ago. The only sounds were their boots crunching and the panting of some of the more sedentary.

'Keep together now,' Yorgos turned around and glowered at his sorry line of would-be soldiers. 'No stragglers.'

After winding around the ridge, they began descending a dense covering of trees in the ravine. Branches snapped, and every few seconds someone could be heard mumbling curses.

'Quiet,' Yorgos hissed. 'They could hear you all the way down in Argos.' But as they drew near the hill where the *andartes* were encamped, luckily a whistling wind sprang up from the east. Whatever noise the militiamen were making was hidden by the rustling of the trees and the snapping of branches broken by the wind.

Ahead, Elias held up his hand until they were all silent and waiting. Then he pointed halfway up the hill, where the pinpoint flare of a cigarette moved back and forth as a sentry smoked through his watch. 'That's the first one.' He pointed toward the crest of the hill, where the others could see nothing. 'The second one should be up there.'

'I don't see anything,' Panayiotis whispered.

'You'll see a flash of something light in the shadows, when he looks this way. *There*!' Elias nodded in satisfaction. 'That's probably where they have their machine gun.'

'Machine gun.' Yorgos dully tried to keep the fear from his voice. No one in Argos had warned them that they might be facing soldiers with automatic weapons. The *andartes* were supposed to be asleep when they burst into the camp, so his men could sneak up and put bullets in the backs of their heads. He was prepared for executions, not combat.

'We'll have to take the sentries first.' Elias looked grimly up the hill. 'Otherwise we have no chance.'

The volunteers nervously looked at one another. No chance?

Yorgos longed for a cigarette. As the officer in charge of this mission, by rights he should have delivered the speech Elias had just made. But he was a trained policeman, not a soldier. He didn't have the faintest idea either how to overrun the enemy camp or how to win back command of this raid. He wetted his dry lips. 'Elia, have you ever been through a situation like this?'

'*Nai*. Against the Italians in Albania.'

'And . . . ?' Yorgos prompted.

Elias shrugged. 'We took it. Eventually. But those were Italians and these are Greeks.' He was tired of talking and so he rooted in the sack he carried on his back until he came up with a leather thong and a handful of grenades. 'We'll use these.'

The others stared at the length of leather and the little grenades the size of the oranges the fieldhands picked in winter.

Elias wound the thong around his neck and pulled the end of the garotte tight with a choking motion. 'That's how I'll get the first one.'

Yorgos brightened. 'You're volunteering?'

In the dark Elias' eyes gleamed like a cat's. 'It will be my great pleasure to cleanse our country of one more bandit. Soldiers they call themselves? Ha! They are common criminals. They killed my daughter's husband. Came down to his village – Midea, it was – dragged him out of his bed and slit his throat with the lid of a tin can. Right in front of my daughter and the children. They are animals.'

'Filthy animals,' Yorgos agreed. An image flashed through his mind of his brother and Marika intertwined in the cave. He could feel the fury building inside him again, pumping through his veins, until his rage overpowered his fear. His next words were crisp with authority. 'If Elias takes the first one, I will take the second. But I'll need help. Volunteers?'

Thanos stepped forward. 'I will, boss.'

'Lieutenant,' Yorgos corrected. But he smiled at the veteran.

'And me.' Panayiotis squared his shoulders and puffed out his chest to make himself appear manlier.

'You?' Yorgos looked doubtful.

'You need someone to throw the grenades.' Panayiotis pleaded like a boy begging another sweet from his mother. 'Always, at football, I am the one to throw the ball. I am the best in Nauplion. Maybe in all the Argolid.'

'He's right,' one of the others chimed in. 'I've seen him. He can throw anything, anywhere.'

'All right, then.' Yorgos clapped the boy on the back. Awash in this novel feeling of masculine camaraderie, he could almost forget that soon some of them might die. 'I need two more. Who's with us?'

A young fellow from Argos put up his hand, along with a middle-aged schoolteacher from a village near Korinthos.

'*Entaxi.*' Yorgos smiled at his volunteers. 'OK, so that's settled.' Gravely he passed the hand grenades to his squad.

'You know how to use them?' Elias held up a grenade and demonstrated how to pull the pin and throw. 'These are left over from the Germans. You should have a half minute after you pull the pin. But only God knows for sure.'

Yorgos turned smartly to Elias. 'As soon as you're sure the sentry's dead, light a cigarette and wave it in a cross. Then we'll take the other one.'

Elias flexed the leather thong in his fingers, turned his back on his comrades, and began snaking up the hill toward the first sentry.

Yorgos and his men stared into the darkness, waiting for Elias to betray himself by sight or sound. But for thirty seconds, a minute, for more than that they could see and hear nothing. Finally, like a beacon, they saw a match flare on the hill, and then a lighted cigarette beckoned in a victory cross.

'*Orea.*' Yorgos' lips were parched. But when he tried to wet them with his tongue, that was dry, too. His eyes raked the faces of the four men who had volunteered for his squad. 'We'll fan out and crawl up the hill, keeping as close to the ground as possible. Then, at a signal from me, we all throw the grenades. *Katalaves?*'

'*Katalava.*' As one, they nodded.

Yorgos turned to the others. 'As soon as you hear those grenades, I want you into that camp before they can get to their guns.'

Then he and his volunteers were on their bellies, crawling over the rocks and up the steep slope. Upward they crept, their movements masked by the wind, until faintly they could see the sentry's silhouette.

Stealthily Yorgos' hand unhooked the grenade from his belt and measured its heft in his palm. Because of the pumping adrenalin he felt bigger and stronger than ever before in his life. He brought his fist into the air as a signal for the others, and hesitated for only an instant before he pulled the pin and threw. But just as the grenade left his hand, he saw Panayiotis advancing on the enemy soldier. The others in his squad, too, had already rained their grenades on the sentry. Just as Panayiotis threw himself on top of the partisan and began to grapple for possession of the machine gun, the first grenade went off in a sulphurous flash of ground-trembling red and orange. Before Yorgos burrowed his face in his arms, he saw a sickening spray of blood and guts in the air. He hid his head and tried not to retch as the second one boomed at some distance from the target, then the third detonated a little to the left, and finally the fourth exploded smack on what remained of the machine-gun emplacement.

Simultaneously from every side, there was the sound of running feet, firing guns, and deep-throated cries as the militiamen charged into the rebel camp. By the uncertain light of a sputtering campfire, his death squad was shooting before most of the *andartes* could grab their guns. One or two fired back, yet in all the confusion at first it was hard to know how many guerrillas were here. But it was clear as they closed in that the militiamen greatly outnumbered the guerrillas.

Yorgos ran in the darkness from one form to another, frantic to find his brother before one of his comrades cheated him of the trophy he had coveted for so long. He squinted into the haggard face of every dead partisan; none of them was Christos. Two of his own men were wounded, but he counted six dead guerrillas, then seven, then eight, plus the two sentries. But at least twenty were supposed to be camped here.

Thanos was wrestling hand to hand by the campfire with the last of the guerrillas, and the other Greek Cross militiamen gathered round and placed bets on who would win. The burly veteran was at least five stone heavier than the young Communist, and his mates cheered lustily when Thanos pinned the partisan to the ground.

But just as Thanos was about the deal the death blow, Yorgos intervened. 'Leave him for me!'

Reluctantly Thanos crawled off, and after a moment the guerrilla sat up and rubbed his arms and neck. Yorgos glared down into the defiant eyes of this bandit who had served under his brother. He didn't seem old enough to be fighting for anyone or anything, but already his face was creased like a man approaching middle age. His hair was unkempt, his clothes were in tatters, and yet there was nothing that suggested defeat or surrender in the way he returned Yorgos' stare.

'Your commander – Christos Kronos, the one they call Captain Prometheus – where is he?'

The partisan didn't make a sound, but Yorgos saw a flicker of recognition in his eyes. He reached down, grabbed the prisoner by his shaggy hair, and held his face to the firelight. 'Andrea!' Back in Panagia, this had been one of his boyhood tormentors. Yorgos smiled, and then he cracked the butt end of his rifle into the side of the prisoner's face. The impact shattered bones and teeth. 'Answer me! Where's my brother?'

Andreas spit out teeth and blood and then one defiant word. '*Poteh*! Never!'

'We'll see about that. *Falange* may loosen your tongue.' The militiamen prepared the guerrilla for that excruciating torture Yorgos had learned in gendarmerie interrogations. First they removed the broken remnants of the prisoner's shoes. While two militiamen held back his arms, another twisted his feet around the barrel of a gun while Thanos – still smarting for the kill which had been denied him – flexed a club in his hands.

'Why not tell us what we want to know now, before we lame you for life?' Yorgos glowered at the village boy who once had broken his glasses in a fistfight. 'You'll tell me where my brother is. In time, you'll tell us everything.'

'*Poteh*!' Andreas was sure he was marked as a dead man. What did it matter if his last moments were as a cripple? Dearly he wished he had obeyed Captain Prometheus' order to leave this camp and carry messages down to Panagia, but he hadn't wanted to miss the news from the party council. Now, *this*.

'Proceed,' Yorgos said softly.

As Thanos brought the club down on his exposed arches, Andreas screamed not words but animal cries of pain. Relentlessly the beating continued – four strokes, six, an even dozen.

Yorgos held up his hand. 'Wait.' He stooped close to his enemy. 'You're ready to talk now?'

Andreas' answer came in a whisper. '*Poteh*.'

Yorgos had just nodded for Thanos to continue, when Elias walked out of the shadows with a knife held to the throat of another guerrilla. 'Look what I found hiding in the bushes.'

'Don't hurt me, don't kill me, I'm not one of *them*! They kidnapped me from my village!' Aris, the Korinthos recruit who had sat around the Panagia bonfire a fortnight ago, had lost his swagger. His greasy hair hung around his emaciated face, and his filthy clothes were in rags. 'Please,' he begged, 'let me go! I'm not a Communist! I swear it!'

'You'll do better than that.' Yorgos rubbed his hands together in anticipation.

'Ari, shut up!' Andreas' scream was as shrill as a woman's. 'They'll kill you anyway. At least die like a man.'

63

Yorgos wheeled back to his old enemy. 'Die like a man? And how, *paidi mou*, does a man die? Perhaps you'll show us.' He nodded to Thanos, who pulled out his butcher's knife and slit Andreas' throat. 'Died like a sheep.' Yorgos turned back to Aris. 'Now, you were about to tell me what happened to your other comrades. And most especially to your commander, Christos Kronos.'

'Captain Prometheus?' Aris' red-rimmed eyes circled the fire, but none of his comrades was alive to hear. Still, somehow the *andartes* would find out. Even if these fascists didn't murder him, the Reds would one day track him down and slice him to pieces if he told all. One thing he had learned in these last horrifying weeks was that both sides were fiends from hell.

'Don't waste my time!' Yorgos held his hand on the hilt of his dagger as he advanced on the prisoner.

'He left,' Aris babbled, his eyes on the knife. 'Left with the others.'

'How many?' Yorgos barked. 'And where did they go and why?'

'Eight of them left for the front up north.' Maybe they wouldn't kill him if he co-operated. He would join up with them, rise in the ranks, and end up on top once the fighting stopped. 'They weren't part of our unit, and orders came for them to move out.'

'Christos – your "Captain Prometheus" – he left for the north, too?'

Aris hesitated. It was one thing to rat on the men from that other unit. But the captain . . . no, not *him*.

Yorgos unsheathed his razor-sharp knife and sliced off his eyelashes. 'Next, your eyes.'

'Oh, God! Oh, God!' Aris wet his pants, and then he broke and blubbered the answer. 'Captain Prometheus and a guide went to Tripolis. For a meeting at party headquarters. The day before yesterday.'

'Tripolis.' Thoughtfully Yorgos stared into the night. The provincial capital was one of the last *andartes* strongholds. There was no way he and his men could root out Christos there. 'And when is he due back?'

'In the morning! Captain Prometheus is due back at dawn!'

Yorgos let out a hissing breath and then made a washing motion with his hands, the Greek gesture to indicate that something is finished. 'Now you can kill the bandit,' he told Elias, who dispatched the prisoner at a stroke before Aris could let out another whimper.

Oblivious to his men who were moving from body to body – pulling off gold rings, searching in pockets for drachmas or gold sovereigns, even stripping the corpses of clothing or shoes that might do for themselves or their friends – Yorgos sat by the fire. It had started to snow, and the flakes fell fast and thick. He rolled a cigarette. He could wait here for Christos or go to meet him in the wastelands between here and Tripolis. Elias knew

64

these mountains as well as anyone. The old veteran could help him intercept his brother. Elias could have Christos' guide. But he himself would face his brother man-to-man in single combat here in the snows of the high country, as though Achilles and Hector again were fighting to death before the gates of Troy.

Yorgos threw his cigarette into the fire, gave Elias his new orders, and then shouted to his men. '*Entaxi*. We're done here.'

But not quite. All this while Thanos had been directing the squad in a grisly business. He saluted Yorgos smartly and presented him with a blood-soaked sack.

'What's this?' Yorgos was so eager to be off on the final leg of his manhunt that he hardly looked at what had been thrust into his hand.

'Ears, sir. Eleven pair. For the collection at headquarters in Argos.'

Yorgos thanked God the light was dim, for it would have been bad for his reputation if his men could have seen him go white as salt. Not for the first time, he wondered what he was doing with these barbarians. Yet he supposed he should be glad they weren't collecting heads like the Turks used to do after a battle with the Greeks. He slapped Thanos on the back and managed to croak out a laugh. 'You tell them yourself. You cut them, so you turn them in. And that's an order.'

'Right, boss!' Thanos grinned from ear to ear.

'Lieutenant,' Yorgos corrected him.

'Right, lieutenant!'

Yorgos watched his men set out with their wounded for the wagon, and then he followed Elias into the night toward Tripolis.

Christos and his aide Apostolis were ankle deep in the fresh snow as they left the lights of the provincial capital behind and silently made their way through the wilderness toward their camp. The night promised to turn still colder and bleaker before they finished their trek through the high passes and finally sank down by their campfire to deliver the sorry news to their waiting men. But Christos had promised to return by dawn at the latest, and after the final showdown at the party council he would have walked twenty kilometres over hot coals to distance himself from what had happened in Tripolis. Better a frigid forced march through the mountains than a knife in the back while he slept beside comrades who had become mortal foes.

Doggedly, as he tramped behind Apostolis, Christos wondered how ripe had turned to rotten. Throughout the lean and bloody years of the German Occupation, bands of guerrillas like his own had lived like wolf packs in the mountains, swooping down to hit and run not only at the Germans but also, later, at rival rightwing Greek guerrilla bands who had become even deadlier enemies than the Nazis. But it hadn't begun with Greeks ferociously devouring their own. In the glory days of the earlier struggle against the Germans, the only ideology in the mountain camps had been to dare all and give all for the beloved *patrida*. But the partisans had fallen out, as Greeks too often did, and hunger and deprivation had sown in some a social conscience that had been eagerly cultivated by the dedicated Communist Party strategists who had ordered their cadres to fight shoulder-to-shoulder with the peasant guerrillas. Leftist and rightwing Greeks had dug in after the Nazi pullout, and for a long while it had seemed that a socialist victory was as inevitable as the sun rising in the east. But just as the Soviets had stopped supplying the *andartes*, the Americans had stepped up their materials for the rightists. It appeared now that the sun would most certainly set in the west.

As Christos marched away from the party betrayals of Tripolis on this moonless night of disillusion and despair, he reflected that far more than the war had been lost. The Party, too, had begun eating its own. Yet not so long ago the comrades had offered a shining alternative to the corrupt leadership of the tired old politicians who had run Greece into the ground. When the Communists had set up schools, health centres, and people's courts in formerly neglected village backwaters at the beginning of the war, they had triumphed not only by force of arms.

Christos wearily paused and looked down over the edge of a precipice. The Party's new marching orders had come, it was said, direct from Moscow. The people's army must abandon the mountain eyries they had won with their blood and regroup near the borders so they could dash to safety after their last stand. Christos had shouted and paced in the Tripolis hall as he tried to persuade the comrades to continue their hit-and-run guerrilla war instead of following the Party's orders for suicidal pitched battles. But Moscow had another agenda, and his entreaties had fallen upon deaf ears. Worse still, before the strategic retreat, the Party was ordering an ideological purge. Rightwing villages were being burnt to the ground. Bands of comrades were raiding isolated hamlets to execute policemen and shepherds and grocers for what they called 'crimes against the people of Greece'. Nearly thirty thousand children were even being taken from their homes by force and spirited behind the Iron Curtain, supposedly for their protection. And within the Party itself, dissidents were being 'liquidated'. In that terrible two nights and a day in Tripolis, the comrades had spent more time denouncing one another than plotting how to safeguard their bedraggled *andartes*. Eighty thousand Greeks had died in this Civil War, and seven hundred thousand men, women, and children – ten percent of the population – had been driven

66

from their homes and become refugees in their own country. Was all this suffering, Christos wondered, for naught?

He trudged on through the swirling snow. Cold as it was, he preferred the pristine purity of this wilderness to the dirty reek of that party council. He supposed he might be lying dead in a back alley even now, if it weren't for the warnings of two old comrades who had taken him aside to whisper that they had seen his name on a cadre death list. What had been happening for weeks up in the north to those who had spoken out against the party line was now beginning to occur here in the Peloponnese. In these desperate last days, the Party wasn't even bothering with peoples' courts or firing squads and instead was ordering their secret police to do their dirty work with a slash of a knife in the night. Already, Christos' friends had informed him, an officer from Koroni and a recruit from Nemea had been murdered with a shoemaker's knife. If Christos knew what was good for him, he and his men would flee to Patras, catch a ferry to Italy, and bide their time until one day it was safe to come home.

Apostolis was far ahead, and Christos was following his tracks in the snow as he considered the alternatives to exile in the West. He faced certain death with the Communists, prison or a firing squad if he surrendered to the rightwing forces, and arrest if he set foot back in Panagia, which was surely doomed to return to government control. But how could he bear to leave Greece? *And Marika; how could he leave her?* Yes, she was Mother Greece. Always he had fought for *her*. He loved her and his country so. Even here, in the dead of this bitter night, this frozen stony earth was so achingly dear to him. He had never been able to understand how his father had chosen to live his life anywhere else. How could mere dollars compensate for the loss of family and country?

With a heavy heart Christos pushed onward. Ever since the scales finally had fallen from his eyes tonight, he had known he would have to leave not only the Party but Greece. Captain Prometheus was no more; that fire was out, and forever. Yet he supposed he would have his father waiting with open arms on the far side of the Atlantic. But he dreaded breaking the terrible news to his men back at the camp. Fairly, however, he would present the alternatives – exile in the East or the West – and let each make his own decision. He would do his best to help those who chose to follow him to Patras and beyond.

Christos stopped, shook a cigarette from his packet, and moodily watched the first rays of the sun light the sky. But *her*, what of her? It had killed him to leave Marika in the dead of that other night, for he had understood that his body hadn't satisfied her wrenching need. Before he left he had debated waking her and repeating his promise to return and marry her as soon as he

67

could, but she had looked so deliciously deep in sleep that he had decided not to disturb her only for a painful farewell. Instead he had tenderly wrapped that shawl around her and stolen away for his rendezvous with his men. He had intended to return in a few days or at most a week, and marry her then if he could talk a *pappas* into performing the sacrament even though it was Lent. But instead he had become enmeshed in the death throes of the war. Before he had set off for Tripolis this last time, however, he had ordered Andreas back to Panagia with a public communiqué for the peoples' committee and a private message for Marika. He had simply counselled both to keep the faith. It would be hard for her to wait a while longer. But at least he knew she would be safely in the bosom of her family. As soon as he was settled in America, he would send for her. It was not the idyllic Panagia future they had dreamed of, but at least finally they would be together.

A shot rang out and, a fraction of a second later, another. Christos threw his cigarette in the snow, swung his rifle into firing position, and stealthily advanced in the fraught silvery dawn light.

Yorgos got there first. Elias and Christos' man were already dead. Just as he had imagined back at that campfire, it would be he and his brother locked alone in mortal combat. He took up position behind a boulder in easy firing range of the Communist corpse and put his eyeglasses in his pocket.

He did not have long to wait. He sensed Christos before he saw him through the veil of pelting snow, and then from nowhere that silhouette he would have known anywhere was crouching over the body of the guerrilla. Through the hairs of his gunsight Yorgos aimed. Christos was thinner than when he had last seen him naked in the cave. Remembering, his trigger finger almost forever evened the score. But then Yorgos eased up on the firing pin. It wasn't enough to gun him down in cold blood. He himself was a real soldier now, not merely a despised provincial policeman. And he wanted Christos to know not only who was delivering the death blow but why.

'Don't move!' Yorgos kept his rifle aimed at his brother as he stepped from the cover of the boulder until he was in point blank range. 'And throw your rifle on the ground.'

Christos had had his gun in firing position and aimed before the first words were out of Yorgos' mouth. But then he saw who it was. 'You!' He had supposed his brother back in Kalamata by now. For a fleeting instant Christos' face was illuminated by the beginnings of a smile, until he saw the menace on his brother's face and the scarlet cross on his shirt. It was bad enough when his misguided brother joined the gendarmerie. But now the Greek Cross? 'You . . .'

68

'Yes, me.' Yorgos waved the rifle barrel. 'Put down the gun. Now!'

Even as Christos kept his sights trained on the target, his voice was as soft as a sigh. 'Why, Yorgo, do you wear that scarlet cross. And why do you come here as my enemy? You are my brother.'

For a long moment, as the brothers stared down the gunsights at one another, Christos wondered how it could have come to this.

He remembered, as if it were yesterday instead of nearly a decade ago, the lighted wick of the oil lamp under his stepmother's favourite icon the night he had sat down for a heart-to-heart about his estrangement from Yorgos. Eleni, that lonely soul, who was too often as sad as the silver-encased painting of the Virgin she kept in a place of honour on a carved mahogany table in the sitting room, had sighed even more heavily than usual after Christos had poured out his troubled heart. For once his stepmother, who rarely stopped working – all day in the taverna, all night in the house – had set aside her knitting and folded her nervous fingers in her lap. Yes, Eleni had nodded, she, too, grieved for the rift between Nikolas' sons. If only your father were here, she had fretted, as she always did when anything went wrong. With a majestic sort of resignation, Eleni had even beat her breast before she had once again sighed and pronounced her judgement with the authority of an ancient oracle. 'Yorgos blames you for how it is with our family.' Eleni's dark eyes had been as accusing as her son's. 'His father never loved him.' Here, Christos remembered, his stepmother's voice had faltered and then broken. 'Or me, either.' Then she had hung her head as though it were too heavy for her weary shoulders. 'He didn't care enough about us to stay.' 'No, no,' Christos had cried out. 'That's not true, *he* loves you both, too.' With less passion but more honesty, he had added in a whisper that he was just as sorry as they were that his father had gone away.

Yet, with his finger still on the firing pin, Christos again felt the same stab of guilt as when he had watched bereft Eleni sigh into the empty spaces of her life. For maybe his stepmother and stepbrother were right to envy him. He had never forgotten how once, when he was very young – five or six, he reckoned, that first magical time when he was old enough to remember his father coming home for a summer visit – Nikolas had announced he was taking his eldest son back to live with him in the rich splendour of America. But Eleni had wept so, and pleaded so hard that he take Yorgos and her along, too, that in the end Nikolas had lost patience and taken none of them. Yet Christos had never forgotten – and he knew that Eleni and Yorgos had never forgotten, nor forgiven, either – that his father had once wanted only him. He remembered, when he had been laid low by some boyish disaster, how he would take that knowledge of his father's love from the secret place deep in his heart. It was a treasure that always comforted him. Even now,

69

with his life in tatters, the assurance of it warmed him. He pitied Yorgos for never having had that paternal security. *That*, maybe, was what was missing inside his stepbrother. Even when he had been six years old, Christos had instinctively known that it was this unforgiveable sin – being the loved son of a loved mother – that had made Yorgos, young as he was, hate him so.

'I forget nothing.' Behind the gunsight Yorgos' laughter was as brittle as the ice under his feet. When still Christos gave no sign that he was about to throw down his weapon, Yorgos wished he had gunned him down when he had his golden opportunity. If he pulled the trigger now, there was an even chance that both of them would fall dead. It might be better to end it as he had planned, with their father's knives. 'It's you against me. But that's the way it always was, eh? So now, here on this mountain, we will finish it.'

'Finish what?' Clearly those Greek Cross thugs had filled his head with their poison. But he had to get that gun away from him before he hurt himself.

'Finish everything. I've been waiting for this moment ever since I could remember. To kill you! Finally to end it!' Yorgos' eyes blurred with sudden tears. 'For the cave, Christo! For Marika and the cave!'

'Ah, so that's it. *Her* . . .' He had figured this mad ambush all wrong. Christos reproached himself for not clearing the air with his brother the first time he had realized Yorgos hankered after her, too. 'I wish to God that had never happened, not *then*, not *there*, with this war . . . and now *you*.' He took a step closer. 'But enough of this.'

'Stay where you are.' Desperately Yorgos wished he could pull the trigger. So long as he took his brother with him, what did it matter, after all, if he died? His index finger trembled and almost he let it click back to his thumb. Yet for the second time he couldn't do it. Why, he raged at himself, *why*? 'We will fight, you and I.' Boldly he gambled on Christos' sense of fair play, and he threw his gun down on the snow. 'With our knives. With the daggers our father gave us.' His hand crept to the sheath at his waist.

Tempted as he was to graze his brother's fighting arm with a superficial wound, Christos decided to humour him with the knives. A cross embroidered on his collar didn't make him a trained soldier. A few feints and swipes, and Yorgos would give up and let him go about his pressing business back at the camp. Christos threw down his rifle and slid out his dagger.

They circled one another in a crouch, their knives at the ready. Yorgos lunged forward, but Christos stepped out of reach as gracefully as though he were dancing. Again Yorgos slashed at his brother, and again the thrust was evaded. 'Please,' Christos pleaded. 'We must not do this. We are brothers.' Yorgos' answer was a savage cobra strike. Christos twisted away just in time, but the blade pierced his left arm and drew blood. Yorgos tried to seize the advantage and thrust again, but this time Christos deflected the blow. 'Please,' he entreated. 'Stop this. Now, before it's too late. In the name of our father, we cannot spill one another's blood.'

Yorgos answered with a snarl. 'I already have!' He cut the air before his brother's face. 'I always longed for this day. Longed for it, Christo! Always it was you against me. For our father! And now, too, for Marika!' Again Yorgos drew blood, this time from Christos' thigh.

'Enough!' For the first time, Christos fought back so he could end this madness and be on his way. Always before when the two of them tussled and wrestled as boys, he had been able to best his little brother without even working up a sweat. But this time Yorgos seemed possessed either of superhuman strength or the devil. Christos was hard-pressed to parry his thrusts. As their blades struck and rang like swords, for a long while it was all he could do to hold off his brother's attack. But experience told, and finally Christos began to beat the other back. He forced him down on one knee, and then Yorgos sprawled back on the snow. Christos leaped on his chest, pinned him down, and in an automatic reflex he held his knife to his throat. Wordlessly he stared into his brother's eyes.

'Now you kill me,' Yorgos whispered. 'Now it is over.'

Christos neatly sliced the Greek Cross from his brother's shirt and then sheathed his knife. 'Kill you? No, not you.' Wearily he got to his feet. 'Go home, little one.' Unconsciously he used the pet name he had called his brother when he was a baby.

'Little one! Little one!' In a frenzy Yorgos tore open the front of his shirt. In his eyes sprang the humiliated tears of a spurned warrior who had been denied even the grace of a noble combat death. 'Kill me! Here! Now! Kill me!'

Christos turned his back and began walking away. But then he looked over his shoulder. 'I'm leaving Greece. I'll send for Marika as soon as I get to America.'

'America?' Yorgos' hand closed again on the hilt of his knife. 'You go to *him*?'

'But first I go to my camp.'

'Why?' Yorgos was back on his feet, his knife was raised, and he was ready to spring. 'They're all dead.'

'Dead?' Christos whirled. 'I don't believe you.'

'It's true. We killed them. At your camp on top of the hill on the far side of the mountain. We got all of them. All but you.' He hurled himself on his brother.

They grappled on the slippery ice. Now Christos fought in a rage that

71

matched his brother's. They slashed at one another, Christos seized Yorgos' striking wrist, and the captain's knife cut deep into the lieutenant's cheek.

'So now we fight,' Yorgos exulted. The blood his brother had finally shed dripped to his lips and he licked it. He closed in for what he supposed was the kill, their knives flashed, and then Christos lost his footing.

Yorgos was on top, he raised his knife, but he faltered as he looked deep into his brother's green eyes. A spasm shook him. 'Christo!' For the third time, he couldn't do it. Around the hilt his fingers slackened, and almost gently the knife slid into the snow.

Christos writhed out from underneath him and was back on his feet. Without a word he sheathed his knife and shouldered his rifle.

'Christo!'

But no one heard Yorgos' anguished cry.

Christos was already gone.

Four

Late on Palm Sunday afternoon, a month after his showdown in the mountains, Yorgos prepared for his triumphant return to the village which surely must now acclaim him as a conquering hero. How appropriate, he reflected, that his homecoming fell on the very day that the pious commemorated Christ's re-entry to Jerusalem. He would have liked to ride into the *plateia* on a donkey and have the people who had once spurned him lay laurel branches in his path. But that, he supposed, would be blasphemy, and a good Greek Christian such as himself would never sink to that. Still, the idea tickled him.

He smiled at his reflection as he stood before his mother's mirror slicking back his hair. Even that scar his brother had cut on his cheek gave him the reckless air of a man who had fought hard and lived to tell the tale, like a pirate perhaps, or a lord who had crossed swords in a duel of honour. He cut quite a figure in the dearly-won Greek Army uniform Eleni had painstakingly pressed late last night when he had arrived on leave for *Megali Evdomada*, the 'Great Week' preceding Easter. He had slept most of the day, revelling in the soft warm bed instead of the hard cold earth he had been camping on these last arduous weeks in the mountains searching for stray *andartes*. But he had loved every minute of it.

Yorgos reached up and flicked imaginary dust off his lieutenant's uniform. When he had parlayed the success of his Greek Cross raid into a transfer from the gendarmerie, he had entered the regular army as an officer. He intended to make a glorious lifetime career of the army. A few more years out here in the provinces, and he would be ensconced in Athens with flunkies jumping to fulfil his every whim. Life was as sweet as the figs from the tree in his mother's garden.

He swept into the parlour as the churchbells began ringing for the evening service. Eleni sat waiting for him to escort her to church.

'How do I look?' He struck a heroic pose.

'*Orea.*' She gazed adoringly up at her son who seemed a changed man more because of the radiance of his expression than that olive drab uniform which had been a devil to iron. Always before Yorgos had been so resentful, even sullen, but now he was euphoric. She had even heard him whistling a military march as he was getting dressed. 'I just wish your father were here to see you.'

A shadow crossed Yorgos' face. He turned his back on his mother as he rolled and lit a cigarette. 'Have you,' he said, far more casually than his racing heart would evidence, 'heard from him lately?' If Christos had succeeded in getting to America, surely Nikolas would have bellowed that news across the Atlantic.

'*Tipoteh.*' Eleni shrugged. 'Nothing.' She repeated the time-worn excuse even she no longer believed. 'But the war . . .' Again she shrugged.

'The war's over.' Yorgos knew that in the larger sense this was not quite true, for the *andartes* were still being mauled in the north. But now that he was home in this self-contained world, his claim seemed on the mark. Not only Panagia but all the Peloponnese had been swept clean of the Communists. Here in the village the partisans who had run the people's committee and the people's court had summarily executed those villagers known to hold rightwing views – including the priest, Father Theo, who had been found with a knife in his back on the side of Panagia mountain. And then the *andartes* had packed up their families and fled for their lives a few weeks ago. The speculation was that by now most of them had slipped over the border to Yugoslavia, but the situation was so chaotic that no one knew for sure. Yorgos was banking on just that.

'I hope,' Eleni fretted, 'that your brother isn't . . . you know?' Her voice trailed off. 'I haven't heard from *him* either.' Even though Yorgos' face hardened like a statue's, she finally asked what she hadn't dared to broach last night. 'Is it true, what they say about your brother?'

'What?' Yorgos betrayed his anxiety only a little, as he absentmindedly flicked his ash on his mother's heirloom Persian carpet. His Greek Cross

73

officers and army commanders had believed his veiled allusions to what had happened atop that mountain. 'Captain Prometheus,' they had demanded, 'did you get him?' In answer, Yorgos had thrown down the bloody ears of Christos' aide and let them believe what they wanted. He was well aware that that bit of theatrical deception had played no small part in his promotion to the army. But his game was up if Christos had returned to Panagia for a visit before he set out for America.

'They say he's dead. That he died in that raid. That you . . .' Eleni faltered and could not finish what she had determined she must ask.

'I'm surprised at you, mama, listening to village gossip.' He ground out his cigarette, this time in an ashtray, and his dark eyes again were alight. So far no one in the village had found him out. With luck, Christos had never made it out of Greece, much less to America. 'If I've told you once, I've told you a thousand times, I will not descend to that level.' Majestically Yorgos stood, smoothed down his uniform, and offered her his arm. '*Pame*. We're already late.'

At dusk on any other evening the *plateia* would have been thronged with villagers out to enjoy the gentlest hours of the day. By this twilight time – six o'clock or so in spring, which the Greeks call *apogevma*, afternoon – everyone had awoken refreshed from the midday siesta. The men had all come back from the fields and the sea. The children had finished their chores and their studies. And even the women had paused in their incessant sweeping and worrying. As dusk fell, one and all, as if summoned by pealing churchbells, liked to gather in the heart of the village for gossip and good fellowship. The women shuffled about buying food and visiting this relative or that neighbour. The children ran wild in shouting packs. And the men settled down in their favourite coffeehouses for a leisurely coffee or raki with those lifelong friends to whom they were capable of talking endlessly about nothing.

But on this particular afternoon, as Yorgos walked through the *plateia* with Eleni on his arm, the square was deserted but for a few *kafeneion* diehards – old leftists, most of them – who stonily watched the lieutenant and his mother hurry to join the crowd of Panagians in church. Only the old women, the unmarried girls, and pitifully henpecked pensioners attended regularly. But the *Megali Evdomada* was the high point not only of the liturgical calendar but village life, and most everyone in Panagia turned out for the moving opening service of this sacred week before Easter.

Marika was standing raptly in prayer near the front of the church, on the left – the 'women's' side – and so she didn't witness the stir when Yorgos entered with his mother. She didn't hear the gasps, didn't see the crowd part, didn't observe the men and women polarize into two camps. Kyria Elefsina,

74

who had just buried her grandson Andreas, glared at the lieutenant and ignored her old friend Eleni's smile of greeting. Argiris the fisherman, whose son had emerged unscathed from the Greek Cross raid, seemed about to kiss Yorgos' hand but contented himself with clapping him on the back. The congregation regrouped, the families whose sons had fought on the left not wanting to be within spitting distance of those families whose menfolk had fought on the right. Yorgos had been dead wrong about one thing back in his mother's parlour. The fighting might mostly have stopped. But here in Panagia as in every village in Greece, the war wasn't over. For some, it would go on forever. Everyone had lost someone, and none would ever forgive or forget. The entire country was caught up in a bloodfeud that would never be altogether avenged so long as great-grandsons and great-great-grandsons and generations even after that could still remember who had done what to whom.

Oblivious to the drama taking place all around her, Marika bowed her head in the prayer she had not ceased to recite for the past five desperate weeks. Bring him back to me, God, please. Let him be safe, please. And above all let him return, and soon, God, please soon. Time was running out. Easter was a Sunday away. Her period was nearly a month late, her swelling breasts were tender, and this morning she hadn't been able to keep down her mother's soothing *chamomili* tea. For anxious weeks she had concentrated all her being on the slightest quiver of change inside her body. All day long, every day, and every night as well, she had gone off to a private place and lifted up her dress – nervously, obsessively, even a bit madly – but no matter how often she had looked, no beautiful red blood had seeped from the place where Christos had been.

She raised her head to her favourite icon of the Virgin, but her eyes fell from this image of eternal motherhood. Babies, everywhere babies. At the conclusion of this morning's service, when the new *pappas* had passed out the *vaya* – laurel, myrtle, and palm woven into crosses, a symbol not only of Christ entering Jerusalem but of fertility as well – she had wished she could throw it back in the priest's sombre face. *His baby*, she was sure that she had to be carrying his baby. What was she going to do if Christos didn't come back to marry her in time? She had heard nothing from him since he abandoned her that night in the cave. The only news had been the rumours that Yorgos had led a Greek Cross raid in the mountains which had wiped out one of the Communist bands. But when she had approached the village people's committee in those last anguished days before the Peloponnese leftist movement collapsed, at first all she'd gotten were distracted evasions and vague platitudes not to lose heart. She had made the rounds, then, of the comrades in arms not only here in Panagia but in Nauplion and even Argos.

75

Those who had bothered to answer her – for they had more on their minds than a jilted lovesick girl – had suggested that Captain Prometheus must be in the thick of the fighting near the borders of Albania and Yugoslavia.

In the absence of any word from him, she had made excuse after excuse for his neglect. On her good days, when she still managed to have faith in her lover, she had told herself he must be doing his duty up in the north. She had wanted to believe that any morning now she would receive the word he must have entrusted with one of his comrades. When, however, still she heard nothing, she had tried to convince herself that somehow, through some mysterious mishap that was beyond Christos' control, his message had not yet been delivered. Even on her bad days, when mostly she had regretted ever having taken him to that cave, she had not quite been able to believe that a man like Christos – so kind, so honourable, so caring – could have left the love of his life in the lurch without so much as saying goodbye.

As the service wound on, Marika could not stop replaying in her mind the terrible account she finally had coaxed from one of the ageing partisans the night before he and most of the other *andartes* pulled out of this part of the Peloponnese. Unlike the others who had tried to sugarcoat reality, Panos had told her what everyone in Panagia would soon know. A few days ago one of the last *andartes* patrols had come upon what was left of Christos' camp. Yorgos' Greek Cross death squad had not only wiped out all of Christos' men but mutilated their bodies as well. 'The ears,' Panos had said, touching the sides of his own head, 'the bastards took the ears! And they carved crosses on their faces! Of my friends, all my friends! Gone, all gone! Dead, like our hopes for a free Greece! It's all over now. Everything, here in Greece, is all over.' But when he had looked over at Marika's stricken face, Panos had assured her, more kindly, that there had been no trace of Christos in that dead camp. 'Maybe he got away to the mountains and is fighting there now. Or perhaps he's already over the border. There is nothing,' he had repeated with infinite weariness, 'left for any of us here.' Yet something akin to a smile had played at the corners of his lips. 'I don't want to give you false hopes. But Christos is not dead, I think. No matter what anyone says, I believe that Captain Prometheus still lives.' Panos had touched his heart. 'Here, anyway.'

As the priest finished his reading and the cantor took up his sonorous Byzantine chanting, Marika's mind wandered through the other shreds of sad news which had been nails in the coffin of her hopes. Once the *andartes* pulled out and the outcome of the Greek Cross raid became common knowledge, those who had taken part had broken the silence they had imposed on themselves for fear of partisan reprisals. Marika's brother first heard their boasts in one of the coffeehouses on the Panagia *plateia*, and delicately he had broken the news to his sister. Just as Panos had said, Christos' band had been slaughtered. But there was more. Yorgos was said to have set out to gun down his brother, and he had walked down alone from the mountain the next day with a pair of severed ears in his ammunition bag. The supposition in the coffeehouses was that Yorgos, who had been off with the army ever since, had succeeded where so many had failed. When later that week the frozen bodies of Panagia's *andartes* had been laid to rest in the village cemetery, some had wanted to mark a grave in Christos' memory. But others, still scandalized at the murder of Father Theo, had threatened to dig up the *andartes'* graves and throw the bodies in the rubbish dump if anyone dared to heap any more honours on these dead godless ones. Marika had been nursing a grudge against the new priest ever since.

The oil lamps inside the church were dimmed. The congregation lit the candles each carried as the cantors began chanting one of the best-loved hymns of the Greek people, 'Litany of the Bridegroom', harking back to Christ being delivered for judgement to Pontius Pilate. Altar boys led a procession with their tall brass candlesticks held high before the *pappas* who carried the priceless old icon of Christ crowned with thorns to the centre of the church, where it would remain for veneration until the Last Supper ritual on Thursday. It was a solemn moment and, like so much of the Great Week liturgy, redolent with the mysteries of faith.

But for Marika the sacred beauty was shattered when her mother nudged her. 'Look who's here.'

Marika turned round where Old Anna pointed and caught Yorgos staring at her in the flickering candlelight. Her eyes fell from the intensity of his gaze.

As one, despite their political differences, the congregation chanted the beloved canticle that closed the service. 'I see Thy bridal hall adorned, O my Saviour, but I have no wedding garment that I may go in.' Marika's eyes filled with tears as she whispered the final stanza. 'O Giver of Light, make radiant the vesture of my soul and save me.'

The next morning Marika killed time by the wellspring, half-heartedly listening to the gossip of the two girls who also lingered here longer than they should. On most late mornings she, Irene, and Calliopi met at the bakery while they waited for their families' midday meals to be pulled steaming from the *fourno* that served as the communal oven. Village houses generally had only a hearth fire and a small one-burner primus stove adequate for soups and boiled dishes. Whatever needed to be baked or roasted was brought to the *artopoion* to be shoved into the oven still warm from the early morning bread-making. When the menfolk picked the olives or the citrus, in return the baker got his fair share. In the subsistence and barter economy of Panagia, where everything, including scarce fuel, was too expensive, it was a way of getting something for next to nothing.

But this was Great Week, a time when even the not-so-pious abstained from meat, fish, eggs, cheese, and oil. When Marika had set out on another of her daily chores, fetching a great jug from the sweetwater spring on the side of the mountain, Old Anna had been preparing their meagre lunch of *fava*, a puréed bean paste; *horta*, boiled dandelion greens; and a thin tomato soup made without oil. But on this morning after Yorgos' return, Marika had so little appetite that she wouldn't have cared if her mother had served up stewed grass.

Usually Marika enjoyed these idle late morning chats with the girls who had been her constant companions ever since she could remember. For the women, the bakery and the village wellspring served the same social function as the *kafeneion* did for the men. But today she was silent and withdrawn. Would Yorgos reveal whether Christos was dead or alive?

'I think,' Irene was saying, 'that Leonidas will finally go to ask my father next week, right after Easter.' For once her homely face – peasant broad, honest as a good day's work, but never pretty – was radiant. 'Maybe the engagement will come soon after.'

'And your *prika*?' Calliopi's cabbage-rose print scarf slipped off her hair as she leaned forward in her eagerness for news she could spread to all the aunts and cousins. None of the women – and the men were as bad or worse – was ever too busy for a tasty titbit that would set tongues wagging on a tedious afternoon or evening. What counted in this village was the price of oranges, the dowries of the girls, and who might be about to give birth to a healthy infant son.

Irene's smile widened as she ticked off her ample dowry on her ringless fingers. 'Four *stremmata* of land, good land, full of olive and orange trees. One donkey and four sheep. And everything we will need for the house that Leonidas told his cousin he will build for us.' She blushed. 'Including a big bed. And of course the trunk with everything I've been sewing since I was a little girl. My sheets, tablecloths, and clothes.'

As modestly she retied her scarf, Calliopi clucked her tongue in apparent delight. But she was disappointed she wasn't hearing anything that wasn't already common knowledge. Since Irene had the good fortune to be one of only two daughters in a family with a rich uncle in America, it was understood that she would be blessed with a grand dowry provided by the profits of a string of Chicago fruit and vegetable stalls. So long as she and her father and brothers were careful to safeguard her reputation and her virginity, that *prika* had been destined to snare her almost any young man she fancied. Still, if Irene had revealed some electrifying new detail – if the preliminary negotiations were stalled on some sticking point such as the exact number of sheep or precisely which plot of land would come with the bride-to-be, Calliopi could have spent a happy afternoon making the nattering rounds of family and friends to spread the word. Yet she rallied and told her friend what she wanted to hear. 'Truly, Leonidas is a lucky boy.'

Irene longed to gush about her beloved's hair, eyes, walk, and talk, but she exerted her maidenly self-control and instead bestowed the ultimate, although understated, compliment upon the young man she had been mooning over for years. 'He is a good boy, I think. Everyone says so.' With the matter-of-fact air of an old man telling his worry beads in a coffeehouse, she recounted what were considered to be his attributes. 'He comes from a good family. His father never dirtied his hands and always worked at a desk over at the Customs House in Nauplion. Leonidas, too, will wear a clean shirt to his job at the post office once it reopens. Everybody says he has a very good character. And he works hard, my Leonidas.' She sighed, and what she really wanted to say burst out of her. 'And he is *poli omorfos*. Very handsome!'

'Yes, you are right.' Calliopi judiciously nodded her head. 'He will make a good husband. Don't you think so, Marika?'

With an effort Marika stopped concentrating on whether, just now, she might have started her period. She forced a smile. The last thing she wanted to hear this morning was more repetitive chatter about Irene's impending marriage to the boy of her dreams. She didn't begrudge her friend an iota of happiness, but it was hard to enthuse about the happy conclusion of a romance when her own had dived perilously close to disaster. Yet Irene had been her closest friend for all their lives. They had been baptised on the same day and shared the same *nonos*, godfather. In the eyes of the church, as well as in their feelings for one another, they were as close as sisters. Arm-in-arm they had skipped off to school every morning, and arm-in-arm on hot summer nights they had promenaded back and forth in the square in the maidenly *volta* parade that was a fixture of village life. 'Leonidas will make you a wonderful husband.' This time Marika's smile was genuine. 'May you give him many sons!'

Irene beamed at Marika, but then she read the worry behind her friend's smile. As Calliopi bent to drink from the spring, Irene formed a silent question with her lips. 'Any word?'

Marika reared her head. She hadn't told Irene *everything*, but her friend shared her anxiety about Christos' disappearance. From this village of less

79

than three hundred, two young men had died fighting the Italians in the World War, the Nazis had killed four more, and another seven had been lost in the Civil War.

Irene mouthed another word. 'Courage!'

As the other two moved on to discuss the wedding dress Irene would be sewing, Marika moodily stared over the flat village rooftops to the white-capped turbulent sea. The sky was as grey and leaden as her thoughts. What did it matter if Christos was dead or alive? He was gone, and her period was twenty-four days late. She had been such a fool to lead him to that cave. But he was a man, and just as her mother always said, the lot of them were brutes. It seemed to her now that when she looked into the eyes of the married women of her village, mostly what she saw were dead hopes and the saddest sort of resignation. It was only the bright-eyed girls, with that dancing way they had of walking, who brimmed with hope and laughter.

Irene and Calliopi now were laughing, just so. Marika felt infinitely older, sadder, and wiser as she listened to Calliopi giggling about a young man from the next village she had seen after church last night walking with one of Irene's cousins in the *plateia*.

'He was laughing so much,' Calliopi said, 'that, I swear, even his little moustache was smiling!'

'You like him, this boy?' Irene shrewdly narrowed her eyes. Now that she was about to be happily married, she wanted to share her good fortune with her friends. None of them were getting any younger. At nineteen, some were already calling the three of them old maids. But with a little judicious matchmaking, maybe the other two would also soon wear the wedding crowns. Perhaps in a season or two, their babies would play together. And in a generation or so, her son might marry Calliopi's daughter. 'If you like him, maybe I will make inquiries. My brother and my cousin always sit together in the *kafeneion* by the cigarette kiosk.' She snapped her fingers. 'By tomorrow or after tomorrow, I will know everything there is to know about this boy with the laughing moustache.'

'What's the use?' Calliopi's smile died. 'You know I have no *prika*. My father says the best he can do is send me to Athens to stay with my uncle's family. Maybe I can get a job. He says I can be a maid, or work in a laundry. Perhaps my uncle can find me a husband there.'

'*Po, po, po!*' Irene puckered her lips in the Greek gesture and sound that indicated not only sympathy but alarm. If Calliopi went to Athens, she would forfeit her reputation and any chance of marriage to a good boy here. Once a girl stepped outside the surveillance of the ever-watchful village eyes, it was assumed she must be doing something she shouldn't. 'Don't go yet,' she counselled. 'Stay a while. The war is almost over. When the boys come

80

back and they see how beautiful you are, maybe one will love you so much that he won't care whether you have a dowry or not.'

'So I pray every day,' Calliopi said. 'I kiss my mother's icon of the Virgin and light a candle and pray, just so.' She shrugged. 'But if my father decides to send me to Athens, what can I do but obey? He says the family needs the money I would send them from my job. My mother is pregnant again.'

'Not again!' Irene did a rapid calculation in her head. At nineteen, Calliopi was the eldest in her family. Like most of the older generation, her mother must have been married at thirteen at the latest. Calliopi's mother was in her early thirties, although after eleven children her sagging figure and haggard face made her seem twice her age. Irene leaned closer to her troubled friend. In the early days of an unwanted pregnancy, a draught of Old Anna's black herbs would empty a woman's womb. But even if a pregnancy progressed a few more months, it was still possible to nip it before it flowered. Abortions, although frowned upon by the church and outlawed by the government, were a last resort. Sometimes, however, the conditions were unsanitary, the abortionist was unskilled, and the woman either died or was left unable to have any more children. Yet still these operations were common enough among those who could afford the fees. Another baby was not only one more mouth to feed but also an additional burden that would keep a mother from working as hard as she should. 'You know, she doesn't have to have this one. My mother had the same . . . problem last year, and she went to Athens and finished it.'

Calliopi shook her head. 'My father wants another son. You know, when someone asks him how many children he has, he always says, "Three children. And eight daughters."'

'He doesn't mean it,' Irene cooed, and then – as she always did when she heard something that disturbed her – she laughed. Her mother had always told her, and she believed everything her mother said, that it was better not to let anyone hear a girl complaining. What man wanted to marry an angry bride? An angry wife, as Irene's mother could attest, was another matter. All a man wanted from a wife, she said, was sons, laughter, good cooking, and nights as hot as the sun. That, and unceasing work while he frittered away his life in the coffeehouses. 'He was just making a joke, like all the men.'

Wordlessly Marika and Calliopi stared back at their more fortunate friend who had six brothers and a dowry big enough to snag her the boy she wanted. What, they both wondered, must it be like to know that your father must have rejoiced – and not all but gone into mourning – when you were born a despised girl instead of an adored boy? Long ago the ancient Greeks had exposed their unwanted daughters on the mountainsides, and there were some modern Greek fathers who might have done the same if the laws allowed it.

But it was nearly one o'clock, and others were approaching for their turn at the spring. The three of them cradled their water jugs like babies as they trudged their separate ways.

Marika hesitated at the path that led up to her house. Dare she steal the time to duck down to the church to light another candle before the icon of the Virgin? Yet she doubted what good one more flickering candle would do. Like her dimming hopes for Christos' return, a candle only burned a few moments before it sputtered, died, and the blackness closed round again. She had been putting matches to wicks and whispering urgent prayers incessantly for too many weeks. If the Virgin was listening, She surely understood by now exactly what – or rather, who – she wanted. If a baby in her womb would bring Christos back and make him stay with her forever in wedded bliss, then she wished she were pregnant. But she had always prayed that, if she had lost him, her womb would be as empty as her life.

Marika contented herself with a little prayer under her breath as resolutely she turned homeward. She was tired of these desperate pleas to a remote God who so far hadn't come to her rescue. She either was pregnant or she wasn't. One more candle wasn't going to alter whatever might have begun inside her. Better, she decided, to go home and see if Vangelis had been able to find out anything about Christos' whereabouts from Yorgos.

She could hear the murmur of voices before she was inside the house.

'He's a strange one,' Vangelis was saying to her mother as she came in the door.

'Who?' Marika set down the jug.

Old Anna and her son exchanged a look, and then the mother nodded for him to tell all.

'Yorgos.' Vangelis all but spat out the name. He wouldn't have set foot in the café where the lieutenant had been holding court all morning if it hadn't been for his sister's urgent need to glean news about Christos. Young as he was, Vangelis hung out at a coffeehouse the *andartes* had called their own. He had never before walked through the door of what his friends called the *fasisto-kafeneion*.

'And?' Marika sank down on the third stool by the hearth.

Vangelis shrugged. 'And nothing.'

'You saw him?' Marika leaned forward intently.

'Everyone saw him. Mind you, not everyone talked to him. I hear Andreas' family is dead-set on revenge. They say they'll get him one day, when he least expects it.' The story of the partisan's torture and death had become a part of village history, complete with Yorgos' contemptuous epitaph that the young man had 'died like a sheep'.

Vangelis went on about Yorgos. 'He made a spectacle of himself, parading out to the kiosk to buy tobacco and cigarette papers and then matches.' Vangelis got up, thrust out his chest, and mimicked Yorgos' rooster strut. 'I never liked him. No one did. But now . . .' Vangelis threw himself back on his stool.

'So what did he say,' Marika pressed, 'exactly?'

'Not much.' Vangelis shrugged his eyebrows. 'Oh, he talked enough. *This* about how the army was making Greece safe for democracy. And *that* about how he had singlehandedly rounded up a band of *andartes* as they tried to make it over the canal at Korinthos. You know Yorgos.'

'We do.' Old Anna stirred the fire. 'But out with it, my son. Don't keep your sister in suspense.'

'About Christos, not much. His friends asked him again and again the same question we all have about what came after that damn Greek Cross raid. But all he did was smile and say his brother wouldn't be coming back to Panagia.'

'Never?' Marika asked.

'He said,' Vangelis reluctantly elaborated, ' "That one won't ever be back here again." About that, I am very sorry to say, he sounded . . . definite.'

'So he's gone then.' Marika's hand crept to her belly.

'Maybe.' Vangelis knitted his brows as his eyes locked on his sister's lap. He had guessed her desperate predicament from snatches of conversation he had overheard in this house. 'But I'm not sure. Yorgos is such a braggart that you'd think he wouldn't have spared us all the grisly details if he did do . . . *that*.' He decided to say one more thing. 'There's something else.' He wetted his lips. 'A scar. Yorgos has a scar, from what seems to be a fresh wound. A deep one. On his cheek.'

'So?' Old Anna was pulling the table up before the hearth and laying out the Lenten dishes. 'Maybe he got it chasing *andartes* across the Korinthos canal.'

'Perhaps. But all the time he was talking about Christos, he kept fingering that scar. As I said, he's a strange one.'

Marika had had enough. 'You eat,' she told her brother, who had already pulled his stool up to the table. As she made for the door, she gave her mother a look. 'I've lost my appetite.'

She was sitting out by the vegetable garden with her head in her hands when, as Marika had known she would, the old one hobbled out for a mother-daughter summit conference.

Old Anna settled down on a boulder and, as she let Marika cry for a while, silently she looked out at the panorama spread before her. Often, in this dreamy seascape that was Greece, the mists of sky and sea were a study in pastel washes of blues and greys, so that only an artist or a native could tell for certain where the water stopped and the air began. But the veils of morning fog had lifted, and the clarities of sea and sky were deeply etched on the horizon. Never was a sea so darkly blue as these calm depths. Never was a sky so lightly blue as these serene heights. Grey and amber clouds raced round the pale sun, and far below shards of light made the sea glitter like diamonds on velvet. The Peloponnese's afternoon wind – hot in summer, cold in winter – raked her face so that she shivered and could almost feel her old bones rattling under her sagging skin. Yet somewhere nearby she could smell basil growing wild between the rocks. Winter was dying, and the resurrecting scent of spring was in the air. Three of the sheep were about to drop their lambs.

Old Anna sighed. 'So, child,' she finally said, 'you can't wait much longer. You have to make a decision.'

'I know.' Marika lifted her tearstained face. But she could not yet bear to speak of Vangelis' news, and so she repeated what she had been saying for weeks. 'Not one word from him! Five whole weeks and no word! Not one word since that morning in the cave! Even with the war, and all his problems with the politics, he could have sent me some word. Anything! He must know how I feel, after what happened in the cave . . . But no, only the silence and the waiting.' Again she started to sob. 'And now they say he is gone. What if he's dead, mama?'

As tenderly she put her arms around her daughter's shaking shoulders, Old Anna's voice fell as if she was talking to herself. 'I knew nothing would come of it. From that night I sent them to the cave, I knew it would all go wrong. But I never thought he would die.' What use, she wondered, were her charms and potions, since she hadn't been able to foresee this calamity in time to forestall it? She should have known better than to nurse Marika's hopes that seducing Christos in the cave would make him marry her. But it was too late for regretful second thoughts. What Marika needed now was practical advice. Again she stroked her daughter's hair in consolation, but then she patted her shoulders in a gesture of finality. 'So, daughter, enough of this weeping. We have a problem, and you must tell me everything if I am to help you. I know your period is late. How much, exactly?'

Marika summoned all her strength so she could sit up straight and look her mother in the eye. 'Twenty-four days.'

'You are sure? You have not mixed up the weeks?'

'You think, on something like this, that I am so stupid?' Marika raised her head in that Greek negative. 'No, mama, I am careful always to keep count.

I thought that when I married Christos, it would help me to get pregnant faster.' Her voice caught. 'They say that some times of the month are better for making babies than others. *Katalaves?*' A pair of tears ran down her cheeks, and angrily she brushed them away. In her bitter eyes, now, there were no more tears. 'They say two weeks after the bleeding begins are the best time. And they say right.'

'Do not be so sure. Maybe it's just nerves. Sometimes the more you think about it, the longer it takes to come.'

'If only that were true!' She paused and considered. It no longer surprised her that there were no bloodstains on her clothes every time she lifted her skirts. She sighed as she dared to voice her fears. 'Somehow, I *know* that I am pregnant. I knew that even the morning after.'

Logically Old Anna wasn't so sure, but she wasn't about to doubt the intuitive abilities of any woman who shared her blood. In the meantime, however, it couldn't hurt to give fate a little push in the right direction. 'It is still not too late to do something about it. I could get the herbs now, and – for sure! – by tomorrow or after tomorrow you would have no problem.'

But Marika shook her head so hard that her kerchief fell from her shoulders to the ground. 'Never! Not Christos' child! Especially not *now* . . .' She was startled by not only her own vehemence but her certainty. Her hand stroked her belly, and she smiled as serenely as the Madonnas in the icons. If he truly were gone, at least she would have this much of him with her forever. If she were carrying his child, she could never kill it. But then, as she looked over and saw the alarm in her mother's eyes, she wavered. A baby was hardly a mere love token, like a wilted flower or the memory of a stolen kiss. Thoughtfully she picked up her scarf and knotted it tightly around her head. 'Or at least I will not even think about those herbs of yours until I'm sure he's not coming back.'

'What proof do you want?' Old Anna was as tough on her daughter as she would have been on herself. 'The *pappas* to give in and assign him a grave?'

Marika flinched, but stubbornly she held her ground. 'Maybe Yorgos is wrong. Maybe Christos will still come back.'

'You believe that, my daughter?'

'Somehow I think I'd know if he were dead. And he isn't! I feel it.' She beat her breast. 'Here!'

'I wish it were so, *paidi mou*. If I could make him come back, my sweet, then I would.' But both of them couldn't live in a dream world. Something would have to be done about this baby Marika was convinced she was carrying. 'But you have to face facts. The best we can hope for is that Christos has gone over the border with his comrades. If he does make it back here, it won't be in time to help you.' The army and the Greek Cross militia

85

were still hunting *andartes*, and island concentration camps were filling up with those who survived the assassination squads.

'I will wait for him forever.' Marika folded her hands over her belly and smiled beatifically at the sea.

'You are young, child. You do not know how long forever is.'

'You are old, mama. Maybe you forget how I feel. Or maybe you never felt it.'

Under her breath Old Anna sighed again as she, too, looked down at the sea and remembered that other time with that other man who had gone away and never come back, at least not to her. No, she had never forgotten Christos' father. She, as well as Eleni, had wanted him for her own when instead he had married Sofia. Had she, by some unlucky trick of the genes, somehow passed that doomed passion onto her daughter? Was this next generation destined to play out that same sad game of love and loss? If so, she would have to do her best to assure a happier ending for her daughter. She shook off her premonition about a cursed love strong enough to span the generations. 'Well, then,' she said with the briskness of the peasant housewife beginning the spring cleaning, 'if you are right, and you *are* pregnant, then we had better very quickly come up with either a husband or a solid marriage proposal. I can't predict what your uncles would do if you became an unmarried mother.'

Marika shuddered. 'I suppose,' she ventured, as she recalled what Calliopi had been saying only that morning, 'that I could go to live in Athens until the baby was born.'

'They live on air in Athens, do they? They eat the air and pick gold bars from trees?'

Marika's face cracked into a smile. 'Remember when I was a little girl, and you told me that story about America, where they pick gold bars from trees? I believed it!' Her chin trembled. 'I always believed everything you said, mama.'

'Then listen and believe me now. Stop pretending that Christos is coming back. He's as gone as your father! And I tell you, do not even think about going to Athens unless you would be willing to give up the baby for adoption as soon as you had it.'

'Never that. Not Christos' child.'

'You are as stubborn as a donkey. You always were. And I suppose you always will be.' Old Anna reached over and stroked the babysoft skin on her daughter's cheek. 'What am I to do with you, my stubborn donkey-girl?' Gently she smiled as she returned to the crux of the matter. 'Like it or not, if you won't get rid of the baby, then you may have to find another to act as its father.'

'Ha!' The very idea was so preposterous that Marika would have laughed if she weren't feeling so bitter. 'Another man? Me? *Ohi*! No! Never that! Even if I wanted someone else – and I am not saying I would – who would have me? If you remember, mother, I have no *prika*. Christos never cared about that, but the others all would. Easier, I think, to find gold bars on the trees of Athens than a husband here in Panagia for a girl who has no dowry.'

And yet that was precisely what she and her mother, with the practised air of professional matchmakers, proceeded to try to do. The two of them already, of course, had whiled away many an hour with their womenfolk speculating about every eligible male any of them had ever heard of or seen. But the wars had winnowed out too many. Of those who had survived, there was one boy who had fancied Marika back in the schoolroom and another who had always made eyes at her when she promenaded on fine nights in the *plateia*. But one of them was off fighting with the government forces, and the other was about to be engaged to a girl from a village on the way to Epidavros. There had to be other possible husbands lurking somewhere – a cousin of one of her girlfriends who lived in a village tucked into the mountainside off the Tripolis road, a friend of her brother's who had gone to find work in Athens, perhaps even a widower who would be eager for a young wife to take over the care of his motherless children. If she scraped rock bottom and said she would marry an old man, one of her uncles' fishermen cronies might be enticed to warm his old bones in her marriage bed. But again, even if she were willing to settle for someone old enough to be her grandfather, she still didn't have a dowry. It would take a long while for the delicate negotiations necessary to persuade even a rheumatic elder to wed a girl without a *prika*, and she could not afford to dally unchurched for so long. If she were to have any chance of passing off Christos' baby as another man's child, she had better get married before another moon waxed and waned.

'But there is one,' Old Anna said, hating to utter the necessary words, 'who might marry you tomorrow.'

Their eyes met. Marika had read his naked desire in that one scorching look in the church last night. Even after all that had happened – his catching her and Christos in the cave and then his supposed murder of his brother on the mountain – she was certain he still wanted her. Whether he would marry her was another question. But even if he would, how could she give herself to the man who implied he was Christos' killer? 'Not *him*. Never *him*.' She hated even to say his name out loud. 'I would sooner slit my throat than marry that one.'

'I do not like him either. But maybe,' Old Anna softly suggested, 'in a little while there will be someone else to think about other than yourself.' She waited a moment for that to sink in. Then, as though this were any other normal discussion about a man's marriageability, thoughtfully she listed the selling points of Christos' brother. 'He comes from a good family, some would say the best in Panagia. His father, as we know so well, is more than a little bit rich. In the summer his mother makes more money with her taverna than most of the men in the village. Yorgos went all the way through high school. And, you will remember, before the wars started there was even talk of sending him to university in Athens. But now he has put away his books and decided to make a career in the army. You would never be hungry if you wore his ring.'

'And never happy, either.'

'So?' Old Anna spat contemptuously into the wind. 'Who in this life is happy?'

'Ah, mother!' Marika's dark eyes were wells of pain. 'To settle for him now! *Him*, after Christos!'

'You must remember your position,' her mother tartly reminded her. 'You will be lucky to get anyone. You could do worse than Yorgos. There are poorer men. And meaner ones, too. But let us not forget the essential point. For you, now, there is no one else.'

Heavily, as though suddenly she carried a great weight not only on her shoulders but in her heart, Marika heaved to her feet. 'I will think about this.'

'Think fast. We have not so much time. Easter is six days away. If you decide it is best to take this other brother, you could be married in time to pass the baby off as his.'

'I suppose.' Marika's face wrinkled up as though she were about to cry again, but instead she stamped her foot as though angry at her own weakness. Was she right to believe that it was too soon to give up her hopes of Christos coming back? 'I will go walk. And think.'

'Do that. But again, I tell you, daughter, do not take so much time with this thinking.'

As Marika paced alone through the sleeping village, she remembered when Christos had trailed behind her on Carnival night. If only she hadn't seduced him, she would still be as free and pure as all the other girls in Panagia. Longing for that lost innocence, she wondered if she would have to pay for that one night of bliss all her life.

Aimlessly she wandered through the shuttered *plateia*, as unsure of where she was going as of what she would do. You must think, she told herself, and then you must decide. There was no time now to mourn either Christos or their love. Yet her mind was such a jumble that she couldn't focus on anything greater than the minutiae of village life: the baker's colicky baby screaming through the siesta, the aged mother of one of the fishermen staring through an open window at the sea, a braying donkey tethered to a bare mulberry tree. For once she, who was accustomed always to knowing what she wanted and how to go about getting it, could hardly bear to think about anything other than how happy she would be if Christos suddenly appeared here as the very human saviour to her divine prayers.

She had wandered out to the woods on the far side of the village before she realized where it was she wanted to go. Suddenly full of purpose, she walked with her customary sure stride down to the beach. She faltered, then, and sighed. It was just here, she reckoned, that I stood in Christos' embrace. She shut her eyes and remembered how his kiss had branded her. But now her arms were empty, and there was only the cold wind to embrace her. Heavily, again, she sighed.

But then she spotted her uncle's rowboat beached just where it had been on that Carnival night. In a moment she was heaving it into the frigid water. As she waded in up to her knees, she hardly felt the numbing cold. She clambered aboard, fit in the oars, and began to row. On the way to the island, it seemed she was the only soul out on the sea. The morning fishermen had already brought in their meagre catches, and those who trawled at night were still home snug under their blankets. It was exhilarating to be one not so much against, but with, the sea. It felt good to pitch her body against the current. After feeling so powerless for so many weeks, it was wonderful to fight something, even the tide, and win. Sharply she wished it were as easy to win at the great struggles of life.

In the silvery afternoon light, the island shimmered ghostly as a mirage on the shining sea. But hard as she rowed, it seemed to remain beyond her reach. Yet that other night even the sea and the tides of the moon had been in league to carry them out on a wave of passion. Or did I, she wondered as she struggled at the oars, imagine that, too? Was everything that night, even the enchanted island, a delusion?

Marika ducked down her head and concentrated all her being on simply rowing, until a long time after, finally she approached the beach. She lifted her skirts, leaped into the water, and shivered as she towed the boat to shore. Out here near the open sea, the water was even icier than back by the shoals that fringed the village beach. Her quivering legs felt pierced with needles, but their ache assured her that this time she was firmly grounded in reality. This afternoon, there was nothing romantic about this wind-swept island of pain.

She stood on the shore looking up at the worn white church on the peak of the mountain. She remembered how she had fancied, when the two of them had slipped inside the chapel that night, that they were plighting their wedding vows. As she had lit a burning nest of candles and the ancient frescoes had seemed alive from those pinpricks of fire, she had imagined that all heaven was witnessing and sanctifying their union. Marika sighed deeply. Maybe all they had been doing in the church that night was making a sentimental visit to an old landmark and lighting a few tapers which had sputtered and died – like her gutted hopes, now – even before they had descended to the cave. She supposed the remains of those candles still must lie in waxy puddles before the icons. She was struck, then, by yet another disillusioning memory. The only icons that had drawn Christos had been St Michael and St George, the fighting saints always on the march against dragons and other evils. I should have been able to read the signs, she thought sadly. But I only saw what I wanted to see.

Tears stung her eyes, and she wished she had not returned to this place where she had been so briefly happy. But she had come this far, and so she would finish her pilgrimage of love and regret. She would creep back into the cave where so much had begun and ended. The wind was rising, and the wet hem of her skirt lashed against her legs. Every step she took, the sharp stones ate into her bare feet. When she turned and looked back, she could see the faint trail of her own blood.

She stared for a moment at the mouth of the cave, remembering how Christos had kissed her just here, how she had fallen on the jagged rocks, and how eager she had been to consummate their union in the Cave of the Great Goddess. Yet something of the magic of that other night still lingered in this place, for her body began to tremble almost as though he were with her still. And he is, she told herself softly. He will never altogether leave me, not while I refuse to let him. If that, too, is a delusion, then so be it. I will never surrender my dreams like all the others in my village who gave up too much too soon.

Suddenly, then, as she felt Christos' presence with her, she was certain not only that what had happened in this place was altogether right but also that she must never allow herself to regret it. Just this afternoon, when she had sat fretting with her mother back in Panagia, she had lost her nerve and told herself that she had been a fool to let him touch her without the blessing of the orange-blossom marriage crowns. But now she was sure that, more than any other single act of her life, it had been right to do as she had done in this place. It was only what had come after – her having to face the consequences of his disappearance alone – that was wrong.

Yet again, as she remembered how he had left her to awaken naked on the floor of this cave, her eyes filled with tears. Never mind the passion and the love and the thrill of it. How could Christos have left her that next morning? She had always been so sure that she would be able to wrest everything she wanted from life. She considered climbing back into the boat, leaving this island forever, and drinking the black tea that would bring at least a part of her predicament to an end.

Instead, as she brushed the tears from her eyes, she reminded herself that she had chosen to live a life that was different from the other girls of her village. Seducing Christos was a gamble that Irene and Calliopi would never have dared. Now that matters had not turned out as she had wished, she had to face the consequences of her own reckless will. Maybe bravery was not exclusively a masculine matter of muscle and brawn. Courage could simply be an acquired art, like cooking or sewing, that could come to a woman with practice. She ducked inside.

Ah, she sighed, as she caught her breath in wonder. Mama was right; it is magic here. Light from outside filtered in faintly, so that the interior was cloaked everywhere in filmy netherworld shadows. The low roof and sloped walls reached round her as though these ancient stones were alive and longed to embrace her. Even the thick air was caressive and redolent of security. Outside she had been exposed to a hostile environment and threatened by a menacing world. But inside she had crawled all the way home, back to the passage to the mother's womb. Here, in this primal space, the rest of the world with all its fears and shoulds dropped away. A realization that was as comforting as a woollen shawl on a winter's night came over her: *I am not alone. Through the ages other women, just like me, have loved and lost. But I, like them, am not defeated, not altogether, not while my heart still beats and my womb still swells.*

As Marika hugged herself in exultation, she could feel a marvellous surge of courage budding within her. She was as sure as she knew her own name that she was strong enough to hold her head high and face her destiny. Always, as her life unfolded, she could trust and depend upon herself. Armed with this surety, she would try never to let herself altogether surrender to despair. She might not always get exactly what she wanted – And Christos! Marika beat her breast at the realization that she might never have her Christos again – but neither would she cease dreaming and struggling for her heart's desires and what she thought was right.

A premonition shot through her. She shut her eyes and could see herself not as she was now, young and fresh and unmarked by life, but with her hair white at the temples and her eyes lined, so lined. She could see herself sitting all alone in a dark place like this – enclosed, underground, with stone walls, too. What was this cell of the future, she wondered. *A cell, yes, that was it exactly.* Marika shivered. Her mother had often warned her that it could be more of a curse than a blessing to see the future. With an effort, then, she pushed aside her foreboding about what seemed to be the prison of her future and instead focused on what she sensed was the essential lesson to be learned from this glimpse ahead. Then, as now, she would be by herself. She was fated to spend most of her life *moni*, alone. Yet in this moment of revelation she understood there were worse destinies.

Marika took a deep breath and looked around again as though memorizing the exact contours of every dear stone in this womb of a cavern. Even though she understood that the bravery of this moment would not last forever, and that there would be other times of weakness and cold doubt, she must take care never to forget nor to lose the courage that she had found – no, that had been *born* – here. She must nurture it like a newborn, for in the hard times to come it would be the cane she would lean on for strength and balance. And whatever the consequences, no matter what awaited her back in the village, she must not lose the certainty that what she had done here with Christos had been right. Even though he was gone now, and because of what had happened here her life most probably would be changed forever – and not for the best – still she would choose to do it all again. She had wanted him, and she had taken him just as much as he had taken her. She flung up her arms over her breasts and, as she embraced herself as Christos had done, the warmth of her own flesh comforted her. No matter what price she had to pay for that night, it was worth it to have been loved so and to love, even once.

On impulse, then, scarcely aware of what she was doing, Marika ripped off her scarf, loosened her hair from its braids, and dreamily began to sway from side to side, then to step lightly to the left, then to whirl from one end of the cavern to the other. Here in the Cave of the Great Goddess, she danced a sensual dance whose steps she had never consciously learned, but which in her heart she must have always known. For here, in this cave that had been sacred to women in the old times, every year the young and the old had come to celebrate their women's mysteries and renew their women's powers. Just so, now, as Marika danced this ancient dance of exultation, as she glided and spun and pranced, her face glowed with a radiance that transcended itself. For one glorious moment, she was the eternal woman, and triumphant.

Marika was panting as she finally sank down, exhausted, on the worn rocks. But for the first time since Christos had left her, her mind was as clear as the sky at midday. *I have myself back again, and I will be all right. Whatever happens, I will be strong enough to do whatever I have to do.*

Still flushed with heady intoxication, she finally admitted what she had long denied, that she shared at least an equal measure of guilt for her predicament. She had seduced Christos of her own free will, and she had done so not from pure lust but from calculated manipulation. He, however, had never pretended he would marry her while this war was on and he was over his head in revolutionary politics. Christos had promised to make her his wife only when their country, and he himself, was at peace. Yet she had wanted him beyond reason. She supposed she had been impatient, and wilful, and confident that she could reshape *moira* to her own specifications. And so she had taken her gamble. Now that she had lost fair and square, was it mean to whine that Christos had treated her shabbily? Did she perhaps deserve exactly what she had gotten?

Marika stamped her foot in anger. No! She had not been wrong, not her, not then, not now. Maybe some other time, when she was old and her bruises didn't hurt so, she could bear to analyse what had happened and apportion blame in a dispassionate way. But, here and now, she would not excuse him for breaking faith and running away in the night. Nor, assuming he was still alive somewhere behind the Iron Curtain, would she try to track him down and beg for marriage. Even though she was a woman, she was a Greek; and she, too, had her pride. She might be pregnant, and unmarried, but she had not lost her essential dignity as a human being.

She looked again at the hoary walls as though they might give her strength to be as stoical as all her people have been since the ancient times. Her heart might weigh like a great stone. But she supposed that in time she would learn to bear that burden without stooping. For her own good, however, she would have to put aside her yearnings for Christos. She would have to wrap up her feelings, like a bride tenderly folds up her wedding dress and packs it away in a cedar chest for safekeeping. But perhaps sometimes in the years to come, again like a wedded woman who wistfully yearns for the hopes she had worn as innocently as her bridal gown, she could quietly dig out those stored memories and remember the glory that once was their love.

Yet she had a lump in her throat. Christos, oh, Christos!

She wanted to throw herself down on the ground and weep, but she did not. If she was to triumph, she had to be strong. Over and over again she repeated those words. If she was to triumph, she had to be strong.

When she was calm again, she forced herself to think through her alternatives.

She could sit tight and wait for him to come back. But Vangelis had said Yorgos had seemed 'most definite' that Christos wouldn't be returning to the village. Whether he was dead or merely living in exile, she couldn't count on him to marry her before the baby was born. So then, what? If she wasn't going to abort either with her mother's herbs or a doctor's help, she either had to leave the village or find a husband.

She could make a new life in Athens. Even though there weren't gold bars on the trees, surely there must be people of decency who would help her. She could say her husband had died in the war. Her father had cousins there, and her mother had a niece. Perhaps she could live with one of the relatives, get a job in an office or even cooking or cleaning, and save up her money for the baby. Even though it would be a hard life, she would be more independent than here in the village.

But then Marika made an impatient 'tsk!' sound with her tongue. No more delusions, she told herself sternly. Just as her mother had warned, she could never manage to work outside the home and, at the same time, take care of an illegitimate baby on her own. Moreover, she had to face the fact that the traditional supports of her family – close or distant – would be denied to her once it was known that she had violated the most basic taboo. There was nowhere to run and hide, and no magical solution. She had to use all the resources at her command to make the best of things in Panagia.

Again she racked her brain for possible husbands, and again she drew a blank except for *that* one.

Marika wrinkled her nose as if her mother were cooking cabbage. All right, then . . . so what about Yorgos?

For a moment her control snapped. Not him, never him! She loathed Christos' brother. Of all the men in Panagia, he was the last she would willingly choose for a husband.

Resolutely she snapped the lid back tight on her emotions. She must think not of herself but the baby. As usual, her mother had been right. She must think of the baby. Because of her lack of a dowry and the haste in which a marriage would have to be arranged, there was no one else but Yorgos.

Yet even as Marika's mouth froze in a hard thin line, she was Greek enough to admit that in practical terms she could do worse. As her mother had reminded her, he had a decent job, came from a good family, and would provide for her and the baby all their lives. There would even be a sort of secret justice to marrying Yorgos, for her son would bear exactly the same name as if she had married Christos. It was the Greek custom to name a newborn after its paternal grandparent. Married to either brother, her son would be Nikolas Kronos. And yet still, no matter how she tried to talk herself into this marriage, it sickened her that Yorgos would have the right, sanctified by the church and written into the letter of the law, to touch her whenever and wherever he wanted. How could she endure a lifetime of nights in his bed?

Marika reached down and tenderly stroked her belly. She might indeed have lost the father. But if she steeled herself to do whatever she had to do to provide their baby with a bright future, she might never lose the son. Their baby would be her living faith in what she had once had in this cave with the man she still loved. She would lavish all her hopes, dreams, and affection on this child who would never leave her as his father had. She would make sure of that, as God – or was it the Goddess? – was her witness.

Under her breath Marika heaved a sigh as she resigned herself to settling for Yorgos.

Again she sighed, even more heavily. If it weren't Yorgos, after all, it would be someone much like him. Prostitutes weren't the only ones who bartered their bodies for survival.

A shudder passed over Marika, and she looked around with a sense of foreboding as she remembered the afternoon she had first heard about this cavern. When mama had made those revelations about the power of this place on Carnival eve, she had warned her – oddly, it had seemed, at the time – that whoever was inside here with her at the crucial moment would be bound up together, and forever. So her mother had said, and so it might be. She, Christos, and Yorgos might be fated to be locked in a triangular passion. Was it inevitable that she would love Christos but marry Yorgos?

Marika shook off her misgivings and stretched as though she had finally shrugged the weight of the world off her shoulders. It was a relief not to have these alternatives racing around her mind like rats on a tin rooftop.

The shadows were lengthening in the cave, and she would have to go soon if she were to row back to Panagia before the night winds were ahowl. She rebraided her hair and fastened her scarf. But before she went off to set this new course of her life in motion, she lingered a while longer with her bittersweet memories. She closed her eyes tight and recalled that exquisite night of love. Where are you, my Christos? Do you remember as I do, or have you already forgotten me and everything that you once said mattered so much?

At last, however, she brushed the dust off her skirt and made her way back to where the rowboat was beached. Slowly she rowed away from the enchanted island, back to Panagia and reality.

Four mornings later on the darkest day of the Greek Orthodox calendar – *Megali Paraskevi*, 'Great Friday', the day Christ died on the Cross – Marika grimly waited in a secluded olive grove for her tryst with Yorgos. Churchbells tolled a funeral knell, flags drooped at half mast, and the fasting village had piously laid aside its work. On every other Great Friday she could remember, Marika had picked a basket of spring wildflowers and then gathered in the black-shrouded church with the other girls to adorn Christ's bier with roses, violets, and orange blossoms for tonight's candlelit procession through the village lanes. But today, when she intended to seduce a marriage proposal from him, Christos' brother was keeping her waiting in this olive grove.

95

She paced under the silvery rustling branches, recalling how, amid the holy hustle and bustle of this Great Week, she had coldly set her trap for Yorgos. She had been forced to move with unholy haste once Vangelis had reported the lieutenant would be returning to his unit the day after Easter. Accordingly, after church on Monday night she had promenaded arm-in-arm with Irene and Calliopi past Yorgos' favourite *kafeneion*. When she had felt his hot eyes upon her, she had forced herself to give him a fleeting glance from the corners of her downcast eyes. And before she had sashayed on her way with her friends, she had smiled just a little.

She watched a bee flitting from flower to flower gathering honey for the queen back in the hive and remembered how she had passed Great Tuesday afternoon buttering up her aunt whose two rightwing sons were back from the army for the holiday. Over tea at her Aunt Zoi's, she had prattled on about how manly Themis and Petros were in their uniforms, flattered her with lies about what she swore the other girls said about them, and complained that Panagia had suffered more at the hands of the *andartes* than the Germans. What a fool she had been, she had sighed to her aunt, to indulge herself with that crush on the likes of Christos Kronos. She had confided that, as she had outgrown her silly infatuation, she had come to realize that his brother had always been far the better man. Finally getting to the point, she had simpered, all ablush with girlish modesty, that she regretted turning down his marriage proposal. Hours later, when again she passed by his *kafeneion* on her way home from church, she had been able to tell by the way Yorgos was preening that – just as she had known she would – Aunt Zoi had passed this delicious gossip onto her sons, who had immediately given Yorgos a verbatim report.

Marika studied a parade of ants marching across an olive root, each patiently carrying a scintilla home to their hill a few trees away. Just so, as anxious as she had been to finish this farce before she lost her nerve, she had wished she could have gone *siga-siga*, slowly, slowly, and kept Yorgos on the boil for weeks instead of days. Instead, conscious of her biological deadline, she had let him catch her smiling when they passed one another on the beach early Wednesday morning, and then she had swivelled her hips a little more than usual when she was certain he would be watching her glide out of his sight. That afternoon in the *plateia*, she had stared at him long and hard before coquettishly covering her mouth with her shawl and turning away. Glimpsing him as she came out of the church that evening, she had audibly caught her breath and then sighed like a lovesick maiden in a cheap melodrama.

Marika listened to the birds chirping as they built their nests in the olive trees. Painfully then she recalled how her desperate courtship had passed arm's-length preliminaries yesterday in a deserted lane out by the Widow Papadakis' house.

She supposed she shouldn't have been surprised when, as a result of her blandishments, Yorgos had contrived to be lurking there just at the hour when she would be passing by with fresh bread for her family's lunch. Never one for subtlety, Yorgos had simply hurled himself upon her. The bread had dropped into the dust as he pinned her against the wall and pressed his lips to hers.

Instead of retching in his face, she had made herself whisper, 'Oh, Yorgo, oh, my dear.' For the count of three seconds she had allowed him a swooning taste of her lips. But then she had wriggled away and hid her face with her shawl. 'You do not respect me,' she had observed as she retrieved the bread and brushed the dust off the crust, 'to treat me like this.' When he had lunged at her again in answer, this time she had evaded his grasp.

'Come here,' he had hoarsely ordered. 'You want it. I know you do. I know how you are. I've seen you, remember, with *him*.'

'You dare to talk to me like this?' And haughtily, as though she were truly an outraged virgin and not the woman Yorgos had seen naked on the floor of the cave a scant six weeks ago, she had muffled the shawl even more closely around her. She had been grateful she and her mother had rehearsed what she must say when Yorgos first threw Christos up in her face. Even so, she had been so nervous playing out this crucial scene that she had nearly stuttered on the next especially difficult words. '*He* is gone – dead, for all I know or care.' Finally she had wrung her hands in the Greek gesture that something is forever finished. 'Do not mention him ever again.'

The blood had rushed to Yorgos' head, and that jagged scar on his cheek had seemed to throb. 'You love my brother.'

She had shrugged and lied. 'Not him.'

'Is it really so?' he had said softly. 'Finally so?'

As she had watched him feasting his suddenly credulous eyes upon her, she had been startled at how easy it seemed to be to deceive this one who had always boasted he was smarter than everyone else in the village. But remembering herself and Christos, she had understood that in this matter of love she, too, had perhaps always been too eager to believe what she wanted to believe. As she had continued to lock eyes with Yorgos, a tenderness had crept into his gaze. He really loves me, she had thought, and from a sense of decency she had almost abandoned her cynical designs. Instead she had dismissed her compunctions and continued parroting the lines she had practised with her mother. 'Come to me tomorrow,' she had breathed, 'and you will know for sure.' As she uttered those words, she had tried to take care that he wouldn't embrace her again.

But he had been too quick for her. Before she could get away, he had wrapped his arms round her, had begun devouring her lips, and had seemed intent on taking her there in the village lane.

'Not here!' She had angled her body away from the hard swell of him against her belly, where his brother's baby was growing. 'Someone will see!'

He had groaned, but that deeply ingrained village reflex always to hide from prying eyes had been stronger even than his passion. He had slackened his hold. 'Then where?'

'In the olive groves up on the mountain behind your cousin's pastures.' She had escaped from his embrace and enveloped herself in her shawl. 'Tomorrow at eleven, when everyone's in church.' Before he could say or do another thing, she had again retrieved the mangled bread from the dust and had begun to edge toward the safety of the corner. Then she had felt like falling on her knees in thanksgiving when she had espied old Kyria Antigoni hobbling in their direction. 'Someone's coming,' she had murmured. 'We must part.'

'Tomorrow, *glika mou*,' he had called out. 'Finally, tomorrow, my sweet . . .'

And so here she waited in the hot spring noontime sun.

She breathed in the scent of basil and wildflowers, listened to an early cicada chirping that summer was coming, and gazed down at the serenity of the blue bay. With a pang it occurred to her that this might be the last time she would be pure enough to feel at one with all of this. On such a day, when all nature throbbed and budded and seemed about to burst into harmonious song, she felt ashamed of the web she had woven. But it was still not too late to back out. She could drink a draught of her mother's black herbs and wait – forever, if need be – for Christos. Or perhaps the bad luck that had dogged her since Yorgos had stalked them to the cave would turn. Any minute now Vangelis might come running up the hill with a message that had just arrived from Christos. She would rip it open and read that he wanted her to join him in exile in Belgrade. In a delicious denouement, just before she left Panagia, she would tell Yorgos exactly what he could do with his slimy reptile body and his palpitating chicken heart.

Marika sighed then, and scaled down her dreams. She would be content if, instead of doing what she feared today, Yorgos would escort her home where once again he would ask her mother and brother's approval for their marriage. Her family would say yes, and the ceremony would take place as soon as matters could be arranged. Yorgos would be a perfect gentleman and never taunt her about Christos.

Again she sighed, even more unhappily. In another yet more preposterous daydream, Yorgos – just as she had seen in a foreign movie one summer in

Nauplion – would go down on bended knee today and beg her to marry him.

Marika burst into bitter laughter at the absurdity of such a thing. For a man to kneel to a woman who wasn't a virgin and didn't even have a dowry! She laughed so hard that she put her face in her hands and cried.

Just then she heard the snap of twigs, and as she looked up through the branches she saw the sickly green flash of his uniform. It was too late to run away now.

As soon as he caught sight of her blue shawl, Yorgos surged over, seized her arm, and all but dragged her deeper inside the enveloping shade of the secluded grove. His hands raked her hair, his lips sucked her throat, his pelvis humped her belly.

'Wait,' she pleaded. 'We must talk.'

Instead he was unbuttoning the bodice of her dress and greedily diving inside. 'Like gold,' he exulted as he beheld the richness of her breasts. He kneaded his hands in them and then buried his head in the cleft. 'Finally mine!'

Rigid with dread that he would rape her if she didn't act fast, Marika coiled all her strength and butted him away. 'Not before we're married,' she gasped.

'Married?' He stopped dead. Clearly on her tearstained face he read not love but desperation. That, and revulsion. He backed away from her. What a fool he had been to believe her smiles, her sighs, and the pretty words she had planted with her cousins. He had loved her so, and he had hoped that at last she had begun to love him in return. He had even talked to the *pappas* about when they could be married. But now as before, she pined after his brother. And now as always, Christos had triumphed. His hand stole up to the scar his brother had marked him with for life. Thoughtfully he caressed it. Three times that dawn on the mountain he had spared his nemesis, and this week he had dared hope that God had awarded him Marika as payment for his mercy. Yorgos' face darkened. He had never been able to best his brother, but Christos' woman was no match for him. '*You* want to marry *me*?' When he took his glasses off, his eyes were as cold as the winter wind from the sea. 'So that's what you're after. Not me, not really. Marriage.'

Stare for stare, she met his eyes.

Just as she thought they were about to begin the negotiations, rage overpowered him. Last week in Korinthos he had visited a brothel. He knew how to treat a girl like Marika. He ripped open his trousers and was upon her again. 'If you want to marry me, you'll have to show me how much.' This time his ruthless hands, lips, and legs pinned her against the gnarled trunk of the olive tree. As he forced her down on her knees, the most primitive woman-to-man fear possessed her. He was bigger, stronger, and he could even kill her if he wanted.

She parted her lips to cry out 'no', but he had pushed inside her mouth before she could make a sound. She gagged as she felt him sliding down her throat. He thrust himself in and out so fiercely that her skull whacked against the trunk of the tree. She concentrated on the impact of her bone against the ridges of the olive bark and the continuous tolling of the churchbells. Do not, she warned herself, let yourself think about what he is doing to you. The churchbells, think of the churchbells. They would not cease ringing until tonight, when Christ's Passion finally was at an end.

'Ah!' he cried out. 'Yes, yes, yes . . .'

She could hardly breathe, she could not think, she felt her gorge rise and was about to vomit. But just then he reared out of her.

Marika collapsed and sprawled down on the earth, still damp from yesterday's rain. At least it's over, she consoled herself. The mud was slick on her face. He can do no more to me now.

But her ordeal had only begun.

Yorgos was rooting in her skirts. Before she realized what he was doing, he had pulled her voluminous knickers down to her knees and was spreading apart her buttocks. With horror Marika remembered first hearing about this particular sexual practice years ago as she and an older girl filled their water jugs at the spring. Brazen Chryssa, who had later married a fisherman old enough to be her father, had confided that she let the boys do it to her like this when they insisted. It keeps them coming back for me, she had said, and still – so long as they don't tell everyone – it will leave me a virgin on my wedding night. When a wide-eyed Marika had asked if she liked it, Chryssa had shrugged and said she liked kissing better. Then she had stopped smiling and said, with the bitterness of one far older than her years, that it didn't matter what a woman liked, did it? She just let the boys do it so they would smile at her, and talk to her, and make her feel pretty. And then one final truth had burst out of Chryssa. Yes, she had admitted, it hurt when they did it in the back.

Marika screamed in pain – just as Chryssa had said – as again he invaded her. It hurt more when she tried to writhe away, and so except for her trembling she lay still.

Yorgos was lying full length on top of her, pumping deeper and deeper, and then he hissed in her ear. 'Did *he* do it to you like this? Did he? Or am I at least the first to be here?'

A shudder passed through her, and she would have traded her soul to be able to crawl away on all fours through the comparatively clean mud. But there was no escape. She cried out when he pounded in still deeper.

'Tell me! Did my brother do this, too?'

Weakly she shook her head.

'Eh? What's that?'

'No,' she whispered into the mud. 'He did not.'

'Good.'

As suddenly as he had been inside her, he was out. She lay where she was until he rolled her over with the toe of his boot. He towered over her. With a sickening lurch of fear, she saw that he was still erect. And he was smiling.

'So you want to marry me.'

She would have preferred death at this moment, but she remembered the baby. She shut her eyes and managed to mutter one word. 'Yes.'

'Why should I marry you?'

Her eyes shot open. A sentiment she and her mother had rehearsed came to her. 'Because you love me.'

'Do I?' He laughed. 'Is this love?'

He has no mercy, she thought. No love, no tenderness, and no mercy. Marika struggled against tears. But if she ever needed her wits, now was the time. She played what she and her mother had decided was her high card. 'It would kill Christos if I married you.' And me, she added to herself. It would kill what is best in me, and forever.

'You think my brother is still alive?' Again he laughed.

Tears rolled down her cheeks. She had been dead wrong in her calculations. Yorgos did not love her and would not marry her. She had let him do these dirty things to her, and for nothing. She could feel a wail of grief, like those the women let loose at funerals, building deep inside her. It started in her womb, retched up to her belly, engorged her heart, and finally burst through her lips. Marika howled like a wounded animal.

For the first time since she had demanded marriage, Yorgos' expression softened. 'Stop that, now,' he said roughly. But when she continued to keen, he knelt beside her and tentatively reached out and stroked her hair back from her temples. 'Stop that,' he murmured as he took her in his arms and held her. She began to cry, and he wiped away her tears with his fingers and rocked her back and forth. When finally she stopped sobbing, he leaned over and kissed her on the lips.

Slowly, then, as she lay limp and unprotesting, Yorgos began to make love to her. He kissed her hair, her breasts, and her thighs. He stroked her and cuddled her. He nuzzled her with his lips, his hands, his hair. He entered her so gently that at first she did not even know he was inside. Against her will, or at least without her conscious consent, she began to move with him. She stared at Christos' scar on Yorgos' cheek until finally he convulsed.

She lay as still as one who is dead.

101

'Marika? Marika?'

After a while she opened her eyes to this strange and violent man.

'So it begins,' he said.

He got up, rearranged his clothing, and brushed his hair back into place with his hands. He took his eyeglasses from the case in his back pocket and carefully polished them on his sleeve before he put them back on. 'I already talked to the *pappas*. We'll be married two Sundays after Easter.' Without another word, he was gone.

Marika lay in the sun under the olive trees for a long while. Then she, too, stood and brushed herself off as best she could before she went home to tell her family that she was engaged to be married.

But just before she left the olive grove, as the churchbells continued to toll, she turned and looked back at the scene of her degradation.

So it begins, she repeated to herself.

Five

'Chris!' The father slammed through the swinging doors from the dining room and impatiently snapped his fingers at his son. Nick Kronos' greying hair was slicked back like in the Brylcreem adverts, and his eyes, shoes, and natty plaid suit were all ashine. His small, newly-opened Boston restaurant had not yet turned a nightly profit, but to him its very existence meant that he had finally achieved the American dream he had been running after for twenty-four years. *Elino-Americanica*, the Greek-American dialect he usually favoured when speaking to his son and the other Greek immigrant staff, boomed over the kitchen. '*Dio chicken ke ena souvlaki*! *Grigora*! *To xeries they hate to wait*!'

'*Eftase*! It's already there!' The English Christos had learned with ease back in his schoolroom was better than his father's, yet from sentiment and stubbornness he insisted on using not a bastardized patois but his real native language when in the company of his countrymen. Fate had replanted him in America, and he meant to make the best of things and take root and flourish here. But he would never forget that his tongue and his soul would always be Greek. 'Right away, *patera*.'

'That's my boy.' Nick beamed like the summer sun over the Aegean. The two pairs of identical green eyes smiled.

Although his tray was already piled high with four heaping dinner plates, Christos adroitly balanced on three more before he sped into the dining room. He had lost much in this past seven months of great changes and greater regrets, but at least he had found the intimacy he had always craved with his father. He would do almost anything to keep this dear one happy. And so he, who had once dreamed of being a cabinet minister in the first socialist government of Greece, tried to be content merely to serve from the left the kebabs, the roast lamb, and the moussaka.

A crisp command issued from the next table of well-dressed diners who had trooped in late after a night at the theatre. 'Ketchup!' One of the women, bossy like so many of them here, sounded as imperious as an Ottoman sultana summoning a slave. 'You forgot the ketchup for the French fries.'

'And they're cold,' another resplendent lady at the table complained. She speared one of the offending potatoes. 'I hate cold French fries.' She wagged the fork at her husband. 'Why we had to come to a Greek restaurant, I don't know.'

Christos smiled as if he meant it as he slid the lukewarm chips back on his tray. What, he wondered afresh as he glided back to the kitchen, would it be like to be married to one of these absurdly dominating women? He and the other Greek exiles all agreed these Americans were beautiful, with their long slim thighs and small high breasts, and even those old enough to be his mother looked young enough to be his sister. But although their men seemed content enough, Christos could not picture how these odd couples must be with one another in the bed. In sex, as in so many things, everything was upside down in this bewildering country.

Yet while he awaited another batch of redhot potatoes in the kitchen, Christos tried to amuse himself by imagining what these couples would be doing in an hour or two between the sheets. He supposed the especially lordly one would insist on being on top, and she might even call out a bored order that her harried husband finish it up so that she could turn over and get her beauty sleep. The impertinent one who had dared wave her fork at her husband in public might, however, be more exciting. By the way she had hungrily looked him over as he stood by their table, she had seemed like a woman who relished her sex more than her food. Yet, considering how quick she had been to send the potatoes back to the kitchen, she might pack her husband off to the divorce court if he, too, wasn't hot enough for her taste.

Christos smiled and meant it, as he emerged from the kitchen with a steaming dish of fried potatoes. These little private jokes were how he kept going night after night in his father's taverna. Better to armour himself with a cynical veneer than to sink down at one of these tables and bury his face in his hands and weep for the loss of his country, his cause, and his woman. Circumstances had forced him to toughen up since he had stalked away from his brother on that Peloponnese dawn and begun the odyssey that had ended in his father's gleaming stainless steel kitchen. Always he told himself that, if he weren't to lose his mind and his soul, too, then he had to wall off the doors to his memory and live in the present instead of the past.

But just then, at the far table by the window that looked out on the bustling Back Bay avenue, a woman with her back to him gave her long black hair an emphatic toss as she said something to her companion. Christos took an involuntary step forward, as if there were an irresistible magnet in that hair that was almost as radiantly blueblack as *hers*. Then the woman turned a fraction further, and he saw the eyeglasses and the pasty skin.

He made a military about-face and retreated to the kitchen. Until he could slow his heartbeats back to normal, he busied himself brewing a fresh pot of coffee and refilling the salad trays.

Yet before he ventured back inside the dining room, he stood at the round window set in the swinging door and stared broodingly at the woman who was not Marika. He thought back to his first day in America, which had begun so auspiciously with his father tearfully embracing him as he walked off the boat in a daze. He had despaired, in the four harrowing months it had taken him to get to that New York pier, that he would ever make it to his father. Getting out of Greece had been the least of it. After evading government patrols and militiamen all the way to Patras, he had used the last of his drachmas to bribe his way onto a ferry bound for the boot of Italy. When he had opened his pockets to Italian immigration officials at Brindisi, instead of identification papers all he had had to prove who he was were his shepherd's flute and that ornate dagger. He had been assigned to a teeming 'displaced persons' camp where he had filled out sheafs of papers attesting that he wanted to join his father, a naturalized American citizen living in Boston, Massachusetts. Then, biting his nails to the quick, he had waited his turn for his application to be weighed and processed. When finally a busy American bureaucrat had interviewed him, Christos had told the first of many lies about his past in Greece. The word in the camp was that Communists – even *former* Communists – were denied entrance to America, and so he had glossed over his war record, admitting only that he had fought against the Nazis. He wanted to join his father, he had sworn, because his village had been destroyed by the Communists and his family ties severed in the war. It had been a common enough story, and one his father had eagerly corroborated, and so after three months in the refugee camp Christos had finally sailed steerage class across the Atlantic to the brave new life he had dreamed he would live there with his father and Marika. All during that arduous crossing, in his mind he had drafted and redrafted the letter he would send her as soon as he arrived in Boston. He had assumed they would be married by the winter, just as soon as Immigration gave the green light and she followed his trail across the ocean. But Christos' house of cards had collapsed before he and his father even took the train to Boston. Over lunch at a Greek-American taverna in Astoria, Nick had filled him in on the family news. Yorgos, he had announced over the moussaka, had married a village girl just after Easter. 'A pretty little thing, at least from the wedding pictures. You'll see them – and my taverna! wait until you see that! – as soon as we get home. Marika doesn't look at all like her mother, that Old Anna. But she's a good girl, Eleni says. But I guess you know this Marika?' Christos had stammered an answer of sorts and then excused himself and gone to the bathroom and bashed his fist into the wall until his knuckles were bloody and the plaster flaked like snow. Still, months later, the hurt had hardly healed. Yet as longingly he gazed at this woman who was a little like the other, Christos was honest enough to wonder if what festered more was that he had lost her or that his brother had won her.

He flexed his empty hand and remembered that terrible dawn on the mountain when he had held his father's dagger to his brother's throat. Fate had presented him with the chance to be rid of the one he now knew as his life's rival, and yet he had let that golden opportunity slip through his fingers with the knife. But that act of mercy had come, after all, before Yorgos had stolen his woman. If some evil genie conjured up his brother and placed that old Turkish stiletto in his hand again, would he make that same choice tonight?

Christos' right hand balled into a fist as he struck his thigh again and again. But it wasn't his brother but the woman who was now his brother's wife that made his blood boil over like a *briki* of Greek coffee too long over the fire. How could Marika have married his own brother? Anyone but Yorgos. But no, that wasn't true. He had wanted her for himself. He hadn't realized how much until he lost her.

His eyes drilled into the black hair that reminded him so of the other's. Perhaps *she* was to blame even more than Yorgos. His mind twisted back to that other night a few weeks after his arrival, when his father had spread open an airmail letter on the kitchen table in the small South End apartment they shared. In that priggish script of his, Yorgos had written that Marika was pregnant and the baby due in the winter. Christos remembered how he had marinated in a jealous rage, counting backwards on his fingers, hardly daring to wonder if that baby could be his. Surely she would have waited and gotten word to him if she was carrying his child. She could not possibly be trying to pass off what was his as his brother's. Yet even as he had ticked off the months since their one night of love in that cave, a small mean thought had taken root in his mind and never altogether let go. Yorgos had said the baby was due in midwinter. If the child was his brother's – as it seemed it must be – then evidently Marika had not wasted much time pining for him. For all he knew, she might have seduced his brother in that same cave the next night. She had been far too eager to give him everything without the blessing of the wedding crowns, so why not his brother, too? Perhaps she had never truly loved him at all. Maybe all she had been after was a lifetime of security as the wife of one of the Kronos boys. She had not had a dowry, and so she might have used her body as *prika*.

His father caught his eye and indicated, by a toss of his head, that his tables needed attention. Christos hid a sigh and tucked away his suspicions as a dog buries a bone to gnaw on another time. But as he tended to his father's business, he couldn't stop himself from stealing hot glances at that woman with the haunting resemblance. He could spend every night until Doomsday trying to convince himself that Marika was a whore, but his heart would remain steadfast. Always he would be tormented by doubts, and might-have-beens, and wishes that matters had turned out differently. Instead of saving his own skin and making for Patras, should he have first risked a visit back to Panagia? Better yet, should he have put love above duty and stayed with her the morning after in that cave? What had his precious politics amounted to, anyway? Last summer Yugoslavia, the last friend of the Greek *andartes*, had closed its border to the beleaguered partisans. Any day now it was expected that the Communists would admit the Civil War was officially over. So much suffering, and for nothing.

Again Christos stared off into space, remembering what he would never forget. After he had left his brother that fratricidal morning, instead of making directly for Patras he had detoured back to his camp to see if Yorgos' boasts were true. The bodies had been mutilated beyond recognition, and he had wept over the remains of those men he had loved. Bent on revenge, he had backtracked to the site of his showdown with Yorgos, but all that he had found there were bloodstains in the snow. That, and the desecration of Apostolis' body. Sick at heart, Christos had determined to leave the bloody graveyard that Greece had become. The Communist Party was riven by dissension and had degenerated into wolves prowling the snowcovered mountains. All he could expect if he went to fight in the last stand in the mountains was a comradely knife in the back. Surveying Apostolis' corpse – Yorgos had cut off the ears and inscribed a cross on the forehead – Christos had understood that he, too, could expect no mercy if he turned himself in to the government forces. And so he had made his way away from love and country – to Patras, and now America.

Christos came out of his reverie when the woman with Marika's hair shrugged on her coat. As she strode into the windy autumn night, Christos felt as desolate as when he had first heard that he had lost the woman he loved to his brother. No, he was sure now, he should never have left her in the cave that morning. But, he pleaded to the court of his own regrets, he had meant to come back to her as soon as he could. Yet there had been a war on, and he and his men had been running for their lives, not only from the army and the militias but also from the brutes who had wrested control of the revolutionary army of the left. But how could she have ignored those words of love he had sent back to her with Andreas? By marrying someone else, she had broken faith with a trust he had thought eternal. Except for an occasional dingy night when he had slunk into the Combat Zone and paid a girl for the use of her body, he hadn't touched another woman since that night in the cave.

As Christos flung open the restaurant door and peered down the street for one last glimpse of that one with the lustrous hair, a terrible doubt crept into his mind. Maybe Marika had never gotten his message. Yorgos had known he meant to send for her from America, but as matters had turned out, his brother had most certainly not pleaded his case. And in those violent days of blood and fire, perhaps Andreas had never made it back to the village. It could be that – waiting, alone, with no word from him, thinking that he was unworthy of any woman's love – Marika had believed herself to be not only betrayed but abandoned. Was that why she had married Yorgos?

Christos bowed his head and quietly re-entered the restaurant. Recriminations and reconstructions and middle-of-the-night wonderings only kept him wallowing in misery. All he could do now was square his shoulders like a stoic of old and get on with this life of his. Whether she had gotten his messages or not, Marika was lost to him.

Nevertheless, some of the best of what he carried inside him from his homeland – the light in his green eyes which, with their extraordinary clarity, were as brilliant as a Greek spring morning – had dimmed as he took orders and served entrees and cleaned up leavings. As from time to time he watched his father solicitously circling the tables, doing everything but taking his customers to his bosom and burping them, he wished that he, too, could be as content in a world as small as this *petit bourgeois* restaurant. At that thought, a new set of worries creased Christos' forehead. What would his father say tonight when he finally broke his news?

It was the wee hours of the morning before the last diner finally paid and left, for it was Nick Kronos' contention that the best way for him to make his mark in the competitive world of Boston restaurants was to keep his

107

prices down, his quality up, and his lights on later than everyone else in this generally early-to-bed puritan city.

And on this night, as on every other, the lights were not switched off merely because the diners were gone. Even after the cooks had scrubbed down the kitchen and the waiters had set up for tomorrow's lunch, the staff lingered. All of them were newly-arrived Greeks who were either bachelors or temporarily had left their families behind in the old country. With no place to go except the bleak tenement rooms they shared with too many other exiles like themselves, the restaurant dining room was the closest any of them came to home. Nick understood and fostered this family feeling. He hadn't been able to bring all of Greece to America, but he did his nostalgic best to recreate a village feeling here in his restaurant. Night after night, as soon as the last diners left, it was transformed into a *kafeneion* back in the *plateia* of Panagia or any one of a thousand other villages just like it. A worn bouzouki disc scratched on the record player, the cigarette smoke grew as darkly dense as rainclouds before a February storm, and Greek olives, pistachios, and a bottle of imported ouzo held pride of place in the middle of the table where the homesick Greeks smoked, played cards, and talked through the lonely hours of the long Boston nights.

Nick settled down at the table with a contented sigh and began rolling himself a cigarette. As he sprinkled the tobacco onto the yellowish paper, he relaxed his insistence on speaking English and began his usual kindly interrogations in the mother tongue. Ever the voluble host, even when these were his employees rather than his customers, Nick plied this one with questions about his family back home, asked that one if he had seen to extending his visa, and expertly nursed recurrent bouts of homesickness. 'So, Stefano, that wife of yours, she has sent you another letter?'

The big-bellied cook slowly brought his shaggy buffalo head up in a wordless 'no'. 'You know I always bring you her letters to read.' He opened his empty hands. 'No letter today.'

Takis the waiter playfully inserted his index finger in Stefanos' bloated stomach and crudely pumped it in and out. 'Maybe she is busy, eh, with one of the fishermen. Or with the schoolteacher who writes her letters to you.'

'She is a good girl, my Maria.' Painfully Stefanos smiled, as he always did when the boys teased him like this. He would never admit that his young wife's fidelity was a constant worry now that he wasn't on the scene to keep his eyes upon her. She lived under the same roof as his mother, brothers and young sister, and he could trust his family to safeguard his honour and her virtue. Yet still he seethed with suspicions. Plump Maria was only fifteen, and as blooming as a garden in May. He regretted he hadn't stayed home long enough to get her pregnant after his family had hastily arranged this match. Again he wondered why they had been so insistent that he marry a village girl before he set off to America. How could they ever doubt that he would return to them as soon as he saved up enough to open his own *kafeneion* back in the village? How could they ever imagine that he would marry one of these strange foreign girls and live in exile forever? His ties to his village cut deeper than a mere wedding ring. Yet he supposed that he would either have to send for his wife or eat into his savings for a visit home. Stefanos' eyes misted over. Yes, he would go home, and not just to spend luscious afternoons and nights with the delicious Maria. The photograph he carried in his wallet in that dear place next to his money was of his mother, his brothers, and his sister.

Nick espied those tears and guessed at the reason. 'I am sure, *paidi mou*, that she is a very good girl.' He patted Stafanos' hand. 'And that she, and your family, will greet you with open arms when you return.'

Gratefully Stefanos gave the boss the sort of trusting smile a son reserves for his father who solves all problems. Observing this exchange, a flash of anger, quickly repressed, surged through Christos. Nick clucked and tsked and nagged and praised his staff like a combination of the *pater familias* and their long-lost mothers. Yet when he and Yorgos were needy boys, his father's tender concern had been half a world away. Christos took a deep breath and shrugged off his resentment. What was past was past. He sank further into gloom as again he remembered what else was very definitely in the past. He hadn't expected that look-alike woman to upset his equilibrium, although this had happened before, just so, when he had caught sight of a woman who walked like her, or laughed like her, or had dark icon eyes.

Nick, meanwhile, was continuing to reassure his cook. 'Your wife is Greek. She will never betray you. My Eleni has been in our village for the twenty-four years I have been here. And never – not once! – has there been the slightest whisper of gossip about her.' Lest his boys think him a fool for placing blind trust in the uncertain virtue of a woman, Nick quickly elaborated. 'Someone, for sure, would have written and told me if she did anything wrong. Believe me, my son, it will be the same with your Maria.' Nick smiled as he prepared neatly to deflect the conversation from the sexual anxieties of Stefanos and onto the sexual expectations of the others. 'Your wife is not like these girls here.'

The men grunted, eagerly cleared their throats, and poured another round of ouzos and ate another handful of pistachios as the conversation inevitably moved onto the sexual availability of these brazen American girls. For in this restaurant, just as in the village *kafeneion*, the favourite topics of conversation were – in this order – how much money everyone else was getting or spending, how much and exactly what kind of sex anyone else was claiming

109

to get or suspected of getting, and, when there was nothing else to talk about, the political fortunes of the village and the motherland. But it was the sex talk they warmed to the most.

'Again tomorrow night I see the blonde.' The aptly-named Adonis preened as he blew smoke rings into the blueish air. 'She is mad for me.' He patted his crotch and laughed. 'She lets me do whatever I want. Everything. Anything. Two, three times a night.'

Takis hungrily gnawed his lower lip. Even though he was fifty and looked a ravaged decade older, it outraged not only his pride but his thrift that he had to pay for what he got in this country. 'Better be careful. I think they have diseases, these girls. They go with everyone.'

'No, no, they are clean, most of them.' As Nick delicately tapped the ash off his cigarette, he reminded himself to have a manicure with his shave at the barbershop in the morning. He fancied that sweet young thing there had been giving him the eye and that she had more in mind than filing his nails. She doubtless would be a handful in the bed and everywhere else, but he was confident that he could have a bit of fun with her without matters getting out of hand. He was fifty-three years old, but he liked to think he was as virile as this young bull Adonis. Yet he worried about his boys being ensnared by these calculating women. He recited his stock lecture about the dangers and pleasures of American girls. 'But the problem is that, just like the girls back home, always they want a gold ring on their fingers.' Nick spoke from direct personal experience. Since he had arrived more than two decades ago, he had formed a string of discreet liaisons, each of which had ended when the girls had gotten too serious. The latest of his ladies was a lonely but willing Arlington widow young enough to be his daughter. For the past six years he had made nocturnal visits to her several times a week. He liked her well enough, yet from time to time there were tearful confrontations about if and when and whether he would divorce his wife and marry her. 'They don't understand that some women – Greek women – are for the marriage. And all other women are for the bed only. I speak to you, Adoni, as your father would. Enjoy your little golden one, but be careful she doesn't trap you into something that is impossible. Do not get her pregnant.'

'*Po, po, po.*' Adonis shrugged off the warning. 'I am not a fool. To marry a girl like that! She let me have her the third time I saw her. The third time! How could I ever trust a girl like that?'

'You don't have to trust a woman to marry her.' Spiros, the morose young one from the mountainous Peloponnese hinterlands who washed the dishes and cleared the tables when the waiters were busy, downed his ouzo in a gulp. 'But that is one way to get your citizenship, eh? Perhaps I go out on the

110

street tonight and look for a wife.' He poured another ouzo and confided what had happened that morning at the immigration office. 'They tell me I must leave in one month. Thirty days! To leave here for *there*!' He arched back his neck, and his heavy-lidded dark eyes almost closed in a despairing negative. 'I cannot go back. There is nothing for me there now. *Tipoteh*.'

The others set their mouths and shook their heads in sympathy. While Spiros had been off fighting in the Civil War on the side of the government, his family and everyone else in his village had been massacred. Some said the men who had swooped down in the night with their heads covered in hoods had been fascists, others that they had been Reds. Spiros contended that it didn't matter who had done it, only that it was done. He never intended to return to Greece. Yet he still carried in his pocket, wadded up in folds of paper secured by a rubber band, a bit of ash and rocky soil he had scooped up from the charred remains of his village.

'If you like, tomorrow I will go with you to the government office.' Nick smiled as he poured his boys yet more ouzo and passed around the olives. 'They know me. There is one of us, a good boy from Lamia, who helps all the Greeks when he can. Maybe we can buy you more time.'

'Or maybe,' Adonis said with a wink, 'we can buy you an American woman. My girl has a sister. She is fat and not so young, but I think perhaps she likes the same things as her sister.' As again he patted himself somewhere other than his back, the others grinned.

Usually Christos endured the crude banter of this male camaraderie that was so reminscent of the old country coffee houses, biding his time until he could steer the conversation onto the political fronts he still relished. But tonight he chainsmoked in silence, waiting to broach the sensitive matter which was sure to ruin his father's ebullient mood.

Finally Takis got out his deck of cards, Stefanos dealt, and the rest began squabbling about who owed what from last night's game and how high the stakes would be tonight. The men huddled over their hands, the cigarettes dangled out of the corners of their mouths, and the smoke and the lovesick bouzouki music hung in the air like ghosts of their lost land.

'*Patera*?' Christos waved to his father's favourite table in the corner. 'Can we talk?'

Nick scraped back his chair, always glad to oblige the son of his heart. But before he settled down with Christos, he bustled out to the kitchen and returned with fresh plates of *mezedes* and two more bottles of ouzo. Artfully he arranged the dishes of olives, cheese, nuts, and salads, one set for the cardsharks and another for him and his son. Just like in a taverna back in Greece, everything his boys ate and drank was on the house.

Patiently Christos lit another cigarette and waited for his father to stop

111

fussing about. He calculated it would be another half hour and two more ouzos before the old man had wound down enough to be able to consider the grave matter he was about to spring upon him.

Nick was just about to take his accustomed seat in the back corner where he could see every move everyone made, when suddenly he darted to the far wall and straightened one of his newly-framed colour photographs of the azure Greek seascape. 'Always,' he muttered to himself in a stream of annoyed Greek, 'I have to do everything myself if it's to be done right.' But when the first picture was realigned, the others seemed out of kilter. He tilted a mountain panorama to the left, and adjusted one of the white pillars silhouetted against a cloudless sky another fraction of an inch to the right. 'Yes, perfect,' he finally pronounced.

With a sigh of contentment the boss at last flung himself down opposite Christos and, as he cracked open a pistachio and popped it into his mouth, he surveyed his son, his workers, and his restaurant. Everything here, he reminded himself yet again with pride, is mine, all mine. He had come to this country as a penniless refugee, and now, by dint of hard work and that canniness about money which was one of the hallmarks of the Greek character, he was the undisputed master of all he surveyed. Still, until Christos had arrived on that blessed boat, his happiness had been built on a hollow foundation. A Greek without his family was like land without water; arid, infertile, incapable of sustaining succulent life.

'Look at it, son.' Lovingly his gaze lingered on chairs, tables, windows, and walls. 'Not bad for a poor man who arrived here with only the clothes on his back, eh? I started standing on the streetcorners polishing rich men's shoes, until I got enough together to buy a horse and wagon and could sell my fruits and vegetables.' Nick shouted his old huckster chant. 'Apples! Potatoes! Fresh ripe tomatoes!' Nick smiled. 'I had the best fruits and vegetables in Boston. But did I stop there?' Nick answered his own question. 'No! As soon as I could get enough money together I opened my own *kafeneion* at night and kept going out to the country at dawn every morning to get those fresh apples. Night and day I worked. And now look at me! I'm a perfect example of what you can do in this country if you work hard! I am the American dream come true!'

Nick beamed at the one who would work beside him all his days and who would one day inherit everything he had slaved for. He was accustomed to lying awake at night, either in the arms of the Arlington widow or alone on his iron cot, dreaming his great dreams of how and when he would fashion his American food empire. He leaned forward confidentially, as though Christos would be hearing all this for the first time. 'And I tell you, this is only the beginning. In two months, six months at most, as soon as I can get the money from the bank, we'll open a bigger and better restaurant on the waterfront.' As Nick looked over his dining room with a suddenly colder eye, the set of his face was scornful. 'It won't be a glorified souvlaki joint like this but a proper restaurant serving fresh fish only. They'll come from as far away as New Hampshire – no, maybe even New York! – to eat my lobsters and my schrod.' He beamed as though the New Yorkers were already queued up on the pier. 'Then maybe we will branch out into frozen foods. Nick's fishsticks! Nick's pizza! Maybe even Nick's ice cream! They'll love it, all of it, you know how they hate to waste time cooking.' His eyes had a faraway look. 'Who knows, maybe someday we'll have a string of restaurants from coast to coast. Take it from me, son, one day I'll be rich and powerful and important.'

Christos smiled at his father's childlike enthusiasm. At some point every night, Nick always harked back to his humble past as a shoeshine boy and conjured up his rosy future as an American food czar. Christos wished he could be as satisfied with his father's comparatively easily-attained goals of money and fame. But he marched to a different music, and he supposed he always would.

Nick poured two ouzos, raised his glass, and clinked it with his son's. '*Yamas*,' he said in the traditional Greek toast, 'to our health!' Now, he thought, all he had to do was find Christos a wife. He had just opened his mouth to confide that soon he would ask Yorgos to find a bride back in the village, when instead he took a sip of his ouzo. Christos turned moody every time he reminded him that it was time he married. It was wiser first to find him a wife before persuading Christos to wear the wedding crown. He would write to Yorgos this very week. Perhaps that Marika had a cousin or a girlfriend who could offer not only a pure young body and heart but some tempting *prika* – orange groves or, better yet, some prime seafront land which could someday be worth a fortune if the tourist industry ever took off as Nick suspected it might. Maybe he could forge another empire in the *patrida* which Yorgos and his children would one day inherit.

Nick poured himself another, and returned to the domestic bliss he planned for Christos. Once he threaded through the tiresome maze of Immigration red tape, Christos could be snugly married to a good Greek girl and a new generation of grandchildren would be on the way. He would buy them all a house out in the northern suburbs, in sight of the sea. The cold grey Atlantic was not the sparkling blue Aegean, but it was the closest he could come to home. Together he and Christos would forge a Greek-American dynasty. Then, as the capstone to his life, one day he would return to Panagia in a shiny black Cadillac and shower largesse on those villagers who had once taken him to their bosom. Since he doubted he would ever go back to Greece for good, in time he might even give in and bring his long-suffering Eleni back here to America.

Nick sipped his ouzo and reconsidered. Eleni was better off in Panagia, running that sweet little taverna of hers. A woman like her, who already looked like an old grandmother in those dark shapeless dresses and that peasant scarf, could never be happy in this country. She didn't even speak English! No, Nick decided. It was better for her and better for me — yes, much better for me — to keep matters as they were. He had enough problems juggling his lady friends without having to contend with Eleni's tears as well.

Christos at last cut into his father's reverie. 'I have something to tell you, *patera*.' Significantly he paused. 'And something to ask you.'

'Anything, Chris.' Nick speared a chunk of feta cheese with his fork.

'I wish you wouldn't call me that.' He knew he shouldn't start off what promised to be a difficult confrontation with this petty disagreement that had sprung up between them since he arrived, but he couldn't stop himself. 'My name is Christos.'

Nick smiled indulgently and savoured the salty bite of the feta. 'And mine is Nikolas. But here in America I am Nick and you are Chris. As I've told you time and again, my son, we have to make our little compromises in this country. America has been very good to me. I'll answer to Nick or any other name they want to call me. So what's on your mind, Chris?'

Christos cleared his throat and decided to switch to English, not so much to mollify his father but to make it harder for the staff at the other table to follow their conversation. 'I have enrolled at Northeastern University. I already took the English test and the entrance examination, and I passed! I'd like your blessing, *patera*.'

Nick had been engrossed in how to finesse the bank loan he needed for his new restaurant, and so he hadn't heard all his son had said. 'School? About time you started thinking about a real American education. What do you think I've been doing all these years but working so you'll have a better life?'

'And I'm grateful, *patera*.' Despite this good start, Christos braced himself for the coming storms. As soon as Nick understood where his studies would ultimately lead, first he would try to bully him into abandoning his plans. Then he would bluster and rage about his ingratitude. Finally, if only Christos had the endurance to outlast him, he would — with very bad grace — begin to accept the new reality. 'If I go to summer school, three years from now I will have my degree.'

'College! You're going to college!' Nick poured himself and his scholarly son another ouzo. He crashed his glass into Christos'. 'To my son the college man!' He brought the glass to his lips and drank. What Greek father could fail to be proud of such a son? He munched another bit of feta. 'So what will you study? Business? Accounting? Or will it be fancy courses in how to run a restaurant?'

'No.' Now came the rough part. 'It's what they call Liberal Arts.'

'Arts?' Nick frowned. Christos couldn't even draw a straight line.

'Government, actually. I'll be in the political science department. Someday I'd like to go into politics, *patera*.'

'Politics?' Nick scowled, and in his mouth the feta took on such a bitter tang that he spit it out into a napkin. He pounded his fist on the table. 'You'll do nothing of the kind. Three years from now, exactly as now, you will be working right here, beside me, in my restaurant! You are my son, and this is your life! Here, beside me!'

Christos raised his head in the negative. 'Next week I begin my government classes at the university.'

'I forbid it! I am your father and I forbid it!'

Christos gave the table of cardplayers a nervous glance, for his father's voice had excitedly risen. He brought his index finger to his lips. 'Please, they will hear us.'

Nick shrugged as though he did not care. Yet the old village habit of keeping family troubles secret triumphed, and his voice fell to an insistent rasp. 'I tell you, son, you will not go to this school to study politics. Business, yes, that makes sense. You could take over doing my books. Be some help to me. But not politics. Not that again.'

'And I tell you again, *patera*,' Christos hissed back just as firmly, 'that my classes begin next week. I will go to the school in the day and work with you here in the night.'

Their green eyes locked. They stared and stared, and finally Nick's were the first to fall. In that instant when the strong younger generation won over the weary older one, Christos felt a wave of tenderness for his father.

Nick, too, sensed what had been lost. For a moment he held his face in his hands in an attitude of despair. But then he recovered enough to begin to rant in a bitter monotone. 'School, he wants more school. He wants to study politics in school. O Holy Virgin, what will I do with this boy? That was the root of all the problems, sending him to school. I stayed only six years in the school to learn to read and write and do my sums, and look at the success I have made of my life! I was a donkey to let him stay so long in the village school. Yes, a donkey! Nikolas the donkey! But he begged and pleaded in those pretty letters, and so I let him do as he liked. Any other father would have pulled him out of school and made him go to work like the other boys. But not me! Here I was, alone, with no one from the family to help me, working night and day not for myself but for my family, and this is the thanks I get! I never should have let him set one foot in that high school!

115

That was my mistake! My deadly mistake!' Here Nick moaned and then began rhythmically striking himself with the flat of his palm to his chest. 'But then, after all of that, the filthy Reds got hold of him in the army! That was the death blow! Death! Yes, death!' Even as he kept beating himself on his heart, Nick's burning eyes came to rest on his son. 'It was there that we lost you, Christo. It was there that you met those monsters.'

Steadily Christos met his father's eyes. He had expected such histrionics and was determined not to be moved by them. In time – perhaps not tonight, but inevitably – his father would have to come round. 'You are wrong, *patera*,' he said gently. 'It was with them that I found myself, and my life's work. Not in the Party. No, that's finished. But in government.'

'Life's work!' Nick balled his hand into a fist and struck the table so hard that the glasses of ouzo jumped, fell to the floor, and shattered. 'Your life's work is here, beside me!'

Christos calmly mopped up the ouzo with a napkin and piled the shards of glass into an ashtray he fetched from the next table. 'No problem,' he called out in Greek to the others who had laid down their cards and were regarding this confrontation with intense interest. 'Back to your game, boys.'

'Your father is right,' Takis pronounced. 'Politics is a curse. And so is too much school.'

'A son should do what a father tells him.' Stephanos recited this family catechism as fervently as though his own father could overhear and benignly smile.

Adonis, too, nodded. 'A father is always right.'

'If only my father were still alive, I would never do anything to trouble him.' Spiros hurled a dagger look at Christos.

Christos hid a sigh by lighting a cigarette. He should have known that the others had understood everything and that they would be unable to resist pronouncing their opinions as though this were a public court of law. Always and everywhere, the Greeks considered it their right to referee even the most intimate of human transactions. They were never content with their shameless eavesdropping and snooping. After they were satisfied that they knew everything, they went on to choose sides, apportion blame, and scold whomever they considered to be the guilty party. He indulged in this national predilection himself, and yet it was galling to have to endure it when the consensus fell so heavily against him.

'Listen to them if you won't listen to me. Your own father.' Nick had taken heart and a second wind from the support of his boys. 'You cannot leave us to go to this political school.'

'I told you before, I am not leaving you or the restaurant, at least for now. I will work with you here while I go to the school.'

Nick snorted in derision, and then again he launched into a monologue, although this one seemed directed more at his sympathetic staff than his defiant son. 'All my life I work so hard, and always for my family. Do I live like a king? No, I stay in the same little rooms for years. Every penny I make I either sent home for my wife and the children or put in the bank so I could open this restaurant. I kept nothing for myself. *Tipoteh*! And what thanks do I get for all my sacrifices? Two sons I have. And the one refuses to work in his mother's taverna, so he can be a soldier. And now the other turns his back on me and says he wants to be a politician.' Again Nick took up his breast-beating. 'Cursed! I am cursed with two serpent sons!' He liked the sound of that, and so he repeated it rhythmically as he hit his chest. 'Serpent sons!'

Christos smoked in silence, waiting for his father to tire of these theatrics. There was more about his ingratitude, and his unnatural behaviour, and how his waiters and his cooks acted more like his sons than his own flesh and blood. Three cigarettes later, when his father seemed to be running out of steam, Christos quietly once again tried to talk sense. 'None of this is new. I always wanted to be a politician. If it hadn't been for the war I would have gone to the university in Athens. You know that. What I wanted to do with my life has never been a secret.'

'A politician.' Reluctantly Nick was considering this hateful idea. He rubbed his thumb and index finger together. 'They make good money, politicians?'

Instead of shrugging and telling the truth, that he didn't care about that, Christos took a wiser course. 'Sometimes very good money.' This was not the time, however, for jokes about bribes and corruption. 'Better than owners of restaurants.'

Nick wet his lips and asked the inevitable Greek-to-Greek question. 'How much, exactly?'

This time Christos did shrug. 'It depends.' He managed a smile. 'I intend to be very good at it.'

'Politics . . .' Nick shook his head. 'A dirty business in Greece and a dirty business here.' Wearily he rolled and lit a cigarette. 'After everything that has happened, after all the wars and the blood, after having to leave your own country, how can you even dream of again the politics?'

'It is what I was born for. In Greece, or here, it is my life.'

Valiantly, one more time, as Nick gazed at the restaurant which was his own dream come true, he rallied and pleaded his case. 'All this will be yours someday. I made this for you, and your children, and your children's children.'

'And I,' Christos said, just as passionately, 'must spend my life working not just for my family. But for *all* the people.'

For the first time since their argument had begun, tears filled Nick's eyes. 'You are making a very big mistake, my son. I can see it, I know it, and yet I fear I cannot stop it. I cry for you, and for the sadness you will bring upon yourself with this madness about the politics.' A cry came from his heart. 'Is there anything worse in this life than to have to watch your child throw away his life?' Fresh tears filled his eyes and coursed down his cheeks. 'This is such a big mistake.'

From out of his pocket Nick drew one of the linen handkerchiefs Eleni had embroidered with his initials. He wiped his eyes and blew his nose. 'Already you have suffered so much – too much! – because of this political sickness of yours. For it is a sickness, Christo, like cancer, and it will eat you up! I listen to you talk about your politics, and I tell myself that this is not the name of your disease. Power, what you want is power! But you didn't get it at home, and I do not think you will get it here.' He lowered his voice, as though unseen but hostile others might overhear. 'We don't really belong here in America, you know, and we never will. So long as we work hard and don't cause trouble, they tolerate us. We're not like the Negroes and the Jews. We're white and Christian, after all. But we will always be outsiders. You won't get far in your politics. There aren't enough of us here to matter. Now, if you were Irish, or Italian, it might be different. But a Greek, in American politics? No.'

Nick sighed, covered his son's hands with his own and looked deeply into those eyes which were so like his own. 'And there is something else I have been meaning to ask you about. I worry so about you, my son. You are always so sad. You smile and you joke and sometimes you even play your pipe or you dance. But I think inside you are always sad. I think you do not tell me everything that happened before you left our country. I think there was something with you and a girl at home. I don't know who she was or what happened, exactly, except that you lost her. Am I right, *paidi mou*?'

Christos bowed his head, unable any longer to meet his father's knowing eyes. 'Yes,' he breathed.

'Do you want to tell me about it?'

'There is no reason.' He pulled his hands away from his father's, rubbed his palms together and then shook them out, empty. 'You said it. I lost her.'

'My boy, my poor boy.' Nick crossed over to the other side of the table, threw his arms around his son, and rocked him like a baby. 'I know how you feel. When I lost your mother . . .' His voice broke. 'It was never the same for me in the village after that.' He stared up at the image of Greek sea and mountains. 'It was easier to go. I thought maybe in this country I could forget. But I never did.' He released his son and drew back so that he could see the tears in Christos' eyes. 'I am sorry that you have this in your life, too. I wanted only good things for you. A beautiful life for Sofia's son.'

Christos looked into his father's brimming eyes and recalled the muggy afternoon years ago, during one of his father's visits to Greece, when Nick had taken him aside and opened his wallet to show him the faded sepia wedding daguerroetype of that beautiful one who, his father had vowed with his hand on his heart, had been the light of his life. Christos had pored over the blurred image of his father and the mother he had never known, looking for clues of what she must have been like in the sweep of her hair and the gaze of her eyes. The young woman in the white bridal dress had a pretty face and a rounded figure, but what had made the most impression on Christos was the way his father and mother had been with one another even in the stiff pose of the formal wedding portrait. Something in the tender possession of his hand on her shoulder and the way her body bent to his proclaimed to all the world that here were a man and woman united by a bond deeper and stronger than matrimony. His father had reinforced that insight when he had kissed his mother's image with that same reverence as the women in the churches kiss an icon of the Virgin.

Now, having lost his own Marika, Christos understood why his father had treasured that photograph like an icon. Never before had he felt so at one with his father. He was so moved that – almost – he was ready to abandon his dreams and cast his lot beside this understanding patriarch who had also lost the love of his life.

Yet he wiped his eyes on his sleeve and hardened his heart. Maybe this compassionate turn of his father's was only another manipulative trick. 'I am asking your blessing for my new venture.'

'So!' Furiously he wiped his eyes. 'That is all you have to say to me?' He rose. 'You are a hard man.'

'I am what my life has made me.'

'No, a man – a real man – always has choices. It is late and I am very tired.' Nick collected his hat and coat. 'I will think about all this, yes, I will think of nothing else. Maybe, just maybe, tomorrow or after tomorrow, I will give you money for that school and even my blessing, so you can go and make more of your big mistakes.' At the door he turned. 'But know this, remember this: you break my heart. You kill me, my son. You kill me.' Nick shambled out the door like a broken old man.

Christos bit his lip to stop its trembling and tried to rejoice for the victory that was surely his. But as he turned round to face the accusing eyes of the others, he felt guilty of the terrible crime of patricide. He did then what he always did when the despair was too much for him. He took down his old shepherd's flute from its place of honour on the far wall, sat crosslegged in a corner, and began playing an ancient dirge that had echoed almost forever from the snowcapped Olympian heights where the old gods had once wreaked such havoc in the affairs of mortal men. Each note was as sad as a tear.

The music rained down on the immigrant Greeks who sat, wet-eyed and entranced, each lost in his own melody of pain and loss. When the last note finally died, for once the men were silent as they trudged out the door to make their way through the deserted streets to their solitary beds that were too far from home.

Marika gripped the side of the bed and dimly, through waves of pain, heard her mother's voice screaming for her to push down, push hard, push as if her life depended upon it, for it did.

'I can't, mama . . .' Marika thought she was shouting, but her voice was a whisper. After so many hours of labour, she was so tired. Her hands let go of the iron piping on the side of the bed. She sighed. She could fight no more. Her body would break into two if she kept pushing like this. It was better to close her eyes and let blessed sleep claim her and this thing that was tormenting her so. The pain subsided, and she let her eyes flutter shut.

'No, no, no!' Old Anna left the foot of the bed and all but flung herself on her daughter's wracked body. 'You can't give up now!'

Dulled with pain, Marika's eyes opened. 'Let me go, mama. I'm so tired. Let me go. *Parakalo* . . .'

Old Anna seized her hands and squeezed them with her bony fingers as hard as she could. 'Just a little more, *paidi mou*. I promise, just a little more.'

'No more.' Marika stared at the icon of the Virgin and Child on the wall at eye level beside her bed. When the contractions had become unbearable, she had asked her mother to move her beloved holy picture closer, from its customary spot over the head of her bed. Marika's eyes misted over. She had so wanted to hold her own baby like that, so close and safe and soft, but she was too tired to keep on fighting. She had been willing to do anything to secure her child's future, but she had not foreseen that it would be the death of her. 'It hurts so, mama.'

'Where's that doctor?' Old Anna spun round and saw the frightful knot of black-shrouded widows who had crowded into the bedroom when her back was turned. She shivered. It was a bad omen that these old crones, led by wizened Kyria Yorgina, renowned as chief mourner and shrieker at every Panagian funeral, had flocked here unbidden. Hooded in their black scarves, they waited like vultures, wringing their hands and keening to the Virgin to

120

help this young woman who seemed surely about to die. 'Out now!' Old Anna shooed them toward the door with the same gesture she used to chase the crows off her vegetable garden. 'Out with you!'

'Mama!' Marika shrieked as another contraction rent her.

'I'm here, I'm here, *paidi mou*. She held onto her daughter's clawing hands. 'Now push! Push hard! Push now!' Why didn't someone come to help? Old Anna had been worried at the early signs, even when Marika's labour had begun yesterday morning. Her daughter had had a difficult pregnancy, and in late summer she had nearly miscarried. Just in case her forebodings were right, last night she had taken the precaution of despatching Vangelis to try to reach Yorgos in his remote garrison in the southern reaches of the Peloponnese. Then, shortly after dawn this morning, when the contractions had begun spacing further apart instead of closer, she had sent Eleni to the next village for the doctor. She herself midwifed easy births, but she hadn't liked the way Marika's condition had deteriorated. Yet it was now early afternoon, and neither the doctor nor Yorgos had arrived. Even if the doctor had been caught up in an emergency, by now he should have responded to her urgent summons. She gave Marika's hands another encouraging squeeze, and with an air of the lady of the manor she strode outside into Eleni's crowded sitting room. After the wedding not only Marika but Old Anna and Vangelis had moved into this imposing three-storey house built over the taverna on the beach. Moved in and taken over, too.

The doctor was drinking coffee and smoking a cigarette as he chatted to three old men who were some connection on Yorgos' side of the family. Eleni hovered anxiously above the men, serving spoonfuls of *kerasma*, the syrupy homemade preserves that were the traditional guest offering. In a corner the old crones whined and wailed like a Greek chorus of doom.

Old Anna pursed her lips as she caught Eleni's eye. Marika's mother-in-law helplessly shrugged as, behind his back, she gave the doctor an Evil Eye look. She had hunted the length and breadth of three villages for him very early this morning, and when she had found him he had demanded a small fortune as a down payment before he would even consent to make the trip through the sleeting rain to Panagia. Yet once he had finally deigned to enter her house a half hour ago, meek Eleni had not been able to persuade, much less insist, that he immediately go to Marika's aid. The doctor was an arrogant Athenian who had come to the provinces to open his practice only last winter after he married a girl in the next village who had a forest of orange groves for her *prika*. Already he was notorious for charging too much for too little grudging care. But even though he was a bandit, he was the only doctor between here and Nauplion, and so the villagers allowed themselves to be held for ransom when they were sick. What else could they expect, they told one another, from a *xenos*, a suspect foreigner from the capital? And there were even some, figuring that you only got what you paid for, who took heart from his fees and even boasted about paying them.

Old Anna was not one of that lot. She wanted to fly at the doctor and gouge at his eyes and kick at his groin, but she drew on a frustrated lifetime of controlling her rage. She put her hands on her hips and tossed her black-kerchiefed head in the direction of the bedroom. 'Please, doctor, my daughter needs you now.' Her words were deferential but her eyes were not. She would get back at him if her daughter died because of his inattention. It wasn't only love charms she could write.

Indifferently the doctor fingered his sculptured Van Dyke beard and puffed on his cigarette. '*Siga-siga*. Slowly, slowly. What's the rush? This is, I think, her first baby. Always the first one is slow.'

'Thirty-four hours, doctor. The pains have been coming for more than a whole day. And now they've almost stopped. She's so weak, doctor. I think she will die if you don't help get that baby out.'

'You can pay?' The doctor's eyes roamed the splendid appointments of the Kronos' *saloni*, the 'best room' parlour where guests were entertained. The walls were lined on all sides with straight-backed chairs, and dead centre sat a square claw-footed mahogany table covered with an exquisitely snowy lace cloth. On it, between two heavy silver candlesticks, rested a finely-cut crystal punchbowl filled with yellowing family snapshots and airmail letters with franked American stamps. Suspended over it was Eleni's pride and joy, a crystal chandelier whose megawatt tulip-shaped bulb lights would one day – as soon as Panagia got electricity – shine strong like the summer sun. The doctor sized up the usual square-jawed brides and grooms and big-eyed babies in the family photographs framed on the wall. But he gazed reflectively at the poster-sized portrait of a dapper and shrewd-looking middle-aged man in a three-piece suit and bowler hat. The *pater familias*' image was encased in a silver filigree frame. 'If it's a forceps delivery, or a caesarian, it will be expensive.' His fingers stole up to his handlebar moustache. He had expected a peasant cottage, not a household grand enough for Athens. Mentally he escalated his fee. 'Perhaps very expensive.'

Eleni stepped forward. 'We can pay. I am the wife of Nikolas Kronos, who has a famous restaurant in Boston. In America! And I am the mother of Yorgos Kronos, who is an officer in the national army.' Even now, when she feared for the life of the girl she loved as if she were her own daughter, Eleni couldn't resist bragging about the promotion her son had fallen heir to when much of the army demobilized after the Civil War had ended a month ago. 'He's a full lieutenant. Only twenty-five and a full lieutenant!'

The doctor was still doubtful. 'A soldier's pay, even a lieutenant's, is not so very much.'

'Dollars! I have dollars!' Eleni looked as though she were about to cry. 'My husband sends me dollars!'

'Ah!' For the first time the doctor smiled. And yet these villagers were sly ones, especially about money. He settled back in his chair and lit another cigarette. 'As soon as you show me these dollars, *kyria*, then I will begin my consultation.'

But from outside there was the sound of a vehicle skidding to a stop and then a bellowing. They could hear Yorgos shouting even before he burst into the house. 'A son? Do I have a son?' The lieutenant stormed in, with Vangelis at his heels. Both men were wet and out of breath, and Yorgos' olive green uniform was splattered with mud high above his leather boots.

Wildly he took in the scene in the *saloni*: his mother and mother-in-law arguing with the doctor, the old men avidly listening as they chainsmoked, the crones recording every detail of this confrontation for the later delectation of the entire village. Yorgos stepped smartly up to the doctor. 'Is it a boy?'

'She is still in labour.' Now that he was talking to a man of the world instead of these tiresome women, the doctor tried to appear solicitous. He shook his head as though he had spent the long day assisting his dearly beloved patient. 'But it is a difficult delivery.'

Yorgos rushed to the bedroom but faltered when he saw her lying as still as a corpse. Yet the sheet was not pulled over her face. 'Marika . . .?'

Groggily she opened her eyes. She could make out only the vague outline of a figure at the foot of the bed. 'Christo,' she murmured in a delirium, 'I knew you'd come. I waited so long, so long, but now you've come back to me.'

The colour drained from Yorgos' skin. For a moment, as his face worked and it seemed he might cry, he stared wordlessly at the wife who would betray him even on her deathbed. In the early days of their marriage he had hoped he could take his brother's place in her heart. He had tried to make up for that first sorry sexual encounter in the olive grove, and at first it had seemed he had a chance. After a lavishly expensive wedding that dazzled the war-wracked village, he had swept her off to Athens for the most romantic honeymoon his father's dollars could buy. They had eaten shrimps by the sea in Piraeus, taken a horse-drawn carriage up to the Acropolis, and dallied on hot spring afternoons in their suite at the King George Hotel. He had made love to her as tenderly as though she were made of glass, and sometimes in the dark she had responded to him as though she were made of fire. In those early days, he would have done anything to please her. Back home in the village, he had even humoured her plea that her mother and brother become a part of the spacious Kronos household. Those first six weeks of their marriage had been halcyon days, and he had been exultant at his virility when Marika announced she was pregnant. But the honeymoon had crashed to an end when that letter had arrived from Boston with its bombshell that Christos was in an Italian refugee camp waiting for clearance to immigrate to America. Yorgos had been so busy bullying his family into keeping that news secret – for his army career had been based on his insinuation that he had killed Captain Prometheus – that at first he hadn't realized its effect on his wife. By the time he had hushed up the news, Marika had turned remote. In bed it had been like lying next to a marble statue, for she had fended off his embraces with a variety of lame excuses connected to her pregnancy. It had been then that Yorgos had begun to wonder who was the father of this baby. By early summer the two of them were so estranged that he had welcomed his transfer to the faraway Mani.

As she was wracked by a feeble contraction, Yorgos' anguished eyes fell to the shuddering mound of her stomach. Was this baby his or Christos'? He supposed, now, that he should have been suspicious about this lightning pregnancy of hers all along. He had seen the two of them in that cave, he had known how she loved his brother, and yet he had wanted her so much that he would have married her on any terms. God help him, he still would remain married to her, still would love her, still would turn himself inside out in the hope that someday she would love him in return. He would move heaven and earth to keep alive this woman who had bewitched him.

His face tightened into an inscrutable mask, as again he stared at this wife whom he passionately loved and sometimes hated – *poli*, too much. Even as she lay here evidently so near death and as vulnerable as any human being can ever be, still she managed not only to wound but to elude him. Christos, she had called out for Christos.

Yorgos bit his lower lip so hard that he drew blood. Marika was the love of his life, but it would perhaps be a blessing if he were rid of her forever. Yet he couldn't let her die, not now, not ever, not so long as there was anything he could do to keep that whorish heart of hers beating. Later, if she lived, he would most certainly hold her to account for that telltale mistaking of him for his brother. But first he would have to make sure that she – and the baby – survived.

Yorgos' gaze softened. The baby might be his, after all. Even though she still had not forgotten Christos, that baby was a Kronos and must live.

He turned on his heel and strode back into the sitting room. 'What are you doing in here, doctor, when my wife needs you in there?'

The doctor tipped his chair back against the wall. 'There is, I fear, some difficulty as to my fee.'

124

Eleni was rushing back from her bedroom with a fistful of green banknotes. 'I offered him dollars, Yorgo, but he said he wouldn't look at her until I brought them.'

'That will not be necessary, mama. Put your money away.' Yorgos reached in his holster, pulled out his revolver, and fired a warning shot at the ceiling. As bits of whitewashed plaster fell like snow, he cocked his pistol at the doctor. 'Get in there with my wife. She dies, you die.'

The doctor was in the bedroom before anyone could say another word.

As the others waited in the *saloni* for the verdict, Vangelis filled in the nervous silence by recounting how he had finally fetched Yorgos. Since the telephones from Nauplion to the Githion garrison had been out of service, a friend with a horse-drawn wagon had driven him to Sparti, where finally he had managed to get a call through to the Mani. Hours later, after Yorgos had careened up in his jeep, he and Vangelis had nearly perished in the dense fog of the tortuous Tripolis mountain road. Once they had nearly driven off a precipice, and another time they had missed a switchback turn and bogged down in the mud. They might still be there, Vangelis concluded, if a lorry full of army recruits hadn't happened along and lifted the jeep back on the road.

When finally the doctor opened the door, Yorgos was pacing back and forth, while Eleni and Old Anna were leading the other crones in prayer.

'Lieutenant Kronos?' The doctor gestured for Yorgos to join him in the bedroom. Firmly he shut the door on the ever-curious others. 'It's not good. The old mother was right. Your wife is too weak. The baby can't come out without assistance. We must transfer her to the hospital in Argos.'

Yorgos was afraid she wouldn't last that long. 'You're a doctor. Cut her open and get it out.'

'It's not that easy. A caesarian – which I suppose is what you're suggesting – is not advisable once the baby has begun its passage down the birth canal.' The doctor wet his lips with his tongue and then said. 'It may not be possible to save both the mother and the baby.'

Again Yorgos whipped the revolver from his holster. 'Then it might not be possible to save the doctor, either.'

'You are mad.' The doctor stared incredulously down the gleaming barrel of the gun. 'In a village of madmen and in a province of lunatics, you are the maddest of them all.' He reached for the door. 'You can't get away with this.'

Yorgos stepped between the doctor and the door. 'Try me. This is not Athens. This is Panagia. My village. Mine! If an unfortunate accident happened here to the foreigner from Athens, everyone – including my cousin who is chief of the police – would be very sorry. *Katalaves?*' With his pistol

125

he gestured in the direction of the bed. 'Now do whatever you have to do to save my wife and my child.'

'You leave me no choice.' The doctor sighed and made a mental vow to move away from these maniacal savages and back to the civilization of the capital as soon as he could. But his forehead creased as he looked back at the bed. He cursed himself for not coming earlier and doing whatever could be done before matters reached this crux. 'I can't make any promises,' he hedged.

'I can.' Yorgos' trigger finger twitched.

'On the other hand,' the doctor said as he rolled up his sleeves and washed his hands in the basin beside the bed, 'I suppose that it might just be possible, with forceps . . .' Aside from his greed he was a good doctor and would do his best for this suffering woman with the insufferable husband. He called out for the mother and mother-in-law to assist him and waited for Yorgos to join the menfolk back in the *saloni*. Instead, when the husband stood leaning against the shut door, his pistol held at the ready, the doctor gulped and went about his work.

Yorgos stood his suspicious watch as the doctor and the two women huddled between Marika's spread legs. He flinched when he saw the doctor immersing the long metal forceps in a basin of boiling water, and he shuddered when Marika let out a bestial cry of pain as the instrument disappeared inside her convulsing flesh. In the next long hour there were enough heartrending shrieks to make an icon of the Virgin weep. The doctor was sweating as they pulled, and Old Anna and Eleni were muttering prayers as they panted and pushed. Marika moaned and begged them all to go away and let her die, and yet the contractions were coming faster now. 'Good,' the doctor kept saying. 'Now more, a little more.' Yet still, even though Yorgos craned his neck to see what was happening, all that came from inside his wife were blood and screams. She seemed more animal than woman as she writhed and twitched, panting, the sweat running down her face like rivulets of tears. The bedclothes were soaked. The bedroom reeked of the sweetish smell of blood. Finally the doctor sterilized a scalpel and wielded it somewhere within her.

This time the way Marika shrieked made Yorgos' heart turn over. Surely, he thought, she could not endure much more. His eyes locked on the image of the Virgin and Child beside his wife's bed. Like all the men, Yorgos was not so religious. And yet after a fashion and when it suited him, he was a believer. His lips moved in a prayer his mother had taught him as intently he stared at the icon. As if this were market day and he was bargaining with a cunning old mountain peasant for a sleek donkey or a barrel of retsina, he tried to strike a deal with the Mother of God. Save her and the baby, and I

126

won't forget it, he grandly promised. When that wasn't enough to produce a miracle – Marika's condition was unchanged – grudgingly he vowed he would light a nest of candles in the church next Sunday morning. Still Marika groaned. All right, he amended, a rack of candles every single Sunday, so long as my wife and the baby live. Yet Marika's thrashings only increased. In utter desperation – she would die very soon, he knew, if that baby didn't come out – he promised the icon the only thing he sensed it wanted to hear, that he would love this child and accept it as his own. Was it only his imagination, he wondered, or did the Virgin, tenderly holding the Baby Jesus, seem suddenly to smile directly at him?

'Yes, yes, it comes now!' The doctor was shouting. 'I have it, all together now, push, one final time . . . yes!'

Marika's scream went on and on.

Yorgos was leaning over the doctor's shoulder, and at first all he could see was the reddened handle of the forceps and more of that sickening blood. But then there was something else in the grip of the instrument, a tiny thing, two tiny things, the unmistakeable shape of infant feet. 'Don't stop now,' Yorgos shouted. 'Now you've got him, get him out!' The miniature ankles and knees slid slowly out, but it took a mighty tug of the forceps before the thighs and the hips were clear. Yorgos stared transfixed at the dearest sight in all his life. 'A boy! My son! It's a boy!' He lunged forward to seize his flesh and blood.

But the doctor butted him away with surprising force. 'Get away, you fool, it's not all over yet.' Expertly, with a great sort of sucking movement, the doctor was pulling out a belly, a chest, arms, and then, with the greatest of delicacy, a tiny head. He held up the infant as though it were a trophy, and he let out a cry of triumph as he hit it in the rump and a tired little sob came from between its lips. 'He lives!'

Yorgos dropped his gun and snatched the baby. Greedily he looked down into his wrinkled red face. Never would he forget this moment. His son! His face was radiant as he clutched his baby to his chest.

An instant later the doctor was cutting the umbilical cord, Old Anna was washing off the infant, and then again Yorgos was holding it and loving it and crooning to it. Finally he seemed to come to as he remembered the one he had almost forgotten in all the excitement. Marika lay in the blood and the afterbirth, her eyes still shut, seeming not even to breathe. 'My wife?' Yorgos demanded.

The doctor leaned over her, put his fingers to her pulse, felt inside the sodden bedclothes, and finally nodded. 'I think she will be all right, so long as there are no more complications.' He mopped the sweat from his forehead and surreptitiously looked at the gun cast aside on a bureau. 'It was touch and go for a while. I needed all my considerable skill to save her and the baby. Frankly, I wasn't sure she would pull through. But I did it.' It was all he could do not to hold out his hand, here and now, for the lavish reward he expected for this miracle of birth. 'You and your wife have a fine healthy son.' Thoughtfully he cocked his head. 'Considering all the trouble she had, he's a bit smaller than I thought he would be. But he seems perfectly formed.'

'He is premature.' Old Anna had been waiting for just this moment. If Yorgos were to accept the baby as his own, he had to believe it had been conceived only seven months ago.

'Perhaps.' The doctor looked doubtfully at the infant, and then knowingly at the old mother who might be willing to pay handsomely if he went along with what was surely a deception. 'But yes, what you say must be true. The baby is premature.'

'About seven months,' Old Anna prompted.

'Yes, I'd say that you are correct. Seven months is about right.' The doctor and Old Anna smiled in concord.

Yorgos registered what was being said even as he gazed up at the icon of the Virgin. In his heart he was sure that it was neither this bandit of a doctor nor his whore of a wife but he himself – and his holy vow – which had saved the day. He held his son close to him. It would not be such a sacrifice to love this dear one, who was surely his own now. Even if the baby hadn't sprung from his loins, he had given it life here today.

Marika's eyes flickered open. 'The baby? My baby?'

'You have a son,' the doctor announced.

'A boy,' she murmured. 'I knew it would be a boy. His son.'

Yorgos stared down at his wife as a wave of doubt swept over him. He had heard that tender inflection in her voice. *His* son. She used that tone of voice only when she referred to Christos. But this time did she mean him or his brother? He fingered the scar on his cheek, and his hold on the infant slackened as it began to cry. Uncertainly, as Yorgos held the wailing baby, he looked back to the icon. Had the Virgin somehow joined his faithless wife in a women's conspiracy to trick him into accepting his brother's son as his own? The Mother's smile seemed suddenly secretive.

Marika held out her hands. 'My son. Give me my son.'

Yorgos took a deep breath and decided. Whether what had happened with that icon was a woman's mean trick to defraud a credulous man or even a twist of his own mind in a moment of high anxiety, still he would keep his sacred promise. He cradled the infant snugly in his arms, then leaned over and passed it to his wife. There were tears in his eyes. 'Our son.'

Steadily Marika's met her husband's gaze. Forgive me, Christo, she thought, for what I am about to say. 'Yes, Yorgo, our son,' she echoed. As for the first time her arms closed around the infant, a look of bliss illuminated her ravaged face. Even though Yorgos laid claim to him, she would never forget that another love had brought this child into the world. In triumph she held Christos' son in her arms.

'I want a photograph of this,' Yorgos muttered. 'Just as soon as you change the bed and get them both cleaned up, we'll take a picture.' He nodded as though infinitely pleased with himself. 'My father will want to see his grandson.' Slyly he smiled. 'And I am sure my brother will want to see him, too.'

A spasm passed over Marika's features, and yet she did not dare meet her husband's insinuating eyes. How could she protest at Yorgos sending a photograph to Boston showing Christos' son as his own? This was only the first but surely not the last time she would have to keep silent as Yorgos claimed a father's prerogative. She sighed as she bowed her head in submission.

Old Anna stood at the foot of the bed, ready to intercede if her daughter needed her. 'You must be careful, now, *paidi mou*.' She looked around the room as though she alone were seeing those things that could not be seen. 'The Fates may be listening. They may come any time now, to write his destiny on the forehead of this little one.'

'Let them listen and let them come!' Yorgos had recovered not only his equilibrium but also his bravado. He was an educated man, not an illiterate peasant like his wife's mother. In a moment of stress he might have struck a holy – or unholy – bargain with a painted image, but he was not about to give in and believe those ancient superstitions about three all-powerful spirits who came to a newborn baby and cast its lot for good and evil in this life. 'Let them try to do as they like.' He was intent on reasserting his mastery over his wife, his son, and his witchy mother-in-law, too. 'But I forbid any of you to indulge in any hokus-pokus superstitions with my son.' As he was struck by a sudden suspicion, Yorgos looked under his wife's pillow. 'Just as I thought.' In his hand he waved a bulb of garlic that the women said helped ease labour pains. 'No more of this!' He pocketed the garlic so they couldn't do anything else weird with it. 'And none of your tokens to keep away the Evil Eye, either. I'll keep my baby safe myself. This is my child. Mine! And I decide its fate. Me. The father!'

Old Anna met Marika's eyes, and the two women smiled the same secret smile as the icon of the Virgin.

As Marika again bent her head over the baby, Old Anna set about readying the bedroom for the visitors who would descend upon it at any moment. As soon as Yorgos' back was turned, she would get out the amulets she had waiting in her wardrobe. She would hang the bed with turquoise

129

beads to ward off the Evil Eye. She would place a tiny silver icon of St Nikolas under the baby's pillow to safeguard his health and guarantee his wealth. She would pin upon his blanket a precious little bundle she had sewed with lucky crumbs from a holy Easter cake and flower petals from the Saviour's bier that had lain in state in the church last Great Friday, when Marika and Yorgos had done what they had done in that olive grove. And tonight, of course, she would light three candles and set out a dish of honey to sweeten the visit of the Three Fates who would surely come to bless her grandson's fortune. Yorgos could bluster and rage, but she and her daughter would continue to do as the women always did.

As the others in the sitting room began pounding on the door, the doctor opened it with a flourish. 'A boy!' In a moment Vangelis was kneeling by the bed to kiss his sister's hands. Eleni was beaming at the baby she assumed was her grandson, as she pronounced the customary sentiment. 'May the Evil Eye not fall upon him.' The old crones were spitting into the air to ward off jealous evil spirits, crossing themselves, and making cooing noises under their breath.

Over it all, the icon of the Virgin and Child serenely smiled a benediction.

Up until the moment when his father showed him the photograph, Christos had been congratulating himself on his best day since he had come to this country.

As he had waited for the trolley from the university to his father's restaurant, he had tried to convince himself this was merely because, for the first time since he had begun attending classes three months ago, he had finally felt less a misplanted alien than a student who belonged on campus. It had been a strain, even though he had thought his English was fluent, to concentrate for hours and absorb complicated abstractions in a foreign language. Like so many of the Second World War veterans in his classes, too, he had felt like a slow-witted old man next to the eighteen-year-old freshmen whose minds were so quick and sure. And yet he supposed what had made his classes magical that morning had little to do with suddenly feeling at home in American History 101. What accounted for his lightning change of attitude was the blonde blue-eyed young associate professor who had announced she was replacing the other lecturer for the rest of the term.

Absently Christos climbed onto the packed Green Line trolley. Instead of taking notes about the Constitutional Congress that had occurred nearly two hundred years ago in Philadelphia, he had sat transfixed by this tall young woman who paced back and forth with an athletic stride, and then swung her lanky buttocks atop her scarred wooden desk, and finally crossed her long legs above the knee. Her hair had been pulled back in one of those absurd pony tails the Americans affected, and on her shiny face there had been not so much as a glimmer of cosmetics. Except for the abstruse concepts that rolled off her tongue at an alarming rate, she had seemed like a little girl who had wandered by mistake into this college classroom. He had been taken by how young she seemed. When sometimes he had tried to imagine himself with a bold American girl, he had always wondered how he or any man could succeed in dominating these modern Amazons. But this one appeared, in her way, as fresh and innocent as a village girl. As he had measured her against his memory of Marika, happily he concluded that this one was nothing like the other. This American had no breasts that he could make out in her smock of a dress, she was probably half a foot taller than he was, and her colouring was pale like the Boston sky rather than sensual like the Greek earth. He had liked the fact that she wasn't sexy. If he wanted any woman at all – and he doubted he did – he most certainly did not want one who would once again lay claim to the essence of his being. Back in Greece, Marika had scorched him with too much heat. This cool little girl with her boyish body and brainy talk could never brand him as the other had.

As the trolley had lumbered toward the Back Bay, Christos had savoured every moment of that wonderful morning during and after History 101.

All through her lecture Christos had smiled benignly and not taken his eyes off her for an instant. When at last she had returned his gaze, her monologue had faltered and she had frowned and looked pointedly at his notebook. The only words he had written during her lecture was her curious name, 'Penny Heywood', which she had chalked up on the blackboard. He had marvelled that here, in this money-obsessed country, they even named their girls after coins. He had supposed that some of them must be called Dime, Nickel and Quarter.

When, a few minutes later, her eyes had returned to him and held his searchingly, he had felt a surge of power race through his body. For a certainty he had known that, if he wanted her, he could have this one for his own. It might take longer to coax an educated teacher like her into his arms than the three evenings Adonis had needed to master his little checkout cashier, but the end result would be the same.

Christos had narrowed his eyes and, with that lazy assurance of a male predator about to pounce, he had looked her over again infinitely slowly, from the sungolden hair that he could almost feel soft against his cheeks to those lithe legs he imagined wrapped around his thighs. He hadn't had a real girl for a very long while. Even back in Greece he had been so over his head in war and revolution that the only woman he had ever had was Marika that one night in the cave. Was it time to begin all that again?

His eyes had fallen, as uncertainly he had retraced her name with his pen. He had vowed he would love Marika forever, and that he would condescend to have no other. She had married his brother, but he had taken pride in the fact that, superior soul that he was, he would still keep faith with that one shining emotion. He would be as romantically idealistic in this matter of love as he had once been with his politics. So what, he had asked himself, was he doing flirting with his teacher?

Miserably he had written 'Marika' in Greek letters and then stared at the two names for a moment before resolutely crossing out them both. He was twenty-seven, and he had a lot of catching up to do if he were ever to make his mark in what they aptly called 'the rat race' here. He should be concentrating on his studies rather than wasting his time with adolescent fantasies of erotic love.

And yet after class, despite his resolutions to the contrary, he had been unable to resist hanging about for a chance to talk to her. Just a few words, he had promised himself, and then he would forget this one. He had waited until the others were gone, and then he had fired the first salvo of what turned out to be a fusillade of personal questions. He had not yet shaken the Greek habit of asking total strangers whether they were married and how many children they had and how much money they made.

She had paused and looked him over long and hard – lingering a telltale second too long, Christos had noted, when she had looked into his eyes – before she admitted that she wasn't married.

He had been so cheered that, after confiding that he was single as well and that he had arrived in this country from Greece the previous spring, he had gone on to enquire about her materialistic name.

She had grinned and told him that actually it was Penelope, as in the wife of Odysseus. Christos had beamed when she had used that crafty ancient mariner's proper name, instead of Anglicizing it into Ulysses like his literature professor did.

Once she had started talking about herself, Peppy – for he had immediately decided to dub her with that modern Greek nickname for those called after Homer's faithful wifely heroine – hadn't seemed to be able to stop. 'Daddy insisted I study the Classics,' she had confided, for her father was a professor of Classical literature at Harvard. Her mother taught archaeology at Simmons. When Christos had commended her for coming from such a distinguished family, she had dazzled him by volunteering the precious information that her uncle was a United States Congressman.

An utterly entranced Christos had hesitated only an instant before asking this pretty young teacher with the perfect family connections to have a coffee. He had been only a little disappointed when she had apologized for having a prior appointment. 'But maybe after class on Wednesday,' she had boldly promised even before he had a chance to ask.

They had smiled a little inanely as they shook hands outside the classroom. And a few paces down the corridor, when he had been unable to resist turning round for another glimpse of her, he had caught her doing the same thing. He had been amazed, then, to see a blush on the rosy face of this American girl who he had assumed must be so sophisticated.

Christos had been so wrapped up in remembering every nuance of that wonderful first encounter with the promising Peppy that he had missed his trolley stop. But he hadn't minded the longer trek back to his father's restaurant, for he had felt like he was walking on air. Yet this was only, he had cautioned himself, a harmless flirtation. He had no intention of ever falling in love again – much less marrying! – for he had learned his lesson back in Greece. A man such as himself could be wedded only to his politics. He meant to join the Democratic Party, apply for American citizenship, and somehow rise in the ranks so that someday he could do the work he had been born to do. He had finished with war, revolution, and the Communist Party. But he had not yet begun to do his part to achieve political, racial, and economic justice in this country that had taken him in when his homeland had spurned him. If later he changed his mind and wanted a wife, he would most certainly never consider a misalliance with an American girl whose background and culture were so at odds with his own. As his father always pointedly said, a man never wore a black shoe and a brown shoe at the same time, but a matched pair; Greeks must marry Greeks. And yet after being so long alone with his sore heart, Christos had felt so happy to have a pretty girl smile into his eyes again.

He had burst into the restaurant, clapped Adonis on the back, and called out greetings to Spiros and Stephanos. He had been all smiles when his father, who finally seemed to have made peace with his political ambitions, beckoned him over to his corner table roost.

Nick, too, had been all aglow as he shouted for Adonis to bring them a bottle of champagne. 'A boy!' he had announced as he handed over a colour snapshot to Christos. 'My first grandson.' His radiance increased. 'They'll name him after me, of course.'

Christos had forgotten all about the girl teacher as he fumbled with his cigarettes to buy time to compose himself. Finally he had lit a match, inhaled, and forced his eyes to focus on the photograph that had arrived in this morning's post.

Marika – how could he have forgotten how achingly beautiful she was? – was lying propped up on a nest of white pillows in bed. Bundled in her arms – she held him so tenderly, there was such love in the curving of her arm and the cupping of her hand — was a red and wrinkled baby. And yet — how could she have married him, *how*? — Yorgos was sitting with his arm possessively around her shoulders. Christos stared mutely at the photograph. Like acid sets a steel engraving, the image was etched in his mind.

Adonis was uncorking the champagne, and Nick was wiping off a pair of fluted glasses. 'Beautiful, eh? Looks just like me, they say. He's small, though. Less than three kilos. Yorgos says he was premature. Even so, Marika had a devil of a time having him. Almost killed her, Yorgos says.'

Yearningly Christos drank in the dear sight of her frail face. Yes, he could see it now, Marika had suffered since he had seen her last, and maybe not just from a difficult labour. Her eyes looked haunted. Again he wondered if she had ever received his plea to wait for him. He longed to bring this photograph to his lips for a kiss which could transcend time and space. But of course that, too, could never be, at least not when his father was watching.

Nick was pouring the bubbly wine. 'They say they'll arrange the christening when I can make it over. And I'll go, yes, I'm overdue for a visit anyway. Maybe next summer, in August. Yes! We can hold the christening on the village nameday festival.' The candescence of Nick's smile dimmed as he looked at Christos. The Greek government had banned the return of all those who had fought with the Communists during the Civil War. 'I wish you could go too.'

Christos hopelessly shrugged as his gaze went from the mother to the child. The baby was so tiny and so swaddled in blankets that he could hardly make out any of his blurry features. But it seemed to him that the infant did indeed have Nick's luminous light eyes. As a sudden thought struck him, Christos more closely examined what he could see of Marika's son. *He has my eyes, too.* Could it be . . .? No, he hastily decided. Nick had just told him the baby was premature. No matter what he might want to believe, Yorgos was this boy's father.

'He's beautiful, Chris, isn't he? He's the most beautiful baby I've ever seen.'

'Ay, yes,' Christos finally managed to say. '*Kuklos*, a doll.'

Nick held up his glass. 'To Nikolas Kronos!'

'Nikolas Kronos!' Christos clinked his glass to his father's. On his tongue, the champagne had a bitter taste as he drank to his brother's son, the infant who should have been his own. He was grateful a moment later when the rest of the staff came out from the kitchen with their champagne glasses at the ready. As they all crowded round and Nick grandly filled their glasses, he hoped no one noticed that he did not appear as happy as he perhaps should be.

Christos' fingers stole back to the photograph. What greater proof did he need that what had once been between himself and Marika was over? She was not only married but the mother of his brother's son. She had made another life for herself, and whether he liked it or not – and he liked it not at all – now it was up to him to make another life for himself as well. 'Antio, Marika,' he said so softly that no one heard. 'Goodbye.'

When finally Christos put the photograph back on the table, face down so he could no longer see it and brood, he felt his last link with his homeland and that one he still held so dear was finally and irrevocably broken.

'Why, Chris, you're crying!' Nick was so moved at this display of familial devotion that he bounded over and hugged his eldest son.

When the two finally drew apart, Nick's eyes, too, brimmed with tears.

Six

The rental Cadillac purred up and down the winding roller-coaster hills that snaked from Korinthos to Argos as Nick bellowed a bouzouki love song more or less in tune with the blasting car radio. He felt the king not only of the Peloponnesus but of all Greece. Never was a land as beautiful as the motherland; never was the sun so warming; never was the light so enchanting. He was so full of his homecoming that he was on the verge of telling the driver to pull over so he could leap out and dance on these sylvan brown hills that baked in the midsummer sun. But even though his family didn't expect him for another fortnight, he was in too much of a hurry to stop now. He had resisted the temptation to telephone Panagia as soon as he docked in Piraeus, for that would have ruined the surprise of his early arrival. At the thought of sweeping into the village in his fancy car, he urged the driver on faster. Already, ahead as they crested a ridge, he could glimpse the mountains that flanked the second most beautiful stretch of sea in the world. Panagia, though his home away from home, had never laid first claim on his heart. Yet, he reflected, it had been his haven after he and more than a million Greeks had been forced from their ancestral Asia Minor villages in that bitter exchange of populations after losing the last war with Turkey in what the Greeks always referred to as 'Twenty-Two'. Could he ever bear, he wondered anew, to revisit his real home now that it had been renamed and repopulated and perhaps even rebuilt as a Turkish hamlet? In his mind's eye he could still see the wrinkle of every hill, could almost hear the slap of every foamy wave on the white pebble beach, taste the sweet clear water that gushed from a mountain spring where it was said that the ubiquitous Aphrodite herself had once bathed.

No. It was better not to return to that dear heartland now it was so sadly changed. A tremor passed through him. Perhaps, too, he shouldn't be going back to this other village which still tugged at his heart. Once he had been so happy there. Panagia had been the joy of his youth. *She* lay there still in the graveyard halfway up the mountain, and one day again he would lie beside her, this time forever. When he sensed his end was near, he would make his way home one final time. He might choose to live as an exile, but he wouldn't die as one.

Nick's hands trembled as he lit one of the expensive American cigarettes which he, a successful restaurateur, now smoked instead of those smelly hand-rolled Turkish ones. It would break his heart, he thought, to make a bittersweet pilgrimage to the lost village of his ancestors, but this sentimental journey home to Panagia would be as sweet as *halva* on the tongue. In a little more than an hour he would hold his first grandchild in his arms. He would cover his tiny face with kisses and gaze in wonder at his ten perfect fingers and ten perfect toes. With the baby in his arms he would stride the length of the village, would sit under a plane tree in the *plateia*, and settle down in a *kafeneion* for the first in a series of endless conversations with greybeards whom he remembered when they were too young to sprout a whisker. Nick longed to let out a long sigh of contentment and do nothing but settle back and once again absolutely belong in this village which had accepted him as truly one of its own. Unlike America, here he didn't have to prove himself every single day and constantly measure himself against impossible standards. Here it would always be enough simply to be Nikolas Kronos sitting in the sun. To sink down and merely exist – like a tree or a flower or even one of the inevitable barren rocks – will be, Nick thought as he sped on home, a state of infinite bliss. And yet, hastily he amended to himself, he loved his adopted country as well. He adored America's excitements, was addicted to its potentials, and lashed himself into a hyperactive frenzy with its neverending ambitions. But he was a Greek, and nowhere else in the world could he be at peace than here in the mottled shadows of his village square. Until he could breathe in Panagia's pure crystalline air and drink in the sight of its dancing blue sea, his soul would not be at rest.

'Almost home!' he enthused to the driver. 'Wait until you see my village!'

'Eh?' The driver shrugged. 'I have a village, too.' Scornfully he glanced out the window at these puny hills which could never compare with the rugged stone mountains of his native Epirus. Hidden in those heights were waterfalls, and secret grottos, and eternal peace. He had lived in Athens since the beginning of the last war and supposed he would remain in the capital until he was too old to work. But then he would retire to that beloved nest of earth, rock, and sky. In one of those lightning mood changes so characteristic of his countrymen, he smiled benevolently at the American. As he took this one home, almost he could imagine he, too, was making a sentimental journey back to his own village.

As the kilometres ticked by, Nick sang and smoked and chattered on about the many changes that had been wrought on this once-familiar stretch of homeland since he had seen it last, thirteen years ago, before the wars. With a proprietary air he gushed that this tarmac road, one of many built by a share of his own American taxpayer dollars since the World War, was a remarkable feat of engineering and a definite improvement over the old dirt and cinder lane that followed an ancient path. He pointed down a ravine at the faint traces of what he swore were roadworks that must have been old when Jesus Christ Himself lived. Once, he confided, when he had been walking just there early on an autumn morning, he could have sworn he heard the clash of armour and the tread of leather sandals. For here, just here, Agamemnon had set out for Troy. And there, just there, the warriors of Athens and Sparta had tramped in their fratricidal Peloponnesian wars. The Persians, the Romans, the Venetians, the Turks, the Italians, the Germans – 'everyone who was anyone', he grandly pronounced – had spilled their blood and guts for this, the most precious soil in all the earth. Greece, Nick swore with a majestic sweep of his arm at the panorama before them, is haunted by the spirits of all those ages long past. 'Look at it! Feel it! Smell it! We are in Paradise!'

But as they twisted through the back streets of the not-so-heavenly town of Argos, still scarred with the evidence of nearly a decade of warfare, he had to bite his tongue. Bullet holes marred unpainted cinderblock walls. What once had been houses was rubble. Shops were still boarded up by flimsy planks. Buildings burnt down years ago lay with their cinders as untouched as though the fires had blazed yesterday. He was reassured only when they came upon the shrill mercantile bustle of the Wednesday fruit, vegetable, and flea market on the far side of the *plateia*. As he watched his countrymen buying and selling everything including sometimes their souls, Nick recalled that – at least in his lifetime – Argos had always been an ugly and sweltering commercial centre; good for shopping but bad for living. Surely, he assured himself, Panagia could not have become as graceless as this.

He breathed easier when they left the dismal town behind and he caught sight of the cleansing sea. Raptly he stared at the azure water. The Atlantic could never be like this, so precisely, purely blue, as though God or the elements had just at this instant been inspired to create this magical colour of sea and sky. The sun flickered on the waves, while near the horizon the peaks of purplish mountains stood their eternal watch. Again he resisted the temptation to stop the car and drink in the calming landscape which never changed.

Moodily he lit another cigarette. The Greek landscape might look the same, he thought, but Greece wasn't the same. Remembering how sadly changed he had found his country since his return, Nick could not be so sure his village would still be as he expected it to be. During the three days he had rested in Athens from the long sea voyage, he had been shocked at how the scarred capital had deteriorated from the vibrant and colourful city he remembered. Athens had suffered badly in the wars. When the Germans had commandeered foodstuffs during the Nazi Occupation, tens of thousands had died of starvation. Horse-drawn carts had rumbled through the streets collecting the bodies. Then after the German pullout, there had been fierce street-fighting and the Communists had nearly succeeded in seizing the city. Even now, nearly a year since the Civil War had officially ended, the neighbourhoods were still chockablock with hundreds of thousands of refugees who had fled the fighting and come to roost either with relatives or in densely packed new breezeblock slums that appeared to have been constructed overnight by blind builders. Once when he had paused for a coffee during an especially depressing ramble through these ramshackle *quartiers*, he had been even more appalled at a *kafeneion* conversation. After smoking three of Nick's cigarettes, a youngish man at the next table had spat contemptuously into the air when he proudly showed him his American passport. 'This for your America!' he had hissed. 'If it weren't for them and their filthy dollars, things would be different here now.' Before Nick could leap to his adopted country's defence, the man had stumped out the door, his empty trouser leg doubled up on his thigh. 'He lost it fighting with the *andartes*,' a fellow at the next table had explained. 'You've been gone a long while,' he had continued, 'too long. Maybe you should have stayed in your America.' As Nick had looked around at the sea of angry eyes in the seedy *kafeneion*, he had hastily backed out the door before the conversation turned even more acrimonious. He hadn't remembered his countrymen being so bitter, and so rock-hard. Surely by now some of the wounds of the Civil War should have begun to heal. The Greece he remembered had been so warm, welcoming, and spiced always with zest and laughter. But the next time he had felt like a coffee, he had taken care to choose a chrome and glass *zacharoplasteion* in a more prosperous neighbourhood where, if there were

138

any leftists at all, they were likely to be sweeping the floor or washing the glasses. But he hadn't had time to do more than take one sip of coffee and one bite of honeycake before, after first ascertaining that Nick lived in Boston, Massachusetts, an old man had slapped him on the back. When the *patrida* had been threatened by the Communist menace – at those words, the fellow had hunched over and looked around as though Reds could be lurking in the painstakingly dust-free corners – it had been Uncle Sam who had come to the rescue. But, he had added, they had stopped short of the goal. 'They should have killed them all, because, mark my words, someday they'll creep back to kill us.' The old man had bared his stained and broken teeth and pounded his fist on the formica table. 'I would like to slit the throat of every Red devil in the world!' Nick had fled that café, too, repelled by the virulence of both the left and the right.

What, Nick wondered again as he stared broodingly at the sea, had poisoned his countrymen? If Christos were here, he would have known the answer. In these past months, Nick had found his dependence on his son increasing. Not, he amended, that he was such a doddering old fool that he needed his son to tell him how to think and act. During the years of his exile, Nick had avidly followed current events by subscribing to a Greek newspaper and sitting night after night with his talkative compatriots. Like all Greeks, he could discourse for hours about everything and nothing, and had yet to find a subject on which he did not hold his own voluble opinion. But he did not know what to make of these changes in his country, and it sickened him to see his homeland so riven by hate. And yet, remembering some late night arguments in his Boston restaurant, Nick admitted that his elder son was just as embittered as those fanatics in Athens.

Nick was so sunk in dark thought that he scarcely noticed when ahead the old Venetian fortress loomed on the cliff above seaside Nauplion. Again he fretted that this homecoming wouldn't be complete without Christos. But because of the Greek government ban against the return of those who had fought on the Communist side, reluctantly he had left his son in Boston to juggle the family business and his university studies. Yet he could not understand why Christos hadn't seemed to mind missing this trip home. Except for the telltale time he had caught him weeping over that photograph of the baby, Christos had been indifferent to Yorgos' letters and pictures. His son had always been strangely reluctant, too, to talk about those troubled last months before he had sailed to America. Yet usually Christos was eager to dissect every nuance of Greek politics. Was he keeping something secret from his own loving father?

As the driver stopped at a kiosk for another packet of cigarettes, Nick gnawed on that intriguing possibility. Even Greeks who sweltered in the rabbit-warren apartment blocks of Athens at heart remained snoopy villagers. Nothing so seizes the creative imagination of the modern Greek's prying nature than a secret, and most irresistible of all is a sexual secret.

Nick was so absorbed in the riddle of his son's sexual past that he didn't see the olive and orange groves flashing by the careening Cadillac. For a long while now, he had suspected his son had left more behind in Greece than his country and his cause. He was a redblooded Kronos, and surely as virile as the rest of his line. It wasn't natural, the way the boy was uninterested in every girl who came his way, with the alarming exception of that skinny giant of an American teacher he had brought to the restaurant a few times. But since the night he had alluded to a broken romance, Nick had not been able to extract any more details about the girl he had left behind. Nick sensed a greater tragedy than merely the lack of an adequate *prika*.

He drummed his fingers on the armrest. He had been away from the village for so many years he didn't even know this younger generation, who had been little girls on his last brief visit. And yet someone in Panagia must know everything about Christos' past; someone always knew everything, and everyone talked. He would discover the identity of this mysterious girl, and then perhaps he would try to rewrite the past and take his son's heart's desire back to America. He had to get him out of the clutches of that bony teacher.

As the driver coursed the home stretch to Panagia, Nick inhaled and let out the cigarette smoke with a sigh. He doubted Yorgos would tell him anything he didn't already know about Christos. His younger son's letters were still studded with barbs against his brother, and he even had insinuated it was better for the family if everyone in the village continued to believe that Christos had perished in the closing months of the Civil War. Nick was sick at heart at the proofs that a feud had sprung up between his boys. If he wanted to understand what had gone wrong in his country, Nick supposed he need look no further than his own sons.

'I think we must be almost there,' the driver said.

Nick came out of his reverie with a start as they rounded a great bend and suddenly he saw the village spread before him.

'Driver! Stop the car!' The Cadillac braked and parked.

Nestled snug at the crest of the bay between mountain and sea, Panagia yawned and slept in the sun. Small houses the colours of milk and butter and bread clustered close to the water, while on the azure sea white boats swung with the waves. Shadows moved on the shore – a fisherman mending his nets, children running on the beach, a figure in black plodding home laden like a donkey. Nick's eye was caught by the glint of a cross shining from the dome of the church, and his heart felt pierced by the green spikes of cypress.

140

The loveliest mountain in the world, high as a staircase to heaven, crowned by a tiara of stone, encircled the village like a mother holds her firstborn son. Blue sky and blue sea shimmered in white light so that the spiny, stony islands strewn with a pagan god's carelessness in the bay seemed something from a dream. He was ashamed that he had forgotten how beautiful his village was. Panagia was so in harmony with the earth, the sky, and the sea that it could have been swept ashore on a morning tide. All that was missing was a rainbow.

'That's it! My village!' Tears ran down Nick's cheeks. He blinked, dazzled by the brightness of the light and dazed by the intensity of his emotion.

Strangely, when again his eyes could focus, he saw not the drowsy fishing village of the backward present but the vision of a tourist mecca of the developed future. There, on the sandy beach fringed by high dunes, he imagined striped umbrellas, canvas chairs, and hot buttered Scandinavian girls lying thigh to thigh on gaudy towels. There, on the barren mountain, his mind's eye built terraced highrises, landscaped holiday homes, and hotels that catered to busloads of sun-seeking vacationers. There, on the mostly deserted *plateia*, he dreamed of smart shops and souvenir stands and cafés that served more cappuchino than ouzo. For the right man, for a canny investor – for *me*, Nick thought with glee – this dirt-poor village could one day be worth a fortune.

Nick mopped his suddenly sweating brow. He would talk this over with Yorgos, and maybe they could pool the family resources and quietly buy up every bit of prime seafront land for peanuts. The wars had wrecked the Greek economy, so surely these village peasants would be desperate for a little cash. Then perhaps he and Yorgos would aim their sights higher and go after acreage up on the mountain where one day the tourists might pay any price for a breathtaking view. He had been wrong before when he had assumed that all that was lacking here was a rainbow. The pot of gold, too, might someday be in the picture.

As Nick smiled radiantly at his village, the most marvellous certainty swept over him. His inspiration of the last moments was a turning point not only for his family's fortune but for Panagia as well. He would skim off the cream for his own, of course, but in time everyone would reap the rewards. Someday these barefoot and illiterate villagers riding their donkeys could be wearing costly Italian leather shoes, sending their children to university in London, and driving cars as grand as the one he had rented in Athens. And someday, when he and his family were all very rich, his children and his children's children would understand that it was his foresight that had made them millionaires. Overcome by a sudden impulse as superstitious as it was pious, Nick wanted to thank God for this materialistic vision and begin the first of many pleas for His blessings upon it.

'Wait for me, driver. There's a church . . .'

Nick leaped out, hared up the path to the crest of the headland, and flung open the door of a tiny chapel sheltered in a cleft of the cliffs overlooking the water. 'Ah . . .' He blinked in the incense-laden darkness lit only by the candles that flickered before the icon of the Virgin that gave the church its name. He leaned over and touched his lips to the hammered silver hem of the Panagia's dress, and then he crossed over and reverently kissed the icons of St Nikolas and St Michael. If there had been a patron saint of money, he would have fallen to his knees and prayed before him, too.

He dropped a coin in an iron box, lit a tall brown beeswax candle, and set it before the sad-eyed Virgin. As his misty eyes met Hers, sentiment overwhelmed his visions of material gain. Long ago, on the day they had decided to marry, he and Sofia had come here to ask the Panagia's blessing. How happy he had been as he held her hand just here, and how certain that they would share a lifetime of continual bliss. For a moment he felt her presence all around him in the thick dark smoky air. 'Sofia,' he murmured to himself, as like a blind man he groped forward in the darkness for the one he would always love.

But there was no one in the church but an old crone with her back to him as she bent almost double sweeping the floor. He supposed she volunteered for this dirty job not for pay but as an act of pious devotion. Still, a flash of irritation prickled him, for he had thought that here in this church he was alone with his past. He scowled at this interloper's shapeless peasant dress. The Greek custom he least liked was this practice of women donning perpetual mourning once someone close to them had died. He supposed this one must be a widow, although she could be wearing the black shrouds for her parents or even a brother or sister. It was anyone's guess how old she was. Sometimes in Greece when he saw what appeared to be an old grandmother holding a baby, he was appalled to see her adjourn to another room so she could breastfeed her child. Scorching sun and the hardness of their lives made women who would be called middle-aged back in America elderly here in Greece. This one looked old enough to be his own dear departed mother.

But, when he could see the sweeper's silhouette as she half turned in the dim light, his eye caught something familiar in the set of her wrinkled features. She moved closer, and the candle he had lit in memory of Sofia illuminated her ravaged face.

'Eleni!' His wife's name escaped his lips before he could call it back. To meet her here, when he had fancied he was alone with the ghost of Sofia . . .

no, this place and this moment belonged solely to the wife of his heart. But then Nick was taken by pity for this poor soul he had married for convenience and left in haste. Even now, at his first sight of her in many years, she was overshadowed by her dead rival. Perhaps the knowledge that she had never been more than his second best wife had aged her so. He resolved, for once, to try to do right by her. He held out his arms. 'Eleni *mou*, it's me!'

'What?' With an effort she straightened up and leaned on the broom. Shyly she raised her deepset eyes ringed in sunken circles. 'What do you say?'

Now that he saw her full face, he fancied that some of the years fell away and she wasn't altogether broken by life. He had never shared the same consuming passion with this homely woman as he had with Sofia. But nonetheless she had been his faithful wife for nearly three decades, and he owed this good woman a certain loyalty. She had given him one son and raised Sofia's boy as though he were her own. Moreover, he knew that she had gone down on her knees and prayed for his welfare every day of her life. Extravagantly he smiled. 'Don't you know me?'

But she was shaking her head. 'Eh?' With suspicion she eyed this plump stranger in the tight city suit.

'It's Nikolas!' When her only reaction was to peer nearsightedly at him, he elaborated. 'Your husband!'

'My husband does not come back yet.' But her hand nervously stole up to the black mourning scarf she wore for her brother who had died in the spring. She had dreamed of this reunion for so many lonely years, and for him to come on her unawares now, like *this*?

'I sailed early. I got to Athens last week and came down as soon as I could.' He laughed. 'I wanted to surprise you all!'

In the uncertain light, doubtfully she looked him over again. The photograph she kept on her bedside table below her favourite icon was of a slim young man with curly black hair and a toothy smile. This one was too grey and sleek. But finally she met those green eyes. Oh, *his* eyes! 'Nikolas?'

Masterfully he closed the distance between them, took her in his arms, and clasped her to his chest. 'Eleni *mou*!' She was so thin and wraithlike that it was like embracing a skeleton, as though – he thought with a shudder – it had been not Sofia but Eleni who had died long ago. Her shoulders shook, and he could hear her sobbing. 'Now, now, enough of that.' He wondered how long decency required that he must hold her like this. His ladyfriends back in Boston were so young and round that, almost when he held them, he felt himself a *pallikari* again. But matched with this ancient one, he, too, felt old. As tentatively he patted her back, again he thought she seemed more like his mother than his wife. Perhaps it would make it easier to be kind if he

143

thought of her as his mother reincarnated. Yes, that was better; a wave of sudden tenderness swept over him and he held her as if he meant it. 'My dear, oh my dear, it's been so long.'

Finally he drew back, wiped away her tears, and steered her toward the door and the waiting Cadillac. 'Now let's go home.'

Early in the morning of the baby's christening, Nick and Yorgos tossed off their coffee at a gulp, ground out their cigarettes, and tried to stride manfully away from the women's frantic preparations for the great feast that would follow the great events. A baptism alone would have had the household in an uproar. But the christening was being held on August fifteenth, the Feast of the Virgin, a great high summer holiday everywhere in Greece but a spectacular one in this village that carried the Panagia's name. On this day every year the *pappas* and the villagers traditionally took to their boats in the morning for a celebratory Mass out at the island chapel, and in the evening there was a candlelight Litany procession through the village and then a fiesta in the *plateia*. Sandwiched in between the Mass, the Litany, and the *fête* were private parties in virtually every family. All the numerous women named after the Panagia – each Maria, Marika, Panayiotia, and Yiota – and every man named Panayiotis, Takis, and Panos celebrated their *yorti*, nameday, in much the same spirit as birthdays were observed elsewhere. The Kronos home was in a delirium of preparations with the christening, the village festival, and Marika's nameday all coming at once.

Yet it was not so easy for Nick and Yorgos to make their escape to the beach. The sitting room was strewn with the sleeping bodies of relatives and friends who had arrived the night before from as far away as Athens. Drowsy heads were raised as the father and son tried to tiptoe to the door. Sloth and curiosity battled, and the less lazy propped themselves up on their elbows. '*Pou pas?*' The eternal Greek question was croaked out by those who had been sound asleep a second ago. 'Where are you going?' As night follows day, the inevitable volley of queries came quickly. 'And why? Why are you leaving us? Is it just the two of you? Wait, we'll come, too.'

Hastily Nick and Yorgos evaded them by ducking into the crowded taverna kitchen. Awkwardly they stood in the doorway. Even Nick, who took a professional's pride in running his own busy restaurant kitchen, felt himself alien in this women's world. He was startled to see his meek wife transformed into a self-assured general commanding her army of chattering female relatives to cut the cucumbers, fry the aubergines, and rush another casserole off to the bakery ovens to be roasted. Eleni seemed to be everywhere at once, tasting this, eyeing that, suggesting a bit more oil or a lot more

144

stirring. In a flash she was at the window, squinting at Old Anna out in the garden supervising a squad of aunts turning the three baby lambs on the spit. Nearby a pig was being readied for the fire, and a henhouse's worth of chickens were sizzling on yet another cluster of spits. Old Anna stood with a sponge dripping with olive oil with which from time to time she would baste the crackling meat. Satisfied that Marika's mother was well in control of the most important dishes – in these hard times, some of the guests would only taste meat once or twice a year, and a hungry man might gorge on a pound of lamb and another pound of pork – Eleni dropped the curtain and turned her attention to the nieces and cousins. Her brother's sister-in-law, renowned for her sweets, was dribbling honey atop a freshly-baked sheet of *baklava*, and her niece was readying another tray of breads she had artfully twisted into curvaceous knots. Mountains of salads were being painstakingly sliced. A season's crop of vegetables were being dropped into the bubbling vats of olive oil. The melons were being trundled from a truck in a wheelbarrow. And great bowls of glistening grapes and ripe figs were being arranged with as much care as though a painter would later immortalize them on canvas. Soaring over it all like a crescendo of operatic music were the women's high-pitched soprano voices; for though their fingers worked fast, their tongues worked faster. Incessantly they gossiped, joked, complained, teased, squabbled, and worried as they readied the platters of food for the feast.

'Enough.' Yorgos tugged at his father's sleeve, eager to be off on what he expected to be a delicious conversation with the man he adored. Since his father had arrived a fortnight ago, he had been jealous of every instant Nick spent with anyone else. He longed for the precious moment when he could have him all to himself. This time, instead of his usual tiresome talk of America, his father might ask about his military career. He would be modest and only boast a little about his exploits in the Civil War and what his superiors had said when they had given him his last official commendation. And then, joy of joys, his father would finally have to pat him on the back and say how proud he was of his favourite son. *Favourite*. Not Christos, but me. '*Pame*,' Yorgos urged, 'let's go.'

'Sure.' Nick couldn't help absently slipping back into the English that now came so naturally to his tongue. Once in a while when either he forgot where he was or he didn't want others to understand what he was saying, he would try to talk to Yorgos in English. But his younger son's schoolbook grasp of the foreign language was far from fluent. Christos, on the other hand, had been such a natural at languages that after only a year in America he spoke English with hardly a trace of an accent. Wisely, however, Nick kept this observation to himself.

Yet he lit a cigarette and lingered in the kitchen, savouring not only the luscious smells of the food but also the lazy pleasure of watching the women do the work. In Boston he was tireless and could chop and bake with the best of them. But here he had immediately sunk into the masculine torpor that tradition demanded. The old ways, he told himself, were sometimes the best ways after all.

When Eleni caught sight of them, she rushed over and pressed them to sample titbits fresh from the ovens and the stoves. Graciously Nick strode here and there, nodding in approval even though this village fare no longer met his more cosmopolitan standards. They ladled on too much olive oil and rained on too much salt for the taste he had acquired in Boston. The farm-fresh ingredients were some of the best in the world, but even a good cook like Eleni had never learned to use what she had with imagination. Still, even though the range of a Greek kitchen was limited, what they did with the old favourites was sometimes inspired. He accepted a hot crusty triangle of *tiropitta*, and said '*Bravo*,' when the cheese inside the flaky multilayered *filo* pastry melted in his mouth. Next he popped in a juicy *dolma*, and his eyes closed in a kind of ecstasy; the vineleaves were straight from the arbour, the raisins succulent, the pinenuts snappy. Finally he pronounced the *baklava poli oreo*, very beautiful. When Eleni seemed about to nip out to the garden to cut him choice slivers of the lamb, Nick held up his hand and regretfully touched his stomach to mime that he couldn't eat another bite.

Beatifically he stood at the epicentre of the kitchen, proud there would be far too much food even if every invited villager ate himself sick. As the host, he wouldn't be able to hold his head high unless there were enough leftovers to feed the next village as well. For years to come, they'd be talking of the grand christening that Nikolas Kronos held for his grandson, and the boys in the *kafeneions* would make their throats hoarse with speculation about exactly how much money he had managed to amass in America. Already some cousins had come begging for loans to buy another grove of olives or finance an ailing wife's operation, for everyone in this dirt-poor village had assumed he must be breathtakingly rich. No one, Nick reflected with satisfaction, would ever guess he had postponed his plans to open the waterfront restaurant and instead taken out a second mortgage on his Back Bay restaurant to finance the high style of this trip: the outside cabin on the ocean liner, the rental Cadillac, the costly presents for even the in-laws, and the entire cost of the village festival to follow in the *plateia*. His dollars went a long way against drachmas, but even so this was an expensive proposition. Yet the extravagance was well worth it. He, who had arrived here as a penniless refugee in his youth, finally had come home like a lord.

Yorgos was still trying to catch his father's eye and hustle him away from the kitchen, when a deep voice called from the garden. 'Ah, there you are.'

146

Marika's brother Vangelis burst in, eager to report the latest about the crisis over the musicians. 'I have news!'

Over a week ago, when Nick had let it be known that he expected music and dancing in his grandson's honour at the village's nameday festival in the *plateia*, Vangelis had been sent to Tripolis to engage a trio famous on all four fingers of the Peloponnese peninsula. Yet late last night, as the old boys had been leaning back in their chairs drinking raki and the old girls had been down on their hands and knees giving the floors of the house yet another fervent polishing, a messenger had arrived to say that the musicians would not come unless the previously negotiated fee were doubled. The men of the family had slammed down their glasses and argued with one another into the wee hours about what was to be done about this attempted robbery. Frantic telephone calls had ensued, threats had been made, and yet the 'foreigners' from Tripolis had stood firm. Finally Vangelis had roared off in the rental Cadillac to confront the musicians. If all else failed, he was to engage another band.

'Success,' Vangelis announced before anyone could even wish him good morning. The three men paced out to the garden and lit fresh cigarettes. 'It was difficult,' Vangelis began. 'Those bandits from Tripolis had heard our American was very rich, and they claimed they were very poor. I suppose it didn't help our case when I arrived in the Cadillac.' In Tripolis, as in Panagia, a herd of screaming children had followed the luxury American car everywhere.

'Is it really so?' Nick tried not to smile at this proof that he had become such a big man that even the lads in Tripolis were eager to fleece him.

'Really!' Vangelis, who had blossomed since becoming a Kronos in-law, punctuated his story by waving his cigarette. As soon as he had finished high school in Nauplion, he had made himself indispensable working beside Eleni and his mother in the taverna. Lately he had even mostly buried his old animosity toward Yorgos. He would get his reward today when he would star as his nephew's *nonos*, the godfather.

'We talked and talked, and even the mayor came and tried to persuade them not to be so silly. By then a crowd had gathered in the *kafeneion* – taking sides, suggesting this, arguing about that. Someone sent for the priest, and I think he must have been a cousin of the pipe player, for he gave them his blessing and told them God was on their side. They were devils! Finally, before dawn, I said *Teliose*, it is finished, and I left them with nothing but a bad reputation. They will never play in Panagia again, in Argos, or in any of the villages in between.'

'So be it,' Yorgos said between gritted teeth. 'I'd like to break their hands so they never play again.'

'Boys, boys,' Nick said, 'it's only music.'

'No,' Yorgos fiercely corrected him. 'It's a matter of *filotimo*, pride. Our honour against theirs.'

Nick hid a sigh. Since he had come home, he had been beguiled by many things he had forgotten in this land he had left so long ago. He loved the slow rhythms of the days blended into weeks, the snug embrace of the family, and the secure certainties that the way of life in this village was the most blessed on all the earth. But sometimes, as now, he was appalled at how his countrymen could let what should be simple matters be twisted into feuds that could last generations. The issue was not honour and revenge but the cost of music for the party. Instead of staying up all night haggling over drachmas, Vangelis should have cancelled their date on the telephone and hired another band. But, because they didn't like it when he acted too American and criticized their primitive roundabout methods, gently he smiled at Marika's brother. 'I know you tried hard and did your best, *paidi mou*, but how will we dance without music?'

'We will dance all through the night!' Vangelis spread his arms and executed an exultant one-two-dip-step-kick. 'I hired three musicians from Nauplion for half what we expected to pay the others. And best of all, the bouzouki player is a distant cousin on my father's side.'

Nick and Yorgos grinned, clapped Marika's brother on the back, and then rubbed their hands together with that special gloating gesture of the Greek who has managed to squeeze out a canny business deal. What made the victory even sweeter was that the money would be kept within the extended family. Paying a relative was the next best thing to getting the music for free.

'Well done,' Nick enthused. Perhaps, he thought, Vangelis knew how best to handle a matter like this after all. He beamed at this in-law who had once again proved his worth to the family. Nikos would be in good hands with this one as his godfather. He was a good boy, Vangelis, and at times during this visit Nick had found himself considering the lad almost like a son. Both Christos and Yorgos had chosen to turn their backs on the family businesses to pursue careers in government and the army, but Vangelis was content to work in the taverna. 'We're off for a walk. Why don't you come along?'

Yorgos tensed up, but relaxed again when Vangelis said the priest expected him for some last-minute instructions about the christening which would be held out in the Panagia chapel on the island later that morning. As the *nonos* rushed off, once again Yorgos tugged at his father's arm. But just then Marika sauntered into the kitchen, the baby in her arms.

'*Chronya polla*,' the women immediately chorused to the nameday girl. 'Many happy returns!'

Nick bounded back to the garden, snapped a red rose from the trellis, and gallantly kissed his daughter-in-law's hand as he presented it to her. '*Chronya polla!*'

As Marika radiantly smiled her thanks, Nick scooped up the baby who would soon carry his name. Up until the moment the *pappas* christened the child, it was bad luck to call it anything but 'baby'.

Yorgos inwardly groaned as his father dandled the infant and made smooching noises with his lips. Now they might never make it to the beach.

Nick was gurgling much like the nine-month-old baby. But he had not forgotten his promise to his son. 'We will take him out with us for a little air, eh, Marika?'

'Of course, *patera*.' She avoided meeting her husband's smouldering eyes and instead sweetly smiled at the father-in-law she had taken great care never to cross. Once again she thanked her lucky stars that, although her relationship with Yorgos was not all it should be, she herself reigned as the young Kronos princess. A girl married not just a man but a family, and so to all outward appearances her marriage was a great success. Many brides were doomed to spend the first years of marriage losing a constant tug-of-war with their domineering in-laws. But she had found a second mother in kind Eleni, and Nick doted on her as the goddess who had given him the adored one. 'Fresh air, yes, what a good idea!' She had intended to settle the drowsy baby for a nap so he wouldn't cry so much during the traumatic ceremony at the church. But instead she immediately bundled the infant in a cotton blanket and handed him back to his grandfather.

'That's a good girl.' Nick fondly patted her cheek. If only he could find a woman like this for Christos! Marika was as beautiful as an Easter morning, and in the first year of marriage she had given her husband a son. What more could any man ask for?

Modestly Marika lowered her eyes, but she looked slyly up between her lashes in time to see Yorgos giving her that glowering look she knew too well. If he even caught her sharing a social *kali mera* with one of her distant male relatives in the street, that night she would have to endure a relentless cross-examination as to whether and how often she was sleeping with her cousin. Yet she could hardly believe that Yorgos was jealous of his own father. Again she glanced at her husband. But this time, as she saw him watching Nick with a look of passionate yearning on his resentful face, she understood he was jealous of the way his father always praised her. He was even more possessive of his father than his own wife.

'Marika?' Eleni's voice called from the far side of the kitchen. 'Your mother wants you to help her with the meat.' Marika gave the baby a final loving pat on his cheek and went off to do as she was told.

Yorgos, too, showed the same filial meekness as he trotted off toward the

149

beach behind his father. Yet inside he seethed with frustration. So much, he thought, for an intimate manly talk. Nick was so crazy about the baby that most likely all he would do now was fondle him and croon to him and praise his every smile and squall. How could it be that his father's love had skipped a generation?

But in the golden morning light, as they walked along the high tide sliver of sandy beach, it seemed that Yorgos would be luckier than he had expected. On this holiday none of the fishermen were mending their nets or beaching their boats, and none of the women were cleaning fish or bashing an octopus to tenderized death on the rocks. Only a few children splashed in the sea, and even the baby co-operated by falling fast alseep. Nothing could interfere with the talk Yorgos had dreamed of for so long.

The two men leaned against the hull of a big wooden *caique* dry-docked on the sand. 'So tell me about yourself, son. Always we talk about the family, and my business, but never about you. When I went away, you were just a boy. Now look at you in that uniform!'

Yorgos did not have to be asked twice. He rolled a cigarette but forgot to light it as he poured out his heart. How frustrated he used to feel in this village that had never given him proper respect and attention. How sweet it was to be in the army where a man might rise as high as his ambition soared. How he loved everything about the military life – the discipline, the order, the tradition, the sense of duty and honour, the power of command, even the uniforms. Especially, he confided, with his eyes all ashine, he loved to fight. Since most of the action had stopped the autumn before, it was tedious to remain posted down at the Githion garrison. Yet from time to time he still took potshots at diehard *andartes* holed up in the mountains. Just the month before he had led a patrol scouring the Taegetus, and he had bagged a ragged partisan who seemed not to have heard the war was over. 'It keeps me fighting fit,' he told his father, 'for the next time we go against the Turks.'

Belatedly, as Yorgos lit his hand-rolled cigarette, he noticed his father now was smoking American filter-tips. He supposed he would make the switch, too.

He went on to confide that, even though he was certain that his decision to make a career of the army was the right one for him, sometimes the life was too lonely. It would be better once he finally wangled an important Ministry posting in Athens. But he admitted that transfer to the General Staff would take years for a young officer like himself with no family connections outside his village, for every soldier sweltering in a provincial garrison dreamed and schemed of a desk job in the capital. He planned to even the odds against himself by getting an appointment to the Military Academy and then the School of War. Meanwhile, marooned an arduous day's drive away in the southern reaches of the Peloponnese, he raced home to Panagia whenever he could. He had considered, but then rejected, bringing his mother, wife, and son down to live in a little house near the fort. The wild Mani was no place for civilized women.

For the first time since Yorgos had begun his monologue, Nick tore his eyes off the baby. 'She is very beautiful, your Marika. I wish I could find a wife like that for Christos. A good Greek girl like yours.'

In anguish Yorgos stared at the one who had failed him once again. He had confided his heart's desires, and his father's response was to worry about his brother and compliment his wife. Yet doggedly, because he had waited so long for this precious *tête-à-tête*, Yorgos let that remark about Christos pass as he returned to his own agenda.

Already, he said, he was trying to pull strings for that coveted transfer to Athens. But in its way the army was as riddled with decay as the rest of the country. Too many other lieutenants – the arrogant Athenians, especially – had better family connections and more money to line the pockets of the greedy commanders. The army, which should be a cleansing force in the country, instead was rife with corruption. 'What Greece needs,' he said, his voice throbbing with conviction, 'is a strong leader. Or perhaps,' he significantly added, 'even a united and fair-minded *group* of true patriots to return this country to the halcyon times past.'

Yorgos glanced at his father to see if the old man had grasped the import of what he had just confided. He had joined a secret rightwing association known as IDEA, an acronym for the Sacred League of Greek Officers. But he hid his disappointment when all he could read on his father's face was bliss to be holding the baby.

But there was more to be said, and so Yorgos continued. Once a strong and forceful government was installed in Athens, then and only then could they set about fulfilling the aims of what was called the *Megali Idea ya Megali Ellada*, 'A Great Idea for a Great Greece'. They would right the wrongs that had stripped the modern *patrida* of too much of its rightful territory and restore it to its Byzantine glories. First and foremost, of course, they would turn their eyes east to that fabled city of cities whose loss Greece had never ceased to mourn. 'Constantinople!' Yorgos shouted, his voice raised in a battle cry that very nearly ended in a sob. When a Greek talks yearningly of the *polis* – the city – he means not Athens but that sacred site which the Turks call Istanbul. '*Aghia Sofia!*' Yorgos cried out, as though before him he saw the dome of the Church of the Holy Wisdom, the ecclesiastical centre of the Eastern Roman Empire which the Turks had profaned into a mosque. His voice fell to a whisper. 'We will again pluck the fruit from the *Kokini Milia*, the Red Apple Tree, from the shade of which

151

the Emperor of the Byzantines once ruled the Eastern Mediterranean.' Like one reciting a sacred vow, he rasped out his promise to the city Constantine had built. '*Pali me chronia me kerous, pali dikia mas thane.* Again in years and times to come, it's going to be ours.'

Yorgos leaned back against the boat, wiped the sweat from his forehead, and continued more matter-of-factly. Constantinople was only the glorious beginning. The army would also have to reclaim the Asia Minor provinces from the Turks and thus free the Greek nation from the shame of having lost that last ill-advised war against the mortal enemy. 'You, then, *patera*, could finally go home to your old village. We'd throw out the Turks, tear down their mosques like they gutted our churches, and once again raise the Greek flag over the lands which had been ours for an eternity.' He paused, hoping that his father would burst out with a chorus of *bravos*.

Instead, not wanting to hurt his son by asking why in the world he would want to leave Boston for a flybitten Anatolian village, Nick remained silent as he stroked the baby's cheek.

The light in Yorgos' eyes dimmed but did not altogether die. He got more response from virtual strangers than his own father. That bright village boy Kostas, for instance, who dogged his heels and lapped up his every word, had been downright adoring last night in the taverna when he had been expounding on the *Megali Idea*. The lad was nothing like his big brother Andreas, who had died so ingloriously in the Greek Cross raid on Christos' camp. Already, at thirteen, Kostas had begun begging Yorgos to help him prepare for an army career. It seemed in that family, too, there had been not only no love lost between the brothers but also a father who strongly favoured his elder leftwing son. In time, Yorgos thought, he might take that kindred soul Kostas under his wing.

But here and now, whether his own father cared or not, Yorgos continued with what he had determined to say.

There would, he supposed, have to be a war – maybe, considering the superior numbers and armaments of the enemy, even a series of wars – to force the Turks to surrender. Then the army would liberate Greeks from the yoke of the barbaric Albanians who had been given half of Epirus at the First World War armistice. After that, the Soviet satellites would have to be persuaded to return parts of Macedonia. The Bulgarians and the Yugoslavs would be forced to withdraw from Greek ethnic territories. And Cyprus, of course, would formally come back where it had always belonged, under the blue and white Greek flag. Then and only then would the real Greece be free and united.

But to accomplish this *Megali Idea*, Yorgos said with a meaningful cocking of his eyebrows, first the Greek army had to be purged of the forces that kept it from leading the *patrida* to its destiny. He was just launching into one of his favourite theories – that the Communists, despite losing the Civil War and being outlawed since its conclusion, had managed to infiltrate every stratum of Greek society and so must be rooted out and exterminated 'like the mad dogs they are' – when his father butted in as though he had not been listening to one word.

'Frankly, son, I've been worried about your brother.'

Yorgos reeled as though he had been struck by a fist. For the first time in his life, he gave his father a look of loathing. There was little respect and no affection in his voice when finally he snapped at his father. 'Is Christos very sick and about to die? Cancer, perhaps?'

Nick didn't even notice the sarcasm. 'No, he's in perfect health. Fit as a fiddle, as we say in the States. But he's not really happy. All he does is work in the restaurant and slave at his studies. Too bad he's not as devoted to business as he still is to politics. But night and day, nothing but work? That's not even natural for a native-born American. And there's something else, son. I think it kills him not to be able to come home.'

Yorgos spat out his next heartfelt words. 'We don't want him, and his kind, in our country.'

'Don't talk that way about your brother.' Nick fixed his son with a steely look. He had had enough of Yorgos' sniping against the brother who was sentenced to a life of exile. Yorgos should be a little generous now that Christos and his cohorts had lost so much. Again, here in his own son, was another example of that rabid intolerance which so repelled him in his countrymen. Maybe he couldn't do anything about the coffeehouse bigots, but he could try to force a reconciliation in his own family. 'I don't want to hear you say another bad word about your brother. He never talks about you like that.' Nick was not about to admit just now that Christos never so much as mentioned his brother's name, which he supposed was just as hateful as Yorgos' ragings. His voice took on a stern hectoring quality. 'I should have put an end to all that business between you when you were children, always at each other's throats. But as I remember it from my visits, you were always the one who started everything. It was your fault then, and I suppose whatever bad blood is between you now is your fault. Well, I won't have it. He's a good boy, my Christos.'

Yorgos had to struggle hard not to burst into tears. Inwardly he boiled at the injustice of his father's attack, and yet he left the bitter words unspoken. Even if his father would never love him, he couldn't make a final break with him.

Nick took his son's silence for capitulation, and so he opened that other matter that was much on his mind. 'And what's all this about pretending your brother is dead? Why I've humoured you so far, I don't know. But after the christening I'm letting the whole village know Christos is right beside me in America.'

'You can't do that.' Yorgos swallowed his rage and prepared to recite the arguments he had primed for just such a moment. If he didn't want to jeopardize his military career, the files on Captain Prometheus had to remain closed. 'With everything as it is now – the continuing trials of the captured *andartes*, the detention camps packed full on the islands, even those skirmishes every once in a while up in the mountains – it's simply not the right time to admit that one of their so-called heroes escaped scot free.'

'Why not? Christos is in Boston. Your men in green aren't patrolling the River Charles.'

'Not yet,' Yorgos mumbled under his breath. But he forced out a barking sound that he hoped sounded like a laugh. 'Trust me, *patera*. I know Greece and I know Panagia. But you can't possibly understand how deeply feeling still runs about the Civil War. It could be bad for the family – and for business – if you spill our little secret at the christening.' He delivered the *coup de grâce*. 'It could rebound on Christos, too. If Captain Prometheus is listed among the dead, it's possible – not certain, but possible – that one day after he gets his American passport he can slip back home for a visit. But if the security forces still have an active file on him . . .' Yorgos made a slitting gesture with his finger on his neck.

'I see, I see. I never dreamed it was like *that*.' Nick didn't notice his son obsessively fingering that curious scar on his cheek. 'I suppose you're right, at least for now. But it breaks my heart to pretend I've lost that boy.'

Yorgos' face was a mask. 'I believe you.'

Nick sighed. 'I worry so much about your brother. Imagine, to be a grown man and live without a woman in your bed! It isn't right to be so alone.'

Yorgos brightened at the thought of Christos in his single bed. Perhaps there was some justice in the world after all.

'But I suppose I should count my blessings. It's better that he stays alone than with that American girl.' Nick freed his left hand from the weight of the baby and fished in his trouser pocket until he came out with a photograph. 'She's a teacher at his university.'

Yorgos studied the image of Christos and a tall, slim girl with blonde hair and a smile like the toothpaste ads in foreign magazines. Marika, he told himself smugly, was twice the woman this one was. As far as he could see, the American had no breasts or hips.

'He says he won't marry her, but you don't know those American girls. It would be a disaster if he married her. *Katastrofe!*'

'Hmmmm.' A sly smile began to play around the corners of Yorgos' lips.

He would like to see Marika's face if she saw this picture. Always when he asked her about her feelings for his brother, fiercely she denied she even thought about him any more. But Yorgos knew that his wife, just like his father, adored the precious Christos. It would torment her to see this photograph of him with another woman. 'I don't have any pictures of my brother.' Yorgos pocketed the snapshot. 'I will take this one to remember him by.'

'Take it, yes, get it out of my sight.' Nick's voice was plaintive. 'And yet, when I try to talk to him about finding a good Greek girl to marry, he changes the subject! Why, I ask myself, *why*? Did something happen here in the village before he left?'

As Yorgos shrugged, in his mind's eye he again saw Christos and Marika naked in that cave. He blinked away the memory. Let his father ask his favourite son about that.

'Think back,' Nick prodded. 'Was there someone he loved and lost, right here in the village? A good girl he couldn't have? Someone maybe like your Marika?'

Yorgos stiffened. What gossip had his father picked up in the *kafeneions*? He could allow no breath of scandal to touch the mother of his son. 'No one in the village,' he said between clenched teeth. 'Maybe he had a girl in the *andartes*. One of those shameless whores who ran off to the mountains, supposedly to fight. The stories I could tell you about those girls!'

Nick decided to let the matter drop for now. Even though he still suspected Christos was hiding a secret love, he hadn't wanted to ply the coffeehouse gossips with indiscreet questions about his supposedly dead son's personal life. It had been a stab in the dark, however, to ask Yorgos. Of course the two of them had never been confidants.

But Nick's mood lightened as he looked out at the sea. He could never get enough of this bay and these islands and those mountains. When he returned to Boston, he would commission an artist to paint a mural of Panagia Bay from his photographs. Again his mind turned to the fortune to be made in the development of this village. 'Have you given any thought to what we talked about the other day? About the tourist boom?'

Sulkily Yorgos grunted. If his father wouldn't give him what he wanted, why should he be eager to indulge his every whim? 'A little.'

'And . . . ?'

Yorgos shrugged his eyebrows, as though such an inconsequential matter didn't even merit a shrug of the shoulders. 'It seems far-fetched. We've always thought this land was worthless. The sea keeps the fishermen alive, and the orange and olive groves keep the farmers from starving. But this

155

land by the sea is too sandy to grow anything. And up on the mountain it's too rocky.'

'But the beauty, son, think of the beauty!'

'You can't eat that.'

'You think not? Mark my words, the day will come when we'll be selling the sun and the sea more than our olives and oranges. One day this land, right here where we're standing, will be worth a million dollars. Maybe *millions*! And it can be *our* millions if we do what I say and snap it up, now, for a song.'

For the first time since his father had broached this daft idea of his, Yorgos considered its merits. He was so accustomed to the sight of the sea, shore, and mountains that it was difficult to imagine a foreigner being bewitched by it. And yet his father, who had lived so much of his life *exo* – outside – might truly have caught the scent of money to be made from those foreigners he knew better than his own kind. Yorgos wetted his lips hungrily. 'You have the money to buy this land?'

'Not here. Not just now.' Nick was reluctant to discuss his personal finances with this moody second son. He smiled as ingratiatingly as though Yorgos had been transformed into his bank manager. 'But I thought you might. Your army connections must be worth something.'

Yorgos nodded. It was true that many owed him favours. But did he want to cash in everything on this wild hunch of his father's?

'Please, son.' Nick reached out and touched Yorgos warmly on the arm. 'Now this time, you trust *me*.'

Bitterly, as the son met the father's eyes, Yorgos remembered locking combat with an identical set of green eyes on that mountain dawn. Why did he still feel so much – love and hate, they were so intertwined – for his father and his brother? And yet, always and perhaps evermore, he himself seemed destined to be the odd man out. But even though he understood that his father was finally being kind only because he wanted something, still it soothed Yorgos' soul finally to have that tender touch. He could not help nodding assent. 'I'll see what I can do.'

At once Nick withdrew his hand and briskly smiled. 'First the beachfront. And then the mountain. Buy it all. Everything!' Nick's smile widened as he gazed possessively at this landscape which one day, like the grandson in his arms, would belong to the family. 'Ours! All ours!' Just then the baby opened his eyes, and he crooned to it. 'Your future is assured, little fellow.'

Was it just his imagination, Yorgos wondered, or did the baby exchange a green-eyed wink with his grandfather? Like all infants, Nikos had been born with blue eyes. But over the summer they had been shading to a greenish cast that one day would be just like Nick's and Christos'. The three generations, all with their vibrant green eyes . . . But was it father, son, and grandson, or – as Marika still claimed – was Christos only an uncle?

Once again Yorgos felt an outcast in his own family. Could it be, just as his father had always favoured his brother, that one day his son would side with his grandfather and his uncle? No, it couldn't always be him against the green eyes. But again, that old uncertainty – was this his son or his brother's – shot through his blood like poison.

And yet, although he could hate his brother and resent his father, Yorgos was helpless to do anything but love this innocent baby. Perhaps with this one, finally his love would be returned in full. In the eyes of the world and in his own heart as well, the child was his. Whether the baby had been started by Christos or himself, it would never have been born if he hadn't been there to wrest it from Marika's body. Surely that counted for something. Too, there was always the secret satisfaction that he had stolen not only Marika but – perhaps – the baby from his brother.

When the infant let out an insistent yowl, gingerly Nick patted its damp bottom and handed him over to Yorgos. He pointed to the boats already massing in the harbour for the excursion to the island. 'I think it's time we made a Christian of the little one.'

Marika took a deep breath and, with a sense of life coming full circle, she stepped onto the island with Christos' baby in her arms.

'Careful.' Her brother reached out to steady her footing.

She leaned on the one who soon, in the old church on the crest of the island, would be godfather to her baby. Vangelis was always a comfort. But it was, she thought ruefully, a little late to tell her to be careful on this island.

Marika looked around the sunny beach at the others who had come out in the lead boat. Father Petros was shaking out the wet hem on his long black robe. Nick was huddled with Yorgos, pointing back to the prime spots on the village shore where he thought clusters of luxury hotels should be built. Old Anna and Eleni were fretting aloud about what still had to be done back in the kitchen. What would they all say, she wondered, if suddenly she announced who was the real father of her baby? Her mother was the only one who knew the truth for a certainty, but sometimes she wondered if others had guessed the secret. Was it only her imagination, or from time to time had those she was closest to given her a knowing smile or a telltale look as if to say that they, too, were in on the conspiracy of silence?

Once, shortly after the baby was born, when they were unpacking a box of clothes she had saved from Yorgos' infancy, Eleni had frowned when she came upon a little sheet exquisitely hand-embroidered with poppies and daisies and roses. 'This isn't mine,' she had muttered. And then, when she remembered whose it was, a look of such sadness had passed over her face that Marika had reached out her arm to comfort her. 'Never mind,' Eleni had said. 'It's only something of Sofia's. She must have made it for Christos.' And then, not meeting Marika's eyes, she had merely handed it over to her along with the heirlooms that had belonged to Yorgos.

Months later then, soon after the baby's eyes had begun to turn from blue to green, Vangelis had casually remarked that he resembled the photographs of his uncle and his grandfather more than his father. Almost then she had blurted out the whole truth. Instead, however, not wanting to burden him with her secret, she had merely bit her lip and looked away. Vangelis had tactfully changed the subject and never referred to it again.

Then last week, when she and Nick had been sitting in the balcony sun enjoying a coffee, she had begun to fear that even her father-in-law knew everything that had transpired here when he had been a world away. 'I want to talk to you about Christos,' he had begun, and she had thanked God that he had been looking out at the sea and so hadn't noticed the flush that had flooded her face. 'I believe there is,' he had continued, 'some sort of mystery in my son's life. A love affair perhaps.' It had taken a great effort of will for Marika to stop her right hand from crossing herself in a plea that the Almighty spare her from Nick's speaking the unspeakable. But then her father-in-law had gone on to complain that he had not been able to uncover even a hint about anything between Christos and a girl here in the village. He had asked Eleni and Yorgos. He had gone to Marika's mother and her brother. He had stopped short only of asking the men in the *kafeneions*, for he had not been away so long that he had forgotten that the most discreet of such inquiries could besmirch the family's honour. 'Christos was always more interested in politics than girls,' she had merely said before she excused herself to go feed the baby. And later she had assured herself, with some bitterness, that she hadn't really lied to her father-in-law.

And as for Yorgos . . . Marika's eyes clouded and she nestled the baby even closer to her breasts as surreptitiously she watched her husband gesturing toward the distant beach as though he were already dividing it into building plots. He was a model father. Yet she could tell by the way she caught him sometimes studying the baby that he still doubted if Nikos was his. And he delighted in tormenting her with taunts about his brother. Just before they had left the house, he had brandished that photograph of Christos and the skinny yellow-haired girl in her face. But now that Yorgos had married her and acknowledged the infant as his son, he would never dare lose face by making his suspicions public.

And yet even though she could count on her family to protect her, it was hard to live this lie. At times she wondered if every gossip in Panagia knew all the intimate details of her life. Of course they knew she had been married only seven months before the baby was born. She supposed the only reason no one so much as alluded to that – to her face, anyway – was that no one dared insult a Kronos. But because she knew they must be whispering behind her back, Marika had begun to feel she no longer altogether belonged here. Even Irene, pregnant by her husband Leonidas, and Calliopi, engaged to marry an ageing fisherman, didn't come to visit so often anymore. She still loved them like sisters, but sometimes now there were silences between even them. Marika was beginning to long to escape from this village where she had expected to live out her life. It could be, she thought, watching the waves rhythmically wash ashore, that once she had broken the taboos and stepped on this very island to seduce Christos, she had become an outsider in her own village. And so she had been disappointed when Yorgos had decided against moving the family down with him to the Mani. Every night she prayed for his transfer to Athens. Already she was preparing for the great escape. Next month she would begin attending night classes at the high school in Nauplion. In five years, six at most, she would have a paper that proved she was an educated lady and the equal of those haughty Athenians. How sweet it would be to walk down the streets of the capital where no one knew or cared about her past!

There were peals of laughter and whoops of joy as the other fishing *caiques* pressed into this shuttle service drew near. As though the villagers had been parted from one another for years instead of fifteen minutes, they waved and hollered to the party on the shore.

'Welcome!' Ever the voluble host, Nick was ruining the trouser legs of his new suit by wading into the water before the boats could make it to the beach. 'Here, yes, here, a little to the left, that's it!'

He splashed out of the water and stood on the shore with his arm wrapped a bit too familiarly around the priest. Father Petros leaned against the rich American's shoulder, and the two heads bent together, laughing. But they had not always been such pals. Father Petros, who still lived in the shadow of the dead but not forgotten feisty Father Theo, had withheld his ecclesiastical favours from this smug *Amerikanos*. Accordingly, when Nick had asked the *pappas* to break precedent and hold the christening on the island, the priest had stroked his bushy beard and refused. Except for today's Feast of the Virgin, when the entire village always took to the boats to honour the patron Saint of All Saints, no services were conducted on the island any more. Yet Nick had set his heart on the baby being baptised in the same church where he and Sofia had been married. Discreetly he had offered a roll of banknotes for vestments, candles, and whatever else Father Petros thought was needed to refurbish the shabby interior of the village church. When still the *pappas* had hesitated, Nick grandly had promised to build him a new church. But, he had hastily added, when the excited priest had all but kissed his hand in gratitude, he wasn't prepared to break the sacred ground just yet. Thinking ahead to the fortune he expected to make one day in the tourist business, however, he had vowed that a big new church – in honour of St Nikolas – would be ready by the time his grandson took a wife. Since then Father Petros had done everything but put an icon of Nick Kronos in the *plateia* church.

The men were leaping into the water, and the women were shrieking as they held high their shoes and waded the final metres in their bare feet. Two burly fishermen began carrying the huge copper cauldron that would serve as the baptismal font up the dirt path to the church. There was no water source on the uninhabitable island, and so another pair of workers were dragging up the jugs of water that would have to be heated before the ceremony could proceed. Children were running like hares to see which of them could first make it to the top, while Father Petros was busily collecting his censers and candles. In a moment the rest of the christening party would begin the ascent.

Yet still Marika lingered on the shore, apart from the rest, alone with her baby and her memories. Here Nikos had been conceived, here she had lost Christos, and here, too, she had decided to make do with Yorgos. The church, the cave, and the betrayal that came after haunted her still. Yet she thought it was fitting that Christos' son was to be churched on this island where his life had begun.

Father Petros led the way, and sure-footed Vangelis came next carrying the baby as the christening party began winding up the path to the chapel. Everyone was talking and laughing and singing snatches of songs as they puffed and wheezed up the steep grade in the searing high noon summer sun.

At the tail of the procession Marika walked with her arm supporting her mother. Old Anna's legs had worsened in the past months. Sometimes now she was content merely to sit with Eleni for hours on wooden chairs outside their house, watching, listening, and gossiping with whomever came their way. The two old crones who had spent most of their married lives without their husbands had become as close as spinster sisters.

Marika's mother stumbled and almost fell when they neared the entrance to the Cave of the Great Goddess.

'You want to rest, mama?'

Old Anna declined. And yet still she hesitated by the mouth of the cave. A smile hovered at her lips. 'Shall we?'

Marika wiped the sweat off her face. The others were nearly out of sight now. Once at the crest it would take a while to get the Mass underway, and the christening wouldn't come until the end of the service. She could not resist the impulse to sit a while with her mother in the cool darkness of that strangely magical women's space. 'Why not?'

They ducked inside, caught their breaths, and let them out in identical sighs as they sank down on a ledge.

Lost in her memories, Marika almost forgot her mother was beside her. Here, just here, Christos had taken her in what she had thought was an act of eternal love. And there, just there, Yorgos had intruded with his lifetime curse. She felt her mother's hand on hers. 'Do you remember, mama, when you first told me of this place?'

'I remember.' In the semi-darkness, Old Anna's wise eyes blinked like an owl's. 'I remember everything.'

Marika's stomach knotted, and there was such a lump in her throat that she had to swallow hard before she could continue. 'I was just thinking what you once said about . . . about what would happen if anyone was in the cave with Christos and me.' Marika blurted out the rest. 'Do you think I'm cursed now, mama?'

Old Anna seemed to smile. 'Do you?'

Again Marika relived the panic of awakening alone that terrible morning in this cave. She brushed away a tear. 'Sometimes.'

This time Old Anna was not going to take her in her arms and kiss the tears away. Marika needed something else from her – and this cave – this morning. It was time her daughter stopped pining for a man who had acted neither worse nor better than men – and women, too – were wont to do. 'Whoever told you, *paidi mou*, that life was supposed to be easy? Or fair? Or even happy?'

Marika recoiled as though her mother had struck her. But she stopped crying, and she listened as Old Anna continued.

'Did I ever tell you that? Did Eleni? Did Father Theo? I don't think even your Christos, for all his fine words, ever promised you what no one can have in this life. You say sometimes you think you're cursed? Welcome to the human race, *paidi mou*.'

'That's hard, mama.'

'So is life.' She let that sink in, and when she spoke again her voice was gentler. 'I know you miss him. I know Yorgos isn't the husband you wanted. But everything hasn't turned out so badly after all. You have the baby. None of us will ever want for a thing, now that we're part of the fancy Kronos family. And you still have your whole life in front of you.'

'I can hardly wait for whatever else is going to happen in this hard, unfair, unhappy life you seem to think I'll have.'

161

'Oh, it won't be all tears.' Old Anna looked around this cavern she had been visiting for most of her life. Once she would have mortgaged her soul to lure Nikolas Kronos to this very site, but she had never gotten so much as a sniff from him. Later, after she had worn the wedding crowns with Yannis, the thrill hadn't lasted much longer than the orange blossoms woven into the garlands that had encircled their heads. 'I've had you. And your brother. I can't say it's been an easy life, no. But it's *my* life. Mine! I have my regrets. But what I'm sorriest about is not that I lost my Yannis but that I wasted too many good years moaning about it.'

Marika bit her lip. Was it another trick of fate that she was learning this latest of life's implacable lessons here in this cave already crowded with memories? Again she sensed these hoary rocks and walls were listening, but today for her there were to be no gifts of passionate love or ecstatic dancing, only an old woman's stoic wisdom. 'Why are you saying all this now?'

Old Anna smiled. 'Maybe your baby isn't the only one who's being baptised today. We'll make a woman of you yet, here in this cave.'

The daughter smiled tentatively back at the mother, and then resolutely she stood and helped the other to her feet.

It was slow going up the final ascent, and when they reached it the Mass had already begun. As Old Anna jostled for a place inside, Nick was at the door urging the overflow crowd to be quiet, to take their time, that there was room for all.

But of course the whole village couldn't squeeze into the tiny church. The only ones inside were Kronos kin. The men lounged under whatever shade they could find: talking, smoking, gesturing, picking up the threads of their *kafeneion* conversations. The women, too, stood about gossiping and fanning themselves with the flat of their hands while their children ran madly about.

Even Marika, the mother of the Christian-to-be, had to follow the custom and wait outside until she was summoned to enter when the baptism was nearly over. She wandered from group to group, absently accepting congratulations not only for her baby's christening but for her nameday as well.

Restlessly she wandered over to the edge of the cliff and gazed at Panagia baking in the sweltering sun. From here, the village shimmered in a haze of white heat. The sea and sky were bleached identical feathery shades of blue, and the mountains, too, were almost the colour of the water and the air. The earth was so achingly beautiful, and yet life too often was not. 'Whoever told you,' her mother had asked, 'that life was supposed to be easy?' For a moment Marika wished she were not a woman bound by duty and fettered by circumstances but a pure white bird which could fly off into this blue infinity and be forever free of all that troubled her. It would be wonderful to soar up into the sky. Almost she could feel the wind whooshing around her.

But where would she fly, and what would she do once she got there? Faintly, from inside the church, she heard her baby crying. The mother in her forgot all about sea, sky, and freedom. Anxiously she ran toward the church but then remembered she couldn't go in just yet. But when she stalked back to the cliff, even though she stared hard at the sea and the sky, that intoxicating feeling of freedom eluded her.

Inside the church's heavy incensed darkness, the air smelled of candle wax, dust, and fresh perspiration. Vangelis held the baby in his lucky right arm while in his left he held high a tapering brown candle. Nick was packed in beside Yorgos while Eleni and Old Anna were testing the temperature of the water in the copper cauldron.

The flickering light glinted on the ornate silver-encased icons of the Virgin and the most beloved of the saints: Nikolas, Michael, George, several of the Johns. Around the peeling walls marched the fragmentary painted images of holy men and martyrs – here an arm or a leg, there a haloed head, in a corner a serene face. Just above, faintly traced on the miniature dome, the faded fresco of Christ the Redeemer gazed solemnly down on the congregation. The years and the elements had worn away His robe and most of His features, but still His dark eyes glowed and His hand was raised in a fierce gesture that was more warning than benediction.

Finally, with a flap of his black robes and a swing of his censer, Father Petros emerged from behind the intricately carved wooden altar screen. As a new musky cloud of incense pervaded the air, the crowd surged closer. The priest's high nasal chant rang out in the Byzantine Greek incantations that were distant linguistic ancestors of the everyday demotic Greek spoken in the village. Yet when the *pappas* asked the crucial question, all fell silent to wait for the godfather's ritual answer. Yes, Vangelis sang out in a ringing voice, in the name of this baby, he renounced Satan and all his evils. The baby cooed and gurgled as if he, too, were casting out the devil. The congregation let out a sigh of relief and smiled at the small one who might now be better able to escape the Evil Eye curses of this world.

Father Petros imperiously beckoned the *nonos* to join him in the sacred secrecy of the inner sanctum. Three small boys tagged behind and stood eavesdropping at the altar screen. The murmuring of the congregation died out, as expectantly they waited for the priest and godfather to reappear with the name of the baby on their lips.

'Nikolas!' Father Petros stood at the screen and shouted as if his paternal grandfather's name were a great revelation. Yet it would have been the talk of the village for months to come, and no one would ever have forgiven or forgotten it, had he been called anything else. 'Nikos! He is called Nikos!'

Yorgos hugged his father, and Nick's eyes brimmed with sentimental tears. Now he could die content that his name would endure surely for another generation and perhaps for an eternity. The circle was complete. One day this little baby would name his own son after his father and that boy would in turn name his son Nikolas Kronos as well. His family would live on. Through his tears, however, as rapturously Nick gazed down at this small guarantee of immortality, a quiver of foreboding shot through him. *My time is over, but his time is only beginning. Now I am old.*

As the villagers closed in even more tightly to offer their congratulations, already the small boys were rushing outside to shout the baby's name to his mother. 'Nikos!' she repeated. As for the first time she said her son's name aloud, never had a word felt so sweet. 'Nikos,' she whispered. 'Oh, my Nikolaki, my little Nikos.' As was the custom, then, she gave each of the little messengers a shining drachma coin. Still she stood outside the church waiting for the summons to come and take her little Christian Nikos. She wanted to murmur his name over and over as she stroked him and kissed him and promised him a thousand blessings in the life he was just beginning.

But inside the church the rites had only begun. Again Father Petros disappeared behind the screen, and when he reemerged he had rolled up his sleeves and donned an apron to protect his vestments. Vangelis, too, slipped on an apron. Then gently he unwrapped Nikos until the baby lay naked in his arms.

In the smoky semi-darkness, Vangelis set Nikos in the copper cauldron and splashed him until the candlelight shone on the infant's wet golden skin. Then the priest held his hand over the baby's mouth and plunged him up and down in the holy water a hallowed three times. Nikos howled and sputtered as the priest anointed the baby with consecrated olive oil. Finally Father Petros scissored four tufts from the baby's hair.

'Ah!' the guests cried as Vangelis held up the infant who gleamed with the sacred chrism. He was one of them now, christened, anointed, presented to God and to man.

Vangelis slipped the lacy white christening robe over his godson's head and fastened a gold cross around his neck. Vangelis rocked Nikos soothingly in his arms as once again the priest began his nasal chanting and the swinging of his censer. Round and round the font the priest and godfather walked as the baby wept and wailed. The sensuous air was dark and sweet, and its heavy scent lay in dizzying clouds. The church had been cool when first they entered, but now it was heatstroke hot. Old women mopped their brows, and girls leaned on their mothers and whispered that they felt faint. In the uncertain candlelight, first the face of a painted saint would be illuminated for an instant, then a weeping old woman in black, finally the fragment of a berobed figure drawn a century ago on the peeling wall. They blended together, these real and unreal faces of the living and the dead and the imagined. At a moment like this, it seemed possible that an icon might weep or smile or work a splendid miracle.

'The mother!' At last Father Petros called for the absent one to join the congregation.

Marika pulled back the curtain at the door and stood blinking in the sudden darkness. Her mother's face floated up before her, then her husband's, finally the *pappas* and her brother. She groped forward for her screaming baby.

Vangelis carefully settled Nikos in her arms as the priest brought a long silver spoon to the tiny lips. The communion wine dribbled down Nikos' chin to his neck.

The candlelight caught and held in the gleam of gold. Marika stared in wonder at the intricately wrought cross, surprised that Vangelis could have kept the purchase of such a costly and exquisite thing a secret even from her. But then her brother whispered in her ear. 'Christos sent it,' he said so low that not even the priest could hear.

At once Marika's face shone with a candescence that had nothing to do with the candles all around her. She had thought he had sent her no message, and yet he had. Whether or not he understood that Nikos was his, he had sent this token of love. She would treasure this cross of gold, and she would take care that Nikos wore it always. She bent her head and softly covered her baby's face with kisses. And then, while they all began to file outside, she kissed Christos' cross, too.

In the bright sunlight, the guests stood chattering on the crest of the island while they waited for the *pappas* to collect the icons for tonight's procession to the *plateia*. One of Marika's aunts was passing out the traditional *bomboniera*, sugared almond candies wrapped in a festive circlet of white net tied together with a baby-blue ribbon. Children played hide-and-seek behind their mother's skirts. The men stood around Nick, smoking and telling jokes and beaming at the very rich American. The women were agreeing that surely little Nikos' life would be blessed with happiness and prosperity.

All this while, a photographer from Nauplion had been trying to round up the family for a group portrait. But no sooner had he succeeded in prying Nick away from his knot of admirers than Old Anna had wandered away to rest in the shade. When he coaxed her back, Yorgos had huddled with that young Kostas who was thinking of making a career of the army.

165

But finally he had them all together. Vangelis stood solemnly at the centre, conscious of his starring role as the *nonos* holding his godson. Marika hovered anxiously by his side, and her hand was cupped around the baby's head with her fingers intertwined in the gold cross. Her other arm was wrapped around her mother, but it was unclear who was leaning on whom for support. On the other side, next to the godfather, Nick beamed proudly straight at the camera. Yorgos squeezed close beside him, gazing raptly at his father as his hand twitched on the scar on his cheek. Eleni came next, and she, too, was giving her husband that same look of adoration.

'*Khamoyelaste*!' the photographer called out. But of all the Kronos family, only ebullient Nick was smiling. The camera clicked, and the moment was frozen for posterity.

Lent

1966-1974

Seven

As usual, Marika lay awake as her husband slept.

She stared at the ceiling of their Athens bedroom and waited for morning. She had spent so many sleepless nights like this, frozen on her side of the marriage bed, that she could judge the time without even glancing at the iridescent hands of the clock on the table beside Yorgos. It had been hours since most of the men had returned home from the *kafeneions*, turned on their televisions for the late movie or their radios for a midnight serenade, and then finally blinked off the bedroom lights and roused their wives with kisses and demands. Then the sputtering of the motorbikes had begun as the big boys reluctantly cruised home in the wee hours of the morning. Always they would lounge awhile on the corners, smoking one final cigarette and exchanging one last round of jokes and insinuations, before finally they went home to their mothers. Some time thereafter the procession of the cheating married men would begin, as furtively the prowling husbands angled their cars into the last parking spaces left on the street. Softly they would click shut their car doors, creep into their houses on the guilty balls of their feet, and sidle into bed to dream of their mistresses. Later still the rollicking bouzouki couple who lived in the new apartment block on the corner would whoosh home, their car radio blaring and their retsina laughter echoing in the cement canyons. But outside now, just as the first dawn was breaking over the Aegean, Athens was as quiet as it ever would be. Yet a motorbike put-putted and died, a car turned a corner on two wheels, and a pair of cats violently courted and mated. Somewhere a woman laughed and a door slammed.

When Yorgos turned restlessly over in his sleep, Marika caught her breath and waited to see if he would wake and want her again. In their seventeen years of marriage she had given him two beautiful daughters in addition to her darling son, and yet this summer he was once more intent on getting her pregnant. Although he continued to treat Nikos as his own, his lust for a son had apparently not been altogether assuaged by her firstborn. During her fertile time of the month he would pump inside her in the mornings, in the afternoons, and of course in the nights. He took pride in his insatiable appetite for this, as for everything else from *souvlaki* to *psari*. She suspected that, in his singleminded drive to plant her with child again, these days he was even neglecting his latest mistress. Just last week, when she was having coffee and a gossip with another of the officers' wives, she had heard that he had been seen in a fish taverna down in Piraeus with a blonde foreign girl who looked young enough to be his daugther. Before that, from signs and clues and gossip, she had suspected a singer in one of the bouzouki clubs and a shopgirl in a boutique along Ermou. But she supposed instead of letting these liaisons upset her as they did, she should be grateful. Her big bull of a husband was more likely to leave her blissfully alone in the infatuated first weeks when he took up with another girl. Still, she wondered at how these other women could find a plump and balding middle-aged man like him so apparently irresistible. He might buy the cheap singers and clerks with gaudy gifts, but what about the succession of educated foreigners he dared to taunt her with sometimes in the heat of their fights? Yorgos most certainly wasn't handsome, but as she knew too well he did have animal magnetism. In his tailored uniform with his medals all asparkle, his girth added to his aura of power and dominance. Even though he was only a colonel, he threw his weight around like a general. Marika would have died rather than admit it, but something dark and unnamed inside herself still responded to the way he was when it was only he and she in this bed. Back in her childhood in Panagia she would never have guessed that despised little boy with the glasses would grow up to become such a scourge of the Athenian ladies.

Her body relaxed when Yorgos began to snore. She still had more precious time to herself before he awoke and the marital charade began again. Like other couples Marika knew here in the city and even down in the village, she and Yorgos tolerated their shell of a marriage. Times were changing, but divorce was still considered so scandalous and the family so sacred that husbands and wives made do with the partners fate and their parents had ordained. Yorgos did his part by providing a good living, and she did hers by taking care of the family and the house. They were seldom alone except in bed. Old Anna and the children were always there, or someone from Panagia was visiting, or they were out together at a reception or nameday celebration where they sat at opposite sides of the room. Caught in the cocoon of the ever-present family and the enveloping military society, the days and the years slid by — and not altogether unhappily. Marika supposed that, if she had found herself surrounded by devoted husbands and doting wives, she might have found it impossible to continue with her own less than idyllic marriage. But as she heard every day in hourlong telephone conversations with the other women in her social set, she was not the only discontented wife in Athens. The men took mistresses wherever they could find them, the women centred their passions on their sons, and the couples continued to stew and simmer in holy matrimony. Maybe it was only at the cinema that love triumphed over all and everyone lived happily ever after.

She scowled at her sleeping husband. Still, it was humiliating to have to lie tensely naked, night after night, beside a man she could never love. She might try to make something out of nothing all day long, but there was no escaping the truth of these sleepless nights. When her insomnia had begun after they finally made the move to Athens six years ago, she had tried to calm what the doctors said were her nerves with camomile tea and hot baths. She had never had trouble sleeping down in the village. But until they had moved to the capital, she had never had to contend with her husband every night and every day; only on weekends, holidays, and during his sporadic leaves from a succession of provincial postings. The doctor had suggested that perhaps the move had unsettled her. So many of his new patients suffered from the unaccustomed stress of city life, and these days the capital's services were severely strained by an urban migration that had resulted in a quarter of the nation's population crowding into Athens. In time, the doctor had said as he wrote out a prescription for sleeping pills, she would get used to it. But Marika had neither swallowed those pills nor gotten used to the compromises of her married life. In time, however, she had made her peace with sleeplessness. She could not banish Yorgos from her bed, but at least she could refuse to let down her guard when the enemy was so near. Better, she had long ago decided, to lie awake and keep watch like a sentry on the front lines of a neverending war. Sometimes, when against her will she did give in and fell asleep here beside him, she felt unbearably vulnerable when she woke in his embrace. Especially she hated all the times when her body betrayed her and her pelvis thrust in time with his rhythms. She was chained to Yorgos by bonds deeper than love or matrimony. At that thought, she remembered lying in Christos' embrace as Yorgos' ghostly candlelit face towered above them. As her mother had warned, she might always be locked together with the one brother she couldn't forget and the other she couldn't escape.

Marika shivered in the sweltering summer's night, but then she dismissed her forebodings of greater evils to come. She was no longer a superstitious village girl. She had just graduated from the university, and today she had an interview for a newspaper job. Yorgos had promised to use his military connections and what he said were his high-and-mighty American friends to persuade the editors to take a chance on her. But she doubted that a mere

171

colonel like Yorgos had much clout. Her husband had an exaggerated idea of his own importance.

Contemptuously her eyes drilled into her husband's spreading flesh. She took pleasure in the fact that time had not been kind to Yorgos. He had gained too much weight around his middle and lost too much hair on the top of his head. Naked in the bed, with the hairy mound of his belly rising and falling, he seemed a harmless figure of fun, the fat man caricatured in paintings on old wine barrels in the neighbourhood tavernas. It was only when he was dressed in his fancy colonel's uniform, strutting here, pointing there, seeing everything and satisfied with nothing, that her fear of him was as strong as her loathing. But asleep without his owlish glasses, his bald pate ashine with sweat and his sleek body splayed across the bed, he resembled a plump and spoiled baby. She indulged in one of her favourite pastimes, imagining her husband reduced to the most ridiculous circumstances. She pictured him helplessly lolling in a massive baby carriage which she wheeled into the main entrance of the Pentagon military headquarters on the outskirts of the city. Lowly coffeeboys would stop and chuck him on the chin. Sergeants would scold him for crying in the corridors. She would change his nappy on a general's desk.

Marika bit her lip and felt like weeping. Nearly two decades of unhappy marriage had reduced her to these adolescent revenge fantasies in which finally he was the powerless one utterly at her mercy. But she had been born for better than this. She had a mind, a heart, and a soul that once had been as pure as her daughters'. She curled up in a ball, cushioned her head on her arm and, as if she needed physical confirmation that she still had a heart, tried to listen to the life beating inside her. She was thirty-six years old, and she couldn't stand the gnawing feeling that she had missed the essence of life. Perhaps, she thought, she might have been able to make do with less if she hadn't gotten the taste for more on that Carnival night long ago. Once – just once – she had felt so complete, as though the two halves of a whole had finally been united. She had lost Christos, and both he and she had married others. But the teasing memory of what she had so briefly tasted still tantalized her. Before she was old and bitter like her mother, she had to try to fill the emptiness inside her. She deserved more than what she had with Yorgos, and somehow, someday, she had to get what she craved.

Her hand snaked out to the packet of cigarettes and the lighter on her bedside table. But she hesitated and looked anxiously at Yorgos. Perhaps a nicotine fit was better than her aroused husband on top of her again. Defiantly then she flicked the lighter and inhaled. She would risk this, and more, to retain her fragile hold on the essence of herself.

As she smoked, she suppressed her welling despair and instead counted her blessings.

First and foremost were her children. Nikos would be seventeen in November, and everytime she looked at him her heart melted and she thought of his father. They had the same limpid green eyes, the same charm and force of character, the same gifts for music and dance. Sometimes, in a certain light, when he was walking toward her on the beach with the sun behind him or as they sat in a taverna with a single candle illuminating that gold cross Christos had sent for his christening, almost she could believe that the love of her youth had come back to her. Was it a blessing or a curse, she wondered, that he was so like his father? She might have laid her feelings for Christos to rest years ago if it weren't for Nikos reminding her of how he had looked, and had talked, and had moved her. Her son was the light of her life, and in time she hoped he might even be her champion. She supposed she was partly to blame for the widening rift between her son and her husband. In the past few years the two had bickered over even the most minor matters. But despite her mother warning her last week not to play with fire, she didn't seem to be able to stop herself from setting them against one another. Someday, she and her son might finally vanquish the figure who so dominated their lives.

She gripped the cigarette so tightly between her clenched teeth that she bit through the filter. In disgust she threw the useless remains into an ashtray by the bed. Her fingers trembled as she lit another cigarette.

And yet, Marika reflected as slowly she exhaled, if she had another chance to lead her life all over again, she would probably make the same choices. She still regretted losing Christos, and even now, when she let herself remember waking alone that morning in the cave, her stomach clenched and she couldn't help bringing her head sharply up in the Greek gesture of denial. But the years had blunted the pain. She had grown accustomed to living with that loss, just as her mother often said with a sigh that she was used to the pain of her ruined legs. Perhaps, too, just as her mother had pronounced the morning of Nikos's christening, everything had not turned out so badly after all. She had entered into her sham of a marriage to provide a home and a place in society for her son, and at least in this matter Yorgos had kept his side of the bargain. His colonel's salary was far from lavish. But supplemented with Nick's continuing remittances and a share of the Panagia taverna profits, in this consumer boom of the past few years she could buy virtually everything she wanted: a television, rotating fans for every room, electric kitchen gadgets that were the talk of their Athens neighbourhood. She haunted the smart shops for the latest fashions for herself and dressed her girls up like pretty dolls.

At the thought of her daughters, Marika's lips curled in a contented smile. Her shy thirteen-year-old – christened after her paternal grandmother but always called Lena – would someday be a serene beauty. Lena loved her ballet lessons, excelled at school, and never caused her mother a moment's worry. Eleven-year-old Annoula – 'little Anna' – was such a lively bundle of curls and giggles that she even wrapped her formidable father around her little finger. Marika supposed her love for her daughters was not so complicated nor as possessive as her feelings for Nikos. And yet what they gave her life was richness and laughter.

From her daughters, Marika's thoughts turned to her mother. Once again she thanked God she had managed to move Old Anna up to Athens with them when Yorgos was transferred here. At the time her arthritic legs had required special therapy at an Athens clinic, and later Marika had said she needed her mother to run the house when she began her university studies. Old Anna still insisted on taking care of the cooking and most of the housework, but what mattered more to Marika was still having the best friend she had ever had soldered to her side. Old Anna had tried to convince Eleni to move up here too, for since Yorgos' mother had suffered a heart attack two years ago she had run the Panagia taverna from an easy chair in the lobby of their newly opened adjoining hotel. But Eleni had refused to make the move. She had been born in the village, she said, and she would die there. If it weren't for Vangelis running the restaurant and hotel, the family might have had to sell out instead of planning to build another hotel and nests of holiday bungalows from the money Nick still sent faithfully from Boston. Planeloads of tourists had begun to flock to Greece, and even though relatively few came to Panagia, Nick still believed there was a fortune to be made from the clean air and placid views of their village. He fired off letter after letter detailing how to exploit his family's place in the sun. As though he were chairman of the board of a multinational corporation instead of only part owner of a small taverna and hotel, already he was plotting just where the children would fit in to what he had taken to calling 'the Kronos tourist enterprises'. Nikos was supposed to inherit the reins of power and responsibility, and even after they were advantageously married the girls would be expected not only to produce a new generation of family workers but also to run one of the restaurants or even the travel agency that Nick was planning to open one day. There would, Marika knew, be a family fight *extraordinaire* when Nikos finally announced that, instead of a military career or hotel management, he intended to become an architect. She had faced the same pressures when, even before they had settled into their modern four-bedroom Athens apartment, she had declared her intention to enrol at the university. Yorgos had been surprisingly open to her taking a

174

degree, but he had wanted her to study something practical like accounting rather than something superfluous like Greek literature. It had taken her more than a year to get her way.

Marika came sharply back to reality when she noticed the first rays of sun filtering through the filmy curtains. It must be nearly six o'clock. She had only an hour or so to herself before the alarm clock clanged and *he* woke again. She supposed Yorgos would want her again before he marched into the bathroom, showered with a blast of cold water, then sprang into his uniform and rocketed off to work in their worn Fiat. When he had decided last spring that they should try for another child, he had assigned Kostas, his hard-pressed little protégé of a lieutenant from Panagia, to provide him with the latest scientific information about fertility in what he insultingly called 'ageing women'. For a month then, the first thing he had done every morning was insert a thermometer in her rectum so he could deduce when she was ovulating. Kostas had drawn up charts, made a graph, and when the data said she was fertile the colonel had flooded her with his semen. Marika calculated she would have to endure another two days of his assaults before he left her alone again. But as soon as he was out the door this morning, she would rush into the bathroom, flush herself out with cleansers and spermicides, and hope that she had drowned her chances of getting pregnant again. She adored her children. But now that she had finally gotten her degree and was seeking a job, she didn't want to be tied down with another baby. And there was, she admitted to herself, something darker to this as well. She had been able to deny her husband the only two things that he had ever wanted from her. She had never loved him, and she had never truly given him a son. All during her last two pregnancies, she had prayed to the Virgin for daughters. She supposed she should make a visit to the church later this morning to light a few perfunctory candles and make a few pleas that the Panagia keep her womb empty. But Athens was an oven just now. The church was on the far side of the *plateia*, which in this ferocious heatwave made it as out of reach as Constantinople. She would light a churchful of candles when she went down to Panagia with the children next month for the summer holidays.

Already the suffocating June heat was too hot for the sheet she had wound round her body in the relative cool of the night. She could feel the sweat pooling under her breasts, between her legs, and at the roots of her scalp. The sheet stuck to the curves of her damp body. Carefully, so as not to wake her husband, Marika inched away the top sheet until her flesh lay free. She sighed with relief when finally she cringed her body even further away from Yorgos, onto a relatively fresh stretch of the bedclothes. Like everyone else in this sweltering city, the heat seemed to excite him. In midsummer Athens, the only things anyone seemed to have the energy for were complaining, sleeping, and rutting on sweaty sheets.

Outside on the street she could hear the jingle of the garbage truck bells summoning one and all to bring out their sacks and litter. Then came the rumble of the refuse truck grinding up the steep roller-coaster grade toward their apartment block. Sleepily she steeled her nerves for the clatter and bangs and curses that inevitably would come next from the noisiest rubbishmen in the world. These men who performed their dirty work while the rest of the city slept seemed to take sadistic delight in creating the greatest possible uproar.

But then Marika sat up straight in bed and almost broke out in a cheer. The garbage strike must be over! The refuse workers had been on strike for more than a week, and the rubbish was piled up on the pavements and spilling into the streets. The stench wafted even up to their fourth floor apartment. There had been talk of the prime minister calling in the army to clean up the mess before an epidemic broke out. But until now – as usual – the weak and vacillating government had dickered, and done nothing. Marika was sick of the strikes that had all but paralyzed not only city life but also the national economy. She sympathized with the workers, but it was frustrating to have essential services turned on and off like a faucet. One day the electricity wouldn't work, the next the buses wouldn't be running. Often this year the children would come home in the middle of the morning with the news that the teachers were on strike, and without warning the trolleys or the taxis would disappear from the streets. The political opposition staged massive rallies and demonstrations which further exacerbated the sense of a country careening out of control. As one Athenian would say to another with a weary shrug, where would it all end? After more than a decade of postwar growth and reconstruction under a rightwing government, a left-of-centre regime had enacted a series of social welfare reforms that had sent inflation climbing. That government had fallen a year ago, and its replacement – hamstrung by the lack of a clear majority in parliament – did little but wring its hands and wait for an opportune time to call new elections. Meanwhile, Greece doddered from day to day like an old man with a terminal illness. As always at times like this, there were rumours, and even hopes, that the army would step in to restore order and the confidence of the nervous business community. Yorgos wasn't the only man in Athens to pound his fist on the dinner table and shout that what the *patrida* needed was a government strong enough to bring order from this chaos. Lately he had taken to bellowing out a popular marching song in his own *saloni*: 'Greece never dies. No threat can scare her. She only rests for a little time. And then marches on to glory again!'

The gears of the garbage truck whined from second to first, the engine let out a screech of machine agony, and Marika listened until the truck seemed to let out an orgasmic moan when finally it crested the hill. She had never thought she would be so glad to hear the garbagemen coming. And yet she couldn't help worrying about what the settlement of this strike would portend. Soon she herself might be working as a journalist, and in her mind she composed an analysis of what lay in Greece's future. If the refuse workers were back on the job, sometime in the night the government must have caved in to their demands. Next week, encouraged by the success of this strike, the trolleys and the buses would probably be out again. The banks would close, and so might the post offices when the civil service employees walked off their jobs. Perhaps the hospital workers, the doctors, or the farmers would call another strike. The teachers would once again take to the streets to demand the back pay they claimed the government was withholding from their spring wages. Yorgos said that if he and men like him were in charge, the workers wouldn't dare step out of line like this. With great relish he liked to quote the old saw – *Theloume vourdoula*, We Greeks need a whip to work. And then he would get out his history books and regale her and the children with citations about how, over and over again even in Classical antiquity, this birthplace of democracy had been forced to resort to dictatorships when the fractious Greek people made any other sort of government impossible.

It was funny, Marika mused as she listened to the cacophony of the rubbishmen working, how often these days her husband was given to grandiose pronouncements that sounded like speeches a politician might deliver in Syntagma Square. He was only a colonel who pushed papers around in a back corridor of military headquarters, but he talked as though he were only a goose-step away from unlimited power. Yet she supposed there was nothing significant about his wild talk. Every Greek man considered it his God-given right to deliver his opinions as though he were prime minister.

Out on the street bins clattered and rolled. Rubbish crunched. Lids thudded and crashed. The loudmouthed garbagemen laughed and joked and gossiped at the top of their lungs as they bashed the heavy metal cans against the back of the truck, then threw them more or less back onto the kerbs. The truck shifted into gear again, and the workers continued on to wake up the next block.

Anxiously she eyed Yorgos to see if the racket would wake him. When his eyes remained shut, she lay back on the pillows and savoured these last minutes of solitude. Once her husband left for work and the children went outside with their friends, she could curl up in bed for a few sweet hours of

177

untroubled sleep. But then she remembered she had her interview today. After that, she had to take the girls to the dentist for a checkup. If there was time, then she would race down Ermou Street to buy her mother some new black cotton cloth. And of course she would have to rush home for lunch. These days Yorgos was always here at the dining room table, fork in hand, at two o'clock. He would bolt down his meal and then give her a meaningful stare before he marched back into the bedroom. She would have to strip and lie there as he went through the motions of love in the spirit of a farmer ploughing a field and sowing seed. When she compared how it was with Yorgos to how it had once been with Christos, it was hard to believe that the essential act was the same.

Yorgos' eyes were open wide and burning into her as though he could read her mind.

Marika couldn't help blushing as he asked her what she was thinking about. 'My job interview,' she lied into his knowing eyes. 'It's this morning, remember? You promised to telephone that editor. You won't forget, will you?'

But his fingers were encircling her wrist as tightly as though his flesh were an iron handcuff. 'Later,' he said thickly. 'After.'

Her wide lips narrowed to a thin line as he rolled over on top of her. His mouth closed upon her. 'Open,' he ordered. When she let her lips go slack, his tongue snaked inside her. She felt him probe her gums, her teeth, her tongue, and she nearly gagged when she felt him invade her throat. He was always so thorough in his assaults. He liked to taste her everywhere. He ran his possessive fingers through her every crack and crevice, as though he were a night watchman checking doors and windows to make sure not only that they were locked but that he had the keys to open them. Like some sort of machine roughly polishing her body, he was rubbing himself against her. His torso ground against her breasts. His hips pushed into her pelvis. His legs imprisoned hers. Still his tongue possessed her mouth. He groaned as he pushed inside her.

She shut her eyes and lay as still as though she were dead. This time she would not let herself respond to him. Please let it be quick, she prayed. She calculated how long he had before he had to be at work. Not so long, she thought. When he pumped harder, she nearly sighed with relief. He was going to let her off easy this morning. In a moment or two it would be over. His fingers dug into her shoulders as he cried out and convulsed.

Marika opened her eyes and met her husband's gaze. He let go of her shoulders, and although he was still inside her, it was as though they were not even touching.

Without a word, he rolled off her and out of the bed. He threw a robe over his shoulders, slid into his rubber sandals, and marched off toward the bathroom.

Marika lay staring at the ceiling and felt dirty as her husband washed.

Miserably Marika waited for the managing editor to remember who she was and why she was here. Sokrates Tritsis was one of those middle-aged little Napoleon Greeks – stocky, balding, and self-important. He reminded her a bit of Yorgos.

But she had been sitting on this hard wooden chair across from his mess of a desk for forty-five minutes as he bellowed into the telephone, joked with his cronies, and drank watery coffee frappés while he held his Marlboros between his nicotine-stained fingers. Was she invisible or simply not worthy of his notice?

As she glanced down at the résumé and writing samples in her lap, she could see that her sweaty fingers had smeared the ink. But she supposed it didn't matter, since Sokrates wasn't even going to look at her work. Obviously it had been a mistake to come here looking for a job. She had only been fooling herself with those university daydreams of bylines and glory. Her professors had said she could write, but this newspaper office was no academic ivory tower. The dusty newsroom was a noisy jumble of desks, typewriters, and rat-tatting wire machines. Pot-bellied men yawned over smudged sheafs of papers, or gossiped as though this were a coffeehouse, or sleepily listened to the telephones ringing like alarm clocks. The only women in this room were two stout ladies with beehive hairdos who were poring over photographs of rich people in ball gowns and tuxedos. To spare herself any further humiliation, she should creep away and be content to take her girls to the dentist and run errands for her mother. Clearly, she could never belong here.

Instead, one last time, she plucked up courage and addressed this rude man who had the power to make her dreams come true. 'Sir?' Repeatedly, since the receptionist had deposited her in this chair, she had failed to get his attention.

But this time, as Sokrates hung up his telephone and picked up his pencil stub, his eyes happened to fall upon her. 'You're still here?' He had thought she would have left by now and spared him the trouble of dismissing her.

'For my interview.' Marika gave him her best smile and smoothed down the skirt of her tailored navy blue sheath. 'Nine-thirty. The reporter's job?'

Sokrates forgot his looming deadlines as he looked across his desk. Luscious breasts. Great legs. Sweet ass. He licked his lips. But this was a newspaper, not a cabaret. 'We're not hiring.'

'That's not what the man at the front desk said. When I made this appointment, he said you were hiring new reporters.' Marika handed him the papers she had painstakingly prepared. 'I've just graduated from university. My professors all said I have what it takes to be a journalist.'

He threw her papers atop a yellowing pile. 'See this stack of résumés? Everyone thinks they can write for us. Sorry, *kukla mou*, but take my advice and stick to making *moussaka*.' Again his eyes rested on the jut of her breasts. 'But maybe we can have a coffee sometime. Or go to a bouzouki club.' Insinuatingly he smiled. 'I might even listen to your telling me what a great writer you are. Who knows, maybe by the autumn we'll need a new reporter. But first we have to get to know one another a little better. How's Tuesday night?'

Marika snatched back her precious stories and was about to storm away when again the editor's phone rang. He seemed to sit up at attention and, after listening for a moment, he waved her back into her chair. When he hung up, he narrowed his eyes at this woman who not only had breasts and buttocks but connections. 'That was about you, *kyria*.'

'Yes?' She caught the significance of his addressing her as 'lady' instead of 'doll'.

This time his smile was deferential. 'Why didn't you tell me who your husband is?'

'Yorgo? That was him on the phone?'

'Not quite. That, dear lady, was my editor-in-chief. Your esteemed husband has friends in very high places. At the American embassy. And in our brave army. It seems that we are hiring reporters after all.'

Marika beamed as she handed back her writing samples. 'I have one piece about what happened to the *andartes* after the Civil War. Another about the failure of the government's economic policies. And a column against the monarchy.'

But he didn't even take them. 'That won't be necessary. If the editor-in-chief says you can write, that's good enough for me.' He nodded a dismissal. 'Come back Monday morning.'

'That's all? That's it?' Again she retrieved the stories she had laboured over so long. The editor was fulfilling her heart's desire, but she felt no sense of triumph. She had wanted to be hired because she had the qualifications, not because her husband knew important people.

'Come in whenever you like. We'll fit you in somewhere.' He tapped his pencil on his desk. 'But now, Kyria Kronos, I'm afraid I have to get back to work.'

Marika, however, was intent on this editor taking her seriously. 'What will I be doing?'

Sokrates shrugged. 'This and that.' He would give her a desk in a far corner and let her file her nails and telephone her girlfriends as many hours a day as she wanted to waste here. Already, Greek fashion, his staff was swollen by cousins of government Ministers, a nephew of the advertising director, and whomever else the publisher owed favours. So long as she didn't get in the way, one more bogus reporter wouldn't matter much. Yet he regretted that, considering the clout her husband evidently packed, he himself would have to keep his hands off her. When his phone rang, again he nodded in finality. 'That's Monday morning. Ten, eleven, whenever you want.'

Marika remained rooted in her chair. She didn't want to owe this job solely to Yorgos. When Sokrates hung up and raised his eyebrows at her, yet again she handed him her writing samples. 'I'm not leaving, or coming back Monday morning, unless you at least look at these. I'm a professional. Or at least I will be if you really offer me a job.'

Sokrates glared, consulted his watch, and then grudgingly took her sweat-stained stories. Anything to keep the editor-in-chief happy. He glanced at a page, looked up at her in surprise, and read on more carefully as he lit a cigarette. When he finished all three articles, he offered her one of his Marlboros. 'Where'd you learn to write like this, Marika?'

'At the university. I told you, I've just finished my studies.'

'Lots of people get degrees, but not many can write much more than their names.' Sokrates leaned back in his chair. 'I should know. I've got a newsroom full of illiterates.' He grinned. 'But you won't be one of them.'

'So you liked my stories?'

'They're a little rough. Need a lot of trimming. But yes, *kyria*, I liked your stories.'

'So I'm hired? *Really* hired? You're not just taking me on because my husband made his friends pester your boss?'

Sokrates nodded. 'You're really hired. Be here at nine sharp Monday morning, and I'll put you to work. But don't expect to be covering parliament or writing editorials, at least at first. I don't need another *prima donna* in my newsroom. You'll have to start at the bottom, like everyone else.'

'Great.' Marika supposed she shouldn't push her luck, but she had one more reservation. She wrinkled her nose in the general direction of the beehive ladies. 'I don't want to work on the women's pages. I want to report real news.'

Again Sokrates revised his opinion of this voluptuous lady who could write. 'Bossy,' he muttered. 'Just like my mother. My wife, too.' But then, again, he grinned. A good reporter was aggressive and persistent. 'It's a deal.'

When Marika collected her stories and rose, her legs were trembling. But she was – almost – a journalist now. Crisply she said goodbye. 'Right, then. Nine o'clock Monday. And . . . thanks.'

As she was leaving, however, she broke out in peals of laughter when Sokrates winked and threw her a mock salute.

Two weeks later she coursed down Ermou Street on a shopping spree to spend the first money she had ever earned. Her white high heels clicked on the uneven pavement as, oblivious to the immobilizing late June heat, she bypassed the pharmacies and eyeglass emporia on the way to the children's shops, fabric stores, and fashion houses. She was going to blow her paycheck on presents for everyone.

Ten paces behind, Irene, her childhood friend from the village, panted as she failed to keep up with Marika's big-city pace. The sidewalk was chockablock with Saturday shoppers who pushed and shoved in their haste to grasp the choicest goods Athens had to offer.

'*Ela*, Irene,' Marika called as she ducked into a children's wear boutique.

When Irene finally caught up, Marika already was imperiously ordering a sullen clerk at the infant wear counter to show her christening robes.

'You're pregnant?' Irene eyed her friends's flat stomach. Since she had arrived on the bus from Panagia the evening before, the two of them hadn't had time for a heart-to-heart.

'I hope *not*.' Marika crossed herself. Now that she had her job, it would be a disaster if Yorgos' sperm connected with one of her eggs. She held up an exquisite white gown sweetly embroidered with pearl-studded flowers. 'I'll take that.' A moment later she presented the gift-wrapped package to Irene. 'For your baby.' Fatoula, Irene's fourth daughter, was to be baptised in August. But ever since the birth, her friend had seemed depressed at her latest failure to present Leonidas with a son.

'No, no, I can't let you buy such a costly gift.' Irene gave the package back to the bored clerk, who merely yawned and waited for her customers to enact the ritual courtesies.

Marika gently pressed the gift back on Irene. 'Please.'

'No, you are too generous.' She handed it back to the clerk, but this time weakly.

'I insist.'

The charade of reluctance enacted, Irene eagerly accepted the package containing the robe which her husband's postman's salary could never stretch to cover. Not, she added to herself, that he would squander their meagre drachmas on something so extravagant for this daughter he didn't want. Four girls and no boys!

'You don't like the robe?' Marika saw the glimmer of tears and put her arm around her shoulders. She had heard Irene crying in the guest room late last night. 'Or is it something else?'

'Later. We'll have coffee and talk.' Irene brushed away her tears and made for the door. 'First let's do your shopping.'

Thus charged, Marika whirled through the crowded shops. For her mother she bought a crocheted black shawl. For Lena, the pink satin toe shoes she had been longing for ever since her ballet teacher said she was ready to go *en pointe*. For Annoula, a fabulous bagful of costly ribbons and bows and glittery bits of fluff to adorn her curls. For both girls, matching red and blue striped bathing suits from California. And for Nikos — the best gift of all for the one she most loved — the guitar he had been swooning over for months. She had intended to buy something wonderful for Vangelis and Eleni — and she had had her eye on a beautifully cut white summer suit for herself, just the thing a reporter should wear on interviews — but she had only a few thousand drachmas left. She stopped at the pedlar pushcarts and made do with a cotton shirt for her brother and a tiny brooch — it was only made of tin but looked like silver — for her mother-in-law. But she had forgotten that other one. She looked in her purse. She would be flat broke after she treated Irene to coffee and cakes. Too bad, Yorgos!

'Whew!' Marika leaned against the cart and wiped the sweat from her forehead as her shopping delirium faded. 'I think we need a coffee.'

Their arms full of packages, she and Irene strolled into the splendour of an elegant turn-of-the-century coffeehouse near Syntagma Square. The village woman's eyes boggled at the sumptuous whipped cream cakes and fancy chocolates displayed like jewels in gleaming mahogany and glass cases. Marika was watching her weight, but she insisted that Irene indulge. Greedily the plump peasant woman chose a triangle of honey-drenched *baklava*, a chocolate meringue confection, and finally after much deliberation a cream cake stuffed with walnuts and calories.

As a snooty waiter brought them Greek coffees and the cakes, Irene looked round at the sophisticated city crowd. Marika, all dressed up in a sleek white dress slashed with a thin red leather belt that emphasized her enviable figure, seemed part of this glamourous élite. Her friend had always been more confident than the village girls, but never so worldly. That job must have wrought the transformation. 'So you really like going out every morning working on your newspaper?'

'I love it.' Marika lit a cigarette and sipped the icy water that had come with the coffees. 'So far Sokrates — my editor, such a dear man! — won't let me write anything. He says I have a lot to learn first. But he says that before

183

long I'll be earning my own bylines. You can't imagine what it's like, how exciting it is!'

'No,' Irene agreed, 'I can't imagine.' She bent over the *baklava* and finished it without raising her head. But then she took a paper napkin and wiped the corners of her eyes.

'What's wrong, *glika*?' Marika stubbed out her cigarette.

'Leonidas.' Irene stabbed the chocolate meringue with her fork. 'He's what's wrong.' Again and again her fork attacked the cake. 'Night and day! Always his criticisms! I'm not respectful enough to his mother. I give his sisters dirty looks. The house isn't spotless. I can't cook like his mother. I'm fat.' Spitefully she took a big bite of the massacred meringue. 'And most of all, he goes on about the girls. It's my fault, he says, that we haven't had a son. When Fatoula was born, he even threatened to divorce me. I wish he would. It's never been really good with Leonidas.'

'Never?' Marika was remembering how Irene once enthused about her husband-to-be. Until now she had believed her friend had a model marriage. How had she and Irene drifted so far apart?

'No, at first I was so happy! I loved him so, at first.' For a fleeting second, recalling those bygone years, Irene's face was alight. 'But it all changed when we got married and I had the first girl. After that, he was never home except to sleep. If he wasn't with the boys in the *kafeneions*, he'd be sitting in his mother's kitchen. She'll live forever, that one.' Thoughtfully Irene took another bite of her cake. 'My own mother says this is what I get for marrying for love. She says I would have been better off if I'd done . . . what you did.'

At that, Marika was so agitated that she forgot her diet and reached for a forkful of the whipped cream cake. 'I don't have a bed of roses, either.'

'No?' Irene finished the chocolate meringue, pushed up the baggy sleeves of her cheap flowered dress, and dipped into the cream cake.

Just as Marika was about to confide how it was between herself and Yorgos, her eye was caught by an ugly black bruise that began at Irene's wrist and disappeared up her sleeve. 'So Leonidas beats you, too.'

Embarrassed, Irene rearranged her sleeve so the bruise wouldn't show. 'You know how it is in the villages.'

Soberly Marika sipped her coffee. In Athens, too, wife-beating was commonplace. Just once, in the early years of their marriage, Yorgos had raised his arm to strike her. But she had hissed that if he hit her she would come at him with a knife when he was sleeping – and he had never threatened her again. 'What are you going to do about it?'

Irene sighed in resignation. 'What can I do? He's my husband.' She looked down at her wedding ring. 'Maybe the next baby will be a boy.'

Then, as she polished off the remains of her cakes, Irene pasted a smile on her face. She had to catch her bus back to the Peloponnese, and she wanted to end their *tête-à-tête* on a happier note. 'You know, don't you, that Calliopi's pregnant again? After those five boys of hers, her husband's actually saying he wants a little girl this time.' Her smile dimmed. 'Funny, how things turn out. I used to feel sorry for you and Calliopi. But now her husband treats her like the queen mother. And you have everything – Nikos, your girls, a husband with an important job, and now maybe even your name in the newspaper every day.'

On Marika's tongue the coffee was more bitter than sweet. 'Not everything.'

Now that she had let her hair down, Irene felt entitled to ask what she had wondered about for years. 'You've never forgotten Christos, have you?'

Marika met her old friend's eyes. 'Never.'

'Maybe you're lucky. Maybe you wouldn't have been any happier with him than I am with Leonidas.'

'Maybe.' Marika signalled for the check and was relieved when the waiter came promptly. She didn't want to share her regrets about *him* with anyone.

But as Irene was about to climb onto the trolley that would take her the first leg of her long journey home, Marika held her tight and whispered a final testament. 'He was the love of my life, Irene. The love of my life!'

Marika rang the bell outside the lobby of Dina's fashionable Kolonaki apartment, aware that she was an hour and a half late. By now, seven-thirty on this sultry summer afternoon, the other officers' wives must have squandered their best gossip, gobbled the choicest cakes, and might even be beginning their farewells. But Sokrates had made her stay in the newsroom until the final edition was closed and he had time to critique her first story.

Dina buzzed her in, and in the lift up to the penthouse – her hostess's husband was a brigadier-general and the scion of an important old Athenian family – she peered into the expensive art deco mirror to fluff up her hair and smooth the wrinkles in her beige linen skirt and blouse. All the other wives would be dressed to kill. But she had come direct from the office, and she looked it. Sokrates had been savage. No byline, but at least he would print an abbreviated version of her piece.

'Darling!' Smashing in a silk jungle-print kaftan, Dina greeted her with cool-as-marble cheek kisses. 'We thought you'd forgotten all about us. The girls were just saying – ' here Dina tossed her mane of platinum blonde hair toward the sitting room, 'that our little Marika must be up to something naughty. We haven't seen you for ages!'

'I've been working,' Marika explained as they joined the others in the

Italianate white-on-white *saloni* which Kolonaki's most sought-after decorator had done up the previous winter. 'I wrote my first piece for the paper this morning, and my editor kept me late to go over it.' But Dina was looking at her blankly. 'My job. At the newspaper? But I told you all about it last week on the phone.'

'Of course, dear.' Dina ordered the young English nanny who doubled as her personal slave to bring the late arrival a coffee. As Marika did her best to settle in a torturous chrome and plastic chair, Dina's eyebrows arched. 'Girls, she wants us to believe her boss kept her late at the office. And now, sweetie, this *editor*. You must tell us all about him. Is he delicious?'

Marika flushed as Mimi, Tula, and Rena simpered on cue. But from habit she tried to do as she had been told. When she had first come to Athens, she had been so flattered that these chic Athenians would bother with a village girl like herself. And Dina, like her husband, was the leader of the pack. 'Delicious? *Sokrates*? Not really. But he's a good editor.'

'Editing.' Dina laughed. 'Is that what they're calling it these days?'

Tula, vivid as ever in a tomato-red sundress with her hennaed hair piled on her head, deftly swallowed the remains of a chocolate eclair and got right down to it. 'So what's new? Taken the plunge yet?'

Marika masked her embarrassment by fussing over the coffee the English girl was handing her. Ever since she had confided her fears that Yorgos was having affairs, 'the girls' had made initiating her into the promiscuous ways of their set one of their pet projects, rather like charity work.

Since, they always said, their philandering spouses were spoiled, selfish, and capable of loving only their mothers, a wife was entitled to look for consolation with whatever masculine morsels came her way: lean students, burly sailors, trendy sellers of furs or jewellery. With the air of officers instructing a new recruit, they had advised her exactly how to take a discreet lover. Mornings, just after their husbands went to work and children to school, were the safest time. Pretend, they had lectured, that you're out shopping or executing any of the interminable errands that eat up so much of everyday Athenian life. It was possible, they had warned, to sneak off for an afternoon assignation only if a woman was blessed with a husband who never came home for lunch and a siesta. As for the question of where, a certain sort of man kept a hideaway one-room *garsoniera* tucked away in one of the farflung neighbourhoods. If a wife carefully selected her partners and took care never to give away her heart, the chances were that her husband would never be the wiser. 'But if Yorgos did find out?' Marika had once naively asked. 'The girls' had quickly changed the subject, not wanting to be reminded of those 'crimes of passion' shootings that even the best families had to hush up from the newspapers. After that, although Marika was tempted to do as they said just to get back at Yorgos, she had only smiled enigmatically when Dina and the others had plied her with questions about her erotic life.

So she gave them a cat smile as she reached for an almond pastry. She had been right. 'The girls' had already wolfed down the best ones.

'You never tell us *anything*,' Rena complained, her heavy brass ethnic jewellery ajingle. 'Last week on the phone I told you *everything* about Sotis – *Four times*! *In two hours*! But he's young, you know, only *nineteen*! – and now all you tell us is that you've been working late at the office. You sound exactly like my husband.'

Mimi fitted another cigarette into the carved ivory wand her latest lover had given her on her nameday. 'I think she's holding out on us. What were you doing, *really*, with this Sokrates?'

Marika was saved by the buzzing of the bell. 'At last!' Dina sprang toward the door. 'That will be Kyria Angella.'

'She reads the coffee cups,' Rena explained.

'And she's good,' Tula added. 'I had her at my house last week. Everyone thought she was wonderful.'

'She's a Greek from the Sudan. Her husband ran a store in the bush.' Mimi rolled her eyes. 'Brace yourselves, girls, we're about to have a little African black magic.'

After that buildup, the matronly widow who followed Dina into the *saloni* was an anticlimax. Kyria Angella looked like every other plump bird of a woman who fought over the best and cheapest tomatoes at the *laiki* street markets. Nonetheless, the girls finished their coffees, swirled around the dregs, and turned the cups over on the saucers. Expectantly, as Dina chattered greetings, they waited for the show to begin.

First, Tula. Kyria Angella frowned into her cup. 'A bird. You've found a bird in your apartment.'

'No, all I have is Mikalis and the poodle. The children and my mother are already on the island for the summer.'

'You *will* find one. Either in your apartment or right outside. A dead bird.' Kyria Angella looked sombre. 'Don't touch it!'

'A dead bird? In my apartment?' Tula shuddered. 'Of course I won't touch it! But what's it *mean*?'

'Darkness.' And despite Tula's blandishments, the *kyria* would say no more.

With some trepidation, Mimi offered her cup. Kyria Angella's frown deepened as she studied the pattern left by the grounds. 'Earthquake. A big one. A bad one. Stay out of Kalamata.'

'There's going to be an earthquake in Kalamata?' Nervously Mimi sucked

187

on her cigarette holder. 'But that's absurd. There's never been an earthquake in my town.'

'There will be.'

'*When?*' Already Mimi was revising her plans for the rest of the summer. She, Haris, and the children would go up to his village in the north.

'The number twenty. In twenty hours, twenty days, twenty months.' The *kyria* paused. 'Or in twenty years. But stay out of Kalamata.'

'Twenty years,' Mimi muttered. 'I can't stay away from home for twenty years!'

Rena, however, was promised a rosier future. Travel in an airplane. The birth of a son. Money. 'But,' the *kyria* warned, 'you have an enemy.'

'*Me?*' The image of her mother-in-law flooded Rena's mind.

'You know who she is. She'll come to your house and offer you something. *Don't take it*! This woman has put the Evil Eye on you. You must get someone to remove the curse.'

Tula cut in. 'I know just who. This one's a man, not a woman. My plumber! Last spring someone put the Eye on my little Sofia. And after Marinas fixed the toilet, he said a few words over her head and she was fine again.'

'Give me his number,' Rena said. 'He can repair my kitchen sink while he's at it.'

Kyria Angella, who was nobody's fool, smiled after she looked long and hard into Dina's cup. 'I see a man. Dark eyes and hair. Young.'

'Yum,' Dina said.

'Maybe she means one of your sons.' Tula, who tended to be catty anyway, was annoyed because the witch hadn't promised *her* a new lover, only a dead bird on her doorstep.

'This young man,' the fortune-teller was continuing as though she hadn't been interrupted, 'will take you on a big white boat. I see flowers. Bottles, green bottles – champagne!'

'I love champagne,' Dina agreed. She leaned forward. 'And then what?'

'Palm trees,' the *kyria* dreamily elaborated. 'Dancing girls. Heat. Hashish.' For a moment, remembering the Sudan of her youth, the fortune-teller almost forgot where she was. But then she came back to reality and told this middle-aged rich lady what she wanted to hear. 'Finally, this one will make you happy.'

'Everyone *said* she was good,' Dina pronounced. She would recommend Kyria Angella to all her friends. 'Now it's your turn, Marika.'

For the first time in this reading, the *kyria* laughed. 'Yours is blond. Blue eyes. Very handsome. And big!'

'You mean tall,' Rena corrected.

188

'No, *big*!' Again the *kyria* laughed. The girls all giggled.

'Who?' Marika was wide-eyed.

'Your lover.'

'I told you she was holding out on us.' Mimi pounced. 'It's that Sokrates, isn't it?'

'My editor doesn't look anything like that.' Marika prodded the *kyria*. 'This . . . man. Where will I meet him?'

'You know him already. But you're about to know him even better.'

'And you'll tell us every detail,' Tula said, 'won't you, Marika?'

But the *kyria* interrupted their fresh laughter. 'He's not the one you love. I see another. He's not clear . . . it's cloudy . . . like a ghost. Someone in your past. I see a cave.' She looked up, and her dark eyes pierced Marika's. 'He will return!'

'Return?' Marika stuttered on the word. '*Now*?'

'Not now. But you're going to hear from him. Hear his voice. Soon, very soon.'

'The girls' were all studying Marika's ashen face.

'Hear from him . . .' Marika's voice trailed off.

'So who's the mystery man?' Mimi's tone was badgering.

'She knows,' the *kyria* said. 'She hasn't forgotten him.' Kindly she looked back into Marika's face. 'Don't worry, dear, it will all come right in the end. And don't lose faith.' She handed Marika's cup back to her. 'But it's late.' She rose. 'I have another appointment down the street.'

As Dina pressed a generous roll of banknotes in her hand, Kyria Angella threw in a final prediction. 'Men in green. Tanks. Flags waving. Power. Change. Look to your husbands.' And with that, she was gone.

In the taxi home from Dina's, Marika chain-smoked as she tried to shake her eerie feeling. Kyria Angella was just another charlatan playing on the hopes of credulous women.

She tried, instead, to concentrate on 'the girls'. She was sick of their hard gloss, brittle laughter, and hollow lives. How could she ever have let them dazzle her so? She was grateful to them for teaching her how to dress like a sophisticated lady, but she had nothing more to learn from the likes of them. The next time any of them called, she would say she was too busy even to talk. In time, they would leave her alone. She would never again be subjected to their insinuations, temptations, and goofy efforts to peek into the future.

And yet . . .

As Marika's mind turned back to the coffee-reading, she remembered Kyria Angella's reference to the cave. That bit about a blond lover was ridiculous, but she had never confided a word to anyone in Athens about the cave.

Yet, after she'd over-tipped the taxi driver and puffed up the stairway – again the lift was broken – Marika forgot about the *kyria*'s predictions as she wondered what she was going to give Yorgos to eat later tonight. Her mother and the children were down in Panagia, so she supposed she would have to cook.

As she fitted her key into the door, the telephone was ringing.

A moment later Nick's voice came on the line. He wanted to give Yorgos some fresh advice about how to maximize their hotel profits. But, Marika explained, her husband was working late. Before she could say more, she heard Nick obviously talking to someone else.

'Take this, will you? I've got to get a phone number. It's here somewhere.' Nick's voice faded, but another came on the line.

'Chris Kronos.'

Marika sank down in a chair. *His voice*!

'Hello? Is anyone there?'

'Christo.' She stared into the black funnel that linked them, if only briefly.

'Who's this?'

'It's me. Marika.'

Silence on the other end. Then, in Greek this time, 'Marika? It's really you?'

She nodded. But of course he couldn't see her. The voice turned urgent. 'Don't hang up!'

'I'm still here.' She waited, just as she had for too many years.

'How *are* you?'

'OK. I'm OK.'

'So Nick says.'

She heard a click, then an inhalation. So he still smoked. She lit one, too. 'And you?' She had recovered enough to be ready to tell him exactly how she was – and had been, ever since he had left her. But then she heard Nick's booming voice. 'Thanks, Chris. But I'll have to cut this little chat with your sister-in-law short.'

Nick came through loud and clear. 'Now, Marika, I have a phone number I want you to give Yorgos. It's – '

Marika's finger hit the button and disconnectd the line. Not now, Nick . . .

In a daze she wandered to her room and threw herself on the bed. *His voice.*

When again the phone rang, she didn't even hear it. Instead, she was recalling Kyria Angella's predictions. She had said she would hear his voice, and she had. Was this only a coincidence? He was her brother-in-law. Sooner

190

or later something like this was bound to happen. Or was everything else the fortune-teller said also going to come true?

'He will return,' she had said. 'Not now. But it will all come right in the end. And don't lose faith.'

Marika stared at her bedroom ceiling.

Eight

By the light of the ripe moon Marika and her family sat at the table on the beach lingering and nibbling and gossiping over their midnight dinner. The last guests at the taverna had finally been served, Vangelis had taken off his apron, and the generations had settled down to enjoy the company they enjoyed most in the world. It was one of those idyllic nights that proved the wisdom of the Greek word for summer. *Kalokeri*, they call that most-loved season: 'good times'. There is even an old saying that exactly captures the national yearning that these spendid high summer days and nights could be spun out forever. 'August,' everyone says, 'my good month, I wish you would come two times a year.'

As though it were indeed possible to slow down the clock and perhaps even stop it just here, when life was so ripe, the Kronos family was taking the longest possible time over their evening meal on the big wooden table precariously balanced in the wet sand a few metres from the black sea. Forks flashed, laughter rippled, a grandmother urged the choicest titbits on a grandson. Sisters put their heads together and whispered girlish secrets. A nephew planned a dawn fishing trip with an uncle. A waiter, distantly related on Eleni's mother's side, came sauntering out with another litre of retsina and another fried *barbouni*, red mullet. An old aunt stopped for a chat with the grandmothers. A pregnant young cousin stood wistfully listening as everyone assured her that of course this time it would be a boy. Calliopi and Irene – almost family – sat down for a while to listen to Marika's tales of big city life. The waiter brought more bread and yet more salads and was sent back for more of the garlicky *tzatziki* yoghurt dip for which Eleni was renowned. Eat, the grandmothers urged; enjoy. On this night, they had all the time in the world. They speared a forkful of fish, broke off a hunk of bread, popped a salty olive into an open mouth – talking, always talking – and then looked round to drink in the sights and sounds of midsummer. The

191

white surf foamed on the silver shore. Pale boats swung on the dark sea. A hot breeze blew in from far Africa. Somewhere near jasmine waved its heavy honey scent in the wind, and a sleepless cicada chirped from a tree. Very faintly on a distant balcony, so softly and so achingly that it seemed more a memory of music than melody, someone strummed a bouzouki and sang of love. On the length and breadth of the beach, the village was more awake now than in the sunny mornings. A newly-married couple strolled by, their arms intertwined. A fisherman trudged home with his catch. Children ran laughing in packs, as though the bright moonlight had bewitched them into believing that this was not midnight but high noon. In the water the winking red and blue lights of a fishing boat glowed like the reflection of stars spread high in glittering constellations. A motor caught; a craft glided out to sea.

The Kronos family leaned back in their chairs, replete with the company as much as the food. The table was crowded with platters of grilled fish, heaps of roasted lamb, and salads dripping with oil pressed from the trees on the Panagia mountain. Everyone here agreed that the most tender lamb in the world came from Panagia flocks. The fattest fish swam in Panagia bay. Also from this village came the earth's reddest tomatoes, the sharpest onions, and – or so it seemed tonight – the sweetest lives.

By the ruddy light of the candles that glowed in the rough red glass globes set on the plastic tablecloth, Marika studied the dear laughing faces around her. Vangelis, as always, was using his dancing hands, his merry eyes and wicked tongue to tell a joke. Nikos was leaning forward raptly listening, a smile already on his face, as his uncle and godfather meandered toward the punch line. Her daughters were laughing so hard that their glossy curls bobbed like the white boats out on the water. Eleni and Old Anna had smiles of contentment on their wrinkled faces as they sat with their gnarled hands folded on their spreading bellies. With the family all here, the rest of the world receded.

But not, Marika amended as her gaze fell on the empty chair in the place of honour at the head of the table opposite Vangelis, quite all the family was here. When her adored son was absent, Eleni insisted on tending his vacant chair like a shrine. Old Anna and the children had packed up and come down for the summer at the end of June, and Marika had arrived at the beginning of August. But Yorgos, like so many of the husbands, pleaded pressing business in Athens and made it down to the village only on weekends. Idly Marika wondered if tonight's urgent business was blonde or brunette. She didn't need a crystal ball to tell her where he must be just now. He would be finishing up a candlelight dinner at a rooftop or garden taverna, snapping his fingers at the harried waiter for the check, and gazing soulfully into the mascaraed eyes of his lady love before they headed off to a nightclub down near Piraeus. In an hour or two she could almost see him – sweating like a pig, prancing like a goat – as he waved a handkerchief and led the *syrtaki* line in the centre of the dance floor. Before dawn this husband who sometimes haggled with her over every drachma she spent for the family's food would be throwing expensive roses at his girl of the hour, ordering another litre of retsina for the parasites he had invited to his table, and shouting '*Opa!*' as extravagantly and in an orgiastic frenzy of destructive glee he threw piles of plates onto the dance floor.

Listlessly Marika toyed with her food and tried to join in the family conversation. But the spectre of her husband had once again broken the spell of this evening. When she was in Athens, she longed to be back in Panagia. But when she was here, a part of her was still up in the capital. Sometimes she wished she had married a simple village man and settled for a predictable life here in Panagia.

Even though everyone still welcomed her back with open arms, she felt herself to be an *Athenian* and almost as much a foreigner as those carloads of British and German tourists who had begun to come here for a week or two in the summer. Yet once she had been as much a part of this rocky earth as a cypress tree rooted on the hillside or that pure bubbling wellspring which miraculously emerged from the barren reaches of the mountain. But, she thought, looking out to sea where the island loomed dark in the moonlight, she had ceased altogether to belong here on that Carnival night when she had violated the village taboos. Yearningly she stared at that island where so much had begun and ended. What was Christos doing now, halfway round the world?

But she joined in the 'ohs' and 'ahs' round the table when the waiter brought out a tray of glistening red wedges of watermelon. Eager hands reached out, shoulders hunched over, and white teeth sank into the red fruit.

Marika set aside her regrets and took a wedge of *karpouzi*. On her tongue the fruit was sweeter than sugar. Perhaps Kyria Angella would be proven right again, and the one with the golden hair would creep up to her balcony tonight.

She had not seen Sakis since he used to sit at the back of her schoolroom with the other dim boys. But when she had come down to the village last spring for Vangelis' nameday celebration, they had talked awhile over cakes and coffee. Sakis had been at sea for years swabbing the decks of the Greek merchant marine ships and was back now – 'for good', he had said with a contented sigh – living with his aged parents in a tiny bungalow halfway up the mountain while he did odd handyman jobs in the village. He had seen the world, he had said, and now that he was home he hated to go even as far as Athens. A man as limited as this, she had thought, should never have left the village womb. And then, when one of her children had called out from the kitchen, she had promptly forgotten all about him.

Thoughtfully Marika took another bite of watermelon. She had been surprised at her reaction, therefore, when she had run into Sakis on the beach this morning. She had been about to pass him with a polite '*kali mera*' when instead she had found herself staring up into eyes which were *galano*, the exact colour of the sky and the sea. Vangelis expected her back at the taverna, but she had not been able to stop gazing into those eyes. Crazily then, she had wondered if she might take this one as her lover. But no, she had warned herself, not in this village of too many eyes and ears. Here there were no secrets. And yet hers about Christos had miraculously been kept all these years. Maybe . . . Sakis had just been swimming, and in fascination she had watched him slowly rubbing his towel over his glistening tan skin. On his broad chest, the golden hair had glistened. She had wanted to reach out to see if that downy hair was as soft as it looked. Maybe, she had thought, if she was very careful, she might be able to get away with a little adventure. For who could forever resist the eroticism of a Greek summer? The heat, the bare skin, the torpor all combined to madden a man – and a woman, too. She had not been able to stop her eyes travelling down his bronze workman's body. Her gaze had lingered on his thick muscled thighs. If, as she suspected – and perhaps Kyria Angella had predicted – more than his mind was thick as well, so much the better. What would it be like just once to let herself go with a sensual male specimen like this Sakis? With him there could be no emotional or intellectual complications. But no, she must be on her way. She could not risk a liaison in the village. Though Sakis had been a lad of few words back in the classroom, she could not trust him to keep his mouth shut now. In the interminable hours he spent talking with his cronies in the *kafeneions*, even a bashful man might not to able to resist boasting about what he had done to a Kronos woman. She had no illusions about the dark side of Panagia life. Everyone might fawn on her family in public, but they would relish slandering them in private. It was dangerous even to be seen talking like this out on the beach. Yet still her gaze had lingered on those golden hairs on his chest. As she stood sweating in the sun and nagging herself to be on her way, instead she had heard her lips and tongue telling him that her balcony shutters needed repairing. Her bedroom, she had said – conscious of the fishermen mending their nets just out of earshot and a woman bashing an octopus on the rocks not more than fifteen feet away – was the one on the right overlooking the sea. Just before he had sauntered off with that rolling sailor's gait she had suddenly found endearing, he had said he might find the time to see to it. Soon, he had added, even tonight.

Hungrily Marika bit into the watermelon. By the looks of him, Sakis might be even sweeter than this fruit.

When Vangelis leaped up to answer a piercing cry from the taverna, she was so involved in her delicious anticipation that she scarcely noticed. Someone was always shouting and running off, and mostly whatever had excited him turned out to be nothing. She was still paying no heed when her brother returned, flushed with excitement and brandishing a bottle of champagne. He had popped the cork, filled the glasses, and was offering a toast before she heard the name 'Christos' and snapped to attention. 'What's this?'

'A baby, mama!' Lena answered before her uncle could.

'Another girl!' Her sister's black curls bounced.

'Didn't you hear?' Nikos grinned indulgently. His mother had been dreaming again. 'Uncle Christos has another little daughter.'

'Nick just called! All the way from America!' Vangelis seemed as excited by the transatlantic call as by the news of another addition to the family. But he kept his voice down. The village still believed Christos was dead. 'Four kilos! A big girl, eh? And he says Peppy and the baby are just fine.'

At the mention of that foreigner who – so far as they were concerned – would never be a real member of the family, three pairs of dark women's eyes glowered.

'Tch!' Keeping an anxious eye on her daughter, Old Anna snorted as though a tragedy had been visited upon them all. 'Two girls and no boys!' It was nothing to her if Christos was the father of a whole regiment of girls, but for Marika's sake she wanted to cut short the hosannas. That night a decade ago, when Nick had called to say that Christos had taken an American wife, Marika had raged to her for hours about the injustice of life and the perfidy of men. And she had been depressed for weeks after the birth of her old love's first daughter. She could tell by the look on Marika's face that she wasn't about to take kindly to this second birth, either. But she hoped her daughter had the sense to mask her feelings while the whole family was watching and listening.

'That poor lost boy. He made a big mistake, marrying that one.' The frown lines around Eleni's creased face deepened. She still loved Christos as though he were her own, and so she had found his taking a foreign wife difficult to forgive. 'A girl like that, I'm surprised she could have even girls.'

'Too skinny,' Old Anna agreed. 'No meat on her.'

'And no boys in her, too, that's for sure.' With the complacency of the wife who had done her duty and presented her own husband with life's dearest treasure, Eleni smiled at Old Anna and Marika, who had also achieved this crowning triumph.

195

'Peppy seems to be a perfectly nice woman.' Vangelis gave the women of his family an exasperated look.

Eleni scornfully dimissed that possibility. 'Why, my Nikolas wrote in his last letter that she can't even cook moussaka right.' Even though Nick had been fiercely against this marriage, in the intervening years his enthusiasm had begun to embrace even his foreign daughter-in-law. Yet sometimes in his letters he still couldn't resist taking digs at her.

'Maybe Uncle Christos doesn't care about moussaka.' Nikos gave Vangelis a macho wink. 'Maybe Aunt Peppy has other good points.' When only his uncle laughed, Nikos wiped the smile off his face. He never could understand why his mother and grandmothers carried on so about Uncle Christos' wife. Lots of people in Athens married foreigners. One of his friends even had a German mother, and she made wonderful chocolate cakes. But so far as this village was concerned, it was a mortal sin to marry anyone who wasn't born and raised right here where everyone knew everything about everyone else. As a little boy he had loved his summers and Easter holidays in this village which looked and felt like Paradise. But in the last few years the narrowness of life here had begun to oppress him. He liked to go where he pleased and do as he liked, and he chafed under the judging eyes of village surveillance. He would be glad to return to the freedoms of Athens next month. Usually he could count on his educated mother to be on the side of the angels. But for some reason tonight she was as stone-faced as his grandmothers. He thought it best, however, to jolly the ladies into a better mood. 'And what's the matter with having another girl, anyway?' He reached over and gave his younger sister's curls a little toss. 'I *like* girls!'

Lena and Annoula gave their adored brother a rapturous smile. 'So do we!' they chorused. But then Annoula's face fell. 'The only thing is, she's there and we're here! We've never even seen our little cousin Sofia. And maybe we won't see this baby, either.'

At that, Eleni began rocking back and forth as though at a wake. 'My own grandchildren,' she fretted. 'And the only way I know them is in photographs!' She continued her familiar litany. 'It's not right, half the family there. It's not natural. If only my Nikolas would come home. And if only Christos would come home, too. Nearly twenty years that terrible Civil War has been over, and still they won't let those poor boys come home. They're a world away, and there's nothing I can do about it.'

'There, there.' Old Anna patted her dear friend's hand and turned to Vangelis in the hope that he would pick up her cue. 'But maybe Nick is coming home this year? Did he say anything about that?'

'No.' Vangelis quickly improvised a soothing excuse. 'But you know how it is. He's busy, remodelling his waterfront restaurant. I expect he can't come home this summer.'

'Another bad year.' Eleni sighed and then she asked what she had been longing to know ever since Vangelis had come running out with the champagne. 'Did he have any message for me, my husband?'

'For you?' When Vangelis once again intercepted his mother's meaningful glare, he told the lonely old woman what she obviously wanted to hear. 'Why, of course! How could I have forgotten? I guess I was so excited, with the news about the baby . . . But the first thing he said when he got me on the line, was, "How is my beloved wife?"'

Eleni's eyes began to shine and tentatively she reached out and took the tiniest sip of champagne. 'He said that? Exactly? He said, "My beloved wife?"'

'He did indeed,' Vangelis lied.

'And what else did he say?' Hungrily Eleni leaned forward so she wouldn't miss a happy word.

'Well, that was it, actually.' Vangelis' imagination ran dry. 'He was telephoning from the hospital. He couldn't talk long. Peppy was just coming to, and he wanted to go see her.'

At the mention of Christos' wife, once again Eleni lapsed back into her litany. 'Why he had to marry her, I'll never understand. My Nick offered to get him a good Greek wife, someone we all know. He was going to have her sent out from Panagia. But did Christos listen?'

For the first time, Marika broke her silence. 'Christos never listened.' Moodily she stared out at the island and gnawed the watermelon rind. So Christos had another daughter. Was he happy, her lost love, with this rich blonde American who had given him two daughters? She looked over at the splendid son who was the product of her own superior biology. It was a pity that everyone — and especially Christos — could never know whose boy Nikos was. But maybe, she thought with a flash of possessive jealousy, it was better that she would never have to share this son with anyone; not really with Yorgos, and not with Christos either. In all the long years that he had been away, he had never sent her even one tender word. Even in that single accidental telephone call, he had only asked how she was. Christos had built an extravagant new life for himself over there in rich America. He had some kind of important job in the city. And of course he had his precious wife and children. He didn't sit around like this, mooning over the past. Instead he climbed into bed every night beside this woman whom he had chosen as his life's companion. Not me, *her*. At this very moment he must be sitting by the hospital bed, holding her pale white hand. Try as she might to convince herself that he must be disappointed by the birth of another

197

daughter, she could not forget how even Yorgos – who had so desperately wanted a 'second' son – had doted on his girls as soon as he had laid eyes on them.

Vangelis was pouring more champagne and calling for the waiter to bring another bottle. Everyone was crashing glasses in toasts to this new Kronos born on the far side of the Atlantic. Marika forced herself to drink, and drink again. But as soon as she could, she made her excuses and crept off to her room.

She took a hard look in the mirror as slowly she wiped off her cosmetics. Except for a faint tracery of fine lines around the corners of her eyes, there were still no wrinkles or sags. Dina and 'the girls' broiled themselves into premature middle age by too much exposure to the sun, but her complexion was still as smooth as a young woman in her twenties. But, she thought as she rubbed an expensive French cream into her face, there was something she didn't like about not only the look in her eyes but also the discontented set of her chin. Even those wives of the leathery skin looked happier than she.

She took a tepid shower, towelled herself dry, and threw herself down on her bed. But tonight, even without Yorgos beside her, there was no merciful release of sleep. Restlessly she turned this way and that. She lit a cigarette but stubbed it out after two puffs. The room was bathed in bright moonlight that poured through the slits of the balcony shutters. The breeze had died down, and it seemed far hotter than it had on the beach. She wrenched off her nightdress and threw it on the floor. When, a few minutes later, she heard the buzz of mosquitos, she cursed, got up, and pumped the Katol spray gun. But as the DDT fumes filled the air, she coughed and opened the shutters so she could breathe.

She prowled the bedroom. On her dresser she paused to stare at the colour portraits of the children. Tenderly she picked up the silver-framed photograph of Nikos. How was it that no one remarked that he looked more like Christos than her husband? She sighed, replaced that portrait, and studied the ones of her daughters. Judging from the photographs that Nick sent regularly in the post, her girls looked enough like their blonde American cousin to be their dark-haired sisters. Again the image of Christos devotedly sitting at his wife's hospital bedside haunted her. She went on with her life, she thought she was all over him, and then out of the blue a phonecall, a letter, or photograph would devastate her.

She stalked to her wardrobe and regarded the clothes she had bought with such pleasure. But now she was bored with them, as with so much else. Tonight she couldn't even take satisfaction in that first byline Sokrates had finally given her a few days before she had gone on holiday. Over on her

198

bedside table, however, was a new volume of George Seferis' poetry. She never tired of her favourite poet. But if she turned on the light to read, every insect in the village would be upon her. She wandered back to the bureau and picked up a hammered silver belt she had bought the week before in Plaka. She wound it round her naked waist, and against her flesh the metal was as cold as a snake. In the mirror her voluptuous body looked the image of some pagan fertility goddess. The island, she thought. She hadn't been back to the Cave of the Great Goddess for years. Sometime – maybe tomorrow – she would row the girls out, perhaps with her mother. But first she would have to endure the sultry hours of this interminable night.

Marika threw herself back in bed and listened to the surf pounding on the beach. Resolutely she shut her eyes and hoped that any second she would be lulled off to sleep. Instead, still, she could almost see that Boston hospital room. Nick would be gambolling about, as proud as though the new baby were his own. There would be fragrant bouquets of flowers and lavish boxes of chocolates. Marika could feel the sweat running down her body. Like tears, she thought. Oh, Christos . . .

Disgusted with herself, she sprang out of bed and flounced into the bathroom. She showered again with cold water and then wandered over to the open balcony door. She stood in the moonlight and tried to think of nothing as the hot wind dried her. Finally, as she closed the transparent curtains, she yawned and stretched. Maybe now she would fall fast asleep as soon as her head hit the pillow. But when she lay back down on the clammy cotton sheet, still she tossed and turned.

It was sometime thereafter – later she calculated that it must have been three or four o'clock – when she heard a thud, then the scraping of rusty metal, and finally footfalls on her balcony. Silhouetted in the backlight from the moon she saw the dark outline of a man. She was just about to call out to frighten off the intruder when she remembered who and what she had invited upon herself that morning.

Oh no, she thought. She must have been out of her mind to tell Sakis which room was hers. The last thing she wanted here and now was a man – any man, but especially this peasant who surely would not be able to keep his mouth shut.

But before she could snap at him to go away, he advanced until he was standing over her bed.

'*Kali spera*,' his deep voice said.

She knew she should be reaching for something to cover herself, but she had thrown the sheet on the floor. Besides, it was hot, and she was lazy. Let him look at what a man like him can never have! When she had heard him at the door, she had raised herself on one elbow, and she still had her hand in her hair. She was on her side, with her legs stretched out provocatively, as though she were lolling on the beach.

'*Orea*' he sighed, 'beautiful.'

Just as she was about to dismiss him curtly, she felt his touch on her thigh. Her skin prickled, and as his fingers trailed up her leg to her pelvis, she looked up at him and reconsidered. Why not? She had been faithful to Yorgos for too long. Sakis was already here, and it would be more trouble to send him away than to let him stay. Besides, he might be a better remedy than those sleeping pills the doctor had prescribed. Surely a few fevered moments with Sakis would be more diverting than brooding until dawn. Yet again she imagined Christos in Boston holding his wife's hand. And by now up in Athens Yorgos would be dancing himself into a frenzy with his latest dolly. To hell, she thought, with both the Kronos brothers.

Utterly conscious of what she was doing, she rolled over a little more on her side so that her full breasts would seem rounder. Seductively, like an odalisque ready for a pasha, she kept her one hand pinned back behind her head. And then, tantalizingly, she slowly began to part her legs at the thigh.

He smiled and gave her another insinuating glance. Then, infinitely slowly, he pulled his shirt over his head, unbuttoned his trousers, and stood naked before her.

In the moonlight she stared at his erection. He was even bigger than she had thought he would be. She was reminded of the erotic statues peddled to the tourists for a few drachmas. She licked her dry lips. The room seemed suddenly hotter.

Languorously she stretched out, thinking he would be in and out of her in a moment. A peasant like this wasn't capable of finesse. But instead of throwing himself on top of her, he merely sat on the very edge of the bed and continued to look her over. She felt his eyes burning into her breasts, her thighs, her belly. Her legs were wide apart, and his flesh was only inches away. He leaned so close to her that she could see that his eyelashes were golden, too. Expectantly she shut her eyes and waited with parted lips for his kiss.

But instead she felt his feather touch on the points of her nipples, first one, then the other. Exquisitely slowly, he ran the balls of his fingers round and round the points of her breasts until the nipples were erect and her breasts felt swollen. Yet still he only touched her nipples. Her heavy breasts were throbbing. She wanted him to suck them, bite them, bury his golden head between them. Her breath was coming faster now, she was breathing in quick little animal pants. Yet still, even though she wanted more – she had to have more, and right now – teasingly his practised fingers only toyed with the very tips of her breasts.

When he stopped even that and drew away, she opened her eyes. She stared as if hypnotized into his knowing blue eyes. She could hear herself still panting.

'You like that,' he observed.

'I like everything.' She was a woman of the world, he only a village handyman with magic fingers.

'Everything?' He smiled. 'We'll see.'

At last his hands snaked out and cupped her breasts. She let out a deep sigh as his fingers fondled the fullness of them, and she cried out when his thumb flicked her nipples. He kneaded them softly, then roughly, until she moaned. Crazily, then, as she stared into those blue eyes, she was reminded of the old myths about one of the golden gods – usually the rampant Zeus but sometimes Apollo – who came by night to seduce a mortal maiden who had caught his wandering eye. But no, she reminded herself with the little conscious thought of which she was capable, this is no god but only slow, stupid Sakis. Don't get carried away. But as finally she felt his lips on her nipple, and his tongue, and his teeth, she wanted to get carried away. Her hand was in his hair, caressing him as he ground his head between her breasts.

He reared back then, and his lips curled up again in a smile as she tried to slow her breath and get control of herself. But she was out of control, and she didn't want to be in control. Why was he taking so long about this? She could see he wanted her. She wanted him inside her, and right now. Greedily she reached for him.

'Not so fast.' He caught her hand and firmly tucked it under her thigh. 'We have time.' Again he smiled. 'It's two hours until dawn.'

Two hours, she thought, of this delicious torment? Her tongue flicked out, and she ran it round her open lips. Her one hand was still behind her head, the other under her thigh. She enjoyed the sensation of being pinned down – helpless, vulnerable, open like this – while this man who had come prowling in the night did whatever he wanted with her. Again she had underestimated this sailor who had come home not only from the sea but from the brothels of the Orient. Sinuously she stretched on the bed, waiting. All her senses were heightened. She could hear the sea pounding. She could smell jasmine on the wind. She was aware of every part of her body: her breasts, her thighs, her belly. Her legs were splayed apart.

She quivered when, still smiling, he reached out his hands and once again cupped her breasts. Expectantly she leaned forward, but this time he only grazed the back of his hands against her taut nipples before his hands strayed first to her waist and then down the length of her. With his twenty dancing fingers he stroked her waist, her thighs, her pelvis, her buttocks. Everywhere she burned. The room was hot, too hot. Beads of perspiration ran down her belly, and that, too, felt like a caress. She was ashamed when she could not keep still. Her body writhed in a motion that was old as the earth. Lightly he stroked the inside of her thighs, and when she could not stop herself from opening them even further, his smile, too, widened. He trailed his hand up to her belly. He traced slow and ever-widening rings around her navel, and then lower. She moaned when he touched her centre. Any second now he would push inside. She panted faster, but she opened her begging eyes when suddenly he drew away.

'You make love first,' he said. 'You only.'

'Me?' Her eyes darkened. She had been embarrassed enough when she had cried out and writhed around like a snake. But she could not bear to let herself go while he just sat there and watched. 'Why?'

'Because I like it.' That smile again. 'And you will, too. You said you like everything. So *let's see*.'

Her mouth snapped shut and her legs, too. She was ready to order him out of her room, when again she felt his hands on her stiff body. Her resolve weakened as his touch leisurely wandered from her breasts to her belly. He stroked her, and teased her, and again she felt the fire between her legs.

'What are you doing to me?' she cried out, as she could not help spreading her legs just a little. His hands were circling her navel again, and lower. She was panting again when finally his fingers were exactly where she wanted them to be. Oh, she moaned, as so lightly, so softly, he probed her moist folds and coaxed her to open wider. She was panting hard, her pelvis was gyrating. 'Yes,' she cried out, 'yes!' She was beyond conscious thought, she was all sensation, his fingers were all the way in her, they were out again, they were caressing the centre of all her pleasure: slowly, slowly, then faster, much faster. 'Don't stop,' she moaned as she careened closer to the edge. He didn't stop, he pushed her further, she was over. She cried out as she convulsed, and when still he didn't let her go she kept jerking as from deep inside her throat she let out a whimper. Finally she sighed and lay as still as the dead.

She was ready to drift off to sleep then. She would have been happy if he had taken away his magic fingers and tiptoed out the door. But instead, a moment later, she felt a brush against her mouth. He wants a kiss, sleepily she thought, and so she parted her lips. Instead she felt something other than lips. Her eyes shot open, and it was his wet fingers he was running over her mouth. He moved his hand higher, and she breathed in the musky smell of herself. When again his fingers caressed her lips and pried them open, she tried to draw away but could not. He inserted one finger in her mouth, and she sucked it at first tentatively and then greedily. She tasted herself on his long wet fingers.

'Good girl.' He ruffled her hair in the same fond gesture Yorgos used with his daughters when they had especially pleased him.

As fleetingly she wondered exactly how many women this man had had, she smiled and stretched. What did it matter, so long as she was the one who had him now? She reached out her hand and ran it over the golden hairs on his chest, in no hurry now for whatever he decided should come next. She all but purred when once again he stroked her breasts and her thighs and her belly.

'You're very sexy.'

She thought of those endless nights lying in her bed as far away from her husband as she could get. Her head reared up in the wordless Greek negative. 'Not so sexy.'

'Shall we find out, you and me, just how sexy you are?'

Trustingly she smiled at this seemingly simple man who was giving her so much pleasure. She was still smiling when at last his lips touched hers in a featherlight caress. Again like a dance to which only he knew the rhythm, he teased her upper lip and then her lower lip with the briefest of touches, until her own searching lips began to let out little animal moans of desire. At last he gave her his lips, and then his tongue. For a long while he kissed her. But when she tried to twine her arms around his body, instead abruptly he pulled away from her embrace.

She had learned a few lessons in these last exquisite moments since first he had touched her. She lay very still, waiting with her eyes shut for whatever he decided would come next. Only dimly was she aware of him moving on the bed.

Finally she felt him against her lips, and she sighed and parted her lips for another deep kiss. But her eyes flew open and she recoiled when she felt and saw that it wasn't his lips that were in her mouth. She hated this particular act which 'the girls' said was the favourite of every Greek man. Even Christos, that one night back in the cave, had been in her mouth for a while. Yorgos insisted on it practically every time he touched her. He would push inside her so far that she would nearly gag, and afterwards she would gargle with mouthwash to try to wipe out the taste and feel of him all the way down her throat.

'You don't like this?' Sakis pulled out and frowned at her.

'Not much.' Suddenly she wanted him to go away.

Sunnily he smiled, stroked her cheek, and then closed his one hand over hers. 'But I would like you at least to touch me.'

'Well . . .' It was a harmless request. She would touch him a little, he would finally come inside her, and then he would go and she could roll over and sleep. With the air of doing a great favour, she let him guide down her hand. Tentatively and without enthusiasm she stroked the length of it, then played with the tip, and finally, when she could feel it pulsing hard in her hand, she rolled on her back and spread her legs so he could get on with things.

He was kissing her lips, his arms pulled her close to him, at last he was kissing her as man was meant to kiss woman. They rolled over on the bed, she was on top of him, she angled herself so he would be inside, but instead again they rolled over so he was atop again. She gasped when he broke away from her, but then she moaned when he was kissing her breasts. His tongue lapped her nipples, his hands kneaded her belly. He was sitting up, bending over her, biting her stomach, his arms were spreading her thighs wide open. Suddenly she felt his lips kissing her there. 'No!' It felt too unbearably vulnerable with him down there like that. She tried to bring her legs together so he would stop, but he had her splayed open. His lips and his tongue probed her, and her body was wracked with sensations she had never felt before. He flicked and sucked and bit. 'Yes, yes,' she gasped, 'yes!' Her lips were empty, her hands were empty, her arms were empty, and to fill them with more of him, blindly she reached out. He was in her mouth, and as she closed around him she couldn't help doing to him what he was doing to her. Greedily she caressed him. She kissed him and licked him and sucked him. She could not get enough of him. She was just about to come, when suddenly he pulled away from her, righted himself, and plunged all the way inside her in the final embrace. She shuddered and convulsed, and still he pumped inside her.

'*Orea!*' he breathed. 'Beautiful!'

He lay still in her arms, and she longed only to be held like this until she drifted off to sleep. But instead, just like Yorgos and all the other village men, he disengaged his arms and rolled out of the bed and into the bathroom. Languorously she stretched as she listened to the sound of the shower. When he padded back, he smiled down at her. 'You were right,' he said huskily. 'You do like everything.'

A moment later, he slipped his shirt over his tanned body. 'I know you'll be here another two weeks. But when does your husband come back?'

She shrugged and let her eyes droop shut. 'I never know.'

'I will come again tomorrow night, eh?'

She turned over and didn't bother to answer. Sakis had been far better than she had expected, but she wasn't going to make a dangerous habit of him. First thing tomorrow she would have Vangelis put a lock on the balcony door and windows. Sleepily she heard Sakis walk out of her life.

Her last thought, as she fell asleep smiling, was that Kyria Angella's second prediction had come true.

Marika did not awaken from the deep sleep of the devils until two o'clock the next afternoon.

After one on that same sultry August morning, the nightclub down by the sea near Kallithea was in full cry. Between the earsplitting and electronically amplified music, the bellowing waiters, and the two hundred or so customers packed in at the tables – every one of them talking, laughing, and singing, all at the same time – the din was deafening even by Athenian standards.

The main act – the popular Manolis Chiotis and Mary Linda – had finished their set of *archontorebetika* love songs. At the epicentre of the elevated dance floor, a singer no one had ever heard of – a bleached blonde in a tight electric blue sequinned dress – held the microphone between her full breasts as she shrieked of love gone wrong. Behind her, gyrating more or less in time with the blasting music, three more girls in racy scarlet minidresses pranced and shimmied and tossed their long teased hair as they winked and pouted at their gentlemen friends panting at the ringside tables. Set back against the wall at the outer fringe of the dance floor the bored-looking bouzouki band played valiantly on, their high and low notes amplified by the most staticky electronic devices money could buy. On the edges of the dance floor goodlooking young sweepers in starched white shirts briskly plied their brooms to clean away the rubble of broken crockery and smashed flowers which had been exuberantly thrown there moments ago when the music and the dancing had reached orgasm.

Yorgos sat thigh-to-thigh with his mistress at a prime table within easy leap and throw of the dance floor. When he had swept in here with Susie a few hours ago, he had slipped the waiter an extra fifty drachmas to clinch this table. He hated to be stuck against the wall with the shopkeepers and the *stenokephalos*, 'narrowheaded' provincial louts in the big city for one heady night. He himself had been born and bred in a village, but he resented how too many of the haughty Athenians still lumped his military friends with the country bumpkins. He liked to see and be seen by all the right people. He was Yorgos Kronos, an up-and-coming colonel in the illustrious Greek army. One day soon, if God and the saints and glorious history was on his side – and he was sure They were – he would stride in here, commandeer whatever table he liked, and the crowd would respectfully part as though he were Moses and they the Red Sea. But for now he was willing to bide his time and shed a banknote or two to secure his rightful place at the forefront of the Tzitzifies supper club where important people came not only to eat fish and listen to music but also to see and be seen.

'More retsina?' Without waiting for Susie's response, he splashed wine in his girlfriend's glass and refilled his own. He frowned, then, at the dregs of the nearly empty bottle. He would have to buy several more if his friends arrived, and he would insist on picking up the tab for their *après*-midnight meal as well. This was going to be an outrageously expensive night on the town, too much for the pittance the army paid him. Even a general in the Greek armed forces made less than a sergeant in the American army. But *then pirazi*, he told himself, never mind, as he snapped his fingers at a waiter running by with a trayful of platters and bottles. His wallet was fat, and there was more where this came from. Besides his private income from his family, he and his friends had not only God but the Americans on their side.

'Thanks, but I don't want any more.' As she pushed away the glass of harsh resinated wine, Susie's thin lips had narrowed to an even thinner line, a sure sign that she was about to be what Yorgos called 'difficult'. 'And it's late, George.' Always she called him by the anglicized version of his name. 'Time to get home. I have to be at work in the morning.'

'So?' In this din, he hadn't been able to catch more than a word or two. But that was no problem, since he could easily read the little that was on her mind. Just as the night was building to a peak, she was beginning to mewl about how late it was. At a particular point every time they went out, always she started looking at her watch as though making her boss coffee and typing letters was a matter of earthshaking importance. Airily Yorgos waved his hand at the other merrymakers who were not yet ready to be tucked into their beds. 'You think you're the only one with a job? I'll be at my desk at nine sharp.'

'I'm tired.' Unhappily she looked around at this fevered mob of sweating, chattering, excited aliens who never slept much less worked. Not for the first time, she wondered what she was doing in this country where she would never belong. She needed her head examined for having renewed her contract for a second year just last spring. But things had been better with George then, she loved the sun, and every time she managed to escape to the dreamlike bliss of the islands she fell in love all over again with the enchanting landscape. And so she had signed up for another year on the job and another impossible course in Greek. She had even almost convinced herself that, if only she could learn to twist her tongue around the gushing polysyllables of their language, she might have the key not only to under-standing but enjoying this country. George always told her not speaking Greek was her biggest problem here. That, and her inability to relax. She went rigid with anxiety every time he ordered her, in that hectoring tone, to relax.

'Your problem is that you don't know how to relax.' Patronizingly he patted her hand. 'Relax! And that's an order.'

Susie's eyes darted around the boisterous nightclub. Relax, here, no, it wasn't possible, not in this country of hot people who were at heart so very cold. Mostly they smiled and jollied up the foreigners only when they wanted something – almost always money or sex – and as soon as they had it they were off, leaving her feeling flat and ravished. One of the bosses at the American construction firm where she worked had told her once that even thousands of years ago, back in the golden days of the Classical era, the Hellenes had so despised all foreigners that they coined the word 'barbarian' to describe anyone not born a superior Greek. In Susie's experience here in this dirty city where nothing worked and often the days and nights were as boring as an Iowa winter, the modern Athenians still clung to that ancient arrogance. Even though occasionally she would be startled by an isolated act of kindness by a stranger in a bus or somebody's cousin who went out of his way to help her, more often the Greeks were shouting, and gouging her – and everyone else, including one another – on prices, and shoving aside anyone who dared get in their way.

But even as that familiar, nagging sense of defeat washed over her, she remembered when it hadn't been like this for her in Greece. She had arrived for her great adventure with such wide-eyed expectations, and at first Greece had been all she had hoped and more. She had felt like the most beautiful woman in the world when those dark hungry eyes had caressed her on every street corner. She had loved walking the winding old lanes of Plaka buying ceramic knick-knacks and intricately worked brass earrings. Time and again she had made marvellous pilgrimages to the National Museum to stare in wonder at exquisite statues and vases. And a little thrill had gone through her every time she had suddenly glimpsed the pure white perfection of the Parthenon when she crested one of the many steep Athenian mini-mountains on which the *quartiers* of the city were strung. But it had been all downhill once she stopped feeling like a tourist. She had begun to believe that, for a certain kind of foreigner, Greece was at its sunny best for a brief holiday.

As the flashing strobe lights pulsated, freeze-framing the play of emotions on her open American face, Yorgos chose not to see her misery and focused on her lustrous blonde hair, her creamy complexion, and her nubile round body. Once again he congratulated himself for his conquest of this pretty young thing. More than anything else about her, he adored how deliciously young she was. He was pushing forty – forty-two, actually, though he knew no one would ever have guessed it – and she a little more than half his age.

207

Anyone who saw them together — and everyone was here! — would know him for the great stud he was. Still, he had to pay a price for her palpitating company. Like so many other demanding foreign girls, she often seemed more trouble than she was worth. She had been more fun in the beginning, before she turned so gloomy. He smiled at the band, grateful that it was too noisy here to talk. Always she chattered on about her silly problems. What did she think, that he was her brother? Even Marika didn't pester him with everyday minutiae.

At the thought of that bitch he was married to, Yorgos' face set like cement. If she treated him as a wife was supposed to, he wouldn't need tarts like this Susie. He had turned himself inside out to please her. He had put up with that witch of a mother of hers, taken her brother into the family business, and never said what was on the tip of his tongue about Nikos. He had indulged what he had thought was her whim about going to the university, and then he had even gotten her that job which now monopolized her so. He made a good living, let her buy whatever she wanted, and despite her many provocations had never so much as slapped her face. Yet always, even or maybe *especially* when their bodies were as intimate as man and woman can be, still she withheld what he most wanted from her. He had hoped, when he first began flaunting his girlfriends, that Marika would come to her senses. The two of them could be so happy! But, his scheme to make Marika jealous had backfired. She had become even more estranged, and his mad passion for her had intensified. How did she continue to bewitch him?

Sullenly he looked over this little *Amerikana* who could never match up to Marika. But at least, under his tutelage, Susie had learned to be magnificent in bed. It soothed his ego, too, to play the same games with her that Marika tormented him with every day. And showing her off in clubs like this inflated his standing with his cronies. Remembering that he was expecting some of the boys from the Ministry any time now, he thought it expeditious to coax her out of this petulant mood. She hadn't been bright enough to pick up much of the language, but she had managed to learn how to pout like a native Greek girl. 'Take it easy, *glika mou*.' His English had improved now that, in his position at the Joint United States Military Assistance Group in Greece, he had so much contact with the American military and intelligence officers posted in Athens. 'Be a good girl for your great big Georgie-porgie.'

Resentfully Susie met his calculating eyes. She hated his saccharine baby talk. But based on her limited social contacts in clubs like this, it seemed that was how the Greeks were with their girlfriends. When she had first met George, she had not had a glimmering that it could ever be like this between them. He had squired her to what he had said were all the best places and had always been so attentive and seemingly bedazzled by everything she did, said, and wore. Looking back now, she was surprised at how eager she, who had always been so sure of herself back in Iowa City, had been to let this man take care of her. But he was old enough to be her father, and her first six months in Greece had reduced her to a dependent child. She had been so naive, assuming she could control not only him but her own emotions. Once in his orbit, it had felt so good not to blunder around alone in this family-rooted culture that she feared would aways remain closed to her. If I knew then what I know now, she wondered, would I have let myself slide into this relationship? He had made no secret of the fact that he was married. But in those first weeks, she had been flattered by how he had acted as though he were crazy about her and yet lulled into a false sense of security by how he had respectfully kept his hands off her. This one, she had told herself, was a cut above the randy Greeks who pressed their crotches against her on the buses and devoured her with their eyes every time she sat in a café. When she had gone off to Mykonos for a summer weekend soon after she arrived, she had been appalled at her brushes with the lusty young Greeks who proudly called themselves *kamakia* – 'spear fishermen' – who fished not the waters but the beaches for one-night stands with tourists. Yet she had grown tired of sitting around in the cafés hour after boring hour, fending off the men and making desultory conversations with the other expatriate girls about the peccadillos of this country and these people. She had come to Greece to take a great juicy bite of the apple of life, not to whine about bad plumbing and armpits in need of deodorant. And so, when George had come striding into the US embassy one afternoon when she was waiting for a girlfriend to finish work, she had let this charming officer talk her into having a drink in a little bar on a sidestreet near the Hilton. She had never suspected she could fall in love with a man so old, who was losing his hair, and who had the squat body of an ageing wrestler. He wasn't a bit like those young men who used to take her to the movies on Saturday nights and talk about football and the latest Beatles' album. Sharply she longed for the innocent company of the boys back home.

Yorgos leaned closer, took her glass in his hand, and held it to her lips. 'Drink up.' He tilted the glass, and either she had to open her lips and swallow or the alcohol would dribble down her chin and stain her new strapless black satin dress that had cost a week's salary on her last shopping expedition to Kolonaki. At home she had never worn anything like this tight slinky sheath. But Greek women going out on the town overdressed like Barbie dolls *en route* to a brothel, and lately she had found in herself a latent taste for rhinestones and *décolleté*. She had known at the time she couldn't afford this dress but she had been so depressed that afternoon; buying it had buoyed her up for at least three hours.

Susie swallowed hard and forced herself to smile so maybe he would leave her alone and go back to ogling the girls at the other tables. She wasn't allowed to let her eye so much as stray to another leering man when she was in his company, but she had to endure him all but salivating when he saw a jiggling bosom or a wiggling backside. She remembered well how jealous she had been the first time she had caught him flirting with a voluptuous brunette behind her back. She, who had never before been especially possessive of her boyfriends, had wanted to smack that other woman's face and tell George he was *hers*, only hers. That, she now knew, had been one of the first danger signs of her growing emotional involvement. I should have broken it off then, she thought sadly, before I got hooked.

'That's better,' he said. 'You look much prettier when you smile.'

But these days, she thought, it was harder to smile and mean it. Yet once she had felt so treasured when George had sent her big bouquets of flowers and taken her to fancy restaurants with linen tablecloths and real crystal wineglasses. She had listened sympathetically when he had confided that he was married to a woman he had never loved – it was one of those arranged marriages back in my village, he had explained, and his wife looked old enough to be his mother. Hearing that, Susie had remembered taking a trip last autumn down to the Peloponnese. As the tourist bus had lurched through some godforsaken village in the middle of nowhere, she had glimpsed an old woman in a black babuska peering suspiciously out of a window in her hut, looking like the wicked old witch in Hansel and Gretel. Poor George, to be married to a crone like that! She had even believed him when he had vowed that he never slept with that Marika any more. She had intended not to let him touch her until he actually went ahead and filed for the divorce he said he longed for, but her resolve had wavered and then collapsed one hot spring night when he had arranged a romantic dinner in the suite of a small seaside hotel on the far side of Glyfada. Susie flushed as she remembered that passionate night. Even now, with all their problems, still their happiest times together were in bed. It was only the rest of it that made her feel so bad.

As expansively – and possessively – he rested his hand on her bare shoulder and gazed not at her but at others, again she wished she had heeded the advice of the other foreign secretaries who had sourly warned her early on never to get involved with a Greek man. When one or another of the girls would treat her to coffee and some well-meant orientation advice, always they had said the same things: never trust a Greek, especially a Greek man; they're all married, and they all stay married; have some fun with them if you like, but never give away your heart; they are poison, these Greeks, and they can break even a strong woman's heart. But she had been so sure that it would be different for her than for those neurotic spinsters-in-the-making who clearly didn't know how to get and hold a real man.

Susie stared at the bouzouki singer fondling that microphone as though it were the most dearly prized part of her lover's anatomy. After that first rapturous night together, George had come to her apartment – twice one week, three times another week, not at all one miserable week – mostly late at night but sometimes in the afternoons. She had waited awhile for him to bring her up to date on his imminent divorce, but finally she had broached the topic herself. Remembering how his face had shut tight against her as he had mumbled that it was 'difficult just now' – Greeks, she now understood, never said an outright 'no' – Susie once again felt the rage building inside her. It had been easy, the next day, to get her girlfriend at the embassy to open her boss's files and find George's home address. It had been degrading to disguise herself in a frumpy black dress and wrap a voluminous black scarf around her hair so she could skulk around his middle-class Pangrati neighbourhood hoping to catch a glimpse of his wife. When at last she had seen the two women emerging from the doorway of his apartment house, at first she had assumed that the old one in black had to be the wife his family had made him marry. But then she heard the biddie shriek out 'Marika!' and turn to the youngish woman beside her. With a sinking heart, Susie had taken in the face and figure of her rival. To her American eye, most Greek women of a certain age had mannish features and thickened bodies. The men here were often more beautiful than the women, for both sexes tended to hawk noses, burning eyes, and moustaches. But George's wife was one of the extraordinary exceptions. She had long rippling black hair, huge dark eyes set in a striking face, and a body that made Susie feel like an adolescent boy in comparison. She had been smartly dressed in a tailored royal blue suit and high heels, and as she took the old woman by the arm and settled her in George's Fiat, her voice had carried. As if she needed any more confirmation, Susie heard the name 'Yorgos . . .' She had thought nothing could make her feel worse, until a handsome boy rushed out the door with a pair of breathless girls clinging to his arms. As the three of them piled into the back of the car, they all had broken into waves of laughter. Watching this happy family pull away, for the first time Susie had seen her relationship with George for what it was. She was the little piece on the side; his real life was in that Fiat. Before she made her way down the steep hill to the Plateia Plastira to find a taxi home, Susie had vomited in the doorway across the street from her lover's house.

She shook a cigarette from George's pack of Marlboros and touched the side of his hand as he liked her to do when he flicked his lighter and she inhaled. She had started smoking a few months ago to keep her hands and lips busy in these interminable hours in loud warehouse nightclubs, until finally he took her home to bed. She hated to think of smoke polluting her lungs, but it did calm her nerves. When loneliness drove her to strike up conversations with tourists, she would stare uncomprehendingly into their blind eyes as they enthused about Greece's serenity. Couldn't they feel the tension in this country? The Greeks were as abrupt, demanding, and impatient with one another as they were with bumbling foreigners. They snapped at one another on the buses, in the shops, and at the kiosks. Maybe, she thought, the rumours she had heard at work were true. Greece could be teetering on the edge of collapse. Because of the constant strikes – one day the buses, another the trolleys, on a third the taxis – sometimes just getting to work took half the day. Nothing worked for long, and on the most mundane tasks – getting money out of the bank, finding a tailor to repair a zipper, convincing her landlord to fix the toilet so it would flush properly – she found herself waiting frustrating days, weeks, or even months on what would have taken her only a few minutes to settle back in Iowa City. Maybe I should go home, she thought. To hell with my contract. The company would have to understand. She wouldn't be the first expatriate to pull up stakes to avoid a nervous breakdown. But she would hate to slink home in defeat. No matter how good a face she tried to put on it, she and everyone else would know that she had failed at her great adventure.

Susie blew smoke-rings into the sooty air of the supper club. She was twenty-two years old, and until she had come to this country she had considered herself a level-headed young woman, competent at most everything she tried to do. Yet here she felt so very stupid so very much of the time. On good days she told herself the problem was Greece and the Greeks; but on the bad days when she double-locked her apartment door and had a good cry, she feared it was her own fault that everything had gone so badly for her in Greece. If she hadn't gotten so obsessed with this destructive passion for George, maybe she could have let this country and these people take root in her soul. Despite everything, what was it about Greece that made her wish she could be a part of it, and forever? It wasn't just the glorious mountains and the intoxicating sea, although she had never been anywhere so soul-satisfyingly beautiful. The radiant sun and the ethereal light combined to bake all the badness out of life. But Greece's powerful pull came from something deeper and stronger than nature and the primal elements. Sometimes – rarely, but unforgettably – an act as simple as sitting under a tree sipping a soda could make her feel so transcendentally *happy*. When she tried to analyse why, the reasons always eluded her. But she could not forget that fleeting contentment. Just so, in her heart of hearts, she suspected that what was best about life here would always elude her. A girl like herself, shackled to a married man, could never experience the warm lap of Greek family life. Doomed to be ever on the outside, she had never been able to pierce the hard protective shell with which the Greeks armoured themselves against a world which they, too, perceived as hostile.

From under her heavily-mascaraed eyelashes, Susie stole a look at her lover. Once again – *why, why?* – she experienced another of those lightning and maddening mood changes that were as much a part of Greece as the sun and sea. George wasn't so bad. He was so exciting sometimes, mostly especially in bed. What was wrong with her, turning against the only person who had been on her side in this country? Even though he was difficult much of the time, and seldom there when she most wanted and needed him, at least he was *someone*. And he loved her, really he did. Every time she pressed him, he said so. She clung to that one thought, and she clung to him.

When Yorgos put his hand atop hers, she let it stay there. He peered at what he could see of her between the flashing throbs of the lights. 'Now that's how I like to see you. Smiling and happy.'

Again her mood somersaulted. Tears stung her eyes, and in another moment they might have spilled down her cheeks if he had said one more word that proved his insensitivity to her feelings. But just then at the door his roving eyes saw the people he had been expecting. He jumped up and frantically waved. 'Here, over here!' The six officers were out of uniform, but their stature was so unmistakeably military that, as they marched purposefully across the room an irrepressible diner at a nearby table couldn't resist saluting.

Susie's heart sank. He hadn't told her they would be joined by a company of his friends. She had thought they would be leaving any minute, but instead they would be staying until dawn. She had endured enough of these encounters to have no illusions about how this one would proceed. After his cronies finished looking her over and saying what she could only guess were insinuating things about her to George, they would acknowledge her presence only by turning occasionally in her direction and – as though she were a dog being patted on the head – asking '*Kala*? Good?' All that would be required of her was to sit rooted like a flower and smile. She considered, but then rejected, making her excuses and slipping home in a taxi. She had done that once, and for two tortuous weeks afterwards George had made her suffer the consequencs of losing face in front of his friends. She had a quick temper but couldn't stay angry for more than a day or two. George, however, was as fierce in his angers as in all his other passions. She felt so unbearably isolated when he refused even to talk to her.

Susie sighed under her breath but prepared to make the best of things.

213

Like it or not, she would be stuck here until he said it was time to go. Hopefully she stared at the approaching officers, but no, they hadn't brought girlfriends. She, of course, had never met any of the wives. But occasionally, when one of the brigadiers or colonels had a Greek girl clinging on his arm, she had hoped that she might make a new friend or at least have someone to talk to at the table. But the girls, who presumably didn't speak much English, never gave her more than a stiletto glance before they shamelessly wrapped themselves around their ageing boyfriends. They held their hands, stroked their thighs, ran their fingers through whatever hair their men had left. When the fellows wanted to be left alone to talk to their buddies, the girls would sulk. Susie supposed, considering past experiences, that she should be glad she would be the only woman at their table.

As the officers arrived, there was the usual clicking of heels, clasping of hands, and a few comradely bear hugs. George was snapping his fingers at the waiters, and a parade of them were arriving with tables and chairs held aloft like offerings to a sultan. Everyone and everything were somehow squeezed in, but she ended up practically in George's lap. He soldered them even more tightly together by wrapping his arm around her bare neck as he made the introductions: one lordly brigadier, three fellow colonels, one lowly and unctuous major, and George's young lieutenant. She had met two of the colonels before, and of course she knew the ubiquitous Kostas. She forced a smile as Yorgos pinched her cheek hard and puckered his lips in a *moue* that was a caricature of a kiss.

In the baritone barrage of familiar '*Yasous*' and even one solitary 'Hi' from the ingratiating major, Susie allowed herself only a fleeting glance at bald pates, thick glasses, and teeth in painful need of a dentist. One of the colonels wore sunglasses even in the middle of the night in this club. She heard a chorus of what she assumed were compliments about her addressed to Yorgos – all she could understand was '*Orea!*', which she knew meant beautiful – and she was embarrassed when the brigadier slapped her lover on the back in congratulation. She lowered her lashes and studied her glass of retsina. Once last month at this very club, she had enjoyed a brief but animated conversation in English with Kostas. But afterwards George had subjected her to a jealous interrogation that had reduced her to tears. It was safer to stay aloof and wait for time to crawl to dawn. She followed the lead of the others and lit another cigarette.

George was barking out orders at a convoy of waiters, and soon more bottles of retsina arrived along with a tray of glasses and bottles of soda and Coke. No sooner were the drinks poured than the starters arrived: three different yoghurty salads, feta cheese, olives, and bread. The fish and fried potatoes would inevitably follow in a quarter of an hour or so. Susie

214

understood eating late made sense in this hot climate, but she could and would not eat supper at two in the morning. Yet she picked at an olive and obediently opened her mouth as George fed her a forkful of feta. Just after the fish and chips were spread on the table, the lights dimmed and Manolis Chiotis and Mary Linda began singing. Susie liked the throbbing gut wails and infectious happy-go-lucky gushes of this particular Greek music. She leaned back, half closed her eyes, and opened them with a start some time later when the house lights came on again. Guiltily she glanced at George to see if he had noticed her nap. But he was deep in whispered conversation.

The waiters were clearing the dinner dishes and bringing more drinks. Two platters of fresh fruit – each grape or bite-sized wedge of melon speared with a toothpick – now also graced the table. Then came the flowers: red carnations, white roses, and even a fragile orchid were piled high on an aluminum dish, the stems cut short to the bud. She was mortified when George dragooned the waiter into replacing the red carnations with white ones. 'No Communist flowers at our table,' he told his approving colleagues.

Idly Susie reached out and toyed with a white blossom. The first time here, she had wondered if the Greeks ate flowers like after-dinner mints. She had heard that in India sometimes the natives munched certain flowers as a digestive, and she had just been about to nibble on a rose when the music changed and everyone leaped up on the dance floor. She had soon discovered that the flowers, like the piles of coarse crockery plates stacked nearby, were a sort of accolade to be thrown at especially graceful feet.

Yorgos was whispering to this one, grinning at that one, and all the while running a possessive finger erotically round the tasty young meat of Susie's shoulder. He was well pleased with who had answered his invitation this evening. As he exchanged conspiratorial winks with the three colonels, part of the great scenario to come, he wondered whether he should discreetly sound out the brigadier as to where he might stand if political and economic conditions in the motherland continued to deteriorate. Of course he would never be so crude as to utter even a syllable about business on a social outing like this. But perhaps he would invite him to an expensive taverna so he could drop a hint about the crying need for stability and discipline if this country were ever to be restored to its rightful place in the community of nations. The brigadier was a true patriot who had fought against the godless Communists in the Civil War. But just in case the slightest pink tinged his past, Yorgos stealthily had managed to take a peek at his CIA file. Except for the usual corruptions – accepting kickbacks from defence contractors, securing lucrative jobs for cousins and nephews, and enjoying an occasional holiday caper on a distant Aegean island with a girl whose fee had been paid by those seeking favours, the old boy was – as the Americans said in that quaint turn of phrase – 'as clean as a whistle'. It wouldn't hurt to have some of the brass on their side when push came to shove.

Yorgos' eyelids drooped as he reconsidered. The brigadier and those like him were old, jaded, and as compromised as the fatcat hypocrites who comprised the current government. Some of the blame for the dangerously leftward tilt of the nation could be laid at the doors of these corrupt senior officers who had betrayed the *patrida* by not defending it fiercely enough. In the very bosom of the army, a treacherous cabal of leftwing officers – *Aspida*, the Shield – had even been conspiring to subvert the nation. The glory days of the brigadier's generation were long past. Greece needed a transfusion of hot manly blood if it ever were to return to the glories not only of the Hellenic Classical Age but also the Holy Roman Empire of the East. The next time he got together with the boys, most probably he would recommend that these old warhorses be honourably retired at full pension. Better to keep the reins of power firmly in the hands of men virile enough to have and hold a nymphet like this Susie. When his hand tightened on the nape of her neck, he was pleased to see her obediently turn her head and look at him with what he took to be smouldering desire. Quick as a flash his own eyes darted around the table – had they seen? – and he exulted when he read the envy on his comrades' faces.

The stars were hitting their honeyed high notes, flowers were raining upon them from every table, and as the professionals swept offstage the band struck a foot-tapping bouzouki favourite that soon caused a stampede to the dance floor. '*Pame*,' Yorgos ordered as he pulled Susie to her feet. The colonel in the sunglasses seized her other hand, and up they went on the already crowded stage.

'Now try to get it right this time,' Yorgos hissed in her ear as he began leading his woman and the line of military men in a simple grapevine step akin to those Susie remembered from back in kindergarten. Cross forward, slide, cross back, slide, hop, kick, hold! Then again, the same combination, only faster as the catchy tempo picked up. They snaked around the stage, Yorgos embellishing the basic steps with occasional extra dips and kicks and lots of extravagant look-at-me wavings of his free arm.

For the first time since she had arrived at this club, Susie began to enjoy herself. When she had no choice but to listen to Greek music blasting on a taxi radio in the impatient heat of a traffic jam, these tunes could give her a headache. But as exuberantly she kept time to the beat, the pulsating music seemed to throb in her veins. Back, forth, up, down, kick! Now, this was as she imagined Greece would be! All around her, packed almost solid on the quivering dance floor, other weaving lines of dancers were at one with the music. She was laughing out loud, her eyes flashed as a darkly handsome young stranger caught her eye and winked, even these portly ageing officers were suddenly transformed into loveable old uncles. What was wrong with her, thinking such evil thoughts about these wonderful people who knew how to have such a good time? She loved them, and she loved Greece! 'Opa!' she exuberantly shouted. She wanted to stay in Greece forever!

Yet an instant later she faltered and missed a step when the sunglassed colonel let go of her hand and slipped his palm down on her backside. Don't get upset, she told herself as she felt his hand slithering over as much of her as he could seize. What did a friendly little pat on the fanny matter when everyone was having such a good time? Yet she hated being pawed by these dirty old men. When she missed another step because she was trying to wiggle out of the colonel's grasp, George jerked up her arm with the same gesture a master uses to curb a dog on a leash. Miserably she tried to keep on the beat, but it was no good any more. She couldn't feel the music, only that sweaty hand on her buttocks. But when in desperation she turned to George to beg him to make his friend behave, she caught him exchanging a sly look of conspiracy with his comrade. She wouldn't put it past him some night to try to get her to go to bed with one of his cronies.

As the roving hands of the sunglassed colonel played over her body, the interminable tune continued its plaintive Oriental quarter-tones. When George led them near the edge of the dance floor, Susie could see a Greek girl standing on a tabletop bellydancing like a slavegirl in a harem. As she shimmied, she let out a hair-raising howl that seemed to sound down from the four hundred long years when this birthplace of democracy was only a primitive backwater of the Ottoman Empire.

It was as hot as a sauna on the crowded dance floor. The satin dress was plastered to Susie's skin. She could feel the sweat running down her face and pooling under her breasts. Then she experienced a new worry when she felt herself almost bounce out of the front of her dress. She looked down in alarm at her bodice which had indeed slipped down a good inch. A few more kicks, and there she would be all out in the open. Oh, God, she prayed, please stop the music before I lose my dress. She let go of George's hand, tugged up the damp satin, and glared at the other colonel as she fled back to the table. She tossed back the full glass of wine. If George tried to force her back up on the dance floor, she would end it with him here and now and fly back home to the States tomorrow.

But she needn't have worried. The band struck up a slow moody melody, and the dance floor emptied as the merrymakers threw themselves back on their chairs and ordered more drinks.

Instead of resting with the others, however, Yorgos stood by the table and wiped the rolling sweat off his drenched face with a linen serviette. He paused only long enough to drain his glass before he seized a fresh napkin and, with the air of a three-year-old boy ordering his mother to witness a cartwheel or a magic trick, he told Susie, 'Watch now. This one is for you.'

Before anyone else could take centre stage in the spotlight, he was back on the dance floor improvising extravagant steps that only sometimes were in sync with the tempo and feel of the music. Like a bullfighter he waved his little napkin as he pirouetted, executed little running steps, and then bent and stretched and froze his torso in attitudes not so very different from a samurai swordsman readying himself for battle.

Lieutenant Kostas, never one to lose an opportunity to butter up the boss, leaped up and threw a rosebud at Yorgos' feet. 'Bravo!'

Susie lit a cigarette. George threw himself from one end of the floor to the other, panting as he kicked, brandishing his napkin above his shining bald head. When he tired of that, he simply roamed round and about the dance floor until he got his breath back. As he began a series of deep knee bends, Susie indulged herself in nasty little thoughts. How long could he keep that up before having a heart attack? Watching him, she couldn't understand why people said fat men made graceful dancers. He was puffing with exertion again, but instead of slowing down he crossed his arms on his chest and began kicking out one leg every time he squatted low. Incredulously Susie stared at this approximation of Cossack dancing. Any second now he would lose his balance and look very foolish when he landed on his rump. Instead, through dogged and heavy-footed persistence, he squatted and kicked faster and faster.

The approving onlookers were on their feet, clapping not in time to the music but on the beat of his kicks. 'Opa!' they shouted in encouragement. 'Ala!'

Kostas was back on his feet buying a vast stack of the plates the waiters had ready for such moments. He seized an armful, let out the sort of warcry that would freeze an enemy Turk's blood, and let them fly at the dance floor. As the plates crashed, Yorgos preened and kicked higher. The colonels got into the act. Some threw carnations, others hurled plates. When Kostas gallantly handed Susie a handful of crockery, grimly she smiled and threw them at her lover. No matter that her aim was poor and the plates missed their target. She reached for another armful of plates and pitched them. Take that, she said to herself. And that, and that, and that, until there were no more plates and she had to be content with roses, carnations, and orchids.

When the music finally stopped, Yorgos gratefully sank down on his throbbing knees and bowed to the wildly applauding crowd. A moment or two later, when he all but crawled back to their table to receive his friends'

218

congratulations, he kissed Susie wetly on the lips. 'Was I good, *glika*? Was I very good?'

'I'll never forget how you looked,' she truthfully answered. She made a point of glancing at her watch, which indicated nearly four-thirty. While he had been dancing, she had been formulating a plan to get out of here. It would never work simply to insist she wanted to go home, but she might be able to lure him out of the club by promising him another sort of diversion.

'I suppose you're tired.' He glared at her and looked back to the scene of his triumph. The sweepers were at work with their brooms, clearing away the broken shards that testified to his matchless grace. 'I'm the one who danced like the wind. But you're the one who's tired.'

She despised herself only a little as she leaned forward and smiled seductively. 'Not so tired as I'll be later,' she whispered as she blew in his ear. 'After . . .'

He laughed and said something that she guessed was coarse to his comrades. Immediately they all rose and hastily made their farewells. Impatient now to be gone, George waylaid the waiter and grandly threw a roll of banknotes on his tray. He whisked her out of the club and into the limousine the brigadier had obligingly loaned him. She cuddled close to him and was almost asleep before the chauffeur let out his clutch. She was so tired that she hardly felt George fondling her as the driver ran red lights all the way to her apartment near the Hilton.

But inside, when she snapped on the lights and shut the door behind him, she revived a little. She always felt better when she was double-locked at home. 'Coffee?' she said brightly as she kicked off her high heels so she wouldn't tower over him when they began the inevitable clinch.

'I'm not thirsty.' He took her in his arms. 'But I'm hungry.'

It was odd, she thought as his lips met hers, that – considering how angry she was at him most of the time – she turned to fire when he touched her. They devoured each other's lips as he unzipped her dress. Like a boy tearing open a birthday present, he peeled it roughly from her sweaty body. She reached up and took the pins from her hair so it fell loose on her shoulders, and then she stood back and let him look at her. She was wearing only the briefest of black lace bikini knickers tied at the hips with ribbon bows, an erotic birthday present from George.

'Where's the camera?' His eyes searched the shelves for the Polaroid he left here to record moments like this.

Throatily she laughed and lied. 'We're out of film.' She didn't like to think why he insisted on taking all those pictures and what he did with them after he left with them in his pocket.

'There it is!' He seized the camera and rummaged through a drawer until

219

he found one of the spare caches of film he had hidden there when she wasn't looking. Eagerly he loaded it and tested the flash.

'Not tonight,' she begged. She wrapped her arms around his neck and tried to kiss him. 'I can't wait. I want you now.'

But he shook her off and went back to readying the camera. 'First a few more pictures of my sexy girl.'

'But, George, I don't like them.'

'I do,' he answered, as if that settled the matter.

She tried to pick up the wreck of her dress and wrap it round her. 'It makes me feel dirty when you take them.'

'Good. That'll make you hotter.' Briefly he smiled. 'Now,' he coaxed, 'be a good girl. Put down that dress and get out the rug. I promise, it will only take a minute and then I can give you what I've been promising you all night.'

She grimaced at the thought of the thick white wool flokati she had bought for a song at a sale on Mitropoleus Street. The last thing she wanted to do, in the middle of this sweltering summer night, was let its scratchy sheep's wool touch her sweaty body.

'Just one,' he wheedled.

Once he got an idea in his head, there was no way she could win. Either she did as he wanted or they would have another of their fights. Then she wouldn't get any sleep at all, and when she went to work her face would be swollen from crying. Sulkily she got the rug out of the closet and spread it on the wooden floor. She stepped onto it. 'OK, take your damn picture.'

'First lie down.'

Gingerly she knelt on the rug. 'This is as far as I'll go.'

'Hmmm. Not bad, not bad at all.' He aimed the camera but then lowered it. 'But you'll have to spread your legs.' She scowled and moved her knees only a centimetre apart. 'I said, spread them!' When she remained immobile, he strode over and jerked her thighs wide apart. 'Yes, yes, like that. Now don't move.' He sprang back and snapped the shutter just as she thrust out her lower lip in a pout. 'Nice,' he said, 'but there's something wrong with the breasts. You'll have to lean forward more.' Before she could scramble to her feet he had slightly hunched her shoulders so her breasts swelled forward. 'Yes, yes, now hold it like that.'

'You said only one photograph.'

'One, two, what does it matter?'

She supposed he was right, that it didn't matter now that she had gone this far. But it seemed he wanted even more.

'Now, one more thing. Your hand's wrong. Put it there, just inside, in the front.'

'Oh, George, no!'

'Please? Just for me?' He came back, picked up her right hand, and pushed it deep inside the crotch of her panties. Unhappily she stared at the camera. 'Now pucker your lips. Yes, like that, beautiful!' He snapped a few more shots. 'Now untie the knickers.'

Tears spilled down her cheeks. 'I can't. I won't. I just can't. I hate it when you make me do this. You make me feel like a prostitute.'

His eyebrows arched in surprise. 'You really don't like this? Other girls – ' He caught himself just in time, and regretfully put down the camera. Some men found tears erotic in pictures like this, but for him the shoot was ruined. Another time, he thought, perhaps on the beach, yes, the next time they would drive north and find a deserted beach. But he'd have to get her drunk first. Champagne, that was it. One bottle between them, and she'd do whatever he wanted. She was difficult like this only when she was still too sober. Maybe he had made a mistake, ignoring her tonight after his associates arrived. But what could he do? Business was business, and pleasure was pleasure. At that thought, as he looked at her kneeling before him weeping, his groin tightened. The pictures could wait. 'My poor baby.' He unzipped his trousers. 'My poor little sexy baby.'

She knew what that deep rasp in his voice meant, so she wasn't surprised when he undid his belt and advanced just in front of her. More than anything, he liked it when she kissed him there. She wiped her tears away with her bare arm and shut her eyes as he thrust himself between her lips. She had grown to like this, too. He moaned, fell forward and tore the ribbons that held together her knickers. In a second he was inside her, pumping hard, while his lips were at her throat and then sucking on her nipples. Wildly she clutched him closer. She had taken a lover or two before him, but none of them had possessed her like this. It was worth all the humiliations and tears just to have him beating inside her. She writhed on the hot wool rug with her legs wrapped around his waist. '*Orea*,' he gasped. Still inside her, he slid his legs down the length of her, shifted his weight backward, and pulled her torso up by the arms so they were sitting face to face. Back and forth he rocked, pressing in deeper. The sweat was running down their bodies as they stared into each other's eyes. Her breathing got more ragged, she could feel herself on the edge, she went over, she groaned as tiny shivers of vibrations shook her insides. She was so far gone that she didn't hear him whisper one word. 'Marika . . .'

Susie would have liked to fall back on the rug and sleep for an eternity, but instead he was egging her on to another height. He leaned way back so she was the one on top. Her tiredness forgotten, her pelvis thrust in a lungeing rhythm, slow at first, then faster and faster until again she convulsed.

'Three or four?' he finally asked, for he loved to keep count.

'Six,' she lied, although it was only two. If she were to get any sleep at all, he would have to finish it off soon. But he wouldn't leave her alone, she knew, until he had bested last week's record.

'So many!' He laughed out loud as he pumped inside her. 'So sexy!' He was thinking of himself more than her.

She knew the end was near when once again, without slipping outside of her, adroitly he managed to be back on top. He seized an ankle, propped it up on his shoulder, and then did the same with the other. He sank in her so deeply that at first it hurt. But as his momentum increased, she passed beyond pain. They thrashed on the rug as together they mounted to a crescendo. As he came shooting inside her, he cried out something in Greek that she didn't understand.

She was asleep before he pulled out of her. Silently he padded off to the bathroom to wash and dress. When he came back and looked at her splayed out naked on that rug, he gave into temptation and took another picture. He pocketed tonight's set of photographs, which were some of her best. Thoughtfully, before he locked the door behind him, he took her alarm clock from the bedroom and set it down beside her so she would get up in time for work.

An hour and a half later, as a fly was biting at her crotch, Susie woke before the alarm sounded. She brushed away the fly, sleepily scratched her arms that itched from the rug, and sat up and looked around. The wispy lace of her black knickers was beside her, and the Polaroid camera was pointing at her where he had left it. Her head ached, and she was drenched in perspiration.

Groggily she stumbled into the bathroom. As the clean jet of water washed over her body, she made a snap decision. Enough of this love-hate relationship with George and with Greece. She would get out today, before she had a chance to change her mind. She towelled herself dry, marched back to the salon, and threw the camera down on the wooden floor so hard the lens shattered. Hurriedly she dressed and packed two suitcases of clothes. The rest – the cheap porcelain vases and ashtrays she had bought in Plaka, the semen-stained flokati rug, the plastic worry beads and the thumbed guidebooks – she left where they were. She didn't need souvenirs to remember Greece. When the alarm clock rang, she turned it off and then switched off the telephone bell as well. She couldn't risk a call from George.

She was at her desk well before her boss and typed out a terse letter of resignation which she left in his 'in' box. Next she cleaned out her desk, checked to see that her passport was in her purse, and took a taxi to the Olympic Airways office in Syntagma Square. She was lucky to get a seat on the early afternoon plane to New York, but she would have to spend a night in a hotel there before she could make connecting flights to Chicago and on to Iowa City. She paid with the Bank of America credit card her father had given her for emergencies. Next she ducked across the square to the bank and drew out the balance, thanking her lucky stars that she had kept her money in a dollar account so that she didn't run foul of the arcane Greek currency restrictions against taking drachmas out of the country. Back at her apartment, she scribbled a note to her landlord saying she was breaking her lease. He could apply her two months' security deposit to her electricity and telephone bills and pocket the remainder.

Susie wandered out on her balcony and listened to the honking of horns and the buzzing of motorbikes. This morning, as on so many other summer days when there was no north wind, a pall of heavy pollution lay heavy over the city. Sometimes from her balcony she could glimpse the Acropolis and a glimmer of the sea, but today she could hardly see the apartment block on the other side of the street. Then she recalled something she had almost forgotten. When she had announced, all starry-eyed, that she was off to Athens to make a new life, her partially senile old grandmother had not been impressed. 'Grease? That doesn't even sound nice.' Perhaps old granny hadn't lost her wits after all.

Finally she telephoned her boss. She said she was sorry to be leaving him without notice, but it was either that or risk a nervous breakdown. He was more sympathetic than she had expected, for he said he had been expecting something like this. She burst into tears because he was so nice. So *American*.

Before she could change her mind, she took a taxi to the airport. She mailed the letter to her landlord, bought a one-day-old *Herald Tribune*, and sat absorbed in it in the departure lounge.

She was the first passenger on the plane. After take off, as they circled the city before heading west, she leaned at the window in the hope of catching a last glimpse of the Acropolis. But smog veiled the city. For her, even to the end, Greece remained elusive. All she could see through her tears was brown earth, blue sea, and blinding sun.

Nine

'The military-industrial complex initiated this war, and continues to foster this war, to provide markets for its arms and a reason for its own being.' The Harvard professor at the podium consulted his notes on the geopolitical realities that had impelled America into the Vietnam War.

Before he could continue, a student lolling on the Harvard Yard lawn jumped to his feet and began waving a placard. He could recite all this like Sunday school catechism, and as one of the committed he could not contain his enthusiam while the professor gathered his woolly thoughts. 'Stop the war machine!'

On the podium behind the speaker, awaiting his turn at the microphone, Christos leaned forward and gave the long-haired student leader with the red scarf wound across his brow a quick V-sign. He himself was one of the regulars at antiwar rallies, teach-ins, and speak-outs all over New England, and a fortnight ago he had shared a ride to Amherst with this young history major from Michigan. Josh was his name, yes, they had joked about his someday sounding a trumpet and the walls not of Jericho but the Pentagon falling down. For three hours they had talked and laughed, and at the end Josh had hugged him and declared that he was 'all right, man, all right!' And then, still holding Christos tight, he had mumbled that he wished he could find the same sort of understanding with his father: 'All he does is tell me to cut my hair, and stop all this hippie stuff, and change my major to business administration so I can be ready to come to work in his factory. Cars! I want to make a new world, and he wants me to make Fords!'

Ah yes, Christos thought, smiling down at the youth who so reminded him of himself twenty years ago. Some things, and most people, never change. He was forty-five years old, and even now he still felt the push and pull of generational strife with his own father. It wasn't that Nick wasn't proud of the way his son's political career had blossomed. Eleven years ago, when Christos had first made a name for himself championing human rights in the American Civil Liberties Union, Nick had carried around newspaper clippings testifying to his son's growing fame. And then, when Christos had won a hotly-contested seat on Boston City Council six years ago, Nick had done everything but hire a skywriter to emblazon the vote count on the grey

224

Boston sky. And yet, Christos reflected as he looked down at that student who had had tears in his eyes when he had talked of his skewed relationship with his father, it was still one of the disappointments of Nick's life that his elder son had chosen politics over the family business. 'Mark my words, Chris,' his father was wont to say over a late night ouzo in his boomingly successful waterfront restaurant, 'your politics are going to get you in the end. One day people love you, and the next day maybe they hate you. But they always have to eat, and they'll come to my place so long as I have the freshest fish in town. And what are your votes compared to money in the bank, land, a business with your name on it? Security, that's the ticket, not your fine words and big smiles and those popularity contests you seem to think you'll always win.'

In the Kronos family, it was not only brother against brother but – sometimes, despite Christos' best intentions – son against father.

Josh grinned back at him and raised his clenched fist in a power salute. 'Right on!' he yelled, more in approval of Christos than the government professor who was making an abstruse point about Great Power responsibilities during the nuclear age.

Christos crossed his hands in his lap and pretended to focus his attention on the speaker's abstractions. But inwardly he basked in the student's adulation. He took pride in the fact that he was as *simpatico* with this passionate young generation of student activists as he had been twenty years ago with his guerrilla band of *andartes* in the Greek mountains. With the campuses on the boil in this long hot summer of discontent, one of the favourite student slogans was, 'Don't trust anyone over thirty'. Yet even though he had weathered into early middle age, he was one of the local gurus of the Resistance movement. He spoke at student rallies, sat up half the night at bull sessions in the dormitories, and even from time to time gave the young folks advice on how to conduct faltering love affairs. Even more than the working-class voters who had elected him to the town council on the Democratic ticket, he thought of these students as his natural constituency.

The professor mopped the perspiration from his face and continued with his speech. As Christos listened to the teacher pressing all the familiar buttons – 'imperialism', 'racism', 'Third World hegemony', and 'the right of the people to refuse to participate in an unjust war', his eyes trailed over the sea of sunburned young faces before him. The girls, as though this were some Hindu festival on the banks of the Ganges rather than a political rally near the banks of the Charles, were colourfully turned out in halter tops, miniskirts, and Indian costumes fitted with mirrors and beads. The long-haired boys wore the modern jeans-and-T-shirt uniform of the young, and some had their guitars resting beside them on the grass. As they listened, a few licked ice-cream cones and many lay back and lazily flirted with one another in the sun.

Christos gazed at these golden children. If, as some said, this new movement were a revolution in the making, mostly it was a gentle one. These three hundred or so students were some of the best and the brightest young minds in the country. A decade ago, in the nose-to-the-grindstone fifties, they would surely have bought into the American drive for material success that had so seduced Christos' own father. Like Nick, their primary concerns would have been landing lucrative jobs so they could buy lavish houses, run powerful cars, and assure themselves a lifetime of consumer bliss. Instead, these students espoused the same idealistic values that had sent him to fight against the Nazis in his own flaming youth.

Remembering those long-ago nights when he had sat around the mountain campfires dreaming with his comrades of a better world, Christos felt the old adrenalin surge through him. The dream had been betrayed in Greece and elsewhere, but perhaps it would become reality here in this goodhearted country where he, too, had come to have faith in the credo that all things were possible to a man of goodwill. Looking out at the rapt faces before him, once again he thrilled to the possibilities of this committed generation. These kids who had cut their teeth on the civil rights marches in the South and come of age demonstrating in the streets against the Vietnam War were capable of transforming the richest country in the world into the noblest one. And yet sometimes he worried that in their young innocence, they, too, might be as easily betrayed as he and his own kind had been back in Greece. He had never forgotten those hard lessons he had learned, to his great cost, in the crests of the Peloponnese.

It was hot on this early September afternoon in Harvard Yard. But remembering that last winter of disillusion in the mountains, Christos shivered. The best and the brightest of his own generation had lost almost everything that mattered in life because they had been betrayed not only by the Soviets, the British, and even the Americans but also – deadliest of all – by their own *naiveté*. In the seventeen years of his exile, he had thought long and hard about why the Communists had lost the Civil War, and had concluded that their ruthless methods and impossible ideology had doomed them to what Trotsky, in altogether another context, had once called 'the dustbin of history'. As fervently as he had once believed in the doctrines of Marx and Engels, his own life experience had turned him just as passionately against those who had exploited those stirring ideas into a new kind of tyranny.

Christos' political about-face, however, was not shared by all the other *andartes* exiles. In his first years in America, occasionally he had been visited

226

by old comrades. It had chilled him to wonder how they had known where to find him. Had the Party sent them to sound him out? If so, he had given earfuls to report back to Moscow. When the one-time comrades broke open the raki, Christos had tried to wake them from the dream. 'Look at Albania,' he would say, 'and Bulgaria and even Yugoslavia. Don't fool yourselves. If the Communists had won in Greece, you'd be eating grass in Athens. And Greece would just be another downtrodden Soviet Balkan republic.' If by then, he and the old comrades had still been on speaking terms, Christos would concede that Western military aid had been the *coup de grâce* that sent the *andartes* into what appeared to be permanent exile. 'But,' he would always add, 'the Soviets bear an even greater bloodguilt.' At Yalta Stalin had cut a separate deal with Roosevelt and Churchill, and in the end the Soviet dictator had sacrificed Greek Communism – and Greek Communists – for free rein in the rest of the Balkans. And then, he had always added, there was the matter of our own fratricide. Remembering that last cadre meeting in Tripolis, Christos would pound the table until the glasses fell and broke into shards as jagged as his own disillusion. 'Is a slit throat in a back alley a socialist solution to a disagreement about party tactics?' In the last few years none of the old comrades had come calling. But on the last visitation, Christos had been surprised to hear himself talking like an American politician instead of a Greek revolutionary. He supposed that was what he was, now. In his own way, he was as much of a successfully transplanted immigrant as his father.

He snapped to attention as the professor relinquished the podium and, before the moderator could introduce him, once more the irrepressible Josh was up on his feet. 'One, two, three, four,' he yelled in the cadence of a cheerleader at a high school football rally. 'We don't want your goddamned war.'

At once the densely packed throng of students sitting on the grass in front of the speaker's platform lustily took up the chant.

As the students kept up their rhythmic chorus, Christos once again studied the girls with their flowing hair and their tanned lithe legs and the boys with their downy beards and their lean surfer bodies. They were as ardent about their beliefs as his comrades had once been, but they were different from those young men and women who had taken to the mountains to fight what they had so believed was the good fight. As he looked out at the childlike American faces – fresh, trusting, unmarked by life's scars – in his mind's eye once again he saw the visages of his comrades: the dark deepset eyes that had seen too much, the scornful lips sealed against crying surrender, the old faces on the young bodies, many destined not to live until middle age. He had never stopped wondering what had happened to those comrades. Many of those who had survived that last bloody stand had disappeared behind the Iron Curtain. Was their idealism intact now in their coldwater socialist flats? And what of those tens of thousands captured by the triumphing rightwing forces and subsequently imprisoned in bleak Greek island concentration camps? Christos ached for the flower of his generation, plucked from the stony Greek soil in the spring of their youths. What had happened to them must not happen to these young Americans.

But he supposed, after all, that this crowd before him was cast from a different mould. Flower children, they aptly called themselves. Instead of having to give their schooldays a miss when they were needed to harvest the olives or pick the oranges, they had grown tall and strong in the privileged suburbs of Middle America. They were rich kids, most of them, and what they knew of the world's suffering came from books instead of the streets. They had never looked into the real-live face of evil, and yet in their confident *naiveté* they were sure they would be able to refashion the world into something wondrous. He supposed what he most loved about these kids was the innocent purity of the revolution they meant to wage with good intentions, folk songs, and those rosebuds he had once seen a beautiful girl sticking into a soldier's rifle barrel at an antiwar demonstration. Being around them renewed his faith in the goodness of man and the eventual triumph of the forces of light.

Christos came out of his reverie just after the moderator had concluded his introduction and the students had begun a howl of approval. His wife got unsteadily to her feet. 'Penelope Heywood Kronos!' The moderator helped the very pregnant speaker adjust the microphone up to her level. She was five feet ten in her stocking feet, and today she was wearing a new pair of stack heels she had bought in the shoe salon at Bonwit Teller's. Turned out in a strawberry pink maternity dress, with her long blonde hair streaming down her back, she looked like a well-groomed American version of a fertility goddess: Mother Earth speaking out against the war.

Penelope grinned as she searched the crowd for familiar faces, waving at this one, nodding to that one. She had been lecturing in American history here at Harvard for the past fifteen years, and she was as practised at public speaking as she was at vegetarian cookery and baking wholemeal bread. 'I wasn't sure I'd be able to make it today,' she began. Wryly she patted her bulging stomach. 'I thought I might have a more pressing engagement.'

As the students goodnaturedly laughed, Christos took his one-year-old daughter Helen onto his lap and held eight-year-old Sofia by the hand. He had insisted on following the Greek tradition and naming the first girl after his mother. He had been willing to call the next one after his mother-in-law, but laughingly Penelope had said – and her mother had concurred – that one

228

Millicent in the family was enough. When tentatively Christos had suggested his stepmother's name, his wife at once had agreed to the American version of Eleni which was also the name of her own recently deceased grandmother. The women in his wife's family were all larger than life. Her old dragon of a grandmother had been a suffragette, and his mother-in-law was capable of scaling any mountain and fording any stream on her archaeological expeditions.

Speculatively Christos sized up the bulging belly of his ready-to-deliver wife. Would this next one finally be a boy? *My son.* He doted on the girls, but as he had tried to make Peppy understand when he had talked her into having Helen as well as the baby she was expecting any day, a man wanted a boy, too. As a Greek, deeply rooted in his genes was the need for a son to carry on not only the family name but also perhaps his own unfinished work. He had so much to share with his unborn son; simple things like how to predict the morning's weather from the way the night wind was blowing over the Aegean and complex matters like how to chart an ethical life's course. Last week, as part of his assiduous politicking, he had stopped for a duty call at a Greek Orthodox church, the heart and soul of the Greek-American community. Nick had long been a stalwart of his Boston congregation and a heavy contributor to the scholarship funds, church refurbishment drives, and every cultural and social date on the calendar. Since Christos' political career had begun to flower, he, too, had become a familiar face in church circles although not so often at services. But last week, when he had gone looking for the *pappas*, the church had been empty except for a bent old widow in black. From habit more than devotion, he had gone through the rituals of obeisance, crossing himself three times and then kissing the hem of the robe of a jewel-encrusted icon. For the first time in a long while, a certain mood had stolen over him as he stood in that darkened church, sparkling with silver and gold, with the smoky scent of incense in the air. Greece, he thought, oh my country! Then, as he had lit a candle in memory of his mother, he had gazed up at the dome where a fresco of Christ glowered in the shadows. He was not a religious man, and yet he had been shaken by an impulse to fall upon his knees. A son, please, he had prayed. I've lost so much that counted in this life, but at least give me a son. He had been surprised when he had felt tears on his cheeks.

Christos affectionately ruffled Sofia's blonde hair and held Helen more tightly in his arms. It was different with girls than boys. A son was for the continuation of the family and the pride of the race, but daughters were simply to love and protect forever. Guiltily he reproached himself for not spending more time with his family. Before I know it, they'll be wearing the marriage crowns and then having children of their own. But I'm out every

229

night. If it's not one of these antiwar speeches, it's a Greek-American souvlaki dinner at a neighbourhood association, or somebody's uncle's cousin's wedding at the Orthodox church, or a Democratic party get-together, or simply a late-running meeting of Boston City Council. But he always found it easier to say no to Peppy and the girls than he did to any one of a number of strangers whose pull on him was more political than personal.

Beside him Sofia was joining in the antiwar chant. Even though Christos despaired that his blonde and rosy daughters were going to turn out far more American than Greek, he took pride that at least in this matter of politics they were destined to be chips off the old block. At this antiwar rally, as on so many speaking engagement in this action-packed year before he hoped to launch the next big leap in his career, the four of them were a family act. Sometimes they even brought their golden retriever dog. Zoi, too, knew how to wag her tail on cue.

At the rostrum Penelope was getting set to deliver more than the usual homespun sentiments of the youngish candidate's wife. As she was fond of pointing out to Christos, she had been active in the Democratic Party while he was still harpooning fish back in his dearly beloved village. Then, and always Christos refrained from correcting her romantic and very mistaken ideas about the life he had lived before he came to his adopted country. He had always been more a fisher of men than *barbouni*. But the less Peppy – and most especially everyone else – knew about his Communist past, the better. He hadn't exactly lied about his activities against the Nazis in the Greek Resistance, but he hadn't told the whole truth about what had come after, either. The Americans never would understand how it had been in that time and place. To them, Communism was the Red Menace, and they couldn't distinguish between the ideals of pure socialism and the realities of Soviet totalitarianism. Better to keep the dead past buried than to risk being hounded out of public office by the kind of Red-baiting hysteria that Senator Joseph McCarthy had trademarked a scant decade-and-a-half ago.

'I want to talk to you today,' Penelope was saying, 'not just about American imperialism in Vietnam, which I think we all know and agree about.'

'End the war!' Josh once more shouted.

'Yes, yes,' Penelope nodded in accord. 'By all means, right now, end the war!' Feistily she raised her right fist as the students cheered. When they quieted, she went on. 'But once that war is ended, we will find, my friends, that our struggle is only begun. The enemy is not only the military-industrial complex who profit by the war machine. The enemy lurks within. We will have to continue to fight to achieve true racial equality, to conserve the environment, and to assure our brothers and sisters in the Third World the same economic, political and social opportunities we enjoy here in America.'

As Christos joined in the applause for this formidable woman who was as much a star of the antiwar movement as he was, he studied his blonde Amazon of a wife. She was half a head taller than he was, and although Christos would never admit it sometimes her size and her ebullient self-confidence made him feel less a man than an uncertain boy struggling on tiptoe to match wits and measure up to this intimidating creature. He supposed, fleetingly, not wanting to probe too deeply into this matter which Peppy carped on too often, that this might be at the root of what his wife seemed to think was his low sex drive. She had been so different, he thought longingly, when he had first met her teaching his history class at Northeastern. Before giving birth to and nursing the girls, she had been as slim as a reedy boy. He had liked her body better then than as she was now, with those melon breasts and strident hips. But after Marika, he hadn't wanted – and he still didn't want – another primal woman. All *that* had finished on Carnival night in the cave. With an effort Christos turned his thoughts away from his first love. Although he could have slept in a different woman's bed every night in the week – these girls, these beautiful young girls, maddened a man with their musky talk of free love! – he had always been faithful to Peppy. Once – briefly, burningly back in Greece – he had loved too much and lost too much. With Peppy he had yearned for the coolness of ethereal shade instead of the passion of scorched earth. Instead it had been his fate to marry a rampant tigress who all but raped him some nights. Would she never let him take the lead in *anything*?

But as he watched her work the crowd, Christos had to admit that whatever the problems in their marriage, Penelope was a definite political asset. She was smart, tough, and she knew everyone who counted not only in the Yankee blueblood world of Old Boston but also in the brainy liberal élite of the Cambridge academic establishment. Moreover, she took great gusto in getting up on a podium and speaking her mind. Still, something in Christos recoiled at the sight of so pregnant a woman raising her fist and sweating like an orangepicker in the sweltering late summer sun. The Greek in him could not help thinking that his wife should be confined at home, sitting in the shade sewing baby clothes as she waited for the blessed event. He shuddered to think what Eleni would say if she could see her stepdaughter-in-law right now.

Under his breath Christos sighed. Why worry about the absent Eleni, when he shared her conservative opinion? This morning, at the elegant Neoclassical Back Bay townhouse her father had given her – not *them* but her, it still rankled that like everything else the house was in her name only –

they had argued whether she should brave the sultry ninety-degree heatwave for another of these student speak-outs. But she had insisted on standing up and being counted, especially here on this campus. Her father had been on the Harvard faculty as long as she could remember, and she had passed her undergraduate years at Radcliffe, Harvard's sister school, before taking her graduate degrees here in the history department. 'When we're invited home to Harvard,' she had said with finality, 'we go together as a family.' After eleven years of marriage, Christos had observed the firm set of her jaw and known better than to continue to argue. He – and she – were so conscious of the high cards she held in their marriage game that it was never necessary for her to remind him that she had brought money, connections, and political clout to the nuptial bed. Much like politics, marriage was a web of compromises. But he had to admit that even these relatively sophisticated Harvard kids warmed to the all-American image of the glamorous candidate who went everywhere with his superwoman wife and adorable children. Penelope was one of the darlings of the Boston media. She was always good for a snappy quote or an endearing photograph. She loved rallies, parades, and even the most tedious ground-breaking ceremonies for roads and hospitals. Sometimes Christos wondered if she should be running for office instead of him. She was as charismatic as her uncle, the soon-to-be-retiring US Congressman whose seat Christos hoped to inherit.

'And there is,' Penelope was saying, 'another issue – and another enemy – that we, someday very soon, are going to have to face.' Earnestly her intelligent eyes raked the crowd as she prepared to get to the point of her speech. 'I mean women.' She flexed her arm in imitation of a bodybuilder. 'Our not-so-much-weaker sex.' Very briefly she smiled. 'I mean the world-wide exploitation and domination of one half of the human race by the other half.' There were scattered groans from the male students in the crowd, but Penelope silenced them with one steely flash of her pale eyes.

Christos kept his face attentive and approving, but inwardly he seethed. He had asked her before not to depart from her prepared text with all this tiresome new talk about women's rights. The struggle was to end the war in Vietnam and, not so incidentally, to get him elected to Congress. Nobody but a few frustrated spinsters wanted to begin a new war between the sexes. Feminism wasn't a popular issue, you could see that from the dubious looks on the faces of students like Josh. But, as usual, his independent American wife did as she liked. For a brief but terrifying instant, Christos imagined this woman who was already too strong, and far too opinionated, and altogether too bossy, accomplishing the mysterious task of what she called 'liberating' herself. Maybe she would grow seven feet tall and be elected President of the United States. Most definitely she could do the job better than Lyndon

Johnson or any other male politician of his acquaintance. Still, it wasn't right, how aggressive she was not only up on this podium but when they were in bed together. He had been born to believe, and he still believed, that a man dominating his wife was the natural order of things. Yet here he was, married to a woman whom it would be impossible to look down upon even if he were as tall as she was. He remembered wondering, when he had first met her, lecturing cold as ice in that history class, what it would be like married to a woman as strong as she was. Now he knew.

Penelope was now hotly into her theme. 'I am talking about the exploitation of women. We must begin the struggle to liberate half the human race! Break those chains! The bondage of Third World women whose minds and bodies have been enslaved for almost forever. Vietnamese women holding their napalmed babies. Indian and African and South American women who have never had a chance to live with dignity and hope.' She leaned forward on the rostrum. 'But let's not get complacent. Women are subjugated here in our own country as well. Here, in the land of opportunity, women are paid less for doing the same jobs as men. They, like blacks, are the last hired and the first fired. We must initiate and legislate equal opportunities for women, just as we have fought – and sometimes won – equal opportunities for our black brothers.' As she spoke, Penelope tried to catch the eyes of the girls in the audience, and when she succeeded sometimes an electric current seemed to pass from the woman at the microphone to the girls on the grass.

Watching that, and suddenly understanding what it might someday mean if women like Peppy had their way, Christos looked with new respect – almost awe – at the wife he had never been able to master. A shaft of insight as blinding as the white light of a July Greek noon shot through him. Theoretically she was right, of course, why had he never seen it before? This issue of hers that he had ridiculed so much had in its way the same sort of burning revolutionary potential as Marxism once had. *To liberate half the human race* . . . The humanist in him had to admit that this cause she was championing was just. If he had been born a woman, he, too, might want to turn the world upside down as she proposed. Yet he was a man, and he didn't like this talk of a revolution that would reach even into his own beleaguered bedroom. He didn't want to risk tearing asunder the everyday fabric of family and social life. And he supposed, not only in his heart of hearts but lower, where his manhood lay, that he didn't want to share the power of his sex with any woman. For the first time in his life ruefully he understood how the rich must feel when they hear the poor screaming for a piece of the economic pie. Why should he surrender what he had so this other could have more? He not only liked things the way they were between men and women but wished his own wife were a lot less uppity. Still, he couldn't help reluctantly admiring the pure radicalism of his wife's political acumen. She could think for herself, this woman, and she had the soul of a hero. Once again he had underestimated not only her but the fire she was trying to kindle in the young women whom just now she was calling, with the same tender timbre in her voice that she used on the children, 'sisters, my sisters.'

The girls were on their feet, cheering this feminist call to action with a fervour more intense than they usually showed at antiwar rallies. Never one to miss a golden opportunity to up the political and emotional ante, Penelope held out her hand to Sofia and scooped Helen up in her arms. Pregnant and glowing, with her daughters she came forward on the platform like a Shakespearian actor about to take a bow at Stratford. The cheering increased. Girls were hugging one another, grinning, all but dancing for joy. Penelope, her daughters, and the girls in the crowd all at once were celebrating one another.

At this magical moment when he witnessed his pregnant wife trying to midwife a new political movement, Christos truly loved this woman. What did he care that he could never dominate her? Can a man tell the sun or the wind what to do? Can he make a tree grow white leaves or rearrange the stars in the midnight sky? Perhaps it was enough just to love the sun, the wind, the trees, the stars, and this startling woman who succeeded in being both so tender and so strong. Maybe, he thought with growing excitement and even a reassertion of his bruised ego, the fates had known what they were doing when they brought the two of them together. It was possible that, if only he could be as true to himself and his ideals as she was to herself and her dreams, then this woman could be his perfect match. He had almost always been more passionate about his politics than his emotional and physical needs. Back in Greece that night when he had stolen away from Marika, he had betrayed the one he had always considered the love of his life because he had believed that the political must always be more important than the personal. Now here, too, in this brave and thoughtful wife, was a kindred spirit capable of the same sort of sacrifice. And yet he wondered if it could be dangerous that the soul of a man lurked inside the body of this woman. Odd, he thought, that I would think of that just now, when I love her more than ever. A foreboding passed over him. Someday Peppy might do to him what he had done to Marika. Was this to be his destiny?

Anxiously he looked back at his wife. But the moderator was at the microphone, and she was gratefully plopping back in her seat. Oblivious to the heat and the mound of her belly, obligingly she let the girls crawl all over her. In an instant his crusading revolutionary of a wife was transformed back into the eternally serving mother. Radiantly Christos smiled at the women in his life. What was wrong with him, imagining that wild nightmare a moment ago? His wife was the very picture of gentle domesticity. On the way to the podium Christos leaned over and tenderly stroked the damp hair back from Peppy's temples. He blew a kiss to his wife and his daughters. And then he turned to the waiting students.

'Chris Kronos!' The crowd was on its feet, cheering.

Christos felt the power surge through him as he stood at the podium. As always, his wife was a hard act to follow. After that womanly call to arms, almost anything he said would be an anticlimax. But he was seized with a sudden inspiration from Greek mythology. He would tell them about Kronos. Not the part every Greek schoolboy knows, about Kronos eating his children. He wasn't about to draw *that* parallel, but another.

'Let me tell you, my young friends, a story that I first heard from my father when I was a little boy, back in Greece.'

'Yes, tell us a story, Chris!' The irrepressible Josh was egging him on.

'It is a story as old as the birth of the world, and yet it is a tale with particular relevance today, when we have assembled to fight the good fight against war, racism, injustice.' He turned and smiled at his wife. 'And sexism.'

'Right on!' The students settled down like the good children they still basically were to listen to the story.

'Long, long ago,' Christos recounted, 'at the birth of creation, the God of the Sky mated with the Goddess of the Earth. Their child Kronos – my family name, which, spelled a little differently, is the Greek word for time – was born, and for a while the world was in harmony. But the skygod Uranus was a tyrant, and like all tyrants – like maybe even our current tyrant Lyndon Johnson – one day he went too far when he waged an unjust war against his own children.'

'Hell no,' Josh yelled. 'We won't go!' The throng of students smiled as one. Already they could tell they were going to like the point of this loose interpretation of the ancient myth.

'So what happened way back there in Greece,' Christos continued, 'was that Mother Earth told Time to bring down the Sky. She gave her son a sickle cut from the moon, and with it one night he snuck up on his father and castrated the Sky.'

'Let's cut off Johnson's balls!' Josh seemed eager to follow his mentor's advice, and at once, not only figuratively but literally.

Christos laughed as he held up his hand to quiet the cheering crowd. 'As Uranus lay dying, blood that dripped from his mortal wound fell into the foam of the sea, and Aphrodite the goddess of love was born. But the struggle didn't end there. After the death of the sky, the world was rent by a

235

great and horrible war. Only after Kronos' son Zeus finally put down the forces of evil was a new and just reign established atop Mount Olympus. Greece, born of the strife between the sky and the earth, man and woman, finally entered its Golden Age. From tyranny was born the struggle, and eventually not only the triumph of freedom but also the birth of love.' Christos paused significantly. 'One of the many morals of this story is that it is possible for you, the modern children of the eternal Mother Earth, to follow the example of Kronos and end the rule of those who oppress the human spirit. It's time, people, it's time! Together we can do it. We can end the war and refashion a brave new world based not on tyranny but on justice.'

'Kronos!' Josh's face was ashine. 'It's time for Chris Kronos in Congress!'

'It's time,' Christos said, 'to do what we were born to do.' Without missing a beat, he began to deliver the speech he had rehearsed about how and when and why to end the war.

As Christos rushed into the hospital room, Penelope was sitting up in bed, one arm around her newborn suckling infant, the other hand cradling the telephone. 'Right, Emily,' she was saying. 'Next Tuesday, that's the twenty-third, in the student union at Columbia. First the speech, then lunch, then the seminars. Got it.' She rested the telephone for a moment on her neck. 'Chris! About time!' She waved to her husband but then put the phone back in place as intently she listened to whatever was being said on the other end.

Christos stared at his wife and the baby. When finally Nick had tracked him down late this morning in Roxbury, his father had only said that Peppy was in labour and would probably deliver sometime this afternoon or evening. He had thought there was no hurry, and so he had finished his inspection tour of the Boston housing developments. I should have come right away, he told himself. I promised her that this time I would be here when she needed me. All those natural childbirth classes, all that practice panting together, all those good intentions about being witness to the miracle of birth, and there I was looking at toilets in a slum when my wife was bringing our child into the world.

At that thought, Christos' eyes focused on the tiny dark head sucking at Penelope's full white breast. He caught his breath. *My son?*

Penelope's booming voice gave him the answer. 'And Emily? One special request. Don't book me too tight that day. I'll have to have time to nurse the baby.' She listened a moment. 'No, not Helen. The little girl I had this morning.' She laughed, 'Yes, yes, I'm fine. And she's beautiful, Emily, really beautiful!'

Christos' shoulders sagged with disappointment. Another girl. Three girls and no boys. Yorgos has a son, but I have only daughters. His brother would have a good laugh once he heard this news. Back in the village, the fellows always made fun of a man who could sire only girls. If a man in Panagia produced only daughters, the coffeehouse consensus was that he wasn't sexy enough to produce real children. But I'm not back in the village, Christos told himself sternly. I'm a modern, educated, naturalized American citizen. I adore my two other daughters, and I'll love this one, too. Yet he had been born and raised in the village, and it was easier to get a new passport than it was to cast away all the old ways. It took every bit of his practised self-control to beam his candidate's smile at his wife and his third daughter.

He was grateful, as he leaned over and gave Peppy a perfunctory kiss, that she was still engrossed in that telephone call. Carefully he drew a chair close and used these precious moments to pull himself together and master his emotions. He had been in America and married to Peppy long enough to know that it would never do to let his disappointment show. Back in the Greece he had left long ago, his wife would be cowering in her bed and his family would all but be in mourning for the birth of a third daughter. Is it the same there now? Christos wondered. He had been away for so many years that sometimes he feared even his memories were warped by time.

As he tucked his misgivings deep inside, his eyes trailed around the sunny hospital room. The bureau, the bedside table, and the rolling food tray were all crowded with expensive arrangements of flowers. There was a heart-shaped gold foil box of imported chocolates on the other side of the bed, and piled by the window were a stack of magazines and today's newpapers. He must have been the last to learn of the birth. On another chair he could see Nick's briefcase, Penelope's father's attaché case, and an expensive black alligator tote bag that could only belong to her mother. The rest of them must have ducked out for a moment. Any time now, Peppy would get off the phone and the others would come rushing back. He must ready himself for performing the role of proud papa.

Glumly, with veiled eyes, he watched his wife still absorbed in the telephone that here, too, seemed grafted to her ear. Any other new mother would be lying back on the pillow, exhausted by her efforts. But Peppy looked as fresh and rosy-cheeked as though she had just awakened from a good night's sleep. When he had left home at eight-thirty this morning, she had already been on the telephone arranging something. In the intervening seven hours she had given birth and immediately resumed her telephone duties. Peppy was extraordinary. She had the Yankee pedigree to prove that she had been born to rank and status, but she was as hardy as a nineteenth-century Greek peasant woman who squatted in a ditch to give birth before

237

she continued to harvest the artichokes. He eavesdropped for a moment to her end of the telephone call. As she nursed the baby, she was booking herself into an antiwar conference in New York scheduled for five days from now.

Christos pursed his lips. Back home in Panagia, a woman didn't even leave the house until the baby was forty days old. Perhaps that tradition was a bit extreme, but surely it would have been more seemly for his wife to postpone her activist duties a while longer. What was he going to do with this woman? If a man couldn't control his own life, was he truly a man?

With trepidation Christos finally dared to look over Peppy's shoulder at the baby. His wife was right, she was a pretty little thing. Not red and wrinkled as the others had been at first, but as golden-skinned as the apricots he had picked long ago on fragrant early summer mornings in Greece. Some of his resentment ebbed. Her hair was different from the others, too. Sofia and Helen had been born with downy yellow hair like Penelope's but this one had a real mop of black curls. Greek, he thought, oh, thank God, this one looks Greek! Eagerly he leaned forward to check the eyes fringed in long black lashes, but they were closed in ecstasy as the baby sucked. Christos ached to take this precious flesh in his arms. What had been wrong with him a minute ago, gnashing his teeth at the injustice of being saddled with a third daughter? He laughed out loud as the baby's lips let go of the nipple, and she gurgled and smiled and fell sweetly asleep.

'Yeah, all right, see ya!' Penelope blew a kiss into the telephone. 'Peace, sister!' She handed the receiver to her husband and grinned down at the baby in the crook of her arm. 'Isn't she wonderful?'

Christos sat on the edge of the bed. 'Yes, oh, yes!' He opened his arms. 'Let me hold her.' As Penelope handed her over, the lines in his face eased and he let out an exclamation of bliss. She was so soft, this baby, so perfectly formed. Tenderly he gazed upon the face of the one he would cherish and protect all the days of his life. Her eyes opened. 'Blue!' Again the stab of disappointment.

'All babies are born with blue eyes.' Penelope was coolly matter-of-fact. She had so wanted him to be here for her in the delivery room. But as usual, she and her needs had come second to his other commitments. As he mumbled some excuse about why he hadn't made it to the hospital until now, she debated whether to make an issue of his late arrival. But then she decided, at least for the moment, that it was better to say nothing. Later, if he gave her trouble about her reasons for wanting to name the baby after him, she would wheel out the big guns. These days, as he waited for her uncle to give him the political endorsement that was his heart's desire, Christos was especially careful to stay on her good side. He hardly ever gave

238

her a hard time about the hours she spent running hither and yon on political errands. He didn't raise an eyebrow when the nanny executed most of her motherly duties. He rarely complained when she served him prepackaged frozen dinners. Best of all, he finally had learned to shut up about how a true Greek wife would act. It wasn't easy being married to a man from such a different culture. She kept telling herself that one of these days she would have to take the children home to that village of his so she could see for herself how things were in that heaven-on-earth he never stopped raving about. Strange, she thought again, that for someone so homesick he always flatly refusd to go back for a visit. Moreover, he wouldn't even discuss the reasons why. Chris could be so open and charming with total strangers, but even after so many years of marriage she sensed that he still walled off his deepest emotions from her.

Yet as Penelope watched her husband caress their baby, she could not stop herself from smiling. As usual, she was quick to anger but fast to forgive. Altogether forgetting was another matter, however. Yet Chris was so good with the children. Just now he was gazing at the infant as though he were the first father in the world and she the first baby ever born. He was so over-the-moon adoring with the baby that once again she felt herself falling back in love with him. She had waged a battle royal with her family to marry Chris, and once she would have done – and had done – anything he asked. She had gotten him his first job at the Civil Liberties Union and then talked the powerbrokers into letting him run for City Council. But for her as for most women she knew well, some of the lustre of her love had dimmed in eleven years of marriage. Yet despite all the miscommunications and failed expectations of their union, still it felt glorious to present her man with this perfect child. At her age, she had worried about birth defects. 'Often a baby's eyes change colour later, honey. Maybe she'll still have your beautiful green eyes.'

'I'd like that, too.' What was it that moved him so about this baby? He had loved the others, of course, but somehow he understood that this one would be a true Greek. Sofia and Helen were little Americans, but this one was born with the light of the Aegean in her eyes and the hot bright Greek sun on her skin. 'My little baby,' he crooned under his breath, first in English and then in Greek. '*Moraki mou.*'

'I've thought of a name for her.' Penelope was regarding him closely as she braced herself. She could have postponed this inevitable confrontation, but she preferred to face it head-on. Naming the baby after him would surely soften the blow. But even if he didn't want to hear what she was about to say, this particular issue was non-negotiable. She wasn't a baby machine; she was a human being with other needs than being a wife and mother. All right, yes, she still loved Chris. But their marriage was an equal partnership and not some primitive Greek autocracy in which he was the master and she the slave. She was well aware, although to his credit he had never said too much about it, that her husband had longed for a son. Yet she could discern no trace of disappointment on his face. Chris was a poor man from a backward country, but he had class. Even though tender feelings for her husband were welling up inside her, however, she warned herself not to give way when she told him how it would have to be.

'I suppose you'll want to call her after your mother,' he said absently as rapturously he examined her exquisite fingers and toes. 'You know you should have named the last one after Millicent. My stepmother was scandalized when you didn't.'

'Yes, well . . ' Penelope leaned over and popped a Godiva chocolate into her mouth. Once again she thanked her lucky stars that except for old Nick, who was a darling, his whole bossy tribe of a family was a world away. She had never met the rest of them, but she was sick to death of hearing Chris worry about what they'd think and say about every little thing. That village of his sounded like it had more social controls than a police state.

She was ravenous, so she ate another chocolate. If Nick and her parents didn't come back soon with the takeaway, she would eat this entire box of candy. 'You know how my mother feels about that. "One Millicent in this family is enough."'

Christos nodded noncommittally. He could tell by the look on Peppy's face that she was about to come up with something he wouldn't like. Maybe she had some weird feminist name in mind. He wouldn't be surprised if she wanted to call the infant 'Man', and be done with it. Or perhaps she wanted to name the baby after someone else in her family, which most definitely ran to girls. Long ago Christos thought he must have met them all, but every year she introduced him to a new one. In addition to her two sisters, her mother had four sisters, her father had three, and she had great-aunts all over New England. He supposed he should have expected, with her genes, that she would have producd a third daughter. But the next one, he assured himself, would have to be the long-awaited son.

'So I was thinking about another name.' She paused until she had his full attention. 'Christina. I want to name her after you.'

'After me?' Christos wrinkled his brow. 'That's a nice thought. But why?'

This was the dicey part. 'Because I think, really, Chris, that this has to be the last one. And I wanted her to have your name.'

'The last one,' he repeated.

'Yes.' Just as always happened when she hit a nerve, his face closed shut against her. 'I mean,' she continued, 'three's enough. I only wanted one, as

240

I'm sure you remember. We waited seven years between Sofia and Helen. But I knew you wanted a son, so finally I gave it another go – not once but twice. Even with the nanny, though, it wasn't easy for me after Helen came. It will be harder now, with this one. I mean, I have my work. The speeches. And I'd like to write a book, Chris. The women's movement needs – '

'I don't care what the women's movement needs. Your work is being a wife and mother.' In his anger, he was holding the baby too tightly. She awoke with a wail, and despite his best efforts he couldn't quiet her.

Penelope took the infant and settled her back at her breast. The wife and husband glared at one another as the baby suckled.

'Look, you've had a hard day,' he finally said, but grudgingly. He was sick of always giving in to her. But she *had* just come out of labour. 'This is neither the time nor the place to talk about this.'

But here and now she wanted to go to the wall. 'I disagree.' Her eyes were steely. She would play hardball if he forced the issue. 'I've already talked this over with everybody. My parents, my sisters, Uncle Jonathan . . .'

At the mention of the retiring Congressman who could make or break his political career, Christos' eyes narrowed. But ambition locked his jaw shut.

She knew she had won, and yet she couldn't resist needling him some more. He had sorely hurt her when he hadn't cared enough to be by her side in the delivery room. 'Sometimes,' she purred, 'my family is very close. Not like *your* family, of course. We're not *Greek*. But we can stand together, too.'

Christos lit a cigarette to keep the hot words from spewing from his mouth. He hissed out the smoke as covertly he studied his wife. She was the very picture of maternal caring as she nursed their newborn, but he wouldn't put it past her to throw a wrench in his political career if he crossed her on this one. He had to have her uncle's political endorsement or he didn't stand a chance in the party primary. But did she expect him to barter his chance for a son in order to get it?

Penelope's anger ebbed, and the vulnerabilities she had been hiding came to the fore. 'I'm sorry, Chris.' Her voice cracked with emotion. 'I know how you wanted a son. I thought, this time, that I'd finally manage it. But I guess a boy just wasn't in the cards.' She bit her lip. 'Everything else aside, I'm nearly forty. This time we just slipped under the wire. But you know the statistics about birth defects in women my age. We'd better stop now.'

He recognized the finality of her words and let out a deep sigh from the gut. What could he say to that final plea? But why couldn't she have put it that way in the beginning? Did she have to rub his nose in the fact that, even if it weren't for the biological clock, her work came before him and the children? And did she always have to remind him how beholden he was to

241

her and her family for his political advancement? But he stubbed out his cigarette and bowed to the inevitable. 'Christina.'

'I wanted to please you, Chris. In something, anyway.'

Before they could say more, they heard Nick approaching down the corridor at high decibel. 'All the way to Kenmore Square in all this traffic, crawling every foot, and then I get a parking ticket, and for what? Garbage! She wants to eat garbage! *Big Macs!*' The way he said it, it sounded like a curse. 'All the good restaurants serving all the good food right around the hospital – or I could have sent down to my place for something beautiful, souvlaki and salads, something *decent*, but instead we go to Kenmore Square for these terrible *biftekis*.'

He and Penelope's parents rushed in the door with armfuls of white and gold McDonald's bags.

'Ah!' Nick cried. From afar his grumblings had sounded bad-tempered. But when he saw his son and the baby, his face shone with a kind of ecstasy. 'Christo!' For once, as Nick took his son in his arms, he forgot to call him by the Americanized version of his name. His eyes filled with tears as he thumped his son on the back. 'She is beautiful, eh, our girl?' Nick didn't seem to mind that his new grandchild was a girl. As he managed to hold both his son and his granddaughter in his arms, he all but danced around the hospital room with the generations in his grasp.

As though they were sitting in the stalls at a second-rate theatre, Penelope and her parents silently watched this latest display of overblown Greek emotions. And then, as Nick's kissing and hugging and endearments showed no sign of abating, the other grandfather picked up the telephone and dialled his office. Millicent broke open the McDonald's bags and efficiently laid out the food on a rumpled corner of Penelope's bed.

Penelope took a chocolate milkshake and greedily bit into a Big Mac. 'He's agreed to everything, Mummy.'

Millicent frowned at her daughter. 'Don't talk with your mouth full. It isn't done, Penelope.' Disdainfully she looked at the cheap, greasy food. She had raised her daughter to be a real lady, and she had never understood where she had picked up this peasant zest. First she had married this Greek immigrant, and now she seemed to have acquired other regrettable tastes. She could understand her daughter adapting to primitive customs as she herself did when she was in the field – say, in Iraq or on the Turkish coast excavating a temple. But in Boston one lived by certain *standards*.

Penelope swallowed, cleared her throat, and repeated her news. 'He's agreed, Mummy! Christina it is.'

'Splendid.' Millicent had been afraid either that Christos would take this news about no more children badly or that he would insist on some outlandish Greek name that no one could pronounce. She took a tentative sip of her vanilla milkshake, and her eyebrows arched in surprise. 'This isn't half bad, you know?'

'Not bad? They're terrific!' Exuberantly Penelope sucked down the thick shake. 'Good for keeping up my milk production!'

'Breastfeeding,' Millicent murmured. 'In my day, that wasn't done, either.' She sighed quietly, then took another thoughtful sip of the milkshake. 'Will we call her Tina, then? There was a girl in my boarding school class called Tina. A big girl, very horsey, but she came from a very good family. Virginia bluegrass, I think. She married somebody in shipping. I hear she lives on Sutton Place now.'

Penelope bit into a french fry, chewed it carefully, then gave her mother her best all-American smile. 'Her name is Christina, and that's what she'll be called. To Christina!'

The two of them touched their plastic milkshake cups together in a toast to this next generation of liberated Yankee women.

The five men in their tailored dark suits sat seemingly at ease in the stockbroker's office. Only Christos chainsmoked Camels. The rest had nicotine, and all other unseemly addictions, entirely under control. It was four o'clock in the afternoon, and they were having tea which had artfully been wheeled into the conference room on a brass trolley by a secretary who held a PhD from Harvard. Only Christos was drinking coffee. The rest of them drank Earl Grey laced, English style, with milk.

The four others – Penelope's father Henry the professor, her Uncle Jonathan the Congressman, her first cousin David the banker, and her second cousin Jason the stockbroker whose State Street office this was – silently watched Christos ladle three spoonfuls of sugar, Greek-style, into his black coffee. He looked up and caught them regarding him as though this were some curious exotic ritual they had read about in anthropological journals. 'Gives me energy,' he said. 'I'll need it for the race.'

The others smiled thinly at his presumption as they sipped their English tea. They had come together to make their final choice of who would be their favoured candidate to fill the seat of Penelope's Uncle Jonathan when Congressman Heywood announced he wouldn't be standing in next year's elections. Of course the position was not exactly theirs to dispose of within the family, as they would a deceased aunt's Revere teaset and Chippendale chairs. They would forward their recommendation to the other Democratic party bosses, then, in the spring primary election, anyone who wanted could have himself listed on the ballot. But in fact if not in theory, these men in the

243

dark suits were the powerbrokers who would decide who went to Washington next year. Jonathan Heywood's seat was from an overwhelmingly Democratic district, and after his thirty-four years in Congress he still carried political clout. He had secured federal jobs for two generations of Boston workers, he had gotten favoured sons appointed to the military academies, he had fixed this and adjusted that, and so no one was going to deny the old man the right to appoint his successor. A cynic might point out that, perhaps even more importantly than sentiment and obligation, what mattered was that his relatives the banker and the stockbroker were heavy contributors to the Democratic Party warchest. Just to be on the safe side, they contributed to the Republicans as well. But in his youth Jonathan had bucked family tradition by enlisting with the Democrats, and so the Heywoods had spent more than a generation solidifying their power in that party. Deciding who would take Jonathan's seat was a family affair.

'So,' Jonathan finally said after some amiable chat about summer holidays on Nantucket and 'Downeast' in Maine, 'shall we get on with it? We have a Congressional seat to fill.'

'Not that anyone could really fill your shoes,' Penelope's father Henry quickly said. He had spent a lifetime bowing to his older brother, and he was not about to break the habit now. 'You don't have to retire, you know.'

'Ah, but I'm seventy-one.' Jonathan smiled deprecatingly.

'There are plenty in Congress older than that.' Though he was Protestant, not Catholic, David the banker also knew how to genuflect. 'Men with experience and wisdom. Men of vision.'

'Men with power.' Jason the stockbroker was not one to mince words. 'You're the chairman of the Armed Services Committee. If it weren't for you, Massachusetts wouldn't have all those defence contracts. Once you go, that's the end of the pork barrel for us. We all know you could have had a Senate seat years ago, but none of us wanted to sacrifice your committee chairmanship. Maybe we shouldn't now, either. Your successor will be a freshman Congressman with no seniority. It will take years – no, decades – to work our man back in place. Think about it, Uncle Jonathan. There's no reason for you to retire . . . prematurely.'

It's only a ritual dance, Christos assured himself as he stubbed out his cigarette and mastered his desire to light up another immediately. The old man won't change his mind and run again. In a moment they'll stop this bowing and scraping and get down to the reason we came here today.

He kept his face composed as he gazed out the floor-to-ceiling windows at the breathtaking view of downtown Boston and the harbour. On the River Charles, tiny sailboats flitted in the wind. The gold dome of the State House glittered like an Oriental mosque. Red and yellow paper kites glided above the trees of Boston Common. Silver planes buzzed in a swarm around Logan Airport, the Mystic River Bridge crouched like a medieval dragon, and as far as the eye could see the navy blue sea sparkled under the sunny New England sky. From up here on the twentieth floor, the city's skyscrapers and motorways seemed insignificant children's toys. Yet it grated on Christos that even in this land that rightly took such pride in its democracy, a congressman was being chosen not by those antpeople down in the streets but these four pompous men in their expensive suits. They sat here like gods on Olympus, deciding the fate of mere mortal men. And of me, Christos thought. Although he took care to hide it, he resented that, too. After so many years of working so hard, all that mattered was his standing in the family clan. Today, here, now, they had the power to bestow or deny what he so dearly wanted.

'No, no, I tell you.' Jonathan was speaking with finality. 'It's time I got out. Catherine and I want some good years to ourselves. I appreciate your trying to talk me out of it. But gentlemen, the answer is no.' He smiled at Christos. 'It's time now for the next generation to take over. And we should make the decision today, so we can get cracking on the run-up to the campaign.'

Four pairs of small grey eyes focused on the man their headstrong Penelope had insisted on marrying. At the time, all of them had been against this *mésalliance*. They had always supposed she would marry a Harvard or Yale man from a good new England family, someone reliable and predictable, someone exactly like themselves. Instead she had chosen this Greek opportunist who they suspected had wanted Penelope Heywood more for her connections than for her intrinsic goodness. The years had not changed their impression that Chris Kronos was a man on the make. But he had been a good boy nonetheless. He had proven himself a devoted family man, and he was a Herculean worker at every task the party and the clan had assigned him. He knew how to play ball with the big boys, and there was no reason to believe that he would forget the ground rules and play his own game once they gave him a starring role of his own. All these factors weighed to Chris's advantage, but the most telling point was that he was Penelope's husband. He had not been born in the family, but he was family.

'So you want to go to Congress,' Jonathan purred.

'I do, sir, yes, I do.' Christos smiled sincerely at these unsmiling Yankees. He had the uncanny feeling that instead of sitting in this penthouse power centre he was back under a spreading poplar tree trying to convince the sceptical *kafeneion* regulars that he was something other than what he was. Just as though he were back in Panagia, where even a man from two villages away was considered a suspect foreigner, nothing he could ever do would

245

earn the absolute trust of these ruthless patricians. Yet he was not some hapless peasant begging a boon from the pashas. His record in public office was exemplary. He knew he cut a dashing figure in all the right liberal circles. And he, just as well as they, had read the glowing newspaper features that called him 'Boston's Golden Greek'. More to the point, there was no one else in the family to fill the seat. They might play cat and mouse with him awhile, and they were sadistic enough to want him to beg for their favour, but in the end he knew and they knew that this candidacy was a foregone conclusion.

Henry cleared his throat and went in to bat for his son-in-law. As though this were some weighty academic matter that needed documentation, methodically he began listing Christos' qualifications: his record with the ACLU and on Council, his media image, his untarnished character.

David the banker cut in. 'What about the Greek vote? We know about the Irish vote and the Italian vote and even, these days, about the black vote. But maybe Chris can tell us if there is such a thing as a Greek vote that would be a factor in the final electoral tally.'

Christos spread his empty hands and shrugged. 'There are Greeks in Uncle Jonathan's district, of course, as there are Greeks all over New England. Mostly the poor ones vote Democratic and the rich ones Republican. But always they vote for another Greek whenever one runs. Generally, however, except in Lowell where generations of my countrymen worked in the textile mills, Greeks have not tended to cluster together . . . in ghettos.'

'Actually,' Jason the stockbroker mused, 'except for Cousin Chris, I don't really know any Greeks. No, I'm wrong. My wife buys cakes at a Greek bakery down on Kneeland Street. And there's a shoe repair shop down on the corner that I think is owned by a Greek. Shoeshine boys, yes, we always used to say Greeks were the best shoeshine boys in the world.'

'That's exactly right.' Christos knew this was not only damning his countrymen with faint praise but also blackening himself in their eyes as a jumped-up shoeshine boy who had risen above his station. Jason personified the fatcat capitalist caricatured in Communist propaganda films, but he would do his best to turn the stockbroker's slur into a plus for himself. 'My father started out just that way, shining shoes on Boylston Street. And look at him now, the most successful restaurateur in the city! But my father isn't so unusual. Greeks are rugged individualists. As soon as they came to this country, they went into business for themselves. Sweet shops, shoe repair shops, flower shops, and of course the restaurants. They work hard, save their money, and they take pride in being patriotic Americans. Next to the Jews, Greek-Americans have the highest income and education levels of all the ethnic groups in this country. But above all, Greeks are canny business-men who know how to turn a profit. You know what they say. "The only one who can outfox a Jew about money is a Greek. And the only one who can outfox a Greek is an Armenian."'

Dryly these White Anglo-Saxon Protestants laughed. It pleased them to think that Penelope's husband could outfox even a Jew. As one, mentally they thanked God – who, of course, had to be an Episcopalian – that at least their kinswoman hadn't taken a fancy to one of the tribe of Israel. Even Jason gave Christos a reluctant smile of approval. He, too, might be able to do business with this Greek who was nobody's fool.

David shot the next question. 'One thing I've never asked you about is details of your war record.'

Christos blanched, but before he could answer his father-in-law cut in. 'I told you, Chris was a bit of a hero, fighting in the mountains against the Nazis. That's quite a point in our boy's favour. You remember how John Kennedy made hay on that U-boat thing. They even made a movie about it.'

David brightened. 'You have any stories like that we can use in the campaign? Blowing up Nazi bridges? Rescuing innocent women and children from the Gestapo?' He had sat out the war as an officer training troops in Texas, but he loved war movies. 'Something like *The Guns of Navarone*, maybe.'

'Afraid not.' Christos thought of the bleak camps in the snowy mountains, the comrades bleeding to death because there were no doctors, the villages burned down not for military or political reasons but because of ancient family bloodlusts. Remembering, he could almost hear the moans and feel the tears on his cheeks. For him, that World War which had turned into a heartbreaking Civil War was not a cinematic adventure but a national tragedy that had blighted not only his own life but that of his homeland as well. 'I was just in the war,' he said. 'Like everyone else in my country.'

'But there must be something we can use in the campaign,' David persisted. 'Think, Chris! Some battle. You know, something heroic.'

Christos tried to smile modestly while inwardly he prayed that they would let him off this uncomfortable meat hook that could spell the end of his American political career. He longed for a cigarette but dared not betray his nervousness by lighting one. None of them knew of his former Communist affiliations, and they had better never learn of them. Yet he had worried for years that, even though so many records had been lost during the war back in Greece, the truth someday would come out. When he first had become active in politics, he had feared that Yorgos might try to sabotage his new career. But he had breathed easier when his brother had continued to remain eager that everyone back in Greece think him dead. As time had passed, he had come to believe that if nothing had come to light so far, there was no reason to believe it ever would.

Luckily for Christos, the Congressman himself came to the rescue. 'I wonder, I wonder . . .' He had only been half-listening to this tiresome talk of war exploits, and now he leaned thoughtfully back in his recliner chair and touched the tips of his fingers together as was his wont when an idea occurred to him. For a moment he rocked back and forth as the others patiently waited for pearls of wisdom to fall from his famous lips. Finally he sprang forward, 'Maybe we've overlooked the obvious. How about Penelope herself?'

'How about Penelope, what?' Her father frowned. *Now* what did his demanding brother want his daughter to do?

'Why, run for Congress.' Jonathan beamed at the others. 'She's a natural. Smart, beautiful, and she can always wrap the press around her little finger. I don't know why I never thought of it before. I know I would have, if she had been a boy.' He and Catherine had no children, and he had always fondly regarded Penelope as his heir apparent. 'But now, maybe, with all this talk about women's rights, perhaps it's the right time for a woman in the family to take over. She'd win if we ran her. I'm sure of it! And then we could keep the seat *really* within the family.'

Christos managed to keep that unctuous smile on his face, but inside his stomach churned. He had worried a little about a prominent Irish lawyer from South Boston and a lot about a Beacon Hill blueblood who was rich enough to spend a million dollars on the campaign. But competing with his wif had never crossed his mind. Penelope in Congress? His wife snatching that coveted seat out from under him? All at once he knew he had lost, and for good. He would end his days as the pet poodle of the female Congresswoman from Massachusetts.

But it seemed Christos had panicked too early.

'I don't know,' her father was saying. 'God knows I think the world of my daughter. But you all know how she can be. Do we really want her in Congress?'

Her cousin the banker laughingly mopped his brow. 'She'd shape up Washington in no time, that's for sure.' He turned serious. 'It's an intriguing idea, Uncle Jonathan. Perhaps in five years, ten years, if this women's thing gets out of hand – '

Jason interrupted. 'Let's hope *not!*'

As all the men laughed, David continued with his thought. 'As Cousin Jason has said so aptly before, none of us wants a government in skirts. But who knows. Maybe women's rights might take off like civil rights did. If it does – God help us! – then maybe we could give old Penelope a go. But now there are still a lot of voters who wouldn't want a woman representing them in Congress.'

'Frankly,' her own father said, 'I'm one of them. Maybe I'm old-fashioned, but I think a woman's place is in the home. Penelope's got the children to take care of, and now, with the new baby . . .' He shook his head. 'Sorry, Jonathan.'

Sagely Jason nodded his concurrence. 'It would be taking a chance.' From his inflection, clearly that judgement was most damning. 'I've never been one to speculate in futures, myself. I like sure things. Bluechips, always. Do we really want to take a chance with *our* Congressional seat?'

'I suppose not.' But Jonathan looked glum. He was accustomed to getting his own way, and he didn't like it one bit when the fellows staged a mutiny. 'I still think she would be a helluva Congressman.' He gave Christos a frosty smile. 'You've got some wife.'

This time Christos did not have to force his smile. The danger now was past, and he hadn't had to say a thing. 'It's like being married to Wonder Woman.'

Jonathan hid a yawn. Now that they had vetoed his idea of running his niece, he wanted to go home to his wife, who never disagreed with anything he said. 'So!' He turned to Christos. 'It looks like it's you, my friend, after all.'

Christos smiled in triumph. 'If you're saying that you want me to run for your congressional seat, then I'm honoured, sir. Honoured.'

With that settled, they shifted gears to what had to be done in preparation for next year's race. Christos would immediately resign his seat on Boston City Council, put the Back Bay townhouse up for rent, and take up residence across the river in Jonathan Heywood's congressional district. Everyone agreed that leafy, sedate Concord would be an ideal place for Penelope and her family to resettle. Cousin Jason's sister-in-law was the best real estate agent in town, and she would start showing Penelope her choice listings that very weekend. Christos meanwhile was to continue his high-visibility antiwar speaking engagements and at the same time begin making the rounds of all the party associations, lodges, and union gatherings in the district. From now until election day, the media would assiduously be cultivated. One month a reporter would be persuaded to write a Sunday supplement feature on the Kronos family at work and play. A little later Chris would write a guest editorial on something of great import to his district. Perhaps Penelope would make an appearance on one of those women's afternoon magazine shows on television sharing some homely recipe for quiche or cookies. Hints, rumours, and speculation about the coming campaign would be planted with all the 'insider' columnists. And every once in a while some shining journalistic light would be granted an 'exclusive' with the new rising star of the Democratic Party from Massachusetts. Finally, just after the first of next year, Congressman Heywood would hold a news conference to announce that Chris Kronos was his own personal choice in the coming election.

I'm in, Christos exulted to himself. Nothing could stop him now.

Ten

In the dimly lit cellar music club in Athens' Plaka, Nikos and his friends listened raptly to the long-haired guitar player in the black turtleneck singing not the usual sappy sentiments of love gone wrong but his own soulful song of lives gone astray. Yiorgos Zografos reached the winter stars in his lyrics. The composition's complicated chords and sophisticated strumming were part of the avant-garde *Neo Kyma*, the 'New Wave' of Greek music performed in these bohemian *boîtes* where the knowing young gathered into the wee hours.

Nikos, dressed like the other regulars in black sweater and black trousers, concentrated on the musician's hands, and as he listened his own empty fingers picked out the tune. When he got home, he would try to replicate the sound on his own guitar.

The musician sounded a final chord and bowed his head. At the tightly-packed tables the in-crowd signified their approval of his performance not by clapping their hands but by tapping their thumbnails together, so that even their applause had a world-weary sound. The coolest of the girls varnished their nails black to heighten the effect.

'*Pame*?' As Nikos put his cigarettes in his pocket, his friends got to their feet. It was late, well after one. But when they got outside and breathed in the balmy spring air, they looked up at the bright stars in the Mediterranean sky and decided it was not too late for another coffee in one of the open-air cafés in nearby Syntagma Square.

Before long they were hunched over the bitter grounds of their expensive but tiny cups of *metrios* at the tables looking out at the street, the park, and the floodlit cream-and-yellow parliament building. It was a quarter to two in

250

the morning, and still this pulsating centre of the city did not sleep. In the sidewalk cafés that ringed the square, knots of young Greeks smoked and drank as they whiled away these last moments until it was time to call it a night. A young man stood outside a kiosk accosting stray foreigners: 'You speak English? You want hotel? Tour? Good tour to Delphi. Or maybe you want Mykonos?' A few feet away two other lads tried their luck picking up the occasional tourist girls who strolled by sampling Athens by night. The traffic, thinner by far than the usual bumper-to-bumper logjam, whooshed by with horns hooting, brakes screeching, and radios blasting. Neon lights from the banks and airlines glared, the fountain splashed, and a few tired men and women in seedy work clothes waited on a nearby kerb for the all-night bus to Piraeus.

Drunk with talk and high on caffeine, Nikos listened to the others enthusing about their first visit to the *boîte* Nikos had been promising to take them to for months. They raved about the music, speculated about the cosmopolitan older girls who flocked there, and could hardly wait to tell their other friends at school tomorrow how they had glamorously passed this night of nights. But, as the conversation shifted back to what they had been discussing before their visit to the club, Nikos made an impatient cutting gesture with his hands. 'So, Stavro, what will it be? You will marry this girl, or not?'

Five pairs of caring eyes watched Stavros shrug. As always, he was reluctant to say or do anything without the approval of his comrades who were dearer to him than brothers. 'What do you think about Nadia?'

The table all but exploded as each voice sounded. No one listened to anyone else. Indeed, no one could hear anyone else. Bemused, Stavros looked from one to the other. Babis was laughing as he wiggled his hands in a crude approximation of the way the girl in question walked. Dimitrios was shaking his head and rubbing his index finger to his thumb as a reminder that she had no money. Grigoris, who had always thought Nadia a snob, had his finger eloquently held to his up-turned nose. Nikos and Alkis were doing their best to drown out the others with a high-decibel argument in which even the soldiers guarding the Tomb of the Unknown Soldier at the other end of the square must have been able to hear not only from Nikos the words 'beautiful' and 'clever' but also – most damning of all comments from the jealous Alkis, 'she goes with everyone'.

Nikos had been the seam binding together this company of steadfast friends since primary school, and now he brought the palm of his hand sharply down on the formica tabletop. In the electric silence that followed, he pronounced his judgement. 'She is a good girl. Pretty. Kind. Everybody likes her.'

'Not everybody.' Alkis, whose father owned a sweet shop where he himself now worked afternoons and evenings, glowered once again as he remembered how Nadia had turned him down two summers ago when he had invited her to the cinema. Always he had suspected that she would have eagerly accepted his invitation if his father had worked in a bank like Dimitrios' or was an officer in the army like Nikos'. It only added insult to injury now that he went hither and yon with Stavros, who only aspired to be a cab driver like his father. Yet he smiled as though bygones were bygones. 'But you're right. She *is* beautiful.'

'Maybe too much.' Dimitrios repeated what his father often said as he looked at his careworn mother. 'It is better not to marry a pretty woman.' He grinned and made a joke in the English they all had studied in high school. 'That is, unless she is pretty rich, too.'

They laughed as though they were experienced men of the world and not just seventeen- and eighteen-year-olds who, despite their best efforts and exaggerated claims to the contrary, had never managed to do more than steal a kiss or two on a dark balcony when they thought no one was looking.

'So, Stavro!' If his friend wasn't serious about this girl, Alkis might try again himself. 'You want her forever?'

Again Stavros shrugged, but this time he pushed back his chair as though about to leave. 'It's late. We'll talk about this another time.'

At once the others reached out, pulled him back into their charmed circle, and made ready to change the subject. None of them wanted to go home just yet. It was better to linger here for another hour. Then two by two they would climb onto their black Solex motorbikes and cling together for dear life even for the short ride home to Pangrati. As they buzzed past the familiar landmarks – the fragrant sprawl of the National Gardens, the peach glow of the Zappeion palace, the stately ancient columns of the Temple of Zeus, the white stone shell of the Olympic Stadium – they would feel so intoxicated by spring and youth that they would execute exuberant and noisy figure-eights the length and width of the boulevards. It was wonderful on the motorbikes late at night, going fast, with the wind ripping through their hair and the moonlight casting shadows from the old marble pillars that still testified to the glories that eternally would be Greece.

'Relax. It's early.' Nikos lit another cigarette, reluctant to leave the snug embrace of this easy camaraderie. Together, always together, the six of them had spun out the easy hours of their childhood and adolescence, the companionship as steady and nurturing as a cane is to an old village grandfather. For a Greek seldom chooses to be alone. In a Greek dictionary the closest definition for 'privacy' – *moaxia* – translates as 'loneliness'.

As the others, too, lit up their Assos *sketos* unfiltered cigarettes, Nikos

252

sang under his breath – '*I Margarita, I Margaro*'. The rest of them chorused the next lines of the popular Mikis Theodorakis song: '*Peristerati ston ourano*', 'A Little Dove in the Sky'. Always these boys were in perfect harmony.

Nikos smiled benevolently at the members of his *parea*, his company of friends, who in their way were as essential to him as his family. He supposed that next autumn, if he passed his examinations and qualified for a coveted place in the polytechnic's prestigious Architecture School of Athens, he would make other friends who shared his interests in music, art, and politics. But the élite students at the polytechnic could never transcend his *parea*. When the boys got together to talk – and they talked even when they had not much to say – there was a shared history not only in everything they said but also in what they did not have to say. They knew one another's uncles and aunts and even second cousins, they had gone along on Easter and summer visits to their families' villages in the provinces, they could recite chapter and verse of what had happened seasons ago when together they stole grapes from a neighbour's arbour or stole glances at nearly naked tourist girls on a beach. For all their lives his company of friends would always ring one another up on their namedays to wish '*Chronya polla*'. And when someday they got married, they might even formalize their affection by serving as godfathers to one another's children.

Stavros, however, sounded a discordant note. 'My father says to expect another taxi strike next week. The fifth one this month. Another day's work lost.'

'Not again!' Dimitrios stubbed out his cigarette. 'Nothing works in this country any more. *Tipoteh*! Especially the so-called workers. Do you know how many strikes we've had in the past year and a half? Like my father always says, every day it's somebody else.' He shook his head. 'With the way things are, he says it's impossible to run a business in this country.'

'*My* father doesn't go on strike because he likes it,' Stavros said mildly. 'If you had to support yourself on what a driver earns – like I'll have to, as soon as I get out of school, you'd be the first to pull your taxi off the road.'

'Maybe.' Dimitrios seemed about to say more, but instead he lit another cigarette. Now that they were about to graduate from high school and go their separate ways, the avalanche of strikes had become a bone of contention between himself and his friends. Stavros was the only one who would soon be in a union. But Nikos and Grigoris fancied themselves as intellectuals, and already they liked to take the fashionable student position in sympathy with the workers. Babis, who had quit school last year and still hadn't been able to find a steady job, always groused as though it were the responsibility of the government to assure his living. And even Alkis, who should know better because his father owned a shop, sometimes joined the unruly workers' demonstrations here in Syntagma Square.

But gloomily Stavros was lighting another cigarette. 'At this rate, I'll be forty years old before I can afford to get married. I don't know why I'm even thinking about getting engaged to Nadia. Maybe I should just sit back and wait until she marries someone else and has a daughter.'

'Then,' Nikos said, 'Nadia would be your mother-in-law instead of your wife.'

As the boys grinned at such a preposterous image, Nikos seized the opportunity to raise the topic uppermost in his mind. 'Maybe the bad times are almost over, Stav. The elections are next month. Maybe this time old George will get a working majority.'

'What difference would Papandreou make anyway?' Babis shrugged. 'The politicians are all the same.'

'Now you're talking sense.' Dimitrios eagerly leaned forward. 'Left, right, what does it matter? They're all parasites. *Paleokomatiki*, with their tired "old heads". And corrupt, every one of them. My father always says that what this country needs is a strong man at the helm. Someone we can do business with.'

'My father says the same.' Heavily Nikos shrugged. The Athens rumour mill was working overtime churning out predictions that this or that one was about to stage an *ektropi*, a 'deviation', which was the current euphemism for a *coup d'état* either from the left, the right, or the king's men. Nikos had asked his father all about this a few days ago. Curiously enough, although Yorgos usually welcomed any opportunity to trumpet his opinions, this time the colonel had only mysteriously smiled. Yet Nikos supposed he should be thankful that he had been spared another brow-beating about the values of Greek religion and what his father called patriotism. 'If what my father has in mind is the country being run like he tries to bully our family, then no thanks.'

'Ah, Niko . . .' Grigoris laid a concerned hand on his shoulder. As long as the boys could remember, Nikos and his father had been at loggerheads. 'So what's he done now?'

'The same as always. "Niko, where are you going? Niko, what are you doing?" He looks at all my books, and sometimes he even calls my teachers when he doesn't approve of what we're studying. He listens to me when I'm on the telephone. He takes away my guitar. He won't even let me talk to my sisters without interrupting, and correcting me, and telling me that everything I say and do is wrong. Then we fight, and my mother stands up for me, and the two of them go in the bedroom and I can hear them shouting.' Nikos' shoulders hunched in despair. 'Last night we had another fight about my going to polytechnic and being an architect. I don't dare tell him that what I'd really like to do is play my guitar in a club like the one we were in tonight. He still wants me to join the army and eventually go to the War College like he did. He says someday he might even get me under his own command. Can you imagine that? *Me* having to obey *him*, twenty-four hours a day! It's the same old thing, all the time. He wants me to be just like him. But I could never be like *him*.'

The other boys nodded in sympathy. Over the years they had suggested everything they could think of to mend Nikos' relationship with his father, but nothing had ever helped for long.

'I listen to all of you talking about your fathers,' Nikos continued, 'and I wonder what would it be like to have someone you admire for your father, someone who had done good things in his life, someone you wanted to be like some day?'

Grigoris smiled. His own father could hardly read or write and worked as a mechanic in his uncle's garage. But when he was young, he had fought the Germans in the Resistance. And then later, after he had taken to the streets of Athens with the leftists during the bitter Civil War, he had served eighteen months detention in an island prison camp. Grigoris was proud of what his father had done in his youth, and – even though next year he hoped to be at the university and one day to be a doctor – he never intended to forget his roots and what he regarded as his father's heroism.

Babis broke in. 'I get along with my father. It's everything else that makes me crazy. Almost one year without work! I go here, I go there, but still no job for longer than a week or two. The government doesn't care anything about people like me.' He spun the ashtray around with his idle fingers. 'Maybe my father's right. I should get a job working on the boats, like my uncle.'

'At least that way,' Alkis reminded him, 'you won't have to go in the army just yet.' He himself was expecting to begin the mandatory two years of national service at the end of the summer.

'The army!' The boys all groaned. Even though some of the older neighbourhood fellows reported the army wasn't so bad, high school boys looked upon their looming military service as a descent into the first ring of hell.

Alkis, however, didn't think being a sailor was much better than an underpaid soldier. 'Yeah, but three or four years, working in some stinking hot boat?' Miserably he raised his stricken eyes to his friends. 'Away from my family. From you. From Greece!'

'Sometimes,' Nikos admitted. 'I think of going away. My grandfather's in

255

America. And my uncle. At least there, I wouldn't have to deal with my father.'

'You would do that?' Dimitrios was incredulous. 'Leave Greece?'

'Don't worry.' Nikos laughed. 'I'm not packing my bags just yet.'

But Alkis was thoughtful as he considered an idea which had just struck him. 'What would you think,' he said to Babis, 'if we went together on the boats? That way I wouldn't have to go in the army just yet.'

'Now, that would be something wonderful!' Babis' eyes were alight.

'Of course,' Alkis mused, 'my mother wouldn't like it. If I'm in the army, I get to come home on leaves. But to be away from her for three or four years? I don't know . . .' He yawned. The cafés in the square were thinning out. It was a quarter after two, almost time to go home.

Dimitrios signalled to the waiter, grandly pulled out a wad of hundred drachma notes, and peeled some off before the rest could even lay hands on their money. They had all lit one last cigarette when suddenly they heard a strange and distant grinding sound.

Puzzled, they looked first to one another, and then, as the noise came closer, they gazed up at the brightly lit parliament building. As they watched, a tank veered down Stadiou Street. Another turned up Panepistimou. A third rumbled down Amalias. Wide-eyed, they watched the tanks pull up before the seat of government. Then, as they broke out in a babble of excited speculation, the military trucks of troops in full battledress careened into Syntagma. Soldiers with light machine guns cocked at the ready piled out into the square. A loudspeaker atop a command car sounded. 'Home! Go to your homes! Now! Clear the square!'

'*Thee mou*! My God!' Nikos stared at the black berets of the armoured division, hoping against hope that he wouldn't catch sight of his father. But he was too far away to see anything but the uniforms, the guns, and most especially the tanks. His voice fell to a whisper. 'It's really happening! They're doing it! Right before our eyes!'

A detachment of soldiers was running down the sides of the square, motioning with the bayonets of their tommy guns for the civilians to get up and go. Nearby, the kiosk vendors were hastily pulling down their grills and locking up. In the cafés, the lights were already turned off. Boys like themselves were standing by their chairs, watching history in the making.

Just before the soldiers reached the foot of the square, Nikos and his friends made a bee-line for their motorbikes parked nearby. The whole way home, as they raced down darkened sidestreets to avoid the tanks and the soldiers, for once none of them said a word.

*

256

Out on the back balcony, Marika tensed up when she heard the front door slam. She had been hoping Yorgos wouldn't be home from that practice alert of his until morning. He had said when he had gone out early in the evening, all dressed up in his military khaki, that he might not return until tomorrow. But if that was her husband, she was in for one of those grapplings which under other circumstances was called lovemaking. Or maybe not. Lately, he had been leaving her alone and even seemed to have forgotten his former rampant desire to get her pregnant again. She supposed he had a new girl and wondered if she was an Olympic air hostess, a bank clerk, maybe even the wife of one of his cronies. But she hadn't heard any gossip about her husband for months. She could call Dina to find out, but she hadn't talked to 'the girls' for a long while and hated to set all *that* awhirl again just to hear about Yorgos' sex life.

'Mama! Where are you? Mama!'

She breathed a sigh of relief that Nikos was home. Since his friends had gotten those motorbikes, she worried so about his lying broken and bloody on an Athens boulevard. The boys were so reckless on those wretched bikes. Yet she knew she would give in and buy him his own shiny black Solex for his high school graduation in June. For months Nikos had been begging for this motorized heart's desire of his, and as usual she knew she would be unable to deny him. She couldn't even bear to tell him not to stay out so late, for she knew very well he was avoiding the man he assumed was his father.

'Out here,' she called, even though she knew he wouldn't be able to hear her from the *saloni*. But he knew where to find her, and so lazily she waited for him to make his way through the apartment to where she always kept her night vigil once the girls and her mother went to bed.

Marika ran her fingers through her hair as though she was awaiting not her son but her lover. Languorously she stretched out and rearranged the folds of the red wool kaftan that kept her warm even outside on these cool spring nights. Now that Nikos was home, instead of brooding here alone she would be together with the one she loved most in the world. Perhaps, for the first time today, she would really be able to relax. The newsroom had been a madhouse today, with all those rumours that the Communists were about to stage a coup. When finally she went to bed, she might even drift off to sleep as soon as her head hit the pillow. But first she and he would sit awhile together, drinking coffee and sharing confidences. But no, Nikos had probably been drinking *metrios* for hours. Instead she would fix him a little meal. The boy didn't eat enough these days. Especially when his father was home and the two of them were at it again, her son was always springing up from the table and dashing off before he had even finished one plateful of whatever his grandmother had cooked. Today her mother had made his favourite *tiropitta*, and there were *dolmades* and roast chicken left over from lunch. She would make him a nice salad, and together they would eat a little of this and a little of that. As they talked and laughed until the sun rose over the sea, they would forget the one who dominated their lives and their fears. They would pretend that Yorgos did not exist.

Worry lines creased Marika's forehead. Her mother always said she should work harder at reconciling Nikos and Yorgos. To try to make peace between the two of them, however, Marika knew that sometimes she would have at least to appear to be neutral. But all her husband had to do was give Nikos one of those dark slashing looks, and she could not stop herself from leaping into the fray in defence of her son.

She lit a fresh cigarette, inhaled deeply, and did her best to exhale all that was wrong in her world. Tonight she would simply be content to have a few tranquil hours with Nikos.

Marika smiled into the dark of this fine and starry spring night. By day honking, sweating, cursing Athens set her nerves on edge, but when the sun went down the capital was transformed into a caressively soft and sensuous Mediterranean metropolis. On nearby balconies yesterday's laundry flapped, cats prowled, and faintly she could hear the strains of a bouzouki record. Farther away she could see lights strung along the spine of Lycabettus mountain, the white shadows of the Acropolis temples, and the winking city sprawl. On the sea, cargo ships were anchored just outside the harbour, and a lone cruise liner was ablaze with laces of fairy lights. She gave Athens a final fond glance and had just gotten up to go to the kitchen when a wild-eyed Nikos burst out on the balcony.

'Where is he? Is he here?'

'Who?' She stared in consternation at her son. Nikos was breathing heavily, his long hair – another bone of contention with Yorgos – was every which way, and he looked as though he were about to burst into tears. A current of fear passed through her. 'What's happened? The motorbikes? An accident? I knew I shouldn't let you ride those things!'

Instead of answering, Nikos opened the sliding glass doors and stepped into his parents' bedroom. 'No, he's not here,' he muttered more to himself than to her. 'I didn't think he'd be home . . . but I hoped.' He heaved a great sigh. 'So he's involved. I knew it, I knew it.'

Marika put her arm around her son and steered him to one of the cushioned balcony chairs. 'Now calm down. You're not talking sense. What's the matter?'

Nikos took a deep breath. 'Sit down. I have news.'

She sank into her chair. 'What?'

'I'm not sure, but I think it's a coup. Or at least an attempted coup. By the army.'

'The *army*?' She herself had written a bylined piece today about the chances of the Communists taking over the government by force. If the military had indeed staged a pre-emptive strike, once again the cyclical pattern of modern Greek political history would be repeating itself. It was always the same, she thought. After a chaotic period of liberal democratic regimes characterized by petty political squabbling and an ultimately para- lysed government and economy, the military stepped in – sometimes only until fresh elections could be held, and sometimes for far longer. In this century alone, the army had triggered a revolution in 1909, took power after the debacle of the Asia Minor disaster in 1922, and staged more coups and attempted counter-coups in the unstable twenties and thirties than anyone but the historians could keep straight. Considering the wreck the politicians had made of the country in the past few years, Nikos' news of a *kinima* – a putsch – was not so surprising. But her son was young, and inclined to take café speculations too seriously. Fondly she brushed his hair back from those eyes which never failed to remind her of Christos. 'I think, my son, that you must have been drinking wine instead of coffee tonight. Or perhaps it was raki that has clouded your mind?'

'No, no, you don't understand!' Nikos jumped up and began pacing as his words came in a rush. 'We were in Syntagma, the boys and I, having coffee. We were just about to leave, when suddenly we saw the tanks. Tanks, mama, in Syntagma! They came right into the square from every direction – three of them, I think, maybe there are more now. Then the soldiers came in open trucks. The first lot jumped out and went into the parliament building. Then there were more trucks, more soldiers. The square was full of them. They started screaming on the loudspeakers for everyone to go home. People were running around, closing up the cafés, not saying anything, just doing what the soldiers said. They didn't fire even one shot. But they didn't have to, I guess, because no one stood up to them. What could we do against those guns?'

Marika's cigarette burned her fingers, and she let it drop on the floor. 'And then?'

Nikos shrugged. 'And then nothing. We came home the long way around, through Plaka, almost up to the Acropolis. Then we looped up and around the back way in case there were soldiers on the main roads. We saw a roadblock on Syngrou.'

'So it's really happening . . .' A coup – no, she mustn't think that yet – an *attempted* coup by soldiers. But which soldiers? The leftists or the king's men? The elections were scheduled for next month, and each side had its reasons for taking by force what they weren't certain they could win at the ballot box. Which of them had made it to Syntagma first?

'Mama, you must tell me. *Him*. Where is he?'

Her eyes met her son's. 'Out.'

'Where?'

She shrugged. 'He left last night shortly after you did. In uniform. He said there was a practice alert tonight. I didn't think anything about it, they do that every so often, you know. And just before he went out the door he said not to wait up for him. I thought that was odd, because I *never* wait up for *him*. And then he did something else. He kissed me. "For luck," he said. Funny, I thought. Your father never kisses me goodbye like that.'

'He hasn't called? Sent any message?'

She brought her head up in a negative. 'You know how he is. If anything's happened, we'd be the last to know. But maybe I can try his office. At this hour there's usually no one there. Maybe no one will answer tonight, either. And in a little while your father will come sneaking home from – ' She had been just about to say, 'from his girlfriend', but had stopped herself just in time. She didn't tell Nikos *everything*.

Without another word, they rushed to the salon. Marika's hand was shaking as she tried to dial his number. Her index finger slipped and the call faulted on the fourth digit. Slowly she dialled again.

On the first ring a voice she didn't know answered. '*Nai?*' Not a polite '*Legete*' or even '*Embros*'. Just a curt 'Yes?'.

'Colonel Kronos, please. This is his wife.' The line went dead. When she dialled again, it was engaged.

Mother and son stared at each other. Nikos strode over to the television, but – as usual at this hour, when the midnight movie was over – nothing was being transmitted. Marika switched on the radio, twiddled the dial, but the only thing she could get was schmaltzy folk music. No voices, no news, only the strum of bouzoukis and the whine of pipes.

When the phone rang, Marika snatched it. After a moment she handed it over to Nikos. 'Sounds like one of your friends.'

Nikos listened intently for a while, bit his lip, and then put the phone back on the cradle. 'That was Dimitrios. He says his father was on the phone when he got home, that everyone in Athens is on the phone right now, that his father wanted to call someone else, that's why he had to make this call so short. Oh, God, mama, he says there really has been a coup! Or at least that the army is trying to take over. They've seized the government buildings and the radio and television. There are troops everywhere! A military truck came down Dimitrios' street – you know, they moved last month to that fancy villa in Psychikon – and one of the government ministers lives right across from

260

them. The soldiers all but broke down the minister's door. They took the poor old guy away in his pyjamas.'

'Did Dimitrios know whose coup this is?'

'You mean, did he know if *he* was involved?'

Marika nodded. She was used to her son calling Yorgos 'he' instead of 'father'. Under other circumstances, this gave her pleasure.

'He says no one knows anything. His father's afraid that if they're leftwing, they might nationalize the banks. Dimitrios says his father would have gone right down to the bank now, in the middle of the night, if it weren't for the roadblocks.' Nikos made a sound that was almost a laugh. 'I wouldn't be surprised if his father's out in the back garden right now, burying money and his mother's jewellery.'

Awakened by the call and the commotion, Old Anna silently crept into the salon from her tiny back bedroom next to the kitchen. 'What's wrong? Something's wrong! I can tell by your faces. Is it Vangelis? Has something happened to my boy?'

'No, no.' As Marika put her arm around her mother, she could feel the old bones inside. She looked even more worn than usual in the frayed grey bathrobe she had worn for years, even though Marika had bought her a fine new one. 'It's just politics again. There was some problem in Syntagma, but it will probably blow over.' She tried to steer her back to her bedroom. 'Why don't you get some more sleep?'

When again the phone rang, they froze. Nikos was the first to recover. 'It's some hysterical woman,' he whispered as he passed over the phone. Even when Marika held the receiver to her ear, Nikos and Old Anna could still hear the shrieking female voice on the other end of the line.

'Have you heard? A revolution! Now, it's happening now!' Marika's friend Nina lived down the street, and often on cold winter nights they played *ekosi-ena* – twenty-one – together. But now Nina broke out in the mourning wail she usually reserved for funerals.

Old Anna sank down on the couch and began wringing her hands.

'Now, now . . .' Nikos perched on the sofa arm and tried to soothe his grandmother as they all listened to the excited, tinny voice.

'What will we do? What will this mean?' But then Nina seemed to get hold of herself, and her voice dropped so that only Marika could hear. 'Your Yorgos? Is he home? Does he know anything? My Pantelis, as soon as we heard the rumours, he said, "Call up your dear friend Marika. That husband of hers, that Yorgos – a fine man, the salt of the earth – if anybody knows what's happening, my friend Yorgos will. Call them!"'

'Nothing, I know nothing.' Since Pantelis and Yorgos had exchanged only the most cursory of greetings at crowded nameday receptions, the reason for

261

all the sudden flattery was chillingly obvious. Marika frowned as Nina began to wheedle, whine, and praise Yorgos extravagantly.

'We've always been such good friends, such very good friends, like family really.' Nina gushed on. 'And I hope you feel the same way. You know Pantelis and I would do anything for you and dear Yorgos. And we certainly hope the two of you feel the same. You do, Marika, don't you? Marika?'

'I have to go now. Yorgos might be trying to get me on the phone.'

'So he's not there? I thought so! But you'll call us as soon as you hear anything?' Shrilly Nina laughed. 'Right from the horse's mouth?'

'*Kali nikta.*' Marika replaced the phone and stared into space. 'She thinks Yorgos is involved. She did everything but ask me to get a job for her son.'

'Coffee. I'll make coffee.' Old Anna shakily got to her feet. 'It will be a long night.'

When she left, again the phone rang, and again Nikos answered it. He talked for a long while, pacing back and forth while his mother anxiously watched him. When he hung up, he shrugged his eyebrows. 'Stavros. He doesn't know any more than we do.'

'Mama! I woke up!'

'Mama! Why is the phone ringing like that?'

Two sleepy girls stood in their nightdresses in the doorway that led to their bedroom.

'Nothing, my darlings. Just your brother's friends calling later than they should.' Marika took them by the hand and guided them back to their room. She had just tucked them in when she heard the phone again. This time Nikos came running to get her. 'It's *him*! He wants to talk to you!'

She ran back to the salon with the girls in her wake. Old Anna came in from the kitchen with a tray of steaming coffees. Marika's heart was beating fast as she held the receiver to her ear. 'Yorgo?'

'You're home, good. And Nikos. The girls are all right?'

'Everyone's home. But you, Yorgo, where are you? We've heard . . . Nikos saw . . . they say there's been a coup.'

'Is that what they say?' Yorgos laughed. 'They say right.'

'You're involved?' Her voice was a whisper. Before he could answer, she heard a door slam wherever he was, and then shouting.

After a moment, Yorgos was brusque. 'I have to go. I just called to tell you to stay inside. Nikos especially. No one will be hurt, I guarantee, if everyone stays inside. We are Christian Greeks, and no one will be hurt unless they make problems. Do not go out tonight! And not in the morning, either, unless I say it's all right. You hear me?'

The line went dead before she could say another word.

Nikos was shouting. 'He's in it, isn't he?'

262

Her voice faltered. 'I think so. Yes, I think so.'

'*Patera mou*? Is there something wrong with our father?' Annoula burst into tears.

The girls went to their grandmother, and she held them close and rocked them like babies. 'Don't worry, *paidia mou*, everything will be fine. Your father will be home in the morning, and everything will be just the same as it always has been.'

Again the phone. Sokrates' voice blasted Marika's ear. 'Cut the blah-blah, *kukla*, and get in here! We have a special edition. Maybe they won't let it get to the kiosks, but we're going to deliver it. I want you – '

But the line went dead. No matter how many times Marika clicked the button, there were no signs of life on the phone. 'Dead!'

For a moment she stared at her mother and children. Then she tore off her kaftan, threw on a dress and – to hell with Yorgos' warnings! – flew out the door to write history.

Twelve hours later on the afternoon of that same day, Yorgos triumphantly marched into the General Staff conference room to take his place of honour among those who now were the rulers of the land. The fifteen members of the inner group weren't scheduled to begin their meeting for another ten minutes, but already most of the colonels were in place, sitting erect with shoulders squared, resplendent in their dress khaki. Greece's new masters were beginning as they meant to continue. Punctuality was a virtue, tardiness a sin. The colonels intended to make sure that nevermore would the government of Greece – or indeed, its lackadaisical citizens – dilly and dally and fret away valuable time. They were impatient not only to save the country from subversives but also to save the Greeks from themselves. One of the colonels, a fierce little fellow from Sparti – where else? – was fond of saying, that, just like a dog or a woman, a Greek needed to be disciplined. The buses were going to run on time. The people would get up earlier and work later. Government ministries were going to act on large and small matters in a matter of hours instead of months. There would be no more strikes because there would be no more unions. The babies who had been coddled far too long in this cradle of democracy were finally going to grow up and *work*.

As Yorgos made his way round the table to his place, he stopped to give an exuberant bear hug to a colonel he had known in his Civil War youth scouring the Peloponnese mountains for the last of the *andartes*. 'It's been a long time, eh?' They thumped each other on their broad peasant backs. He gladhanded another he had befriended in the School of Artillery more than

263

fifteen years ago. 'We finally did it!' He flashed the V-sign and beamed at other clear-eyed comrades he had come to know over the past twenty years at provincial garrison camps, at the War College, or in these last tedious seasons holding down desk jobs here at military headquarters. Some had enlisted in their struggle to purge the nation and restore a 'Greece of Christian Greeks' more than twenty years ago in the clandestine IDEA, Sacred League of Greek Officers, others had come aboard later in another secret society, ENNA, the Union of Young Greek Officers. Most, like him, were self-made men in their mid-forties or early fifties. They had been born and bred in the dirt-poor villages of the hinterlands, and they resented that all their lives they had struggled against the odds. Unlike the clannish old power élite of Athens, they didn't have feudal family connections, snobbish degrees from foreign universities, or the aristocratic airs of those who tangoed in royal circles. But last night, when push had come to shove, they had had what mattered more. Tanks in Syntagma. Soldiers in Omonia. Roadblocks in Syngrou.

Yorgos took his seat in the straight-backed chair, adjusted his thick black-rimmed glasses, and skimmed the neatly-typed communiqué his efficient Lieutenant Kostas had readied atop a sheaf of papers on the table before him. Just as soon as the new civilian figurehead government was announced over the radio – with the king's reluctant stamp of approval – this statement would follow. Martial law had already been declared in a proclamation the colonels wanted the world to believe had been signed by the king. And soon the waiting country was going to be informed that civil liberties were being suspended while more than a thousand subversives already caught in the military police net went on trial for their crimes. The communiqué also castigated Greek's former political leaders for very nearly betraying the country into the hands of the Communists. Henceforth, the communiqué said, there would no longer be conservatives and liberals and centrists, '. . . only Greeks who believe in Greece.'

Yorgos read that last stirring phrase to himself, and for a moment he wished that he could have been the one to read his own words into the radio microphone. But then he cleared his throat and shut his mouth. Long months ago when he and his comrades sealed their pact, they had agreed that once they struck and triumphed they would strive to remain faceless men in uniform for as long as they could. They would appoint a civilian figurehead to do their bidding during those crucial first weeks until the opposition was either under lock and key or in exile. For a while, too, they would even invite other civilians to serve in the government along with a constellation of high and middle-ranking military officers. Meanwhile, this hardcore cadre of 'revolutionary group' colonels would continue to pull the strings and play the music to which the nation would learn to dance. Only when their power was absolutely solidified and the opposition silenced would they step out of the shadows and into the blinding Greek sun. Sometime thereafter they would hold new elections and return power to a civilian government. This was not really a revolution but an *epemvasis*, an 'intervention by the army' to save the country from ruin.

The conference room was abuzz with activity as the last few colonels strode in. Sweating lieutenants came racing with their despatches and their sheafs of papers.

The phones never stopped ringing. But it was an orderly pandemonium. Their regime, like their *coup d'état*, was going to work like a finely-calibrated Swiss watch. Around the table, even though none of them had slept the night before, the colonels sat upright and austere, conscious that here and now they were making history. The operation had been almost perfectly executed. Two girls and a boy had been shot by mistake as the infantry and artillery units seized the telephone and broadcasting centres, surrounded the king's country residence, and rounded up political and military leaders. But otherwise there had been neither resistance nor bloodshed. Literally and figuratively, they had struck while the country slept.

Yorgos leaned back in his chair and lit his cigarette with a flourish. We did it, he gleefully told himself yet again. With the help of God and that precisely detailed NATO contingency plan, we won the hour, the day, and the future. 'Operation Prometheus' – Yorgos liked the irony of the plan's code name being the same as his brother's *nom de guerre* – had been drawn up to stabilize Greece in the event of an imminent Communist takeover. Another fine irony was that the military brass had actually assigned George Papadopoulos – the mastermind of this coup, the colonel his cohorts had long ago nicknamed 'Nasser' – to design 'Operation Prometheus'.

Yorgos thoughtfully rubbed the sweaty palms of his hands together. What now? The colonels were dedicated patriots. But until now mostly they had commanded provincial battalions, freezing in shabby breezeblock command centres in the winter, perspiring in dusty flyblown camps in the summer. They knew how to whip new recruits into shape, but could they work the same miracle on a country? Over the years, as they had complained to one another about the cancers eating away at Greece, they had come to some firm conclusions about who and what had made their country sick to death. The politicians – all of them on the take, none of them with any moral fibre – were the greatest culprits, and so of course one and all would have to go. The rabid leftwing – unconsciously Yorgos fingered the scar on his cheek as he thought of Christos, how unfair it was that he was so successful now in Boston! – had not been dealt with sternly enough since the end of the Civil

War. It would be one of the most heartfelt aims of the new regime to exterminate those traitors once and for all. As for the rest ... absently, forgetting for a moment where he was, Yorgos scratched his head. Last week one of the colonels had declared they must 'fashion a New Man with the strength to do Absolute Good'. Another had extolled the virtues of 'Hellenic-Christian civilization'. And Papadopoulos himself, who had coined the memorable phrase 'Greece of the Christian Greeks', was fond of comparing Greece to a sick man who needed to be encased in plaster until he mended. Some of the colonels fulminated about how Greece was being ruined by decadent Western influences, and so they wanted a crackdown against miniskirts, beards, and hippies who polluted the loveliest beaches in the world with the drugged smoke of their marijuana cigarettes. Others, who maintained that the problem lay in the collapse of religious and family traditions, wanted everyone in church on Sunday and oil lamps flickering in front of an icon in every home. What were they to do about the galloping inflation, the faltering farm industry, the fluctuating value of the drachma on the world market, and the low level of capital investment? How would they stimulate industry and tourism? What would they do about the festering problem of Cyprus, the nervous American alliance, and the ever-present danger of the Turks massed at the border? So far the people had been as docile as lambs in the pasture, but Greeks were volatile and fierce fighters once roused. Even with right on their side, the colonels couldn't keep the country under lock and key forever. An ugly little demon of doubt gnawed away at Yorgos. Did he and his comrades have the administrative experience and the political canniness to transform the *patrida* into the glorious world power it could and must be?

The stocky balding colonel didn't need a gavel to call his meeting to order. George Papadopoulos merely raked his comrades with his eyes, pursed his lips, and waved his hand to the wallmap of Greece where blue flags marked the disposition of military forces. 'The country is ours.'

'*Bravo*!' Yorgos banished his misgivings and raised his fist with the others. He let out a cheer that came from his gut.

'The city is ours.' Papadopoulos looked out the window where a helicopter whirled into the sky, ferrying another batch of political prisoners into the special detention centres and remote hotels which had been in operation since two-thirty in the morning. The eyes of the other colonels followed their leader, and to a man they smiled.

Papadopoulos smiled, too. 'And the future is ours.'

Any other Greek would have been unable to resist this opportunity to orate about exactly what had been accomplished in these first hours of the new regime, but Papadopoulos was not a *kafeneion* raconteur babbling a lifetime away over cups of coffee. Briskly he called his men to account.

Brigadier Stylianos Pattakos, the number two man in the coup who had just been sworn in as the new Minister of Interior, reported that the only resistance had been brief and quickly suppressed student demonstrations in Ionnina and Crete. Tanks guarded every Athens crossroad. The police, who quickly had gone over to the colonels, were patrolling the streets where all other vehicles were forbidden to circulate. The telephones were dead, only a few newspaper editions had hit the kiosks, and the banks and Stock Exchange were closed. Nearly all the party political leaders and three-quarters of the former members of parliament had been arrested along with most of the ministers of the last government. In addition, a mixed bag of intellectuals had been detained – lawyers, writers, journalists, actors, poets and students. 'Everyone,' Pattakos said, 'who would have liked to see the red flag flying over Constitution Square.' Soon, he added, the military courts would begin their work, and those convicted would be shipped to concentration camps on the islands.

'All as planned.' Next Papadopoulos reported on foreign reaction. It was too soon, he explained, for recognition from ambassadors and heads of state. But now that the king had appointed a new civilian prime minister, their regime had an air of legitimacy. He had already been privately assured by his CIA contacts that, aside from diverting a scheduled shipment of tanks from Greece to Turkey and perhaps imposing a temporary arms embargo to soothe ruffled liberal feathers in Washington, the Americans would not intervene in this Greek domestic matter. He expected other governments to follow suit. As for the international press, Papadopoulos eloquently shrugged off their significance.

The next to report was Colonel Nikolas Makarezos, the new Minister of Coordination who was to be responsible for overall policy. A series of emergency regulations would authorize arrest and detention without any time limits, forbid bail for political offences, ban public or private assemblies, abolish trade unions and strikes, authorize search and seizures everywhere and at all times, impose press and broadcasting censorship, and institute court martial tribunals with the right to try political offences and censorship violations.

Yorgos carefully kept a smile on his lips and in his eyes as covertly he stared at this triumvirate of Papadopoulos, Pattakos, and Makarezos who had quickly managed to clench the reins of power in their hands. Had the colonels gotten rid of the politicians, neutralized the king, and rounded up the subversives only to find that they had created these three all-powerful new masters? Yorgos looked across the table at what he had always regarded as the sinister visage of Brigadier Dimitrios Ioannides. *Four* masters, he amended to himself. Ioannides was quiet today, but surely not for long.

Still, Yorgos took care that none of these thoughts were reflected in his carefully veiled face. He hadn't come this far only to condemn himself prematurely with one careless word or glance. Yet the colonels were supposed to be announcing a series of popular measures to win the people to the side of this transitional regime. Prices of everyday commodities – food, housing, and utilities – were supposed to be fixed, pensions increased, and land in the countryside redistributed. Resources were supposed to be allocated to the neglected villages. Roads were to be built, electricity installed everywhere, the telephone system broadened, and education revamped. Corruption was to be eliminated at all levels, so that the government functioned as smoothly as a regiment. And last but not least, tourism had to be stimulated and foreign investment encouraged. Instead, all Papadopoulos seemed to have on his mind was the consolidation of his own power by a thorough suspension of civil liberties.

But, Yorgos seethed as he kept his eyes discreetly lowered, the agreement had been that they would take power, clean up the country, get rid of the lemming politicians, and then return the *patrida* to civilian control.

As if he could read Yorgos' mind, Papadopoulos looked up from the phoenix he had been doodling on the paper before him. 'Of course we want to restore democracy in Greece. Let no one ever forget that democracy is a Greek invention. Now that our country is back in the hands of God-fearing, family-loving Greeks, we will strive to restore the motherland to the glories of Helleno-Christian civilization. But it would be a mistake to return to democracy . . . prematurely. Greece, whom we have here on the operating table, is a sick man. And if the surgeon does not strap him down for the duration of the operation, there is a possibility that instead of the operation restoring his health, it may lead to his death. We must take care that the politicians never have the opportunity again to ruin this Greece of Christian Greeks. *Poteh*! Never! Do you all understand?'

As one, the colonels nodded. Papadopoulos consulted his watch. 'Time for our little judge – no, it's *Prime Minister* Kollias now – to read our communiqué to the people eh? Meeting dismissed. We'll convene again tomorrow at oh-nine-hundred hours.' Abruptly he got to his feet and marched out the door.

In the sudden silence, the colonels did not look at one another as they collected their papers and followed the one who was obviously now the big boss out of the door and back to their offices.

Once he had shut the door behind him, Yorgos heaved himself down in his chair. Papadopoulos had turned into a dictator who meant to rule Greece just as he had ruled the colonels.

He lit a cigarette and thoughtfully inhaled. He could go along with this new order of things, or he could subvert it. Tonight he could begin sounding out the other colonels – those he had known almost forever, those he could trust with his life – and they might be able to oust Papadopoulos before he had the time to solidify his pre-eminent position. But then, as mentally Yorgos ran through the roster of colonels, he wondered if he truly could trust any of them with his life. Any of them might be tempted to betray him if he so much as breathed a word of dissent. After biding his lifetime waiting for the chance to *be* somebody, he might even end up rotting in one of those infernal island concentration camps. Perhaps he would be a fool to risk everything for niceties such as the civil liberties of strangers. His first responsibility was to himself, his family, and maybe – if finally the Panagians learned to treat him as they should – his village.

He let his mind wander back to the bad old days in Panagia when he had skulked like a wolf outside the charmed circle of those who had spurned him. Those boys who had made his childhood a misery were only fishermen now, and today he had helped to form a new national government. Those fisherfolk would never understand that here at policy meetings in Athens even he had to run and fetch and do his masters' bidding. But if he was smart – and Yorgos had never for a moment in his life doubted his own intelligence – he could use his position to play king back in Panagia. He could get everyone jobs. He could pave roads. He could light up the night with electricity lines strung to the most remote shacks on the mountainside. In time, he might even be able to build Panagia into a tourist mecca that would make millionaires not only of his own family but also of anyone else who showed him the proper respect.

A discreet knock sounded on his door, and when he barked out a curt '*Nai*?' Lieutenant Kostas came in carrying a tray with a cup of hot coffee and a glass of cold water. 'Thought you might like it, sir.'

Yorgos smiled benevolently at this young officer from Panagia who was rising on his coat-tails to the top. It was a pity that more of the villagers hadn't shown him the devotion that this lad had demonstrated since he had become his protégé. Kostas' exemplary record and faultless service was even more extraordinary considering the rotten family tree from which he had sprung. Back in the dark days of the Civil War, his own father had been one of the first to welcome the *andartes* when they took control of Panagia, and his older brother had died with Christos' band in that Greek Cross raid. Once long ago Kostas' father had even vowed revenge for Andreas' death. In the ten years that Kostas had been his aide, he and Yorgos had sometimes had a good laugh about the preposterous bloodlust boast of the old man who was now lying in Panagia's cemetery. Kostas sometimes even said, with tears in his eyes, that Yorgos had become like a father to him. It was too bad, Yorgos thought, that he didn't get the same filial devotion from Nikos. But he would take care of Kostas as if he were truly his son. He would see that the lad got his captaincy in the next list of military promotions.

'Anything else, sir?'

'Not just now. But I'll have a report for you to type. Once that's done, you can lock up and go home.'

'Right, sir.' Kostas lingered an instant in case the colonel, as so often happened, wanted to share his thoughts with him. He dearly would have liked to have heard his conclusions about the momentous events that had happened today not only in the streets but also in that conference room. But when the colonel said nothing more, the lieutenant softly closed the door behind him.

Yorgos took a sip of coffee, washed it down with a draught of water, and came to a decision. He would cast his lot with the winners. He feared what Papadopoulos might do to the motherland; nevertheless he would strive to be a loyal member of the new order. At least for now, he would carry out the boss's command. Never would he call negative attention to himself with idealistic prattle about human rights. If later Papadopoulos and his cohorts went too far, he would reconsider his position. But for now he was going to look out for number one.

And yet, instead of studying his draft of new guidelines for the tourist development which was going to be his administrative fiefdom, Yorgos stared into space and thought of Christos. What would his brother do, if he found himself behind this desk? Sourly Yorgos smiled. Of course that so-called hero would be the first to man the barricades, fighting to the end even if he was destined to lose. But Christos had always been a loser. He had lost not only the woman he loved but also his country. If Christos had been in Greece last night, he would have been on the list of those to be arrested and sent to the prison camps.

Yorgos lit another cigarette. But Christos wasn't here to get what he so richly deserved. Once again his brother had eluded the punishment which should have been meted out to him. Life wasn't fair. Christos had married a rich blonde American, completed his university studies with honours, and then embarked on what from all reports was going to be an illustrious political career. If those newspaper clippings Nick sent were to be believed, this autumn Christos might be elected to serve in the US Congress.

Yorgos smoked and fumed. Here he was, one of the colonels who ruled

Greece, still worried that his older brother again would finish first. He couldn't stand it if Christos was elected to Congress. He couldn't – no, he wouldn't! – stand for it.

He twirled the combination lock on his safe and extracted the file he had compiled on his brother long ago. It was all here – the date he had entered the Communist Party, the engagements he had fought against the government forces, how and why he had finally taken ship from Patras.

He took a fresh sheet of paper and began rapidly writing the letter he had been considering for years. In a few moments, every incriminating name and place and date was there.

Yorgos consulted a paper on which he had already noted the address of a Boston newspaper and copied it out on an envelope. Should he mail it today, while he was still flush with the success of the coup, or should he stash it away and wait until the precise moment when it could hurt Christos the most? But a scandal like this would bring shame on the family and embarrassment upon himself.

Yorgos slipped the unsealed letter into his 'Christos file' and stashed it back in his safe. He supposed he would never mail it. He had written and shredded two or three just like it over the years, but always – just as back on the Peloponnese mountaintop – something kept him from delivering the death blow.

With a sigh he went back to his memorandum on tourist development. When he finished, he buzzed Kostas and instructed him to type it up and duplicate it for tomorrow morning's meeting. Yorgos hid a yawn. He should wait for Kostas to finish so he could lock it up for safekeeping, but the sleepless night had caught up with him. 'Put all the copies in the safe when you've finished,' he told his lieutenant as he donned his hat and made for the door. There was such an air of conspiracy here in the General Staff now that he didn't want to leave anything lying around on his desk. 'And make sure it's locked before you go.'

'Of course, sir. Goodnight, sir.'

Kostas wanted to pounce on that unlocked safe as soon as the colonel was out the door, but he had waited for this moment for years and so could wait a while longer to be sure Yorgos was truly on his way home. He took his time typing the report and then making fifteen copies for the other members of the *junta*. Yorgos had been gone for forty-five minutes before Kostas finally ransacked the safe.

He shuffled through the insurance papers, the personal legal documents, and paused to read the confidential memo about his own performance and Yorgos's recommendation for his captaincy. Hungrily then he fell on the folder documenting Colonel Kronos' own complicity in last night's coup,

271

and he set that aside for duplication. One day next month, next year, or even ten years from now, the evidence in this file might convict Yorgos for plotting to overthrow the legally elected government of Greece.

Kostas was about to copy those papers so he could shut the safe before someone caught him redhanded, when he picked up one last file mixed in with the boss's personal papers. He scanned the particulars of Christos Kronos' political and war activities and then opened the letter addressed to the American newspaper.

Got them, he exulted. Now I've got them *both*!

Finally, after all these years licking the colonel's boots, he had the weapon to bring down the Kronos brothers. Christos, who had led his big brother to death in the mountains, who had saved his own skin by fleeing to America, and then who had turned his back on the Communist Party and betrayed the people and the cause – *my cause*, Kostas reminded himself – which 'Captain Prometheus' had once vowed to defend with his life. And Yorgos, who had not only tortured Andreas but blackened his memory by taunting that he had 'died like a sheep'.

Quickly Kostas photocopied the letter and the two sets of documents, returned them to the safe along with the report on tourist development, and checked again to see that everything was arranged as it had been. Finally he snapped the safe shut.

He stuffed his photocopies inside the front of his shirt and buttoned them in tight before he turned out the lights and locked the office.

All the way home to his modest *garsoniera* in Kypseli, he rejoiced that finally today he had grasped the means to fulfil his deathbed promise to his father. One day soon, his family's honour would be avenged. Today, when the colonels had staged their coup, he, too, had achieved a coup of his own.

Eleven

Christos leaped out of the back seat of Penelope's station wagon and hit the ground running. His campaign aides sped behind him in a harried pack. It was six-forty in the morning, almost time for the shift change at the East Cambridge macaroni factory. He stationed himself at the gate and began gladhanding the workers in their hardhats. 'Hi,' he said. 'I'm Chris Kronos, and I'm running for Congress.'

'Yeah, yeah,' one grizzled middle-aged man in a workshirt said as he looked Christos over. The candidate was turned out in an open-necked striped shirt and dark trousers, for the image he had sought to cultivate was that of a man of the people. 'I saw your picture in the paper.' The man hesitated and then took one of Christos' leaflets. 'Can I have your auto-graph?' He flushed when the fellow behind him hooted. 'For my wife, I mean.'

'Glad to.' Like a movie star, Christos smiled. 'What's your wife's name?'

'Candy. Candy Chiavaroli.' Patiently he spelled the last name.

Christos scrawled his best wishes to the lady, pumped the millworker's hand, and without missing a beat greeted the next in line. Ever since the colour photo spread in the Sunday paper, he had grown accustomed to being treated as a celebrity. The pictures of Penelope, the children and the dog had been endearing, but what had caught the public's fancy was the newspaper dubbing him 'The Greek Kennedy'. That kind of publicity, as Uncle Jonathan assured him, couldn't be bought for love nor money. Already the family and the party were predicting that his plurality in next week's primary elections would set a district record.

Tirelessly Christos shook hands, met smiling stares, and did his best to slip in a word or two about the wonderful things he intended to do in Washington to help these working-class men and their families. He loved the adrenalin rush of the campaign, but it was frustrating that there was so little time to talk policy on the brutal split-second schedule his manager presented him with each morning. He would have loved to talk at length to these weary men with calloused hands. *The people*. He had turned his back on the Communist Party forever, and mostly he had given up his romantic notions about the intrinsic primitive goodness of the working class. But what remained from his youthful idealism was the sense that his mission in life was to work for the betterment of all the oppressed: the blacks, the workers, the disadvantaged of every colour and ethnic group and class – even, as Penelope was taking such care to convince him, the women. He itched to get to work and finally do what he had been born to do. Once, long ago in Greece, he had been so close to real political power that he could smell it. Now, again, he had the scent.

The knot of workers was thinning out, and already James, the young Harvard graduate who was one of his aides, was plucking at his shirt sleeve. 'C'mon. Let's go. We have to get in another factory and then be at a coffee in North Cambridge by seven-forty-five.'

The driver was racing the engine, and he started up before the back door was closed. They whizzed up sidestreets. Again Christos bounded up to a gate, his smile and his leaflets at the ready. He shook hands, he small-talked, he signed three more autographs.

There was only time for one cigarette in the car before they pulled up at the Victorian three-decker wooden house on the tree-lined street. Matthew, another of his Harvard graduate aides, consulted his ever-present clipboard. 'Barbara Kleeblatt. Lecturer in government at MIT. Americans for Democratic Action, American Civil Liberties Union, Women for Peace and Freedom. Big in the antiwar movement. Her husband's a doctor at Mass General.'

'I know Barb.' Christos hastily snuffed out the cigarette. This woman, who was one of Penelope's many activist friends, was a no-nonsense sort who never allowed anyone to smoke in the house. 'Who will be there?'

'The usual Cambridge types. All women, I expect. Professors, graduate students, social workers. Maybe a writer or artist. All very *earnest*. They'll want to hear about how you will single-handedly end the war.' Matthew yawned. For him, this penny-ante Congressional race was only a warmup for this autumn's Presidential election. If he distinguished himself on this campaign trail, he could expect a plum assignment in the national sweepstakes. Cynically he looked out the window at the house with its tricycles on the porch and its labrador retriever barking in the yard. Doubtless the Kleeblatts jogged together every morning at seven, never ate meat, and would never cross a picket line. He had been born and raised in jaded Manhattan, and he was bored with uptight, do-good Cambridge. 'But at least we'll get good coffee. And probably homemade cake. Ten to one it'll be made with wholemeal flour and nuts and raisins. But it'll be better than those awful rock-hard cookies the Portuguese ladies give us.'

'Will my wife be there?' Lately Christos had hardly seen Penelope, for the managers booked her into a schedule of her own. They appeared together only for the major rallies like Saturday night's speech on Cambridge Common.

Bud, the aide in the front seat, swivelled round and consulted his notes. 'No, she's out in Lexington by now. One of her aunts booked a whole morning of coffees.'

'Good.' Christos imagined Penelope kissing babies, petting dogs – actually, the crowds liked it better when she fussed over the dogs rather than the babies – and saying exactly the right things to those rich dowagers with the blue-rinsed hair. 'That should sew up Lexington.'

The three aides parted their lips in identical gleaming white-toothed smiles. Christos reflected that these bright, efficient, articulate boys were the grease that made his well-oiled campaign run so smoothly. But as always when he was in their capable hands, Christos felt more like a puppet on a string than a candidate in touch with the people. Yet he had learned to do as he was told. Uncle Jonathan had hired one of the best political consultants in the business, and everyone assured him that his glossy image was sure to win the day. Once you get to Washington, they all said, then you can get down to the real work of government. But first we must have our little circus.

Together they strode up the steps, rang the bell, and Barbara herself opened the door. 'Chris! Right on time!' They touched cheeks in that cool halfway kiss of social acquaintances, and then she guided him into the sitting room that was already crowded with long-haired women in vivid Marimeko print dresses, maternity smocks, flowing Indian cotton shifts, and the inevitable bluejeans. As he waved to those he already knew and began systematically working his way round the room meeting others for the first time, his eye registered all the hallmarks of a middle-aged Cambridge activist home. There were plants everywhere – trees in Mexican terracotta pots behind the off-white cushioned sofa, creepers and vines and ferns hanging from the ceiling by macrame ropes, fledgling cuttings artfully drooping on the mantelpiece next to the framed crayon pictures the children had drawn in kindergarten. The floorboards had been sanded down to bare wood, and upon it lay colourful folkloric carpets the Kleeblatts had picked up for next to nothing when they had served in the Peace Corps in Guatemala. The walls were crowded with posters in bright primary colours calling for an end to the war, racial equality, and assorted chic liberal causes. And yes, on the butcher-block table stationed against the far wall, he could see the homemade cakes studded with nuts and raisins. Again the feeling that he had come to visit another homogenous village washed over him. Americans took such pride in their individualism, but they conformed to their own group norms just as his neighbours had back in Panagia.

Someone got him coffee, and Barbara herself served him a slice of the breakfast cake she had made at the crack of dawn that morning. 'You'll like it,' she said. 'It's stuffed with cream cheese. My grandmother's secret recipe.'

As he wolfed it down – she was right, it was delicious, he had developed quite a taste for these Jewish pastries – he fielded questions from all sides. Yes, he would work to establish daycare centres. No, he didn't think the civil rights movement was dead. Of course the environment must be saved, nuclear reactor plants must not be built, and the country needed a coherent medical insurance system. These women were intense, assertive, and none of them asked for his autograph. But it was exciting to talk to them. They, as much as he, were concerned more with the issues than the way he – and they – styled their hair.

But as he made his way toward the upstairs bathroom, he was waylaid in the narrow hallway by a young graduate student in very tight jeans. She snaked her arms around his neck and kissed him soundly on the lips. 'There,' she breathed, 'that's for openers.' He smiled politely and tried to disengage her clinging body, but exuberantly she kissed him again. 'Right,' Christos mumbled as finally he escaped and ran up the steps. He had grown accustomed to such encounters by campaign groupies who collected kisses and hugs as though he were a guitar player for the Rolling Stones instead of a candidate for Congress. It was one of the campaign hazards, for even old Uncle Jonathan joked that he could have had a different girl every night if it weren't for his devotion to Catherine and a certain lack of stamina. But Christos couldn't get used to all those breasts and behinds thrusting at him when he least expected them. He wasn't a piece of meat. He was a politician running for office.

And, almost as soon as he returned downstairs, he was off and running again. His aides sprinted ahead of him to the car, the doors slammed, and they sped away. 'What's next?'

'Two more coffees.' Matthew consulted his holy clipboard. 'One in Arlington. Another in Watertown. Housewives, this time. Mostly Armenians in Watertown.' He pulled a face. 'Icky honey pastries, for sure. But some of them may speak a little Greek. Try a word or two on them, they'll love it. As for Arlington, they're assorted ethnics. They won't care what you say. They just want to be able to tell their friends they met you.'

'And maybe steal a few kisses.' Bud rubbed his hands together. 'The one who was after you back there was really something! You could have had her right there, on the stairs! A candidate has all the luck.'

Christos lit a cigarette and exhaled. 'She was almost young enough to be my daughter.'

'So?' Bud arched his patrician eyebrows. 'That's a problem? If you don't want her, pass her on to me.'

Christos forced a smile, even though he hated such banter. He had not spent his youth in prep school locker rooms like these sporting Harvard lads, and even back in the *kafeneions* of Panagia he had never liked that coarse sort of joking about girls which so much of the masculine world seemed to think so manly. Still, he supposed he should work on cultivating his sense of humour. Uncle Jonathan said he was too serious, that he should laugh more, that the journalists as well as the voters liked a laughing candidate. He made a mental note to try to relax and be one of the boys, but just now he was more intent on today's schedule. 'So what's up after that?'

'OK,' Matthew said, 'once we knock off the coffees, we begin lunches. A Lion's Club back here in Cambridge. You'll speak first, and we'll leave before they eat. We should have just enough time to get to a Rotary Club lunch in

Medford. First you eat, then you talk. Business. They want to hear about what you'll do for business. Talk about your father's restaurant and how you worked your way up from arriving here as a penniless immigrant.'

Christos sighed. The lunches would be an ordeal. He would have to put on his coat and tie and curry favour with men he did not much like. 'And then what?'

'A small antiwar rally at U-Mass Boston. Not much. A few hundred students at most. But the media may be there.'

'Television?' Christos took a deep drag on his cigarette.

'We hope so. The assignment editor at Channel 4 said he might send a crew. No promises, you know how the TV boys are. But we told the guys at 5 and 7 that the competition will be there, so they might send someone. If we're lucky, they'll all turn out in force. And we can count on the print boys.'

Christos nodded. Obviously this rally was the high point of the day. He would have to pace himself so he was fresh for the cameras. 'And is that it until tonight? Or do we have to go somewhere for tea, too?'

'Not today. Tomorrow we have three teas. But today, thank God, we give them a miss.' Matthew was solicitous. 'But we have something else. I know it's a lot, but this is the last week of the campaign. If there's time – if the rally doesn't run over – we want to get in two more factories at the shift change.'

'All right.' Christos leaned back on the seat and stretched. 'And tonight's the get-together at the Greek Orthodox seminary in Brookline.' He had been looking forward to relaxing with his countrymen all week. They would speak Greek and eat Greek and maybe, if the mood was right, he would even play his pipe. No doubt it would wend on until the wee hours, and most certainly there would be dancing. He would link arms with his compatriots, and for a while as they laughed and pranced and danced he would forget his weariness and recapture his zest for life. No one would ask him about ending the war or setting up daycare centres, and there was not a snowball's chance in hell that a good Greek girl would corner him in a hallway for stolen kisses. Of course there would be politicking. The archbishop would be there, and so would his father's business cronies. Nick, who was taking the night off from the restaurant, would be everywhere at once as he praised his son the candidate to the skies. One more time he would tell everyone how he himself had come to the shores of this country with only five dollars in his pocket. Little did I know, he would say, that in forty years my own son would be about to be elected to the United States Congress! Then, at a certain point in the evening, all the men would get together and argue heatedly about the *junta* which had taken power in Athens just over a year ago. Christos' eyes darkened. Since the *coup d'état* he had been so busy with his own political fortunes that he had not had time to grieve as he should for the disaster that had befallen his country. How could his brother be a part of that gang of thugs which had turned the motherland into a police state? The American and European papers were full of ugly rumours about the torture of political prisoners in Greece.

'Right. The seminary. We'll have you in Brookline at nine – ten o'clock at the latest.' James was glad that he and the other two aides did not have to endure another of those interminable nights with the candidate's Greek constituency. They were so overwrought, those Greeks, so terribly out of *control*. They were always shouting and hugging and making too much of inconsequential matters. James narrowed his eyes as surreptitiously he studied the candidate, who, despite his ethnic roots, was a cool one. Night and day for the past two months, he had been one of Chris's shadows. But still the man kept himself aloof. One of his own secret assignments was to report back regularly to Jonathan Heywood everything the candidate did and said in public and in private. It irked James that he had found so little to say. Chris was smooth, amenable, and he always performed like a well-rehearsed actor. But even after all this time together, the essence of the man eluded him. Yet James shrugged off his reservations. What was it to him if there was something not quite right about this candidate who had married into a political dynasty? 'But first you'll have cocktails on Beacon Hill. One of your wife's friends is throwing a little do. Very posh. Lots of money people. I think the Congressman himself will be there. And maybe the mayor, too.'

'All in a day's work.' Christos was used to Penelope's rich friends. Little would be required of him except good manners, a suave appearance, and what passed for wit in their circle. As he smiled and sipped his Scotch whisky, his radiant wife would adroitly steer him from this stockbroker to that industrialist. Uncle Jonathan would act more like the father of the bride than the uncle-in-law of the candidate. The mayor would playfully spar with him, and the two of them – as though they were the best of friends rather than bitter foes – would joke about last year's contretemps about missing funds in the housing authority. The minutes would crawl by, but finally he would be able to escape to his Greeks in the Orthodox seminary hall.

'OK, the Arlington housewives await.' As the car screeched to a stop, Matthew was the first one out of the door. Christos and his aides ran up the pavement to meet the next crop of voters.

*

278

Flushed with the undoubted success of the rally on Cambridge Common, it was nearly eleven o'clock on Saturday night when Christos and Penelope – arm-in-arm and laughing – all but danced inside Nick's waterfront restaurant. Just behind them Uncle Jonathan's limousine pulled up, and a pack of his henchmen helped the senior statesman and his wife inside the front door of the candidate's father's establishment for the reception which – three nights before the election – had the air of a victory celebration.

'Son!' Nick greeted Christos with open arms and for a moment they rocked together in a wordless embrace. Then Nick kissed Penelope exuberantly on both cheeks. 'Oh, my dear,' he enthused, 'everyone says you were wonderful tonight, just wonderful! A goddess! A real goddess!' As Nick took Congressman Heywood's hand, for an uncertain moment Christos worried that his father might bend to kiss it. But then a third car pulled up and two overexcited little girls burst into the restaurant trailed by Penelope's parents. '*Paidia mou*! My children!' Nick swept his granddaughters into his arms and, although he was short and slight and not so strong as he once had been, he carried the girls into the dining room on his shoulders.

'Christina,' Penelope said to her husband as she slipped away to get the baby in the makeshift nursery Nick had set up this afternoon near the kitchen. 'It's long past her feeding time.'

Congressman Heywood threw a possessive arm around his heir apparent's shoulder as the two of them strode into the dining room. At once, the assembled throng of wellwishers broke out into wild applause and then began a rhythmic chant. 'Kronos for Congress! Kronos for Congress!' Together the old and the new politicians held up their free arms in a V-sign. Camera strobes flashed, and the Congressman who was and the one who would be posed like film stars on a set.

The two separated then to work the dining-room crowd. This had been supposed to be a small family dinner. But as the momentum had built during this last heady week of the primary campaign, it had been impossible not to invite everyone from party bosses and ward leaders to sympathetic journalists and leaders of the Greek business community. Yet even though there were more than a hundred supporters packed in the dining room, the crowd had a family feeling. There were more embraces, kisses on cheeks, and warm manly handclasps as the party faithful and the family intimates congratulated both the Congressman and the candidate on the splendid success of tonight's rally.

And it had, Christos reflected as he was swept from one grinning face to another, been the capstone of the campaign.

From Harvard Square to the university campus, the park had been packed with party and student supporters. Antiwar posters and 'Kronos for Congress' placards had waved in the wind. The young people from the campuses had turned out in force, but so had the ethnic Italian, Portuguese, and Irish voters from the district's working-class precincts. Though the predominantly black wards of Roxbury weren't in this Congressional district, the city's civil rights leaders had remembered Christos' support of their needs on City Council and sent a busload of their people to form a united front with the man of the hour. The Greeks had been there, too, and the blue and white flags of Christos' homeland had fluttered among the stars and stripes. A loudspeaker had blasted music: Bob Dylan singing 'Blowing in the Wind', Joan Baez delivering 'We Shall Overcome', Mikis Theodorakis strumming the theme from 'Zorba the Greek', and finally the Boston Pops playing 'America the Beautiful'. As the crowd had waited for the speeches to begin, some of them had sung along with the music. When the Greek bouzouki music had sounded the students had snaked on the outskirts of the crowd in a line dance that looked more like the conga than a *syrtaki*. High above the crowd, a kite emblazoned with 'Kronos for Congress' had flown.

After the mandatory introductions from party leaders, Congressman Heywood had kicked off the speeches with an emotional oration calling for the torch to be passed to a new generation. As he had in essence bade a fond adieu to the constituency which had sent him to Washington for a glorious thirty-four years, some of the more sentimental old women in the crowd had been moved to tears.

Then Penelope had swung into action, recalling her student days a stone's throw away at Radcliffe, her coming of age right here at Harvard, and finally – casting a fond glance over her shoulder at Christos – her meeting her handsome husband in another classroom just across the river at Northeastern University. 'It was love at first sight!' The crowd had applauded as though this were a family get-together rather than a political rally. Only when she was sure she had them in the palm of her hand had Penelope launched into a hard-hitting addressing of the issues. The war, of course, and civil rights; national health insurance, the protection of the environment, a lessening of Cold War tensions. But she had not forgotten the meat-and-potatoes issues of the working-class voters who cared less about Vietnam than the shrinking value of their dollars in the supermarket. New programmes must be instituted to help the elderly live in dignity, housing must be built for the poor and the homeless, crime in the cities must be decreased, the unions must be strengthened so that those who worked so hard for their paychecks could be assured a reasonable standard of living. To Christos' relief, she had refrained from her pet theories about women's rights and instead, to the cheers of the people, had finally introduced 'My husband, the man you are about to send to Washington!'

Like members of a royal family, they had kissed for the cameras. And then it had been Christos' turn at the microphone. Uncle Jonathan's professional campaign manager had decreed last week that in this rally they would leave the issues to Penelope and the emotional appeal to Christos. Talk about arriving here as an immigrant, he had been told. Pull out all the stops, wave the flag, do everything but sing 'The Battle Hymn of the Republic'. By now everyone knows what you stand for. Now what you want to do is speak from the heart. Woo them as you would a woman. Make them love you, and next Tuesday they'll all but be pulling bodies out of the graveyards to vote for you.

At the podium Christos had striven to do as he had been told. 'Eighteen years ago I came here from the cradle of democracy,' he had begun, 'and when I stood on board that ship in New York harbour and saw the Statue of Liberty, I never dared hope that one day I would be here asking you to send me to Washington as a representative of this city which you so proudly, and so aptly, call the Athens of America.' Delighting in Boston's self-styled soubriquet, the crowd had cheered. There had been more of this — the immigrant's determination to succeed as so many others had 'in this land of immigrants and the sons and the grandsons of immigrants', amusing anecdotes about how in those first years he had striven to transform his accented schoolbook English into the fast idioms of American slang, truly heartfelt sentiments about how comforting it had been to return to the snug embrace of his father, and how he had finally had tears in his eyes the day he was sworn in as an American citizen.

Listening to himself recite the catechism that the voters loved to hear, Christos' soul had trembled as he had remembered the darker moments he dared not mention: how he had looked at the grey Atlantic and longed for the blue Aegean, how his Greek pride had been outraged when boys in the street had mocked his foreignness, and how he had never been able to believe that he was anything but a Greek making the best of things here only because he was forbidden to return home.

Nonetheless, he had laid aside his qualms and gone on with his prepared speech. He had worked long and hard for this day, and he was not about to turn aside now just to soothe his troubled conscience. But despite what he had heard his enemies whispering, he was not a ruthless opportunist. He hadn't merely married Penelope for her money and her connections. Even back home, a man considered a girl's dowry before he took her for his wife. He would not let himself be ashamed of the way he had conducted his life in this country that truly was the land of opportunity. The good works he would

281

do in Washington justified the small compromises that were rolling off his tongue tonight.

Christos' voice had throbbed with conviction as he had told this crowd everything they wanted to hear about what he loved in America. He had praised his adopted country's ideals of liberty and the openness of this society where even an immigrant could aspire to national office. And finally, turning to blow a kiss at Penelope, his voice had fallen to an intimate whisper as he had told his followers how he had felt he finally belonged here when he married his beautiful American girl and they had established a family. 'It's the American dream come true! And now, after this country has given me so much, if you send me to Washington, I will do my best to repay the debt I owe to America and to you the people!'

Penelope had bounded up to embrace him, Uncle Jonathan had thrown his arm around his shoulder, and the love feast between candidate and people had concluded with shouts and chanting which a hyperbolic television journalist reported could be heard on the far side of the River Charles.

Over the heads of his enthusiastic supporters in the restaurant, Christos caught sight of Penelope at the head table with baby Christina in her arms. Hastily he finished his rounds and took his seat beside her. Instantly Nick, who had been rushing about seeing that his army of waiters got everyone drinks and were ready to begin serving dinner, sat down and began whispering in his son's ear. 'A great night, a fine night, to think I lived to see this blessed night! I take back everything I ever said about your politics! Proud, son, you've made me so proud! Oh, if only your mother were here, if only Sofia had lived! May the Panagia bless her and her soul rest in peace forever!'

'Easy, father.' Christos put his arm around the old man and tried to calm him down.

But Nick had something else he wanted to say. 'And this is only the beginning, *paidi mou*, the beginning! Who knows what will happen next?' Triumphantly he reached into the box he had waiting under the table and unrolled an architect's drawing. 'I didn't tell you my big secret before, I kept my great idea to myself for years! I would have told you last month when I went to the architect, but you're so busy now with the campaign, I didn't want to bother you. But I can wait no longer! Here, son, is my great idea!' To Christos' astonishment, he pointed at the drawing of a building which had an amazing resemblance to the Parthenon that sat on the Acropolis atop Athens.

'I don't understand.' The old man, Christos thought, must be losing his marbles. Why else would he pay an architect to copy the Parthenon?

'For the restaurant! For here!' Nick rapturously pointed out the window

282

to the long lawn that stretched between the horseshoe-shaped restaurant and Boston Harbor. In good weather, Nick filled it with chairs and tables so his patrons could dine *al fresco*. His accountant and even his waiters had been telling him for years that this was a waste of prime real estate, but Nick had refused to build another dining room on the site. Only now was the reason apparent. 'I'll build it right out there. I've dreamed of this for years, *paidi mou*, for years! Why else would I have had the restaurant built all around that empty space? You think I care about grass? No, no, that land out there will be Nick Kronos' Acropolis! I've talked to the builders, and they tell me they'll have it up by this time next year.'

Bemused, Chris stared at his father. On this night of nights, he didn't think anything could steal the thunder of his campaign. But he had never dreamed his father could come up with a scheme like this. 'You're telling me that you're going to build a replica of the Parthenon here, right in the middle of Nick's Boston Fish House?'

'No, not in the middle, I'd have to tear down the restaurant. Actually, that was my original idea. But the architects told me it would cost too much.' Patiently Nick once again pointed outside. 'It will be right out there, just on the water. We'll put floodlights on it at night, and you'll be able to see it from Revere. The pilots will point it out as they circle Logan Airport. Think of it, son, our own Parthenon!'

'Just an empty building?' Christos was so stunned he didn't know what else to say.

'No, no, we'll use it. For an oyster and clam bar.' Nick's finger stabbed at the architect's drawing. 'There, inside, where the Statue of Athena once stood. I was going to have someone build one of her – maybe use Peppy as a model, who knows? – but the architects thought that would be . . . too much. Then I thought, why not use the space constructively?'

'I see.' Christos took a sip of water. 'You're going to build a miniature Parthenon and sell fish inside it?'

'You bet. And not only that. In no time at all, it'll be a tourist attraction. People will come from miles around – from California, Hawaii, you name it – to have their pictures taken on the steps of Nick Kronos' Parthenon.' Cannily his eyes gleamed. 'But of course they'll have to have dinner here to do it.'

'That's some idea.' Gently Christos probed the extent of what had to be his father's delusion. 'You will build . . . this thing . . . of Athenian marble?'

'I'd like to, but the architect says it would be too expensive. He suggests cement blocks with a plastic overlay. Maybe some laminated tiles on the top that look like marble. He says they do great things with plastic these days.'

283

The *maître d'* rushed over with an urgent appeal that Nick come to the kitchen, and before Christos could say another word his father was gone.

Penelope leaned over. 'What was that all about?'

'You won't believe it.' Christos shook his head. 'My father never ceases to amaze me.' He was just about to show her the architect's drawing when there was a commotion at the door and two of his campaign aides came in with a stack of the newly-printed editions of tomorrow morning's newspapers. 'Ah,' he said, carefully rolling up his father's precious plans. 'I can't wait to see what they say about the rally.'

But as Matthew and James made their way toward the head table, Christos saw the looks on their faces and was struck by a foreboding. Never before, in the two months that he had been in the company of these young men, had he seen any expression on their faces other than bland competence and occasional amusement. How could it be that the two of them looked about to burst into tears?

He wondered no longer when wordlessly Matthew flung down the early edition of the Sunday newspaper with the page one headline facing Christos.

'Kronos: The Red Greek!'

Later Christos was to try to reconstruct his exact emotions when he first caught sight of this newspaper which was so to change his life. But then, and later, all he could recall was a great dark blankness. For a terrible long moment, he merely stared at the headline.

It was Penelope, looking over his shoulder, who was the first to read the sensational article spread below. How it had come to light, 'by a team of award-winning investigative reporters sent by this newspaper to Athens, Greece,' that the erstwhile Democratic candidate Chris Kronos had been what they termed 'a card-carrying member of the Communist Party'. How he had led a team of 'Red terrorists' fighting in the mountains against the established government. How they had first been tipped off to what they called 'Kronos' traitorous secret' by a letter sent by 'an unimpeachable source, a prominent member of the current Greek government'. How presumably Kronos had lied about his past on his US immigration application. And how 'this Red Greek mole' had compromised the antiwar movement and now was attempting to infiltrate the highest governing body in the land. There was more about treason, a spy ring, and 'an intricate Communist plot'.

Penelope read it all, then quietly turned to her husband. 'Tell me this isn't true.'

Briefly Christos met her eyes, and then in anguish he looked away. 'Some of it's true,' he answered in a whisper. 'And some of it's not.'

284

'About the war? What you did in the war? That you were . . .' She could not quite bear to say the word.

'It's complicated,' he hesitantly began.

'No it's not. You were either a member of the Communist Party or you weren't. I have to know. *Now*! Before all hell breaks loose here.'

Miserably he finally nodded. 'I was. But I left the Party before I came to America. I did, Peppy, I did.'

'Right.' A lesser woman would have broken down there and then, but Penelope had the breeding to rise to the occasion. With rigid self-control she put aside her own feelings. Her survival instinct warned her that this was definitely neither the time nor the place to face the recriminations of the supporters her husband apparently had betrayed. But until she knew the extent of his culpability, she would not sit here and allow these people who had assembled to hail the conquering candidate turn into an hysterical lynch mob. She had some serious questions to ask her husband – oh yes, and this time he would tell her the truth! – but she would wait until they were safely at home to hit him with them. What would happen after that would depend on his answers. Even if she decided this spelled the end of their marriage, she, Penelope Heywood Kronos, would hold her head high and never falter in public. First, however, she would have to get her family home, and fast. Above all, she must protect her family. All around the dining room, a silence had fallen as copies of the newspaper were passed from hand to hand. In a moment they all would be on their feet demanding answers. She leaned over and touched the Congressman's arm. 'We're going home, Uncle Jonathan. I'll call you first thing tomorrow, and we'll talk.' Without further ado, majestically she rose with the baby in her arms. 'Come, children.' Obediently Sofia and Helen joined her. 'Let's go, Chris. *Now*!'

Before anyone had a chance to say a word to them, they sailed out the door and into the safety of their car.

In the forty minutes it took the driver to whisk them home to suburban Concord, Penelope did not speak to her husband. Instead she sat in the far corner of the back seat with her children around her, promising the disappointed girls an ice cream if they were good. She crooned soothing noises to the baby.

Christos sat hunched in the other corner. Landmarks flashed by. The Mystic River Bridge. Charles River Park. The Hatch Shell. The Mall. The River Charles. Fresh Pond. Route Two. Think, he ordered himself. What are you going to do? But try as he might, he – the smooth political operative, the man who always had all the answers – couldn't focus on anything other than who had blown the whistle on him in Greece. The newspaper had attributed its facts to a tip from 'an unimpeachable source', someone in the government of the colonels itself. *Yorgos*; it had to have been his own half-brother. But surely even Yorgos would never stoop so low. Nick's other son would not bring such dishonour on the family. But then, as if it were yesterday instead of nearly twenty years ago, once again Christos saw his brother's face contorted by hate as they had struggled with that knife on the Peloponnese mountaintop. His own hand balled up as though once again he held that Turkish stiletto. If he had killed his brother when he had the chance, how different his life would have been! Maybe he would have married Marika after all, and perhaps he would even have found a way to stay in his homeland. Instead, this . . .

As Christos looked over at his wife, for a crystal clear moment he forgot his dashed political hopes and instead a tenderness for this good woman washed over him. How could he, even now, betray her with thoughts of Marika? This woman who had given birth to his three children deserved far more than he had ever given her. She and their daughters – more than his relatives in Greece and even his irrepressible father – were his family now, and yet until this instant that essential truth had never dawned on him. How could he have wasted the prime of his life on brooding memories and vainglorious hopes? He had lived so many lies for so many years that he wondered if it were too late to begin anew and honestly love Penelope as a man was supposed to love a wife. She had been magnificent back there in the restaurant. But he had to admit that Penelope always had been magnificent. Inside he seemed to shrink. *Another betrayal.* Once he had betrayed Marika, and now he had done it again with his wife. How had his life gone so wrong?

As they came through the door, the telephone was already ringing. The first thing she did when it finally stopped was to tell the answering service to intercept all incoming calls. They would pick up their messages in the morning. Then she gave the girls their ice cream and put the baby to bed.

Christos was sitting in front of the unlit fireplace petting the dog and sipping a seven-star Metaxas brandy when finally she returned from tucking in the girls. He poured her a Scotch and soda and ran his fingers through his hair. For the first time, he noticed that it was thinning. He braced himself for a torrent of recriminations and accusations. She would shriek and cry, of course her family would arrive and join the fray, and most probably she would leave him in the dead of this night with the children. 'So . . .'

Without looking at him she sank down on the other armchair pulled up before the fireplace. 'I suggest you start from the beginning. I want to know everything about your activities. First, before you left Greece. And second, since you've come here. And no lies, Chris. There's no time for lies.'

'OK.' The calm and measured tones of her voice registered on him. But of course, he reminded himself, this was Boston, not Greece. Was it better, or worse, that apparently the two of them were going to try to be civilized about all this?

Christos stared into the dead fireplace. It had been a hot May evening, but now it was cold, too cold. A shiver ran through him as haltingly he tried to conjure up that bygone time, how it had been fighting against the Nazis, how the feelings of comradeship and commitment had grown among his men, how gradually – day by day, skirmish by skirmish – their radicalism and their sense of oppression had grown. Thinking back, he could not honestly tell her exactly when he had begun to believe in Marxism as Greece's answer. He remembered a young man with burning eyes who had come to them from Athens with answers to all their wretched questions about why this world of fire and blood was as it was. 'Maybe he convinced me. Or maybe I came to the Party myself. Because for me and for so many others, in that time and that place it was *right*!' And then his voice which until then had been soft and apologetic had taken on a defiant timbre. 'How can you understand what I mean? You, who have lived your rich American life? Have you ever been hungry? Have you ever lived without hope? Have you ever seen the charred remains of a village gutted by the fascists, with women and children burned alive in their own houses? You can't imagine what it was like, Peppy. You can never imagine it.'

'After all these years with me, you still think I have no heart and no mind?' Her pale blue eyes flashed. 'Spare me, please, any more about how a rich American could never understand a suffering Greek. I can understand if you make me understand.'

He gazed at this woman who perhaps, after all, was capable of understanding. If she had been born his contemporary back in Greece, she might have been one of the first of those fervent girl guerrillas to take to the hills to fight against the Nazis. A smile played around his lips.

'You find that funny?' Penelope was not smiling.

'No, I was just thinking what a comrade you would have made. I can just see you in battle fatigues, with your rifle primed. You would have been quite a comrade, Peppy.'

'I have always been your comrade. Even here, in capitalist America.' Now she was not only smiling but looking at him straight in the eye. 'And I am still your comrade.'

He grinned and gave Zoi the dog the caress he didn't dare try yet on his wife. It was easier, then, to tell Penelope how it had been when he had joined the Communist Party and how, in those first years of fighting, the ideal of socialism had inspired him to make such gut-wrenching sacrifices. His voice dropped to a whisper as he described the seasons of betrayal, and how finally old comrades had told him his name had been placed on a death list. 'It was then that I left the Party,' he said. 'And I left it for good. I swear to you, Peppy, that I have never had anything to do with the Party since then. I am not a Communist mole and not a Communist spy.'

Intently she stared into his eyes, and then she nodded. 'I believe you. So far I believe you. Maybe no one else will, but I do. But let's get back to Greece. What happened after you left the Party? For good, as you say.'

'I decided to come here to join my father.' For a moment he fell silent, remembering how he had stood on that Tripolis mountaintop and made the decision temporarily to abandon both Marika and Greece. Was it true, what his political enemies here in America said about him, that he was a rank opportunist? Did he richly deserve what he had gotten tonight in that newspaper? With an effort he cut off such conjectures. Later, if the consequences of that article were as he feared, he would have all the time in the world to ponder what might have been if he had made different life choices. He returned to the answers he owed his wife. If he had stayed in Greece, he explained, he either would have been salted away in a government concentration camp or gunned down by his former comrades.

But Penelope did not let him so easily off the hook. 'I presume that every Communist dissident didn't leave Greece for America? That some chose to stay and fight? And others went to the prison camps for their beliefs?'

His eyes were hooded. 'Yes.' If she dared to say another word about this particular matter, his nerves would snap. He was not ashamed of once fighting with the Communists then turning against them. But he would never forgive himself for abandoning that one he had cherished most in the world. Marika . . .

For the moment she let this drop as she turned to another troubling matter. 'And after you made the decision to come to America, what did you say on your immigration papers? Was the newspaper right? Did you lie about your Communist affiliations? Correction, your *former* Party membership?'

'You know, and I know, that I would never have been able to set foot in America if I had told the whole truth.'

She let out the breath she had been holding in a hiss.

'They may revoke your citizenship and deport you, you know. Perhaps even put you in prison. I'm no lawyer, but clearly what you did was against the immigration laws.'

'I was desperate, Peppy. Desperate men do desperate things.'

'Apparently so.' She was so caught up in what to do about his immigration problem and what to say about all this to her family – not to mention the reporters who would be camped outside the front door in the morning – that she forgot how angry she was at him and absently, like a good wife, she refilled his glass of brandy. 'Maybe, if Uncle Jonathan's still speaking to us after all this, we can get you a pardon.' She poured herself another Scotch and soda. 'OK, I can follow what you've said up to now. Frankly, I'm not the least bit happy about it – '

'You think I am?'

She flared. 'Those were your choices and your life. Not mine. Or the children's. But now we're all in the mess you've created. Don't forget that.' She stared at him until his eyes fell. 'But what I can't understand is how – with a past like yours – you dared to run for public office. Something like this, it had to come out sometime.'

His face set in grim lines. 'It didn't have to come out unless someone made it come out. So many records were lost in the war. Greece is not like America. So many things can get lost there. Even people.' His voice dropped an octave. 'I think it was my own brother who tipped off the paper.'

'Yorgos?' Her husband had always been strangely closed-mouthed about his half-brother. The little she knew about him she had gleaned from Nick and newspaper clippings about the rightwing dictatorship. 'The little colonel?'

'The very same.'

Thoughtfully she shook her head. 'You Greeks are funny. You always carry on about your families like they're holier than the church. And now you can't wait to point the finger at your own brother.'

'I'm sure it was him. You don't know him.' Christos' right hand balled into a fist as again he remembered coming within a hair's breadth of slitting his brother's throat. 'What he's done. What he's capable of doing.'

'Must run in the family,' she muttered to herself. She shook her head. 'This gets uglier and uglier.' Again she shook her head. 'But you still haven't told me, knowing what would happen if the truth about your past came out, why you ran for public office.'

Earnestly he leaned forward. 'It was what I was born to do, Peppy. To serve the people. That's what I wanted to do in Greece. And when that went wrong, that's what I wanted to do here. I would have been great in Congress. I know it, I know it.'

'I'm afraid we'll have to take your word for it.' She paused. 'Because there's no way you're going to Congress now.'

He took a deep breath. Finally she had said what he had known the instant he had seen the headline. He nodded once, as a man will when he first hears of a death in the family. 'It's all over, then.'

'Completely.' She let that sink in, and then as neatly as a surgeon suturing a wound she sewed up the rest. 'Of course you'll have to withdraw from the race. I suppose we'll have to hold a news conference and bow out as gracefully as we can. I'm not sure what exactly we should say, but we'll think of something. We'll have to talk to the lawyers first, so we don't say anything that will make the immigration thing even worse.'

She swirled her drink until the remains of the ice cubes tinkled. 'The election's Tuesday. We'll have to have the news conference on Monday.' She downed the dregs of her drink. 'I'll have a terrible time with Uncle Jonathan. He never liked you much anyway, you know.' She shrugged. 'Well, he's the least of it. Him and everyone else. You realize, don't you, the repercussions this could have? Aside from compromising yourself and the family, you've laid the whole antiwar movement open to the worst sort of attack. A lot of good people – and a cause that I happen to believe in with every fibre of my being – are going to suffer because of this.' She shook her head in despair. 'Well, I suppose there's nothing to be done about that now. We're going to have our hands full just keeping you in this country.'

' "We?" You keep on saying "We". Does that mean you're still with me?'

'That depends.' She had taken him for better or for worse, but she had never dreamed of a catastrophe on this scale.

He waited for her to say more. But when she continued to stare silently into the empty fireplace, he repeated his question.

Finally she looked at him. For the first time since she had sat down with him her voice was hoarse with emotion. 'Chris, why didn't you tell me all this before?'

The dog whined and Christos hung his head. Yes, now the hysteria would begin. 'Look, before you say anything, I know I have shamed you with your family. And betrayed your uncle and his political friends.'

'To hell with the family and politics.' Her voice rose a decibel. 'What about *us*?'

'Us?'

'You know . . . me, you, *our marriage*? We've been married twelve years, and now I discover you have a whole secret life you never told me about. Do I really know you, Chris? Do I know anything that matters about you?'

He shrugged. 'Does any human being ever really know another?'

'Don't give me that line. I'm not one of those cute little starstruck coeds who are always throwing themselves at you.'

'I have always been faithful to you, Peppy.'

'With your body, maybe. What little of it you've grudgingly given me. But there are other, maybe more important ways that a man can betray a woman.' In despair she hid her head in her hands, and when finally she straightened up she looked more tired than he had ever seen her. 'I suppose what really kills me about all this is not what you did when you were young. I can understand and, in a way, even admire that. But what I don't think I

290

can forgive is what came after. *Here*. How you lied to everyone. How you did your best to exploit everyone – including me. And most of all how you never trusted me enough to tell me some of the essential facts of your life. Trust, Chris! And intimacy. I'm talking about the most important thing between a man and a woman. You are my husband, and yet you are a stranger to me. Twelve years, three children, and I'm no closer to you than one of your campaign aides. That's what kills me, Chris.'

He bit his lip. In this country where he would always be foreign, he remained a stranger with everyone except possibly his father and his children. Yet he did love Penelope. Until tonight, he had not realized how much. He reached over, took her hand, and spoke the words so difficult for a Greek man to say to anyone but his mother. 'I'm sorry.'

She looked into his eyes. 'Yes, I do believe you are.' Her voice fell, and she seemed to be talking more to herself than to him. 'But I wonder if you're sorry for the right reasons.' She sighed.

The sound of her sigh cut him deeper than a knife. He didn't remember ever having heard her sigh before.

'I am so tired. So very tired.' Again she sighed. As she stood, she looked down at her husband. He looked so small and vulnerable in that great wing chair that had been in her family for generations. Pity for him washed over her. Life was short and full of brutal surprises. But perhaps she could muster the strength to be kind to this wounded but still proud man who, she sensed, needed her tonight much as the children needed her in all their waking hours. After all this, she didn't know whether she would want him beside her forever. But maybe they could comfort one another tonight. She had been going to tell him to sleep in the guest bedroom, but instead she held out her hands. 'Time for bed.'

Gratefully he took them. He looked at her slim white fingers, and for a moment it seemed he might kiss them. Instead he clasped them to his cheek and leaned against her thigh like a small boy trying to take refuge in his mother's skirts.

Does it always come to this, she wondered, between a man and a woman? They say they are strong and we are weak, and yet here we are, the eternal mother and son. She stroked his thinning hair.

Christos put out the dog. And then, arm-in-arm, slowly, like old people, they walked up the staircase to their bedroom.

At eleven o'clock on Monday morning, Christos looked straight into the television cameras as he read his prepared statement that he was withdrawing from the congressional race.

291

His voice was firm and controlled, and he did not sweat under the bright lights the news crews had turned upon him. The carefully-worded statement, which the battery of lawyers from his wife's family firm had worked out in his sitting room the night before, said as little as possible about the charges and insinuations which had first been levelled against him in the Sunday newspaper. The lawyer's advice had been to admit nothing, to avoid directly addressing the charges, and to be the first to call for a public investigation. In the meantime, they had counselled, say you plan to file a libel suit against any newspaper which continues to slander you. Above all, they had stressed, no matter what the provocation, do not say one word to the press except what we write in your statement. And then, before the media has a chance to devour you, get the hell out of that news conference and stay out of sight and incommunicado while we do what we can to limit the damage.

'For the good of the Democratic Party and in the interest of the voters who will go to the polls tomorrow,' Christos read, 'I will withdraw from public life until the distressing published smears about my alleged activities in Greece are laid to rest.'

As the cameras rolled, the strobes flashed, and the reporters scribbled, beside him Penelope sat dressed in a conservative navy blue suit with white piping around the collar. No one else was at their table with the microphones in the Statler Hotel conference room. Congressman Heywood had refused to compromise himself further with his niece's husband, and not a single Democratic Party official had dared let himself be photographed with the disgraced candidate whom the Monday morning newspapers had called 'Red Chris'.

Attentive but distant, as though she were listening to an uninspired church sermon instead of the death knell of her husband's career, Penelope recalled all that had happened yesterday, her personal Black Sunday. She and Chris had planned to go to her uncle's house in nearby Ayre first thing in the morning, but by seven o'clock their manicured front lawn and even the vegetable garden by the kitchen door had been crowded with reporters, photographers, and television crews. She had telephoned her uncle, quickly apprised him of the situation and a little of what Christos has told her the night before, and finally convinced the Congressman to come to their house for an emergency family conference. No sooner had she hung up the phone than a key had turned in the front door and Nick had burst in with Penelope's mother and father in tow. Penelope had firmly pushed back the reporters and relocked the door. As Christos and Nick embraced and gabbled to one another in high decibel Greek, she had steered her parents into the sitting room, served them coffee, and had no sooner started to answer their questions when an insistent pounding had begun on the back door. A

292

moment later Congressman Heywood had stormed in with a squad of the relatives in his wake.

Penelope's makeup was flawless, and except for the tightness around her eyes, there was no visible sign of the strain of the last thirty-six hours. But the confrontation with Uncle Jonathan had been hell. At first her family had insisted she simply get a divorce and leave her husband to 'get what was coming to him'. Congressman Heywood had raged at Christos for disgracing the family, sullying his own political reputation, and betraying everything that a man of honour held sacred. At one point she had feared her uncle and her husband would come to blows. But when finally the limousine of lawyers had pulled up the driveway, calmer heads had prevailed. Nick had whipped up lunch, and by the time they had eaten and digested the situation, their course had been set. Uncle Jonathan had grudgingly agreed to assure the party bosses that Christos most definitely would withdraw from the race. 'For the sake of Penelope and the girls, not for you, you Red bastard,' he had shouted at Christos, he would do what he could to keep his niece's husband out of jail and in the country. The lawyers would hammer out the public statement. Then immediately after delivering it to this news conference, Christos, Penelope, and the children would leave directly for the family's summer place at the far end of Cape Cod. They would remain isolated inside the security fence around the ten-acre grounds while the lawyers handled everything. There would be no private interviews with reporters and no statements to investigators without the family lawyers present.

Adroitly Penelope avoided the searching looks of the journalists she once had treated as friends. She held her head high and stared intently at an oil painting of a sailing ship on the far wall. All afternoon and evening Christos had sat with the lawyers. First they had grilled him about his political past in Greece. Was there any written proof of his membership of the Communist Party? Were there any living witnesses who could stand up in court and identify him as a Communist? Exactly what had he done in Greece – they wanted names, dates, circumstances – when he was a Party member? Then they had moved on to not only his reasons for coming to America but the papers he had filed to gain entry to this country. Christos had rooted through his office and produced his documents, and for a long while the lawyers had pored over them. When they dryly asked him if he had any more secrets about further Communist activities since he had arrived in America, at first Christos had shaken his head. Then he had recalled occasional social evenings with old comrades who also were exiled from Greece. Again they had asked for names, dates, and places, and Christos had hauled out his old appointment books and tried to reconstruct the past eighteen years of his life. It had

293

been long past midnight when finally, after drafting the statement he was reading now, the lawyers had finished working out a strategy for how to handle the press and US governmental authorities.

Sincerely Christos gazed into the cameras. 'Ladies and gentlemen, I will not allow myself, or my family, to become the victims of a witch hunt that is not so different from a regrettable and recent chapter of American history. You all remember how former Senator Joseph McCarthy ruined the lives and careers of hundreds of loyal Americans with his unsubstantiated charges about their alleged leftist affiliations. Are we to let that happen here and now, *in Massachusetts*?' He paused. 'I will not be tried by the press. This is a government of the law, not of the media.' He looked straight into the red light of the camera. 'Already,' he said, 'I have contacted the Federal Bureau of Investigation, the US Department of Justice, and the Immigration Service to offer my full co-operation in what I hope will be a thorough investigation of the unsubstantiated rumours which have blackened my name, caused my family grievous embarrassment, and made it impossible to stand for public office at this time.'

Blandly Penelope stared at the sails of the oil-painted schooner. Not only Christos but she, too, had battled with Uncle Jonathan and the lawyers about how to handle this crisis. The two of them had wanted to tell the truth and throw themselves on the mercy of public opinion and the courts. But the Congressman and the attorneys had insisted that, considering the facts, honesty was very definitely not the best policy. At one point Jonathan had even run up the stairs and come down with the baby in his arms. 'Do you want,' he had shouted, holding up Christina before the assembled tribe and lawyers, 'to ruin the future of this helpless child?' When the baby had started to cry, hastily he had handed her over to her mother and continued with his diatribe. 'No one in this family, not Christina, not Sofia, not Helen, not you, Penelope – and not me, either! – will ever live down this scandal, especially if that husband of yours admits the truth!' And then, breathing heavily, he had sunk down in an armchair and held his chest as though he were about to have a heart attack. While Catherine and the rest had huddled around the Congressman loosening his tie, getting him a glass of water, and soothing him with pats and murmurs, Christos and Penelope had adjourned to the kitchen for their sharpest exchange since the scandal had broken. 'Don't ever tell me again that my family is hysterical and yours is a model of breeding,' he had told her between clenched teeth. And she had shot back: 'At least my family doesn't send poison-pen letters that may ruin all our lives.' Yet after his father and her mother had broken down and wept, finally Christos and Penelope had caved in and agreed to do as the lawyers advised. Yet as she listened to her husband dodge and evade the issues, Penelope wondered why

294

it was that so often in life a man or woman had to choose between doing what is right and what everyone else says is smart.

'Ladies . . . gentlemen . . . thanks very much.' Christos and Penelope stood and made for the door behind their table.

'Not so fast!' A reporter was shrieking. 'Are you a Red or aren't you?'

'Is it true you're still a member of the Communist Party?'

'Are you still in the pay of Moscow?'

'How many others in the antiwar movement are in your cell!'

'Who do you think you're fooling with this, anyhow!'

At the door, Christos paused. 'No comment,' he said. 'I do not want to prejudice the upcoming investigations. Until this matter is resolved, I will have no further comment.'

'No more questions!' A phalanx of young men in dark suits suddenly stood between Christos and Penelope and the press. The last thing the two of them heard before they escaped into the next room was a wail from a reporter.

'You won't get away with this! We'll find out! We'll find out everything!'

Twelve

His eyes still shut, Christos reached for her with a need that was stronger than love. His fingers caught strands of satin hair. His hand skimmed velvet skin; her swollen nursing breasts, her taut belly, her undulating thighs as in her sleep she turned toward him in unconscious response to his touch.

'Peppy . . .' He groped closer to her. He had to touch her everywhere. He had to make them one, for it was no longer enough to be only himself. Home, he had to get home, where it was warm and tight and safe. His lips were on her neck, his fingertips on her nipples, his hips over hers.

He opened his eyes to her tan skin, gold hair, and those porcelain breasts the sun had never seen. He suckled like an infant and drew strength from her font of mother's milk. He could feel himself swelling, not just between his legs but inside, where his need was strongest.

'Chris, oh Chris.' By the silvery morning light filtering in the bedroom window of their Cape Cod hideaway, she watched his black hair buried in her breasts. Then he lifted his head and covered her lips with his, tenderly at first and then with an urgency he couldn't control. His tongue was inside, his legs were parting hers, and then all of him was inside. Home! His hands were under her pelvis pulling her closer, he went deeper, they gasped and thrust in the pounding primal rhythm. Fiercely he kissed her. 'More,' he murmured, 'give me more.' All her body took him in. He sank deeper in her heat. The fever increased, they held on to one another as first she came and then he followed in a convulsion that went on and on.

Afterwards, they clung to one another like frightened children.

'Mummy! *Dad*! Let us in!' Excited barks, then a baby crying. Sofia wailed: 'C'mon! Get up! We're going to Greece, *remember*?'

In the bed, their eyes met; then his fell. He turned over and pulled the sheet over his head. The alarm clock sounded. Eight o'clock. 'Mummy!' Little Helen was pounding on the door. Peppy swung out of bed. 'Coming!'

'Who's ready for another one?' Less than an hour later, Penelope stood in front of the sizzling grill. Pancakes for Sunday breakfast were a family tradition, and on this – the morning of the day that she and the children were leaving with Nick for Greece – she was determined to maintain the illusion that all was right around their kitchen table.

'Me!' Greedily Sofia sopped up the last bit of her pancake with the maple syrup on her plate and held out the dish as her mother slid another one on it.

'And me!' Helen had not yet finished her last one. But anything her big sister got, she wanted as well. As her mother flipped a pancake onto her plate, she looked over to make sure that Sofia's wasn't bigger.

Penelope buttered her two-and-a-half-year-old daughter's pancake, poured on some syrup, and slid another pancake off the grill. 'Chris?' She frowned when she saw that he hadn't touched his last one and was smoking a cigarette. 'Done already? But you've hardly eaten a thing.'

'I've had two.' Better that she didn't know he had fed even those to the dog. Zoi loved pancakes. But he had never been able to develop a taste for these sticky sweet breakfasts. And today, when his wife and children were leaving him behind and going off to the one place in the world he longed to be, he had even less appetite than usual. But he, too, wanted this last morning together to be a happy one, and so he forced a smile. 'Better eat up, girls.' He tried to joke. 'When you get to Greece, you'll have to do with a little bread and a glass of milk in the mornings.'

As Sofia polished off her pancake and held out her plate for the one her father had spurned, anxiously she looked at her mother. 'No pancakes? But they'll have Coco-Puffs, won't they?'

Penelope ruffled her daughter's curly blonde hair. 'I'm taking two big boxes with us, just to make sure.'

But this news that there would be no pancakes in Greece had alarmed Sofia. What else – besides her father, who for some strange reason wasn't going with them – would be missing in this faraway place? 'And peanut butter? And Spaghettios? And Oreo cookies? We'll be able to eat there, Mummy, won't we?'

Christos laughed. 'Of course you'll be able to eat. Greek food is very good.' He stared off into space, remembering. 'Wonderful, really.'

Doubtfully his daughters looked at him. Helen piped up. 'Will there be a McDonald's? And will the ice-cream truck come around like in Boston?'

Christos' face clouded. 'I'm not sure. I've been away a long time.' He stubbed out his cigarette. 'Too long.'

As Penelope busied herself reassuring the girls that they would have everything they wanted, and more, on their two-week holiday, out of the corner of her eye she watched her husband moodily staring out the window at the pounding Atlantic. In the two weeks they had been holed up here after he had dropped out of the Congressional race, Christos had withdrawn more and more into himself. At first he had jumped to answer every ring of the telephone, but none of the political men and women he had thought were his friends had ever dialled their number. He had been helpful and polite when the lawyers came to call with their briefs and depositions, and he had tried to hide his impatience when they insisted on staving off the pending government investigations for as long as they could. But the isolation, and the stress of so much unresolved, was clearly getting to him. He had seemed his old self only when he was playing with the children, but even with them he had begun to show an alarming new side. He was fine when he was off with Sofia and Helen fishing or romping in the surf. But in the evenings when he insisted on trying to teach them his native language, he turned into such a stern Greek *pater familias* that sometimes he reduced the girls to tears. With the baby, however, he was more tender than she had ever seen him. It had tugged at her heart to observe him simply holding Christina for hours on end as he whispered long soliloquies to her in Greek. It had seemed to her that he had clung to the infant even more than she held on to him. Penelope might have left the baby here with him if she had been altogether weaned. She had hated to stop breastfeeding this last of her children, for she, too, could feel middle age closing in.

As for how Christos was when it was just her and him together . . . Penelope brewed another pot of coffee and stared unseeing out the window at sailboats tacking against the wind. She had hoped their ordeal would draw them closer together. Repeatedly she had tried to get him to open up and talk not so much about their predicament but their relationship. Yet he had preferred to suffer in silence. Sometimes when she pressed him she had thought, although she couldn't be sure, that she had seen tears welling up in his eyes. But that old Greek devil *hubris* – the same stiff-necked, prickly pride that had wreaked such havoc in so many of the ancient tragedies – was once again shadowing their marriage. Intuitively she understood that, even though he didn't show it much, his love for her had grown stronger. Or maybe, she reflected, it was only his dependency that had increased. There was something disquieting in the way she would find him dogging her footsteps as she worked in the kitchen or tidied the family room. Just as it had been this morning, in bed together, too, he ached in her arms. Yet proudly he insisted on keeping his pain to himself. He took long restless walks alone on the beach, he closeted himself in his study and played wailing Greek records for hours on end, and some mornings he did not get out of bed until noon. She couldn't bear to see him so listless and defeated. Maybe in Greece she would find some answers to the enigma of the man she had married.

'OK, girls, drink your milk, and then it's upstairs with the two of you for your baths.' Penelope cleared the dishes off the table. 'Your nanny's waiting. And don't dilly-dally. Our bags are all packed, and we'll be leaving for the airport in an hour.'

As the girls pushed away their half-full glasses and ran up the stairs, Penelope poured two fresh mugs of coffee and sat down at the table. Again she doubted if this delicate mission to Greece was a good idea. Christos had turned even more melancholy since the lawyers had come up with this plan to sabotage the investigations at their source. For it appeared that his suspicions of his half-brother's role in the scandal might have been on the mark. A source at the newspaper had admitted only that their initial tip-off had come from an anonymous letter posted from Athens. They had sent reporters to Greece to confirm the story before they printed it, but apparently – from the lack of details and attributed quotes in the first exclusive and subsequent followups – they hadn't been able to unearth enough to convict Christos anywhere but on the pages of a newspaper. The lawyers reasoned that if Colonel Yorgos either was behind the anonymous letter or knew who had sent it, Nick and Penelope might be able to talk him out of co-operating with the American investigators. Anything they could do to stonewall the story would increase Chris' chances of escaping prosecution and staying in America. When they had first broached this idea to Nick, he had eagerly agreed. He had been planning a trip home anyway, for back in Panagia a family wedding was in the offing. Vangelis, the brother of Yorgos' wife Marika and a partner in the family enterprises, was marrying a Greek girl from Australia the Saturday after next. They would tell everyone that

Penelope and the girls were taking this opportunity to come along for a long-postponed trip to meet their Greek relatives. Once there, Penelope would try to use sweet reason on her brother-in-law. If this failed, Nick vowed he would simply put his foot down. Yorgos might be one of the colonels who ruled Greece with an iron fist, but within the family he was the eternal boy who would have to obey his father's wishes. Or so Nick hoped.

'Well.' Penelope poured cream in her coffee and spooned sugar into her husband's. 'Any last-minute advice for me?'

He lit another cigarette. 'Since when do you need advice from me about anything?' He exhaled. 'You always have all the answers.'

She sipped her coffee and controlled her temper. He was in yet another of his difficult moods, the one she always thought of as the Grand Greek Sulk. By rights she should leave him to pout and pollute his lungs with those cigarettes, but she could never leave whatever was unfinished between them when he was morose like this. As always, despising herself a little but unable to stop herself, she tried to jolly him out of his mood. 'Just think! Finally I get to see that village of yours!' When he did not respond, she prattled on. 'And your family.' Hastily she decided this was not the strategic moment to mention Yorgos. 'Your stepmother sounds really nice. In the photographs she has such a sweet face. And that Marika and her children – the girls can't wait to meet their cousins. Why we didn't go before this, I don't know.'

'You didn't go because I didn't want you to go.' He stubbed out his half-smoked cigarette. 'And because I can't go. As you know now, Greeks with my . . . past associations are not allowed back in the country.' He lit another cigarette. 'I still don't want you to go. It's a waste of time, money, and effort. Yorgos will never agree.'

'Chris! We've been all over this before. It's our best shot at nipping all this in the bud.'

'You think so?' Again that image of Yorgos' contorted face as the two of them had struggled with that knife swam up in his mind. 'But you don't know what you're in for. Yorgos!' He spat out the word.

She leaned forward. 'What's he like?'

Contemptuously Christos shrugged. 'You will see.'

'It might help if you prepare me. From what you say, I need all the help I can get if I'm to wrap him around my little finger.'

'Fat chance of that.' But forewarned was forearmed. He searched for words to describe that one who had tried so hard to ruin his life. 'He's short, round, wears glasses – you wouldn't look twice at him in a crowd. Or at least you wouldn't have, years ago, before he became so important. But I've seen his pictures in the Greek newspapers. He looks the same, only older and fatter.' Christos did not try to control the loathing in his voice. 'As for what is called *character* in other people, my half-brother is a bully. He was a little fascist even as a schoolboy. But don't make the mistake of underestimating him like I suppose I always did. To think that I used to feel sorry for him! Poor, pathetic Yorgos, the little boy no one liked. I expect people still don't like him. But probably now everyone in the village kisses his hand or whatever other part of his anatomy he prefers.' Christos blew smoke-rings. 'One thing for sure is that Yorgos is smart. He always was smart. Maybe, as things have turned out, he was smarter than me.'

'Oh, Chris!' She bit her lip but did not dare to reach out and cover his hand with hers. 'Don't go on like that, so bitter.'

Wearily he shrugged his eyebrows, then he took a deep drag on his cigarette as something disturbing crossed his mind. He reflected, and then, for her own good, he shared it with his wife. 'Watch out for him. He can be deadly. I even wouldn't put it past him to try to seduce you.'

'Come on, Chris, now you're going too far! I know you don't like him, but this is too much.'

'He's tried to take everything away from me that's mattered, so why wouldn't he go after you, too?' First Marika, and perhaps next Peppy.

'You don't honestly believe you have anything to worry about on that count, do you?' She was as gentle as when she was crooning to the baby. Something in his voice had told her that this preposterous fear was a cry from his heart. 'What would I want with a short, fat fascist when I have my very own former Communist?' She laughed just like she did when the children were worried about ghosts in the cellar.

His eyes darted to hers, and after an instant he tried to laugh away that primal fear. But then, as his thoughts returned to his wife's mission, Christos shook his head. 'I still don't think you'll be able to do anything with him. Whatever is going to happen, will happen. Your going to Greece isn't going to change anything. *Ti na kanoume*? What can we do?'

'But we have to try, Chris! We do!' More than anything, she hated this fatalism that had settled over him like a shroud. 'Even if we fail, we have to keep on trying!' When he gave her a pitying – even a patronizing – look, she gritted her teeth and once again put on a defensively bright social face. 'And besides, I'm really looking forward to Panagia. It looks so beautiful in that mural Nick has had painted on the restaurant wall. And you've talked about it so much, I feel I know it already.'

'You will never know my village.' Again he looked out the window at this ocean which was so unlike his sea. 'But maybe I don't know it any more, either.' He sighed. 'Look, Peppy, I worry about your going there. Especially without me.' Imagining her there and himself still here, he couldn't stop the resentment from creeping into his voice. 'You don't speak Greek, and the girls don't either. Why you never managed to learn, and how the girls are growing up without knowing – '.

She broke in. 'Sometimes I can understand when I hear you and Nick talking. And I can even speak it a little.'

'Very little. You won't understand how little until you get there.' He flicked off the ash of his cigarette. 'And another thing. It's not just the language. Panagia's another world. And a world that will always remain closed to you. You're a foreigner, and my people are very suspicious about foreigners. Everybody will be watching you, judging you, and – sorry to say this, but I must – I very much doubt that they'll like what they see.'

So that was it. For some strange reason that he had never let her know before, he was ashamed of her. She had a PhD from Harvard, and yet he was afraid that these illiterate peasants in his remote village would look down upon her. She pursed her lips. 'I see.'

'No, no, I didn't mean they wouldn't like *you*. Everyone always likes you, Peppy, you know that.' Genuinely he smiled at his wife. 'I meant they don't like anything that's different from them. They won't approve of how you dress, and how you talk, and what you say and do. You can't imagine how critical they are. Minding everyone else's business. It's the village sport.' He shook his head. 'It would be different if I could go with you. I could protect you – shield you – and maybe they wouldn't talk about you so much.'

'I think I can take care of myself.' She squared her shoulders. 'Besides, this is 1968. Greece is a modern country. It's in Europe, for God's sake! They won't expect me to live locked up in a harem. And if what you're worried about is my having a *man* to *protect* me, I'll have Nick.' Brightly she smiled. 'I'm sure you're over-reacting. From everything I've heard, read, and *know* about Greeks, they're very hospitable. I'm sure your family will welcome us with open arms.'

'Of course. Not just the family but everyone in the village will make a great fuss over you. But don't be taken in by their smiles. Be careful what you say and do. Be cool – even cold – to the men. And don't be too open with the women, either. Assume when you're talking to anyone, even in my family, that everything you say will be repeated. Even the most casual conversation is like being interviewed on the radio.'

She wrinkled her brow in disbelief. 'You make it sound like some police state.'

'Greece under the colonels *is* a military police state.' For an instant there was the ghost of a smile on his lips, and he seemed the Chris she still loved. Then he added another warning. 'My village is rigid, conservative, and it can be very rough there if you break the rules. Most especially there are many restrictions about what a woman can and can't do. You'll hate that.'

'Patriarchy,' she mutterd. 'Keep the women barefoot and pregnant, while the men rule the roost.'

He made a *tsk* sound of annoyance with his tongue. '*Everybody* has to conform. My God, Peppy, in this day and age grown men and women still submit to arranged marriages. Even the *men* can't violate the codes of behaviour.'

'And yet your brother apparently did what he did.'

His eyes were hooded. 'I told you before, Yorgos is different.'

'He must be really something, this brother of yours.' Her eyes narrowed. She would put that one in his place, and fast. And she would take her husband's warnings about his village seriously. But surely she would get along with some of his family. 'That wife of his sounds interesting. Nick says she's working for a newspaper in Athens. And that she speaks English. That note she sent you was so *caring*. More than you got from any of our old Boston *friends*.'

Christos did not dare meet her innocent eyes. Peppy had torn open that short letter from Greece before he'd even seen it, and she had been touched by Marika's terse words of condolence about the scandal. He, too, had been moved by her reaching out to him after all those years of silence. He had run his fingertips over the thin blue paper, wondering what message she had really intended to send.

But Penelope was gushing on. 'At least maybe I'll be able to talk to her, woman to woman. Bring a little sisterhood to Panagia. After all, we have a lot in common.'

More than you think, he said to himself. To hide his agitation he took a gulp of coffee and scalded his tongue. Of them all, Marika would be the worst. Maybe another woman would have forgiven and forgotten by now, but not Marika. Or at least, he amended – recalling the kindness of her note – not the Marika he had once known. American feminist sisterhood was most definitely not on the cards between his wife and his first love. He had a momentary impulse to confide what had once been between himself and his half-brother's wife. If ever he was to tell her, now was the time. He took a drag on his cigarette, and the moment passed.

Under his breath again he sighed. With an effort he put aside his misgivings and, for the first time since they had begun to talk, he looked his wife in the eyes and spoke from the heart like Americans do. 'I just wish I were going with you. I'd always hoped that someday they would let me go back. I wanted to be the one to show you all the places. To take my children to their grandmother's grave. And now I stay here and you go there.' His uncertain smile was a kind of apology. 'I guess that's why I'm acting like this this morning.'

'You think I don't know that?' Radiantly she smiled at him. 'I just hate to leave you here alone.'

'It will be a long two weeks.' He stubbed out his cigarette and took her hands in his. 'You've been great, Peppy.' He glanced around the lavishly appointed summer house which had become their gilded prison. 'All this is my fault. Being stuck here, not even able to go to the supermarket, sending the nanny out for supplies and the mail. And on top of that, I know I haven't been so easy to live with. But you've never once thrown all this up in my face. There aren't many women like you.' His voice was thick with emotion. 'At a time like this, a man finds out what's important in life.'

She let her hands rest in his. Finally, a breakthrough. If only they could resolve these investigations and return to a normal life together, perhaps now it would be different between them.

Penelope was just about to try to put her feelings into words when the phone rang. As she held it to her ear, even across the table Christos could hear his father's voice. 'All set? You'd better leave early. You know the traffic! And don't forget your passport!' The man and wife smiled at one another as the old man continued his ebullient fretting on the telephone.

When finally she hung up, Christos consulted his watch. 'He's right, you know.' From upstairs the children were calling for their mother.

'OK, OK.' Reluctantly Penelope got to her feet. Why, just as they seemed about to draw closer, did something or someone always intervene to keep them apart? But she really did have to rush to make that plane. As she passed her husband, she reached over and stroked the thinning hair on the top of his head. 'It'll be all right, honey. It's only two weeks. And don't you worry about that brother of yours. Or that damn village. They're not going to get the best of Penelope Heywood Kronos.'

A half hour later, as he stood in the driveway kissing his wife and children goodbye, Christos kept his emotions tightly under control. Only when he held Christina did the tears shine in his eyes.

'We'll call you as soon as we get there,' Penelope promised as she kissed him. There was another flurry of kisses and hugs, a last-minute checking to see that they had everything, then Penelope climbed into the driver's seat. 'Kalo taxidi,' he called out in Greek, 'Good journey!' The station wagon wended its way down the long driveway to the security gate and fence.

For a while Christos stood watching the spot where the car had disappeared. When he heard the gate clank shut, he felt that the key in his prison door had turned. He sighed deeply, wiped his eyes, and whistled for the dog. The golden retriever bounded beside him as he walked down to the beach slowly, with his hands in his pockets, as an old Greek fisherman will. The salt spray of the Atlantic stung his face as he looked at the far eastern horizon. He had never felt more alone.

Penelope's first thought when she caught sight of Colonel Yorgos striding toward them in the baking heat of the Athens runway was how much he reminded her of her husband. They had the same confident bearing, the same white-toothed smile, the same air of being born to command. Yorgos walked cockily, just as Christos had done until that newspaper headline had taught him to slump. But she had been expecting someone short and fat. This man, although stocky like her husband, looked fighting fit and taller than she had expected. She heard the click of heels and, as the colonel came closer, she stared at the elevated soles of his shoes. Her eyes trailed over his smartly-tailored khaki uniform. His barrel chest and wrestler shoulders were bedecked by so many medals, badges, stars, and epaulettes that it seemed Yorgos had singlehandedly won every war ever waged on earth. He sparkled in the sun as, followed by an entourage of uniformed lackeys and airport guards, he walked smartly up to his father, clicked his high heels, and bent to kiss Nick's hand.

The old man threw himself into the colonel's arms. 'Son! Son!' The two men rapturously embraced, kissing and hugging and babbling in high-pitched Greek. Penelope held the baby tighter as Sofia and Helen huddled close to her watching their weeping grandfather enveloped by this stranger in uniform. All the way from Boston Nick hadn't had a kind word for his younger son, and here he was greeting him as though he were the dearest soul ever born. Later these two might all but claw each other's eyes out, but for now they were stars in the melodrama of the moment.

As she waited for this reunion to conclude, Penelope looked around the busy airport of her husband's homeland. Planeloads of brightly-dressed holidaymakers were debarking from airliners which flew the flags of England and Germany. En route here, she had read in the Olympic Airways magazine that the government of the colonels had made tourist development a top priority. Despite adverse publicity about political repression in Greece, record numbers of visitors were expected for this year's high season. It seemed all of them were arriving just now.

'I'm hot, Mummy,' Sofia pawed at the skirt of her mother's dress as she whined.

'Me, too.' Helen put her thumb in her mouth, a sure sign of impending tears.

'We'll be going in a minute.' The baby and the girls had been good on the all-night trans-Atlantic flight from New York, but now they were turning cranky. And no wonder. When she stroked the blonde hair back from Helen's face, her hand came away wet with the sweat that was pooled at the roots of the little girl's hair. As soon as the stewardess had thrown open the airplane hatch, a wall of heat had hit them. Now, on this oven of a runway, the stack heels of Penelope's shoes seemed to sink into the tarmac. Her lemon yellow sundress clung to her skin. She felt slimy with perspiration. A sultry wind, hot as a hair dryer, whipped her skirt above her knees.

Yet still Nick and Yorgos were embracing and exclaiming. As Penelope did her best to quiet her fretting children, she looked past the airport perimeters at what she could see of this ancient city she had always dreamed of visiting. When Penelope was a child, her scholarly father had told her bedtime stories not just about Red Riding Hood and Snow White but of the gods and goddesses of Greek mythology and the doomed protagonists of Greek tragedy. Her archaeologist mother had made the crumbling sites of ancient Greece seem as familiar to her as New England's Plymouth Rock. Somehow, irrationally, she had expected toga-clad philosophers still to be striding about in their coarse sandals here in the olive groves of Attika. And so, as they had circled before landing, Penelope had peered out the window trying to pick out the white temples of the Acropolis among the beige sprawl of flat-topped buildings that seemed to sizzle in the blinding glare of the sun. But from the air Athens, sunk in a deep bowl between a hug of bare brown mountains and a blue sweep of sea, had been shrouded by a rusty haze of smog. 'Ten years ago,' Nick had told her, 'the Athens air was as clean as a mountaintop village, but now look at it! Too many cars, too much industry, and probably no north wind today to blow the pollution out to sea. But we'll be off to Panagia as soon as we land. There a man can really breathe!'

Penelope coughed as she took a deep breath of the dirty air. She and the children were so tired that she had considered trying to talk Nick into spending this first night in Athens. But now she, too, wanted to escape this sweltering city. Even Los Angeles' smog wasn't this bad. A plane rumbled down a nearby runway, and another taxied to a stop not far away. Somewhere near she could hear an angry hooting of horns. The heat, the noise, the pollution, and the jet lag made her dizzy. She staggered over to the colonel's grinning minions who were demanding the family's luggage from the airplane's crew who until now hadn't realized VIPs had been aboard. All of Yorgos' men were in uniform, all wore dark sunglasses, and all but one paused in what they were doing long enough to give her body an insinuating once-over.

305

'Welcome to Greece,' the exception said. 'I am Colonel Kronos' aide. Captain Kostas, at your service.' He smiled at the pretty thing 'Captain Prometheus' had married. Obviously that letter to Boston had made her come running fast. From the foreign newspapers he knew that Christos' political career was shattered, but his only regret was that he had not been able to bring Colonel Yorgos down with him just yet. When his own Communist Party bosses had found out about that letter he had sent on his own initiative, however, they had vetoed his plan either to blackmail Yorgos into co-operating with them or to blow this matter of his resurrected brother into a scandal that would force Yorgos to resign from the government in disgrace. Not only Yorgos but Kostas himself, the Party had decided, was more valuable to them where he was. When the 'Red Chris' story broke in Boston, the colonel had gotten off with a mere dressing-down from an outraged Papadopoulos. But the *junta* protected not only its own but its own self-interest. Papadopoulos hadn't wanted one of his men made the laughing-stock of Athens, and so the news had not even been reported in the censored Greek press. When those American reporters had come nosing around for more dirt, no one in the government had told them a thing.

Penelope smiled back at this courteous young officer as she waited for Nick and Yorgos to draw apart.

Finally the colonel called out to her. 'Ah, so at last I meet the very dear wife of my brother! Peppy, my sweet!' He held out his arms as though to embrace her, but instead Penelope coolly extended her hand. As Yorgos bent to kiss it, deftly she turned it and seized his palm. Firmly she shook it. As men will do, they measured one another by that handshake.

'Enchanted,' Yorgos murmured like an endearment as still he held tight to her hand. 'Call me George. All the tourist girls call me George.'

'Yorgo,' she replied as she wrested her hand away.

He said something to her very fast in Greek, and when she knitted her brows in consternation his smile widened to show red gums. 'Still haven't learned the language, eh?'

So, she thought, trying but failing to see through his sunglasses into his eyes, this then was the enemy. Close up, she was struck by how different he was from her husband. What with the opaque glasses and the visored military hat emblazoned with more marks of his rank, all she could see of his face was swarthy tanned skin and that smile which didn't waver. She couldn't read this one. A disquieting thought struck her. Had she ever been able to read Chris, either?

But when he bent over the baby in her arms, the colonel seemed the doting uncle. Richard III, Penelope thought, as he clucked his tongue and tweaked Christina's cheek, and the baby gurgled for him just like she did for her father. He was solicitous of the older girls, too, rumpling their fair hair and promising them an ice cream as soon as they cleared the airport.

But then he beamed that mask of a smile back on Penelope. 'I adore little girls. I have two angels like yours myself. Some would say that a man who can produce only girls is not really a man at all, but they are old-fashioned. And yet a real man yearns for a son.' Before she could draw away, he had leaned closer and patted her flat stomach. 'Perhaps next time a boy, eh?' His voice lowered. 'As that brother of mine must have at least *told* you, Greece is a very hot country, and we are a very hot people. But maybe my brother's not so hot now.'

Her temper snapped. 'He was fine until *someone* wrote that letter to the editor.'

He laughed as though she had made a pretty joke, but then he turned his back to her and threw his arm around his father as he steered him toward one of the two black official limousines pulled up on the tarmac. Man to man, father and son chattered away in a Greek so rapid Penelope could not catch a word. For a moment she stood abandoned with her daughters clutching at her skirt. Yorgos and even her father-in-law were ignoring her as though she – a lowly woman, the mother only of inferior girls – suddenly were of no account. She had half a mind to march her children into the airport and find her own way down to Panagia. But not knowing Greek and how to go about things here, that prospect was daunting. Besides, the girls were hot and exhausted and about to burst into tears. I'm just tired, she told herself. I must not blow this out of proportion.

'Here,' Captain Kostas said. 'Let me help you.' He took the hands of the daughters of his enemy.

'*Ela, ela!*' Nick was already at the car. 'Come, come!'

Gratefully she allowed that thoughtful Captain Kostas to settle them in the waiting car. Crushed in the back seat with Nick and the children, she looked around in bewilderment as the limousine lurched ahead. Gaily the father and son nattered on until the car screeched to a stop outside the terminal. 'Give him your passport,' Nick ordered, and when she did her father-in-law continued his racing incomprehensible chat. Captain Kostas bounded inside with the passports and returned in a moment with them stamped. '*Pame!*' Nick shouted with the elan of Anthony Quinn about to launch into a dance in *Zorba the Greek.*

Sofia eagerly translated one of the phrases she remembered from her father's lessons. 'That means, let's go.'

'*Pame!*' Helen repeated.

But they drove only a mile or two before their limousine pulled over and Yorgos jumped out. With what Penelope supposed was a mocking salute to

307

herself and the girls, Yorgos leaped inside the second car with Kostas. His driver shot off in a cloud of dust that made Penelope cough again. She hated not knowing what people were saying and what they themselves were doing. Never before in her life had she let herself be swept here and there like so much excess baggage. They wouldn't treat me like this if I was a man, she fumed to herself. She didn't try to control the anger in her voice. 'All right, Nick, what was that all about?'

For a while her father-in-law didn't answer. First he busied himself climbing into the front seat, then he said something that sounded chummy to the driver, and finally he adjusted the sun visor and turned on the radio. But as the limousine slid into the fast lane of a wide crowded highway, finally Nick – who back in Boston never smoked any more and was inclined to lecture others about the dangers of what he called 'nicotine addiction' – lit one of the driver's Greek cigarettes and turned to the women in the back. 'My son wanted to drive down with us, but he has an important meeting with the Prime Minister. He'll come down tonight, and we'll have a real family reunion.' Thoughtfully Nick exhaled. 'He's really something, isn't he, in that uniform? With all those soldiers, and these cars! He's an under-secretary in a very powerful government ministry. Imagine my son, one of the men who rules my country!'

Penelope stared at her father-in-law. My country? In America Nick delighted in being American. How had he managed such an instant about-face? And how could he enthuse so about his son the fascist? She, along with all her liberal friends in America, had felt an innate repulsion when Greece had fallen victim to military dictatorship a year ago. It was bad enough when that happened to Latin American banana republics, but one expected more in the birthplace of democracy. Her compulsion not only to help her husband but also to probe his past had been stronger than her political compunctions. Still, she felt guilty, as though even being here were crossing a picket line. Try as she might to relax, her nerves were ajangle as, horn hooting and brakes screeching, the limousine wove a reckless path through the clogged traffic of Athens. She caught a glimpse of stalwart white pillars in the centre of the city – was that the Roman Agora, vaguely she wondered, or the Temple of Zeus? – before again the car was swallowed up in a bumper-to-bumper jam. It was so hot she thought she might faint.

After smoking another cigarette in silence – all the while hungrily looking out the window at signs in Greek, listening to the radio wail music in Greek, drinking in the smells and noise and bustle that most certainly was Greek – Nick seemed to shake off the mood that had seized him as soon as he had set foot in the homeland. The next time he turned around, once again he was the doting grandfather and solicitous father-in-law. 'What do you say we stop a bit and have a little rest and a big ice cream. And then, *paidia mou*, we'll go home to our village.'

Nearly four hours later, as the limousine bumped down a rough road a few miles from Panagia, Penelope awoke with a start. She had been dozing in this white heat, on and off, since Athens. Groggily she looked around at the dusty orange groves on either side of the road. Would this ride go on forever? Would the scathing sun never set? And the sea, where was the sea?

Once, hours ago, when she had awoken and looked out from their cliffside highway upon a vista of blue sea, blue sky, and blue mountains, she had caught her breath. Just as, when in France, even a bit of cheese, a crust of bread, and a sip of wine had made her feel that she was tasting the apotheosis of these ordinary substances, so now she felt as though every other bit of blue in the world would henceforth have to be measured against this quintessential shade of sea, sky, and earth. The Greeks, Nick had volunteered, even had a word for this colour. '*Galano*, we call it, and we even use it on our flag. Beautiful, eh?' When Penelope had yawned then and asked him where they were, she had perked up after her father-in-law informed her they were overlooking the Bay of Salamis. Penelope had gazed down at these now calm waters where, more than two millennia ago, the Greeks had routed the Persian navy and thus ushered in the Golden Age of Classical Greece. After that, she had wanted to keep her eyes open wide and ask a million questions. I should get out my map, she had nagged herself, to follow this historic route where once armies marched and cultures clashed. But despite her best intentions, the heat had made her heavy eyelids close. Christos had told her to make sure she showed the girls the narrow chasm cut through sheer rock at Korinthos, but they were all asleep when the limousine cruised over the isthmus to the Peloponnese peninsula.

When the driver stopped a while later for cold drinks and petrol, the terrain had changed into wooded highlands of olive trees, vineyards, and tobacco fields with no glimmer of the sea on the horizon. 'Mycenae must be around here somewhere,' she had said to Nick. Back at university, she had been fascinated by the bloody tale of the doomed House of Atreus, and when she had studied the road map before setting out for Greece, it had looked like they went right past the ancient palace of Agamemnon and Clytemnestra. But Nick, engrossed in animated talk with the driver, had merely pointed ahead: 'Mykenae,' pronouncing it with a hard Greek 'k'. Soon after they had set off again, Penelope had drifted back to sleep with the children nestled around her like puppies.

A while later she awoke, looked at her watch and reckoned they must have passed Mycenae – or *Mykenae* – long ago. 'Where are we?'

'Almost there.' Nick was his usual chipper self. 'Prepare yourself. Paradise awaits!'

Gently Penelope shook the girls awake and felt the baby's bottom to see if she needed another change. Helen and Sofia stretched and rubbed their eyes, and Christina began those soft little cries that meant she was ready for a feed. Penelope rooted in her bag for the bottle she had prepared the last time they stopped. It, along with everything else in this stifling car, was hot. The baby sighed and began to suck.

In the front seat, Nick was tensely leaning forward for his first glimpse of the village. 'Now look, girls, as soon as we round this bend, you'll see it.'

Not only the little girls but their mother, too, craned their necks.

'There!' Triumphantly Nick pointed to the cluster of beige houses on a curve of beach just ahead. 'Panagia!'

'There?' Sofia wrinkled her nose. 'Daddy comes from *there*? It's not very big.'

'Small beach,' said Helen. She was used to the giant dunes of Cape Cod, but this strip of sand wasn't much wider than a sidewalk back home.

'It's lovely,' Penelope quickly said so as not to hurt Nick's feelings. But she needn't have worried. Much as Christos had taken to doing in his summer-house exile, Nick was muttering a soliloquy in Greek. The old man held his hand to his heart as he drank in the sight of this world he was about to reclaim.

As Penelope looked closer at her husband's village, she, too, was taken aback by its size. She had heard so much, for so many years, about Christos' birthplace that somehow she had expected a site of suitably mythic proportions. But there couldn't be more than a hundred or so ramshackle cottages perched on the bridge of land between the sea and the mountain that rose behind it. The tiny boats loosely anchored inside the harbour seemed to outnumber the houses. Her wandering eye was caught by the outlines of a whitewashed building that was familiar to her from the family photographs. Larger than the rest of the houses but still not very big, the Kronos taverna stood in the place of honour at the epicentre of the curving beach. She supposed the family must be awaiting them there now.

She licked her dry lips. Her experience at the airport had unnerved her a little, and she wondered what she would do if the rest were cut from the same cloth as that strutting little colonel. Even if her in-laws were wonderful and welcoming, what could they do with one another other than smile and exchange a few halting phrases? She reproached herself for never having made the time, in the twelve years of their marriage, to learn more than a

310

word or two of Greek. So far as she knew, aside from Nick's grandson, Yorgos' wife, and Vangelis' bride, no one in the family spoke much English. What was she going to do in this remote little backwater for two weeks? Her mind caught on the matter she had been avoiding since their encounter at the airport. Yorgos had been worse than she expected and, just as Christos had warned her, she doubted if she could move that one with reason or anything else including her fair white body.

She smoothed down the rumpled skirt of her dress, adjusted the bottle in the baby's mouth, and resolutely returned to her contemplation of the visual delights of Panagia. From afar there was a pleasing symmetry about this unspoiled hamlet tucked between that tall green mountain and the wide blue sea. Surely strong and simple people lived out decent lives in this pretty place. Perhaps Nick had been right back in Athens; here a man could truly breathe. But she couldn't help wondering whether a woman could breathe here, too. Somewhere along the road they had overtaken a young man riding an old donkey, while trudging ahead leading the animal by a rope was a middle-aged woman in a shapeless black dress with a black scarf pulled low over her forehead like a hood. *Aha*, Penelope had thought, and she had pitied that poor woman and all those like her condemned to lives of misery.

She tried to put her honed feminist point of view on hold. She didn't want to meet her husband's family with a large chip already on her shoulder. Instead she made an effort to see Panagia through the eyes of her absent husband. Was this what Christos was looking for when he gazed out at the Atlantic? What must it be like to call a self-contained little universe like this home? And coming from such humble beginnings, how must it have felt to have – almost – suceeded in snatching a very grand piece of the American dream? In a rustic way this village was truly charming. But it looked like a place which had fallen asleep centuries ago and might never wake up.

As the limousine shot closer to the village, however, Penelope first noticed the steel skeletons of three- and four-storey buildings perched a few yards from where the sea washed the sand. She counted six – no, seven – half-finished structures which only could be destined as tourist hotels. And now she could make out sunbathers stretched on the beach. Soon, next year or surely the year after, Panagia might look less like a fishing village than a tourist colony.

And yet, as they rounded a turn and raced ahead toward the village, she forgot her misgivings as for the first time she beheld the enchanting seaview that Christos must have gazed upon every day of his youth. Again, yes, here was that incredible bewitching *galano* blue. At the head of a calm lapping bay, Panagia looked out at an expanse of sea and sky and mountains which blended in a filmy shimmer of dreamlike blue. A trick of the light made it hard to distinguish where the land stopped and the sea and sky began. Here there was no horizon, only that haunting blue. But Panagia Bay was more than a mesmerizing study in azure. The sea was studded by marvellous little humps of islands that seemed as playful as seals romping in the water. She wouldn't have been surprised to see mermaids floating, or Aphrodite emerging from the sea, for there was something deliciously sensual about this seascape. At the far end of the harbour, not far from the family's hotel, she could glimpse an island with a chaste white church glinting in the sun atop it. Penelope shut her eyes and tried to record in her memory the exact tints and shades of her first glimpse of this world. 'Yes,' she echoed, 'it really is lovely.'

But as they made their way down the only street of the village, Penelope grew apprehensive. Battered pickup trucks were parked in front of an unlovely strip of storefronts selling the necessities of life, and the men she saw getting into them looked rough and hairy. She didn't see a single woman. Except for an occasional souvenir shop selling postcards, rubber rafts, and reed beach mats, most of the buildings seemed to be men's coffee shops. She had ample time to record all this, for Nick kept telling the driver to stop as he spotted one of his cronies lounging outside a *kafeneion* or emerging from the bakery with a loaf of bread under his arm. Repeatedly Nick bounded out of the car for cries and embraces.

As he tarried with one of his old friends for an animated chat, Penelope looked out the open window at what evidently was the square. *Plateia*, that was the Greek word for it, she remembered. A weatherbeaten old church stood dwarfed by tall cypress trees. She couldn't read the signs above the shops, but she picked out what seemed to be a hardware store, a grocery, and a shop that sold dusky fabrics. It was six o'clock in the evening, and apparently most of the villagers had not yet risen from their afternoon siesta. Only a few old men sat in the cafés. A pair of sunburned tourists wandered about with their beach mats under their arms. A little boy rushed into a shop, a tray of small coffee cups and tall glasses of water held aloft. A very old man bent over his cane as he walked slowly, infinitely slowly – how was it possible, she wondered, for anyone to move so slowly? – from one side of the square to the other. The sun beat down on this dusty, sleepy village. Two weeks, Penelope thought again. What am I going to do in this place for two weeks?

Her answer was waiting at the very end of the road. News of the limousine's arrival had preceded them, and already the Kronos family were assembled to give a proper greeting to the American branch of the family. As Nick leaped out and was promptly engulfed by weeping women in black, Penelope fixed a smile to her face and climbed out of the car with her children. At once grinning faces surrounded them, affectionately possessive hands stroked the little girls' gold hair, and she heard repeated shouts of the Greek word for welcome. A face detached itself from the rest, and with relief she heard English. 'Welcome, Aunt Peppy. I'm Nikos. Yorgos' son.' She put out her hand to greet her nephew, but instead Nikos gave her a warm hug and kisses on both cheeks. She looked into the face of a young man who bore a startling resemblance to her husband. He had the same build, the same hair, and most of all the same intent green eyes. Yes, he was wearing that gold cross Chris had sent long ago for his christening. Just as, at the airport, she had taken an instant dislike to the father, now she instinctively warmed to the son. 'Your cousins,' she said, introducing the girls. 'I'm afraid none of us speaks much Greek.'

'No problem. It will be my very great pleasure to be your translator and guide.' Exuberantly Nikos kissed his cousins and then steered the girls to his own sisters. The teenage girls smiled at their American cousins. Tentatively Sofia and Helen tried to use their halting Greek.

Watching them, Penelope was relieved to see all four girls smiling. In a moment, without a backward glance, her daughters ran off with them toward the beach. Other faces swam out of the crowd. A jolly round youngish man took her hand and pumped it hard. 'I am Vangeli,' he said in heavily-accented English, 'and I am so happy you are here.'

A slight, dark-haired woman with an equally likeable face was next to seize Penelope's hand. 'And I'm Vasso,' she said, in the broad unmistakeable accents of Australia. She grinned. 'We go together, me and Vangelis.'

'The wedding is the Saturday after next,' Nikos explained, in case Penelope had forgotten the ostensible reason for her visit.

'Of course.' Gratefully Penelope beamed at these three who – thank God! – spoke English. But before she could say more, two wizened old women in black set upon her with happy cries. Penelope looked down at these wrinkled crones with black raisin eyes. Neither of them could be more than four feet nine or ten. They seemed so small and frail that she had a momentary impulse to pick them up and cradle them as once she had done with her dolls. Carried away by the mood of the moment, she embraced them and then let them take the baby. They cooed over Christina, they kissed every inch of her face, and finally they carried her away as though she were the most perfect souvenir that had ever come from America.

'My grandmothers,' Nikos explained. 'Nick's wife Eleni, and my mother's mother, whom everyone calls Old Anna.'

'They look like sisters,' Penelope ventured. 'I don't know if I'll ever be able to tell them apart.' But as she saw one of the old women standing with the baby in her arms, looking raptly up at Nick, she knew she would never again confuse this one with another. Eleni was old and bent and so skinny that she seemed a bag of bones, but the way she looked at her husband! Penelope's heart went out to this woman who so evidently had spent her life waiting for her long-lost man.

There were other aunts, cousins, uncles, and in-laws to meet, to hug, to grin at, to try and fail to communicate with in her pigeon Greek. When it seemed that at last she had worked her way through the welcoming committee, Penelope eagerly looked around for the one she had already decided would be her bosom buddy in the family. That Vasso seemed nice, but she wanted to befriend a real Greek woman here in Greece. 'And where,' she asked Nikos, who had obligingly stationed himself beside her to interpret as best he could, 'is your mother?'

Nikos broadly smiled and blandly lied. This morning his mother had threatened to cut short her holiday and go back to work in Athens at once so she never had to meet her sister-in-law. But she had most definitely been overruled by her mother, her mother-in-law, and solid ranks of aunts and cousins. The demands of hospitality required that she be here with a happy face, but instead Marika had remained in her room. 'She must still be asleep. The heat, you know. I'll tell her you're here.' Before leaving, he carefully entrusted his American aunt to the capable hands of his Australian aunt-to-be.

Meanwhile, locked in her bathroom, Marika was glaring at herself in the mirror as she put on her makeup to meet the woman Christos had married instead of herself. She slapped on the moisturizer, caked on the foundation, piled on the blush. As she leaned closer to begin work on her eyes, she stared critically at the face time and God had given her. The hot Aegean sun had cut tiny lines around her eyes, and her skin wasn't so soft any more. Would her rival be more beautiful?

Carefully she outlined her eyes with a stark black line. She stepped back from the mirror and nodded in satisfaction. Yes, her eyes were her best feature. Christos once said she had icon eyes. Artfully she painted her lids with gold shadow and began applying the first of four thick coats of mascara. In her pictures the *Amerikana*, like so many of the foreign tourists who had begun to fill Panagia's beaches in the summer, looked mousey. She seemed to dress in muted clothes without ruffles or plunging necklines, more like a man than a woman. When Marika had surreptitiously used a magnifying glass to examine her face in the photographs, it had seemed that she didn't even know how to make herself look a little better with the right cosmetics. No discriminating Greek in the sidewalk cafés of Kolonaki would give a woman like her a second glance. Dina and 'the girls' would even call her frumpy.

She pouted her full lips as she used two different shades of lipstick to make them redder, and then she picked up her brush and began to stroke her rippling blueblack hair whose silver roots she now had to cover with a black rinse every six weeks. But as she remembered the other one's fair mane, Marika's confidence crumbled. The *Amerikana* looked younger than she did. Her hair was a golden halo, her babysoft face was as pretty as a girl's, and even those shapeless clothes couldn't conceal how firm her body was. No wonder Christos had married her. They looked happy in the pictures. Try as she might to convince herself that Penelope was sexless and inferior in every way, there was no getting around the fact that even in those family snapshots she always seemed to keep a possessive hold on Christos. And why not? He was her husband. Christos had stood up in church and worn the wedding crown linked to hers. Not *me*, but *her*.

'Mama!' Nikos rushed into the bedroom and rapped on the bathroom door. 'They're here!'

Marika gave her hair a final caressive brush and threw open the door. 'How do I look?'

His eyes widened at the sight of his mother in a tight white dress with a wide belt and a neckline cut low to show off the cleft in her breasts and the tan of her skin. Brass bracelets slid halfway up her arms, golden candelabra earrings shone through the fall of her hair, and her white patent leather stiletto heels made her appear taller and slimmer. Accustomed to seeing her here in Panagia in a bathing suit or perhaps a cotton kaftan, Nikos whistled. '*Orea*. But I didn't know you were going out.'

'I'm not.' She cast a final glance at the mirror. 'I just wanted to give the new arrivals the sort of welcome you all seem to think is so necessary.' Again she fluffed up her hair. 'You've seen them?' She lit a cigarette, for she intended on making an entrance and would wait until the rest of the family had finished with their kissing and hugging and exclamations.

'Grandfather was so excited, I thought he would jump out of the car before it even stopped. You know him!' Nikos laughed. 'It was wonderful to see grandmother's face when she caught sight of him.'

'And the rest of them?'

'The little girls are beautiful. Like blonde dolls. But they don't look Greek. And they can hardly speak any Greek at all.' Nikos looked worried. 'They ran off to the beach with my sisters, but they're just little girls and Lena and Annoula are in high school. I don't know what we're going to do with them for two weeks.'

'They'll manage.' Furiously she puffed on her cigarette. 'And your father? Did he come down with them?'

'No, he won't get here until tonight. But he sent them down in one of the cars from the Ministry.'

'I see.' She hissed out her cigarette smoke and finally asked. 'And the other one?'

'Aunt Peppy?' Nikos whistled appreciatively. 'Wait till you see her!'

Marika did just as he suggested. She sat down to postpone the hateful moment of truth for as long as she could. As she waited, she cross-examined her son. 'What does she look like? Exactly?'

Dreamily Nikos stared into space, remembering. 'Like a movie star. No, a goddess.' At his mother's exclamation of impatience, dutifully he did as he had been told. 'She looks a little tired from the trip – they all do, actually, and no wonder – but still, in that wrinkled yellow dress, she is very beautiful.' As his mother stubbed out her cigarette and lit another, he tried to describe the American aunt who, for some reason he didn't fathom, had antagonized his mother before she even set eyes on her. 'She's taller than I am. Nice figure. Thin, but big where a woman's supposed to be big and small where she should be small. I can't wait to see her in a bathing suit.' As his mother glared at him, hastily Nikos went on with the required description. 'She's pretty. Her hair is long and very blonde and curly. She's got these wonderful eyes. And freckles, just like I've seen on some of the tourists. She hardly wears any makeup, but still she's beautiful. Like an angel, really. And not so old. She could be one of the girls in my classes at the university, even though I know she must nearly be your age – ' He stopped short when his mother aimed a dagger look at him. 'And she's nice, mama, you should have seen how she was with my grandmothers. Already everybody loves her. Tonight I want to teach her how to dance.' He executed a little *syrtaki* preview. 'Tonight I dance with an angel!'

Marika blanched at the very thought of her son, who looked so like his real father, dancing arm-in-arm with the woman Christos had married. If I'm not careful, she told herself, this horrible woman will steal my son just like she stole his father. She ground out her cigarette and sailed forth on Nikos' arm for her first encounter with the woman she had been born to hate.

By this time the family had moved down to the taverna tables set under the awning on the beach. Marika stopped dead and took in the sight of the golden-haired foreigner in the very centre of the family grouping. Everyone appeared to be fawning on her. Eleni was lovingly smoothing back her hair. Vasso was running toward her with an iced coffee frappé in her hands. Her own traitor brother Vangelis was evidently telling one of his funny stories. Her very own treacherous mother was holding that baby of hers in her arms.

316

And everyone else was simply sitting there staring at the novelty of this newest addition to the family circle.

For Nikos had been right. She did look like an angel. An innocent, rich, presumptuous American angel who had been born to win at everything, even love. Marika's feet dragged in the sand as she forced a smile and held out a reluctant hand to this winner. 'You must be Penelope.'

Still smiling at Vangelis' joke, Penelope looked up into the lush dark suffering eyes of one of the most beautiful women she had ever beheld. Maybe she once had been pretty, this woman, but she wasn't any more. Her features were too strong and bold: her flashing eyes too large and deepset, her passionate mouth too full of secrets repressed, her nose too arched from looking down all her life at lesser mortals. She seemed a larger-than-life woman – as likely to do bad as good, a flawed woman, but a woman such as those who had once inspired the classical playwrights.

Penelope couldn't tear her eyes off Yorgos' wife. A woman like this could never passively wait in human bondage for fate and a handsome prince to kiss her to life. This one would dare, would act, would even damn herself and those she loved for a mad passion that lashed beyond the bounds of her control. A woman like this could have caused the Trojan war like Helen, could have killed her own children to spite her husband like Medea, could have let herself be buried alive to prove a point of honour like Antigone. Her hair, dark as night, black as sin, framed her extraordinary face. There was nothing of the nubile virgin about her; clearly, this one had taken her carnal pleasures wherever she wanted. And judging by her ember eyes, she had suffered the consequences of too much reckless desire. Her fertility goddess body – the jutting breasts, the rounded belly, the insistent hips – must drive men to obscene acts. Women, too . . .

Gazing up at her, Penelope was as stirred as when she saw a man with animal magnetism on the beach. Quickly she suppressed that odd wayward feeling. She appreciated this sister for the work of art she was, that was all. Why, Penelope wondered, retreating to the safety of intellectual abstractions, did so many artists choose soft, blurry, pastel women as their feminine archetypes? If she were a sculptor, she would immortalize this powerful panther of a woman for posterity. Surely there was a tender side to Marika. When she was young, before whatever had happened to her had happened – and by the look of those ferocious eyes, early on something shattering had made her as she was – Marika must have been the sort of mortal that had tempted the Olympian gods. But forever after, in the books of feminist thought Penelope intended to author, when she wrote of the dark side of eternal woman – rampant lover, clutching mother, vengeful harridan,

317

implacable queen – the primal image she would carry in her head was of Marika.

Impulsively Penelope got to her feet and swept the other into her arms. Ever the quick study, she kissed her on both cheeks as seemed to be the custom here. She smiled into the wary dark eyes. 'At last we meet!' She linked her arm in Marika's and, wondering why she seemed so reserved – even hostile – she redoubled her efforts to win over this reluctant sister. 'I can't imagine why my husband never told me how beautiful you are. The photographs don't do you justice.' She steered her sister-in-law over to the chair the ever-obliging Eleni had vacated. 'I just know we're going to be great friends! And you must call me Peppy, just like Chris does!' Confidentially she lowered her voice. 'I must thank you for that note you sent us. We really appreciated it.'

'*You* saw *that*?' An earthquake tremor passed over Marika's face. She had agonized over those heartfelt words of love and had carried that letter around in her purse for days before finally mailing it. She had not expected an answer, but she had never dreamed he would share it with his wife. The two of them must be so close, so happy together. Maybe Christos had even told her all about Carnival night in the cave. But no, she thought, she would have been able to see that in Peppy's eyes. No woman could be so warm to a rival, even to one who had lost.

Gingerly Marika sat down thigh-to-thigh with the woman who had married the love of her own life. As she listened to her gushing on about how beautiful her children were, how fine a boy in particular Nikos was, how moved she was finally to meet her husband's family, Marika fought hard to retain the grudge she had so long borne against this other. But it was hard to resist Penelope's overpowering goodwill and electric energy. Even though she must be exhausted, she was infectiously laughing, she was talking a mile a minute even to those who didn't understand a word she said, she was charming the entire assembled clan. As the *Amerikana* leaned forward and pointed fondly toward the kitchen where Nick had his arm around his adoring wife, Marika couldn't help sharing a smile with this new member of the family. Penelope seemed so irrepressibly *good*. There was an artless innocence about her, the sort a trusting baby had when it looked up into the face of a stranger expecting love and therefore being granted it. On her open American face there were no dark shadows. Nikos was right; she *is* nice. As Marika sipped a frappé and listened to Penelope's amusing version of their hair-raising drive through Athens traffic, she was surprised to hear her own throaty laugh. She wasn't prepared to love Christos' wife, but perhaps she would be unable to resist liking her just a little.

Hours later, after naps and baths and settling into their rooms with

318

balconies that looked out upon the sea, Penelope and her children sat at the long table of relations on the beach a stone's throw from the water. A full moon beat down on the shimmering waves, a gentle breeze swept in from the sea, and from inside the taverna a record of happy bouzouki music exactly caught the mood of the feasting Kronos family. Exactly as Nick did back in his Boston restaurant, Vangelis darted here and there delegating his squad of waiters to bring in the lamb he himself had roasted on the spit. There were all the usual accoutrements of a Greek feast, so familiar to Penelope from those barbecues and church dinners she had attended with Chris in Boston: smooth spreadable salads of roe and eggplant and garlicky yoghurt, gleaming salads of tomatoes and cucumbers and onions, mountains of fried potatoes and deep dishes of oil-drenched greens and beans, thick-sliced peasant bread, and tall pitchers of resinated wine. But all of it tasted even better here, *in situ*. Penelope ate, as she always did, with gusto.

Wedged between Marika and Nikos, with Vasso across the table chatting to the girls in English and Nick and Eleni taking turns dandling the baby, Penelope beamed at this family who seemed to have accepted her without reservations. No wonder Chris yearns for all this, she thought. Her own tightknit family was close by American standards. But at home always there were undercurrents of stress and competition, needle remarks that left her wondering the next day what her uncle or cousin had really meant when they bestowed a loaded compliment. Here she could detect none of that. Everyone seemed so wonderfully affectionate and accepting of everyone else. She felt as if she were floating in a warm scented bath of love. And yet she reminded herself that families were essentially the same everywhere, and so were people. Chris, after all, had warned her not to trust anyone, even his dearly beloved family. She supposed that, handicapped by her ignorance of this language and culture, she might be missing subtle slurs and barbs behind the radiant smiles. But it was impossible not to be seduced by these warm-hearted people who had welcomed her with all possible embraces. A rush of love for these men and women flushed through her. I'm drunk, she realized; intoxicated by Greece and the Greeks.

When Vangelis turned up the music and Nikos got up to dance, for a while Penelope watched him and a line of slim young men dip and prance and kick with the grace of young animals romping on an African plain. They were so lithe, these boys, with their strong warrior bodies and their proud princely faces. How erotic this country is, she thought, as her eyes were insistently drawn to their thighs and their buttocks. Was it only the hot heavy air that made her so conscious of her body and everyone else's? Barely repressed currents of desire swept around her like the scent of jasmine from the bushes outside the kitchen. Sharply she wished her husband were here.

Without him tonight, she would toss and turn on the starched white sheets of her single bed.

Everyone clapped when Nick gamely came forward, waving a handkerchief as he performed a wavering old man's solo dance that brought tears to Eleni's eyes. Penelope surprised them all when she leaped up and snapped pink rosebuds from a nearby trellis and showered her father-in-law with these scented accolades as she had seen her husband's friends do at the Greek dances at the Orthodox church. '*Bravo!*' she cried, and '*Bravo!*' everyone chorused, as much for her as for Nick.

Then the patriarch beckoned to the others, and laughingly they joined in, forming a single line joined cousin-to-aunt at their triumphantly-raised hands. They wove round and round in time to the music. Penelope watched for a moment, and then she broke off another rosebud and snugly tucked it behind Nikos' ear as she linked her hand in his and joined the dance without missing a step. Nikos grinned at her in delight when he saw that she could *syrtaki* with the best of them. Vasso joined in, so did Vangelis, and then the grandmothers – even crippled Old Anna – came up and joined the line.

Marika smoked and watched for another long moment as warring impulses fought inside her. Experience had schooled her not to trust anyone overmuch, and most especially she did not warm to other females who were her eternal competitors for the smiles and favours of capricious men. When she was very young she had traded confidences with the village girls, but she had never told them all her secrets or given them all her trust. Why then, she wondered, was she so drawn to Christos' wife? She had so admired her pretty gesture of throwing flowers at Nick and adorning Nikos with the most beautiful rosebud of all. No wonder Christos loves her ... Marika was surprised that thought did not hurt as much as she supposed it should. A moment later, softening still more, she had another thought: if I couldn't have him, I'm glad at least someone like her got him. Still later, as she sprang to her feet, she turned the final corner that was to seal her strange friendship with her sister-in-law. It's not *her* fault that Christos didn't marry me. *He* was the one who left me in that cave. What have I been doing all these years hating an innocent woman when it's he who did me wrong? She joined hands with Penelope, and they threw back their heads and laughed as the music wove on and on. Faster they danced, kicking off their shoes and feeling the cool sand on their bare toes. The music swelled, the tempo increased, the whole united family danced faster than the wind.

It was then, at this midnight moment of supreme happiness, when suddenly the music stopped. The dancers looked around, and standing in the moonlight was the dark figure of Colonel Yorgos in the full regalia of his uniform. For an instant everyone froze, as if guilty of being caught in the act of

320

something sinful like joy. But then in a body they surged forward to welcome the most famous, the most important and, Penelope was beginning to suspect, the least loved member of the family. They kissed his hand, a few of them hugged him, and the rest merely crowded round at a respectful distance uttering shrill cries of anxious welcome. But it seemed to Penelope, looking from face to face, that the atmosphere now was tinged with fear. She shivered as if the night had suddenly turned cold.

So much did Colonel Yorgos dominate this scene that at first Penelope thought she was the only one to hang back from the rest. But then she saw Nikos disappear into the kitchen, and she heard a throaty noise near her that sounded almost like a growl. In surprise she turned just in time to catch a look of naked loathing on her sister-in-law's momentarily unguarded face. *Of course.* How could a woman like *her* be married to a man like *him*? Clearly, everything in this family might not be exactly as it appeared. Soberly she recalled her husband's warnings. Careful, she told herself. Remember why you're here.

Penelope hovered on the fringes of the circle, waiting for her turn to pay her respects to one of the dictators of Greece, and of this family.

Nearly two weeks later, in the early morning of the day when Vangelis was to take Vasso for his bride, Penelope and Marika rowed their daughters toward the island where the Cave of the Great Goddess awaited.

It was hot and sunny, like all Greek summer mornings, and under their loose cotton dresses the women wore their bathing suits so they could swim later. As she stroked with the current away from Panagia, Penelope felt a sense of relief. After a fortnight here, she didn't know what to make of this alien, emotional, disturbing backwater. Even though never once had she deviated from her best behaviour, almost everything Christos had warned her about had come true. After that first heady day of welcome when it had seemed that everyone loved her and that everything was possible in this primeval paradise, the village had gradually but inevitably closed around her like a cage. That next morning she had awoken early, donned her bikini, and set off for the harbour to hire a powerboat so she could waterski on that delectable bay. How free she had felt, skimming the water with her long blonde hair streaming in the wind! But that had been not only the last time she had waterskied but also the end of her feelings of untrammelled freedom. No one had exactly forbidden her to hire that powerboat again, for – as she had already learned from being married to Chris – Greeks were too subtle ever to utter a blunt 'no'. But Nick had tactfully told her that, even when on holiday, a Greek married woman of her age usually spent her mornings

321

sedately watching her children paddle in the sea. Or perhaps, he had suggested, she might like to spend some hours in the kitchen, learning to prepare real Greek food under the tutelage of his wife? Then Vasso had offered to lend her one of her modest one-piece bathing suits. She, too, she had explained, had packed her bikinis away as soon as she and Vangelis had seriously begun to plan a future together. It was a small compromise, the Australian had explained with the light of new love shining in her eyes: 'You don't know the Greeks like I do.' And when defiantly Penelope had gone to the dock in the late afternoon for another independent sweep of the bay on skis, the boatman had said he was sorry but he had been chartered for not only the day but the next two weeks. In Panagia, Penelope had fumed as she sat fettered on the beach watching other foreign men and women waterski, no one dared to cross the Kronos family.

In anger Penelope rowed hard, her toned American muscles rippling under the sun. She would have liked these people better if they had said straight out what she could and couldn't do now that she was under their sway in this family fiefdom. Instead, subtly they had tried to manipulate her into conforming to their very definite ideas of what was acceptable conduct for a woman who was one of them by marriage. She had thought it sweet at first when Eleni had fussed over her before she went walking through the village. Once she had insisted on giving her an antique family brooch to join tightly together the slightly low-cut neck of her dress. Another time, her stepmother-in-law had deftly swept her provocative fall of golden hair up upon her head in a matronly bun. And after a few days Penelope had realized there was a pattern to how the women of her family had praised her severe navy blue shirtwaist but dissuaded her from going out in one of her sensational new summer dresses. Once Eleni had even gone as far as to cover her from shoulder to waist in a dark cotton shawl so as, Vasso explained, to keep her from catching cold in the evening breeze. But the only time she had been chilled in this village was the evening when she had appeared in the taverna in her new black dress. Aghast, the Greeks had stared at her. Old Anna had even made the sign of the Cross on her chest three times to ward off the Evil Eye, lest this mourning dress prompt the gods to take one of the family across the Charon. They were so superstitious, these people. So ignorant and so superstitious.

Furiously Penelope rowed. As long as she stayed home – in the house, on the family beach – mostly she could do as she pleased. But when she took a stroll with her children through the streets in the cool of early evening, always one of the family was by her side to make sure she did not transgress. If she wanted to sit down at a men's coffeehouse, Nikos or Vasso or even Marika would make some excuse: this was a dirty place, or the family was

322

feuding with its owner, or Eleni was waiting for them back home and it would insult her to drink coffee someplace else. Penelope began to notice that eyes followed her everywhere as she paced the boundaries of the village in the custody of her relatives. Even when the faces were wreathed in smiles, those dark all-seeing eyes were hard with suspicion and even malice. The family introduced her to no one. And when passersby waylaid them with what seemed to be questions about her, she listened in vain for Chris's name to be mentioned. Finally, when she had asked Nick why this was so, her father-in-law had admitted that so far as the village knew, she was a family friend from America. 'You see,' he had revealed with some embarrassment, 'none of them thinks Christos is . . . well, still alive. With feelings as they still are about the Civil War, Yorgos thinks it's best they don't know all our business.' When Penelope had retorted that the news of Chris's scandal had been widely reported in the American newspapers, Nick had reminded her that the censored Greek press had not printed a word of it. 'Try to understand,' he had pleaded. 'That *we* know what's best in *our* village.' Watching those suspicious eyes, so alight with speculation, Penelope had wondered if the villagers knew more than the family thought. Nevertheless she had fallen in with the Kronos conspiracy to keep her husband's secrets buried. She was surprised that she, an ardent feminist who was prepared to unite in sisterhood with all women – most especially with oppressed women from a traditional culture like this – had quickly learned to shrink away from the prying, judging eyes of those witchy old women who sat outside their whitewashed cottages eternally knitting and crocheting and stitching like modern Greek descendants of Madame Defarge.

As the village receded, Penelope felt the tenseness leave her body. From here, how beautiful Panagia appeared! A tourist on holiday might long to chuck her humdrum life back home and go native, imagining endless seasons of simplicity in the sun. Penelope supposed just such yearnings might have played a part in seducing a woman like Vasso into voluntarily turning her back on the freedoms of Australia. For Vasso did her capable best to act even more Greek than those born and raised in Panagia. She dressed mostly in drab dark colours, and sometimes when she ducked out to the market she covered her head with a scarf. She had her bedding out on the balcony to air before any other woman in the village. Her busy hands never stopped working at bits of embroidery even when she took a break from her eternal dusting and cooking. With her mother-in-law Old Anna she was as respectful as a convent girl before the Mother Superior, and scrupulously she kept herself aloof from all men except her husband-to-be. After a few days of observing this circumspect behaviour, Penelope had taken the other foreigner aside and asked her how she could stand it. Vasso had looked up from the

323

fussy flowers she was cross-stitching upon a pillowcase and radiantly smiled at Vangelis who was openly flirting with a tourist as he filleted a fish at her table. 'I wanted to marry him,' she had said simply, 'and this was the only way.' She had met her fiancé four years ago while backpacking through Greece with her mates, and her intended four days in Panagia had stretched to three sunny months. 'Such a summer,' she had sighed to Penelope. 'We went everywhere together, we were so in love!' After she had returned to her family in Melbourne in the autumn, she had telephoned Vangelis every month, written every week, and counted the days until she returned for a holiday the next July. But her second coming to Panagia had been stormy. Vangelis had criticized her clothes and her freewheeling ways, and he had warned her that sometime soon – 'maybe this winter' – he would bow to family pressure and submit to an arranged marriage with a girl from the next village who would bring six *stremmata* of orange groves as her dowry. In desperation Vasso had countered that her father owned a lucrative string of fruit and vegetable shops in Australia, and she had returned home committed to do whatever she had to do to win the man she loved. When she returned to Panagia the next summer, Vasso had changed her demeanour, her appearance, and her attitude. She had spent the winter polishing her Greek to near fluency, and she no longer had even a coffee at the cafés in the square. Perhaps more importantly, as matters turned out, she had her father's promise in writing that – on her wedding day – he would settle upon her the share of the family business she would have inherited one day anyway. At a stroke, Vasso had out-trumped the village girls with their orange groves. She and Vangelis had become engaged that August, and she had been living with the family ever since. 'That hotel down there,' she had said to Penelope, looking up from her needlework to indicate the shell of a building rising a hundred metres away from where they sat, 'is my *prika*. I'm building it with my share of my father's shops.'

Thoughtfully Penelope had watched Vasso stitching her future on that pillowcase. If she came back to this village in ten years, would this transplanted Australian still be thriving in this alien soil? Vangelis seemed a nice enough fellow, but was he worth Vasso's soul and her *self*? Yet she had supposed it was always easier to see the marital compromises in someone else's life. She, after all, had practically done this same thing. She had never kidded herself about how her political connections had weighed in Chris's marriage proposal.

As Marika chattered to the children, Penelope remained lost in thought. When this disquieting visit was over, the budding writer in her would have vivid new material about the conditions of women in our time. That poor old Eleni was pathetic the way she trailed around Nick as though he were

324

God made man. And unless Penelope was much mistaken, Vasso was about to seal herself into a living tomb. Even the undoubtedly strong Marika was yoked to a man far inferior to herself in every way that mattered.

Penelope breathed easier as Panagia grew smaller. She supposed she shouldn't harp so on her anger at the subjugation of Greek women, for her visit was hardly a feminist fact-finding tour. On those occasions when she had escaped from the confines of the village, she had thrilled to be in this country which had given birth to so much that stirred her creative imagination. True to his word that first night, Nikos had escorted her wherever she wanted. Together they had climbed the eerie ruins of Mycenae, and when she had shut her eyes there on that barren hill she had almost felt the cursed ghosts of the House of Atreus beside her. Another day they had driven over Tripolis mountain and then south to Mistra, where delicate Byzantine mosaics testified to the faded glories of a lost civilization. And they had gotten up before dawn another morning to drive across the achingly beautiful Peloponnese mountains to Olympia where she had been enthralled not so much by the extensive site of the ancient temples and stadium but by the beauty of the sculptures in the adjacent museum. But best of all had been her first Saturday night in Greece, when she and Nikos had driven to Epidavros to see a Greek company enact *Trojan Woman* in the ancient theatre where it might well have been first performed more than two thousand years ago. As black-swathed Hekuba had let loose with a heart-rending wail at the death of her son, Penelope had looked beyond the stage to the tree-covered mountains where just then a forest fire had glowed; for a magnificent, wonderfully destructive moment, it had seemed as though ancient Troy still burned from the sacking of the Argive army.

As she rowed, Penelope remembered what else had made that night with Marika's son so memorable. It was when Nikos was driving her home from Epidavros that she had gotten into her first and what she suspected would be her last political discussion in Greece. Every time she had asked anyone about the *junta*, all she had gotten were smiles and exclamations about how Yorgos' government had saved the motherland from the corrupt politicians, how much more smoothly the *patrida* ran now, and how much better it was for business. Until this night her nephew, too, had kept his silence. But driving through the black night, Nikos had suddenly opened up after she ventured another comment about what she had read in America about the political repression here. 'Yes,' he had said, 'it's all true.' After the coup thousands had been detained and despite some much-publicized releases many were still languishing in distant island concentration camps. But Nikos had said that was only the tip of the iceberg. The army, the civil service, and even the academic world had been purged of all those thought to be against

325

the rule of the colonels. As his own mother could attest, the press was strictly censored. Even at Nikos' polytechnic lecturers were careful what they said. Yet aside from an occasional bomb exploding, mostly in the capital, there were no signs of a popular revolt. At the first rumour of resistance, the efficient military police rounded up the conspirators. After the king had staged an abortive counter-coup and fled the country last December, the colonels had seemed only to grow stronger. Papadopoulos had made himself Prime Minister, most of the colonels had demobilized and become civilian Ministers and, despite the new head of state's assurances that democratic elections would be held sometime soon, the country had settled down to what appeared to be long-term military rule. Virtually every nation in the world had recognized Papadopoulos' regime, the tourists had begun flocking back to Greece, and foreign investment had increased. One the whole, Nikos had said, his countrymen were satisfied with the government God and the colonels had given them. 'And you?' Penelope had probed. As Nikos had taken his eyes off the road, again she had been struck by his uncanny resemblance to her husband. 'I hate them! And I'm not alone! When the time is right, we'll bring them down! But not yet, when we're still too weak. For now, we must shut our mouths and wait. But I promise you, we will not wait forever.' And then, Penelope had realized later, he had revealed the reason for his candour. 'Uncle Christos, is he doing anything to help? Groups are forming "outside" – in Sweden, England, maybe even in America. Maybe you could ask my uncle – not just for me, but for all of *us*, for Greece! – to do what he can. Will you, Aunt Peppy? Will you?' Of course she had promised to carry that message home to America.

As their boat neared the island, the current quickened. Though they rowed harder, the island remained the same tantalizing distance. At this new frustration, Penelope's thoughts turned to the exasperating Colonel Yorgos. Two weeks here, and still she hadn't succeeded in cornering him in a talk about her husband. His comings and goings were less like visits than lightning raids. Sometimes, like that first night, he arrived at midnight and was gone again before dawn. He turned up when she least expected and left without uttering a word to her. She would hear that he had come in the night to go fishing in the bay, and when she asked to see him she would be told that he was asleep. Even when he presided at a family dinner, smoking like a disdainful lord as his mother tried to tempt him with his favourite dishes, he would not speak a word to Penelope. Yet often she caught him fingering that scar on his cheek as he stared at her, and that look of his would make her adjust the bodice of her dress or recross her legs. When she had asked Nick if he had talked to his son yet, her father-in-law would pat her patronizingly on the cheek. 'Patience,' he would say, 'this is Greece,' as though she needed any reminders of where she was. But they were leaving early tomorrow morning after the wedding feast, and still their mission was unaccomplished.

The boat twirled in the current, and now the shore was in striking distance. Marika leaped into the shallows, and Penelope followed suit. Lena, Annoula, Sofia, and even little Helen towed the boat to shore.

'So this is it,' Penelope said, looking at the rocky island. One of the surprises of this visit was what Marika had told her by chance one lazy afternoon as they lay side by side on Panagia beach. As usual Penelope had been talking and Marika silently smoking. Try as she might, the American had not been able to get her sister-in-law to talk about politics. That sole outpouring from Nikos had been the only breach in family solidarity in support of Yorgos' regime. But they did while away the hours discussing everything else under the sun. This time the American had been exclaiming about the museum copy of an ancient statue, an exquisite terracotta with protruding breasts and arms like wings, she had bought the day before in Nauplion. Her archaeologist mother, Penelope had been explaining, believed that such statues were proof of Mother Goddess worship in the Mediterranean world. Millicent had uncovered statues like this when excavating near the Euphrates in Iraq. Some academics believed such figures were mere burial totems of servants and relations, but Penelope's feminist soul thrilled to the possibilities of an ancient race where women had once ruled in an era of peace and benevolence. 'Ah, the Great Goddess,' Marika had murmured as familiarly as though she ran into the Earth Mother at the bakery every morning. Her interest piqued, Penelope had spent the rest of the afternoon relentlessly drawing out her sister-in-law. Hours later, when the sun was almost setting, her efforts had been rewarded when finally, with the air of a mother telling a daughter a bedtime story, Marika had confided bits and pieces of the tale her own mother had told her about the cave on the island. After that, nothing would do but for Penelope to see this wonder for herself. She had begged and pleaded and pestered, and finally, as a sort of goodbye present, Marika had consented to take her to this secret rendezvous. As an afterthought, she had invited along their daughters. She had been meaning to bring Lena and Annoula to the cave for years, but something had held her back from fulfilling that promise she had made long ago to her mother. Today not just Christos' wife but Marika's own daughters would be introduced to the wonders of the cave.

'It's up here,' Marika called back as she hared up the steep trail. If the *Amerikana* couldn't keep up, perhaps that was for the best. Now that she was on the shore of this island where so much had begun and ended, she wondered what had possessed her to share this intimate site with this woman so linked to her by fate. But maybe, Marika thought, her breath ragged from too much smoking as she scaled the difficult path, it was inevitable that she share this, too, with the woman who now slept beside Christos. In Greece it was the same now as it had always been. Who can fight *moira*?

Above, in a cleft of rock, Penelope could just make out the mouth of a cave. She looked behind her at the two hummocky hills. They were aligned exactly like a woman's breasts and vagina. A thrill coursed through her. Maybe there was truth to Marika's tale. The ancients had been masters at choosing natural phenomena like this to prove a symbolic point.

Marika was first in, then the girls. Penelope ducked her head inside the cave. All stood blinking in the dank, dark cool. Marika made the formal introduction. 'This, *paidia mou*, is the Cave of the Great Goddess.'

With the air of a mother telling a bedtime story, Marika told the girls what once had happened in this place so beloved by their ancestors. The dancing. The mysteries. The glory. She left the erotic details for when they were older, but nonetheless the magic caught and held all four girls. Annoula touched the rocks in wonderment. Sofia and Helen joined hands in a romping dance. But it was fifteen-year-old Lena who seemed most affected. Until now she had always claimed she wanted to be a ballerina, but as she gazed shiny-eyed at this cave she announced she wanted to be an archaeologist like Penelope's mother.

Penelope, meanwhile, sat apart, musing in the womblike cave. Was it possible that, millennia ago, women had come here just as they had flocked to that famous cave outside Athens at the end of the Sacred Way at Eleusis to celebrate the eternal 'mysteries' of the triumphant female? She, too, reached out and stroked the stones that might hold so many secrets. An eerie mood overtook her. She shut her eyes and imagined dancing women circling round a fire, their bare thighs flashing as they cast leaping shadows on these hoary walls. Almost she could hear their voices, smell their perfume, taste their frenzy. When she opened her eyes, she felt shaken. What exactly had happened here long ago? 'A place like this,' she said to Marika, 'anything could have happened here.'

Marika was dreamily gazing at a flat rockbed in the far corner of the cave. 'Christos said the same thing, that anything could have happened here.' Christos had said nothing of the kind, and she wondered why she had said that just now. Because everything did happen here, she added to herself. And maybe I want *her* to know it.

Penelope shook off the mesmerized mood that had seized her since she entered this cave. Sharply she stared at her sister-in-law. '*Christos was here?*'

'Once,' Marika said, in a soft and faltering voice Penelope had never before heard her use.

Penelope's eyes drilled into her sister-in-law as she had a flash of intuition

– was that a gift of the cave, she was to wonder later? – which illuminated everything. So that was it. Marika and Christos. *Of course.* That explained everything, or almost everything . . . Penelope had always suspected that her husband had left a secret love in Greece. He had been twenty-seven when he arrived in America, after all, and it would have been odd if he had passed the years of his young manhood without attachments. But despite all her artful probing, she had never been able to get him to talk about any women in his early life. In her heart of hearts, she had always felt threatened by his reluctance to confide the secrets of his emotional past. She had told him the little there was to tell about her own boyfriends: prep school lads, a lifeguard one summer at the pool, and, more significantly, the intense bearded graduate student to whom she had given her virginity at the age of twenty-three.

Penelope continued to stare at the woman she suspected her husband still might love. She had come to Greece in search of clues to Chris's elusive character, and the answer to the riddle had been sitting next to her for these past two weeks. Now she thought she understood not only why Marika had seemed so hostile when they first met but also the reason for the ravaged look in the other's eyes. Sometimes she had caught that same look of anguish in her husband's eyes.

Penelope fought back tears. I married him, but he was never mine, not altogether, and he never will be. Maybe she hadn't had a chance against the ghost that stood silently beside her in this woman's cave. She longed to sink down on these stones and weep aloud, but she cringed away as if they would burn to the touch. Had her husband and Marika lain together just here?

Another even more wrenching thought smote her. She did a rapid series of calculations in her head. When had Chris left Greece, what year had Marika married Yorgos, what month had Nikos been born? The figures did not quite gel, but she supposed this woman like so many others over the eons could have lied a little for herself and her child. Could Nikos be her husband's son? Ah, yes, that was it; intuitively she knew it; yes, now she was sure. Marika had given Chris the one thing he wanted most, the one treasure she had never been able to deliver.

Surreptitiously Penelope wiped her eyes with her fingers, and when she looked over again at Marika she saw her sister-in-law doing the same. For once the American could not think of a thing to say.

Without another word these women who shared too much gathered their daughters and turned and left behind the darkness of the Cave of the Great Goddess.

*

It was after sunset, but still the church on the *plateia* was stifling hot. Just last week Nick had finally kept his promise to Father Petros and broken ground for the grand new church that would tower on the hillside of Panagia Mountain, but Vangelis and Vasso had to make do with the old church that had served generations of villagers. Relatives stood wedged in between icons and candle stands, friends were packed from altar rail to vestry, and the overflow spilled into the square with its panorama of the bay. Inside, the lingering scent of incense and the waxy smell of burning candles made it even harder to breathe. Vasso, radiantly sweating in her thick white satin gown, and Vangelis, even more sodden with perspiration in his new grey striped suit, might have fainted from the heat if the crone twins Eleni and Old Anna had not been behind them on tiptoe energetically moving the thick air about their heads and shoulders with homemade reed fans.

Penelope stiffly stood as far apart as she could from the uncles and cousins and aunts – and especially Marika. She had been so eager to witness this wedding, and yet now all she longed for was tomorrow's departure to America. After they had anchored the rowboat back in Panagia, she had gone straight to bed and slept like the dead. She had, however, awoken in time to finish most of the packing. Except for the clothing she and the children were wearing tonight and would need for the morning, she was ready to go. She had had more than enough of Greece and this village and – most of all – old family secrets she wished she had never learned.

Yet still, as the raspy voice of the Orthodox priest chanted on, she could not help craning her neck to see what was happening inside the altar rail. The *pappas*, who looked like God the Father in a long white beard and grand multicoloured vestments, was busily intoning this and waving that as he rushed back and forth from the sanctuary to a kind of second altar draped in white satin and festooned with ribbons which had been erected in front of the bridal couple. At one point he seemed to be asking for something, and Nick – who was the *koumbaros*, the best man – presented him with the modest gold wedding bands. Father Petros inscribed crosses in the air above the bride and groom, then on their chests, then again here and there before finally he slipped the rings on their fingers. He swept back to the altar, singsonging in his deep melancholy voice as the bridal couple waited for him to pronounce them man and wife. Penelope thought back to the double ceremonies of her own wedding day. In the spirit of compromise which was so to characterize their union, she and Chris had been married first in the Harvard chapel and then in the Greek Orthodox church, with a tasteful reception afterwards under a marquee in her parents' garden. But what had their marriage amounted to anyway? Her husband had left his heart elsewhere. She glanced over at Marika who stood shoulder-to-shoulder with

330

Nikos. Perhaps she herself had never had a chance against these clannish people, this closed culture.

Marika's daughter Annoula plucked at her sleeve, and Penelope looked absently at the beribboned basket she was carrying from guest to guest. So engrossed was she in her memories and her longing to be gone from this place, that she took a handful and carried it to her lips as though it were some form of ritualistic candy. Just in time she caught the scent of roses and peered down in the semi-darkness at the handful of petals and rice. She recalled, from the countless times she had accompanied Chris to Greek weddings, that later the guests would shower the bridal couple with these symbolic good wishes.

'What's that, Mummy?' Helen turned her questioning eyes on her mother.

'I told you before,' Sofia loftily answered, 'it's for throwing. Just like at home, only here we do it in the church.'

Lena, too, came by passing out those artful, decorated handfuls of sugared almonds that the Boston Greeks always had at their weddings.

'And do we throw these, too?' Helen asked.

'No, silly,' Sofia answered. 'This is a *bomboniera*. For good luck.'

Penelope kept a possessive hand on the shoulders of her daughters who had taken to their father's homeland as though guided by genetic memory. To her surprise, they had picked up more of the language than she herself had been able to manage. She was a little afraid of this sudden Greekness of her American girls. What was it, she wondered, about the power of this country? How did it take hold of all who stepped onto its shores? Even she could feel it, although in her present mood it seemed more of a clutch than a caress. She supposed she shouldn't be surprised that her daughters had felt their blood calling. She had hardly spent an hour alone with them in these last two weeks, for always they had been running in a pack of their new-found friends. Christina, too, had been petted and pampered by a succession of doting old women. Jaded as she now was, Penelope had to admit a Greek village was a children's paradise. How the Greeks enjoyed life! That *joie de vivre* began young and never really ended. The children played until they dropped, watched over by a succession of adults who seemed ever-eager to indulge their every whim. She would have to do her best to be especially kind to her girls when they got home. She suspected they were going to have trouble readjusting to the discipline and demands waiting in America. But this Greek hiatus was only a holiday. She would see to it that they grew up to be as American as she was.

Up on the altar, the priest held aloft two shining silver crowns, garlanded with flowers. They were yoked together with a wide white satin ribbon, and he arranged them so that they formed a perfect sphere as once again he inscribed a series of crosses in the air over and around and in front of the marital couple. Finally he pulled the crowns apart, fitting one on the bride, the other on the groom, and then changing them around, so she wore his crown and he hers. 'Ah,' sighed the crowd as they moved forward for everyone's favourite part of the service.

Nick leaned over the shoulders of the bridal pair and deftly fitted the crowns more tightly on their heads as the priest joined hands with Vangelis and he with Vasso. The three of them danced around the little white altar as Nick nimbly kept his hand on their two crowns lest they slip off in a portent of bad luck. 'Now!' Sofia prodded her little sister as the family let loose with a shower of rose-petals and rice. 'Good luck,' Penelope called out in English, hoping against hope that Vasso would be happy in this otherworld that was so strange and yet so compellingly beautiful. For the church, just then, leaped alive with joy and fire. Icons encased in silver glowed a benediction, and bits of burnished brass on jewelled censors reflected the flickering candlelight. As the couple circled in rapture, Penelope glimpsed the bride's shining face as she laughed into the eyes of her beloved. For her, Penelope wished this dance of love would never stop. Round and round wove the priest and the bride and the groom in a soft rain of flowery rice, until finally Father Petros led his parade out of the church and into the evening cool.

Long hours later, amid the feasting and dancing at the family taverna, Penelope stood on the fringes of the crowd trying to catch what breeze there was from the sea. She was glad she no longer was in the spotlight of the family's attention, for on this last night in Panagia she had no heart for pretty gestures and winning ways. Yet only two weeks ago she had stood just here and showered her father-in-law with rosebuds. She remembered that glorious night of intoxication with Greece and the Greeks. Which was real and which was false, that wonderful first impression or this wary disillusion? Her feelings for this beautifully deadly village and her husband's cloying family were so bittersweet. What still fascinated her was the dark side of their humanity, not their virtues but their sins. Lust, greed, sloth, envy – the Greeks excelled at them all. How fiercely they loved and hated here: Christos, Marika, Yorgos . . .

She felt a force close beside her. 'A drachma for your thoughts,' Colonel Yorgos said.

'*Tipoteh*,' she answered, 'nothing.' Not for all the money in the world would she tell this one anything. For two long weeks he had ignored her. It was too late now for a *rapprochement*.

'Funny, but I believe you wanted to talk. May I suggest a *volta* on the beach?'

Penelope shrugged as indifferently as a Greek. 'Why not?' She hadn't seen the colonel up at the church, and – not that she cared much any more, after the cave – she had supposed she would go away without accomplishing the real purpose of her coming. And yet, presented with this opportunity, she could not resist it. She had some hard thinking to do about her feelings for her husband, but loyalty was a value she still lived by, and so she steeled herself to go through the motions of pleading her husband's case. There was an inevitability to playing out the next act, as though the drama of the lives and loves of the Kronos brothers would be staged next week at Epidavros. With a feeling of doom she slipped off her high-heeled shoes and walked beside Yorgos in the sand.

Only a faint sliver of new moon shone on the sea. Tonight even the stars seemed dim in the heavens. The black water lapped the grey sand. She had opened her mouth to begin the speech she had long rehearsed when Yorgos pre-empted her.

'Not much to look at yet, this village.'

'Oh, but it's so beautiful.' She was surprised at how quickly she leaped to Panagia's defence. How could it be that this place tugged so at her heartstrings? There was so much here that repulsed her – the hypocrisy, the ignorance, the superstition, and most especially what she perceived as the oppression of women – and yet against her will this village had fastened a hold on her. She loved it and hated it, but most certainly she would never forget it. A sudden sadness washed over her. This time tomorrow, she would be gone.

'But it is poor and backward! And it is still underdeveloped in its facilities. Have you noticed that the hot water runs out every afternoon, that the electricity comes and goes in spurts, that the road from Nauplion is little more than a dirt track? There's not a single first-class hotel in this village, and the level of service is far below anywhere else in Europe.' Before she could answer, he excitedly thrust his arm ahead to indicate the skeletons of the new hotels rising from the sand. 'But that's all about to change. This time next year, we will be able to handle four, even five thousand more tourists a day. I'm personally making sure that a wide new road will be paved from here to Argos, and those electricity lines will be faultless!'

She had caught the significant pronoun. 'You?'

'Yes, I, Yorgos Kronos!' He pounded his chest. 'Soon it will be announced that I will be the new Minister of Tourist Development. Not an under-secretary, a full Minister! And I can assure you, dear Peppy, that Panagia is one of the up-and-coming tourist meccas of Greece. In two years, three years, five years at most, you will not recognize this place. There will be pedalboats from one end of the beach to the other. Umbrellas and rubber rafts for rent by the day or the week. Bars that serve Western cocktails.

333

Restaurants that specialize in schnitzels and fish and chips. Charter jets from Germany, England, Austria, and everywhere else that matters will land at Athens early every morning, and we will have them packed on our beach that same afternoon. Think of it, Peppy!'

Penelope thought that she was glad she had come here in time to see the sleepy fishing village rather than the honkytonk Greek Coney Island the colonel predicted.

Yorgos dropped his voice as the Greeks always did when talking about money or sex. He rubbed his thumb and forefinger together. 'They will be worth their weight in gold, those tourists! And the family will get the lion's share. With the help of my dear father's American dollars, we will have three new hotels open for next year's season. And that is only the beginning. We will break ground for bungalows on the side of the mountain, tavernas down here by the sea, and souvenir shops on the *plateia*. We will be as rich as kings!'

She trudged beside the fascist colonel who imagined himself a king of schlock. 'I came to talk to you about my husband.'

Yorgos made a hissing sound between his teeth. '*Him?* On such a beautiful night, here with me, you want to talk about him?'

'Precisely.' She stopped walking and faced her husband's nemesis. She would not beg, just flatly state her demand. 'I came here to ask you not to co-operate with any American investigators who want to know about Chris's activities during the Civil War. You've already ruined his political career with that letter you sent to the Boston newspaper. Enough is enough.'

Yorgos drew back as if his prickly Greek pride had been outraged. 'Again you bring up that letter? Again you insult me with your childish accusations? The first thing you say to me at the airport and now the last thing here on the beach?'

'Naturally. That's why I came.'

'Peppy, my Peppy, have you learned nothing about us in your two weeks here?' He turned away from her and resumed his military pace down the beach. When she followed him after a moment's hesitation, his voice rose. 'You dared to throw those ugly words at me as soon as you stepped off the plane! But I thought that by now you might have learned some manners. Against my better judgement, finally I decided to give you another chance. And what do you do? Again you insult me!' He halted. 'You may get away with that in America. But this is Greece, and here we are *civilized*!'

On the tip of her tongue were hot retorts about the most *uncivilized* political detentions and tortures so widely reported in the Western press. But for Christos' sake she left that unsaid. With iron self-control she mostly succeeded in keeping the anger from her voice. 'So you still contend you had nothing to do with that letter?'

Yorgos held his hand to his heart. 'I swear by all that is holy – I swear by the flag, by the Bible, by the glories of Helleno-Christian civilization – that I had nothing to do with that.' He smiled. 'I won't say I was sorry it happened. A man like my brother . . .' Eloquently he shrugged. 'But I paid for that letter, too, you know. It was more than a little embarrassing when the *New York Times* reported that my brother was not dead but very much alive.'

She looked into his dark calculating eyes. Maybe he had sent that letter and maybe not. 'Then who mailed that letter?'

Again Yorgos shrugged and made an airy gesture with his hand. He was not about to admit that he had dispatched Kostas on a wild goose chase to discover who had sent that letter. His aide had come up with a list of suspects: envious Panagians, vengeful exiled Communists, even a conspiracy of *junta* colonels who wanted to discredit the up-and-coming Minister of Tourism. Kostas had been eager to follow his hunch that treacherous Brigadier Ioannides was behind it all, but Yorgos had prudently muzzled his assistant and let the matter drop. 'Who knows? Anyone in the village could have.'

'But Nick says they all still think Chris is dead.'

'So they *say*. But what they think, now that is maybe different.'

Again Penelope remembered her husband's warnings that nothing was as it seemed in the village. She was getting nowhere in her effort to make Yorgos come clean. 'All right, then. Let's try to forget about that letter. But can you at least promise me that you'll keep the lid on all this when the American investigators come to Athens?'

Archly Yorgos smiled. He was not about to tell her all that was already stonewalled. Why should he worry about the peace of mind of his brother and his wife? 'My dear, what can you be suggesting?'

'That you protect your brother. And the family.'

'Would you have me perjure myself? Would you have my government refuse to co-operate with the representatives of our dearest ally? *Tch*! I'm surprised at you! Maybe that sort of thing goes on in America, but here we have standards of behaviour in public office.'

Her eyes flashed, but again she kept her mouth shut. Clearly she was wasting her time with this one. And yet valiantly she cleared her throat. 'And I want to ask you to do something else.' She had not discussed what she was about to say with her husband. But in her weeks in Panagia the certainty had grown in her that he would never be whole – and if their marriage was to continue, she had to be able to share her life with a complete man, not the haunted shell of a husband she had – unless he came home and laid the ghosts of his past to rest. She was fighting for her marriage now, so a note of urgency crept into her voice. 'Let him come back to Greece, Yorgo. At least for a visit. You don't know how it kills him not to be able to come home. Just this once, make an exception to the ban against anyone with a Communist past.' She swallowed a little of her pride. 'You can do it, I know you can. *Please*! Everyone says you can do anything you want, now that you're so powerful.'

'They say that? That I can do anything I want?' He preened. He had richly enjoyed baiting her about his brother, but this begging was even better. She said 'please' so nicely! 'Powerful, yes, they all know that now.'

She regretted having resorted to the flattery he so evidently loved. 'Yes or no, what will it be?'

'That depends. You want something from me. And I want something from you.' In his elevated shoes, Yorgos was level with her eyes. 'Perhaps we can make a deal.'

'I don't understand.' But she did. It took her breath away, what she suspected he was suggesting.

'My cousin has a little apartment right here on the beach. Very private. Altogether discreet. Come with me, my Peppy, and I will take you to Paradise as we seal our little deal.'

'How dare you!' Two weeks of suppressed anger shot through her, up from her stomach and her heart through her throat and to her mouth. At her great cost she had learned more than she wanted to from these Greeks, and one of those lessons was that there was an insult which could never be forgiven or forgotten. After she did it, she and Chris could expect no quarter from the colonel. But she doubted if he would have kept his part of this sordid bargain even if she had let him strip her naked and pump inside every orifice of her body.

In her mouth she sucked the saliva into a pool, then she puckered her lips and spat into his face. For a moment they stared into one another's eyes without blinking.

Then she turned and, as though not only his mocking laughter but also the hounds of hell were following her, she ran all the way to her room. She wasn't going to give him a chance to get back at her. Before anyone knew what she was about, she would be gone. She slipped down to the hotel lobby and dialled the number of the taxi company in Nauplion she had taken care to jot down in case of an emergency like this. Efficiently – God, it was wonderful, after the stupor of this passive fortnight under the thumb of the family, to take charge of her life once again and do as she wanted – she consulted her guidebook and telephoned the Grande Bretagne Hotel in Athens to book a room for the night. Quickly she gathered up the girls and the baby back in their room, and then she heard a horn hooting outside. She gave Christina to Sofia, took Helen by the hand, and told the taxi driver where their bags were.

She saw the flutter of the taverna kitchen curtain as the driver made a fuss about the suitcases. And then as they finally pulled away, Nikos burst out of the taverna and ran shouting behind the taxi most of the way to the *plateia*. She was hardly surprised that she hadn't been able to escape undetected, but she doubted if they would try to follow her all the way to Athens. She didn't care if the family would be outraged that she had left without a word of farewell. Let them think, and talk, and judge, as they would. Her husband's family was nothing to her, only trouble.

It was three o'clock in the morning before they reached Athens. Christina and the girls had slept most of the way, and it was easy to transfer them to the hotel beds. First thing in the morning, she hired a car to take them all up to the Acropolis for the one sight she had come a world away to see. Without enjoyment she tramped over the site and even paid a tourist photographer to record their visit. Once they'd finished that, she was ready to leave Greece forever. She and her daughters checked in at the airport early. They were already strapped into their seats when she saw one of Colonel Yorgos' limousines cruising onto the runway. By the emotional goodbye Nick and his son seemed to be sharing on the tarmac, she guessed that her father-in-law had succeeded where she had failed. Man-to-man, the patriarchs must have struck a new bargain. She supposed Nick must have promised to build Yorgos another hotel or two, or perhaps a truly royal castle, in exchange for his silence about Chris's past.

But Penelope hardly cared about the Byzantine interworkings of the Kronos family. Here and now, to her, all that mattered was that this jet quickly carry her up and away from this festering old world of dark secrets.

Thirteen

Penelope barrelled down Storrow Drive in the fast lane, her foot flooring the gas pedal of the battered station wagon she still refused to trade in for a newer model. She was late for the feminist gathering at the sister's house in North Cambridge. She had been running at full throttle all day, starting with a breakfast meeting with her literary agent in the Ritz Café, then out to

Concord Academy for midterm consultations with her daughters' headmistress, after that down to Loch-Ober's for a dour luncheon with the men of her family, and finally a lightning assault on the bits and pieces of everyday housewifery: collecting the dry cleaning, cashing a cheque at the bank, filling a prescription for Chris's cold at the pharmacy, and coursing through the lanes of the Government Center Stop & Shop filling her cart as though she were a beat-the-clock contestant on Supermarket Sweepstakes, picking Christina up at her playgroup and dropping her off in the care of her nanny at home. She had hardly had time to change from her constricting striped business suit to her comfortable jeans and sweater. I've got to slow down, she told herself.

But she kept her foot firm on the accelerator. In this, the heady autumn of 1970, how could a woman put on the brakes? The feminist movement had caught fire in radical East and West Coast circles, and before long the conflagration would rage in every household of the nation. Her long blonde hair streamed behind her in the wind, and she felt free, so free, as she changed lanes and headed over the bridge to Cambridge. Her publisher had loved the manuscript. There would have to be what her agent had delicately called 'a few cosmetic revisions', mostly on that troublesome chapter about the psycho-sexual roots of women's obsessive love, but with a little bit of luck and lots of midnight oil she should have the book ready in its final form in a few months. If she turned in the revised manuscript in early December – by the end of January at the latest, her publisher would be able to get it into the bookstores in time for next year's Christmas sales. *My book!* Forgotten for the moment were the two hard and lonely years she had sat hunched over her typewriter writing, it had seemed, dull theoretical paragraphs no one would ever read. Her publisher said it was a landmark work that would cause a sensation, possibly even hit the nonfiction bestseller list. The women's issue was hot, her agent had said, and he was sure it would hot up even more. He had talked grandly today about an auction of the paperback rights, sales to England and translations in German and French, and maybe a promotion tour that would include a coveted slot on the 'Today' show. *My book! Me*, an author!

Penelope felt like abandoning the car where it was stalled in rush-hour traffic and dancing the rest of the way to North Cambridge. Walking on air! Now she understood that old cliché. Life was so very good ... She remembered a drawing she had seen last month at a feminist gathering, of a nude figure curled in a fetal position. 'I am a woman giving birth to myself', had been lettered below it. A thrill had raced down her spine when she had seen it, and again she felt that prickle like electricity. Every day in every way, I am growing, opening up, blooming in ways I had never dreamed possible.

How exciting it was to be a woman in this time and place! And yet, she thought, we women must take care not to repeat the destructive patterns of millennia of male dominance. We must not fall into the trap of becoming little men, letting ourselves be selfish like them, and hard like them, and wrong like too many of them have been for too long. As we shake off the bonds of our oppression, we must not forget how to be soft and kind and nurturing; that took strength, too, maybe more than it did to rule the world with an iron fist. She had said so herself, at convincing length in her manuscript. That was why she was so drawn to the haunting poster image of that woman writhing in labour. There had to be – and there was – pain in liberation. For everything gained, something had to be sacrificed. Or someone.

Penelope stared at the glaring red traffic light. She would have to do something about Chris, and soon. They couldn't go on like this forever.

The light flashed green. She spurted ahead, eager to escape not only the traffic but the one thing which was wrong in her world. Her reprieve, however, was short-lived. She screeched to a halt at the next corner, hemmed in again by the usual bumper-to-bumper crawl of Harvard Square. How and when would she tell him she wanted a divorce? It wasn't like her to put off an onerous task or shrink from a confrontation. Every night before she went to bed she made a new list of what she had to accomplish the next day – big things like revising a tricky chapter or having a serious talk with Sofia and Helen about ending their sisterly spats, small things like phoning the wine shop for a new case of her favourite vintages or remembering to post greeting cards for everyone's birthdays and anniversaries. Efficiently she crossed these matters great and small off her list the next morning as she despatched them one by one. And yet in this one matter she had not been able to find the heart to say what had to be said.

The light in the centre of the square changed from red to green and then to red again, and still the grid-locked traffic didn't budge. Her father was always going on about how something had to be done about the congestion in Harvard Square. She should have gone to Kate's the back way, through Watertown and around Fresh Pond, and then she wouldn't have been stuck here worrying about how best to extricate herself from the stalemate of her marriage. Surely Chris must have an inkling that their days together were numbered. She supposed she had been hoping, in the two-and-a-half years of their essential estrangement, that he would find someone else and make the break of his own accord. Instead, he had clung to her. She had been the one to find solace elsewhere.

Penelope hit the horn, impatient to be up and away from all this. Greece, she suddenly thought, as she hooted like an Athenian fuming in the frustration of stalled traffic between Omonia and Syntagma. It had been all over with her and Chris since Greece – or maybe a few weeks before that, when she and all their world had first become aware of the secrets of his past. Oh, in those first weeks after Chris had dropped out of political life she had tried to gloss over her disenchantment with a grand show of forgiving and forgetting. She had swallowed her angry resentment and been the perfectly loyal wife. She had comforted him that first night not only as a devoted mother holds a son but as an adoring wife embraces a husband. She had sat by his side at that news conference when he had pulled out of the Congressional race. She had flown off to Greece and tried to dance her way into the hearts and minds of his family. And later she had sat in those courtrooms listening to him saying what had to be said to squash those proceedings which had threatened his deportation. But for her, essentially their marriage had ended as soon as she had realized that he had never trusted her enough to tell her the things a husband must tell a wife. What had killed her, and their marriage, was not the fact that Chris had once been a Communist or even the suspicion that in his youth he had been madly in love with another woman. What she couldn't forgive was that he had held back the essence of himself from her. How can you love a stranger? Penelope sighed. Maybe women and men were fated always to be strangers. Perhaps there was a reason that their relationships were so often called 'the war between the sexes'. But now she for one had chosen to make not war but love. A shudder – or was it a shiver? – ran through her body. She, too, now had a secret. When she ended it with Chris, should she tell him everything or only part of the truth?

The dirty white van in front lurched forward, and she surged ahead adroitly through the traffic, past the kiosk, down the underpass, beside the campus, and then turned off Mass Ave into the street where the sisters already were assembled. She threw open the car door, grabbed the magnum of champagne she had brought to celebrate the good news from her agent, and ran up the wooden steps of the fashionably rundown three-storey house and rang the bell. At once a trim figure in a blue workshirt and jeans opened the door. 'We started without you,' Kate said, 'but you didn't miss much. We're only getting to the good stuff now.'

Penelope tucked the champagne in the refrigerator and quietly entered the room crowded with the women she sometimes spent more time with than her own family. Even though it was not yet six o'clock and some of the regulars were still at their jobs, the sofa and all the chairs were full. She jack-knifed down on the floor, sitting crosslegged on the patterned Afghanistani rug Kate had bought in the mid-sixties when she and her husband had gone overland to India. In the intervening years Kate had disposed of her Harvard

340

Law School professor husband, but still her living room was chockablock with the bazaar buys of their roving married life: copper pots from Turkey, primitive weavings from Guatemala, brass gods and goddesses from India and Nepal. Like so many Cambridge households, Kate's resembled a folklore museum; no Chippendale and Sèvres here. Penelope smiled as she took a big stoneware mug of coffee one of the women had poured her.

As she took a tentative sip she tried to get the gist of whatever was being hotly debated. Interest rates, shares, portfolios; they sounded like her uncle and her cousins at lunch today at Loch's. She looked from one rapt face to another. They were all sizes and shapes, these women, but most of them were wearing the utilitarian bluejeans that Penelope, too, now donned for her feminist gatherings. Except for Martha, who was in her sixties, and Judy, just out of Radcliffe, they were in their late twenties, their thirties, or early forties. 'In our prime', as the sisters were fond of saying, sometimes with a raised fist. Penelope reflected that only a few years ago, in what sometimes seemed to her the dark ages before her own awakening, she would never have thought she had much in common with these women who were so careless of their appearance but so careful of their politics. Moreover, had she walked into a room like this, immediately she would have judged them by their hair, clothes, faces, and figures, and she would have been unable to stop from comparing herself to them, most especially wondering which of them were what a man would call *attractive*. Mirror, mirror, on the wall, who's the prettiest of us all? She remembered once, at a consciousness-raising meeting a few years back, saying just that, and how they had all laughed at how crazy they had once been, appraising one another through men's eyes, not being able to take off the blinkers and see into the sisterly souls that so united them. Penelope grinned at frizzy-haired Carol who was trying to talk Boston University into establishing a women's studies programme, at porcelain-featured Margaret who was making a film about menstruation, at square-jawed Joan who was a junior partner at one of the best law firms in the city, at motherly Linda who ran a progressive daycare centre in Cambridge, at plump Ginny who fought daily against entrenched male chauvinism in her Boston City Hall job.

Penelope finally let her eyes fall on the one whose presence she had felt since she first crossed the threshold of this room. Liz sat smoking in the corner, her slim boyish body even slimmer in that black turtleneck and those faded jeans and high black boots she wore everywhere but in bed. She met Penelope's eyes and arched her eyebrows in an unspoken question. Penelope flashed her a V-sign with her fingers, and Liz broke out in a smile; she had been trying to get Penelope at her Back Bay townhouse all day to find out how the meeting with her agent had gone.

341

But back to business. 'The problem,' Liz said as she tore her eyes off Penelope and leaned forward intently, 'is that we can't operate a bank – even a women's bank for our sisters' money – without going down in the muck ourselves.' As she sucked on her cigarette and blew out the smoke, her thin white face was all angles and hollows, the pale image of the ascetic poet. Already, at twenty-six, she had published three slim volumes of verse. But she talked less like a sensitive artist than the streetwise union organizer she was in her paying job. 'OK, suppose, just suppose we manage to get enough capital together to get incorporated and do whatever else we have to do to open for business. What then? You think we'll be able to lend a thousand bucks to every woman we like, or every sister who has a worthy project? No way! Our depositors are going to want interest, not right away maybe, but in a year or two they will. And then what will we do about those loan payments that were never made by the woman who was going to cut a feminist record or open a feminist health foods store? Are we going to foreclose on our sisters?' Again she paused for a puff, and as she exhaled she jabbed the cigarette in the air for emphasis. 'And another thing. Exactly what do we propose to do with the capital deposited in our bank? Keep it in a sock under a mattress? No, like every other bank in the country, we'd lend it to other banks – Chase Manhattan, Bank of America, all the big boys, and I do mean 'boys' – or we'd invest it. But how would we keep our sisters' money from going to support the racists of South Africa or fuelling the war machine here? You roll around in the mud with pigs, and you get dirty.' Her voice softened as she smiled at Joan who had been slaving for months on this plan to open a Boston Women's Bank. 'I'm sorry, Joanie. You've worked so hard on this, and I know how bad you want it. But I think we should spend our energies on issues we can control a little better. Money, at least the money in banks, is the backbone of – ' contemptuously she spat out the words ' – white capitalist male America.'

At once the room exploded, as almost everyone let loose with an angry torrent of words. Penelope contented herself with exchanging a silent look of total accord with the one who had said it exactly as it was. Liz never minced words. In this meeting, as in all meetings, she took the hard line that usually carried the motion and the day. Yet there was a softer side to this union-organizer-cum-poet. Last night, when she should have been working on her manuscript, Penelope had instead found herself trying to pen a poem to this Liz who was the lover of women. No, a woman.

Penelope unfolded her cramped legs and wondered if she should tell Chris everything. He hardly deserved her total candour, and honesty had never been the *leitmotif* of their marriage. Even now, years after the scandal that had changed their lives, he still kept silent about the reasons he had chosen to wall off his past from her. She supposed, in a way, that she should be grateful to that monstrous Yorgos or whoever had leaked the story of Chris's past in that letter. If someone hadn't blown the whistle on his brother, she might never have found out the sort of man her husband really was. So why now, as their time together most definitely was drawing to a close, should she tell him the sort of woman she really was?

Penelope leaned her aching back against the sofa. It would kill him if she told him the whole truth. He might once have been radical in his politics, but in his personal life – particularly when it came to issues of women and men and the family – he was as conservative as those old men she had seen sitting in the village *kafeneions*. After all that had happened, she had no desire to wound him more. He, even more than she, had never altogether recovered from his fall from grace. Sure, sometimes she still resented the waste of those years they had limped along together in a marriage crippled by his deceit. But she had done her best, in the weekly catharsis of her consciousness-raising sessions with the sisters, to work her way through the anger she had repressed for so long. Now that she was happier than she ever remembered being, she could be generous enough to feel sorry for Chris. He wasn't a bad man, just not the right partner for her. And they had shared good years along with the bad. Maybe, if she didn't tell him the absolutely whole truth, they could still be friends?

Sitting on the floor like this might be egalitarian, Penelope thought, but it killed her spine. As she tried and failed to relieve that ache, she reverted to her old habit of trying to give her husband the benefit of the doubt. Perhaps he had tried to make a fresh start with their marriage after those messy political enquiries and immigration hearings had finally been brought to the best conclusion the family lawyers had been able to arrange. Yorgos, or *someone* in league with him in Greece, had stonewalled the evidence of his past. When the dust had settled, Chris had been allowed to stay in America but had been barred from political office. Since then, he had worked in his father's restaurant and new frozen food division like a dutiful Greek son, and had come home every night and gone through the motions of being a model American husband. The only time there had been glimmerings of the old fiery Chris was when he sporadically was involved in helping to organize Greek-American resistance to the *junta* in Greece. But Penelope had always wondered whether his new devotion to his father and her and the children was because of a fundamental change of heart or because he didn't have anything else to do. She supposed it said something about how far apart they had grown that she didn't even know what motivated her husband. No, she would have to get a divorce. She would talk to him soon, perhaps even tonight. Or maybe, she hedged, she should wait until after the first of the year, so the children would have one last Christmas securely in the bosom of what they must suppose was a happy united family. Oh, God, how was she going to tell her daughters?

Penelope sat up straight and massaged the small of her back. Sooner or later she would have to deliver the *coup de grâce* to their marriage. Liz and the sisters were right. Already she had waited too long. Maybe, in fact, she should have done as her family had wanted and left him flat after the scandal first broke. But she supposed that if she could hardly face doing it now, she never could have done it when she still had been nursing hopes of a phoenix rising from the ashes of their marriage. Even after she had returned home from Greece, there could have been a chance for the two of them to make it together if just once he had opened up and poured out his heart to her. Instead, he had remained elusive. Even when he was by her side night and day, she had felt alone in his presence. For a long while their marriage had been dead. The right thing was to give it a proper burial.

As the debate about priorities and capitalism and resources raged round her, Penelope thought back to the first time she had seen Liz leaning against the refrigerator at a party at Carol's house in Brookline. That had been more than two years ago, when the members of their consciousness-raising group were still dragging their husbands and boyfriends along for an occasional Saturday night get-together. Penelope smiled to herself. How things had changed in those revolutionary two years! Last week, at Margaret's shabby Inman Square apartment, they had actually debated whether it was permissible for the sisters to bring their little boys along to meetings when they couldn't arrange for daycare at home. There was no question, of course, about daughters being welcome, but among some of the sisters – the gay ones in particular – avenging anger against men cut so deeply that one or two wanted to bar even Sally's two-year-old son Alexander.

Belatedly Penelope looked around the room for Sally, who had left in a huff last week when the debate had been at its most heated. Penelope the perpetual peacemaker had meant to telephone her the next morning to assure her that in the end sanity had prevailed; the hardliners had given in, and the group had decided that small sons could continue to accompany their mothers. But Penelope had been so wrapped up in her manuscript that she had forgotten to make that placating call, and now she worried that Sally might never return to this particular nest of sisterhood. It had happened before with this good woman or that, especially in the past months when the gay-straight split had begun to sunder the solidarity all of them had worked so hard to build. Factional infighting was the curse not only of the women's movement but every other liberal-to-left cause Penelope had ever joined. Still, she regretted that she hadn't spoken up at last week's meeting and said

344

how ridiculous, how divisive, and how counterproductive it had been to waste time in such foolish debate when there was a whole world out there so badly in need of concrete action to improve the status of women.

Again her eyes trailed over to Liz, who had been one of the ringleaders of the antiboy movement the previous week. It was because of her that Penelope had held her tongue instead of taking Sally's part. Just that once, she had felt it important to show her solidarity with the sister who was to her the dearest of them all.

Penelope tuned in again to the banking debate, listening not to the arguments, but to who was aligned with whom. Martha, Carol, and Kate were firmly in Joan's middle-of-the road camp. Margaret, Judy, and Linda were heart and soul with radical Liz. Ginny, like Penelope herself, was so far abstaining from the fray. It was doubtful, with the group so split, that they would be able to battle to consensus today. Under her breath Penelope sighed. In theory she believed in the righteousness of working collectively, arguing everything out, and never shirking from the energy it took to bring the entire group to accord. But sometimes she longed to cut short these interminable debates with a dictatorial shout: 'Shut up! That's enough! We'll do it, and that's that!' Pure democracy was a beautiful ideal, but it took too much time to make it work.

Around her she could hear the voices tiring. Everyone had said her piece. The lines were drawn, and consensus was nowhere near. She glanced down at her watch; nearly seven, almost time to wind this up, for most of them were going on to what promised to be a provocative lecture at MIT on the influences of patriarchy on the great Western religions.

'It seems to me,' Penelope said, 'that what we have here is not so much a difference in politics as in strategy.' Benevolently she smiled at Joan who was sunk in despair on the deep cushions of the sofa. 'I personally have always loved the idea of a women's bank. Money is power, we all know that, and what better way to flex our muscles than to open up a bank of our own?' When Joan gave her a grateful look, Penelope made a bid to co-opt a few more of the sisters. 'Setting up our own bank is part of the plan to establish parallel institutions catering specifically to women's needs. The blacks have been doing it in their communities, so why don't we? Already we have a women's bookstore and we're about to get a women's restaurant. We're compiling a directory of women doctors, dentists, and lawyers. I think we can all agree that we want to broaden the women's support system.' She looked from face to face until she saw accord on all of them. 'But the question, as Liz was saying when I came in, is one of resources and priorities.' Liz had said nothing of the kind, but nonetheless she smiled benignly at Penelope. She, too, was aware that no decision would be taken on the banking question at this meeting. 'Maybe,' Penelope went on, 'we should make the women's bank our number one goal, and maybe not. I, for one, have to have a little more time to think this over. But, look. It's late, and that lecture's due to start very soon. Would anyone object to carrying over this debate for next week?' She grinned. 'And besides, I can't wait one more minute to tell you my news.' Dramatically she paused. 'My publisher loves the book! They're going to bring it out before next Christmas!'

'Right on!' Liz brought her fist up in a power salute, and Ginny leaned over and gave her a hug. A smile lit every face, and there was a soprano chorus of happy exclamations. Once more they were united, proud of the success of one of their own.

At that moment Kate emerged from the kitchen with a homemade carrot cake and the champagne. Carol and Martha ran out to help with plates and glasses, and the rest gathered around to congratulate Penelope. No, she assured them, her editor didn't want her to change anything that the sisters regarded as politically important. 'And, can you believe it, they think it might be a bestseller!'

Liz was wresting the cork from the bottle and then pouring the foaming champagne. 'To our Penelope!'

But before they could drink, the budding author amended the toast. 'I'm dedicating the book to all of you. I couldn't have done it without your support. To *us!*' As they clinked their glasses and drank, her gaze trailed from face to face, and then her brimming eyes held Liz's.

It was after ten, and Penelope was giving Liz and two others lifts home from the lecture. As she cruised over the bridge toward Boston University to drop Judy off on Commonwealth Avenue, she listened to the others excitedly hashing over the woman professor's theories about how the Judeao-Christian tradition was riddled with the most primitive sort of male chauvinism.

'I can't believe I never put all this together before,' enthused Ginny, a lapsed Catholic. 'It's always God the Father. Christ, of course, was God made Man. And all the apostles and writers of the Gospels were men.' She looked up at the cloudy Boston night sky as though the very heavens were in league against women.

'Paul was the worst.' Liz leaned around to address the back seat. 'All that stuff about evil women tempting man to sin and damnation. The so-called Church Fathers have a lot to answer for in my book.'

'In my book, too,' Penelope said. The others laughed.

Judy spoke up. 'But let's not forget, that particular mindset didn't start with the Christians.' She had been raised in a reformed Jewish household, and she had not forgotten the lessons of Hebrew school. 'How about Adam and Eve? God created man, but woman was an afterthought put together from his rib. And of course it was *her* fault that they both got run out of Eden.' She snorted in derision. 'And, for women, it was downhill after that. No women rabbis or priests. All those taboos about menstruating women being dirty and forbidden to set foot in holy places. You know what religious Jewish men do every morning? They thank God they were not born women!'

'I thank God they weren't too.' Liz grinned. '*She* wouldn't have chosen inferior souls like that as Her females.'

Again the women laughed. All during the lecture, the professor had repeatedly said '*She*' to refer to the deity.

'I don't know about the rest of you,' Penelope said as she threaded her way through the stop-and-start traffic of Commonwealth Avenue, 'but what fascinates me the most are those theories about how, long before Moses went up on the mountain, everyone worshipped the Great Mother Goddess. Every time my own mother goes on one of her digs around the ancient world, she comes back with more evidence to support those claims. I mean, those terracotta figures she finds everywhere most definitely have breasts.'

'Do you really believe all that?' Ginny had her own bones to pick with the male power élite of the Catholic church, but she was reluctant to go off the deep end and subscribe to what, to her, were farfetched and wishful feminist fairy tales.

'I'd like to,' Penelope answered honestly, as she pulled in front of Judy's building. She put the car in neutral. 'And I really think there's something to it. Remember what I told you about that strange cave someone took me to back in Greece?'

'Marika,' Liz muttered. She lit another cigarette and did not look happy.

'What's this about a cave?' Judy had just joined the group the past spring and had missed the play-by-play of Penelope's trip to Greece. 'Look, maybe we should go upstairs and have some coffee. The place is a mess, but that's nothing new.'

'Sorry, but I'd like to do some work on my manuscript when I get home.' But Penelope couldn't resist filling Judy in a little about that expedition with Marika. 'I was visiting my husband's family in Greece, and one day on the beach I got to talking to my sister-in-law about Great Mother worship in ancient times. "Oh, yes," she said, "the Great Goddess," as though She were her next door neighbour. You see, there was this cave on an island not far from the village. They actually called it the Cave of the Great Goddess, if you can believe that.'

'So?' Judy was rapt. 'Did you see it?'

'Of course. We rowed out to it.' She paused as once again she remembered

347

what she had guessed about her husband and Marika in that cave. She had been sorely tempted, when she returned home, to tell Chris exactly what she suspected about his relationship with Marika and his parentage of Nikos. But she, perhaps just as much as he, had learned to keep her silence about those things that mattered most in their marriage.

'And?' Judy prompted.

Penelope shrugged, sorry now that she had brought up ancient history. She had succeeded in forgetting about her husband for three happy hours. 'It was a cave, that's all. Small, dark, damp. But what was weird was the way you felt inside it.' She shivered, remembering. 'Energy forces, I guess.'

'Spare us,' Liz snapped. 'I had enough of that spacey "energy forces" and "groovy vibrations" talk out in San Francisco.' She looked at her watch. 'And besides, it's late.'

Penelope knew that testy tone. 'Right.' She smiled at Judy. 'Another time, huh?'

After a chorus of farewells and reminders about coming meetings, Judy banged shut the car door and Penelope eased back into the traffic. On the way to Ginny's apartment near the Boston Museum in the Fenway, Penelope and Liz were silent as Ginny mused about the Blessed Virgin Mary's possible connection to early Earth Mother worship.

At a traffic light Penelope looked out of the corner of her eye at Liz smoking and staring straight ahead. She went into a funk every time the subjects of Chris, Marika, and Greece were mentioned.

Penelope thought back to her first impression of Liz leaning against the refrigerator in Carol's kitchen. Then as now, she had been wearing that inevitable black turtleneck and jeans, and then as now, abrasively she had been making short work of someone else's doubts – in that case, Martha's Catholic qualms about abortion. Who was that impossible woman, Penelope remembered asking later. Carol had told her the aggressive newcomer was a radical feminist poet who had already made a name for herself not only in her native San Francisco but in New York. Penelope had been impressed but wary, as Bostonians always were of anyone or anything with a New York stamp of approval. Some of the New York sisters were ferocious; ideologically pure, of course, but frighteningly strident. Moreover, even to Penelope's then-innocent eyes, it had appeared that Liz, with her short blunt-cut hair and even blunter manner, might be a lesbian. Although she would never have admitted it to anyone, least of all to the women in the group, in those early days of the movement Penelope had shied away from the man-tailored sisters. It wasn't that she didn't like them – or some of them, anyway; even though it made her a little nervous to be around them, she admired their uncompromising strength. They had committed themselves totally – heart, mind, body, soul – to the women's movement, while she still dressed up in Bonwit Teller clothes and slept each night beside her shell of a husband. And looking back, she supposed that somewhere in her heart of hearts she had been revolted at the thought of what these women did with one another when they were alone. Somehow it had always been easier to accept homosexual men than homosexual women. Gay men were witty and urbane, but to her there had been something almost sinister – or was shameful the right word? – about these harsh women. In the beginning with Liz she had never felt that rush of impulsive attraction that she remembered with, say, Marika, back in Greece.

She wound through the sidestreets of the Fenway toward Ginny's building, wishing she had never broached the subject of Greece and Marika. If she read the look on Liz's face correctly – and these days they were so close that words often seemed irrelevant – they were going to have another go-around about her asking for a divorce as soon as Ginny was out the door. Marika and Chris, Marika and Liz . . .

Penelope hardly listened to the other two discussing how long it would realistically take for women to be ordained as priests in the Episcopal church. Except for her raven hair and dark burning eyes, Liz didn't look anything like that Greek woman who had seemed to leap to life from the ancient tragedies of Euripides and Sophocles. But lately she had wondered if all *this* had in fact begun back in Panagia the first time she laid eyes on Marika. Was it possible, as some said nowadays, that every man and every woman had the innate capacity to love members of his or her own sex, and that whether or not this ever came to pass depended not so much on genes as simply meeting the right person at the right time? And that the only thing that held a man or woman back from such a relationship was fear of violating one of the greatest taboos? Maybe. Although she had always thought herself strong and brave, it had been many months before she dared to admit even to herself what sort of feelings she had begun to have for Liz. And it had been another year before she had given in and done anything about it. Such had been her resistance to embarking on this unconventional way of life that she supposed, had she not been so swept along in the deep currents of the women's movement, that she simply would have repressed her yearnings for Liz just as she had suppressed what she now acknowledged as her attraction to Marika. But with politics thrown in for good measure, this final commitment had grown to seem not only right but inevitable and all of a piece. The reasons for what she had with Liz could be all these things or none of these things. Perhaps, she thought, none of us has any real choice about whom we will love. Maybe we just should be grateful for the great gift love is when and wherever we find it.

'OK,' Ginny was saying as she leaped out of the car, 'see you Thursday night.' Just last week there had been a rape on this street, so Penelope waited until her friend was safely inside and the lights of her apartment winked on, off and on again in a prearranged signal before she pulled back into the traffic. Now it was just she and Liz on the way to her place in the South End. 'Good meeting,' Penelope ventured after a moment to fill the oppressive silence. 'And a great lecture.'

'You think so?' Liz frowned. 'The lecture was all right. Good, in fact, although I've heard it all before. But as for the meeting, we may lose Joanie over this banking thing, which would be a damn shame. She's such a good woman. And very determined. If anyone can pull off a women's bank, she can.'

'So why not back her?'

'As I said, money is dirty. And we want our movement *clean*. We start compromising now, and in five or ten years, we'll just be tired old liberals cutting deals with everyone else. As I told you before, Penelope, I don't like compromises. And I, at least, don't live lies.'

Here it comes, Penelope thought. One of the qualities she most admired about Liz was how, unlike Chris, she never compromised her beliefs. She braced for the fireworks. But Liz said nothing more until they were on her street. 'Coming up?'

Penelope shook her head. 'Chris will be home at eleven. And I haven't seen him for days.'

'Suit yourself. I wouldn't want to intrude on your quality time with your husband.' But she lit a cigarette and made no move to get out of the car. 'We should talk, you know. We haven't done even that for days. There's a parking space at the end of the block.'

Another confrontation, Penelope thought. But she parked the car.

'So when are you going to tell him?' Liz demanded before Penelope had even switched off the ignition.

'Soon. I told you before, I'll tell him soon.'

'Soon is a four-letter word.' Liz fixed her hawk eyes on her lover. 'What I'd like to hear – now! – is that you're going to tell him tonight.'

'I tried to do it last week. But he was working late every night, and then he got that terrible cold.' Penelope was embarrassed to hear herself sounding like a meek little wifey. 'It's the children,' she blurted out. 'I hate to think about what this is going to mean to the girls.'

Liz sighed. 'Yeah, that's a real problem. There's no way to help hurting the children in a divorce.' She stubbed out her half-smoked cigarette and turned to face Penelope. 'Is it them, or is it me? If I were a man, and you were in love with me, would you march right home and tell your husband you wanted a divorce?'

Penelope stared into those dark eyes that, despite her tough words, were full of tears. She felt an impulse to take her in her arms and comfort her as a mother would a daughter. Sometimes she was the strong one to hold it all together, and sometimes it was Liz. That was what was so wonderful about what they had together, the softness of it, and the caring. Liz always *understood*. Even when she was fierce and demanding, she could empathize with exactly what Penelope was feeling. And – unlike Chris – she always talked about her feelings. After living with an elusive alien for so many years, it was a relief to have someone who was so like herself. She felt so sure, when she was with her and the other sisters, that this all-woman life was what she wanted. But Liz was right, it wasn't just the children that kept her from making the break with her old life. She put her palms up to her temples and pressed in hard, as though to squeeze out her doubts and fears.

'Now look what I've done!' Liz' voice was pitched so low that it seemed she was talking to herself. 'Oh, God, why can't I shut my big mouth for once?' She wiped her eyes and forced a smile. 'Sorry, Penelope. We should be celebrating the news about your book tonight.' She tried to change the subject. 'Imagine how you're going to feel the first time you hold that book in your hands. Or see it in the bookstore.'

'Yes, it's like giving birth again. I'll have three daughters and one book.' It would be so easy to take this opening to sidle away from the subject that troubled her so, but now it was Penelope's turn to be hard on herself. It was always this way between them, each so eager to please the other that they switched forward and backward, always striving to see things through the other's eyes. 'But let's not get sidetracked. You're right. I have to talk to him. The way things are isn't fair to you or to me. Or even to him. But it's hard, you know?' Her voice broke.

'I know. Give me credit for a little bit of sensitivity. I was married, too, remember.'

'But you didn't leave Bill for another woman.'

'No, *he* left *me* for another woman.' Still, after six years, her expression was very sad as she remembered the pain of that time. 'I was like everyone else, thinking marriage was forever. And then the axe fell. If it weren't for the sisters, and the support they gave me then, I don't know how I would have gotten through it.' She lit another cigarette. 'But later, when I was living with Sylvia and he found out how I'd changed, you would have thought I had insulted his precious manhood. *Men!*' She took a drag on her cigarette and reconsidered. 'I don't know, maybe you shouldn't hit Chris with the whole thing at once. Maybe it would be easier for you, and for him, to take it in steps. First the divorce, then later, when you're both a little stronger, *me*.'

'But I'm so tired of all this sneaking around. It's not like you and I are committing some sort of *crime* together.' But it is exactly like that, she amended to herself. In the eyes of society, we are the underworld of love. She liked that phrase, 'the underworld of love', and mastered her writer's compulsion to pull out a notebook and write it down before she forgot it. Doggedly she went on. 'OK, suppose I tell him I want a divorce and ask him to move out. You think he's not going to find out that you've moved in?' She paused. 'Him and everyone else.' She would have to tell her mother and father, the rest of the family would eventually be informed, and once it became common knowledge she would have to endure even having acquaintances look at her in a certain way when she ran into them on the street or at parties. *Lesbian, gay, dyke.*

'I know, that's the other thing. The social stigma.' Liz wished she could take Penelope in her arms and tell her none of this would wound her. Better yet, she wished she could shoulder her lover's pain herself. If it would help, she would volunteer to tell Chris how things were and tackle that uptight family of Penelope's as well. But some passages a human being has to make alone. She sighed. 'We've all had to go through it, and it's never easy. My father cried when I told him. Tough as nails, worked on the docks all his life, and he cried like a baby.' Again her own eyes filled with tears, and almost angrily she wiped them away. 'Coming out of the closet, they call it, as if it's as easy as opening a door.' She would try to offer this woman she loved a ray of hope. 'But think of it this way. Who wants to live cramped up in a dark closet all her life? Once you're out in the sun, you're free. And take it from me, you'll feel better once you've done it. That is, *if* you decide to do it. You don't have to, you know.'

'Oh, I'll do it. I can't go on like this.' If she didn't do it soon, she might lose Liz. 'I know you won't wait forever.'

Liz threw her cigarette out the window and reached over to take Penelope's hands in hers. 'There's something you still don't understand about you and me. You've spent all your life loving men, so you think I'm going to threaten to leave you flat unless you do what I want. Control, power, dominance, manipulation . . . that's how it is between men and women. They play the masters and our role is the slaves. If we don't tow the line, off they go. And often, even when we turn ourselves inside out for them, they take off anyway. But I'm not putting that kind of pressure on you, Penelope. OK, I hate the thought of you going home to *him* every night, and I get jealous as hell every time I think of that Marika. I love you, after all, and I want you all to myself.' Her ardent grip on Penelope's hands slackened, and now their palms were intertwined like comrades. 'But we're friends, too. Sisters, Penelope! *Women!* I want what's best for you. I don't want you to do something that's going to make you miserable. You're all grown up, and you have a right to make your own decisions about how you're going to live your life. If you can't or won't commit to me, if you need more time or just decide this whole thing's too hard, I'll understand. It will break my heart, but I'll understand.' She bent and kissed Penelope's hands. 'Courage, sister.' And with that she was gone.

Penelope watched the dark figure fade into the shadows and disappear inside the doorway.

Before she even had the front door shut, Christos called out from the living room. 'Is that you, Peppy?'

God, she thought, I've always hated that Greek nickname that makes me sound like something between a hot tamale and a jumping bean. 'Yes.' Despite her feeling that she *should* talk to him, she had hoped she would be able to slide into bed and be fast asleep before he got home. But no such luck.

'I came home early.' He had thought she would, too, to tell him her news. 'I've been here since nine-thirty.'

He sounded lonely. Reluctantly, and with a feeling of guilt – she was late and he had been waiting for her while she sat with her lover talking of how to divorce him – she trailed into the room where he was listening to that sad Greek flute music he loved. Christos put down his Greek newspaper and smiled expectantly. He had built a fire before the two wing chairs. On the table before him was a bottle cooling in a bucket of ice and two fluted crystal champagne glasses. The dog lay curled at his feet. 'Surprise!' He peeled the silver wrapping off the bottle. 'I've been trying to get you on the phone here all night. Your mother called about six to see if you were at the restaurant, and she told me what your agent said. That's great, Peppy. You should be very proud.'

'Ah, yes, the book.' She was so preoccupied with what Liz had said that she had almost forgotten the news from New York. She sank down in her chair and was reminded of their confrontation, sitting in these very chairs more than two years ago, the night the story of his past had broken in the Boston headlines. But they had been living out in Concord then. After Greece, they had sold that house and moved back to this Back Bay townhouse. Yet much more than their residence had changed in that span of time. The melancholy music hung in the air. Should she try to get this all over with tonight, or not?

353

Oblivious to her mood, Christos was prying off the cork. 'Your mother said she's been trying to get you all day. Or at least all afternoon, ever since your father found out about the book when he saw you at lunch. She seemed to think she was the last to know.' As he held the bottle between his knees and pulled at the cork, reproach crept into his voice. 'But I told her no, that it was news to me.' The cork popped, and Christos held the bottle up like a trophy. 'To the author!' He poured the glasses, gave one to her, and held his up for a toast. 'And to wonderful new beginnings!'

And to amicable endings, she amended to herself. But she clinked glasses with her husband and drank. He had been sweet to think of the champagne. In these last years, as her own emotional involvement had lessened, Christos had turned more thoughtful and anxious to please. She listened to him enthusing about the book and was startled to hear him even asking to read it in manuscript. Liz and most of her group had critiqued her work chapter by chapter as she had written it, but until now Christos had evidenced no more interest than if it had been some bit of embroidery a village wife was sewing in her spare afternoons.

'You might not like it,' she ventured, although she was certain he would not be happy about her radical feminist ideas. Every time it was her turn to have the sisters here, Christos had made it his business to stay away until he was sure the last of them would be gone. He had taken a particular dislike to Liz. Penelope had wondered if he had intuitively known what a deadly threat she was to their marriage. *I've got to tell him.* But I hate to do it tonight, when he's being so nice. Also, she could see by the box of tissues beside his chair that he was still nursing his cold. Maybe she should wait until he was feeling better. But would there ever be a *right* time?

Christos was still doing his best to ignore how cool she was acting. She was just tired, that was all, from running around at those constant meetings. He remembered how he used to feel when he was so busy. A pang much like homesickness shot through him. In the old days – his time in the sun, he thought of it now – there had not been enough hours in the day to do everything that had to be done. He had felt so exuberantly alive, then. Watching his wife so involved now in that women's movement of hers, he yearned for what he had lost. Now that he lived in the shadows it took all his energy to pretend interest in his father's frozen food business. His work for the Greek resistance to the *junta* helped, but it seemed the Athens regime was so entrenched that nothing he said or did here in Boston mattered much. And even though he tried to pretend enthusiasm, he did not exactly bask in his wife's feminist glories. 'Your mother said the book will be out before next Christmas. And that they think it will be an even bigger bestseller than Nick's Fried Clams.' Engagingly, as though he were still running for office, he smiled. His world, since his legal and immigration problems had finally been settled, had revolved around marketing Nick's Fishsticks, French Fries, and especially his New England Fried Clams. That, and arranging parties and catering to his father's every whim. 'As soon as I talked to your mother, I knew we would have to have the publication party down at the restaurant.'

These days, Penelope thought as she sipped her champagne and listened to him elaborating about the party he would throw for her, Christos seemed to take luncheons and dinners as seriously as once he had taken politics and elections. The committed young man she had loved and married had dreamed such different dreams. It was a measure of how far apart they had grown that she didn't have the faintest idea what he felt now. *Why don't I know my own husband*? A sense of failure washed over her. A welling tenderness for this middle-aged man who had lost so much and was about to lose even more saddened her. Perhaps, she thought, I should have tried to love him more. She supposed she was every bit as much to blame as he was for how it was between them now. Maybe she should try again? But no, it was too late. She had another life now, and what she had to do was let go so he could start afresh as well. Perhaps it would be a mercy to end this pretence of a marriage. But how could she find the words to tell him? She felt so very sorry that she was going to have to hurt him so much.

'And if all goes well,' Christos was saying, 'our little Parthenon will be ready by then. Maybe we'll even unveil it at the party for your book. It would be great publicity for the restaurant. I talked to my father already, and he thought that was a great idea. You know Nick. He still wants you to model for the statue of Athena. He even said today that instead of having you hold a spear, maybe you could have an open book in your hands.'

She winced. 'I thought we'd heard the last of that.' In the aftermath of Christos' political scandal, her father-in-law had seemed to forget his plan to erect a plastic Parthenon on his restaurant lawn.

'No such luck. He told me last week that, now that I've got the frozen food division on its feet, he wants me to get to work building his little bit of Athens right here on Boston Harbor. But I told you that. I must have told you that. Or maybe Nick did.'

'I haven't talked to your father in ages.' To herself she added that she wanted to keep it that way. Ever since Greece, she had done her best to distance herself from her father-in-law and all things that reminded her of that visit. But Nick seemed hardly to have noticed how she absented herself more and more often from family get-togethers and Greek functions of every sort. Aside from occasionally reproaching her about how hurt the family had been when she left without saying goodbye, the old man had continued to dote on her. 'But let me get this straight. He wants you to build a plastic

355

replica of the Parthenon and sell oysters and clams inside it. And he actually thinks that I'm going to model for some ridiculous statue of Athena, holding my book?' Despite her worries, she laughed.

So did Christos. At that sound, Zoi woke up and began wagging her tail. 'I know, Peppy, it's too much.' His eyes caught hers. 'It's good to share a laugh again, eh?' He seemed his old confident self as he refilled their glasses and gave the dog a few ebullient pats on the head. 'I can't remember when we've laughed like that.' Or made love, he added to himself. Since last winter, he had hardly touched her. But with her sometimes staying up until two or three working on her book, it had made sense for Penelope to move into a separate bedroom so they both could get a good night's sleep. Yet all that was over now. Except for some minor revisions, the book was finished. He had been very patient, but it was time to resume a normal married life. 'From now on, Peppy, it will be different. We're going to spend more time together not only as a family but as man and wife. I thought, now that I've got out from under the frozen foods and you've wrapped up your book, you and I can get away for a real vacation. Just the two of us.' He reached into his pocket and brought out the airline tickets he had bought that afternoon. 'I've booked us on a flight down to Jamaica for Saturday morning. And reserved rooms at what sounds like the most romantic hotel in the West Indies.' He refilled their glasses and raised his. 'To *us*, Peppy.'

She stared at her husband and did not move to take the glass. It was now or never. If she drank to their future, she would be agreeing to more than a second honeymoon. One thing would lead to another, and she might never ask for a divorce. Besides, she knew that gleam in his eye. She had used every excuse known to woman to keep him out of her bed for as long as she could. Tonight she did not dare even to let him touch her hand. She would burst into tears if he took her in his arms. Once, in another lifetime, they had been happy together. But she could not bear to go home again, into his arms. Her eyes filled with tears, and she said the hardest word she had ever spoken. 'No.'

'What do you mean, no?' He was still smiling, but not with such certainty.

'I can't do it.' She knew she should blurt out the rest and be done with it. But instead she sat silently listening to his broken-hearted music.

'What's the problem? More of your meetings? A conference perhaps? *Or that damned book.*'

Her eyebrows arched. That damn book? Was that how he really had felt about her work all along? 'That's part of it,' she said slowly.

He tossed back his glass of champagne and slammed it down on the table. He looked at her in her jeans and rumpled sweater. When had he last seen her in a skirt? She wasn't wearing makeup, and her hair was a mess. He tried and tried to make their marriage work, but she had let herself – and what they used to have together – go. The resentment he usually succeeded in repressing boiled to the surface. 'I don't understand you. I try to do everything right. I'm sick and tired of having to watch everything I say to you. "Don't say girl, Chris, say woman, or better yet, person!" Sexist this and chauvinist that! You never let up! But still I try to be what you're always saying I should be. *Supportive*, that's the fashionable word, isn't it? But I'm not some concrete pillar holding up a roof, I'm a *man*. Your husband! I hardly see you for months, but do I complain? No! And then you finish that . . . that *thing* you care about more than me and your own children, and you don't even have the courtesy to tell me that in New York they think it's the best thing since sliced bread. I have to hear it from your mother! You've been running all over Cambridge all night telling every one of those dykey friends of yours all your business, but once again you forgot about me. I don't feel very good tonight, I should have gone straight to bed, but instead here I sat waiting for you – like the dutiful *wife*! – with my bottle of champagne and my tickets to the Caribbean. And now you won't even drink to our future? I don't understand you, Peppy. I don't understand you at all.'

She sighed. 'Chris, we've got to have a serious talk.'

'Serious? I wouldn't call what we're doing right now a barrel of laughs.' All at once, his anger seemed to fall as flat as the champagne in her untouched glass. 'What's wrong with us, Peppy?'

'Ah,' she said so low that it was a whisper, 'so you know.'

'Know what?' Chilled by a premonition that things were worse than he had thought, he got up and began pacing back and forth, the dog at his heels. 'I know that we have problems. I know that we hardly spend any time together. I know that you pick at every little thing I say and do. I know that you turn as cold as that ice in the bucket if I so much as kiss you. Yes, I know that, too. But what I don't know is why all this is, and what you intend to do about it.' He stood still and faced her. 'Suppose you tell me.'

'All right.' She looked him straight in the eyes. 'I want a divorce.'

He sagged back into the chair. 'A divorce.'

'I think it would be the best for both of us, considering . . .'

Christos had cut down on his smoking – that was to please her, too, he thought to himself as he shook out a cigarette from his packet – and as he held a match to it he saw that his hands were shaking. He had not thought that relations between them had deteriorated so far that she was even contemplating *this*. He inhaled deeply, but bent over double in a coughing fit. Blindly he reached for the champagne, took a swig from the bottle, and as soon as his coughing stopped he took another drag of the cigarette. The

357

nicotine spread through his bloodstream like a deadly balm. Finally, then, he recovered enough to repeat that word. 'Divorce.'

Now that it – or most of it – was out in the open, Penelope was eager to say the rest and be done with it. 'You said it yourself. We have serious problems.' She attempted not only to be generous but to try to keep the discussion on an abstract political level. If it was at all possible, she thought, she didn't want him to take the divorce personally. The absurdity of that hope! 'I know it hasn't been easy for you these past years. First the scandal and then the women's movement. It's been the same with all the sisters who have relationships with men.' Careful, she warned herself, you're getting too close to that other thing. 'I mean,' she continued, 'we're in the middle of a real revolution. A social revolution. As you no doubt remember from your Communist days, you can't make an omelette without breaking eggs.'

'An omelette? Eggs! You dare to misquote Lenin to *me*?' He, too, had recovered his powers of speech. 'And it's this way with the rest of the girls, is it? Men and marriage are passé?' He shook his head. 'No, Peppy, I won't buy it.'

'Won't buy what? My political ideas? You just said you resent my work and the time I devote to what I consider the greatest issue of our time. How can I stay with a man who doesn't respect these things which are so important to me? Chris! Think back how it used to be when you were so politically involved, not just here, but in Greece. Unless I'm very much mistaken, you, too, once put politics before your personal life.'

For a moment he smoked in silence as he thought the irony of that one over. Was he, who had left the love of his life for the cause he once had thought paramount, now being paid back in kind? Maybe so, but somehow his wife's glib political excuses didn't entirely ring true. Penelope was passionate about her women's movement, but she wasn't so fanatically singleminded that she would sacrifice her marriage on the altar of women's liberation. Something else was at the root of this. 'Politics? Your work?' Again he shook his head. 'I won't let you off the hook that easily. If you want,' he hesitated, unwilling to say that word again, 'what you just said you want, you're going to have to tell me why.'

She took a deep breath. 'You'll have to admit that we haven't had a real marriage for a long time,' she began, 'not since – '

'It was your idea to move into that other bedroom,' he snapped. Furiously he puffed on his cigarette. 'And let me tell you, I don't know another man from my country who would have put up with that.'

Grimly she nodded, remembering oversexed Greece. She tried to hold back her temper. She wanted a civilized divorce. She wanted it to be possible for them at least to part as friends. 'I didn't mean just sharing the same bed. I meant *marriage*. Communication. Sharing. Intimacy.'

'More of your fashionable words.'

She threw her hands up in the air. 'It's impossible to talk to you. It always was impossible to talk to you.'

'Always?' He looked into her eyes, remembering a time when he had been able to read her thoughts by what was reflected in her candid eyes. But now her eyes were veiled. 'You're hiding something.'

Her eyes fell, and when she raised them again, she said the things she had hoped she would not have to say. 'OK, you want to know why I want a divorce? All right, I'll tell you why. Because of your lies, Chris. Because you never trusted me enough to tell me about what had happened to you in Greece. Because of the way you manipulated me and my family into helping you fulfil your ambitions. Because of the way you betrayed everyone who ever meant anything to you, not only here in America but back in Greece, too. I can't trust you, Chris. I thought I could, once, but not now.'

He let out a deep intake of breath. 'So that's it. Yorgos and the letter. You've been holding that against me all this time.'

'Don't blame it on your brother. Blame it on yourself. All those years together, and you never told me what mattered most about yourself.' She hesitated, and then she blurted out another accusation. 'And there's something else. Back in Greece. Marika. You never told me about you and her.'

He froze in the act of reaching for a tissue. It was his turn then to avoid her eyes, as slowly he took that tissue and blew his nose. 'What about my sister-in-law?'

'Come *on*, Chris, I know all about her and you. And why you *really* left Greece.' It was on the tip of her tongue to ask him how he could have abandoned not only Marika but the child she was carrying, but just in time she kept her mouth shut. She didn't want to open the issue of Nikos, she wanted to get her husband to agree to a divorce.

He swallowed hard. 'She told you?'

'I guessed. You didn't have to be a genius to put that one together. You never got over her, did you?' She was surprised to hear the hurt in her voice. She had not realized that she still cared enough to be jealous of that other woman.

'I never pretended to be a virgin when we met. And I might remind you that you weren't one, either. But I don't sit here throwing those old Harvard boyfriends up in your face.'

'Perhaps because I'm not still in love with them. And that's just it! You never told me anything about what you really thought and felt. You've always built walls around yourself.'

'And you? You haven't done the same thing? For more than two years this has been eating away at you, and you never said a word to me.'

She shrank from his eyes, aware that she had to share the guilt for how it was between them now. 'I couldn't. I didn't want to hurt you.'

'And now? What's different now? All of a sudden you can't wait to hurt not only me but the children. Have you thought of what this would do to them? We're a family! Maybe this doesn't mean anything to you, but I was brought up to think that the family was something sacred.' He tossed his used tissue on the table. 'You can't throw what we've built together away, just like that!'

'Don't, Chris.' Another time, when both of them had calmed down, they would settle the issue of custody of the children. If he came to his senses and agreed to an amicable divorce, she was prepared to let him keep Christina while she took Sofia and Helen. But now was not the time to hammer out the details. She stood. 'Look, it's late. I've had a hard day, and I can't take any more of this. I'll just go up and look in on Christina. Why don't you think all this over, and we can talk again in the morning.'

'Not so fast. Sit down, Peppy. I want to get to the bottom of this.' When she hesitated, his voice rose. 'And as for Christina, she's just fine. While you were out at your important meeting, I told her a story and put her to bed. When's the last time you did that, Peppy? Or is motherhood passé in your avant-garde circles now, too?'

'Don't make this any more difficult than it already is.' Gingerly she sat on the edge of her chair. 'There's no point in getting ugly about all this.'

Intently he was studying her eyes. 'You didn't answer my question. What's different now?' He stubbed out the cigarette and seemed to come to a conclusion. His jealousy now was even stronger than his fears for the welfare of the children. 'It's someone else, isn't it? That's why you moved into the other bedroom. Who is he, Peppy?'

Now or never, she told herself again. With an effort she said the words. 'Not he.' Defiantly she met his eyes and threw caution to the winds. 'She.'

'She? *She!*' Incredulously he stared at his wife. 'No. Oh, no.'

Now that it was out, she wanted to tell him everything. 'Liz.'

'Her?' His mouth dropped open. 'That *dyke*?'

For a moment she thought he might strike her. Instead he got up, went to the liquor closet, and poured himself a tumbler of Metaxa. His mind was a blank. Inside he was altogether empty. He drained his glass in one gulp. The fiery brandy scorched his stomach and branded his brain. A *woman*? How was it possible? She was his wife and the mother of his children. He had loved her, honoured her, and now . . . He poured another brandy and sipped it, willing his mind to function. He could feel his heart hammering in his chest. What could he say? What could he do? Home, he thought. I wish I could go home to Greece. I wish I could stand on Panagia beach and let the cool pure sea wash all the dirt of life off me. Dirty, she was dirty. Slowly he came back, slid into his chair, and without looking at her reached for a tissue to wipe away the tears that were streaming down his cheeks. He blew his nose and lit a cigarette. He was conscious that the record of his flute music had finished some time ago. The room was deadly silent. He smoked his cigarette without saying a word. What was he going to do? By rights he should be beating her half to death, but it made him sick to his stomach to think even of touching her with his fists. How could she have done this? She had insulted not only their marriage but his manhood. His *filotimo*, his Greek pride, had been shattered. The shame of it! His own wife! And what of his daughters? Was she going to make all three of those innocent little girls sick like her? But no, he thought, even though they were growing up in America, they had his Greek blood. Once they grew up and married and had a man inside them, they'd be natural women. Not like *her*. Not like this *dyke*. He took another sip of the seven-star brandy. He had all the time in the world to think this over from every possible angle, to dissect her character and behaviour for the telltale clues that this was how it would end between them. But here and now, tonight, there was only one thing he had to do. She had taken most of his pride away from him, but he would gather the tattered remains and end this thing with what dignity he could muster. He stubbed out his cigarette and once again wiped away his tears. Finally, still without looking at her, he spoke. 'OK.'

'OK, what?' She was watching him with frightened eyes. She had never seen him cry before.

'OK, I'll give you a divorce. After . . . this, I don't want you as my wife.' He made the Greek gesture of washing his hands. 'Finished. It . . . everything . . . is finished.' He drained his glass, got to his feet, and carefully attached the leash to Zoi's collar. He would take the dog tonight, and tomorrow he would come back for Christina. If she fought him about that, he would go to court and win custody of Sofia and Helen, too. 'I'm going to my father's. Your lawyers can find me there.'

'Chris? Chris!' She got up and followed him to the door. 'Don't take it like this, Chris. Wait! We'll talk some more, I have to make you understand.' She touched his shoulder, and he wheeled to face her.

'Don't touch me.' For the first time since she had said her fatal words, he looked her straight in the face. His eyes were cinders. He had loved this woman. She was the mother of his children. Together they had founded a family. But as he looked at her, he had an impulse to insult her with that greatest gesture of contempt known to a Greek. He wanted to spit in her face.

Instead, as he had done with the Communists, he merely walked out and slammed the door shut on his married life. Then when he slid into his car and hunched over the steering wheel, he wept not for lost pride, not for the shame of it, but because he had forever lost a woman who had been dear to him. For a long while he cried in the car with only the anxious dog to comfort him. Finally, when he thought he had no more tears, he put the key in the ignition. What was left in his life now? For the second time, he had lost everything that mattered. What was he going to do?

It had started to rain, and so he put on the windscreen wipers and pulled out of his parking space. Tomorrow or the next day, somehow he would find the strength to pick up the pieces and once more start again. Maybe, in time, he thought, he would even see the irony of it all. He had lost his country, both women that he loved, and not one but two political careers. It was possible that all he would succeed in doing in life was building his father's plastic Parthenon.

He wasn't even aware that he was still crying as he drove through the rain toward his father's house.

Fourteen

Nikos was always to remember the first time he saw her, in late March of 1972, striding in the soft early spring sun up the flower-lined pavement toward the National Museum. She was tall and slender, like so many of the tourist girls, and she walked in long graceful ripples. Like a dancer, he thought, admiring the way she held back her shoulders and rotated her hips, so proud. She was dressed all in black, the snug trousers tucked into high boots, the narrow sweater and wide belt drawing his eye again to those high full breasts. There was music in those thighs of hers, and he felt a strange sensation in his hands, as though he longed to strum her like his beloved guitar and coax melody from the rise and fall of her pretty breasts. She was too far away at first for him to see her face. But the sun caught the lights in her honey-coloured hair and the wind tossed it round her face like the halo in an icon of a saint. Maybe it was her swinging walk or perhaps it was her breezy hair, but he had the sensation that what was coming his way was freedom made woman. She looked so young and confident. She was nothing like the Greek girls in his class at the nearby polytechnic. Those sultry, round, chattering young women travelled everywhere in gossipy packs, their noses – though not necessarily their breasts – up in the air. It was easy enough to get almost any of them to go out for a coffee once they'd heard that his father was one of the colonels who ran the country, but they were looking for husbands, not just happy times or even love. One coffee, and they were all but ordering the wedding crowns. But this one was of another breed. He could not take his eyes off the proud young animal walk of this beautiful foreign girl.

Next to him on the steps Stavros caught him staring and saw at what. 'Nice.' He looked back at Nikos and grinned. 'I think you're in love.'

'*Tch*!' Carelessly Nikos tossed his head back in the Greek negative. He and his old friend were killing time, that was all, before Stavros had to take his taxi out again and he had to be back at school for a late afternoon class. But still his eyes were locked on this girl who moved like a tawny lion.

'Well, if you don't want her, maybe I'll make a try.' Stavros squinted at the girl. 'She looks Swedish.' He had forgotten the little English he had learned in high school, and so his encounters with foreign girls were limited to trying to cheat them on taxi fares. But he had fantasized a lot as eagerly he had listened to luckier boys tell their seductive stories. 'And they say they're the easiest. Like rabbits. Of course the English and the Germans are supposed to be hot, too. I'd like to take *this* one for a ride. Look at those legs!'

Nikos scowled at his old friend who was talking about this lovely creature as though she were a piece of meat that any boy could pick off the hook and devour at leisure. Down in Panagia in the summer, he had played the luscious game of romancing the tourist girls. But this one was different. He was surprised at how protective he felt of her. Possessive, too. 'I saw her first.'

Stavros nodded. In their *parea* of fast friends, it was part of the code never to steal one another's girls. But there was nothing wrong with making the chase into a game. 'Bet you fifty drachmas you can't get her over to that café for a coffee.'

'That one's worth more than fifty drachmas.' He could see a little of her face now. She had very pale skin and delicate, almost fragile, features. A girl like that must have every boy in Athens running after her. Were her eyes light or dark behind those sunglasses? 'Maybe all the money in the world.'

'I'll settle for a coffee.' Stavros clapped him on the back. 'You go to it.' He gestured toward the café on the side of the museum grounds. 'I'll be waiting over there, eh? And I won't pay the bill unless or until I see you coming over

363

with her. But you'd better make quick work of it. I go back on duty in an hour.'

At last she was coming up the steps in graceful little running steps that made her breasts bob. She didn't seem to be wearing a bra. Belatedly Nikos took a step forward, but she glided past him into the museum.

He lurked near her as she queued for her entrance ticket. Up close her windblown hair was all soft goldish curls. He breathed in the scent of her, a perfume sweeter yet lighter than jasmine. She was just his height. If she were to turn around and he kissed her, their lips would fit together perfectly.

He would have followed her anywhere, and so docilely he trailed behind her into the main exhibition hall where the golden treasures of Mykenae were displayed. Just like his grandmother Eleni drawn to her favourite icon on her daily pilgrimage to church, the tourist girl made a beeline for the solid gold death mask that occupied the place of honour in a glass case. Obviously this wasn't her first visit to the museum.

Nikos came up behind her. 'That's the Mask of Agamemnon,' he said in English.

'Hmmmm.' Without answering or even turning to see who had spoken, she inched away from him.

Hoping that she wasn't German or French or some other nationality that might not understand his only foreign language, he tried again. 'It's very famous. And very beautiful, don't you think?'

Still she ignored him. She gazed as if transfixed at the ancient gold mask.

Nikos looked at it, too, desperately wondering what else he could say about this old piece of precious metal beaten into the shape of a man's face. If the two of them were down at a club in Plaka where the music never stopped, he could lean over to her table and say any one of a thousand wonderful things that would make her smile for him only. He could raise his rich deep voice to sing along with the music, and before long she would be his. But for the life of him he couldn't think what to say about this mask she was staring at so raptly. He, like virtually all of his countrymen, took pride in what his ancestors had accomplished. From the first to the last year of school, the greatness of Classical Greece was drummed into every student's head. Nikos had been nine years old before he had altogether realized that Zeus and Aphrodite and the rest of the Olympian gods did not really exist, for to him they had been more real than the Panagia and St George. And yet sometimes now he resented how the foreigners fawned over his brilliant forebears. How could he or any modern Greek live up to them? He was embarrassed to hear the tourists extolling the glories of Ancient Greece and then shaking their heads at how it had degenerated. Greece wasn't a fossilized relic that existed only for the edification of over-educated foreigners. With his country suffering under the yoke of a brutal police state, what did old trinkets and columns matter? How could the tourists ignore everything that had happened in his country for the past two millennia and instead all but worship a culture that had perished long ago? Yet still, ransacking his mind for another gambit, Nikos wished he had total recall of what his teachers had said about Mycenean culture. Unless he said something, she would slip away. 'They found it at a place called Mykenae down in the Peloponnese. Not far from my village.' He took a step closer to her. Even though she had removed her sunglasses, with her head turned away he still couldn't quite see the colour of her eyes. Her cheeks and nose, however, were covered by masses of freckles. He wanted to kiss every one of them. 'My name is Nikos, Nikolas Kronos, really.'

'Honestly,' she muttered more to herself than to him, in the posh vowels of upper-class English, 'I'm fed up.' Two months in this bloody country, she fumed to herself, and I can't sit down and have a drink or get on a trolley or – now – even have a few minutes' peace in the museum without one of these fellows pestering me. *Kamakia*, they called themselves, 'spear fishermen' whose prey were girls. In her first days here she had been flattered by the attention – England was nothing like this, so blood-rushingly sensual – and it had been fun to have a little flirt or two. But she had learned that a smile could easily lead to a wrestling match, and so before long she had begun to try to brush them off politely. Such niceties, however, seemed lost on randy Greeks. She intended to make short work of her latest admirer. Still not taking her eye off the golden ornaments, she turned her head slightly toward him. 'But since you insist on trying to make conversation about the objects before us, let me point out that this isn't really the death mask that Agememnon – if there really was such a king – wore.' Her tone of voice was as frosty as only one of her class and country can make it. 'Most archaeologists agree now that when Schleiman found it there in the shaft graves, he jumped to a wrong conclusion.' At Oxford she had read history and politics, but she had dabbled in the Classics as well. 'It was a king's funeral mask, but not Agamemnon's.' That, she thought, should put this one in his place. For good measure, she turned to give him a steely drop-dead look.

Instead she gazed into his startling green eyes. Extraordinary, she thought, I've never seen eyes like this on a Greek. It wasn't polite to stare, and so her gaze fell. An instant later, however, she couldn't help looking up into his green eyes again, this time with the intensity she had previously reserved for the death mask. Those eyes were set in a handsome tanned face framed by thick black hair long enough to curl on his shirt collar. He was young, her age or maybe younger. She had time enough only to register the smile – not predatory, like most of them, but engaging – before she recovered her wits and tore her eyes off him. She tried to focus again on the mask, but another tourist had pushed in front of her. Without being aware of where she was going, she wandered over to a display case of Mycenean jewellery against the wall.

Her imperious disdain had been lost on him, but he had not missed the import of her being unable to resist a second look into his eyes. He was encouraged enough to follow right behind her. When he stopped, he was one breathless step closer to this goddess who, on the evidence of her speech about that mask, must know everything. Her eyes were grey. From somewhere in his schoolboy past, a memory stirred. Like Athena's he thought, remembering how Homer had always referred to the deity who had steered Odysseus through trials and tribulations. 'The grey-eyed goddess.' He had thought he was only thinking, but to his chagrin he was speaking out loud.

'Athena?' Out of the corner of her grey eyes she glanced at him. She, too, remembered her Homer.

'Not Athena.' Soulfully he gazed at her. 'You. The grey-eyed goddess.'

She laughed and turned to him. 'Well, I have to hand it to you. That's original.'

Happily he laughed, too. She was even more beautiful when she smiled. And her laughter was like . . . All he could think of was that it was like the most wondrous music he had ever heard. 'What's your name? Or shall I just keep calling you Athena?'

Again, as happily as though she were back home among old friends, she laughed. It felt marvellous to laugh again, instead of having to walk around scowling to keep the boys at bay. This fellow seemed a cut above the others. Sweet, really. That line about her having Athena's eyes had tickled her. And she liked looking into those eyes. 'All right.' She extended her hand like the foreigners always did. 'Liberty Penn-Nevard.'

With reverence, aware that this was the first time ever that he had touched her, gravely he shook her hand. 'Nikos Kronos,' he repeated. 'But your name – Liberty – I have never heard a foreign girl called that.'

'Neither has anyone else.' She laughed. 'I suppose I'm one of a kind. My parents always say that, anyway.'

'Oh, yes!' How perfect her name was! She, who walked so proud and free, was even called Liberty. 'But that is a Greek name, you know. *Eleftheria*. A little girl on my street in Pangrati was called Eleftheria.'

'Eleftheria,' she repeated, massacring the consonants.

They both laughed, and then – conscious that he was still holding her hand – gently she disengaged it.

'Maybe sometimes I will call you Eleftheria.' When she smiled noncommittally, from habit he launched into the inevitable boy-meets-girl round of Greek-to-tourist questions. 'You are American?'

'Oh, God, do I sound it?' Again Eleftheria laughed. Why, she asked herself, can I not stop laughing? At home in London everyone said she had a champagne laugh. But matters had not gone as well as she hoped since she arrived in this country, and she had lost most of her effervescence. Yet if I don't stop this silly laughing, this fellow will either think I'm a total fool or that I'm leading him on. Am I? she asked herself, stealing another look at those eyes of his. But it was dangerous to flirt with a Greek. She should nip this in the bud, before it got harder to get rid of him. In a moment he would be asking her out for a coffee, and more. But even though she was lonely and he looked like a nice enough chap, she couldn't let herself be picked up by a stranger. She wasn't a tourist out for a holiday fling; she was here for a serious purpose. And yet she answered him. 'No, English.'

Radiantly he smiled. Yes, she liked him, he was sure of it. 'How long are you in Greece?'

'Too long.' But when she saw the light in his eyes die, again – what was she doing, encouraging him? – she gave him a more civil answer. 'Sorry . . . Nikos, is it? Yes? OK, sorry, Niko, I've been here since January. And I do like Greece, or some of it anyway. But I get so fed up with always these same interrogations and being followed everywhere I go.'

'Followed?' He took a protective step closer to her as he scanned the exhibition room, wondering why the security police had her under surveillance. To him she appeared just like any tourist making the obligatory pilgrimage to this museum, but perhaps she was in some sort of trouble. And she had mentioned interrogations. 'Look, if there's something I can do to help, you must tell me.' He lowered his voice. 'I, or rather my father, can probably fix things for you. That is, if the security police don't want you for anything big.'

'Security police?' Although this was a deadly serious subject and one that in fact did have something to do with her reasons for being in Greece, she threw back her dazzling hair and laughed again as she realized the misunderstanding. He really was sweet. 'No, no, all I meant was that men keep following me everywhere. But not police. *Kamakia*.' Her tone was lighthearted, but she, too, glanced warily around the gallery. Was it possible that police really had begun to follow her? So far she had hardly been able to find anyone who would talk to her for the series of broadcasts she hoped to sell to the BBC World Service. Mostly all she seemed to do here was sit around waiting and drinking coffee. That and plod through her evening classes at a *frontistirio* where she taught English to Greek children. But you never knew.

367

One of her tentative contacts – with someone who knew someone else who was reported to be active in the Resistance – could be in the pay of the secret police.

'Oh.' Of course someone like her must already have a boyfriend. Maybe many boyfriends, or even . . . 'Are you married?'

'Not yet.' She always gave that stock answer with an enigmatic smile, but this time – oddly – she said it soberly as she looked him full in the face.

For another spellbound moment they stood together – close but not yet touching – in the musty main exhibition hall of the National Museum, saying nothing with their lips but everything with their eyes.

Then Nikos managed to croak out an invitation. 'Coffee? You want coffee?'

Her tawny hair swung loose as she shook her head. 'No. Or at least not yet.' She suddenly seemed to come to and realize where she was and why. 'I wanted to go upstairs and have another look at the pottery.'

'When?' She hadn't said 'no,' she had said 'not yet'.

'Well, now, actually.' She looked at her watch. 'The pottery section closes in an hour.'

'No, I meant when can we have a coffee?'

'Ah.' She had been right, he was just like the others. One coffee, and he would want to take her sightseeing on his motorbike. Then he would want to walk around Plaka, and it wouldn't be long before he tried to get her in a bouzouki club which would be a brief prelude to his bed or perhaps even a little roll-around in the bushes. Really, she should save herself a lot of aggravation and simply turn on her heel and leave him without another word. Yet she could not stop herself from looking into his mesmerizing eyes. She knew she shouldn't do this; she didn't really know this fellow at all; she would probably regret this later. But what was the harm in a coffee? 'Shall we say in an hour?'

'Oh, yes! An hour!' He wanted so to be dashing and say something clever, but all he could do was grin at her. 'I'll be in the café just outside.'

It was an automatic reflex for Liberty once again to extend her hand. He took it in both his hands and held it as though her fingers, palm and wrist were something precious. He was still standing there with his hands held prayerfully in front of him when she smiled and walked away toward the staircase.

In a daze Nikos wandered outside, down the steps, and over to the café. Stavros had to call his name twice before he heard him.

'Ah, well,' Stavros said as he sat down, 'never mind, there will be other girls.' When Nikos said nothing and simply gazed at a bed of spring flowers on the lawn in front on him, he took pity on his friend. Grandly he gestured for the waiter to bring another *kafe*, and generously he told Nikos that despite their bet he would pay for the coffees.

Finally Nikos snapped out of it. 'But she's coming in an hour!' He had thought those sixty minutes before he saw her again would stretch for an infinity. But a Greek, especially a young Greek who has just been enraptured by a pretty girl, can spin out a tale of love and longing for more than a mere hour. If Liberty had spent a weekend examining every pottery shard in that museum, Nikos would still have been sitting there gesturing and sighing and confiding his hopes and dreams to Stavros, who would have forgotten all about returning to work. When she finally emerged from the museum, he was still repeating every detail of their encounter: what he had said, what she had answered, how she had laughed, what her laughter had sounded like, how her hair had caught even the filtered light, how beautiful her eyes were, how she had goddess eyes.

By the time she came over to his table, however, Stavros had obligingly melted away. She was smiling as she sat down, and then without his having to say a word once again she laughed into his green eyes.

The white sailboat cut through the azure water as the two of them lounged on deck, laughing, as always, even when neither had said anything funny.

'I still can't understand why you won't tell me where we're going.' Liberty tossed her lioness hair. The ferocious white midsummer sun beat down on her tanned skin as she stretched out before him in her black bikini. She liked how it made her feel to have him looking at her. His eyes caressed her shoulders and the cleft between her breasts. Her arms and legs felt so heavy. She was very conscious of the rise and fall of her breasts as she took each languid breath. She could feel her nipples harden, and the heat spread through her as his gaze wandered the length of her. So hot. Greece was so hot. Drowsily she thought how England was so cold, the colours there so muted, damp greens and shivering greys. The men were cold there too, not like Nikos. Lazily she smiled at the one she had kept waiting for four long teasing months in Athens. But she was going to make him wait no longer. As soon as the deep delicious rocking of this sailboat stopped, she was going to give him everything.

'I told you before, because it's a surprise.' He glanced up at the billowing sail and then back at the rudder which was attached to the automatic pilot. Two hours ago, after catching the early morning flight from Athens, they had left Rodos harbour in this boat he had borrowed from his old friend Dimitrios. If the wind held, in another hour they would near the Turkish coast and begin tacking toward their destination. Sailing windward against the *meltemi*, they would arrive at Symi island long before sunset. There wasn't another boat on the horizon, and ahead it was clear sailing.

'But I want to know where I'm going.'

Nikos kept his hand firmly on the rudder as he adjusted the automatic pilot. He struck an exaggerated *macho* pose, leered, and twirled the imaginary end of a moustache. 'To Paradise,' he answered, in that hackneyed Greek seductive boast, and they both laughed at his parody of a *kamaki* closing in for the kill. He, too, was so sure of what would happen once they got to Symi that he could joke about it. But he was not about to rush it. She had kept him waiting for months. Now it was her turn to wait. They wouldn't anchor in that secluded cove he had circled on the map for hours. He had plotted out every detail of this day of seduction so the first time they were together would be perfect. If everything continued as it had begun between them, someday – perhaps on the day after the fall of the dictatorship – they would be man and wife. His family would be dead set against his marrying a foreigner, but in time they would have to come around and accept the inevitable. He wasn't about to waste his life with an empty arranged marriage to a cow of a girl whose biggest asset was her dowry. In a little while he would take Liberty home to meet his mother. But he would keep her away from his father for as long as he could. Always his impulse was to hide whatever was most precious to him from *that* one.

Liberty's eyes held his. 'Come and kiss me then.'

He released the automatic pilot and took the rudder. 'Not now.' He was staring expertly at the wind furling the sails, adjusting the rudder a bit to the lee. He had learned to sail as a boy in Panagia bay, and there were few things he loved in life more than the heady freedom of skimming over the sea with the wind in his hair. He had hoped she wouldn't be one of those squealing girls who got seasick in a blowing wind, and in this, as in so much else, she had not disappointed him. She had learned to sail in the English Channel, and she could trim a sail or chart a course nearly as well as he could. But even so, he wouldn't kiss her just yet. He allowed his eyes to light on her for only a second. 'Later. When I'm ready.' Let her wait, he thought. The sun was hot, and it would get hotter. So would she.

Again she laughed and stretched out even more languorously. She shut her eyes and surrendered to the sensuality of the sun, the wind, and – yes, she could feel it, he was looking at her again – his gaze. What did it matter which secluded Aegean cove was their destination? All that counted was what would finally happen once they got there. She sighed as the late morning sun baked her skin. She had known, that first time she looked into his eyes by the Mask of Agamemnon, that it was only a matter of time before she would take him as her lover. She had considered, later that afternoon as

370

they had sat together sipping a frappé, whisking him straight back to her flat and getting it over and done with fast; easy come, easy go. She was twenty-five, and she had come of age in swinging London. Someday she supposed she would marry and start a family, but she could wait for all that. In the meantime she had not wanted a real love affair, especially with a Greek. These sexy dark men had such bad reputations for being careless in love, and the last thing she had wanted to do was crash and burn here in this scorching country. She had come to Athens to make her reputation as a serious journalist. She would stay six months, a year, however long it took to make her mark as a foreign correspondent, and then she would go back home and pick up the threads of her freelance writer's life in London. She had no time for a man like Nikos. And yet, sitting there, playing with the straw of her frappé, against her will she had found herself caught in the web of her most intense conversation since she had come to Greece. She had liked how his face lit up when he told her about his love for music and then later, when they lowered their voices and began their first veiled and hesitant talk about politics, she had been moved when she had seen something like grief in his eyes when he referred to the military dictatorship. This one, she had thought, was too good to kiss off with a one night stand.

Liberty leaned over, took a cigarette, and lit it while still lying down. Smoking with her eyes shut, she looked back on the months of their courtship. Of course he had tried to get her in bed at once, but he had seemed almost pleased when she had held him at arm's length. So they had started out slow and easy, as though all they wanted from each other was friendship. She was tied up teaching at the *frontistirio* until ten every night, and he had early morning classes at the polytechnic. Often during the week they would only meet for afternoon coffees and rambling chats. When he had confided who his father was, she had caught her breath; finally, here with this lovely boy, she might have found the political source and mentor she had been looking for since she arrived. As the weeks had passed and their trust in one another had grown, she had urged him to stop merely talking about resisting his father and the *junta*. Surely, she had whispered, from his years hanging on the leftist fringes at the university, he must know how to make contact with the Resistance? And so the two of them had flirted not just with one another but with danger. In this, the fourth year of the military dictatorship, the *junta's* hold on the country seemed as invincible as on the first night they had taken power. The colonels kept assuring their American allies, who were negotiating for homeport facilities for the Sixth Fleet in Greece, that democratic reforms were in the offing and elections would follow. But still the repression continued. The year before, while more than two hundred politicians were released from prison, a new lot had been sentenced by the military tribunals. A villager was imprisoned for playing a Theodorakis record, a man convicted for 'insulting authority', and a poet jailed for publishing slurs against the army. Censorship was formally relaxed, but a new 'code of ethics' went into effect along with a new list of banned books including titles by Chekhov, Brecht, and Gorky. Then finally this past spring, hairline cracks had begun to appear in the regime's foundations. University students began demonstrating for the right to elect their own representatives to college boards. Forty of them were arrested in May, and the Cypriots among them deported. In America and Europe, Greeks and their supporters had begun pushing harder for a change in regime in Athens. The time seemed pregnant not just with romance. Over cheap *souvlaki* pitta and jugs of rough *retsina* wine, Liberty and Nikos had put their heads closer together as they tried to figure out what they could do to help save Greece from itself. He would be the hero, she the scribe who recorded his courage for posterity. Liberty supposed, looking back on the fragrant assignations of that heady honeysuckle spring, that it was this shared dream of perilous adventure that had made her fall in love with Nikos. That, and his green eyes.

   She tossed the end of her cigarette overboard, locked her hands behind her head, and abandoned herself to the caresses of the sun and Nikos' eyes upon her. She was so glad they had waited so long for what would happen once the sailboat anchored. On every spring weekend, when they had gone out to neighbourhood tavernas for simple food and deep conversations, she had been the one to hold back and dance away from what was building between them. She would allow him a kiss or two at the door of the flat she shared with two roommates. She would let his hand rest for a moment on her shoulder, as if by accident, when they sat for too many hours on those uncomfortable wood and rattan taverna chairs that ate into their thighs. But, apart from occasional lingering erotic glances, she had been cool with her hot-blooded Greek. Matters had taken a different turn in June, when both of them had finished teaching and Nikos had begun spending extended weekends down in Panagia with his family. Wandering alone in Plaka, she had found herself missing him more than she had anticipated. Wasn't he ever going to invite her down to meet his family and see that village he talked about so much? I'm in over my head, she had admitted to herself as she paced past the shops chockablock with plastic statues of ancient gods and brass keyrings and posters of whitewashed houses set against the turquoise sea. Then later in the summer when he was back in town, on sultry evenings they would sit close together sipping ouzo and eating pistachio nuts under a chestnut tree in the *plateia* near where she lived. Now she was as likely as he to let a hand graze against a thigh. Her eyes, too, held his in looks that

372

burned. They went everywhere on his motorbike. They would bake on the beaches on the far side of Glyfada, and sometimes he would bring along his guitar and serenade her with songs he had written just for her. They would zoom to Sounion for ouzo sunsets, to a seaside taverna for grilled fish, to an open-air cinema to watch last year's comedies, and maybe end up in the market district at three in the morning to eat *patsa*, pork belly soup, with the night owls. On the motorbike she would wrap her arms tight around his waist, and sometimes she couldn't stop herself from rubbing her hair against the back of his neck until he almost purred. But Nikos continued to leave her at her door with only a goodnight kiss. When one night in early July she had asked him in for a coffee, he had shaken his head and merely said, 'Not yet'. Caught in the erotic heat of a Greek summer, she had begun to long for his touch.

Liberty could feel the sweat pooling under her breasts. As soon as he had suggested this weekend away from Athens, she had known its significance. She had half expected him to sweep her off immediately to a Rhodes hotel, but instead he had surprised her with this sailboat. Did he mean to seduce her here in the cockpit? She was achingly aware of exactly how far away he was from her at every moment. Why wouldn't he touch her here and now? How could he drag this out? Her voice was throaty. 'How long did you say it was to this island of yours?'

'Ours,' he corrected her. 'This island of ours.' He laughed. 'Depends on the wind. I'd say five hours. Maybe six.'

'So long and so far.' She opened her hungry eyes. 'There's nothing closer?'

'Some things, and some people, are worth the wait.' Steadily he held her eyes. 'Besides, I like to take my time. I'm a very patient man. But I almost always get what I want.'

Liberty was conscious of each breath she took, how it filled her lungs, how her breasts fell as she exhaled. She could feel her every eyelash. She burned for this man. She turned on her side, propped her head on her arm, and tried to keep her hands off him. 'We could have just stayed in Rhodes, you know.' If we'd stayed in Rhodes, she added to herself, we could have been in bed together all morning. She crossed her legs. 'It looked beautiful, with those old walls and that castle.'

'Trust me.' He laughed. She was like an impatient child who couldn't wait to tear open a nameday present. 'Where we're going is even better than Rodos.' Just then he caught sight of the cape looming off the Turkish coast, and he asked her to take the rudder as he readied the sails. 'Hang on,' he advised. 'From now on it's bound to be a bit choppy.'

Nikos was as good as his word. As they neared the brooding dark coast, the wind picked up and the boat keeled over. Gone now was the drowsy lassitude of their morning sail on the bathtub waters off Rodos. Wildly they rocked over the waves, both laughing for the sheer exuberance of being young and together here in the sun and on the water. Onward they sailed over the wine-dark sea.

Much later, when finally they eased into calmer waters, he went below for the ouzo and *meze* snacks he had bought in Rodos. They clinked glasses and sipped the milky licorice-flavoured liquor. Liberty popped a black Kalamata olive into her mouth and savoured the salty pulp with her tongue. Nikos sliced through crusty bread, a hunk of feta cheese, and ripe tomatoes. He brought a succulent wedge of tomato to her lips. She fed him a hunk of feta, and he sucked the brine from her fingers, one by one, very slowly. They put their heads close together and laughed at everything and nothing as they devoured the simple fare that was so quintessentially Greece. He put the automatic pilot back on, came over to sit beside her in the cockpit, and slid his arm around her shoulders. He poured more ouzo, and again they clinked their glasses and toasted the sweetness of life.

'Happy?' he murmured.

Contentedly she took his hand in hers. 'You know I am.'

'Still love me?'

'Of course.' She kissed him.

'*Agapi mou,*' he sighed. 'Eleftheria, my love.'

They rested snugly like that, each dreaming the same exquisite dream, until ahead on the horizon appeared a spiky mass of dragon-back peaks.

'That's it,' he said.

'Paradise Island?' She laughed and kissed the palm of his hand.

'Yes. But on the maps they call it Symi. There's a myth about it, you know.'

'There's a myth about everything in Greece.' Was that, she wondered, why this place and these people stirred her so? The light, the air, the water, the mountains, everything was mythic. Nikos too . . .

'It's a creation myth. All about beginnings. They say that long ago, when the world was younger than we are, Prometheus made the first man out of clay here, just ahead, on one of those rocks. But when Zeus found out, he got into one of his rages and turned Prometheus into an ape. That's why it's called Symi. And that's why I wanted to bring you here, the first time. Because we're starting something new, too. You might say that Symi's a real Greek Garden of Eden.' Shyly he smiled at her, and they kissed and clung together another moment as the boat rocked onward.

Then with a sigh he began preparing the boat for the port. He hoisted the sail, turned on the outboard, and took the rudder. 'First stop is Ghialos town. But let's not stay long. We have another half hour's sail ahead after the port.'

She slipped on a T-shirt and shorts and stood leaning on the mainsail as the boat cruised into one of the most picturesque harbours in the Aegean. Small, tight, snug Symi port was carved out in a perfect circle at the base of a steep mountain shooting up to the sky. The mid-afternoon sun turned the creamy Neoclassical shipbuilders' houses into mansions of gold, and the crescent of the waterfront was lined with tavernas and stalls selling sponges and spices. The port bobbed with colourful *caiques* heaped with sponges, nets, and great vats of fish caught in the night. 'It's magic,' she breathed.

As they chugged toward the wharf, doubledecker boats were loading up herds of tourists and casting off. 'Daytrippers from Rodos,' Nikos explained. 'They come here to buy sponges and have lunch. Then it's back to the boat for a quick trip to the monastery on the other side of the island.' He was pleased that he had timed their arrival exactly right. On other occasions when he had sailed here with Dimitrios, they'd learned that the quiet charms of this out-of-the-way island were at their best once the tourist boats were gone. With satisfaction Nikos scanned the almost deserted quays. He had wanted this stopover in the port to be perfect, too.

He deftly piloted toward the pier, and she fixed the rubber fenders to the side of the boat and cast the ropes ashore to a boy who wound them round a post. Nikos shut down the engine, and together they leaped ashore.

'I reckon we have just enough time for an ice cream and a little shopping for sponges,' he said as he walked down the wharf with his arm around her. They stopped here and there, admiring the fluffy bins of yellow, gold, and tan sponges that generations of Symi men had always wrested from the deep. '*Melita* are the best,' Nikos explained. 'In Greek *meli* means "honey", and these are the softest in the world.' He picked out a smooth handful of sponge whose surface was bored with lacy pinpoint holes. At once the grizzled pedlar dipped it in a bucket of water and handed it to Nikos with a flourish. Slowly he ran it over Liberty's face, neck, and arms, like a caress. She shivered in the heat, and their eyes were locked in another of those scorching looks.

Greece, she thought, oh Greece! This country and this man were in her blood. She wanted to take that sponge and run it all over his body. Later, she thought, as she contented herself with a laugh. Together they rummaged through bins of sponges buying presents for their families, and then Nikos haggled fiercely for a good price.

Arm-in-arm they climbed up the backstreets of the steep hillside. Here and there they passed the ruined remains of stone villas, once the pride of the Dodecanese. 'Less than a hundred years ago this was one of the richest islands in the Aegean,' Nikos told her. 'At the turn of the century Symi was more important than Rodos town. They made their money building ships, and they still turn out some of the most beautiful boats in the Med.' It was four o'clock, and almost everyone was home sleeping. They didn't pass another soul on the narrow cobblestone lanes. It seemed, as they sauntered past whitewashed cottages, rusty oil cans overflowing with red geraniums and vivid scarlet bougainvillaea that spilled over everywhere, that they were wandering through a whitehot dream. All of this – the flowers, the houses, the shadows of bygone times – seemed created just for them.

But lovely as it was, Symi port was also oven-hot. They made their way back to the waterfront and gratefully sank down under the awning of a harbour café. Nikos ordered frappés and chocolate ice creams, and they ate and drank with the appetite of the young.

'God,' she said, when finally she finished the ice cream, 'I'd love a swim.'

'Now?' He frowned.

'Of course now. It's the heat of the day. Everyone goes swimming. That, or they take naps.' Hastily she veered away from that subject. Now that the time of togetherness was obviously drawing near, she felt like some silly blushing bride. What if he didn't like her, that way? She wrinkled her brow. 'Why don't you want a swim?'

'Oh, I'd like a swim, all right. But what I had in mind was a special swim. Have you ever gone . . . what the Americans call skinny dipping?'

'Without clothes, you mean?' It was her turn to frown. She was not a prude, but she *was* British. She had never even gone topless on a beach, let alone swum naked.

'That's what I mean.'

She looked around the drowsy harbour. Most of the shops were shuttered for the siesta hours, and only a few people were staggering along in the paralyzing heat. 'Isn't this a bit . . . *public* for that sort of thing?'

'Oh, not *here*.' He signalled for the waiter and paid the check. 'I mean the next time we stop. First I thought we'd have our private little swim. And then we'll anchor in another harbour – Emborio – for the night. There's a great taverna there.' He gave her a steamy look. 'But first the swim.'

'Oh.' She smiled into his green eyes. 'I've never been swimming like that.'

He lowered his voice and covered her hands with his. 'There's always a first time, Liberty. For everything.'

In a hurry now, quickly they cast off and chugged out of the harbour. She took the rudder, and he set the sails. They tacked against the wind. Liberty stripped down to her bikini and stood by the sail with her hair blowing behind her. Watching her, Nikos thought she looked like a figurehead carved on an ancient boat. And very soon, as soon as they eased into that perfect little cove, she would be his.

'There,' he pointed to piles of rocks ahead. 'That's where we're going.'

'But there's no harbour.'

'Sure there is. But it's very private.'

He took down the sails, turned on the outboard, and slowly they vibrated into a secluded moon of a cove. Surrounded on three sides by sheer cliffs with only a tuft of pebble beach at its core, the inlet was hidden from the sea by a natural bridge of rocks.

'A secret cove,' she breathed.

'For us only,' he murmured.

Carefully he piloted the boat into the epicentre of the harbour, then shut down the engine and let down the anchor.

'So,' he said as he took her in his arms.

But now that they were here, she was shy in his embrace. She broke away after allowing him only a slighting kiss. 'A swim. You promised me a swim. It's so hot.'

He gestured toward the turquoise sea. 'After you. But remember what we said back in the café.'

She hesitated but then smiled. 'Right.' Nervously she smoothed out her bikini. 'But don't look. Turn your back.'

Obediently he turned around, and she reached behind her and untied her bathing top. Quickly then, she slid out of the other piece. In a second she was poised at the edge of the deck with her arms gracefully arched above her. He stole a glance at her bronze body with its slashes of milk-white skin. Yes, she was sleek and slim and round, all at once, so beautiful. He caught his breath as she dove into the water. Her long blonde hair streamed behind her, and he watched the white spheres of her buttocks disappear in the depths. 'Fantastic!' she called out as she surfaced. Before her in the shimmering water, her breasts floated as if on a tray. He couldn't tear his eyes off those breasts, so full, so white against the rest of her. In the water they glowed like neon. 'Come on in, Niko!'

He kicked out of his trunks, tensed on the deck, and dove toward her. But she swam away before he could reach her. She cut through the water with a clean sure stroke, laughing all the while in sheer delight at the sensations caressing her everywhere. 'Wonderful,' she called out, 'this feels wonderful.' She could feel the cool slide of the water all over her body, and she wriggled in the water like a golden dolphin. Free, she thought, I feel so free! For a moment she forgot all about Nikos and simply revelled in the feel of the water whooshing the length and breadth of her, against her breasts, between her thighs, everywhere water, everywhere freedom. She turned over on her back, looked up at the sky, and luxuriated as she bared most of her body to the man floating nearby, watching her swim circles around him. Here, just as on the boat this morning when she had lain splayed out before him, she could feel his eyes all over her. But now there was an innocence about his gaze. Marooned here, naked in the sea, with only the sun as their witness, they were primitive man and woman. The Garden of Eden, she remembered suddenly, he has truly brought me to a floating, dazzling, delicious Greek Garden of Eden.

She turned over, in no hurry for the inevitable touch of him, and once again began cutting through the water in a graceful crawl. He swam off after her, and lazily they circled the cove, stealing glances at one another as they came up for air, altogether at one with the elements and with each other. Still in the deep water, at last she turned over on her back and lay still and floated on the crest of the sea. He came near and let his gaze wander the length of her, admiring those breasts and the swell of her belly and the flow of her golden thighs. Then he turned over on his back and floated beside her, touching only her finger tips with one hand. For what seemed like a long while they lay like this in the dual embrace of the sea and the sun, and then he let the current carry him closer. Infinitely softly he let his hand run down the length of her, and in the water she shuddered and looked over into his green eyes and smiled.

Without a word he drifted away from her and purposefully swam toward the pebble beach. She watched him between half-closed eyes, and when she saw him standing in the chest-high shallows she knew she had to go to him there. She swam tantalizingly closer, but again she turned shy. For long moments she swam widening circles around him. She wanted to go closer, she wanted to be as close as it was possible for two human beings to be, and yet at the same time, contrarily, she wanted to be free and alone. Two, not one. As she circled this man she wanted to take as her lover, never before in her life had she savoured her own freedom so much. She felt the pure cool water caress her every pore, and she loved her independence. She wanted to keep herself alone forever, she didn't want to give herself to anyone, not even this man she loved. Always she wanted to swim yearning circles around him in the water, not touching, not giving.

And yet, she could not resist swimming just a little closer. His rippling bronze skin was so enticing. She wanted to taste it in her mouth. She wanted to feel his arms round her.

Undecided, she looked from him out to the sea, so wide, so infinite, and again she loved her freedom.

Without being aware of it, however, she was now so close to him that if he had reached out he could have crushed her close against him. Yet he remained motionless, unwilling to take what she didn't want to offer. He waited for her to come of her own volition into his embrace.

She swam around him in her own personal mating dance in the water, until finally she came to a decision and reached out and came snug into the harbour of his arms. He looked into her eyes, then brought his lips to hers. She wrapped her arms around his neck, and for the first time ever they felt their naked flesh taut against one another. He kissed her lips and neck, and she held on tighter and kissed him back as they wriggled more tightly together. In one quick, fluid, caressive motion, then, he reached down and pulled her legs up round his waist. 'Oh,' she whispered as he slid inside her. With eyes open wide, they made love in the turquoise water, slowly, then faster, until finally together they cried out and convulsed.

A little later they swam back to the boat, embraced on the deck, and then drank an ouzo toast to their baptism of love.

Sitting in the back seat of the taxi next to Nikos on the way to Neo Psychicon, Liberty smoothed down the hem of her beige silk dress and wondered again if she were dressed properly. After six months of keeping almost constant company, she had finally succeeded in convincing him to take her home to meet his mother. Would this woman whom Nikos seemed to regard as some sort of beloved and almighty empress be more favourably disposed toward her if she had worn a simple sweater and skirt instead of this smart tailored dress, her good pearls, and her best high-heeled pumps? At home in understated England, overdressing was a social crime. After all, this wasn't high tea at Buckingham Palace, only a reluctant invitation to have coffee at Nikos' house.

But here, Liberty thought as distractedly she looked out the window at the coursing, hooting, fuming afternoon traffic, everything was so different from the way it was at home. When she had first come here, she had believed this was a European country much like any other. But eight months here had convinced her that Greece's Western veneer masked an Eastern culture whose values had more in common with Istanbul and Cairo than London or Paris. Even Nikos, who spoke such splendid English and seemed so European, sometimes surprised her with passionate pronouncements about the importance of family, tradition, and – most of all – personal honour. The deeper she probed, the more alien and maddeningly elusive this country and these people became. She simply didn't know what to make of the Greeks. They said one thing, did another, and always remained utterly unpredictable. What was it going to be like married to a Greek and settling here for the rest of her life?

As they crawled through the logjam of traffic, Liberty studied the lettering of the incomprehensible Greek signs above the bustling shops. Since September she had been struggling through a Greek language course, and in time she supposed she would learn to get by in it. But she was less optimistic that she would ever be able to decipher, much less master, the complex layerings of family relationships. From listening to Nikos, it seemed to her that, no matter what people said about how patriarchal this society was, the importance of the mother and son bonding must never be underestimated. She remembered a joke she had heard not once but several times here in Athens, purporting to prove that Jesus Christ could not have been anything but a Greek. At the time of His death, after all, He had been thirty-three years old and still living at home, His mother thought He was God, and He thought His mother was the Virgin Mary. Here and now, on the way to meet Nikos' mother, she found that joke more chilling than funny. Her foreign friends had already regaled her with horror stories of how ferociously possessive and protective Greek mothers were of the little princes who had sprung from their wombs. What was she going to do if Nikos' mother hated her on sight?

'Are you sure I look all right?' Liberty tried to crane her neck to see her reflection in the driver's rearview mirror. This meeting was altogether her own idea. Nikos had advised they wait a while longer – sometimes she thought he would have been willing to wait until their tenth wedding anniversary before introducing her to his family – but she had insisted on getting to know at least his mother now. When Nikos had continued to balk, they had had their first major fight. Was he ashamed of her, or what? Didn't he love her? She was willing to give up everything for him – home, family, country – and he wouldn't even let her past his own front door? Gradually she had worn him down, but now that it was too late she had second thoughts. Perhaps they should have simply eloped to London next summer and presented his family with a *fait accompli*.

'You look beautiful.' Nikos took her hand and squeezed it. How could he tell her that it wouldn't matter to his mother how she looked? Weeks ago, when he had announced that he intended to bring his foreign girlfriend home, his mother had raised holy hell. He had always known she had a temper, of course, for her rows with his father had been the talk of their old neighbourhood in Pangrati. But even when he had done something naughty as a little boy, his mother had hardly ever raised her voice to *him*.

'What if your mother doesn't like me?'

'How could anyone not like you?' But even as he did his best to smile reassuringly, Nikos could not quite look the woman he intended to marry in the eye. He had never before brought any girl – much less a blonde foreigner

380

– home to his mother. And though he had tried to prepare the way for her favourable reception, the best he could hope for was that his mother would be coolly polite.

He had been careful, in the first heady months of their courtship, never to mention Liberty's existence to his mother. But two months ago, after Symi, he had been unable to stop talking about her. At first his mother had been indulgent about this foreign girl who seemed to have made her son so happy. But all that had changed when he confided that he was serious about this one.

At once his mother had gone on red alert marshalling the inevitable arguments against marrying one not of their kind. He had already admitted this English girl was three years older than he was, and of course his mother used that as prime ammunition. 'Three years, Niko! Three whole years! You already have one mother, so why do you need another?' From this she had moved on to the matter of Liberty's not speaking Greek. 'So how,' his mother had continued, 'would she ever be able to understand how things are here?' Furthermore, she had said, he would never be able to communicate with her like he could with a Greek girl. 'It's not just the language. It's our values, how we grow up, what we want from life.' When that had not seemed to shake Nikos, Marika had fit her next arrow in her bow. 'Look what happened to your Uncle Christos when he married that Peppy.' Terse as it was, Nick's letter announcing the scandalous divorce – the first in their family, and only the third one in recent memory in their village – had been full of recriminations against his former American daughter-in-law. He hadn't revealed the whole shocking story until he had come for a visit the next Easter, and the family had listened open-mouthed to this sensational tale that only reinforced their prejudices against intermarriage. Peppy's behaviour in Panagia had again been minutely dissected, they had speculated about whether she had sneaked off for trysts with other foreign girls, and she had roundly been condemned once more for leaving in the dead of night like a criminal. Marika had seemed to take especial delight in throwing Christos' disastrous marriage in Nikos' face. 'You see what happens when a Greek goes against his family and marries someone no one knows? Nick tried to talk him out of it, but did Christos listen?'

Not wanting to dwell on this affair of Uncle Christos', Nikos had been quick to point out that his Uncle Vangelis, too, was married to a foreigner, and that Vasso was a model wife.

'But Vasso is *Greek*. An Australian Greek is still a Greek. Eh, but this Liberty – she will never be one of *us*.'

Then she had reached out and stroked back the unruly hair where it curled against his temples. 'Niko,' his mother had purred, 'listen to what I tell you.

381

You like this girl, OK, so have your fun with her. You're young, much too young to get married. You still have to finish school. Then you have to go into the army. And after that you'll be looking for a job. Then and only then you can think about getting married to a good Greek girl and having a family. But understand, Niko, that it is not possible for you to stay together all your life with someone like her. I think only of you, *paidi mou*, and what is best for you.'

Feeling that beloved hand touching him with such tenderness, Nikos had wavered. He had thought his Aunt Peppy an angel, and look what she had done to poor Uncle Christos. Sometimes, too, it was such a relief to go out with his Greek friends and speak his own language instead of searching for the right words to say to Liberty in English. But then, as only for an instant he considered the possibility of ending it with Liberty, his soul had rebelled and stubbornly he had shaken his head. If his mother made him choose between her and Liberty, then he would.

Seeing that in his eyes, Marika had gotten up and begun pacing. 'He meets this girl God knows where, she bewitches him, and now he talks of ruining his life with her. Panagia! It is too much! Twenty-three, he is only twenty-three, too young to get married, especially to an *old* foreign girl.' His mother had wheeled on him, gripped the side of her head with her hands, and run her fingers through her hair in a melodramatic gesture of despair. 'Niko! You are a donkey!' She had seemed unable to stop the hot words from rolling off her acid tongue. 'You know how those foreign girls are, they go with everyone. The ones who can't get a man from their own country come here looking for husbands. They meet a nice Greek boy, and they make them crazy. They try to trap our boys into marriage! And this girl of yours, she's probably heard we have money. Is that what your grandfather and your father have worked their fingers to the bone for all their lives, so you can buy diamonds and furs for your little English girl? Snap out of it, Niko! There's nothing wrong with a little discreet fling with a foreign girl. It's cleaner than going to a prostitute, after all. But let's not hear any more talk about marriage.'

Under his breath Nikos sighed. In the tense fortnight since their confrontation, neither he nor his mother had given way and taken the first steps toward reconciliation. But two days ago his mother had suddenly announced she was willing to meet the foreign girl. Had she suddenly had an uncharacteristic change of heart, or this afternoon did she mean to say or do something irrevocably insulting? Looking over at Liberty's anxious face, Nikos wondered how he could ever have been persuaded to bring the two women he loved most in the world together. His mother was right about one thing. He was a donkey. The meeting would be a *katastrofe*.

Defiantly Nikos tightened his grip on Liberty's cool hand. As always, the touch of her heartened him. Whether his family liked it or not, he was going to marry her next year. And maybe Liberty was right. It was better to get this initial meeting over with, for in time his mother and the rest of the family would have to learn to accept her. He had talked all this over endlessly not only with Liberty but with his *parea*. Even though mostly boys married girls their families approved of, everyone knew someone who had been strong enough to risk all for romantic love. In most cases, after a distraught period of recriminations and estrangement, the families had been forced at least outwardly to accept their new daughters-in-law. Relations in the family usually remained tense and highly problematical until the babies started coming, but after that gradually the in-laws began to accept the foreign wife. Dimitrios, however, knew one fellow who had settled with his wife in Hamburg and never even telephoned his mother at Easter. And Stavros told a terrible story of another boy's father who acted as though his son had died when he married a French girl.

Again Nikos sighed. First he would tackle his mother, and then, if she finally came around, he would begin the even more perilous proposition of his father.

Nikos gnawed his lower lip and wondered if Liberty would be able to help him get a job in England. His father, even more than his mother, would be violently against marriage to a foreigner. If his father had his way eventually he would pair off with one of the Panagia girls whose family was as rich as their own. Ah, well, Nikos thought, *ti na kano*, what can I do? 'We're almost there, Neo Psychicon.' Nervously he repeated what Liberty already knew. 'We moved there nearly four years ago, right after the coup. My father didn't think the Pangrati apartment was good enough any more.' Unhappily, as they turned off the main road into a shady complex of sprawling villas and embassies, Nikos longed for the noisy, crowded, yeasty middle-class neighbourhood of his childhood. Only rich people and government ministers who had learned how to become rich at the public expense lived in this newly-built northern suburb well away from the congestion and heartbeat of real Athenian life.

'It's quite lovely,' Liberty said politely as she tried to remember everything Nikos had ever said about his mother. She was strong – yes, there was not only affection but awe in his voice every time he spoke of his mother – and she had to be intelligent, for in these past few years she had begun writing not only front-page bylined pieces but also a widely read thrice-weekly column in one of Athens' most influential newspapers. Obviously she wouldn't be one of those dumpy village matrons who slumped around the house in baggy black dresses, eternally dusting the end tables. But would she be one of those chic bleach-blonde Athenian ladies dressed to kill in gold jewellery and Parisian couture? And, most important of all, would she be an ally or enemy in the coming marital campaign she and Nikos were determined to wage? For the umpteenth time that afternoon she reminded herself that, whether their families liked it or not, she and Nikos were going to get married. Yet what if his family absolutely refused to accept her? Even though Nikos vowed he would marry her anyway, she had been in Greece long enough to understand that here the power of the family was often stronger than the power of mere romantic love.

Liberty's thoughts trailed to her mother, father, and brother back in England. Her father was a Mayfair lawyer, her mother a fashionable decorator, and Peter was still away at school in Devon. None of them would be overjoyed when they learned that she meant to marry a dark Mediterranean type and make her life so far from the West End centre of the universe. It would not sweeten the pill when she told them that Nikos' father was a member of the *junta*, for in London sometimes it seemed that everyone but the Foreign Office diplomats blanched at the excesses of the military dictatorship. Tales of torture and detentions without trial filled the newspaper columns. Then when Greece had withdrawn from the Council of Europe two years ago just before it was about to be kicked out, even wellborn true-blue Tories had raised their eyebrows about Greece's fall from grace in the community of nations. Like most other English public school gentlemen, Liberty's father was a Philhellene who did not take kindly to the colonels perverting the ideals of the Age of Pericles. He was not likely to approve of his only daughter marrying into such a family. And yet it irked her that, although she had never mentioned her family's probable opposition to their marriage, she and Nikos had squandered countless hours worrying only about how to win his own family's approval.

The taxi pulled into a long driveway, cruised through landscaped grounds, and then stopped before a low white stucco house that sprawled behind a screen of blooming scarlet bushes. 'Welcome to my home,' Nikos said as he threw open the taxi door. As hand in hand they walked toward the entrance, Liberty noticed a slight flutter of the draperies behind a picture window. Nikos had seen it, too, and he waved to the unseen eyes that most surely belonged to his mother.

Marika threw open the door as they approached the threshold. Her lips were smiling and her arms were outstretched, but was that welcome in her glittering black eyes? In an instant the two women sized up one another.

Liberty's heart sank as she stared at the voluptuous dark woman who seemed, at first impression, to be all hawk eyes and raven hair. She looked younger than she expected, and more beautiful. Her sleek black dress clung to her curves, and at her throat and on her earlobes a jeweller's window of gold flashed. She had that polished chic look of the Athenian ladies who shopped at Kolonaki, but there was nothing frivolous about this formidable woman who seemed to be staring into her very soul. Why, Liberty wondered, didn't Nikos make me understand that his mother, without even knowing me, had already branded me as the enemy?

Marika's eyes continued to bore into the intruder. She had been prepared for a girl as pretty as this one, for her mother's pride would not allow her to think that a boy like Nikos would court an ugly duckling. She was, however, a little surprised at the refined tailored clothing, those heirloom pearls, and that patrician posture. It would have been easier to dismiss Liberty if she had looked like what she undoubtedly was, a foreign adventuress out to trap her son into a marriage that could never work. It wasn't possible that she was as angelic as she looked, with that fair cloud of hair and that rosy skin which even the Greek sun couldn't wilt. Marika was pleased to see, however, that her adversary's boyish hips were too slim to carry on the family name with a tribe of sons. But she wished she didn't have those full pillow breasts. It was going to take all her wiles to wean her boy away from this one.

Marika set about trying. She had lost Christos to another blonde, but she wasn't going to lose her son the same way. She wrapped one possessive arm around Nikos and stiffly held out her other hand to Liberty. 'Welcome,' she said in rapid-fire Greek, as though the sentiment burned her tongue. 'My son has told me very much about you.' She used the Greek word *poly*, which meant 'too much.'

As Liberty touched her hand to Marika's, desperately she tried to remember the Greek she had so painstakingly learned. But she was so nervous that the foreign words utterly eluded her. She looked in consternation at Nikos, who had told her his mother spoke English.

'She says that you're very welome, and that she's heard a lot about you.' Still on the doorstep, unsure whether to go inside or leave in a huff, Nikos was glaring at his mother. 'But perhaps she can tell you that herself. My mother speaks very good English.' Without giving any sign that she had understood, Marika ushered them in the door. She still had her arm firmly around her son, and as she led them through the hallway into the salon, Nikos mumbled under his breath to her in Greek. 'Black, eh?' He hoped Liberty wouldn't realize that his mother had dressed for this meeting as though she were in mourning.

Marika merely shrugged her eyebrows and turned a wintry smile back on the girl she would never truly welcome into her house, much less her family.

Liberty trailed behind the evidently inseparable mother and son. 'What a beautiful house,' she said, taking note of the regal scale but what her own mother would call the doubtful taste of this Greek *nouveau riche* household. The hallway had been wallpapered in some expensive gold-embossed pattern, carpeted in some even more costly scarlet Oriental rug, and was lit by an extravagant Bohemian cut-glass chandelier big enough for a hotel ballroom. As they passed into the salon, she caught a glimpse of other overdone rooms leading off in all directions. 'And what a spectacular salon,' she said as they entered a sitting room as big as a basketball court. Still, as she threaded her way through nests of furniture – mammoth crushed velvet sofas, massive brocade easy chairs, sweeping marble and teak and brass-encrusted coffee and end tables – she wondered at how Nikos' mother had managed to make this grandiose space look so poky.

Marika gestured for Liberty to take a heavily upholstered armchair while she nestled close by Nikos on a facing sofa. For a moment all three busied themselves lighting cigarettes, and then Marika leaned even closer to her son and said something in Greek.

Nikos flushed and chose not to translate that his mother had said Liberty looked young for her age. He thanked God that his grandmother was down in Panagia for a visit. It would have been worse if Old Anna, too, was giving Liberty that same Evil Eye stare as his mother. But he had to say something. 'So.' Miserably he smiled. 'Here we are.'

'Yes.' Back home, in such a stilted situation, automatically one would chat about the vicissitudes of the weather. But here what could one say about months of invariable sun? Valiantly Liberty strove to be civil. 'You have quite a remarkable home here, Kyria Kronos. It's quite extraordinary, really.' Her face was a polite mask as she took in the floor-to-ceiling dark mahogany wall units chockablock with brass and silver-framed family photographs, fussy German porcelain, gaudy Venetian glass, and assorted chunks of heavy Victorian china. What wallspace was not taken up by this bric-a-brac was hung with gilt-framed oil paintings of English country life: fox-hunting, threshing, fishing. But there wasn't a book to be seen. Nikos was so sensitive and artistic. What a shame he had a mother like this one. Over the marble fireplace hung a portrait of a portly officer who could only be Nikos' father. Liberty's depression increased as she studied the arrogant bearing of this soldier-turned-despot. A shame about the father, too.

As again Marika let loose with a torrent of Greek, her eyes drilled into Liberty. No, her son was not going to follow in his real father's footsteps. She hadn't been able to prevent Peppy from taking Christos away from her, but she was determined to make quick work of this Liberty. This girl might even make him go live in London! It had been better to invite her here once to show her how it was and always would be with Nikos' family. Still, she was confident enough of ultimate victory that she could afford to feel not only ashamed of her own ruthless conduct but also a little sorry for the girl. It couldn't be easy for her, having to sit there and endure the kind of treatment she was going to continue to dish out. Any Greek mother would do the same! Yet Marika had to admire the way the girl held her head high and hid the hurt she was surely feeling. She looked and acted like the lady she obviously was. If Liberty had been Greek and endowed with a bountiful dowry from a good family, Marika might even have considered encouraging this alliance. Already, from the way she had seen the two of them looking at one another, it was obvious that they were in love. Remembering how she herself had once looked at Christos in just that way, Marika felt a stab of pity for her son and this girl. It wasn't going to work out for them, either.

'My mother says she doesn't like this house much herself. And neither do I. All this — ' with a sweep of his arm Nikos indicated everything the eye could see, 'was my father's idea of what the house of a government minister should look like. This is only our formal salon, the one we use for receptions and for guests we don't know very well.' Too late Nikos bit his tongue. 'I mean,' he explained, 'most of the time we spend in the other rooms. But of course we couldn't take you there. I mean, straight off. On your *first* visit.'

As she smoked in the leaden silence, Marika considered but rejected breaking down and speaking to this girl in English. This was how it had to be, now and always. She was fighting for her son! It was worth an uncomfortable hour in this stuffy salon so Nikos and Liberty would both understand that on this matter she would never soften. She gave Nikos another loving pat on his knee, and then without so much as looking at the girl she rose and swept out of the room. 'She's just going for the coffee.' Nikos waited until he was sure his mother was out of earshot, and then earnestly he leaned over the cold marble expanse of coffee table. 'Look, Liberty, I'm sorry. I never dreamed she'd be like this.'

'It's fine, really.' She tried to laugh, but she couldn't. For the life of her, she couldn't understand why Nikos' mother wouldn't give her a chance. Back home she came from a good family, she had a splendid education, and she was willing to turn her entire life round and settle in this foreign country to make Nikos a good wife. If the truth were told, in the eyes of the world Nikos was the one who should be worried about winning acceptance from *her* family. But apparently, here in Greece, other assumptions ruled. She recalled hearing similiar cautionary tales about encounters like this from other European girls who had tangled with chauvinistic Greek families. But it was absolutely no consolation that others had endured this treatment.

Marika sailed back in, and behind her was a young woman carrying a laden copper tray.

'This is Loula,' Nikos explained. 'From Panagia. My village.'

387

The girl smiled at the foreigner and stepped closer so she could better examine her hair, her face, and her clothes. She would be returning to the village next week for a visit, and she wanted to be able to pass on every detail about this young woman of Nikos' who actually had been invited into the Kronos home.

But, mentally cursing her husband for insisting they employ her old friend Irene's oldest daughter, Marika waved the one she always thought of as the village spy out of the room. She didn't want even Irene to know about this English girl.

Then she allowed a fleeting smile to curve her lips as graciously she poured the guest a coffee and asked Nikos if she took it with milk or sugar. Now that she had let Liberty know how it had to be, she was prepared to fulfil the demands of hospitality. 'Nescafé,' she consented to say directly to the woman her son was not going to marry. She handed Nikos his Greek coffee and put the second tiny cup of it in front of herself.

Liberty stared at her large china cup. Even this serving of the two different kinds of coffee reinforced the message that there were two separate species of humans sitting here. Liberty had an impulse to flee this woman and this room, but a glance over at Nikos changed her mind. He was worth even her own pride. She gritted her teeth and redoubled her efforts to fight for her man. 'Nikos tells me that you're a journalist, Kyria Kronos. That means we have something in common. In addition to Nikos, I mean. I work for the BBC. Or rather, I do some work for the BBC from time to time.'

Just as Nikos was translating that, the telephone rang in a nearby room. After a moment, Loula came running into the salon and shouted something in Greek. Hastily Marika followed her.

'I shouldn't have come,' Liberty said as she lit yet another cigarette. 'You told me how it would be, and I should have listened.'

'Never mind.' Nikos smiled with more certainty than he felt. 'It will get better. I'm sure of it.' For himself as much as for Liberty, he redoubled his efforts to sound convincing. 'She'll come around. As soon as she returns, and we start talking about your work and her work, everything will be fine. Besides, if she wants to, she'll be able to introduce you to people who can help with your broadcasts.' Since they had met last spring, Liberty had managed to file two reports which had been aired on the World Service. One had been on summer tourism and another on the continuing Greek demands that Britain return the Elgin Marbles to the Parthenon. She didn't expect that either of them, although professionally executed, would win any journalism awards. But she hoped the sensational piece she was working on now, an exposé on victims of political repression, would make the producers in London sit up and take notice of her.

388

'Maybe.' She didn't have the heart to say that the only thing Nikos' mother was likely to want to help her do was buy a oneway airplane ticket back to London. Yet she couldn't give up so easily. 'Look, Niko, you know her better than I do. If you think the time is right, ask her to – '

Before Liberty could finish, they heard shrieks from the other room and then the rat-tat sound of high heels running on the marble floor. Marika burst back into the salon and began shouting at Nikos in Greek. Liberty watched his face change and then he, too, began screeching back in the same language. He leaped up, threw his arms round his mother, and strove to calm her. Marika broke away, lit a cigarette, and began pacing back and forth between the furniture. Then she wheeled and disappeared again into the other room. A moment later they could hear her raised voice on the telephone.

'What's wrong, Niko? What's happened?'

Distractedly Nikos looked down at her as though he had forgotten she was still there. He ran his hands through his hair in a gesture of despair. 'It's my uncle. My mother's brother. Down in Panagia. Uncle Vangelis has been arrested for subversion.'

'What!' Liberty had heard much about this loveable uncle who was married to an Australian. But Nikos had never said anything about Vangelis being political.

'That was my grandmother Eleni who called. She said they think Uncle Vangelis is in the jail in Argos. And my mother's mother – Old Anna – collapsed when she heard the news.' He seemed to forget Liberty again as he listened to his mother's voice yelling on the telephone. 'She's trying to get my father, so he can *do something*. But it sounds like he's not in his office.' He listened another moment. 'And no one seems to know where he is.'

When Marika came back a moment later, she was wearing a jacket. '*Pame*, Niko.' Without waiting for him, she rushed for the front door.

Before he could follow, Liberty tugged at Nikos' sleeve. 'What's happening now?'

'I think we're going down to Argos to see what we can do.'

She put her cigarettes in her handbag. 'I'm coming, too.'

'You?' He reared up his head in the Greek negative. 'Why?'

'Why not? Maybe I can write about it.' And perhaps, she was thinking, in the process I can not only learn something about Nikos' family but take a giant step into winning them over.

Outside Marika was sounding the car horn. For good measure, she screamed out his name. 'Niko!'

Nikos looked out the door at his mother and then back at Liberty. 'OK. *Pame*.' She leaped up, and together they ran out to the car.

389

Marika scarcely seemed to notice Liberty's presence. Before their doors were altogether shut, she was off with a screech of rubber. As she expertly wove her way through the stalled lanes of Athens traffic, hooting at this one, cutting off that one, she all the while kept up a high decibel harangue in Greek.

Now that she didn't have that other woman's ferocious eyes upon her, Liberty was able to concentrate on getting the gist of what she was saying. From a word picked up here and there, she gathered that she was mostly angry with her husband. 'Too much!' she shouted. 'This time he goes too far.' Could it be, Liberty wondered, that Nikos' mother suspected her own husband of having her brother arrested?

By the time they had cleared Athens and were whooshing down the National Road toward Korinthos, Marika had cooled down enough to stop shouting. Yet still she talked on and on. She told Nikos she couldn't believe this had happened. Oh, she knew there were arrests. Everyone knew *that*. She herself had been able to move up so far and fast at the newspaper not only because of her talent and her husband's influence but because some of the veteran journalists either had been jailed or dismissed for their liberal sympathies. So far she herself had always kept away from the fray. But she had never dreamed the repression could touch her own family. Yet, remembering her brother's sympathy for the *andartes* during the Civil War, she wouldn't put it past him to have done something foolhardy with the Resistance. They might be torturing her poor dear little brother at this very moment. '*Vangeli!*' she shrieked.

As they careened along, Liberty watched the roadside emblem of the colonels flash by: a phoenix rising from flames before the black silhouette of an armed soldier with the words 'Greece' and '21 April 1967', the day of the coup which had brought Nikos' father and his cohorts to power. Sitting in the back, listening intently, it seemed to Liberty that the Greek woman was trying to find out if Nikos knew anything about her brother's alleged activities in Panagia.

Nikos answered only in monosyllables until he turned on the car radio. 'I wouldn't put it past *him* to bug the car,' he explained in an aside to Liberty. Then, as he launched into a long explanation to his mother in Greek, Liberty distinctly heard the Greek words for 'boat', 'last summer', and 'Italy'. Eagerly she leaned forward on the front seat. 'Maybe I can help. That is, if you tell me what's going on.'

Marika took her eyes off the road long enough to stare into the foreigner's eyes in the rearview mirror. 'This is family business,' she said loud and clear in English.

'Liberty is family.' Nikos' voice was firm. 'Or at least she will be.' Without waiting for an answer, he turned around to include her in the conversation. 'My mother was just asking if I knew anything about Vangelis' work.' He hesitated but then went on. 'In the Resistance.'

'Niko!' Marika seemed about to pull the car off the road, but she thought better of it. A sigh escaped her, but then she shrugged. Her anxiety about her brother was stronger than her aversion to this interloper. 'OK,' she said in English. 'Have it your way. Just this once.'

Triumphantly Nikos smiled, and then he continued in English for Liberty's benefit. 'From what we can gather, they picked my uncle up on suspicion of helping political dissidents escape from the country. By boat.'

'To Italy?' Liberty wanted to let them know that she had, after all, understood at least a little of their Greek conversation.

'Yes,' he answered. 'And to Yugoslavia.' As the car streaked down the busy toll road, Nikos revealed that Vangelis had, in fact, been involved in a Peloponnese unit of the Resistance for the past two years. In Athens and Thessaloniki the network working for the downfall of the *junta* busied itself trying to organize an effective movement against the dictatorship. In August there had been a symbolic guerrilla attack on the US embassy in Athens, in September a rash of bombs had exploded in Athens, and in October ringleaders of a group called the 20th October Movement had been arrested and sentenced. Secret cells of activists were forming at the university and within radical groups of workers and liberal circles of professionals. But the military police had paid informers everywhere, and it seemed that no sooner had a group begun working than the police vans came to arrest them all. In conservative provinces such as the Argolid section of the Peloponnese, the most a man of conscience could do was occasionally help shuttle wanted activists out of the country before the secret police could get them. Vangelis' contribution was to pilot a fishing *caique* down to a remote inlet in the Mani. From there a bigger boat took the dissidents across the open seas either to Italy or Yugoslavia.

'How, Niko,' Liberty asked, 'do you know all this?' In the mirror Marika's eyes sought hers, and the two women who loved Nikos exchanged a look of shared concern.

'Because I was Uncle Vangelis' contact in Athens.' As his mother erupted in another explosion of Greek, Nikos reached over and patted her arm. 'It's OK, no one knows. Or at least I think no one else knows. I've been very careful. Mostly I just carried down messages. I only went out with him on the boat once. And that was just to Mani.'

'If they know about Vangelis, they know about you.' All the colour had drained from Marika's face. 'How could you do that, *how*? You know your father. Once he finds out . . .' She bore down harder on the accelerator. First she had to save her brother, then she could concentrate on her son.

'You never told me about this.' But Liberty was remembering all those summer weekends when Nikos went down to Panagia. What she had assumed had been holidays in the sun had been political assignations. And she had thought he had always told her everything!

'I'm telling you now.' Nikos looked from one to the other. 'Both of you.'

'Yorgos,' Marika mused aloud with some satisfaction, 'would never get over this.' To herself she added that over in America his real father would be very proud of his son. She took her right hand off the steering wheel and reached over and touched Nikos' long dark hair. If she had done nothing else that was right and good in her life, at least she had given life to this brave boy. But then, as she pulled off the highway at Korinthos and began snaking toward Argos on the two-lane road that she knew so well, again fear overwhelmed her pride. She had thought that nothing could be worse than the arrest of her adored brother, but what would she do if Nikos were languishing in the Argos jail?

'*Paidi mou*,' she whispered in Greek, 'oh, my child.'

Nikos leaned over and patted her hand on the steering wheel. 'It's OK, mama. We're very careful. We're *all* careful. And I'm a man. I'm only doing what I have to do.'

Marika turned her icon eyes upon him. Hadn't Christos said the same thing to her years ago? Was she to lose the son as she had lost the father? Abruptly she pulled off the road. 'You drive now. I'm tired.'

In the back seat, Liberty watched the other woman surreptitiously wiping her eyes as Nikos climbed into the driver's seat. Impulsively she reached out and touched Marika's shoulder. The older woman stiffened and turned her head to meet Liberty's eyes. Again the two women looked at one another with something other than mistrust and fear. Then they both sighed and sank back in their seats and waited in silence for the young man they loved to take them to the jail where they assumed Vangelis waited.

It was getting dark when they threaded their way through the rundown back alleys of Argos and finally pulled up before a dirty small building with iron bars at the windows. 'I'll do the talking,' Marika said in Greek as she was first to leap out of the car.

Inside, three tired policemen were slumped at cluttered desks, smoking cigarettes, drinking Greek coffee, and listlessly talking to one another like habitués in a *kafeneion*. They did not even look up as Marika stormed inside and demanded to speak to whoever was in charge. When she raised her voice and repeated her demand, one of the policemen merely inclined his head toward another room. Marika swept into the back office, and after a moment's hesitation Nikos and Liberty followed her.

'I am the wife of Colonel Kronos of the Revolutionary Council.' Haughtily she looked down at the middle-aged policemen who was sitting at his desk munching pumpkin seeds. 'And a journalist.' She threw her press credentials on his desk. 'I have come here for my brother. Vangelis Papageorgiou. From Panagia. Our village.'

The sergeant popped another handful of *pasatembos* in his mouth, spat out the husks, and stared back without blinking at the arrogant Athenian lady who was under the mistaken impression that she could treat him like a peasant. 'Wait outside.' He yawned. 'Someone will take care of you there.'

Instead Marika advanced a threatening step closer. 'I will not wait! You will tell me about my brother, and now!' She reached for the telephone. 'Either that, or I'll call my husband. I can promise you that he will not be so pleasant as I am.'

As the policeman insolently stared back at Marika, Liberty clutched at Nikos' shoulder. Clearly the other woman was making a grievous mistake. In another moment, the policeman would have all three of them under arrest.

But she was wrong. The policeman's eyes fell, and slyly he licked the pumpkin seed salt off his lips. He knew all about the Kronos family, and ever since they had arrested that one this afternoon he had been expecting some of them to come storming into the station. Yet he was glad this wasn't a purely local matter. If the Panagia man had been arrested as a result of his own district's work, he would be quaking in his boots just now. But the arresting military police had come directly from Athens and taken the prisoner straight back to the capital. Again he congratulated himself that he had nothing to do with this messy business. He popped another pumpkin seed in his mouth. 'Your brother is not here.'

'Then where is my uncle?' Nikos advanced and put a steadying arm around his mother.

The policeman shrugged. 'That is not my problem.'

'Where is my brother!' Marika pounded her fist on the desk.

The policeman smiled as he spat the seed husk into an overflowing ashtray. 'What happens to all the traitors?'

'Dead?' Marika was shrieking. 'You've killed him? You've tortured my brother to death?'

'Easy, mama.' Nikos had his arm around her shaking shoulders. 'Athens?' he asked the policeman. 'Have you taken him to Athens?'

Again the policeman popped a pumpkin seed in his mouth. 'If he is not here, where else would he be?'

'Athens. All the way down here for nothing. Vangelis is in Athens.' Marika

393

spoke very low, as though she were talking to herself. Framed on the wall above the policeman's head she stared at the colour portrait of George Papadopoulos, the head of the military dictatorship who was now Regent as well as Prime Minister, Minister of Defence, and Foreign Minister. Her terrible suspicion that her own husband had been involved in her brother's arrest was growing stronger. That must be why she hadn't been able to get in touch with him at his office. Her mind raced. Did Yorgos know about Nikos, too? Was her son to be the next to go? Should she try to spirit Nikos out of the country now, before he suffered the same fate as his uncle? Don't worry about that now, she told herself. There was nothing more to be done here with the peasant of a policeman masticating his pumpkin seeds. Vangelis was in Athens, and the key to getting his release was her own husband. First she would have to go to Panagia to collect her mother. Eleni had said on the phone that she'd collapsed when the police took Vangelis away, but her mother was as strong as an ox. Together they would return to Athens and face down Yorgos. When she spoke to the sergeant again, she had herself tightly under control. 'Tell me one thing. The arrest order. You must have known what was happening in your own district. What exactly did the arrest order say?

The sergeant shrugged and popped another handful of pumpkin seeds in his mouth. Contemptuously he spat out the husks.

Without another word, Marika turned and, still with Nikos' arm around her, walked with a leaden step back to the car. Liberty followed them.

Thoughtfully, still sitting at his desk, the police sergeant picked his teeth free of pumpkin husks. Then he snapped to attention and dialled a number in Athens. Yes, he reported, everything had gone exactly as predicted. The colonel's wife and son had arrived, and a young blonde foreign girl had been with them. No, he said, he didn't know who the girl was, she hadn't said a word.

In his ministry office, Yorgos hung up the phone. His wife and son had been given their warning. But who was that girl they had brought along on such an intimate family mission? Nikos, he suspected, had been keeping not only his traitorous political work but also his blonde foreign girlfriend secret from his own dear father.

He hit the inner-office buzzer. 'Kosta,' he ordered as his aide promptly appeared, 'call the Brigadier's office over at military intelligence. They owe me a few favours. See what they can dig up on a little blonde girl who's been seen with my son.'

Then Yorgos rubbed his hands together in satisfaction, put on his military cap at a jaunty angle, and picked up the suitcase he had brought to the office that morning. On the way out, he left a telephone number with Kostas.

Under no circumstances, he ordered, was Kostas to disclose his whereabouts to his wife or any other member of his family. Only if there was official business could he give out the number of his hotel in Crete.

Yorgos sang a little love song under his breath as he went to pick up his own little blonde girlfriend on the way to the airport.

Fifteen

Forty-eight hours later, on Sunday evening, Yorgos took his time strolling through the Athens airport with his bleached-blonde lady love on his way back from their tryst in Crete. Aware that all this time his wife, son, and in-laws must have been trying to track down not only his but Vangelis' whereabouts, he savoured the knowledge that by now their anxiety had surely escalated to panic. They must learn their lesson the hard way. He, not to mention his hardline colleagues who held a firm grip on the government, would no longer tolerate sedition in the bosom of his own family. Making an example of the unfortunate Vangelis would assure that his wife and son towed the line.

Three paces behind him Katerina wobbled in her high heels as she tried to keep up with his military stride. 'Yorgo? Yorgo, wait!'

He cast an irritated glance back at the heavily-made up twenty-five-year-old who served during the week as a receptionist in his office and on occasional weekends as his mistress. She was better in bed than on the phone, but being cooped up with her for two days had gotten on his nerves. Between her and those repeated calls he had made to Averof prison where Vangelis was being interrogated, he hadn't been able to enjoy his weekend in the luxury Cretan bungalow whose use was another of the perquisites of his Ministry post. Katerina had been alternately demanding and petulant, as though her three month tenure in his bed had made her his surrogate wife. Disdainfully he eyed how tarted-up she was in that tight black skirt and clinging orange sweater. How could a girl like her ever imagine that he would put up with behaviour he barely tolerated in his wife? He intended to kiss her off when he dropped her at her Nea Smyrni apartment. If she raised a fuss, he would either have her transferred to another department or sent to a provincial office where she would never trouble him again. He already had her successor waiting in the wings. Myrto, a secretary in accounting, had

395

eyes and hair that reminded him a little of his wife's. With her, maybe when he dimmed the lights he could even pretend that it was Marika he held in his arms. Perhaps that little secretary would give him the respect, passion, even adoration which his wife had always denied him. It was Marika's fault that he wasted himself on these cheap, big-breasted dollies.

Yet he was in no hurry to get home to his wife's hysterics. When he spotted the newsstand he bought his favourite Sunday newspapers, skimmed the headlines, and as an afterthought bought a copy of Marika's newspaper.

'Yorgo? Are we going to stay in the airport all afternoon? I'm tired, Yorgo.'

He ignored Katerina's wail and leisurely sauntered over to the coffee bar, ordered a *metrios*, and leaned against the counter sipping from the miniature plastic cup as he leafed through the pages looking for Marika's column. Odd, he thought, when he saw another writer's piece in her accustomed slot. He supposed she'd been so upset by her brother's arrest that she had missed her deadline. But then his eye was caught by an item in the news columns under her byline. Quickly he scanned it, banged his cup down, and balled the paper up in a ball and threw it in a trashcan. How dare she have written this veiled reference to political dissenters in the Peloponnese! He was beginning to think the military police had arrested the wrong member of his family. He was going to have trouble about this article as soon as he got to work tomorrow morning, and he couldn't afford to draw any more negative attention to himself. First his Communist brother resurfaced in Boston, then Vangelis and his son dabbled in treason, and now his own wife danced dangerously on the edge of what it was permissible to write in the newspaper. Yorgos took a deep breath and told himself not to get upset. At his last checkup the doctor had warned his blood pressure was far too high and ordered him to stop smoking, lose weight, and avoid all stress. Obviously his wife was trying to kill him with her reckless writing. Well, he would fix *her*. He would make her quit her job, stay home, and begin acting like a dutiful wife.

'*Pame*,' he barked, eager now to get home and engage the enemy. Without waiting to see if Katerina was following, he marched out of the terminal into the parking lot. He had the motor running by the time the girl puffed up wheeling her luggage on a trolley. He let her struggle by herself to get her suitcases in the back.

On the way into town, Yorgos tuned out Katerina's whines that he was acting like he didn't love her any more. Stuck in the inevitable traffic jam, he seethed at the trouble his family was causing him. He had had a devil of a time over the past weeks explaining away his brother-in-law's Resistance activities. Vangelis' dossier, painstakingly prepared by military intelligence, had been as thick as a book. How could his wife's brother have ever thought he could get away with his harebrained sea escapes? The military had been tipped off to his initial run to Mani two years ago. Since then, they had tracked Vangelis' *caique* every time it pulled out of Panagia harbour. The only reason they hadn't picked him up before was that they were using him as bait to bigger fish. But now that they had netted two important Communists after Vangelis dropped them in Mani, Marika's brother had served his purpose. If he had been a nobody like most of the fools in the underground with their homemade bombs and laughable stratagems, Vangelis would be facing bleak years in a desolate island concentration camp. But Yorgos had pulled strings on his behalf and cut the best deal he could with the military police. In another week or two, after Vangelis had been thoroughly questioned and the rest of the family had been suitably intimidated, the prisoner would be provisionally released. Meanwhile, the security police had promised not to use their more painful persuasions on a brother-in-law of one of the original *junta* members. But just to be on the safe side Yorgos had telephoned the prison warden five times this weekend for assurances that Vangelis wasn't suffering anything worse than fear, indignity, and a few strategic punches. Afterwards, there would be no trial or sentencing. Instead, Yorgos himself would see that his brother-in-law left the country at once. He supposed Vangelis would go to Australia, where his wife's family could provide a job and a future. Yorgos would be spared all further political embarrassments from at least that rotten branch of Marika's family.

'Yorgo, why are you acting like this?' Katerina's eyes welled with tears. 'Yorgo, why won't you talk to me?'

He looked over and saw that familiar pout on her face. All he had to do to bring her around was pinch her cheek or give her thigh a little squeeze, but instead he lit a cigarette and went back to his brooding. His brother-in-law's sedition was the least of his problems. Far more serious was the complicity of his son and possibly even his wife. How could Nikos have let himself be duped into treason, carrying messages for the Resistance and attending those clandestine meetings at the polytechnic? Even though his doctor had advised him to take it easy and not get excited, Yorgos had been apoplectic when he had read the account of how his only son had compromised not only himself but the entire family. Papadopoulos and the other officers on the Revolutionary Council had ordered him either to clean up his house or resign from office. He supposed he would have been in a far more tenuous position if the booming tourist business hadn't been bringing so much badly-needed foreign revenue into the country. Despite the international press's adverse publicity about repression in Greece, four times as many tourists came to Greece now compared to a decade ago. This past summer alone forty percent more tourists had arrived than in the previous year, and the figures for next year's season again were expected to break all previous records. Still, considering the infighting now raging among the colonels who had triggered the Revolution, the last thing he needed right now was a seditious family. Last year a conservative faction among the *junta* colonels – unhappy with continuing problems in Cyprus and budding domestic resistance to the regime – had tried to oust Papadopoulos from his pre-eminent role. But Brigadier Ioannides, the powerful head of military intelligence, had sided with the boss. Shortly thereafter, all the government ministers had been forced to turn in their portfolios, and when a new Council of Ministers was announced a number of the original colonels had been reassigned to provincial posts. Then again this past March, Papadopoulos had once more purged his inner circle. Yorgos had barely survived both power struggles, but he didn't want to risk being branded a security risk because of his family.

Stalled at a traffic light, Yorgos gazed longingly at the mothers, fathers, and children walking arm-in-arm on the crowded pavements. To all of them, the family was the axis on which their lives turned. How had it happened that he, who had achieved such glorious professional success, was cursed with a family that caused him more shame than pride? After all these years of stalemated marriage, Yorgos didn't think anything his wife could do would surprise him. But for his only son to fail him like this! And it wasn't only his political activities that rankled. He had wanted Nikos to become a career military officer, marry a good girl from the village, and spend his life where he belonged, by his father's side. Instead Nikos frittered his time away playing frivolous music and consorting with traitors. The fact that he was studying to be an architect at the most prestigious school in the country didn't sweeten the pill. An architect was still an artist: expendable, decadent, even unmanly. He had so wanted a soldier son, a young man he could point to with pride as following in his footsteps. Instead Nikos was turning out to be the greatest disappointment of his life. What's more, Yorgos' attempts to convince Nikos to agree to a suitable marriage to a sensible Panagia girl had fallen upon deaf ears. Last summer, while his son was sneaking around ferrying traitors on his uncle's boat, Yorgos himself had delicately begun to sound out the best families of Panagia in the first preliminary marriage negotiations. But he had not been able to convince Nikos even to have coffee with the fathers and brothers who had been eager to solder an alliance with the illustrious Kronos family. At the time Yorgos had thought the boy, who was after all young for marriage, was only shying away from commitment and responsibilities. But after that phone call from the Argos police sergeant, he had understood his son's reluctance to court a village girl. Again he wondered about the identity of that pretty blonde foreigner who had come down to the Peloponnese with his wife and son.

As he pulled up in front of Katerina's apartment building, expectantly she sat there not making a move. 'Coming up, Yorgo?'

He kept the motor running. 'I have no time.' But to forestall another of her scenes, he leaped out of the car, opened the back door, and carried her cases onto the pavement.

Reluctantly she slid out of the car. 'Yorgo? We should talk. Please, Yorgo.'

'I'll see you at work tomorrow.' When she went to embrace him, he snaked away. 'Not here, We're back in Athens. I've told you before, a man in my position has to be discreet.' He was back in the driver's seat before she could say another word.

As he pulled away, Yorgos forgot all about Katerina and went back to worrying about his son's entanglement with that foreign girl. He would get to the bottom of this latest disturbing mystery, and the rest of his family's sins, as soon as he walked through his front door. Once and for all, they would learn who was boss. He would spare none of them, beginning with his renegade wife. Apparently she knew all about Nikos' romance. After all, she had taken the girl along to Argos for all the world to see, as though she were already an accepted member of the family. It would be just like her to encourage this relationship to spite him, for she knew very well that he wanted Nikos to marry a girl from the village. That one would stop at nothing. It was bad enough that she was meddling in his dynastic plans, but he would not tolerate her using her newspaper to make a fool of him. After all he had done for her – picking her up out of the gutter and making an honest woman of her after his brother had used her and left her, and then letting her go to the university, and even getting her a powerful job – how dare she taunt the government in that column of hers? If she continued like this, he would be the laughingstock of gossipy Athens. Had she no sense of shame or decorum? Well, he had made her and he could break her. He was sick of turning himself inside out to please her. By rights he should have changed tactics and gotten tough with her years ago. But it wasn't too late to begin. One more false move, and he would get her fired and then installed back in Panagia in the taverna kitchen. Or perhaps he would even send her to jail. Just the threat of a prison term would cool her off, most probably permanently. She'd be on her knees pleading for mercy. And he supposed – God help him! – that he'd grant it. Why could he never rid himself of his passion for this impossible woman who never would love him?

Yorgos' frown deepened when finally he pulled into the deserted driveway. He had expected the whole family to be anxiously waiting for his return. But

Marika's car was gone, none of the Panagia vans or trucks were there, and Nikos' motorbike was leaning against the garage door where Yorgos remembered having seen it when he left for work Friday morning. Where else would they all be but here?

In vain he rang the doorbell. Even the maid was gone. He had to fumble for his key, and as he came in the door he heard the telephone ringing. He dove for it. But before he could even say '*Legete*', he heard Marika's voice screaming on the other end.

'Yorgo! Is that you!'

He exhaled in a deep sigh of satisfaction. Now this was more like it. 'Where are you?' He was determined to seize and hold the offensive.

'Where am *I*? Where were *you*?' Before he could answer in kind, her voice took on an urgency he had never heard in it before. 'Yorgo, listen to me. I'm in Panagia. We'll all here. We've been frantic! Yorgo! It's my mother! She's dying, Yorgo!'

'Your mother?' He sank down in a chair. 'Old Anna?'

'The doctor said she had a heart attack. Friday, when they took Vangelis away.' Marika was sobbing. 'It's been terrible, Yorgo. She's so bad, the doctor wouldn't even risk moving her to hospital. She keeps asking for my brother. You've got to help. I've been calling and calling, but that Kostas wouldn't tell me a thing. Yorgo, you've got to get my brother out. I can't let her . . . go . . . without seeing him. My God, Yorgo, she keeps asking for my father, too! She hasn't mentioned him for years, but now she keeps asking where he is. First she cries out for my father, and then for Vangelis. I can't let her . . . go . . . without seeing my brother.'

'But that's impossible.' His voice was very gentle. 'I can't do that, my dear.' He had not called her 'my dear' for years and years.

'Please, Yorgo! *Please*! Do this one thing. For me, Yorgo!'

They had been married for nearly twenty-four years, but never before had she begged him for anything. The only time he remembered her ever even saying 'please' like this was that Great Friday in the olive grove when she'd pleaded with him to marry her. A few moments ago in the car he had been willing to have her carted off to prison, but now . . . 'I'll see what I can do.'

Marika let out a great sigh of relief. 'But you'll have to be quick, Yorgo. The doctor says she won't . . . he says he's surprised she's lasted this long. But you know mama. How strong she's always been.' Again she broke down in sobs.

'I'll call you back as soon as I know anything. The military police have him. In Averof.'

Quick as a flash, her voice changed. 'So you *do* know where he is?'

'I've been doing all I could, Marika.' The tenderness in his voice hardened.

'I've been in touch with the authorities, and all I can tell you is that your brother is being routinely questioned.'

'Tortured?'

'No. I have been assured that is not the case. May I remind you that Greece is a civilized country. No matter what lies they print in the foreign press, we do not torture those detained in our jails.'

She started to say something, but then she seemed to change her mind 'Just get him out, Yorgo. *Please*!'

'I'll let you know.'

When he put the receiver back on the cradle, Yorgos lit a cigarette and considered. There had never been any love lost between himself and his mother-in-law, but at a time like this loyalty to the family was paramount. Honour required that he respect the old woman's deathbed plea. Knowing Old Anna, too, she'd haunt him forevermore if he didn't give her the chance to say farewell to her beloved son. And yet despite his assurances to his wife, he had second thoughts about even trying to intervene in a matter of treason. Vangelis had been caught redhanded in his sedition, and already Yorgos had used up most of his bankroll of personal favours to secure the promise of his brother-in-law's eventual release. But, remembering the sound of his wife's begging, Yorgos knew he had to try. She wasn't much of a wife, but she was his wife. As head of the family, he had to protect her. No matter what the cost, he could not refuse to try to grant her request. Whether he would succeed was another matter.

He pulled a little book of numbers out of his pocket and hesitated. Should he go straight to the top and phone Papadopoulos or start with Brigadier Ioannides who was the head of the military police? It would take longer if he went through the big boss. But if Ioannides wanted, he could get Vangelis released for a mercy visit with a single phone call.

He dialled the Brigadier's home number.

Old Anna lay in the bed as Marika sat beside her keeping the deathwatch. It was the middle of the night, and she had sent everyone away for a few hours' sleep. The old woman's eyes were closed, and her faltering breaths came as weakly as the flickering candle burning low on the bedside table. Always when death was near, the Greeks lit a candle to guide the soul's path to the other world.

Outside in the hallway Eleni's clock striking three sounded like knocking on the door.

Old Anna's eyes shot open. 'He's here? He's finally come?'

Marika held her mother's hands more tightly. 'Not yet, mama. But he's coming. Yorgos called. He says he's on his way.'

The old woman's eyes leaped with hope. 'Finally! He comes! Everyone told me he was never coming back, but I waited and I waited and now he comes. My Yannis!' She tried to sit up, but she couldn't raise her head. 'My hair. My face. I'm not ready.'

'Oh, mama!' In these fraught two days since her heart attack, the worst moments had been when her mother called out for the husband who had abandoned her nearly forty years ago. At first when she had said that name which hadn't passed her lips for years, Marika had thought her mother was about to pass away and was seeing her father's shade. When it had dawned on her that her mother's mind was wandering and that in her heart the old woman had never given up hope of her husband's return, Marika wept for the pain she must have suffered mostly in silence.

Old Anna squinted at Marika. 'And who are you?'

'Your daughter. Marika. You remember, mama.'

The old one's eyes cleared. '*Paidi mou*!' Her fingers were like claws on Marika's hands. 'My good girl.' She looked round the darkened room. 'But where's my boy? My Vangelis!' A spasm contorted her wrinkled face as she remembered the police coming and taking her son away. 'My boy!'

'Easy, mama. He's coming. I told you before. Yorgos called from Athens. He's bringing Vangelis. They'll be here soon, mama.' As her mother's eyes shut again, Marika's eyes went to the icon of the Virgin that had stood guard over Old Anna's bed for as long as she could remember. Please, she prayed, let her live until Vangelis comes. 'Hold on, mama. Don't give up. He'll be here. He's coming. Just be quiet and wait.'

'Wait,' Old Anna echoed. 'My whole life waiting, and now I must wait for my death, too.' On the pillow her head jerked from side to side, and the bag of bones that was her body seemed to writhe, but weakly.

Watching her, Marika remembered the old wives' tale about how God sends his messenger Charon to collect souls and bring them safely to the other side, and how sometimes Charon has to wrestle with those unwilling to go before they gave up the ghost and surrendered the known for the unknown. Before her eyes her mother seemed locked in just such a struggle. Marika leaned closer, and she slipped her arm around her mother's shoulders. Charon would have to fight her, too.

After a moment, the old woman lay still and opened her eyes. 'Water.' When Marika had lifted her head and poured a few drops between her lips, her mother seemed stronger. She looked Marika straight in the eyes. 'So it's time.'

'No, mama, not yet. We have to wait for Vangelis. And then you'll feel better. Just as soon as you're a little stronger, we'll be able to move you to hospital. The doctors can work wonders these days. You'll be up and about in a week.'

'No,' Old Anna said flatly. 'I will never see another dawn.' Her eyes were infinitely sad. 'No more sun and no more moon. No more flowers and no more birds. No sea, no mountains. And no you, *paidi mou*. Ah, that's the hard part!' She tried to smile. 'But you know what they say, the first day in the other world is the worst. The soul cries and cries, and all the other souls laugh at so many tears. But then they take the new soul to the well of forgetfulnes, and as soon as you drink you forget everything in this life and you laugh at the pain of the shrieking soul.' Old Anna's voice fell, so that Marika had to lean closer to hear. 'But they lie. Never, for all eternity, even if I drink that well dry, will I ever forget *you*, my child, my joy, my Marika . . .'

'Oh, mama!' Marika's shoulders shook with sobs as she clutched onto her mother, fearful that these were her last words.

But the old woman rallied. 'Don't cry. Don't cry for *me*. It's a hard life, so hard . . .' Her eyes closed, and when they fluttered open a moment later they were not so lucid. 'Yannis, where is Yannis? He's coming?' On the pillow fretfully she shook her head. 'I asked him not to go so far away. Australia! The other side of the world! Even America is not so far. Why he couldn't be content to go to Argos or Korinthos or even Athens to find work, I don't know. But that's the men for you! Off and away! First Nikolas, then Yannis.' Her eyes fell on Marika, and her mind cleared a little. 'And Christos. *He* left, too. The morning after the cave. You remember, *paidi mou*?'

'Of course. The night that changed my life.'

'The Cave of the Great Goddess!' Old Anna's face was alight. 'Such a place! Such a night!'

Marika assumed her mother must be talking about her own Carnival night with Christos. 'My Nikos came from that night in the cave. I lost so much that night. But it was worth everything to get my Nikos.'

'Nikos?' Old Anna looked bewildered. 'Who's talking about Nikos? *You*, Marika! That's where I took Yannis that night you were conceived.'

Marika stared at her mother. 'You went there with my father?'

Old Anna smiled so broadly that she showed all her gums. 'I was young once, too. Never so pretty as you were, but I *was* young. When Nikolas married Eleni after Sofia died, I thought my life was over. He never even gave me a sniff! But my mother sat me down – just like I did with you – and she told me about that cave and what I had to do to get a man.' She broke off her narrative. 'Don't forget to take your girls there. The cave must not die with us! You promise? Yes?'

403

Marika didn't have the heart to remind her mother that she had already rowed her granddaughters to the cave. 'I promise, mama.'

Old Anna sighed and went back to her remembering. 'Of course Yannis wasn't Nikolas. He was never much to look at, Yannis, and people always said he would never amount to anything. But I was old – nearly twenty – and he was my last chance. The moon was full, he was willing, and here you are. My great gift from the cave!'

'There, in the cave?' Marika was remembering the dark recesses, the eerie womblike feeling she had always had there, how it had felt that inside she was coming home.

'I always wondered, after I sent you there with Christos, whether it was a blessing or a curse that I did that.' Old Anna's eyes sought her daughter's. 'Which was it?'

'Oh, mama! How could anything that created Nikos be anything but a blessing!'

'Good.' The old woman sighed. 'I always wondered . . .' Her voice trailed off.

'Mama! Mama, don't go! Don't leave me, mama!'

'It's time, *paidi mou*. I'm tired, so tired. So many years waiting. I can't wait any longer.'

Outside Marika heard car doors slam, then the taverna door being thrown open and heavy footsteps on the stairs. 'Vangelis! He's coming, mama!'

The door burst open, and Vangelis raced in with Yorgos and four armed guards in his wake. He stopped a few paces from the bed, saw his mother's eyes still open, and threw himself down on the floor at the side of the bed. 'Mama!'

She did not have the strength to move her hands to caress his hair, but Marika placed her hands in his black curls. 'My son. So you came. Ah, good. I can go, now that I know you're . . .'

'Get the doctor!' Yorgos stood in command at the foot of the bed. 'Anybody can see she needs the doctor.' He wheeled on one of the military guards and shouted. 'Get the doctor!' The guards backed out of the room.

Old Anna's eyes opened again. 'Who's that? Yannis? Is that Yannis?' Her eyes could not altogether focus. 'Yes, *Yanni*! You came! I knew you would! I knew you'd come back finally, if only I waited, Thank God I waited. Thank God I hung on.'

Yorgos and Marika exchanged a silent look, and then Yorgos came close enough to hold his mother-in-law's hand. 'Of course I came. But I was far away, and it took a long time to get back.'

Old Anna made a sound like a laugh. 'You always were late. Late for our wedding. And now almost too late for . . .' A choking noise came from her

404

throat, and Marika and Vangelis leaned closer and held on to her more tightly. 'Yanni? Where are you, Yanni?'

'Here.' Yorgos sat on the side of the bed and kissed the old woman on the lips. 'I'm here.'

'Finally,' she murmured. 'Finally all together.' She shut her eyes and heaved a great contented sigh, and she did not breathe again.

Marika was sobbing as she kissed her mother's hands, Vangelis was smoothing the white hair back from his mother's temples, and the room was filling up with the rest of the family. Yorgos and Nikos had their arms around Marika, Eleni let out with a mourning shriek, Vasso ran in and threw her arms around Vangelis, and Lena and Annoula stood in their nightdresses weeping for their grandmother.

Eleni was tearing at her hair as she began improvising a *myriologion* dirge for her old friend. 'Why did you leave us?' Her voice had a weird singsong tone that was as sad as the grave. 'How can you go? Where did you go so soon? How can we live without you?'

Marika lifted her tearstained face and in a broken voice she took up the rhythmic lamentation her mother-in-law had begun. 'We cry for you, we weep for you! Go in peace, my wise one, my good one.' Her voice rose in a shriek. 'I will look for you on the crest of every wave, on the petal of every flower, at the rising of every sun! My mother, oh my mother, where have you gone without us, your children?'

'No more,' Eleni wailed, 'will together we sit in the sun. No more will we rock in the shade. You have left us, you have left us. What will we do? What will we do!' As she sang her mournful lament, Eleni took the coin she had ready in her pocket and placed it between her old friend's lips in case Charon required it to take her where she had gone. 'Oh, my friend! Oh, my sister! Wait for me, Anna!'

Liberty stood near the doorway. Forever after, she would be haunted by the terrible bewitching women's song which was to her the very sound of death. Tears filled her eyes as she watched her lover's family grieve for the old woman who had endured such a sad life but been blessed with a death as happy as her united family could make it. As was the custom here, she and Nikos would name their first daughter Marika. But someday, she promised this one whose death had so moved her, they would name another of their daughters Anna.

As the churchbell tolled on Tuesday afternoon, the funeral procession wended its doleful way through the silent village streets from the church to the cemetery on the side of the mountain. Even before they could see it, the

405

villagers could hear it. The mourning shrieks of the women echoed in the lanes. First came a boy carrying aloft the lid of the coffin covered in white silk, followed by the altar boys brandishing the Cross and their ornate banners which fluttered in the late autumn wind. Father Petros in his vivid liturgical robes marched to the beat of the mournfully tolling bells. Behind him Nikos was among the six young men in black carrying aloft the open coffin in which Old Anna, her body washed in wine and dressed in snowy white like a bride, was propped up so that all could bid her farewell. Behind the cortege the family walked, all in black: Marika and Yorgos, Vangelis and Vasso, Eleni with Lena and Annoula. Liberty was somewhere among the mass of cousins, aunts, and uncles. Just behind Vangelis, the armed soldiers who had escorted him from Athens marched like a guard of honour. At the tail of the procession cousins passed out the traditional *kolliva* funeral sweet, a mixture of boiled wheat, sugar, pomegranate seeds, raisins, and sugared almonds. As every villager took a bit of it, they murmured, 'May God forgive'. The mourning shrieks of the women continued unabated. Some struck their heads, and an old woman collapsed and had to be carried home.

As the procession approached, the villagers shut tight the doors and windows of every shop and house not only in respect for the passing of one of their own but also so that wily death could not gain entrance to another household. Old Anna's soul must pass safely over the threshold to the other side and not slip by mistake inside another door where she might eternally wander, seeking rest and consolation.

It was a dark late October morning, and on the mountainside the cypress trees bent in the wind as Father Petros prayed over the grave. One by one the family bid farewell to Old Anna. Marika wailed as she threw herself on her mother's body, and Yorgos had to pry her hands away and help her to her feet. Vangelis kissed his mother on the lips but then stood dry-eyed and manly as Vasso cried as though she were burying her own mother. Eleni shrieked her *myriologion*, and she was joined by the other old women who had shared the joys of their youth and the pain of their age with the one who was leaving them. A pillow of earth was placed under Old Anna's head, the lid was fitted on the coffin, and slowly the casket was lowered. When the grave was filled in, a candle was left burning upon it. As the mourners made their way down the mountain, the churchbell continued to toll.

But still the ordeal wasn't over. Virtually every man and woman in Panagia brought a candle or a bunch of flowers to the wake at the Kronos house. As the villagers drank *sketos* – coffee without sugar – munched *kolliva*, and sat awhile for a visit, the family set aside the bones they had to pick with one another.

Sometimes in the afternoon, however, in the siesta lull before the next wave of villagers came for the evening visits, the soldiers who had escorted Vangelis from Athens took the colonel aside and discreetly reminded him they had to return the prisoner to Averof.

Yorgos nodded. The family knew Vangelis was due back in Athens, and he hoped he could spirit his brother-in-law away without anyone causing a scene. They were all overwrought from the funeral and the deathwatch which had preceded it. By now they probably would be in bed for their siestas. But his heart sank when he found Vangelis in the *saloni* flanked by Vasso and Marika. Nikos and the blonde foreigner were on a nearby sofa, while Eleni sobbed as she prayed before an icon of the Virgin. Yorgos caught his brother-in-law's eye and gestured to the soldiers waiting in the next room.

Vangelis had promised to return without a fuss. He paled as he gave his wife's shoulder a final pat and stood.

But Marika grabbed his hands before he could go. 'Not yet. Don't *you* leave us, too.'

'Marika, you know he has to go.' Yorgos spoke softly, as if to a sick child. Her mother's death had devastated her. She had deep blue circles under her eyes, and she had all but collapsed at the cemetery. Last night he had held her in his arms for hours before she finally fell into a fitful sleep. And yet, since she had pleaded with him on the telephone to secure her brother's temporary release, between the two of them a tenderness had been born. After her mother had died, Marika had even kissed his hands in gratitude for having eased Old Anna's passing by pretending to be her long-lost husband. Yorgos didn't know whether this was only a short-lived truce or a permanent change in their relationship. He, however, was eager to continue as they had newly begun. 'Let him go. *Please*.'

'Not yet, Yorgo.' Marika did not loosen her grip on her brother. 'One more night. That's not so much to ask. You'd like that, Vasso, wouldn't you?'

'Can he, Yorgo?' Vasso's face was swollen from weeping, and again the tears were running down her cheeks.

Eleni broke off her devotions. 'Vangelis stays. Yorgo, call Athens and tell them he'll be up tomorrow.'

Yorgos looked at the tearstained faces of his women, then at Vangelis, and finally at the next room where the soldiers waited. 'I can't.' Already the prisoner had stayed longer than he should. Yorgos had promised to send him back to Athens as soon as Old Anna was buried.

'You can if you want to.' Nikos joined the nagging chorus. 'You're always telling us how important you are. Why don't you *show* us?'

'Niko!' Marika held a warning finger to her lips. Not now, she prayed. She couldn't stand it if her husband and son got into another of their rows.

Yorgos' gaze flickered over to Nikos sitting thigh-to-thigh with the foreigner. He would deal with his son and that girl as soon as Vangelis left. That, and the matter of the boy's treasonous politics.

'Since when do you − any of you − tell me what to do?' Yorgos' anger built as he looked at the faces arrayed against *him*, their saviour. The only one who had ever shown him proper respect and affection was his mother, and even she was beginning to act like the rest of them. 'I told you that he had to be back in Athens right after the funeral. So he goes. He goes now. *Pame!*'

Vangelis broke away from Marika and followed him to the door.

'Yorgo?' Vasso put up her hand as though she were back in the schoolroom. 'What's going to happen to my husband?'

Benignly he smiled. He had left the great news until now. 'Nothing. A few more days − perhaps a week − of routine questioning.' With his hands he mimed an airplane taking off a runway. 'And then the two of you will be up and away.'

Vangelis frowned. 'I don't understand.'

'When the authorities at Averof finish with their questioning, you will be released. Not court-martialled and sentenced. *Released*. I personally will escort you and Vasso to the airport, and off you'll go.'

'*Exo?*' Vasso's lip trembled as she said the word that meant 'outside' the motherland.

'Precisely.' Yorgos smiled at the Greek-Australian. 'Perhaps you can take him home with you.'

'Home?' Bitterly Vasso brought her head up in a negative. 'My home is here.' She touched her belly. 'I am carrying his child. He . . . we . . . can't leave now.'

'As you like.' Yorgos nonchalantly shrugged, but inside a slow boil was beginning. He had come close to laying his career on the line for his brother-in-law, and all he was getting in return were demands that Vangelis violate his parole and accusing looks about his upcoming exile. 'If you want your husband to stay in prison, then so it shall be. He's guilty of treason. Others who have done far less have been on islands like Yaros for four years.'

Eleni dried her eyes and hesitantly got up and laid her hand on her son's shoulder. 'Can't you *do* something?' Vangelis had become as dear to her as a son. 'Surely you can change their minds.'

'My dear mother, I already *have* done more than I should. Vangelis has been treated with kid gloves since his arrest. They didn't hurt you in Averof, did they?'

Vangelis met his brother-in-law's eyes. 'They didn't torture me like they torture others, no. At night I could hear their screams.' He bit his lip. He did not want to set the women off on another round of weeping. 'They asked a lot of questions. They roughed me up a little when they first took me there. And they made . . . threats. But now you're saying I have you to thank for special treatment?'

Yorgos rocked proudly back on his heels. 'I'm saying I did the best I could for you.' Now, he thought, he would get the gratitude he deserved. 'And believe me, it wasn't easy.'

'What I'd like to know is who blew the whistle on my uncle in the first place.' From the way Nikos was glaring at Yorgos, his insinuation was clear.

'Niko, *please*.' The mother and son exchanged a look, and sullenly Nikos lit a cigarette.

Vasso wrung her hands and broke the electric silence that had fallen in the room. 'So we have to leave Greece?'

'I'm afraid so.' Vangelis came back and embraced her. 'I'll see *you* at the airport.' Next he kissed Marika goodbye and hugged Eleni. Nikos held him tight. And then, before he altogether lost his composure, Vangelis left the *saloni* and surrendered himself to the soldiers. Eleni and Vasso fled the room in tears.

Yorgos sat down next to Marika. That business of his brother-in-law had not ended as well as he had expected, but he wasn't going to put up with any nonsense from his son. 'Now,' he said, turning to Nikos, 'what were you doing on that boat to Mani last July?'

For a moment Nikos faltered. Despite his mother's warning, he had not believed his father knew anything about his Resistance activities. 'I don't know what you're talking about.'

Yorgos slammed his fist on the small table before him so hard that the cups on it fell and broke on the floor. 'Enough of your lies, and enough of your treason! You were with your uncle on one of his little adventures on July the eleventh, to be exact. If it weren't for me, you'd be in jail right now, too. And you still may, unless you promise me here and now that you will cut all ties with that underground cell of yours at the polytechnic. Then you will either begin your military service at once or return to Panagia and take your uncle's place in the family business.'

Liberty could restrain herself no longer. That funeral had been grisly, and she still couldn't get over what Nikos had told her, that in two years they would dig up his grandmother and put her bones in the family crypt. Then, back here at the house, the family had mostly ignored her while strangers had stared at her as though she were a carnival freak. All that had been bad enough, but Nikos' family had been shouting at one another in Greek for more than half an hour. Did these people never tire of their screeching melodramatics? And now the colonel was obviously starting on Nikos. It was driving her crazy, not understanding what was happening around her. 'What's he saying, Niko?'

Yorgos shifted his attention to the one he had so far done his best to ignore. 'And *her*. I want her out of this house and out of your life *at once*!'

'Niko.' Marika had a splitting headache. So they'd stop this screaming, she broke precedent and took her husband's side. 'Maybe she could take a little nap while you talk to your father. This is family business.'

'Liberty's family.' Nikos took her hand firmly in his. 'Or at least she will be. I told you before, mama. We're getting married next year.'

Yorgos fixed a deadeye stare on the interloper who was no doubt responsible for his son's political sins. She reminded him a little of that American secretary he had taken those delicious pictures of years ago. Sally? Jane? No, he remembered it now, Susie. He couldn't fault his son for dallying with a girl like this. He himself wouldn't mind snapping her up for awhile. Doubtless she was good in bed, but *marriage*? She must have cast a spell on him. But the family witch had just been buried under the cypress trees, and Yorgos was not about to welcome another one in her place. With his thumb he pointed to the door. 'Get her out of my sight.'

'Yorgo, your heart.' Marika knew the signs of one of her husband's impending rages, and she couldn't face one now. 'And Niko, think of *her*.' She still wasn't any more in favour of this match than her husband was, and her presence would only antagonize Yorgos. 'Maybe she should wait in her room.'

Uncertainly Nikos looked from his mother to the colonel, and then gently he touched Liberty's shoulder. 'Could you wait upstairs? Really, try to understand. It's for the best. Just this once.'

Liberty understood more than he thought. In these last dreadful days she had done everything she could think of to win over Nikos' family, but now she wished she hadn't come. With what dignity she could muster, she sailed out of the *saloni*. She was English, and she, too, had her pride. She would not so much as give that tinpot dictator of a father of his a glance.

As soon as she was out of earshot, Yorgos rounded on his son. 'You should never have brought her here.' He was not about to absolve his wife, either. 'And Marika, you should not have allowed it.'

At the blink of an eye her stoked resentment flamed. But before she could say anything, Nikos beat her to the punch. 'Leave my mother out of it. This is between you and me.'

'Oh, yes.' Yorgos turned his attention back to his son. 'I'm still waiting for your explanation of what you were doing on your uncle's boat last July eleventh.'

Defiantly Nikos met his father's glare. So what if he knew everything? He would never kowtow to this man again. If worse came to worst, he would leave home and go underground. Others had done it, and so could he. 'I will tell you nothing.'

'A little time in the prison may change your mind.' Yorgos could feel the blood pounding in his head. 'Perhaps you and your uncle can share a cell.'

'You wouldn't dare!' Marika had been doing her best to maintain the rapprochement with her husband, but now her frayed nerves snapped. 'Even you would not do that to your own son.'

'Wouldn't I?' Yorgos' eyes narrowed, and his hand stole up to the scar on his cheek as he, too, slipped back into the adversary role he had sharpened for years. *Your own son*, she had said. Always he had tried to forget his old suspicion that Nikos was not his but his brother's. But still the gnawing doubt – or was it a certainty? – remained. If he had had other sons, good boys a real man could be proud of, he would have no compunctions about cutting this one out of his life and his heart. But Nikos was the only son God and this wife had given him. Even though he seemed to be turning out all wrong, a bad son was better than no son at all. And yet . . . as he stared at Nikos once again he reflected that this boy was more like his brother than himself. They had the same green eyes, the same love of music, and apparently the same radical politics. Nikos seemed bent on marrying a foreigner, too. At that reminder, Yorgos' blood rose. 'And another thing. You will never see that little whore of yours again.'

Nikos raged back at his father. 'She's not a whore!'

'I said,' Yorgos repeated as once again he slammed his fist on the table, 'that you will never see that little whore again!'

'Careful,' Nikos warned, 'how you talk about the woman I am going to marry.'

'Niko! Yorgo!' For so many years Marika had fanned the animosity between these two, but now she had to stop this before it went too far. 'Stop it, both of you. How can you carry on like this today, with my poor mother not even cold in her grave?'

As though she hadn't spoken, relentlessly Yorgos continued. 'Marry?' He barked a sort of laugh. 'That will never happen. *Poteh*. I'll see to it. One way or another.'

Nikos did not hide his feelings as he met the eyes of the man he despised. 'Over my dead body.'

'That too,' Yorgos retorted, the hot words coming out of his mouth before he could stop them, 'can be arranged.'

411

In the silence that followed, Marika crossed herself. But before she could fly to her son's defence, Nikos rose and stalked out of the room. They could hear his steps on the stairs, and then his calling Liberty. A moment later, a car pulled away.

'He'll be back,' Yorgos said, as much to reassure himself as Marika. He had not meant to say what he had said, but the boy had defied him and had to be taught a lesson. Still, he was shaken. 'As soon as he comes to his senses, he'll be back.'

Marika held her head in her hands. First her mother, then Vangelis, and now Nikos. Was she to lose everyone she loved? Slowly she raised her head until her burning eyes met her husband's. 'I'm warning you. Leave *my* son alone. It's time I told – ' Just in time she caught herself. Almost she had blurted out the old secret.

Yorgos' hand shook as he lit a cigarette. *My* son, she had said. Was what he had always suspected true, then? Had he been raising Christos' son as his own?

Slowly his index finger ran down the scar on his cheek as he inhaled and watched her leave the room with the bowed and hesitant step of the old woman they had just laid to rest on the mountain. Again, Christos! How could it be, that all his life was shadowed by his brother? Time and again, he had thought him vanquished. And yet, even though he had not seen Christos for many years, still his ghost haunted his marriage. He had raised the other's son as his own. He had loved him, nurtured him, staked his dreams upon him.

And yet perhaps now, Yorgos reflected, Nikos was as dead to him as the ashes of his cigarette. With his heel he ground it out on the floor.

Sixteen

On a Friday evening two weeks later, Liberty and Nikos were getting ready to leave her apartment for an important Resistance meeting in Thessaloniki when a knock came at the door.

They froze and exchanged a nervous glance. Since the evening when Nikos had stormed away from the village, mostly they had avoided being together here until late at night when they fancied the chances of being observed were lessened. Once or twice they had thought they were being followed. She had wondered about a man she had spotted hanging around her *frontistirio*, and he had taken note of a pair of burly fellows who got on and off buses right behind him. Liberty's roommates, too, before they left for a long skiing weekend up in the north, had reported that old Yangos, the crippled Civil War veteran at the local kiosk, had confided that strangers had been around asking questions about the foreign girls who lived on the next street. But Liberty and Nikos had tried to laugh away their fears. Surely, they had reasoned, the colonel wouldn't turn his own son's fate over to the military police. And, to their knowledge, no one in Athens except Nikos' mother and a very few stalwart members of the Greek Resistance knew about the sensational piece Liberty was working on for the BBC. There was no reason to panic. They were being paranoid, that's all. And yet neither of them wanted to answer the door.

'Your motorbike?' She moistened her dry lips with her tongue. 'You didn't park it outside?'

Nikos lifted his eyebrows in a definite negative. 'I left it near Patission and took the bus here.' When he hadn't been sleeping at Liberty's, he had been bedding down at a succession of his friends' houses. Although he had telephoned his mother almost every day, he had not been home for a fortnight. 'Maybe it's your landlord, or the plumber coming to fix the toilet. It's been broken for weeks.' But it was ten o'clock, late for even an Athenian plumber's housecall.

'Maybe it's just the driver.' They were riding north through the night to Thessaloniki. But they didn't expect the courier for another hour.

Again the knock sounded, this time more insistently. Nikos stood close behind her as Liberty turned the key which these days she always kept in the door just for an added sense of security. She didn't trust her sneak of a landlord. If the police had been around asking questions, gladly he would have opened the door and led the search of her rooms himself. At least with the key in the door, he couldn't get in when she was home.

Cautiously she opened the door. A slim dark youth in blue jeans and leather jacket stood waiting. He looked enough like Nikos to be his brother.

'Aleko!' Nikos welcomed the comrade he had known since his first year at the polytechnic. '*Ela mesi*, come inside.' He had his arm on his friend's shoulder. 'This is Liberty. I told you about her.'

Alekos touched her outstretched hand in the usual glancing Greek hand-shake, and then his eyes darted around the foreign girl's *saloni*. 'It is safe to talk here?'

Nikos shrugged. 'As safe as anywhere.'

'The radio,' Alekos said, 'turn it on.' As the whine of bouzouki music

413

blasted, they sat down and lit the obligatory cigarettes. Then Alekos explained there had been a change of plans. He and Liberty would leave for Thessaloniki, but Nikos must stay in Athens.

Nikos frowned. 'What for?'

Alekos grinned. 'I think it may have something to do with your songs.'

'Niko, that's wonderful!' Liberty beamed at him.

'My songs?' Nikos had been strumming his guitar for years but lately he had tried his hand writing folk songs against the dictatorship. But he had only sung them for Liberty and a few friends including one fellow who had recorded some of his favourites on a beat-up cassette player. 'How do they know about that?'

Alekos' smile widened. 'May I remind you that this is Greece. Here everyone knows about everything.' He meant it lightly, but all three looked to the door and the windows. Alekos consulted his watch. 'We'd better go. It's a long way to Thessaloniki.' He rose 'I'll take you to Omonia, Niko. Someone will meet you there. Then tomorrow morning you'll come up to Thessaloniki in another carload of our people.'

'I don't know.' Nikos looked at Liberty. With things as they were, he hated to be separated from her for even a night. Two days ago his Uncle Vangelis had finally been released from the prison, and according to his mother Yorgos had personally escorted him straight to the airport. He and Vasso must be in Australia by now. But his mother reported that the colonel was still in a towering rage, and that most of his fury was directed at Nikos and Liberty. 'Maybe you should wait and drive up with me.'

'Absolutely not. I can't miss what might happen up there.' Politicians and intellectuals who had been living underground would be making their way to Greece's second city for this meeting. It was even possible that some exiles would be filtering back over the border to make contact with their brethren. If she waited until the morning to drive up with Nikos, she might lose some important interviews. 'Really, Niko, don't worry about me.' With a pang, she wondered if Nikos wouldn't be at greater risk here in Athens, where even the highest levels of the Resistance sometimes were infiltrated by police informers and spies. Was this musical rendezvous of his a set-up? But Niko trusted this Alekos. She supposed she was only being paranoid again.

Alekos laughed. 'I always take good care of all the pretty girls.'

'That's what I'm afraid of.' Nikos laughed, too, as though the only worry he had was losing Liberty to his old friend.

'So it's settled.' Alekos made for the door. '*Pame*.'

'I'll just be a second.' Liberty went to her bedroom. As she turned to come back with her case, Nikos rushed in and took her in his arms. Ardently he kissed her. As always, the touch of him drove everything else from her mind. She dropped her bag and flung her arms around his neck. They kissed as though for the first time. And then they kissed as though they were going to fall down on the bed and make love all night long.

'Nikos!' Impatiently Alekos called from the sitting room.

'Oh, God,' Nikos groaned as his hands travelled down the length of her and pressed her closer to him. They had spent all afternoon in bed, and yet he wanted her again. His voice was husky. 'Stay tonight.' Was it his imagination or was there real danger in the air tonight? 'I'll come back after my meeting, and we'll go up together tomorrow.'

But gently Liberty pulled a little away from his embrace. One of them had to have some self-control. 'Tomorrow,' she whispered. 'We can be together tomorrow. I've never had you in Thessaloniki.'

'I want to have you here, there, everywhere.' Passionately he kissed her lips, her eyes, her nose, her lips again. 'I want to take you everywhere, have you in every bed in the world. That's what we'll do for our honeymoon, go all around the world, yes?'

'Oh yes!' She laughed and reached up and tousled his hair. 'But first we have a dictatorship to overthrow.'

'Niko!' Again Alekos called out.

'I love you,' Nikos told her again.

'And I love you. More than anything. More than life, death, anything!'

They kissed one more time, and then arm-in-arm they walked out of the bedroom and followed Alekos down the staircase to the car. They were all silent as they drove toward the centre of the city, and when they arrived in the crowded square Alekos told him his contact would be waiting in the underground station near the Pro-po lottery vendor. He would be tall, with dark hair and a moustache, and carrying a Longman English proficiency textbook.

Nikos had the door open while Alekos waited for the traffic light to flash green. He leaned forward and for an instant touched Liberty's hair softly, very softly. 'Until tomorrow.'

'*Avrio*,' she echoed, and from the window she blew him a kiss. But just then a foreboding struck her. She would never see him again. 'Niko!'

But he had already disappeared down the escalator to the underground.

'Something wrong?' Alekos' eyes were kindly.

'Just nerves, I guess.' But still she stared out the window. Should she go or stay?

The light changed, and Alekos screeched away from Omonia Square.

*

The old guy with the cracked leather face was arguing with two young men in jeans and sweatshirts when Nikos finally walked in the door of the dingy two-room apartment on a grimy back alley in a working-class neighbourhood not far from the quarter where he had grown up. It was half-past midnight, and as the three men fought on with raised voices, they nibbled on *souvlaki pitta* takeaway spread over the kitchen table on the same greasy paper bags it had been wrapped in at the shop.

Abruptly they all fell silent as they stared suspiciously at the young stranger. But then Nikos' courier followed him into the room. 'Ah, Ari!' The old man grinned. 'You had us worried, *paidi mou*. You should have been here an hour ago.'

'Can't be too careful,' Aris said. From Omonia, he and Nikos had hopped the underground to Piraeus, then taken the long bus ride in heavy traffic back to Monasteraki. From there, they had climbed on another bus toward Metz, where Ari had left his motorbike. Just to be sure no one was following, he had woven through the back streets of Pangrati before finally making a beeline to this safehouse in Kaseriani.

The old man grunted. 'That's what I was trying to tell the boys here. But they think they know everything. Youth! I remember, back in the Civil War ...' He broke off his reminiscence and turned his attention back to Nikos. 'And this, I presume, is our very own Greek Bob Dylan.'

Nikos flushed. When they were cruising the streets on the motorbike and he was certain no one could be eavesdropping, Aris had told him why the urgent summons and tight security. Resistance leaders had heard a home-made tape of Nikos' songs, and they were considering using them to galvanize Greeks to throw off the yoke of the tyrants. But first an old leftist the colonels had been trying to catch for years insisted on hearing Nikos perform. Riding through the darkened streets, Nikos had tried to control his growing excitement. He could do it, he knew he could! In Greece the power of music was perhaps stronger than mere lying words. And now here was this man comparing him to Bob Dylan! 'I'm Nikos Kronos.'

'I know. And you can just call me Takis.' He raised his shaggy white eyebrows at Aris. 'You filled him in?' When the courier nodded Takis picked up another *souvlaki* sandwich, belatedly offered some to the newcomers, then pointed to a guitar leaning against the wall. 'So let's hear if your songs are as good in the flesh as they were on that tape.'

Nikos picked up the guitar, draped himself over a wooden chair, and strummed a moment to get the feel of the instrument. Hesitantly at first but then with elan, he played a catchy foot-tapping tune whose lyrics lampooned the dictatorship.

When he finished, Takis lit a cigarette. 'Another!'

Nikos grinned. Takis and the others were as spellbound as Liberty always was when he played. He settled into his chair and his music. He delivered one of his favourites, a sad song with a haunting melody about a defiant young man who refused to break even in the torture chambers of Averof prison.

When he had strummed the last chord, Takis looked reflective. 'You know, I heard a voice and music like that once, long ago, when I was with the *andartes* in a camp high in the Peloponnese.' He shook his head as though he were seeing old ghosts. 'Are you by any chance related to one of my old comrades? Don't know his real name. But we always called him Captain Prometheus.'

Nikos' head jerked up from the guitar. 'He was – is – my uncle. Christos Kronos.'

'Your uncle!' Takis regarded him more closely. 'Looked just like you, as I recall. Quite a resemblance. Well, well . . . Captain Prometheus' nephew!'

Nothing would do, then, as Takis reached for the Metaxa and poured stiff measures for himself and the boys, but for Nikos to recount a little of Christos' life since he had gone into exile in America.

'Ah!' Takis exclaimed when he heard of his comrade's political misadventures. 'It was one disaster after another with so many who left Mother Greece. Your uncle should never have gone away like that. He should have stayed and fought like we did, like we are still doing. Even, or maybe especially,' Takis said, 'those who went *exo* to the Soviet Union and the Eastern Bloc had not fared much better than those who had fled to America, Europe, or Australia. But *ti na kanoume*? What can we do?' Takis' dark face grew even darker and sadder. 'And still we need them here. Still we miss them here.' He raised his glass. 'To Captain Prometheus! And to his heir, our Nikos!'

As the old leftist kept pouring, he told Nikos what was required of him. He must make tapes of Resistance songs so they could be scattered the length and breadth of the country. They would record the music in the basement of a comrade's house here in Athens and duplicate them at another trusted worker's home in Patras. In a month, six weeks at most, Nikos' songs would be playing behind every locked door in Greece.

But in the meantime, Takis warned him, he must lie low and do nothing to excite the attention of the authorities. Nikos was more valuable to them as a musician than a messenger. Instead of going up to the Thessaloniki conference, he must stay in Athens and do nothing to attract the attention of the military police. He would have to continue his classes at the polytechnic and even patch up what he claimed was his irreconcilable rift with his father.

417

Nikos balked at that final directive. 'I can't do it.' He never even thought of his mother's husband as his father any more, just 'the colonel'.

But just then, outside there were running steps, shouts, a banging on the door.

They all froze. Then Takis went for his gun. The leader waved a pistol that looked even older than he was. 'You said you weren't followed.' His accusation to Aris was as fast as a bullet.

Then a key turned in the door. As Takis took aim, a little girl poked in her head. 'Ari, mama says to come home. Our father's drunk again, and you have to help her put him to bed.'

Takis and the boys laughed as sheepishly Aris bid them goodnight and hastened to follow his mother's orders.

The old leftist yawned and looked at his watch. 'It's late, and we'll have to get out of here at first light.' He turned to Nikos. 'You bed down here, too. We'll get started on these tapes first thing tomorrow. And I don't want to hear another word about how you can't pretend to get along with your father. We're at war, boy, and this is an order!'

'All right . . .' Reluctantly Nikos agreed to try to gull the colonel into a false sense of security.

In a spirit of exhausted comradeship, Nikos rolled up in a blanket and stretched out on the floor with the others. How happy he felt, lying on the hard, honest wooden planks! What an idiot he had been, nursing a sense of impending danger back at Liberty's apartment! He just wished she'd been here to be a part of all this. She would have been so proud of him. Always she said he sang like a angel. Nikos thought of his love, safe with Alekos. By now they should be over halfway to Thessaloniki.

Nikos stretched out his arms as though Liberty were lying in his embrace.

Liberty was the last in the car to notice the monster truck bearing down on them.

In the back seat, next to a kinky-haired girl who had ignored her since Alekos had picked up her and that other fellow, Liberty yawned as she tuned out the voices nattering on in rapid-fire Greek. Again she wished Alekos hadn't stopped in that rundown western Athenian district for this girl and that Vasilis, sitting in the place of manly honour in the front. She and Alekos could have passed the time in comradely conversation, but instead Liberty had whiled away the hours dreaming of Nikos. In her mind she had replayed those erotic stolen moments in her bedroom while Alekos had been urging them to be gone. Remembering, her lips had felt bruised. She had reached up a finger and shuddered as she ran it over her lips. What did she love about

418

him the most, she had wondered, how he made her feel when he touched her or how she admired the political fire and creative zest of him? He was all sweet music, that man, soft and hot and hard and pulsating, all at once.

Liberty had nodded off to sleep soon after their old white Fiat had hit the wide toll highway of the National Road a little north of Athens, and she hadn't woken until three hours later when Alekos stopped at an all-night café near Lamia. Inside, she had ordered a double Greek coffee, determined to stay awake for the final four or five hours of the drive along the mostly empty highway. At the wooden table she had studied her companions. There was nothing special about the haughty girl called Nasia. At rush hour every Athenian trolley had a pack of young women just like her hanging from the straps, most of them carrying armfuls of books. Liberty had guessed she must be a university student, although to be invited to this conference apparently she filled a key role in the Resistance. The other had the self-important air of one accustomed to being the centre of whatever group he deigned to grace with his presence. He was balding, plump, and his round pink hands had never done the manual toil of a factory worker. Possibly he was a lawyer or politician, maybe even one of those who had been living a hunted life underground until he could slip over the border to safety. Still, by the looks of him, Liberty had thought he hadn't been suffering overmuch. As the coffees arrived, he had caught Liberty staring.

In perfect English, Vasilis had addressed her. 'Alekos says you work for the BBC. But I said no, you look like you're still in school.'

Annoyed, Liberty had flicked the ash of her cigarette in what she had hoped was a worldly gesture. 'Actually, I'm a stringer. At least for now, I just do occasional pieces.' She had patted her handbag which held her miniature cassette recorder. 'For the radio. The World Service.'

'I see.' Vasilis had cleared his throat. 'And what are you planning on doing up north?'

Liberty had shrugged like a Greek. 'It depends.' She did not much like this man who had not bothered to speak to her until he had a glimering that she might be able to help bolster his reputation. She had met publicity hounds like him in London as well as in Greece. Given the chance, she suspected Vasilis wouldn't be much different from Nikos' ruthless father.

Again she had remembered cynical political conversations with weary Athenian intellectuals who despaired that, human nature being as it was and politicians being as they were, things wouldn't be any different here even with a change of government. Some even went so far as to say that only second-raters went into politics, while the best and brightest went where the big money was, in shipping or tourism. At least, they would add, the *junta* manages to keep the country from chaos. Liberty had once assumed that in this country, which had midwifed democracy long ago, those ideals which had inspired all the world would still burn brightly. Instead, those who bothered to think much about these issues were so jaded that next to them often she felt herself a naive and simple-minded child.

As she had looked across the table at Vasilis, she had wondered why she always argued so passionately against political cynicism. If the alternative to the military dictatorship was a government comprised of fatcat hacks like this one, maybe Nikos and his friends – and herself, too – were fools to risk their lives as they did. But it was the middle of the night, she was still half-asleep, and so she had told herself she was being unfair to this man who was taking the same chances as everyone else in the Resistance. Yet still she had wondered what, besides love, had made her get over her head in a struggle whose currents she sometimes doubted she would ever understand. She had arrived here convinced the colonels were the villains and the resisters the heroes, but familiarity with the Greeks had taught her that reality was not so black and white. The dictatorship remained popular with ordinary folk who wanted little from their government except to be left alone to raise their families and make their money. Along with the hardcore left and university students, it was mostly those in the liberal professions who had suffered from the *junta*'s crackdown on personal liberties and individual expression. Too, as she had delved deeper into the Resistance, she had been appalled by the petty rivalries and deadly in-fighting of these men and women she had so admired from afar. Nikos and his idealistic young friends were cut from a different cloth than oily demagogues like this Vasilis, but unfortunately the leadership was more like this middle-aged lawyer than Nikos and his arty friends. Soberly she had drained her coffee to the bitter dregs. She had made her choices, and she would hold fast to the belief that they were the right ones.

Back in the car, moodily she had smoked in the darkness. Once in the summer she and Nikos had driven this way in a friend's borrowed car. The landscape here was rolling farmland, not steep mountain gorges like so much of the Greek terrain. Still, like virtually everywhere she had been in this country, the land they were crossing was very beautiful. When she and Nikos had passed Mount Olympus, they had vowed to climb it after the summer heat had passed. But in this autumn of surreptitious meetings, there had been no time for the heights of Olympus. Maybe they would finally do it in the spring, perhaps in May when the mountains were carpeted with wildflowers. Dreamily she had stared into the night.

More than an hour later, as they approached Larissa, even Alekos had seemed to tire of conversation. He had turned on the radio and speeded up as the bouzouki sound swelled in the car. Nasia had cracked a smile and sung

420

along, and even Vasilis had tapped his heavy gold signet ring in time to the music.

To herself, Liberty had sung the words Nikos had taught her. She had supposed, by then, that he had discovered what his mysterious meeting in Athens was all about. Recalling her premonition back at Omonia, again she had worried for her lover. To drown out her fears, she had raised her voice in Nikos' song.

Nasia had swivelled her head. 'You know this?'

So she, too, spoke English! Liberty had sung louder in answer. Nasia had grinned and begun belting out the words. Alekos had joined in, and even Vasilis had sung off-key. Shooting down the highway, for the first time since Athens, Liberty had felt at one with these Greeks who, dissimilar as they were, were all fighting the good fight. On her lips the lyrical Greek words had felt like a caress. She had loved this country, these people, and this moment. It was, she had reflected, so very Greek to love the moment, to forget all else but the here and now.

A sense of peace had settled over her as she gazed out the window at the grey sky shot with pale silver light that, even as she watched, the alchemy of sunrise was turning to gold. It was going to be such a glorious morning. Twisting around and craning her neck, she had just been able to make out the peak of Olympus towering in the sky. It was early November, and the crest of the mountain had been capped in a shimmer of snow. How easy it must have been for the ancients to believe the gods lived there on the heights. Never could she leave the place she had found here in the sun.

But sharply then the highway had changed. For the last few monotonous hours, the National Road had been a flat straight asphalt ribbon. But here it narrowed to snake through the mountains to the coast. Alekos had taken a bend too fast and had slammed on the brakes. Good thing, Liberty had thought as the car careened almost to the edge of a precipice, that nothing had been coming on the other side.

But Alekos had hunched over the steering wheel as he reached out and snapped off the radio. In the sudden silence, tensely he had asked Vasilis to light him a cigarette. The others had looked attentively at the driver and then the road ahead. All the way from Athens, Alekos had been lighting his own cigarettes and driving with one careless hand. Why the caution now?

From behind them came a piercing light. The beams were high, too high for a car. Liberty looked round at the huge truck which was gaining on them too fast for the twisting road. Nasia turned too, and then Vasilis looked and winced.

'No problem,' Alekos said. But he stubbed out his newly-lit cigarette and held tightly to the steering wheel with his white-knuckled hands.

421

'Is that the same one?' Vasilis asked.

Alekos nodded. 'The same number plates. Greek.' Except for worried glances in his rear view mirror, he did not take his eyes off the road.

Again Liberty looked around at the lorry. She had not quite been able to follow their Greek. 'What are you talking about?'

'Oh, nothing.' Alekos managed a grin.

But Nasia answered. 'That truck pulled on the road behind us after we stopped for coffee. He's been following us ever since. Sometimes a few kilometres back, sometimes closer. But never as close as this.'

Smoke hung heavy in the car as the three anxious passengers lit cigarettes.

'Well, then.' Vasilis bent over, clicked open his case, and began leafing through a file of papers. Calmly he extracted a handful, passed half of them back to Nasia, and flicked open his gold-plated lighter. He lit the bottom corner of the papers. As they slowly burned, Nasia set hers afire as well. When all that was left was a blank upper margin, the two of them blew out the flames and tossed what was left out the window. Liberty shut her eyes and fought her rising panic. What she was thinking couldn't be true. Vasilis and Nasia were being melodramatic. The Greeks were always blowing everything out of proportion. Perhaps they were even playing a joke on her to break up the boredom of this trip; yes, that was it, they were just trying to scare her.

But this was no joke, she thought, as in terror she clutched onto her seat. Alekos was keeping a steady pace, but he had to brake when the road began a convoluted series of arabesques. The tyres screeched as the car rounded a turn too fast. Except for the lorry, the road was deserted.

'Maybe you should pull over as soon as you have a chance,' Liberty worried out loud. 'That way he can pass us, if he's in such a big hurry.'

No one bothered to answer her. Four nervous pairs of eyes were focused first on the bends ahead, then on the lorry barrelling toward them from behind. The truck was gaining on them.

Ahead the road dipped in a steep descent and then swung wide in an aching double-S curve. But instead of slowing down, Alekos hit the accelerator as the truck all but panted on their bumper. It hit them once; the second time it whacked them, the car swayed. Alekos hung onto the steering wheel and braked to the floor. They screeched around one bend then took another too fast. The car spun wide, almost off the road, but Alekos managed to pull it back just in time. But again, on the next curve, the truck slammed into them, this time harder. The car fishtailed on the precipice. Alekos struggled to hug the road as the car wavered on the edge. For a breathless moment it seemed he would make it again. But then the car shot clear of the road, into the clear mountain air.

'Niko!' Liberty shouted into the dawn. For an instant, as the Fiat flew straight as a jet, flashes like a strobe lit her mind. Her mother holding her brother at his christening, long ago. Her father grabbing her hand as they narrowly missed being hit by a red doubledecker bus crossing Piccadilly. Graduation day at Oxford. Recording her first piece at the BBC. Nikos and the Mask of Agamemnon. The wind in her hair on his motorbike. The harbour on Symi. His gold body. The blue water. The feel of him inside her. His eyes, his green eyes.

Then, as the car fell, she heard his grandmother's deathly shriek and saw the pillow of earth under Old Anna's head. Again, as the car plummeted to the depths, she held fast to the vision of his green eyes. 'Niko!'

Nikos gunned his motorbike engine at the traffic lights and was hardly conscious of what he was doing when he saw a break in the Athens traffic and coursed ahead before the signal changed. Home, he had to get home, the colonel would be there now, and this time there would be no holding back between the two of them. On the motorbike handlebars Nikos' hands itched to close around the colonel's neck. Almost he could feel his bull neck constricting, his breath coming in gasps, his eyes bulging. Tighter he would press, he would pay him back for all he had done. All . . .

Ahead on Alexandras Boulevard a yellow trolley was letting on a mob of commuters. Yet Nikos did not stay waiting in his lane. Recklessly as he wove past the trolley, he narrowly missed a battered van whose driver let out a screeching blast of his horn. Let him hit me, Nikos muttered to himself. What did it matter whether he lived or died, now that Liberty . . .

Oh, God, he moaned, oh God.

Again he wove around the stalled traffic, again he jumped a red light, and as he spun down the boulevard an image darkened his mind: Alekos' old Fiat careening down a mountain road, the truck behind it, the road narrowing, the car losing control, the precipice looming.

Nikos risked wiping his tears from his cheeks with the sleeve of his leather jacket as he darted the motorbike from lane to lane. He concentrated on banishing the unbearable thoughts of *that*. Automatically he turned north to Neo Psychikon. He had to get home, he had to wreak vengeance where vengeance was due. In that last confrontation down in Panagia, hadn't the colonel as good as threatened Liberty? But he never would have imagined that even *he* was capable of what had happened on the National Road in the early hours of this morning. Just as his henchman had surely killed Liberty, he would kill the one he no longer thought of as his father.

He scooted down an underpass, wove in and out of the traffic, and turned into the leafy parkland surrounding the expensive villas of Neo Psychikon. Again in his mind he heard the shattering ring of the telephone that had woken him from his sweet dreams of love and glory. Funny, he thought, how only that one urgent late morning telephone call had roused him from deep sleep. Curled up in a ball facing the wall, vaguely he had been aware of other sounds this morning – garbagemen banging and cursing, engines roaring to life, and intermittent rings of that same telephone. But perhaps a sixth sense of impending doom had made him sit straight up and listen when that one call had come from Thessaloniki. One of the boys who seemed to hang around the house had picked up the receiver and passed it wordlessly to Takis, who was already up pacing while he let the boys sleep off the Metaxa. The old leftist had listened intently, interrupting only for terse bullet questions – when, where, *are you sure*, absolutely *sure?* – before he had hung up and sunk down in a chair with his head in his hands. After a moment, then, he had looked up and found Nikos' eyes upon him. Slowly Takis had shaken his head and then beckoned Nikos to his side. 'Sit down,' he had said, 'and have a cigarette.' He had ordered one of the boys to bring them coffee, and then tenderly he had broken the news to Nikos. How there had been an 'accident' on the National Road, how there had been no survivors, how hours later the security police had burst into the Thessaloniki hideout and arrested virtually all the participants in the northern leadership conference.

Nikos drove round and round the traffic circle that was the green shady hub of Neo Psychikon. 'Liberty?' he had asked. And Takis had brought his head up in a final negative. For a moment the young man and the old one had stared into one another's eyes, and then Takis had taken Nikos into his arms and rocked him like a baby.

Nikos turned off the roundabout and headed down the road to his house. Too bad, he thought, recalling the comfort of those manly arms around him, that someone like Takis wasn't his real father. He roared up the driveway, and his teeth bared in something other than a smile when he saw the colonel's official limousine parked in front of the villa. He cut the engine and swung off the bike.

His mother, dressed head to toe in the black she would wear for the next two years for her mother, was framed in the doorway.

'You know?' he asked, for it seemed to him there was fresh grief in her black eyes.

In answer she opened her arms. '*He* told me. Oh, *paidi mou*, I am so sorry.'

Briefly Nikos endured her embrace. Another time, maybe many other times, he would enfold himself in his mother's arms and cry away his pain. But here and now he had another mission. 'Where is he?'

Her eyes darted toward the family sitting room, but before he could break away she held tight to him. 'Don't be crazy. I'm afraid, Niko. Afraid for you. My God, when I first heard, I thought you were in that car, too. You were supposed to go to Thessaloniki with her! It could have been you, Niko, you!'

'I wish it *had* been me.'

'Don't say that! And promise me you won't be crazy! Be careful, Niko! He says he had nothing to do with it, but – ' She was talking to herself. Already Nikos had lunged away to where the colonel waited.

Yorgos sat in the tufted centre of the regal gold velvet sofa as he held the telephone to his ear and listened to Captain Kostas giving him the latest bulletin about the aftermath of that 'accident' which could turn out to be an international incident.

When he had first been told of Liberty's death at work early this morning, he had been able to master his agitation only with the greatest effort. The lieutenant sent over to the tourist ministry by Brigadier Ioannides had informed him that his son's girlfriend had surely been one of the fatalities, for they had found her British passport intact in the burned wreckage of the Fiat. My poor son, Yorgos had thought, remembering the way he had seen the boy looking at her. It was a pity that one so young and pretty had to die as she had.

But then a current of dread had passed over him. What if Nikos, too, had been in that car? When Yorgos had asked for the names of the others who had died, the lieutenant had only shrugged and waved his hand as though rubbish like them were not worthy of his attention. The victims, he had finally revealed after further prompting from Yorgos, included a diabolical Athens lawyer the police had been looking for for months, another girl who hadn't yet been identified, and the young driver whose body had been damaged almost beyond recognition.

Yorgos' stomach had turned over and his blood pressure had risen at the thought that the boy might even now be lying on a slab in the Thessaloniki morgue. Whether Nikos was his son or Christos', he had raised him as his own and, despite everything, he loved him.

Still, Yorgos hadn't dared let the lieutenant guess he suspected his son might have been in that doomed car. More was at stake even than the life of his son. It had taken much of his political capital to survive the seditious behaviour of his brother-in-law, but he might have to turn in his ministry portfolio and could be posted to some God-forsaken provincial garrison if his Nikos had died in that carload of dangerous anarchists.

After the lieutenant had left, Yorgos had called in Captain Kostas to

425

make a series of surreptitious telephone calls to make certain that Nikos hadn't been in that Fiat. As always, Kostas had been solicitous and efficient. Only when he was sure Nikos hadn't been involved and was presumably still unharmed had Yorgos sunk back in his chair and taken long deep breaths to calm his rapidly beating heart. He had been so relieved that the boy hadn't died with that girlfriend of his. But also, as he sat massaging his aching chest, he had resented being put through all this anxiety. He had forbidden Nikos ever to see that girl again, and yet, according to the surveillance reports Brigadier Ioannides had been supplying, they had all but been living together since he left the village in a huff.

He took a sip of sweet Greek coffee. At mid-morning, when Marika telephoned to see if he would be home for lunch, he had broken the news of Liberty's death but assured her that Nikos had apparently been nowhere near the accident.

She had caught her breath and let it out in a hiss: 'You did it, you did *that*?'

It had taken Yorgos an instant to understand her meaning and longer than that to deny her preposterous insinuation. Maybe it was true that the military police had arranged the 'accident'. It wouldn't be the first time political assassination was carried out on the slaughterhouse of the country's roads. But Yorgos had little or nothing to do with the military police. At Council of Minister meetings he heard the Brigadier's reports, and from time to time he rang him for a favour like investigating his son's foreign girlfriend. But military intelligence was no more his bailiwick than the agriculture or education ministries.

Yorgos had tried to talk sweet reason with his wife. OK, he had admitted, there had been no love lost between him and that girl. And yes, he had threatened to have her removed from Greece. But all he had meant was having her deported on a technicality such as not having her residence or working permits. Or, if her papers were in order, it could have been arranged for small quantities of hashish to be found in her apartment. But he hadn't ordered her murder. Even if he had that power, he would never do a thing like that.

Still, he had told his wife, he could not pretend that he wasn't glad she was no longer a threat to his career and his household. She had had no business meddling in not only the affairs of another country but also the pulsebeat of his own family. But fate had dealt with that girl.

To himself he had added that *moira*, in conjunction with Brigadier Ioannides' minions, had saved him the trouble of getting rid of her himself.

And yet, as Marika had continued to hurl accusations at him, Yorgos' head had started to pound with fury. How could she believe that he had connived to have the girl killed? 'What do you think,' he had screamed into the telephone. 'That I'm a psychopath?'

She had hung up the phone in answer.

Yorgos lit another cigarette. After that, matters had gone from bad to worse. Someone in the Brigadier's office, rereading the file on Liberty Penn-Nevard, had noticed that, although she wasn't accredited by the press ministry, she was a stringer for the BBC. Ioannides himself had immediately telephoned Yorgos for details, he had been forced to ring back Marika, and Yorgos' head had begun to pulsate with worry when she had informed him that at the time of the accident Nikos' fiancée had been working on a piece about the Resistance. The last thing the *junta* needed was the blood of a BBC reporter on their hands.

Yorgos' next series of phone calls had left him red-faced and shaken. Ioannides had screamed on the telephone. Papadopoulos himself had been cold as ice. Yorgos had told them everything he knew about the girl and promised to inform military intelligence the moment he had any inkling of his son's whereabouts. Before the international media got wind of this story, the *junta* wanted to guarantee the silence of everyone involved.

'I'll call you back, Kosta, the moment he gets here.' Yorgos had heard the motorbike in the driveway, but he wanted a few moments alone with his son before he summoned the authorities.

He hung up the phone, stubbed out his cigarette, and rubbed his aching temples as he readied himself for the confrontation. He had been certain that Nikos would come home. At a time like this, of course he would want to be with his adoring mother.

A flash of jealousy shot through Yorgos at the thought of his wife and the one he had always treated as his son. Thick as thieves, those two had always been. They had always had their heads together, and he didn't doubt they had been plotting against him for years. Well, this time they had done a job not only on him but themselves. He had no choice but to turn in his own son. And, unless he was sadly mistaken, his wife, too, would go to jail if she dared to write a word about this. Last but not least, he was sure that his own days of power in the government were numbered. And all for that damned girl!

As Nikos stormed in, Yorgos carefully set the cup down on the copper tray resting on the heavy marble coffee table. He opened his mouth to give Nikos the tongue-lashing of his life, but the look on the boy's face silenced him. Nikos' eyes were dark pits. Recalling again how the young lovers had looked at one another, the colonel's eyes fell.

427

'You killed her,' Nikos said, his voice deadly quiet. He clenched and unclenched his hands in fists. 'You killed Liberty.'

Yorgos looked up. 'What?' In all the hysteria about the possible repercussions of the dead girl being a BBC reporter, he had almost forgotten his wife's bitter accusations about his role in the death.

'Come *on*. You *know*. The so-called accident. The National Road. The truck. You said you'd get rid of her, and you did.'

The colonel coolly took a puff of his cigarette as he collected himself. 'Ah, the accident. I heard of it on the radio.' He shook his head. 'That part of the highway, as I recall, is most treacherous. And in the early morning hours, perhaps there was fog.'

'There was treachery, all right. But it had nothing to do with the weather.' Nikos advanced on the colonel. 'You did it. You!'

'I had nothing to do with it.' If things had been different between them, he might have hinted that others in the regime had engineered the accident. He might even have told the whole truth, that Ioannides had been after that lawyer. No one had even known Liberty was in that car. But if he said one word about all that to Nikos, he might read all about it in tomorrow's *New York Times*. He could see that it would get him nowhere to try to talk sense to his son. He reached for the telephone to summon the military police.

But just then Marika rushed in and stood between her husband and her son, unsure whether to join in the attack or do her best to defuse the confrontation. For years she had fanned the rift between these two, always hoping that one day Nikos would be strong enough to vanquish Yorgos. But now she wished she had left Nikos out of her marriage wars. He was still too young to fight and win. Yorgos could crush him just as he had Liberty. She put a restraining hand on her son's shoulder.

'Stay out of this, mama.' Nikos brushed her hand away.

'Yes, go!' The colonel snapped his fingers at his wife. A fine family they were, so eager to believe that he had ordered that girl's murder. He could feel his blood rising. After all he had done for both of them, this was how they repaid him? Don't get excited, he told himself. The doctors said not to let yourself get out of control.

Yet as he looked at this woman who had never loved him, never honoured him, and most certainly had never obeyed him, his face reddened and his breath came in shallow pants. Had she been pregnant with his brother's child when she married him? And did she, even now, still yearn for Christos? A pain shot through his chest.

He dared to snap his fingers at her like a servant? Marika rounded on her husband and shrieked. 'He's right! You killed that poor girl!'

Yorgos lifted his eyebrows in a nonchalant denial, picked up the telephone,

428

and dialled Kostas' number. When the captain answered, he merely said the code words that meant his son was at the villa. 'I'll be working at home tonight. You can send the reports over now.' He hung up the phone and smugly turned his attention back to his son.

'And now,' Nikos said as he towered over the colonel, 'you're going to have to answer to *me*.' But before he let his hands close around the other's throat, he had more to say. 'You and your kind, we've all had enough of you. It's started already, the Resistance, and it's growing every minute. Soon – tomorrow, after tomorrow, but soon! – you're going to get what you deserve. And I can promise you there will be no mercy! We'll do to you exactly what you did to Liberty!'

'Mad,' Yorgos muttered with difficulty, for in his mouth his tongue felt thick, so thick, 'you're mad.' Stay calm, he warned himself.

'No, I'm saner than I've ever been in my life.' Nikos' voice had fallen to a whisper. 'For years I've watched everything you've done not only to our country but here in the family.' He jerked his thumb toward his mother. 'How you've treated her.' Nikos eyes softened as he looked at his mother. 'I don't know how you've endured it.'

'Niko! Enough, that's enough! None of this will bring Liberty back.' Again desperately she clutched at her son's shoulder. Then she pleaded with her husband. 'Please, Yorgo, don't pay any attention. He's upset, that's all. The girl! You know, he's not himself – '

'Oh, I'm myself, all right. Never more.' Gently, once again, Nikos disengaged himself from his mother's restraining touch. 'Now, go away, mama. This is between him and me.'

'Niko!' she cried, 'stop *now*!'

But he had turned back to the colonel. 'I despise you. I always have, ever since I was a little boy. I used to look at you and wonder how God could have cursed me with a father like you.'

'You little bastard . . .' Yorgos tried to struggle to his feet. He was head of this family, and he had to put these two in their places. But his legs buckled, and as he sank back on the sofa his breathing was ragged.

With difficulty he focused on the boy. For a moment Christos' face swam before him, and when he looked harder at Nikos it was Christos he once again faced. The two of them were at the snowy crest of that mountain, they were struggling with the knife, Christos had him pinned down, and yet those green eyes – Christos' eyes? Nikos' eyes? – had been blazing with contempt as he held back the fatal blow.

Yorgos reached up and waved his hand before his eyes to cast off that memory. But, strangely, his vision clouded over. Everything was going dark, his chest hurt, the shadows were closing in. With a great wrenching effort he managed to hold back the darkness. Yet as he glared at Nikos and saw that same blazing contempt in those same green eyes, his certainty grew that this boy was the son of his brother. Even now, more than twenty years since Christos had slunk away from Greece, not only his spirit but his true flesh and blood were still here to haunt him.

He swung his glance to Marika, the font of all his troubles. She had betrayed him with his brother, and then she had betrayed him a hundred times over by deceiving him with his brother's bastard. And now, after all these years, this mother and son who hated him so stood in league against him.

'How dare you,' he tried to mutter, but the words came out garbled. To himself he raged on. How dare they accuse him of engineering that accident! He wasn't sorry that girl was dead, and the other traitors deserved exactly what they had gotten. But he had had nothing to do with it, nothing . . . he shook his head once, twice, but again everything was swimming before his eyes.

Nikos put his hands out and reached down for the colonel's neck. But just as he was about to close in for a choking hold, Yorgos let out with a gasp and reeled head first onto the marble coffee table. He lay there without moving.

For an instant Nikos and Marika stood frozen in place, and then wordlessly they looked at one another.

'His heart?' she said finally.

'He has no heart.' Nikos was not to be turned aside by a pretended seizure. But when he reached out and touched the prone body, Yorgos did not respond.

Gingerly Marika crouched down and took Yorgos' wrist in her hand. Was he dead? She felt for the pulse. 'He's still alive.' She looked up at her son. 'But I think he's had a stroke or a heart attack.' She let go of the limp wrist. 'I'll call the doctor.'

'Why?' Still the rage boiled inside Nikos. Had the colonel and his kind shown any compassion for their victims? 'Just let him be.'

'Niko! Of course I have to call a doctor.' Remembering how tenderly he had eased her mother's passing, she reached for the telephone.

'It's probably just another of his tricks. In a minute he'll sit up and laugh at us.' But as Nikos uncertainly stared down at the inert body of the colonel, shame flooded his face. A moment ago he had been as heartless as those he was pledged to fight against. He sank down on the sofa and brought up his hands to cover his face.

Marika leafed through a book looking for the doctor's number. When she found it, hurriedly she dialled and exchanged a few urgent words. 'An ambulance, yes, send one at once.'

As soon as she hung up, she eased Yorgos back on the sofa and loosened the neck of his shirt. Then she sat down next to Nikos and took his hands in hers. 'You'll have to go into hiding. Right away, before the doctor and the ambulance even get here. *They'll* really be out to get you now. I know you don't believe this, but *he* did his best to protect you. But now . . .' She looked back at her husband and took a deep breath. 'Even if he lives, I think you might have to leave Greece.'

Nikos' eyes blazed. 'Never.'

Her talon hold on his hands tightened. 'It's not safe for you here any more.'

'Safe? You remember that old Cretan slogan in their uprisings against the Turks. Kazantzakis used it for the title of his best book. *Freedom or death*! What do I care now if they kill me? Others have died. *She* did.' His voice broke. 'Do I love my country any less than she did?'

Looking into those green eyes which were so like his father's, Marika faltered. Once she had seen that same look on Christos' face. First the father, and now the son. Her woman's heart ached. Men, deluded with their stubborn selfish dreams of glory! Why wouldn't they understand that all that mattered was love and family and living a decent life? In the end, what had Christos' dedication to politics come to? He was eking out his exile life in his father's restaurant. But she had wanted so much more for her son.

Under her breath she sighed. A good life was not necessarily a safe life. Never had she loved her son more than at this moment, and never had she been more proud of him. 'At least take some of the money Nick left for emergencies.'

'I don't need dollars where I'm going.' He stood. 'But you're right about one thing. I can't wait here for them to come for me.' He held out his arms, and when she threw herself into them they held each other tight. He stroked her hair and she clung onto him for dear life. But then he pulled back and held her at arm's length. 'I'll telephone when I can.'

When she heard the motorbike engine catch, she bit her lip so hard it bled. She was still standing alone in her mourning black, above the unmoving body of her husband, when the military police beat the ambulance to the villa.

431

Seventeen

Tensely Marika crouched by the radio, listening to the students at the Athens Polytechnic call the nation to stand up and be counted against the dictatorship. 'Down with Papadopoulos! Down with the *junta*! Tonight will be the end of them! Fascism will end tonight! Education, freedom, bread! Down with the dictatorship!' Through the heavy static of the pirate shortwave station the students had begun transmitting on two nights ago, she listened to the exact timbre of the reedy voice that crackled with excitement. No, that wasn't Nikos on the radio. Relief flooded her, but a moment later she hunched even closer to the radio. Of course Nikos wouldn't be sitting at a desk speaking into a microphone. Her son would be one of the leaders who delegated that task. But she was sure he was at the core of the student occupation of the polytechnic. He had been enrolled there for the past six years, although he had stopped attending classes a month ago when he went underground after Liberty's death and his father's stroke. But she was certain he would have surfaced to join the sit-in at the first scent of trouble on his own turf.

Listening to the broadcast, she tried to imagine what her son must be doing at this very moment: arguing strategy in a leadership meeting, pacing the roof to see if the police and the army were ringing the school yet, shouting slogans into a megaphone, or perhaps whispering to foreign correspondents who had thronged to the school from all over the world. For in the heady two days and nights since the student occupation of the polytechnic on Wednesday, not only national but world attention had been focused on the Neoclassical building in the heart of Athens. Finally, after six and a half uneasy years of military rule, Greeks had once again dared to shout 'Ohi! No!' It had happened before, in the dark days before the Axis invasion in the Second World War, when the Greek premier had answered the Italian ultimatum to surrender with that one defiant word of denial, 'Ohi!' Although it seemed, in the long siege of the *junta*'s rule, that Greeks had forgotten how to say 'no' to dictatorship and fascism, some had remembered. Every autumn, on the anniversary of that defiance which had immediately been followed by the Axis invasion, Greek schoolchildren march in the centre of Athens shouting 'Ohi! Ohi! Ohi!' And now, too, the children

432

of Athens were repeating that cry inside the beleaguered gates of their college.

'Radio Polytechnic! Radio Polytechnic! The station of the free and fighting students, the voice of the free Greeks in their struggle! Help us! Join us! Radio Polytechnic! Radio Polytechnic!'

Marika twiddled the dial until she got the government station. A cool voice was reading an announcement that citizens should remain indoors until order was restored in the city. In alarm she switched back to the student station.

'Education, freedom, bread! General strike, general strike! Let us not bow down to them! All of us together, at last it's now or never!'

Marika frowned at the radio. The students had been calling for a general strike for two days, but so far the only takers had been the students at Patras and Salonika Universities who had forced those institutions to close. Athens University had been shut down even before the polytechnic sit-in had begun. Strangely, too, a group of farmers had heeded the call and sent a parade of tractors to demonstrate in Omonia Square. But what could a few farmers and even a legion of outraged students do against the combined might of the military regime?

'Join us! Help us!' Marika thought she heard a new desperation in the student's voice. 'We need doctors and medical assistance of all kinds!'

When the telephone sounded at just after ten o'clock, she froze for a long moment. Since Nikos had left home, their only contact had been hurried calls he placed from newspaper kiosks scattered round the city. A week after his father's stroke, a notice had been delivered cancelling his student deferment and ordering him to report for military service at once. A few days later, when the police arrived to arrest him, Marika and Eleni had honestly been able to report that they didn't know where Nikos was. All they had been able to gather from his cryptic messages was that he had channelled his grief into a passionate drive to unseat those who had killed Liberty. From key whispered words, Marika had understood that he had been up in Thessaloniki and over in Patras organizing students. Here in Athens, too, he had been at work not only on the campuses but in some clandestine recording studio making copies of a series of protest songs he had written after Liberty's death. But so far as she knew, most of those recordings had been confiscated by the security police. Nikos' naive dream of changing history with the strumming of his guitar had come to nothing. What were songs against tanks and guns?

She picked up the telephone on the third ring. 'Niko?'

'No, no, it's me.'

Marika let out her breath. It was only her mother-in-law calling from the military hospital outside Athens where her son had been languishing since his stroke. Yorgos was still paralysed from the waist down, but he had managed to recover most of his powers of speech. Every time Marika's sense of duty sent her there for a visit, she had endured his poisonous accusations. His stroke was Nikos' fault and hers. If it hadn't been for his seditious family, he would still be sitting pretty in the government. But now the doctors doubted if he would ever be able to return to work. Her 'damned son' had made him a cripple. That was all the thanks he had gotten for a lifetime of taking care of that boy, giving him everything money could buy, investing all his dreams in him. And yet, when Marika had been sitting by his hospital bed the day after his stroke, Yorgos had opened his eyes and searched the room not for his wife or mother but the one who was not there. She thought she had seen Yorgos' lips trying to form the word 'Nikos'.

Eleni spoke so low that it was hard to hear her. 'Marika! Yorgos says the army is going to move on the polytechnic! Papadopoulos is replacing the police with the army! The tanks will be on the way any time now! If Nikos is there, you've got to get him out!' Before Marika could answer, there was a click and the line went dead.

Marika stared at the silent telephone. What did Yorgos know that everyone else still didn't know? Even though his illness had removed him from the centre of power, the telephone he had installed by his bedside kept him connected to his old friends in the government and the army. In the first weeks after his stroke, he had taken extended leave. But when the doctors had said there was no chance of a full recovery, he had surrendered his portfolio and what was left of his political power. Sometime after the new year, too, his retirement from the army would be official. Day after day, as he had lain in that hospital bed, faithfully tended by his devoted mother, he had denounced his son, his wife, and the ill fate that had stripped him of so much. And yet now there was this warning on the telephone. Crippled as he was, Yorgos was too sly to let his mother overhear anything he wanted to keep from her. Was this his roundabout way of saving Nikos?

Whatever Yorgos' role in this was, Marika grabbed the handbag she had stuffed with Nick's dollars. But at the door her daughters were waiting with plastic sacks of medicines.

'If you're headed for the polytechnic, we're going with you,' Lena said. She was studying archaeology now at Athens University.

'I can help,' Annoula added. 'They're saying on the radio they need doctors and nurses.' She had just begun her medical studies at the same school.

'Isn't it enough that one of my children is inside?' But then Marika reconsidered. Maybe it was time every Greek, her daughters included, stood up to this regime. Tonight at the polytechnic her girls might learn more about what was important in life than they would in all their years at the university. '*Pame!*'

As starry night fell on the city, the streets in their northern suburb were strangely quiet, not hushed – for Athens is never hushed – but tense and expectant. For two days the metropolis had been riveted on the polytechnic. Behind those shuttered balconies, Marika wondered how many radios were tuned to the polytechnic station. When the students had occupied the school, at first it had seemed that this protest would end as quickly as the others had earlier this year at the law school and the main university. Instead, it had come to the boil. On Wednesday night students had barricaded the gates, brought in food, and set up a co-ordinating committee to oversee the coming siege. Slogans had been painted on the façade. On Thursday the polytechnic faculty had affirmed their support and warned the police not to invade the school. Groups of workers had joined the occupation and held a joint news conference with the student leaders. But before dawn this morning on November the sixteenth, tanks had already been spotted moving into strategic positions in the outskirts of the city. By mid-afternoon police had halted two crowds of demonstrators marching from the polytechnic toward Syntagma Square, and another angry mass of demonstrators had taken up position outside the Ministry of Public Order. By five o'clock police had begun lobbing tear gas canisters outside the polytechnic, and the first wave of students beaten by police truncheons had been carried into the hospital emergency rooms. In the early evening the focus of violence had shifted to the Ministry of Public Order. Reportedly the workers and students had tried to storm it with sticks and stones and petrol bombs, and the police had begun firing on the mob. At the polytechnic, too, police sniper fire had begun.

When they were stopped at a traffic light on Alexandras Boulevard, Lena pointed out a glitter of light on steel. The mother and daughters peered down a blocked sidestreet and saw soldiers in military formation. Yorgos was right, the army was getting ready to move. Marika prayed she would get to the school in time to warn her son and the others to get out.

When they neared the polytechnic, ahead on Patission Marika spotted a roadblock manned not by police but soldiers. She turned onto a sidestreet and parked the car up on the pavement. She grabbed her handbag, and the girls took the sacks of medicines. Avoiding the main thoroughfares, they threaded their way closer to the school. No cars moved on the streets which were crowded with clusters of the young and the not so young. Every time they saw a knot of police or soldiers standing with their truncheons and guns at the ready, they detoured to a safer path until finally they worked their way near enough to smell the tear gas and hear the bullhorns and the shouting. On a normal night it might take twenty minutes to drive from their villa to the school, but tonight it had taken nearly two hours to cross the city. They rounded a final corner and beheld the chaos of the boulevard in front of the polytechnic.

The smoky street was thronged with people and lit by bonfires. The students had set tyres afire to counteract the tear gas. Acrid smoke filled the hellish air. Marika doubled over, coughed, and brought her hands up to her streaming eyes. Annoula rooted in one of the sacks for vaseline and the three of them smeared it around their eyes and below their noses to lessen the effects of the gas. From the rooftops, the police were shooting tear gas canisters into the street. Rimming the school were knots of foreign reporters scribbling on notepads. A huge sign hung on the main gate of the polytechnic; 'When the people aren't afraid, the tyrant gets frightened.' Beside the gate 'Get out of NATO' was scrawled, and on the side of the building 'Out with the Americans' was painted. The balconies fronting on the avenue were crowded with onlookers, some hooting the students, some joining in the chants that came from behind the tall gate enclosing the polytechnic. The din of the screaming students was deafening. 'Down with Papadopoulos! Down with the *junta*!' They hung on the school gates shouting their defiance of the military regime. The only perches bereft of students were the dusty palm trees in the forecourt. Marika had second thoughts, now, about bringing her daughters into the danger zone. But it was too late to send them home now. They would stand – or fall – together.

Marika continued to stand looking at the thousands of students enclosed in the cage of the school. Her gaze swivelled to the darkened nearby streets where, just out of sight, the lines of police and soldiers were standing in the shadows. These vulnerable young people were penned in like animals in a zoo. If Eleni's warning was right and the military was about to attack, what could they do to save themselves? Nikos had to be somewhere inside.

Frantically she and her daughters pushed and shoved their way forward until they were near enough to see the front gate manned by students questioning all those who tried to get inside. She asked a young long-haired fellow in front of her what was the problem, why weren't they welcoming all who wanted to join them?

'Police spies, I guess. And *provocateurs*. I hear military intelligence has sent their agents, and the word is that the Communists are trying to exploit the situation as well.' Nervously he looked over his shoulder at where the police and the army surely waited.

Marika was at the gate begging a muscular student to let her in at once. She waved her press credentials.

But the guard wasn't impressed. 'No media inside. Get your story outside the gate like everyone else.'

'My son's inside!' Desperately Marika pulled at the bars of the gate. 'I have to get to my son!'

He brought up his head in a firm negative. 'We all have mothers. And fathers. We can't let them all in.' He, too, glared into the night at the unseen enemy.

'But you must let me in! I'm Marika Kronos. The mother of Nikos Kronos. You know him, you must know him! I have an urgent message for my son.'

'Nikos?' The student looked uncertainly at the determined woman. Everyone who wanted in claimed to know someone. But then, as though Nikos' name were a secret password, he seemed about to open the gate.

Then Lena intervened. 'Alki, it's *me*! I came as soon as I could.'

The guard, who knew Lena from meetings at the university, gave her a power salute and opened the door.

Marika, Lena, and Annoula were inside before he could change his mind. No time now, Marika thought, to cross-examine her elder daughter about her possibly radical student life. Was every student in Greece engaged in clandestine political activity? Tonight it seemed so.

As they raced toward the building, they saw the old Mercedes parked lengthwise in front of the main gate as a second barricade in case the military tried to crash the gate. Around it students chanted their slogans, and some of them climbed high on the railings and shook their fists at the soldiers crouching on the nearby rooftops. But Nikos, she thought, where was Nikos? If she knew her son, he would be at the epicentre, perhaps up on the roof where the leaders could watch the military and the police watching them.

Marika charged up the stairs into the polytechnic. Lying on the floors of the corridors she could see wounded students being tended by their comrades. Some were bleeding. She stood looking down at the wounded. Yes, the student radio claim was right. The police had begun firing on the college. She raced up a stairway, trusting her instinct to find her son. On the second floor, she ran down a hallway. In one room a middle-aged doctor was tending the wounded. In another students were lettering more placards. In a third others were frantically clustered around a telephone trying to rouse the foreign consulates to send observers as witness to what everyone feared would soon happen.

At the end of the corridor again she ran up flights of stairs until she emerged on the roof.

'Get down!' She heard the warning scream just in time and ducked back into the shadows as she heard the whizzing bullets. Snipers poised on nearby rooftops were shooting at the students. 'Niko! Oh, Niko, where are you?'

437

She thought she heard an answering call and, heedless of the gunfire, she edged onto the roof. Keeping to the shadows, she inched along to where she thought she could hear her son's resonant voice. Yes, just there, crouched on the parapet, she could see him huddled with three others. On all fours, she crawled forward. 'Oh, Niko!'

He turned and saw her. 'Mama!' For a moment exasperation and something like embarrassment flickered on his face. At a time like this, the last person he wanted by his side was this quintessential Greek mother who would follow her adored son to the ends of the earth and even onto the firing line. But then, taking care to shield her with his body, he embraced her. 'You shouldn't have come,' he said roughly.

'I had to, Niko, I had to. Lena and Annoula came too. They're down helping with the wounded.'

'I knew they would.' Nikos smiled. 'So we're all here.' At a word from him, the other students melted away.

As soon as they were alone, urgently Marika whispered her news. 'Your grandmother called from the hospital. Yorgos says the army is coming in. With tanks. They're already moving through the city. You've got to get out!'

Grimly he looked out at the dark night. 'Yes, we know they'll come soon. We just heard it on the police radio.'

'You can still get away. Now, before they come!'

'Leave here? No, mama.'

'But Niko,' she pleaded, 'think! They've been looking for you for weeks. And if they get you, this time your father won't be able to help.'

Nikos grimaced. 'That one? *He* never helped me.'

'One thing's for sure, no one will be able to help you if the police get you this time. They'll kill you.'

A bullhorn crackled somewhere outside. 'Attention! Evacuate the polytechnic! You have one half-hour to evacuate the building!'

'See,' Marika said, 'they're coming! You've got to get out.' She clutched at her son. 'What good will it do for you to die here, or in one of their wretched prisons?'

'Others have died so.' He shrugged. 'Why not me?'

'Because,' she answered fiercely, 'it would be suicide for you to stay here now. But if you go – and I don't mean just get out of this school, I mean if you get out of Greece – you'll be able to keep fighting. And maybe, just maybe, you'll be able to make a difference.'

'I can make a difference here. With my body. With my blood.'

'But to sacrifice so much, and for nothing?'

He gestured with his hands at the students packed inside the polytechnic.

438

'Nothing? There are five thousand students inside the gates, my sisters included. This is nothing?'

'You can't win if you stay here now. But if you go, and if you continue to fight, then you will win, Niko, you can! This is the beginning of the end of the dictatorship. And when the nightmare is over and you come back, you can help build up Greece into something great again.'

He looked down at the flaming street, the shouting students, the massed police and now the soldiers. 'Maybe.'

She dug in her purse and produced a wad of bills. 'From your grandfather. Dollars. They'll help get you out. You can go to him in Boston. He and Christos, they'll help you.'

'*America*? Go to *America*?' Ever since the *junta* took power, the Resistance had claimed the CIA was to blame not only for the *coup d'état* but also for the dictatorship's continued hold on the country. The colonels had given the Americans home port facilities for the Sixth Fleet and a secure base for its military in the eastern Mediterranean. 'No. Not *there*.'

'England, then. Or to your uncle in Australia. I don't care where you go, just get out! For *me*, Niko. Do it for me!'

With resolution he stood. 'All right then. I'll go, and I'll take as many as I can with me. We can't let them get us all tonight.' He held out his hand to her. '*Pame*. We'll pick up Lena and Annoula on the way out.'

'No, you go, and I'll follow with them. I'm a journalist, remember? This is the biggest story in the past six years. I have to write about it for tomorrow's paper.'

'I'm not leaving you here. Or my sisters, either.'

'It's better if we separate. We'll just hold you back. And they're after you, not us.'

'Niko! Niko!' The others were calling him.

Again he hesitated, and then quickly he embraced his mother. She held him tight, feeling the strength of his young *pallikari* warrior body. Keep him safe, God, she prayed. A moment later he edged away towards his comrades, and then their dark shapes descended from the roof.

From the shadows of her cover, Marika stood looking out at the chaotic street. The bonfires were dying out, the crowd in the street had thinned, and inside the iron gates of the polytechnic some students were still shouting slogans while others milled around debating what to do if and when the attack came. The main gate remained shut, but she could see a stream of students racing out two side entrances. Hard as she looked, however, she could not distinguish his form among so many others. Please, she prayed, don't let him change his mind and stay.

Nevertheless, she took a deeply thankful breath that at least this once he had appeared to listen to reason. When she had given him the dollars, she had hoped he would agree to flee to Boston and be reunited with his grandfather and Christos. If he had, truly the wheel would have spun full circle. As she had listened to herself pleading with her son to go into political exile, a strange sense of *déja vu* had stolen over her. Long ago, when Christos had been confronted with this same decision, he, too, must have been gripped by the emotions Nikos was feeling tonight. Her thoughts trailed back to that night in the cave. For the first time in all these long years, she had an inkling of what it must have cost him to leave her as he had. Now, a generation later, she had urged the same flight on their son. Perhaps she had been wrong to lose faith in Christos as she had. If somehow she had waited and gotten the news of her pregnancy to him, they might have been able to salvage everything. Perhaps . . .

Her ruminations were cut short by blinding arcs of light and a low threatening earthquake rumble that sent shivers up her spine. She peered down and saw the lumbering line of tanks approaching the main gate of the polytechnic. The students were still hanging on the fences, and she could hear them calling out to the soldiers in the armoured cars behind the tanks. 'Brothers! Help us! Join us! You are our brothers!'

Inexorably the line of tanks moved dead straight at the main gate. She looked down at her watch. Only ten minutes had lapsed of the half-hour the government had given them to evacuate the polytechnic. Surely they weren't coming in now, before those who wanted to go had a chance to get out. Desperately again she stared down at the side gates. Was Nikos in or out?

Below she heard a thunderous crash. The lead tank had smashed through the gate, it was grinding forward over the parked Mercedes, troops of commandos were racing inside with their clubs held high. She heard the rat-tat of bullets and watched in horror as soldiers ran the students to ground and clubbed them with a savagery that made her want to vomit. Screams pierced through the gunfire.

Armoured cars were screeching inside where once the main gate had stood. She could see a stream of soldiers pouring into the polytechnic. With a jolt she came to. This wasn't some violent film playing at the Odeon, this was real, and she and her daughters were as vulnerable as those students down in the courtyard. Through the open door, she could hear the panicked cries from the students on the lower floor. Soon the soldiers would be up on the roof. Being the wife of one of the original *junta* colonels and a columnist on a daily newspaper wasn't going to help her once the commandos were upon her with their clubs and guns. Was it better to wait here for them to find her or go to meet the enemy? And what about Lena and Annoula? She had to find them! Cautiously she inched toward the door, slipped inside, and catapulted down the stairs to the floor where she'd left her daughters.

Students were running pell mell. A young man was holding a girl in his arms who was not much older than her younger daughter. Children, she thought dully, they're only children. How can the soldiers be attacking their own flesh and blood? How can these Greeks be eating their own children? She spied her daughters huddled together. Annoula was crying, and Lena was doing her best to comfort her. Marika threw herself between them, encircled them with her arms, and held them so close that she thought she could hear their racing heartbeats.

She wrapped her arms around their faces so they wouldn't see the first wave of soldiers haring up the stairs. Under her breath she let out soothing rhythmic noises, holding them closer, rocking them in her arms. 'Murderers!' the students were screaming. 'Assassins!' At first, as the soldiers went after the moving targets of the young men who tried to fight them with their naked fists, she thought that perhaps she and her girls would escape notice. But there were so many soldiers, too many still were pouring up the stairs, and at last one tramped with his heavy boots in their direction. When he was towering above them, he began kicking hard, again and again. Marika screamed, the girls howled, and at that the soldier raised his club and brought it down. Marika heard the crunch of bone, she smelled the scent of blood, again she screamed before finally everything went dark.

Hours later, sometime in the late morning, an unlit cigarette hung out of the corner of Marika's mouth as she sat over her typewriter banging out an eyewitness account of the nightmare at the polytechnic. For once, she would not mince words. Finally, she would write from the heart. Others had risked so much – again almost she could smell that blood and hear those screams – so this time to hell with the consequences. No matter what the government 'guidelines' were for the press, she would write the words that had to be written.

'From the roof of the polytechnic, I could see the tanks coming towards the main gate. In the first wave there were eight of – '

She stopped, threw her cigarette into the overflowing ashtray, and propped up her throbbing head on her hand. Before she passed out, she remembered taking one blow on the crown of her head from the soldier's club. But from the bruises on her arms and legs and the gash on her thigh, she assumed they had struck her there, too. As she recalled regaining consciousness in that ambulance, listening to the moans of the seriously wounded lying all around her, she was almost ashamed that her injuries were so slight. Her body would ache for a day or two, but her sore heart was another matter. Some of the students had been beaten bloody, and others had been riddled with bullets. Lying next to her on the floor of the ambulance had been a boy who couldn't have been more than fourteen or fifteen. As the blood had gushed from a gaping bullet wound in his stomach, he had called out for his mother. 'I'm here,' she had crooned as she had tried to encircle him with her bruised arms, but then he had let out a long sighing gasp and died with his eyes wide open. How many, she wondered, had lost their lives last night? Nikos had said there were five thousand students inside the polytechnic. Even if hundreds or perhaps at most a thousand had managed to escape, so many more had been caught in the savage attack of the soldiers. Her daughters had not been in that ambulance, and she had been frantic until she saw them – like herself, nursing only minor bruises – at the police station.

But Nikos, she wondered again, what about Nikos? Was he at this moment under police interrogation, rotting in some crowded cell, or even lying cold and unmourned in a makeshift mortuary?

She pulled her telephone close, dialled home for the fourth time that morning, and again shot that one question as soon as her mother-in-law answered the phone. 'Have you heard from *him*?' When Eleni answered, 'Not yet', Marika hung up the telephone. If he were safe, surely by now he would have called home.

For her son, and for those other sons and daughters, she continued her eyewitness account.

'The lead tank rolled over the main gate, and in its wake were a fleet of armoured cars and commandos who fired at will at the unarmed students fleeing in panic before them.'

Again she stopped, lit a cigarette, and stared into space as she remembered what had happened when the ambulance finally screeched to a halt. She had assumed they were heading for a hospital emergency room. But instead they had pulled up at a police station where the wounded had been roughly carried or herded inside. She didn't know what had happened to that dead boy in the ambulance and the others killed in the attack. But she and her daughters had had a tearful reunion. A little later, when the police had begun questioning all those who could speak, there had been no signs of the bodies of those who had not survived.

As she had sat waiting with her daughters on the crowded corridor floor, Marika had debated whether to reveal her identity or say nothing. But she still had her identity and press cards in her pocket, and there had been no chance to get rid of them under the watchful eyes of the police. When her turn had finally come and she had been led into a bare room to face two harried policemen, she had mustered what dignity she still possessed and demanded that she be released at once. She was Marika Kronos, a columnist for one of Athens' most respected newpapers, and her husband had been one of the key movers of what the *junta* liked to call the Revolution of 21 April 1967. When she had presented her papers, the officers had drawn aside for a whispered consultation and then left her alone in that room for nearly two hours as they telephoned their superiors to see what was to be done with this woman who claimed she was above their reach. When at last they had returned, they had admonished her as a stern father does a mischievous child that someone like herself should never have been inside that den of subversives. But then they had seemed eager to be rid of not only her but her daughters. One had given her a pen, and the other had waved a paper at her. Once she had signed her release, she had been free to go.

Outside, in vain she had wandered about looking for a taxi on the streets which were empty but for tanks, police vans, and soldiers entering apartment blocks. Lena and Annoula had sought refuge in a friend's house nearby. Then, on her long solitary walk to the newspaper office, she had seen young and old being hustled into police cars.

At work, when she had cleaned herself up as best she could in front of a cloudy mirror in the ladies' toilet, she had found out in the newsroom that the city was clamped under martial law. Then she and Sokrates had huddled for a heart-to-heart, and she had talked him into co-operating with what she had decided must be done. But she was so tired now that she didn't know if she could finish her story. I should go home, she thought, as again she leaned her aching head on her hands. I need a bath, and sleep, and Nikos.

When her phone rang, she lunged for it.

'He called,' her mother-in-law said.

'He did! He called!' Marika shut her eyes in relief. As soon as all this was over, she would go to church and light every candle in the rack in thanksgiving. 'Where is he?'

Her mother said nothing, but Marika could almost hear her shrugging. What did it matter, after all, where Nikos was, so long as he was safe?

'His father called, too,' Eleni continued. 'From the hospital.'

'And you told him what?' Marika chose her words carefully. Of course her telephone at home was tapped, and the newspaper lines as well. If the *junta* ever fell, hundreds of thousands of police spies and informers would be out of work.

'Nothing. Except that you're at work and that you'll be home soon. You will, won't you? And the girls, they're really safe at their friend's?'

Every time she had talked to her mother-in-law this morning, she had assured her that Lena and Annoula were safe. But she said it again, and then she returned to her despatch.

An hour and a half later it was ready, just before the edition was about to close. The newsroom was even more ahowl than usual. Reporters were scurrying about with their stories, copy boys were running down to the composing room, and editors were screaming into telephones. Across the room she caught Sokrates' eye, and a moment later he pulled up a chair beside her. When she handed him her piece, he took it as gingerly as though it would explode.

'You're sure you want to do this, *kukla*?' His dark eyes were solemn.

'I'm sure. But what about you?' She did not care about the consequences for herself. But when her story was printed Sokrates, too, would be liable for prosecution. The government had formally stopped censorship prior to publication a year and a half after the coup, but since then the press had been policed by a vague 'code of ethics' which the government selectively enforced. One month in one newspaper a reporter might get away with a veiled reference to the excesses of the dictatorship. But the very next month in another newspaper, journalists might be arrested and sentenced for a few unwary words. Considering the ferocity of the government sack of the polytechnic, however, Marika did not think the *junta* was going to be in a merciful mood once they read her story.

'I told you,' Sokrates said, so low that no one else could overhear, 'my cousin's daughter was inside the polytechnic. We still don't know how she is. Or where she is.' He stood with the sheaf of papers in his hand. 'I owe her this.' And yet he couldn't resist shaking his head. 'I never thought it would come to this, when you came sashaying into the newsroom that first time dressed up like you thought this was a fashion show. And now look at you!' Fondly he regarded the bruise on her arm, the cut on her neck, the rip at the shoulder of her dress. 'But the question is, which of us is Dr Frankenstein and which the monster?'

For the first time today, Marika smiled as she watched him saunter over to his desk, bend over her papers, and scrawl on a headline and printing instructions for the typographer he had already alerted down in the composing room. We couldn't get away with this, Marika told herself again, carefully watching two of the other editors who were said to collect a second salary from military intelligence, if they had even an inkling that finally I have slipped the leash and said what I should have had the courage to say long ago. Sokrates took a quick phone call, shouted something to a fellow editor, and threaded his way through the desks to the doorway that led down to the composing room.

When he was gone, Marika let out a deep intake of breath. If her luck held, in a few moments her burning words would be hot lead. In less than a half hour her piece would be set into the waiting page. In an hour the edition would be running off the presses. She supposed that, just as soon as someone from the military or the government noticed that she had written not only a condemnation of the polytechnic attack but a clarion call for return to democracy, all the copies of the newspaper would be confiscated and destroyed. But there was a good chance that first they would be distributed to kiosks throughout the city. She imagined her account hung up by clothespins stretched on a line outside newpaper stalls in Syntagma and Omonia. Crowds would congregate. Eager hands would snap up the newspaper and hustle it home to be passed from house to house and read and reread. She had done her part for Nikos, for Lena and Annoula, and for all the sons and daughters who had made their stand in the polytechnic.

Wearily she laid her head on her desk and slept. Some time later, when Sokrates shook her awake, she looked him in the eye. When he merely nodded, her face cracked into a smile. She collected her things, gave Sokrates a hug, and tucked the freshly-printed newpapers he gave her under her arm like baguettes of bread hot from the oven. Only when she finally managed to snag a taxi and was on the way home did she open the newspaper and reread the story she had been born to write.

She was asleep that evening when the military police came to arrest her.

Six weeks later Marika sat on the hard wooden courtroom bench as she patiently awaited her courtmartial for violating the press 'code of ethics'. She had been aware, the morning after the government crushed the occupation of the polytechnic, that, as surely as winter follows summer, she would one day sit in this dock and be judged and convicted for flaunting the press's self-censorship guidelines. Writing that article had been not only a conscious choice but one of the two great decisions of her life. And now she awaited the inevitable with something that felt almost like contentment.

She rearranged the folds of the black dress she wore not only in mourning for her mother but for Greece. She knew she had Yorgos to thank for her having spent only one night in prison before she was sent back to the Psychikon villa to await trial. The four soldiers assigned to guard her there hadn't been much older than Nikos, and mostly they had seemed more interested in Eleni's home cooking than making Marika feel like a prisoner. But still those weeks under house arrest had been fraught. Conditions in Greece had deteriorated from bad to worse since the fall of the polytechnic. Only nine days later rightwing elements in the army, masterminded by Brigadier Ioannides, the head of military intelligence, had ousted Papadopoulos in a bloodless middle-of-the-night mutiny that had been a replica of the colonels' coup more than six years ago. At first, believing that Ioannides and his gang had deposed the former dictator for the polytechnic massacre in which an uncounted number of young people had died, Greece had welcomed the new regime and believed its promises of liberalization and upcoming elections. But within days its iron fist had smashed such illusions. Ioannides and his hardline cohorts had taken power because Papadopoulos had replaced most of the original *junta* colonels with civilian politicians and had been bent on holding elections early in the new year. The Brigadier had indefinitely imposed martial law, locked shut the offices of a critical newspaper, and reopened the most infamous island concentration camp on Yaros. Marika supposed they would send her there after sentence was passed upon her today. She doubted if Yorgos' waning influence could help once the judges delivered their verdict.

As she sat waiting, she looked around the packed courtroom of strangers. Some wore military uniforms, and many others had either the bulldog look of policemen or the sly faces of paid informers. But she presumed, since her family wasn't here and neither were the press, that the proceedings were closed to the public. An English phrase – kangaroo court – came to mind, and her thoughts trailed to her brother, beyond the reach of farces like this, somewhere in what she supposed was the wilderness of Australia. What was Vangelis doing now, at this instant? Before the polytechnic, and her subsequent arrest, he had written homesick letters from where he had settled among the Greek community of Melbourne. They were living with Vasso's parents. He was cooking fish and chips in a takeaway restaurant, and she was working at a hotel reception desk while she awaited the birth of her baby next month. Vangelis' child would be born in an alien land.

But at least, she thought, gazing at this courtroom of lackeys and spies, her brother's child would be born in a free country. If the baby didn't or couldn't at some point come home, he would still be able to fashion a life of dignity and honour – saying what he wanted to say, reading what he wanted to read, doing what he wanted to do. And yet, thinking of that unborn child, Marika reflected that, for a Greek, exile in some ways was even more wrenching than a lifetime in a barren island prison camp. How tragic it was that still, despite their love of homeland, so many were gone now! Greece was a field lying fallow in the scorching sun. In her moments of deepest despair, she could almost believe that all the best were gone and that nothing good could grow here now. Her own family had been pruned of its strongest branches. Old Nick and her own father had been compelled to go by hard times and limited opportunities, Christos had been forced out by that thirst for political vengeance that poisoned the country still, and Vangelis and Nikos had been driven out for the same reason.

At the thought of her son, Marika gave the courtroom another nervous

446

glance. Always, as soon as a door opened and a new prisoner shambled in, she caught her breath and didn't let it out until she was certain the newcomer wasn't Nikos. Since her son disappeared the night the polytechnic fell, the only word she'd had from him had been that lone telephone call her mother-in-law had intercepted the next day and a cryptic postcard from Liberty's parents in London. She prayed that her son remained safely tucked away from all this madness. She dearly hoped that he was in England with Liberty's family, in America with his grandfather and his true father, or even in Australia with his uncle. Please God, she prayed, let him remain safely out of Greece. If something happened to Nikos, she couldn't bear it. The decision that had led to his birth – as if it were yesterday, she remembered leading Christos to that cave, and throwing herself in his arms, and making him love her, if only for that one night – had been the transcendent act of her life. Even though she had lost her gamble with Christos, she had gained something greater and finer in his son.

And yet, now, alone in this courtroom, she faced the second greatest crisis of her life. But perhaps, she reflected, she wasn't altogether alone today. A fortnight ago her telephone had rung in the dead of night. And when she had sleepily answered, Christos' voice – she would have known the sound of him anywhere! – had come on the line. Tersely, without saying his name to alert whoever was doubtless tapping her phone, he had delivered words of support and, maybe, love. 'I'm so proud of you,' he had whispered. 'And I, and so many others, are with you still.' Before she could respond, the line had been cut. Since then, every time her courage had faltered, his message had renewed her strength.

She looked beside her at her lacklustre attorney, yawning as he waited for her name to be called. He had appeared at the villa four days after her arrest to say his services had been engaged by the court. She would have preferred to hire someone she knew and trusted, but the military authorities had ignored her requests for a lawyer more to her liking. He had advised her to plead guilty, apologise contritely, and hope that sentiment for a helpless woman and fear of her well-connected husband would move the judges to be lenient. And yet her attorney had cautioned her to expect no mercy from the new regime. But what, she wondered, looking at the thickly curtained windows which shut out the cold January light, were the Greeks thinking, believing, and perhaps even plotting? As surely as spring follows winter, the season of the tyrants was drawing to a close. The polytechnic students had cracked the glacier. Soon, now, when the avalanche began, the young would have their revenge.

But not quite yet. As another name was called out, her head swivelled to the raised platform where the seven judges in military uniform sat stonily

447

watching a lawyer approach the bench with his arm touchingly around his client's shoulders. For a moment she assumed the attorney must be a brother or cousin of the accused. But then, when the defendant stumbled and nearly fell, she looked at his ruined legs – or was it his feet, had they been using the old Ottoman falange technique of beating him on the soles of his feet? – and then she lowered her eyes in shame. This one, like so many others, had spent too long in the torture chambers. That one terrible night in her cell she had heard their screams and trembled on her iron cot waiting for them to come for her. As soon as she had heard the lock turn in her door, she had looked around the small dark cell and shivered as she remembered her premonition of this moment years ago in the Cave of the Great Goddess. Strangely, that recollection had steadied her. But, aside from a gruelling interrogation the next morning about not only her own subversion but also her son's, the authorities had left her alone. Though Yorgos, still recuperating in hospital, had never so much as sent her a word of concern, she supposed he had been protecting her nonetheless. Even if her husband hated her now, his pride of possession would never have allowed his wife to be tortured. Lying untouched in her cell, she had been frankly grateful for the special treatment. It had been one thing to write that column in the white heat of her indignation after the polytechnic, but quite another matter to lie in the dark listening to the military boots march down her cellblock. As she had cringed when they paused at her door, she had come face to face with what she had told herself were the limits of her courage.

And yet, watching the prisoner standing as straight as he could manage in front of his judges, she reconsidered. This man didn't look so very different from those she had seen every day of her life buying cigarettes at a kiosk or playing cards on a coffeehouse table. Maybe he, too, had surprised himself with his own bravery. It could be that sometimes a man didn't break, that instead he called on hitherto unsuspected reserves of strength to become as strong as his destiny required. Perhaps the limits of courage were as elastic as the boundaries of love. *Christos*, she thought, *Christos*! As though she had just bolted a shot of Metaxa, warmth flooded through her. Since that furtive phone call, she had felt him with her again. She had had ample time, pacing the villa grounds in these last cold winter weeks of captivity, to reflect on what had happened so long ago between them. Now that she had finally dared to put political justice ahead of her personal safety, at last she had understood how he could have left her to wake alone in that cave. She had even put pen to paper and tried to share all this with him. But she could not re-write her past or reshape her own *moira*, and in the end she had torn it to shreds and thrown it away. But perhaps, she thought, Christos understood anyway.

Absently she listened to the charges being read out to the prisoner leaning on his lawyer, and then the judges swiftly sentencing him to eight years in prison. Her turn would come soon. In prison she would have all the time in the world to ponder these unanswered questions about herself and Christos.

Then Marika's heart sank as a new prisoner was led into the courtroom. Sokrates! Until this moment she had not known that they had arrested her mentor, too. She tried to catch his eye as he walked past her with the hopeless stride of a doomed man, but Sokrates kept his head bowed. Marika had hoped the two of them had covered their tracks so well that her friend and editor would not have been called to account for his complicity in the publication of her article. Had they tortured Sokrates, too?

Her conjectures were cut short by the President of the Court calling the next case.

But before Marika's name could be read out, there was a stir in the back of the courtroom. The doors were thrown wide, heads swivelled, and all eyes were on Colonel Yorgos as Captain Kostas wheeled him into the chamber. Behind them marched two greying men with the officious air of attorneys.

Marika held her head higher. Had he come to gloat or help? As she watched her husband being rolled in her direction, she tried but failed to read his closed face. With a sense of high drama, Yorgos had dressed in his most resplendent uniform complete with medals, ribbons, and badges. Marika reflected that this was probably his last public parade, for his army retirement would be official at the end of the month. And yet he looked more pathetic than impressive. The uniform that used to fit him like a second skin now hung as if on a wire hanger. He had not only lost weight but had aged since she had last seen him in his military hospital bed. His skin was the colour of the belly of a dead fish, and his aura of bullish power had altogether deserted him. And yet, as Kostas wheeled him closer, she saw that something of the old Yorgos remained in the glint of his steely eyes.

Marika looked down at the wedding band she had continued to wear, mostly for the sake of her children. As the captain drew Yorgos up next to her, she slipped off the ring and put it in the pocket of her dress. Later she was to wonder about this gesture. Had she intuitively guessed what was about to happen?

He was parked inches away from her in the aisle between two banks of seats. And yet, as though they were commuters thrown too close together during the rush hour on the metro, he was doing his best to ignore her presence. Why, she wondered again, was he here? Despite everything, maybe he was still going to try to wield his waning influence to help her. It could even be, she thought, remembering how she had never altogether shaken off her passion for Christos, that still he loved her in his way. Or maybe what

449

had brought him here was only simple loyalty to their twenty-five years of marriage. Whichever it was, here sat her glowering invalid husband; but her husband nonetheless. For her, too, old habits died hard, and the wife in her was unable to resist leaning over and touching him on the arm. 'Yorgo?'

With an effort he tried, but failed, to turn his head toward her.

'He can't talk.' Kostas leaned forward and whispered. 'He had another stroke. He can hear, he can sometimes manage to write down what he wants done, but he can't speak.'

'Since when?' Eleni had told her none of this. She had gone to the hospital every day, but her mother-in-law had carried this burden alone.

'About six weeks ago.'

'Ah!' After the polytechnic, Marika thought. When Nikos left the country, I wrote my article, and Ioannides took over the government. She stole another glance at his sunken cheeks and unhealthy pallor. She asked herself if she cared what had happened to this man who had been a tyrant not only of Greece but of her own life. She surprised herself by answering that she did care. For most of their adult life they had battled. But, seeing him so diminished, she felt no sense of victory.

The two men she assumed were lawyers had taken seats behind her, and they were leaning forward to say something to her when the court officer called the next case.

'Marika Kronos.'

She snapped to attention. Out of another old habit, quickly she crossed herself three times. But to her surprise her attorney remained rooted to his seat, as instead the two men who had come with Yorgos made ready to escort her up to the judges.

Marika balked. 'Who are you?'

'Your attorneys.' They flanked her, and each of them took her by her arm as though ready to drag her up to be judged.

Marika's eyes flashed, she shook off their grip, and she walked ahead of them to the front of the courtroom.

The President of the Court barked out a command. 'The charges.'

A court officer read the indictment. Violation of the censorship laws. Inciting to insurrection. Lies against the state. Danger to national security.

Smoothly, before the bailiff even had time to sit, one of Yorgos' lawyers approached the bench and presented a paper to the judges.

'Ah, yes.' The chief judge took the paper as though he had been expecting it. He glanced down, nodded, and passed it to his colleagues. 'All in order, except for that other document.' Yet even without it, he seemed about to close her case.

'Just a moment.' Marika stepped forward. 'What's going on?'

Mildly the judge in charge peered over his glasses at her. 'Motion for dismissal.'

'My attorney filed no such petition.' Marika had her hands on her hips in the peasant woman stance of growing anger. Every Greek mother's son knew that posture.

'Don't make problems,' one of Yorgos' lawyers said.

'It's for your own good,' the other chimed in.

Marika stepped closer to the bench. 'There seems to be some mistake. These two,' she said, giving a contemptuous tilt of her head toward the two lawyers behind her, 'are my husband's attorneys. They do not represent me.' She pointed to the paper they had passed the judges. 'And neither does that document represent my wishes.'

'*Kyria*, please!' The chief judge wearily shook his head at the shrewish wife of the highly-placed colonel. But Brigadier Ioannides himself had called him at home at seven o'clock this morning with specific instructions about this sensitive case, and the judge was not about to countermand the Brigadier's orders. 'You are obstructing the business of the court. We are overtaxed, and we have no time for domestic disputes between a husband and wife.' Again he appeared impatient to be rid of this case. 'Now, if you will present me with that other document, we can move on.'

'What other document?' Marika was glaring at Yorgos' attorneys, and when they did not answer she turned back to the judges. 'I demand that I be allowed to consult with my counsel.'

The judge's eyes went to Colonel Yorgos, then to the two lawyers before him, and finally to this irate woman who looked just like his mother when nothing on heaven or earth could move her. 'Ten minute recess.' Without another word the judges filed out of the courtroom.

Marika marched back to where her lawyer cowered. 'What is all this?' Before he could answer, she rounded on the other two attorneys who had followed at her heels. 'And suppose you tell me who you are, what was on that paper, and what's that "other document" the judge is waiting for.' Her eyes fell on Yorgos. 'Or maybe I should just direct all my questions to you.'

Faintly Yorgos seemed to smile. He inclined his hand toward the attorneys he had brought with him.

Thus cued, they bent close to her and began talking in turns.

'Your husband is having the charges against you dismissed,' said the first.

'And,' continued the second, 'having you remanded into his own custody.'

'It is his idea,' said the first, 'that you will immediately return with him to Panagia.'

'That is,' interjected the second, 'tomorrow, when he is released from his treatment in the hospital.'

451

'Of course,' qualified the first, 'all this is conditional upon your signing a document.'

'It's not an important paper,' explained the second, 'just a legal technicality. You know our bureaucracy. Papers, always papers, so many papers . . .'

When they finished, Marika pursed her lips. 'Exactly what does this paper say?'

'What does it matter what it says?' cooed the first lawyer.

'It only matters that you sign it,' added the second.

'I'll have to see it before I sign it, won't I?' Marika held out her hand. 'Show it to me now.'

At a nod from Yorgos, the first lawyer produced a sheet of paper. Quickly Marika scanned it. Phrases leaped out at her. 'With utmost contrition . . . Under extreme stress, as a result of the violent and dangerous actions of my son . . . Didn't know what I was doing . . . Condemn the illegal occupation of the polytechnic by its misguided students . . . Hereby resign from my position at the newspaper . . . Promise never to publish my work in this country again . . . Pledge my loyalty and devotion to the government of Greece . . .'

She looked at the document that would allow her to walk out of this courtroom and go home to her village. There would be no more prisons and no more trembling in the night waiting for the torturers. She could forget any of this had ever happened. She could bake spinach pies and knit sweaters and gossip with Irene and Calliope. She could also achieve the same purpose and simply check herself into the hospital and have a lobotomy. 'Ohi,' she said, 'no.' She looked Yorgos in the eye as she ripped the document in half.

'Kyria, kyria, don't be so hasty.' One of the lawyers produced what she assumed was another copy of the document.

'I'll tear that one up, too.' She reached for it.

But before she could grab it, the second lawyer stopped her dead. 'It's not what you think. It's your divorce papers.'

'Divorce?' Marika paled. Her eyes rested on Yorgos. In all the long and unhappy years of her marriage, she had wondered if it was only the fear of scandal that had kept him from divorcing her. Now finally the ultimatum.

'It's one or the other,' the first lawyer gratuitously explained.

'Prison and divorce, or the village and marriage,' elaborated the second.

'I see.' Marika faltered, sank back in her chair, and looked longingly at the curtained window, beyond which the Greek sun surely shone. Almost she could feel that sunshine on her pallid skin. Often on January mornings like this down in Panagia, the sun sparkled so on the water, and the brilliant light was so pure and clean that it seemed there could never again be darkness in the world. Oh, to be there now, instead of here! And she could

452

be there, it would be so easy to agree to what they asked. All she had to do was sign her name, and it would be done. They were offering her freedom. She could go home to the village, she would have her daughters and her mother-in-law near her, she could walk along the beach and wait out the months until the nightmare was over and her son and all the others could return. No one would blame her if she settled for this bargain. What was the difference, after all, between fleeing the counry like Nikos and Christos, and fleeing back to the village? She had done her part when she had written that article. What further good would be served by rotting mutely in a cell, cut off from family and friends?

Slowly her eyes trailed around the courtroom. She looked at those who served this government: the men who reported on their neighbours, the officers who unquestioningly obeyed orders. How had it happened, exactly, that each of them had made that first crucial decision to do what was expedient instead of what was right? She supposed they all had families, and responsibilities, and that they, too, had been persuaded that it wouldn't matter much in the end, either for Greece or their own souls, if they went along with the authorities and made the most of every opportunity for their personal advancement. But, she asked herself, do I want to be like these men?

Her eyes fell on Sokrates and the others, the prisoners like herself who had come to this courtroom to face the consequences of their political actions. Most, like poor Sokrates, were glassy-eyed as they slumped on their hard wooden benches. None looked particularly brave or defiant. Yet she supposed, gazing again at these trembling prisoners, that perhaps this was what the face of courage looked like. Maybe it was only in books and movies that heroes and heroines sat tall on white horses and died with a proud scream of exaltation on their lips. In real life courage could be sad, and wavering, and riven with fears and regrets. But it didn't matter if a man or woman was afraid. All that mattered was that he or she did what was right.

Marika reached in her pocket, fished out her wedding ring, and took Yorgos' hand in hers in what – she could see it in the triumph in his eyes – her husband took for her final surrender. But a moment later, when she withdrew her hand and left the symbol of their marriage in his palm, she saw his eyes change, as once again they locked onto hers in combat.

But his attorneys did not realize the game was up.

'Think, *kyria*, of what you are doing.' One of them clutched at her arm.

'The paper,' the other hissed, 'just sign the paper and you can go free.'

Proudly she brought her head up in the Greek negative, and defiantly she vowed to keep her head that way. Yorgos had never been able to break her, and neither would these lawyers or this court.

453

Now the attorneys were turning desperate. The judges were filing in, and soon the matter would be closed.

'*Kyria*! You can't do this!' One of the lawyers was digging his fingers insistently into her arm. 'The publicity! The international press! The shame!'

Ah, she thought, so that's it! Somehow, someway, the news had gotten out. It was even possible that abroad – 'outside', where the press and men and women were free – she had become a *cause celèbre*, maybe even a political embarrassment. She was, after all, the wife of one of the original members of the *junta*. She could imagine how the foreign press might make her into a martyr. That's why Yorgos had let himself be wheeled into this courtroom. As his final act of service to the regime, he had been told to bring his erring wife back into line. And almost, she thought, it had worked. She had come within a hair of acting like the docile wife who did her husband's bidding.

'*Ohi*,' she told the laywers. '*Ohi, ohi, ohi*.' Never before in her life had she felt so close to Nikos. And to Christos! Then, with her head still high, she rose and went to say that one shining word to the judges. For she knew that in this closed courtroom, stirring speeches about freedom and dissent did not matter. It was enough merely to say, 'no'.

But of course Yorgos and the court had come prepared for this response, too. Her husband's attorneys put aside the divorce papers and whipped out yet another copy of her contrite confession. But this one, she saw, had her signature forged at the bottom. The judges smiled as they entered it into the court record.

'The defendant is remanded into her husband's custody. Two officers will escort her to her village and remain there for her protection. Case closed. Next!'

Eighteen

On a rainy evening in late March, Nikos stood backstage at the Albert Hall. He clutched his guitar in his arms like a baby as he waited for his turn to walk on the London stage and sing out his heart in this fund-raiser for the Greek Resistance. He, who had never performed for more than ten or twenty of his friends, soon would have to step out there under the lights and bare his soul to tens of thousands of strangers. He could feel the sweat pooling on his scalp. When the time comes, he told himself, just go out there and pretend you're sitting on the balcony of a friend's house in Nea Smyrni.

'You're on next.' The young blonde girl with the clipboard led Nikos to the wings, gave him a bright smile and a matey touch on the shoulders, and then speeded off to make sure the next act was primed and waiting.

From where he stood, now Nikos could see as well as hear the Cypriot band from North London's Kentish Town, incongruously costumed in wide dark pants and swashbuckling boots, as though they were Cretan warriors of another century. Any moment now they would get up, link arms, and begin shuffling back and forth in one of those old-time folk dances that television producers in Athens filled time with on Sunday afternoons.

To avoid thinking about his own approaching performance, desperately he focused on those others out there under the lights. They were good boys, he supposed, and they did their best to play the kind of music tourists remembered from their summer holidays in Greece. But to him these musicians seemed as different from his real countrymen as cottage cheese was from feta. Their ancestors, like most of the Greek community in Britain, had hailed from Cyprus instead of Greece. But what mattered more was that their families had taken root a generation ago here in England. Homesick for a real conversation in his native tongue, several times he had tried to talk in Greek with two of the bouzouki players. Both, however, were second-generation Londoners who could only speak a few heavily-accented Cypriot clichés in their grandparents' language. When Nikos had given up and switched to English, one had said he worked in a takeaway restaurant and the other painted houses for a living. For them, as for most of the players in this band, Greek music was a way to make extra money working weekends at weddings and fancy nameday celebrations. Watching them sweat on stage, Nikos wondered if he was looking at what he would become in a decade or so. Unless there were a change of government in Athens and he could go home, someday he, too, might become a caricature of what foreigners thought was Greek.

As the band warmed up the audience for the main acts to come, Nikos craned his neck to look out at the sumptuous gilded concert hall that was the most prestigious music venue in England. Tonight it was standing-room only. So far as Nikos could see, there wasn't an empty seat anywhere. The hall was packed with those who had paid up to ten pounds apiece to raise money for the Resistance movement against the military regime in Athens. Already last week, due to advance bookings that had been heavier than expected, the earnest middle-class British Philhellenes who had organized this event had pronounced the concert an unqualified success. As he had ducked in the stage door, he had even heard scalpers trying to sell tickets for twenty or thirty pounds. How had the Greek cause become so trendy? Remembering how cold he had been since he arrived in this damp grey country, he supposed this fondness for Greece could only partially be explained simply by memories of sun-drenched vacations. Now Nikos understood how right Liberty had been when she had maintained that British currents of affection for Greece ran warm and deep.

Against the blinding footlights, Nikos shaded his eyes as he gazed at the rapt audience. Even if he made a fool of himself out there tonight, they would probably goodnaturedly applaud. Tonight in the Albert Hall a Greek could do no wrong. He had been surprised, since he had arrived here in London, at the sympathy the British showed to his own and his nation's plight. Not only at sherry parties organized by one well-wisher or another but also when he fell into casual conversation in a pub or shop, Greece was a popular cause. The colonels were the bad guys, and anyone who stood up against them had to be a hero. Without even a strum of his strings, he himself had become more a personality here in London than he had ever been in Athens. His mother's arrest had been widely reported in the press, and Liberty's death on the Thessaloniki road had become a *cause célèbre* with members of parliament demanding an international investigation. Some of that dark glamour had washed over him, and soon after he had arrived he had become much in demand at West End parties where the hostesses begged him to bring his guitar and play them a song. No one seemed to mind, however, even if he was moody and melancholic and refused to sing for his supper. After all, this young green-eyed singer in the baggy sweater and jeans was not only an artist but a Greek who had suffered too much at the hands of tyrants. And yet Nikos had no illusions. He hadn't been invited to sing at this benefit because of his music. He had been given star billing because of how Liberty had died, because of how his mother had been arrested for writing the truth about the regime, and because the British had a sentimental attachment to the long-ago golden age of Classical Greece. They would have loved him to stride out on stage in a toga.

Nikos sighed. In a little while he would do what he had promised to do. And yet, waiting for his turn to go on, he resented – a little – the misplaced emotion the British invested in a modern Greece that had so little to do with the time and place of Pericles. Greece, to him, wasn't only crumbling white pillars. It was the heavy musk of incense, the salty tang of Kalamata olives, and sun, always the sun; his dry skin itched for the sun. Greece, he thought with longing, was his family gathered together on somebody's nameday for cakes and animated conversation about weddings and babies. It was a tiny dark church lit by flickering oil lamps and waxy candles and the shine of silver icons. It was sitting down on the beach with his friends for a midnight dinner of fresh fish. It was rapier wit and belly-shaking jokes. Sun and laughter, that was Greece. It was also caressive summer nights under a chestnut tree at an Athenian taverna, when the air was redolent with jasmine and passionate secrets. It was, too, short tempers, petty jealousies, and Evil Eye superstitions; not all good, certainly, often maddening, but his country nonetheless, and fiercely he loved it as much for its faults as its pleasures. Greece was daredevil whizzing through a traffic jam in Syntagma as horns impatiently hooted. It was interminable gossip about everyone and every-thing – 'where is he going, what is he doing, *look*, that's Katerina on the back of his bike!' It was old widows in black shapeless dresses and young *kamakia* in tight black leather jackets gathered around a kiosk reading newspapers stretched out on a line like inky laundry. It was strikes, surly clerks obstructing progress in government offices, and most of all the tanks crashing down the main gates of the polytechnic. *That* was his country, and *those* were his people, not a collection of statues built twenty-five hundred years ago by men who had about as much in common with modern Greeks as tree-worshipping Druids had with the British of today.

Nikos leaned against the red velvet stage curtain, held his guitar more tightly, and fought against the homesickness that raged through him like a fever. What was wrong with him, finding fault with these foreigners? He was grateful for their support, and they had been so kind and welcoming that he wondered how they had gotten such a reputation for being cold. Was it a crime that they were still inspired by what his ancestors had once dreamed and written and created? Some of the English he had met knew more about Greek mythology than he did, and a few could even remember some Classical Greek from their schooldays. For a certain sort of upper-class Englishman, Greece was not only a beloved country but a pure, gleaming, golden ideal. Perhaps more importantly for the Resistance, many even seemed personally outraged that now, in the birthplace of democracy, a man or woman could not speak out without risking arrest and perhaps torture. More than once, a new British acquaintance had surprised him with an informed opinion about how and when the *junta* would fall. What did it matter why these English were such ardent advocates of his cause, so long as they supported Greece in her hour of need? The Resistance needed not only money but publicity. It was remotely possible that international pressure against the Athens dictators would one day contribute to a change in the regime. And yet, no matter what the man in Oxford Street might feel, British foreign policy fell in line with Washington. Maybe he was too cynical, but he thought it unlikely that even the newly-elected Labour Party government would come down hard against the military masters of Greece. True, last week the British had cancelled a Royal Navy visit to Greece to show its disapproval of the

Ioannides regime. But gestures like that would hardly bring down the dictatorship. Still, he supposed every little helped. Besides, even though the British affection for Greece was romantic and had not much to do with what he himself loved in his country, he could not help warming to these people who so admired his homeland. And how, after all, could he fail to be grateful to the country who had produced his Liberty?

If only she were here tonight! If only she were still here! She had been gone now for more than five months. He had not held her for so long . . .

In his arms the guitar felt cold and hard; it was not flesh and blood – certainly not *her* flesh and blood – and yet since he had lost her his guitar had been his only real comfort.

He stroked the strings as tenderly as if they were her hair. In a way, he supposed, it was because of Liberty that he had made London his first stop after he and three student comrades had fled over the northern Greek border into Yugoslavia. He could have joined his grandfather in America, his uncle in Australia, or his friends who used some of his grandfather's dollars to get to Paris and Stockholm. But instead he had hopped a plane to Heathrow and gone directly to her parents' Mayfair flat. Considering their grief, they had made him feel as welcome as they could. They had taken him to the churchyard where they had buried Liberty in the family plot after the Greek government had finally shipped home her remains. He had drunk tea with her mother in their garden and whisky with her father at his private club. Later they had gotten out the old family photograph albums to show him baby pictures of Liberty and girlhood snapshots of her with their now-aged English setter. Sitting in front of the fireplace in the grandly tasteful parlour where Liberty had grown up, Nikos had felt momentarily with her again. But after a few days with her family, it had hurt too much to be surrounded by mementos and memories of Liberty. He had made his farewells and found a bedsitter in North London, where most of the Greek Cypriot community had settled. Kentish Town wasn't Athens, but at least the Greek markets smelled like feta and olives and home.

He stared into the lights until he was blinded and had to look back at the band. Valiantly they played a medley of Greek tunes familiar not only to every sun-loving tourist who had ever spent a holiday on the islands but to every movie-goer who had ever watched Antony Quinn dance the *syrtaki* and Melina Mercouri lock her sultry eyes into the camera. Tonight London loved 'Zorba the Greek' and 'Never on Sunday'. Their British reserve was forgotten as they clapped along to the infectious beat. But it was easy, Nikos thought, to nod their heads in time to music as accessible and simple as those homogenized hits. The happy-go-lucky melodies conjured up a blithe peasant culture of endless sun and clinking glasses of retsina. It seemed that any

458

moment now the audience would be out of their seats, linking arms and swaying in the aisles with a grapevine step.

Yet as Nikos stood waiting for his turn in the spotlight, something grew cold and still inside him. Music like this, at a time like this, was like playing wedding songs before the open grave at a funeral. This was a time for dirges, not for the clapping of hands. Festive tunes like this belonged to the Greece of carefree yesterdays, to innocent summer nights down in his village when families were whole and united, not to the police state of torture and repression which Greece was now. If his life depended upon it, he could not coax music like that now from his guitar or his throat. He who used to be the first to tuck a rose or a sprig of basil behind his ear and link arms on the dance floor could not do that any more now, either. In those first lost weeks after he had fled to London, he had even been afraid that he had lost the capacity to sing. For him, he had feared, the music had stopped forever when Liberty had died, his mother had been arrested, and he had gone into exile from everyone and everything he held dear.

Closer he clutched his guitar to his heart, as though its wood and strings were the stony soil of his homeland. His knowledge of himself and his music had deepened in those first lonely days of exile when, at his wits' end what to do in this alien nation of Liberty's, late one night in his bedsitter he had picked up his guitar and begun strumming chords. At first every note had rung false. From his despair, then, slowly at first, he had coaxed music as aching as his heart. After a while he had begun experimenting with tempo and melody. Some of his compositions were angry, others were sad, and when he played the ones with a hard, driving beat again he could see those tanks rolling toward the polytechnic just after he and his friends had escaped out a side gate. But Nikos worried whether this audience would respond to the darker strains of his own new music. Especially he wondered if they would take to the new song he had written about Liberty. Maybe he should keep that one to himself, to be played only when he was alone. What it meant to him was sacred and perhaps should never be shared this side of the grave.

The band was reaching a climax, the audience was clapping, and all the Albert Hall needed to be transformed into a Plaka taverna were stacks of plates crashing joyously on the stage. The Cypriots were bowing and then scampering away to the other wing. A stool was placed before a microphone in the centre of the stage.

The blonde again had materialized beside Nikos. 'Go!' She gave his shoulder a pat and all but pushed him out of the wings.

Nikos had never felt so vulnerable as when he walked those excruciating twenty paces out in front of those thousands of waiting foreigners. From

459

where he had waited offstage, he had been able to peer down into the audience. But here in front of the blinding lights, all he could see ahead of him were the sound technicians recording the concert for a disc to be sold later to raise more money for the Resistance. He sat on the stool, adjusted the microphone, and wished he had followed the concert producer's advice and dressed up in something fancy instead of his faded Levis and the green sweater Liberty had bought him the week before she died.

'*Lipon*,' he breathed into the microphone, 'so . . .' To himself he added that this – all this, his songs, his life, everything – was in memory of Liberty.

So inspired, he started out slow and dreamy with one of the instrumentals he had written in that burst of lonely creativity in his London bedsitter. It had more in common with the old melodies shepherds have played since time immemorial than with the *opa*! favourites the Cypriot band had just performed. But when he finished, the applause rang in his ears.

Startled, he gazed out at the audience he could hear but not see. It seemed they liked his music, and when again he strummed his guitar he began to feel the same old assurance that had always come to him when he was playing only to his very best friends. He had meant next to sing them an old Cretan song of war and death, but instead he leaned closer to the microphone. 'This one's for my mother,' he said as he sounded the first chords of another of his new London songs. 'And for all the other political resisters.' Almost he could hear the audience sigh in anticipation, for they had assembled here tonight not just to listen to Greek music but to show their solidarity against the regime in Athens.

Nikos squinted soulfully into the glaring light, and began to sing about a woman with blueblack hair and raven eyes who had not been afraid to dare all for what was right. The Greek words were as simple as a child's nursery rhyme and the melody as uncomplicated as an advertizing jingle on the television. But Nikos' voice throbbed with emotion as he sang his mother's story, how she had begun her life walking barefoot in her seaside village, how she had followed the dictates of her time and place and married and had children, and how finally in her middle years she had grown tall as a cypress, solid as a block of marble, and shining as the Greek midsummer sun. When he was finished, the applause went on and on.

Nikos grinned and began to enjoy himself. Again he departed from what he had planned to play and instead launched into a raunchy tune he had heard a few times in a down and dirty *rebetika* tavern in Piraeus. The original lyrics lampooned a balding buffoon who was being cuckolded by his young wife, but when he had played this for his friends in Athens he had substituted new verses that poked fun at the pretences of the colonels. 'This one,' he informed the audience, 'is for those who are about to fall in Athens.'

The lyrics, which were all about whores and lies and treacheries repaid in full, were in Greek. But the mockery needed no translation, and the audience was on its feet, stamping and cheering, when he sounded the last chord.

He had planned four numbers, for after him there were three more singers and another band. Should he, he wondered, as the applause rolled on, share Liberty's song with them? In a way he wanted to hug it only to himself, for playing something like this in public was like letting the whole world into his soul. And yet, not only for Liberty but for the cause, for *Greece*, he decided to do it. He held up his hand to signal for silence, and then he cleared his throat. 'This one,' he said, 'is for my Liberty.'

There was a hiss of whispers from the audience, as those who knew the story of the death of the British journalist who had been Nikos' fiancée repeated the tale for those who hadn't heard it. When finally the hall grew silent, Nikos leaned over his guitar and played 'Liberty's Song'.

The melody started out as light and graceful as she had been that fine spring day when first he saw her gliding up the museum walk. The words, when he began to sing about her hair, her eyes and her laugh, were in English, and in them Nikos chronicled the teasing innocence of first love in a fragrant Greek summer: all light and water, sun and kisses. But then, subtly at first, the mood changed as Nikos began to sound a driving beat as threatening as a raised club or even a truck butting a small Fiat on a dark and winding mountain road. The two strains of the music ebbed and flowed as the softness of the woman struggled against the brutality of the forces careering toward her. The beat grew stronger, more implacable, and yet under it still, albeit faintly, the melody that had been the best of Liberty still played on. Now the tempo swelled, raced, thumped until finally, in a crescendo of a crash, it seemed for a moment that the sweet music underpinning it all had forever been silenced. Heavy as a boot, the beat marched on. But then, as hesitant as a sigh, the ghost of the melody began to weave an intricate musical web that grew so strong and powerful that it overwhelmed the beat. The last gentle stanza was a melancholy echo of the first, the innocence dead and buried, but the music rich and true and eternal; Liberty triumphant.

When it was over and Nikos bowed his head and hugged his guitar, for a moment the Albert Hall hung in silence. Then, as one, the audience was on its feet, shouting, stamping their feet in rhythm, begging for more. But Nikos was too blinded by tears to sing another note. He wiped his eyes, fled to the wings, and would not even come back on stage for a bow.

As the concert organizers buzzed about him, congratulating him on his triumph and hatching plans to release 'Liberty's Song' as a single record which they thought might even make the pop charts, Nikos hung miserable and aloof, wishing only that they would leave him alone. Finally, when another Greek orchestra trooped onstage and a popular Athens bouzouki singer took the microphone, he was able to steal away to a quiet corner.

He set down his guitar and huddled by the red plush curtain. He would have liked to wrap himself in its suffocating folds and never sing again. He had not thought it would devastate him so to sing of her as he had, but the words and music had made him relive her death all over again. Behind his shut eyes, hot tears stung. He braced himself to slink out of this hall and get a taxi back to his rented room. He would pull the covers over his head and seal himself away from the world that hurt too much.

But that was not to be.

'Niko!' A familiar voice called out, and arms that he had known for most of his life suddenly were wrapped around him.

He opened his eyes to the grandfather that held him. 'You? Here?' When he had talked to his grandfather just last week on the telephone, Nick had said nothing about coming to London. He hung on for dear life to his father's father, and now he was not ashamed to cry.

'*Paidi mou*!' Old Nick rocked his grandson in his arms as he crooned to him. 'It's all right, my child, it's OK, we're here, we flew in this afternoon for the concert as soon as we heard you'd be here. All day we wanted to see you, but we waited until now, to make for you a big surprise. You didn't see us out there in the front row? No? Oh, *paidi mou*, you were wonderful! We were so proud of you, so proud.'

Nikos pulled back, wiped his eyes, and looked around. It couldn't be! By some miracle, had his mother gotten out of Greece and flown here in time to hear him sing her story? 'We?'

'Your Uncle Christos and I.' Nick beamed at his firstborn son, who stepped forward and smiled at this young man he was seeing for the first time in his life.

Nikos gaped at the one his mother had talked about so much that, to him, Christos had always been almost a mythic figure. As a boy he had thrilled to his mother's stories of how 'Captain Prometheus' had fought in the mountains, first against the Germans and then against the rightwing government forces. Later he had followed his career in America and wept when he had been forced to withdraw from political life. When he first had begun his boyhood fights with his father, he had even wished that instead of Yorgos he could have had someone like Christos to emulate and love. More recently, too, when that old leftist Takis had recalled the magic his uncle had once coaxed from his flute, he had wondered if his own gift for music had come from this glamorous relative. But until now, his uncle had only been a face in faded photographs and a name scrawled at the bottom of airmail

462

stationery. Christos was dark and stocky, like all the Kronos men, and he had those same green Kronos eyes that stared back at Nikos in the mirror every day. As he looked from his grandfather to his uncle, he thought that, a thousand kilometres from Panagia, the generations were finally complete. Nikos had an impulse to hurl himself in the arms of this long lost uncle, but instead shyly – they were in England now – he held out his hand. 'Uncle Christo.'

But Christos had no such inhibitions. He folded Marika's son in his arms and hugged him in a tight embrace. 'Niko, Niko, at last, my Niko!' He murmured the endearment that every Greek lavishes on anyone beloved. '*Paidi mou*! My child!'

A shiver of intuition shot up Nikos' spine. But no, he thought; it can't be, that's crazy. Yet still, with Christos' arms around him, he felt so whole, so *right*. Again the feeling that now the family circle was complete. But he supposed this concert and *that song* – 'Liberty's Song' – had just unleashed too much emotion. He warned himself not to get carried away. This is my uncle, not my father.

Yet as Nick burbled on – he and Christos were staying at a suite in the Savoy, and they would go to the hotel now for a midnight supper, it would be just like old times down in the village, only better – Nikos stood with Christos' arm snugly around his shoulder and felt happier than at any moment since he had first heard of the disaster on the Thessaloniki road. As the three Kronos men made their way out of the hall and into a taxi, it seemed to Nikos that even the soft early spring English rain was a caress. Life, he realized anew, was lush not only with sorrow but joy.

They celebrated not only Nikos' triumph at Albert Hall but their family reunion in a sumptuous meal in the gilt and mahogany splendour of the Savoy dining room. Nick ordered enough food for all the absent members of the family, and as best he could he tried to coax Greek foods from the traditional English menu. There was roast lamb and new potatoes, grilled liver and kidneys, salads of every description, and even bottles of retsina he had laid in earlier in the day from a Greek shop in North London. They clinked glasses and toasted the future.

But here, just as in his own popular restaurant in Boston, Nick could not stay seated at his table. Three of the waiters were Greek, and time and again the old man leaped up to joke with them as they glided about their work in the far reaches of the dining room.

During one of those spells when it was only he and Nikos at the table, Christos leaned closer, as though what he were about to say was some intimate matter that could only be spoken about in a whisper. 'Your mother . . . how is she?'

Nikos shook his head. 'You know she's back in Panagia? With *him*? I don't dare write to her, nor she to me. But my Uncle Vangelis in Australia keeps me posted. She's all right, I guess. At least *he* kept her out of prison. But it sounds like she's under house arrest.'

'Nick says the same. He telephones, you know, and he says she's in good spirits, considering . . . It took a great deal of courage to write what she did about the polytechnic. Your mother is a remarkable woman. She always was, even as a girl. But I never thought, never dreamed, that one day she would be as she is.'

'What do you mean?' Nikos was closely watching the play of emotions on the other's face.

Christos smiled in a dreamy way, as though he were transported back to another time and place. 'She was so beautiful, Marika. Why I remember . . .' He stopped in mid-sentence. 'That song of yours, about your mother. How did you know how she once was? Listening to you, I could almost see her walking down the shallows of Panagia beach, with that hair of hers, and those eyes.'

He loved her, Nikos thought. Yes, once Christos loved my mother. And yet he had left, and she had married Yorgos. Before he could ask about that, Christos broke into his thoughts.

'And that other song, about your girl.' Christos reached out and put his arm around Nikos. 'I'm so sorry. I know what you must be feeling.' His eyes were hooded. 'Believe me, I know what you're feeling. And what you've lost. I, too . . .' He lit a cigarette, inhaled, and said no more.

He means my mother, Nikos thought, not Penelope. Yes, somehow he was sure he had guessed right.

But before he could ask what was on the tip of his tongue, Nick returned to bombard him with questions about the future. 'So, *paidi mou*, when do you come to Boston?'

Nikos had been dreading this inevitable query. The moment when he could have asked Christos about himself and his mother passed.

'So,' Nick was pressing, 'you'll come back with us tomorrow? It was touch and go about getting your visa without even having your passport. But I pulled every string I could. I'll be giving out free lobsters to the whole Boston Immigration Office for a year and a day. They'll bankrupt me, those bandits, but never you mind. I got the visa! I've already booked you a seat with us on the afternoon flight. First class! Only the best for my grandson, the star!'

'I'm afraid that won't be possible. I have more concerts to do here in England next month.'

'So?' Nick snapped his fingers. 'Fly back for your concerts. What's six hours? You'll go back and forth like an eagle. They have direct flights every day from Boston.'

Nikos had intended to put off his grandfather with the excuse, which really wasn't a lie, that his work here in England still wasn't finished. He had promised the concert organizers that he would play another series of benefits in Bristol, Manchester, and Birmingham. And after the success of his performance tonight, one of them had alluded to other appearances he might have to make if 'Liberty's Song' took off and became a hit on the European charts. But instead Nikos blurted out the truth. 'I can't go to live with you in America. Anywhere else, but not America.'

'You make a joke, eh?' Nick scowled at his grandson. 'Of course you will come back with us to Boston. We're your *family*, and your place is with *us*. If it's singing you want, I'll set up a place for you in my restaurant. Maybe inside my Parthenon, yes, that's it, I'll change around the oyster bar and make it into a cabaret! Wait until you see the temple that your uncle built. A little bit of Athens, right in the heart of Boston. You'll love it. You're an architect, after all, so you'll really appreciate what your uncle managed to do with that plastic. Everyone loves my Parthenon.' He pulled an envelope of snapshots from his pocket and laid them out on the linen tablecloth as though they were a winning hand of aces. Nikos looked at the Americans posed on the portico of a white edifice that did, indeed, look like a scale model of the Acropolis shrine to Athena. Nick rubbed his hands together. 'Yes, that's what we'll do. You'll play your songs in my Parthenon. It's all settled.'

'Sorry, grandfather.' Nikos reared his head up in the negative. 'I'd go with you and Uncle Christos anywhere else. But not to America.'

Nick was so busy deciding where to relocate his oyster bar so Nikos could sing inside the plastic Parthenon that he hadn't been listening to a word his grandson said. But Christos was leaning forward intently. 'Why not America?'

Nikos eloquently shrugged. 'What can I say? The CIA was behind the '67 coup. They're the ones that have kept the *junta* in power. And now, after what happened at the polytechnic, how can I go to live in America?'

'What's this I hear you saying about America?' At last the import of his grandson's words were getting through to the old man. He glared at Nikos. 'What are you, some kind of Communist?' His scowl extended to Christos. 'I just get you straightened out, and now this young one starts?'

'No, no, I'm not a Communist.' Nikos wished now that he hadn't brought any of this up. His grandfather was never going to let it rest. 'It's just, as I said, that I can't set foot in a place that has caused my own country so much trouble.'

465

'You don't like America? *My country?*' Nick's hand was over his heart, as though he were about to recite the Pledge of Allegiance. 'But it's a wonderful place, a paradise, really. The land of opportunity! America has been very good to me, and you will see when you get there that it will be very good to you.'

'I'm not coming.' Patiently Nikos tried to explain his politics to his grandfather. 'So much that's happened in *my* country, in *Greece*, is because of the policies of the American government. The *junta* came to power because the Americans wanted it in power. And the only reason it still stands is because the American government, and in particular the CIA, wants a regime it can count on in Athens. The dictatorship gave them their precious homeport facilities for the Sixth Fleet. We're a military base for them, that's all. An American satellite! Everything bad that's happened to my country is the fault of the Americans.'

'You *sound* like a Communist.' Again Nick glared at Christos as though his past was responsible for his grandson's present.

Under his breath Christos unhappily sighed. But then he launched into a lecture. 'I know where you're coming from, Niko. But believe me, world politics are a lot more complicated than the slogans you kids hung outside the polytechnic. I'm not saying what you did was wrong, not at all. I'm proud you were a part of all that. But you and everyone else in Greece have got to stop blaming Washington for everything that's gone wrong in Athens.' As Nikos intently hung on his every word, Christos warmed to his subject. 'It's true that Greece, like other small countries, depends on the patronage of a great power not only for its external security but its economic survival. That's what power politics are all about. But it's about time that Greeks accepted responsibility for their own shortcomings. The *junta* has most definitely been supported not only by the Americans but also by the great mass of the Greek people who – until now, anyway, when you laid your lives on the line at the polytechnic – have cared less about their civil liberties than their pocketbooks. Think, Niko! The dictatorship will fall only if and when the Greek people have finally had enough of it. And I pray, *paidi mou*, that thanks to what you and your friends did at the polytechnic, that day will come soon.' But when he saw the uncertainty on Nikos' face, Christos decided that this was neither the time nor the place to continue to explain the intricate shadings of right and wrong to this young man who had so clearly swallowed the same sort of black-and-white simplicities and do-or-die slogans that he himself had once taken for catechism.

But Christos needn't have worried about embarking into such deep waters. Nick was shaking his finger at his grandson. 'Listen to your uncle if you won't listen to me. I don't know what we're going to do with you. Because you believe these dirty lies about America, you expect to stay all alone here, in England, away from not only your country but your family?'

'No.' Nikos was surprised at the answer that came so quickly to his lips. 'In a little while, as soon as I finish whatever work the Resistance wants me to do with my music, maybe I will go to Australia.'

'*Po-po-po!*' Contemptuously Nick dismissed such a preposterous idea. 'Kangaroos! Boomerangs! What else is there in that place?'

'My Uncle Vangelis.' Now that he had said it, Nikos was warming to the idea. 'You know he and Vasso live in Melbourne with little Yannis.' The baby had been born last month and was thriving. 'It's very Greek there, they say, and they're going to open a little hotel. It's not Panagia, of course, but it's as good a place as any to wait out my exile until I can go home.'

As Nick continued to sputter on about the superiorities of America and the ingratitude of his grandson, quietly Christos leaned closer to the young man. 'You won't reconsider? It would mean a lot to me if you'd come back with us. Seeing you . . .' Christos touched Nikos' hand. 'It brings a lot back. Brings everything back.'

Nikos wavered but then held fast. 'Maybe one day we'll all be able to go back. Go home. But, for now, for me, I just can't go with you to America.'

After that, there was little more to do but pay the outrageous bill. Nick of course insisted that Nikos stay the night in their suite, and they made their way up to the resplendent rooms with their glancing view of the Thames. Yet still Nick refused to admit defeat and stayed up most of the night trying to convince his grandson to return to Boston with them. Late the next morning, Nikos went to see them off at Heathrow.

At the airport, however, as he stood in the queue with them waiting to check their baggage, Nikos had one of those lightning changes of heart to which all his countrymen are so addicted. A Greek will lay elaborate plans and vow up and down that he will not be dissuaded, and then at the last minute he will take enormous pleasure in casting those plans aside and following the impulse of the moment.

Just so, as Nick was about to step up to the reservations clerk, Nikos wondered what had been wrong with him, stubbornly putting student slogans before his feelings for his family? He was a Greek; and although politics mattered, the family mattered more. Nikos' thoughts raced. Christos, who once had been such an ardent revolutionary, had made sense last night in that impromptu lecture of his. He wanted to have more such talks with his uncle. Maybe he could even find out if his hunch about him and his mother was right. Christos could undoubtedly help him with his music. And he could hardly wait to have a look at his grandfather's plastic Parthenon.

He cast aside his reservations about America and decided he had to follow these dear ones wherever they were going.

He pulled out his wallet to make sure he had his passport. Then he tapped his grandfather on the shoulder and simply handed him the document.

'Bravo!' Nick threw his arms around his grandson. 'That's my boy! I knew you'd come to your senses!' He exchanged a radiant smile with Christos and then, as he reached the front of the line, he gave the clerk all three passports. 'Kronos. Three of us. First class to Boston!'

They linked arms and, to the astonishment of all those patiently waiting in the queue, they executed an exuberant *syrtaki* step as they danced toward the departure lounge.

The old man bent almost double as he methodically swept the gleaming marble floor of the Melbourne Greek Orthodox Church. There was a christening this windy late July morning in suburban West Bend. The old widows who watched over the cleanliness of the *ekklesia* as though the fate of their mortal souls rested upon its perfection would skin him alive if they spotted so much as one dust mote under the high heels of the rich parishioners who were baptising their baby boy today.

'Over *there*, Barba Yanni.' Kyria Aphrodite stood with her hands on her wide hips as she pointed to a speck he had missed under the ironwork candle stand.

The old man straightened up with a groan and leaned on his broom as he squinted in the shadowy semi-darkness. He had just swept there, but he supposed his eyes had failed him again. Obligingly he bent over the broom and gave a swipe where he had been directed.

'No, no, not *there*.' Kyria Aphrodite grabbed the broom and wielded it with the elan of Saint George spearing the dragon. 'Over *there*.' For good measure, she reswept the entire corner, her tongue lashing as she worked. 'For the life of me, I will never understand why the *pappas* lets the likes of *you* help take care of the church. For twenty-three years Kyria Maria, Kyria Dimitra, and I have done our best to make this church the cleanest in all Australia. And then last year, out of the blue, Father Alexandros tells us *you* will be giving us a hand with what he said was "the heavy work". Right away we knew it was another of the *pappas'* crazy ideas. A man can't do a woman's work. As Kyria Maria said at the time, "Can a bird pull a cart?" All it's done is made more work for us, cleaning up after you. That, and another mouth to feed. And another load of laundry to wash and iron. It wouldn't be so bad if that wife of his was well enough to look after the two of you. But the next time Father Alexandros has another bright idea like this, let him tell it to the icons instead of us.'

The one they all called *Barba* Yannis – Uncle John – slyly watched the old woman doing his work for him. For the thousandth time mentally he thanked Father Alexandros for keeping what he knew about his past from Kyria Aphrodite and those two other hags who so oppressed his life. He had served six years of his ten-year prison sentence for larceny and fraud, and his parole had been conditional on his performing community service for at least a year. Sweeping the church, polishing the icons, and acting as the good-natured priest's servant had seemed a far better deal than rotting in that jail cell. In his heart of hearts, too, Yannis had even welcomed the opportunity to square matters with God. He was sixty-nine years old, and his scoundrel life would not go on forever. But when he had agreed to come to work in this church, he had not reckoned on Kyria Aphrodite being part of the bargain. He supposed now that he had served his required year here, he should be moving on. It hardly mattered where he went, so long as he was away from Kyria Aphrodite.

While her back was turned, he stuck out his tongue at her. She and those two other crones who always dressed in black with their babushkas pulled low on their foreheads reminded him of the pictures back in his Greek schoolroom of the mythological harpies who had tormented some hero or another. Yannis tried to remember whether their victim had been Herakles, Odysseus, or maybe Jason? But he had spent only a few short winters in school, and that fact along with so much else that once had been part of the fabric of his life back in the *patrida* was altogether gone now. Sometimes when Kyria Aphrodite and her cronies flew at him, however, clearly he could remember the garish picture of the ugly winged harpies swooping at a virile young man. He supposed there might even be a sort of malignant women's justice in his spending his last years here in this church doing the bidding of these three hags. He had left two of his wives – one in Greece and another in Africa – and been abandoned by the last of them here in Australia. Now it was as though these old girls were repaying him for the ancient wrongs his harpy wives would doubtless have maintained he had done them. By a trick of fate, instead of eking out his sunset years in humble and solitary penitence, God and the parole board had put him once again under the thumb of three bossy women who were enough like his ex-wives to be their sisters.

Kyria Aphrodite was proceeding to sweep the rest of the floor. In a better mood now that she had her beloved broom back in hand, she seemed to forget her contempt for Barba Yannis as she settled down to her second greatest passion in life, after sweeping. 'This should be some christening! I heard Father Alexandros saying this morning to his wife, when I brought in

469

the fresh bread, that back in Greece the baby's father's family owns half the Peloponnese. They came here just last year. Some sort of political problem. I suppose they'll be going back soon, now that it looks like the colonels are on the way out. Mark my words! They'll never survive this Cyprus disaster. Gave the island – *our* island, a *Greek* island – to the Turks on a silver platter! It was bad enough when that snake Ioannides tried to have Archbishop Makarios assassinated. A saint, that one, a real modern Cypriot saint! But then when the Turks landed and took nearly half the island before anyone could stop them, that was the end of the colonels. And high time, too, in my estimation!'

Barba Yannis nodded knowingly, although he had only a vague idea what she was talking about. Since when had the old hag become an expert on international affairs?

But to Kyria Aphrodite the rise and fall of governments – even a Greek government – mattered less than the ins and outs of local gossip. Without missing a broom stroke, she returned to the star players in this morning's christening. 'The mother's a West Bend girl, although she got married back in the Old Country. Vasso's father is old Mikis who owns all those fruit and vegetable stands. He's worth a fortune, too. But nothing like the young fellow from the Peloponnese.'

'Is that so?' Barba Yannis trailed along beside her in the attitude of a small boy dogging his mother. So long as he kept her talking, she would finish his morning chores. 'How rich?'

Kyria Aphrodite paused in her sweeping long enough to hold up her right hand and twitch together thumb and index finger in that Greek gesture that means *lots* of money. 'I heard him say they own hotels, restaurants, and enough orange groves to feed the whole state of Victoria. He says they just about run a village not far from Nauplion.'

'Nauplion?' Barba Yannis couldn't resist repeating the name, which hadn't passed his lips for so many years. The ship's captain who had originally been supposed to take him to Australia had been from Nauplion. Poor old Stavros, dead and buried in heathen Africa! Everything might have turned out differently if his freighter hadn't blown its engine off Mombassa, and then Stavros hadn't gotten malaria while they waited in that fever-ridden port for a replacement engine. Desperation wouldn't have forced Yannis to take that black cow for a wife, he wouldn't have gotten stuck in Kenya for the duration of the Second World War, and he wouldn't have had to escape Numa and those three squalling dark children of theirs as soon as the war ended and the freighters began calling at Mombassa again. He wondered, very briefly, whatever had become of black Numa. If she and Anna had ever met, they would have made quite a pair! Barba Yannis nearly shuddered at that ghastly thought. They had both been witches – Anna with her Evil Eye and Numa with her black magic – and he had been terrified of them. No one could blame him, really, for having left the two of them flat. Though, considering how everything had turned out, one or both of them might have marked him for life with one of their damned curses. It would be just like them to haunt him to his dying day. Yannis hadn't thought of his first two wives for years. Tula – the third one, the love of his life, the young she-devil who had ruined him with that land scam of hers – now *her* he still thought of every night. He had heard she was working in a bar in New Zealand now, dancing topless. Yannis sighed at the thought of her watermelon breasts now on display for all those lucky Kiwi sheepherders. But then, willy-nilly, the word 'Nauplion' hanging in the air turned his thoughts back to the far less lovely image of Anna. Homely, she'd been, and she hadn't even had any *prika* to sweeten the deal. He would never have married her if she hadn't bewitched him that night in that bat-infested cave. Women! They were all mad as hatters! Yet at the thought of not only her but Stavros, Barba Yannis shut his eyes and could almost see the Venetian square and that old castle on the Nauplion cliffs. Other images flooded his mind. Little Marika sitting on his lap begging him to tell her a story. And the baby, the long-awaited boy, little Vangelis . . . Barba Yannis reopened his tear-filled eyes to see Kyria Aphrodite's bright black eyes speculatively watching him.

'Say, aren't you from somewhere near Nauplion?' She took pride in never forgetting the smallest personal detail anyone had ever been rash enough to confide to her.

'That's right.' If he didn't keep her talking, he would have to finish the floor himself. Barba Yannis' lips parted in a sort of smile that showed gums instead of teeth. 'A little fishing village.' Usually he was closemouthed about his past. But if he didn't answer her question, she'd flounce off and he'd have to kill his back with that broom again. 'Panagia. A pretty place. But dirt poor.'

'Panagia! Why, that's the village I heard Father Alexandros mention. I remember it distinctly, because my husband's family came from a village also called Panagia over by Patras.' Kyria Aphrodite had been born and raised in a Greek mainland village in Euboea and after the war had come to Australia to marry, sight unseen, a friend of her uncle's. But despite her twenty-five years in Melbourne, she still looked and acted and thought exactly like a Greek village woman, circa 1949.

'There are many villages called Panagia.' Barba Yannis dearly hoped the old lady had gotten the name or location of that village wrong. It had been forty years since he had encountered anyone from home, and the last thing he wanted this morning was to be found humbly sweeping this church by

471

someone who might be able to hold him to account for his past. And yet he wondered if he would recognize the name of this particular family. 'But still,' he said, unable to resist asking, 'even though I left there long ago, and it's probably not even the same village, did you happen to catch the name of these people you think might have come from Panagia?'

'Father Alexandros told me, he must have told me, but I can't remember. Old! I'm getting old!' Kyria Aphrodite frowned and handed him the broom. 'I don't know, but I'll find out.' She was muttering to herself as abruptly she left the church to clear up what for her was a matter of personal honour.

As Barba Yannis gingerly resumed his work with the broom – taking a shortcut or two, carefully scattering Kyria Aphrodite's sweepings under the chairs on the far wall – he tried to master his rising panic. Even if the old crone had gotten the name of the village right, the chances that anyone in this christening party would remember him were remote. He had left four decades ago and in the intervening years had never so much as sent a postcard. By now his family would assume he was dead, and he wanted to keep it that way. He might feel differently if fate had been kinder to him since he'd left. If he could have showed off a big shiny car and flashed a fat bankroll, he might even have braved Anna's wrath and returned for a lordly visit. He would have liked to have seen their eyes pop when he rolled into Panagia in a Cadillac. No one in that wretched village had ever appreciated his true worth. But for one of *them* to find him now, reduced to sweeping up a church!

He leaned his broom against the wall, surreptitiously lit a cigarette, and reconsidered. He had changed his name twice since he'd left Greece, and even Father Alexandros didn't know his real family name.

Carelessly he flicked ashes on the clean floor and then stealthily scattered them with his shoe so Kyria Aphrodite wouldn't browbeat him about the mess. Even if some of the christening guests did come from his village, there was no way they would know his true identity unless they recognized him.

Yannis shambled over to the church's most treasured relic, an icon of the Archangel Michael studded with jewels and encased in glass. He stood so he could see his reflection superimposed over the saint's halo. His head was as bald as a newborn baby's, his haggard face was all wrinkles and folds, but he fancied he did not look so very different from the winter's day when he had left Panagia for good. He had been a handsome devil then, too. A little weathering only enhanced a man's virility.

He heard Kyria Aphrodite's approaching bustle in time to deposit the forbidden cigarette behind the sacred icon, and when she reappeared he was once again pushing the broom.

'News!' she shouted. 'It's all over the radio! Greece! The dictatorship has

472

fallen! Today! Just now! All the ministers have resigned! And Karamanlis has been called back from Paris to form a new government! They're dancing in the streets in Athens!' As though she, too, were among the crowds in Syntagma, she executed a frisky little kick-step right there in the church under the dome with its fresco of Christ the Redeemer.

When she tried to link arms with the old man, however, Barba Yannis adroitly eluded her grasp. He knew these old widows were still hot for a man like him between their legs, and he was definitely not going to let himself become a four-time loser. 'Please, *kyria*. This is a *church*.'

'But a *Greek* church.' She pranced over to the icon of Archangel Michael and gave his feet a smacking kiss. 'Today even the icons should be dancing. They've promised to release all the political prisoners. Free! Once again the *patrida* is free!' She whirled like a dervish.

Patiently Barba Yannis asked the only news that mattered to him. 'And the name?'

'What name?' If that old fool wouldn't dance, Kyria Aphrodite would have another. She grabbed the broom and tangoed with it.

'The name of the *family*? At today's christening?'

'Oh,' she said. 'Papageorgiou. The baby will be baptised Yannis. And the father's Vangelis Papageorgiou.'

When she dipped and turned, Barba Yannis had fainted on the marble floor.

Two hours later, when the christening guests were gathered around the baptismal font, Barba Yannis lurked in the dark shadows of the church.

He had let Kyria Aphrodite and Father Alexandros believe that he had fainted because he had been overcome with emotion at the great news from Athens. The *pappas* had been touched that the old reprobate, who until now had never shown much affection for the motherland or anything else, had demonstrated such a wellspring of love for the Old Country. Solicitously he had suggested Barba Yannis spend the rest of the day in bed. But after going back to his room for only a few minutes, he had insisted on heating the water for the font. And then he had stood waiting on the church steps until the christening guests had begun to arrive.

In his sweaty hands he had clutched the old photographs he had retrieved from the box he kept locked by his bed. He and Anna on their wedding day. Marika in her christening dress. Himself holding Vangelis on the beach, with Panagia Island looming behind them. He had stared down at the fuzzy images, blurred by time, which were all he had left from the life he had walked out on too many years ago. Would he even recognize his family when finally he saw them again?

He had assumed, when the first car had pulled up, that the one carrying the swaddled baby must be his son. The beefy young man with the fair hair and thick eyeglasses didn't have the family resemblance, but he supposed the boy must have taken after Anna's ugly relations. When he had last seen his son, he hadn't been much bigger than the infant in his arms. But then Barba Yannis' heart had raced when a tall young fellow with a mop of black curls had bounded out of the next car, and he had heard someone calling out to him, 'Vangeli!' It had been like looking at himself in a forty-year-old mirror. The young man had his athletic build, his luxuriant hair, his merry eyes.

Impulsively Barba Yannis had taken one hesitant step forward and was about to clutch Vangelis to him and murmur, 'My son, my son. Oh my son!'

But he had been too late. Vangelis and the others had swept past him into the church. I am forty years too late, Barba Yannis had told himself.

He had stood rooted on the steps. After all that had happened, how could he now lay claim to the past? Yet, watching the other guests arrive, intently he had listened to them call out to one another. Which of these women was little Marika? And was one of these old crones Anna? Once he had thought he'd spotted his daughter in a pretty, youngish woman with dark hair and eyes. But then another girl had taken her arm and he'd heard her call her Gelly. A few moments later he had cringed against the church door when he caught sight of a formidable hatchet-faced old lady in black, but he had breathed a sigh of relief when he realized she was half a foot taller than the wife he had fled from a lifetime ago.

As he had listened to the sounds of the sacramental ceremony beginning in the church, Barba Yannis had debated whether to slink back to his room and let the past remain decently buried. But again he had studied the old photographs, and the memories had come back as clearly as if all *that* had happened only yesterday. Fishing with Nikolas Kronos in a leaky old *caique*. Anna that night in the cave. Marika's laughing eyes. The babies they had buried in the cemetery under the cypress tree. The first time he had held Vangelis in his arms. Anna's tears the night of their parting.

As though Father Alexandros' chanting was a siren's call, he had been unable to resist entering the old church with a faltering step. But he wouldn't intrude on the family's affair. He couldn't risk the humiliation of their contempt not only for what he had done but also for what he had become. But no one could blame him for bearing silent witness to his grandson's becoming a Christian.

Barba Yannis lurked in the dark shadows of the church, his eyes locked longingly upon the son who was a stranger to him. In the dim light, candles and oil lamps cast a golden light on Vangelis. He was so fine and strong, this young man who had grown up without a father. Shame overcame Barba Yannis. When this man had been a needy little boy, he himself had been lying in the fat arms of Black Numa under a starry African sky. When this man had been a tender adolescent, he himself had been whoring around the Australian outback and crawling in the fleshpots of Sydney. When this man had worn the wedding crowns, he himself had been married to a girl young enough to be his daughter. No, now that his son had grown strong and he himself was weak, he could not expect mercy, much less love, from this one he had failed when it had been his turn to be vulnerable. He was unworthy even to stand here spying on this moment of familial joy. And yet Barba Yannis could not tear his eyes off his son. What sort of man had he turned out to be? Kyria Aphrodite had said he was very rich but that he had left Greece for political reasons. Was his son a lawyer, a journalist, or some sort of spy for the Americans or the Russians? Maybe he was only a fisherman – or an owner of fishing boats – whose political crime was shooting his mouth off once too often about the government in Athens. Barba Yannis supposed he would never know. In a little while his son would walk out of his life. But now that he had been granted this glimpse of the family he had forfeited, how could he endure the loneliness of his iron cot in the *pappas'* house?

'Yannis! He is called Yannis!' As Father Alexandros announced the baby's name, the old man's eyes misted over. His grandson's name was his own. The generations had come full circle. Even though he would never know this baby, even though he would never hold him in his arms and sit with him in the blessed sun of Panagia's *plateia*, he would live on in the life and hopes and fears of this baby who carried his name.

Barba Yannis slunk further away from the charmed circle of the family he dared not claim as his own. His legs shook, and he sank down on a chair in a corner by a candle stand. A trembling seized him, the tears spilled over, and as his head sank down in his hands he dropped the photographs he had been clutching to his heart.

His shoulders shook as he silently sobbed. He couldn't bear it if they knew he was here. He was so ashamed of abandoning them. He could still see Anna's eyes, how she had wept so, how he had promised to send for her as soon as he got work in Australia. As he had lived his cheating life of lies and deceptions, he had thought the family he had left behind meant nothing to him. Even when he had vowed to Father Alexandros that he regretted his dissolute life, that, too, had only been another lie to secure release from prison. But now, face to face with his family who evidently had prospered in his absence, Barba Yannis wept for all he had lost. He had thought he was so smart, eluding the clutching demands of his family. *Families*, he amended to himself, remembering black Numa and the three children he'd sired on her. But what he wouldn't do now to have his son's strong arms around him! He was old, so old, and afraid to die alone so far from home. Greece, he thought, oh my country! He had betrayed everything that mattered in life: his wives, his children, his homeland, too. He was a Greek, and yet he had run out on his own flesh and blood.

But one attentive pair of ears and one sharp pair of eyes had heard his sobs and seen his despair.

Kyria Aphrodite, at work in a near corner giving the brass another obsessive polishing even while the baptism was underway, squinted at the old man weeping in the wooden chair. *Now* what was the matter with Barba Yannis?

She tucked her polishing rag in her pocket and tiptoed near enough to see the photographs scattered on the floor. She picked them up, pursed her lips, and did a doubletake at the one of the young man holding the baby. She looked from Barba Yannis over to the rich man from the Peloponnese – grinning as the baby was dipped in the baptismal water – and then back at the snapshot. Could it be? She recalled Barba Yannis' curiosity about the family from Panagia, and then his falling into a dead faint when she'd repeated their name. She let out her breath in a hiss. *Yes.*

For an instant she stood irresolute. Should she confront Barba Yannis with her suspicions, hand these photographs over to the rich Greek from the Peloponnese, or go back to her polishing and keep her nose out of what was most definitely not her business?

Of course she put her hand on his heaving shoulder. 'Barba Yannis?'

He looked up in alarm. But when he saw it was only *her*, he shrugged off the gnarled hand. 'Go away, old woman.' Again he covered his face with his hands.

She looked over at the family clustered around the font. If she hesitated, the ceremony would be over and the opportunity lost. It was her Christian duty to get to the bottom of this mystery. Armed with the photographs, she sailed across the floor and tapped the rich man from the Peloponnese on the shoulder.

His face was radiant as he turned away from the sight of the priest anointing his son. 'Yes?'

'I believe these are your father's.' She handed him Barba Yannis' snapshots.

'What did you say?' Vangelis frowned at the interruption. But he was incredulous when he looked down at the same yellowed photographs his mother had shown him a thousand times. 'How did you get these?'

'I think from your father.' She pointed at Barba Yannis sobbing in the corner.

'My father?' Vangelis reared up his head in the Greek negative. 'But my father's dead.'

'That one looks alive to me.'

Again Vangelis stared down at the photographs, then over at the old man. No, it wasn't possible, not after all these years. His father must have died long ago. 'What's his name?'

'We just call him Barba Yannis. But I know he's from your village. Panagia, right? In the Peloponnese? Not far from Nauplion?'

'But what's he doing here?'

'Not much, I'll testify to that. Eats like a horse. But he's lazy. And a mean one, too. A good for nothing, if you ask me. But what he's *supposed* to be doing here is helping to clean up the church. He fainted dead away this morning when he heard your name. And your son's.'

At that reminder, Vangelis looked back to the baby, who was now dressed in his christening robes and being placed in his mother's arms. In a moment they would be leaving the church and going home to the christening feast which would be a double celebration because of the glorious news from Athens.

He looked back to the old man weeping in the corner. Even if the *kyria* was right in her hunch, what did he owe a father who had abandoned them all more than a generation ago? Some things a man can never forgive. But then, remembering how his mother's face had been illuminated at her moment of death when Yorgos had pretended to be her long-lost husband, he thought that maybe there are some things a woman can never help forgiving.

Just then the old man raised his head and met his eyes.

Him, Vangelis thought, it's *him* . . . The face he had studied all his life in these same photographs was in ruins. But even in the dim church light, he knew this was no ghost. This was his *father*. He supposed he owed this old man nothing. But Vangelis was after all his mother's son. For *her*, he would do this.

Slowly he closed the distance between himself and his father. And then he reached down and took him in his arms. As the old man clung to him as a child will, Vangelis felt the frailty of the old bones. Pity for his father washed over him. Gently he held him.

A moment later, he drew apart and smiled through his own tears. 'Come now,' he said, his arm around the old man's shoulders as he steered him over to the rest of the family. 'It's time we took you home.'

Kyria Aphrodite wiped the sentimental tears from her withered cheeks. And then, as she watched the look of wonder on Barba Yannis' face as he reached out his hand to the baby, she prepared herself for a long day and night of sensational gossip. First she'd tell Kyria Maria and then Kyria

Dimitra. After that, the *pappas'* wife. Or maybe she'd better tell Father Alexandros' wife first. By tomorrow the whole Greek community of West Bend – or maybe all Melbourne – would know that she, Kyria Aphrodite, was responsible for this happy ending.

She *loved* a happy ending. And who knew? Maybe the very rich young man from the Peloponnese would give her a handsome reward for reuniting him with his father. Now that, she reflected, as she bustled off to tell the *pappas'* wife before Father Alexandros disrobed and could tell her himself, would be an even happier ending.

Easter

April, 1975

Epilogue

In Panagia on Easter Eve, although the women of the family wore their aprons instead of uniforms and brandished their paring knives, sieves, and cauldrons instead of weapons, Marika paced the taverna kitchen like a general reviewing the troops. Everything had to be perfect for the reunion tonight. She looked at the clock over the refrigerator. By now *they* would be halfway here from the Athens airport. Or maybe, despite the inevitable holiday traffic jam on the National Road, even closer. Nikos drove like a maniac. If she knew her son, he and Vangelis would have Nick and *him* back in the village in another hour. Sixty minutes. After waiting for twenty-five years, this last hour burned.

She paused beside Vasso, who was up to her elbows in the dough for a belated batch of *tsoureki* Pascha bread. Marika gave it a little knead and then patted her sister-in-law on the back. 'Couldn't do better myself.' She and Vasso had become as close as sisters since the Australian branch of the family had come winging home last autumn, after the new government of national reconciliation in Athens had not only released all the political prisoners but also declared an amnesty for those in exile. As soon as the doctor had confirmed her new pregnancy, Vasso had confided her great news to Marika right after she'd told her husband. Already Vasso's stomach bulged with the twins who would be born in the summer. That fancy new test she'd had in Athens had confirmed not only that the fetuses were fine but that they would one day be named Eleni and Anna.

By the sink Marika watched her own girls at work on the ingredients for their grandmother's soup. Lena was patiently cleaning every grain of rice, and Annoula was washing the fresh mint and dill. '*Bravo*,' Marika pronounced.

As her daughters smiled, she reflected that before long they, too, would be getting married and having babies. Or perhaps not, she amended, remembering how airily they had dismissed the stern telegraphic note their father had written them just last week on that pad he kept always on the arm of his wheelchair: 'Marriage! Good village boy! Now before too late! Old maids?' Her daughters had merely laughed, given their father kisses on his cheeks, and gone back to their animated discussion about college life with their brother. Lena was nearly twenty-two and deeply engrossed in her archaeology studies at Athens University. At twenty, Annoula had just begun the second year of her medical studies at the same institution. The last thing either of them seemed to have on their minds, as they returned to the village for their Easter holidays, was wearing the wedding crowns. Marika reflected that this younger generation of liberated Greek girls was so very different from how she and her friends had been at their age. If she hadn't been so worried about being a spinster, maybe she would never have seduced Christos to that cave. She glanced up at the clock. Fifty minutes.

'Like this, mama?' Annoula, who one day would be a surgeon and already had the technique, showed her the first bits of herbs she had sliced on the cutting board.

'A little smaller,' Marika answered, remembering how her own mother had first initiated her into the ways of the kitchen, and of life. Sometime this week, before she and Nikos and the girls went back to the Athens villa, she would take them back to the Cave of the Great Goddess and tell them the cavern's secrets they had been too young to hear on their first outing there. Not, she amended to herself, that her blooming, confident, quite liberated daughters needed the cave or any other sort of magic to lure the men of their choice to the altar. But Lena, with her passion for archaeology, would thrill to all the particulars of the tale Old Anna had told her long ago. All the girl wanted to talk about these days was the dig she'd be working on in Cyprus this summer. For the past year or so, Lena's interest in that troubled island had become such a compulsion that sometimes she even talked with a Cypriot accent. Marika gave her daughter a speculative look as she sifted the rice through a sieve with the same attention that those of her profession sifted dirt for clues to lost civilizations. She wouldn't be surprised if Lena had a young man somewhere on Cyprus.

When Lena felt her mother's eyes upon her, she glanced up and blushed. Woman-to-woman, they exchanged a certain look.

Marika, on second thoughts, decided that maybe her archaeologist daughter just might have her own reasons for wanting to be initiated into the cave. If Lena was having man trouble, her dear mother had an answer of sorts a short row away on the island. Liberation or not, maybe some things never changed between men and women. The one she wanted seldom wanted her – at least *right now* and *altogether* and *forever* – whereas the ones she didn't want refused to take no for an answer. She herself had loved the one and married the other, and here she was at the ripe old age of forty-four watching the clock as nervously as a teenage girl waiting for a promised telephone call. Forty minutes, or less. By now maybe they were in Argos.

Killing time in the ancient woman-to-man waiting game, she turned her attention back to Annoula. Her younger daughter acted as though she were more interested in her chemistry books than a nice young man. Yet last week, in search of her own black designer blazer – both girls had the annoying habit of borrowing her clothes without bothering to tell her – in Annoula's wardrobe she had found not only the missing jacket but a packet of photographs in its pocket. The whole roll of film had been of Annoula and a long-haired boy in a black leather jacket who was so handsome that Marika would have turned to give him a second look if she had seen him passing in the street. Maybe, after a visit to the cave, both of her daughters would break their silence about the men in their lives. She had so many regrets in her life, but the one that only lately had begun to rankle was that she had given such comparatively little attention to her daughters. She had always been so obsessed with Nikos and her tangled relationships with the Kronos brothers that her daughters had grown up almost without her notice. But she vowed she would find the time to make amends, starting this week with the cave. Sharing that, after all, had been one of the secrets that had made her mother and herself so close. *She* had been gone for a year and a half. Marika would continue wearing black for her mother for at least another six months. She looked again at her daughters. Perhaps getting closer to them would help fill the gap the loss of her mother had left in her heart.

But Marika's demeanour changed when finally she came over to old Eleni, preparing the *mayeritsa* soup for tonight's late supper. She herself might be the inspecting general for Vasso's, Lena's, and Annoula's culinary skills. But in the kitchen, as everywhere else in this household, her mother-in-law was ever the Commander-in-Chief. Eleni expertly scooped the simmering sheep innards from the skillet. She minced the heart, liver, intestines, and lungs. And then with a flourish she sauteed the bits in olive oil along with a dozen spring onions.

'*Orea*!' Marika's mouth watered for the traditional soup that would break the family's Lenten fast tonight when they returned from the midnight church service. Eleni's *mayeritsa* was the second-best in the world. At the reminder of whose had been the best, Marika smoothed her black sweater down over her black skirt.

As if Eleni could read her thoughts, she sighed over the soup pot. 'Ah, but it won't be as good as *hers*. If only Old Anna had lived to see this day! Finally all of them – my Nikolas, too! – will be back.' She paused, savouring the knowledge that this time her husband had promised to stay in the village for good. But then the sadness was back in her eyes. 'All but *her*.'

Marika put a consoling arm around her mother-in-law. But as Eleni began to weep the ever-ready tears of the aged, she wondered if it would ever be possible for her mother-in-law to break her lifetime habit of grieving for the one who wasn't here instead of rejoicing for those who were. Poor soul, she thought, poor sad old soul.

'Daughter!' A now-familiar querulous call came from the balcony. 'Did you forget our coffees?'

Eleni rolled her eyes, and with a sigh Marika got out the *briki* and measured in the water, coffee, and sugar for yet another round of *metrios* for her father and her husband. Since he'd returned with Vangelis and his family, old Yannis had become the most demanding although most definitely not the most beloved member of the Kronos household. He had passed the winter playing high-stake cards with what Eleni and Marika suspected was grocery money that mysteriously had begun disappearing from its jar by the kitchen sink. When he wasn't in the least reputable coffeehouse in Panagia's *plateia*, gambling or telling preposterous yarns about his alleged adventures in Africa and Australia, he sat on the balcony ordering the women about like a lord. And yet Marika's father was good not only with his grandson but also his son-in-law. For some reason no one could understand, Yannis and Yorgos had become inseparable companions. The old man had even taken to wheeling his son-in-law down to the *kafeneion* every morning for a glass of ouzo and a game of cards.

The coffee foamed, Marika poured it out, and remembered to ready the glasses of cold water on the tray. Vangelis had told her in great detail about the sorry state in which he had found their father paroled in Australia, and yet Yannis was most insistent about being served like a family patriarch instead of a man who had chosen to turn his back on his wife and children when they had most needed him.

Her father was holding the baby, showing him the faces on a garish deck of cards, while Yorgos glowered nearby in his wheelchair. The depression that had gripped him since his strokes had deepened since the fall of the *junta* the previous summer. But a month ago, when the summons for his upcoming trial had been delivered, he had turned despondent. He was accused not only of treason for plotting to overthrow the elected government of Greece in the 1967 *coup d'état* but also of corruption in the siphoning off of many millions of tourist development drachmas for his private benefit. His trial, along with that of other prominent members of the *junta*, would convene in Athens next month. The only concession the prosecutor's office had made to his invalid status was that, instead of awaiting trial in prison along with the other members of the dictatorship, he was under house arrest here in Panagia with two soldiers stationed outside the taverna.

Yorgos continued sullenly staring at the sea as she set down the tray and carried his coffee to the table beside him. Of all the reforms enacted by the new government in Athens, the one he most hated was the legalization of the Communist Party and the decree allowing the return of all Greek Communists who had gone into exile after the Civil War. *He* would be home any minute. Yorgos' pen moved on his notepad. 'When?'

Accustomed to the code of his written demands, Marika looked at her watch. 'Soon. Fifteen minutes or so.'

Yannis took a lip-smacking sip of his hot coffee, washed it down with a swig of cold water, and lit one of the expensive American cigarettes he now smoked. 'It's been more than forty years since I saw Nikolas Kronos. I remember the day he left with not more than the shirt on his back. But they say he's been on a lucky roll since then.'

Briefly Marika's black eyes rested on the old man who had crawled out from under his Australian rock. If it had been her instead of Vangelis who had found him, she would not have been as compassionate as her easy-going brother. She knew what it was to wait the best years of her life for a man, and she would never forget how her mother's dying face had been illuminated with joy when Yorgos had pretended to be her long-lost husband. His abandonment had embittered – even poisoned – her mother, and Marika was enraged that he had returned to a life of ease and comfort now that Old Anna was gone. In the six months he had been back in Panagia, he had never even visited her grave. And yet, as Marika's thoughts returned to her mother's deathbed, on this balmy spring afternoon of homecoming she could understand that look of joy which had transformed her mother's worn face. It was the same, now, for herself. In the years that *he* had been a world away, her yearning love had sometimes curdled to something akin to hatred. And yet now the wheel had turned again. To see his face! To touch his hand! Easy, she told herself. Remember how he left you, how he married another, how he forgot what no man ever should. But she couldn't stop herself from glancing out the window to see if the car was approaching.

'They say,' Yannis continued, putting down his coffee and executing a professional riffle of the cards to the delight of his grandson, 'that Nikolas is a millionaire. And that's in American dollars, not drachmas. Imagine getting your hands on *that*! When he goes, I suppose that will be split between his sons. Yorgos and that other brother who's coming back today . . . what's his name?'

Christos.' That name on Marika's lips hung in the air.

Yorgos turned his dark beseeching eyes from the sea to his wife.

485

Marika couldn't stand the accusation and the pain in those eyes. It had been easier to hate her overbearing husband than it was to endure the pitiful invalid he had become. Every morning when she bathed him, dressed him, and set him in his wheelchair as though she were a mother settling her baby in his stroller, she had such conflicting emotions for her husband. They had never been happy together. But now that he was so obviously vanquished, Marika could be generous enough to admit that Yorgos, who had lived for twenty-five years with the knowledge that she had never loved him, had perhaps gotten the worse of their marital bargain. Yet she couldn't fault him for his honourable support of herself and his devotion to the children – even or maybe especially Nikos, the son she now suspected he had never believed to be his own. And now, too, after these personal heartaches, Yorgos had to face the shame of being humiliated in court. How galling it must be, after all this, to sit helpless in his wheelchair, waiting for the triumphant return of the brother he had warred against all his life.

She was about to return to the kitchen when outside on the road she heard the sounds her ears had been straining for these last anxious minutes. The new Volvo screeching to a stop. Nikos exuberantly sounding the horn. Car doors slamming. But just as she was about to run to the hotel lobby where already she could hear Eleni calling out fervent welcomes, Yorgos deftly wheeled himself between her and the door.

A moment later, when Christos emerged from the lobby door, she still stood with Yorgos' wheelchair blocking her.

Marika caught her breath when finally she saw him: older, stockier, balding, silver at his temples, but nonetheless Christos. Her heart was beating so fast that her hand crept up to her breast as though to contain it.

Christos stared from *her* – the blueblack hair, the voluptuous figure, the eyes as black as a moonless Aegean night – to *him* – pale, sick, shrivelled in that wheelchair.

For a second, just like the last time the three of them had been together, back in that cave when Yorgos had surprised Marika in Christos' arms, they froze like the figures on an ancient Greek vase.

But then Nikos appeared behind Christos' shoulder holding his seven-year-old cousin Christina by the hand. 'Mama! Can you believe it! Finally, he's back!'

The years dropped away as she looked into the green eyes of the love of her life. And when belatedly she glanced down at Yorgos, she saw the shine of tears on his cheeks.

*

486

The Kronos family was so intoxicated by their reunion that they almost missed the midnight service in the splendid new village church Nick had built halfway up Panagia mountain.

They had whiled away the afternoon and evening with introductions, reminiscences, and the heady camaraderie of those tied by blood and affection. After that first electric meeting, Marika and Christos had been shy with one another. But always, whether she was pouring another round of coffees or serving up her own newly-honed political opinions, Marika had been conscious of where Christos was sitting, what Christos was saying, how Christos' eyes shaded with laughter and grief and speculation. As repeatedly she had caught those limpid eyes upon her, she had known it was the same for him. How could it be, she had wondered, that a generation had passed – Nikos had grown to manhood, and democracy in Greece had suffered and nearly died and finally been reborn – and still, by some miracle, the connection between the two of them was unbroken. Frayed, maybe, she had amended to herself, for she could not altogether shrug off a twenty-five year-old separation, but still hanging by something stronger than a thread. With a sense of growing wonder, she had listened to her laughter mingling with his.

But of course those first hours of reunion had not been all jokes and exclamations. They were Greeks, and their country and family had just passed through one of the darkest passages in its history. When the conversation had inevitably turned to the politics on which the Greek world revolved, with great gusto the family had squabbled and bickered as their ancestors had done for millennia. Nikos, whose recording of 'Liberty's Song' had become not only an international hit but nearly a national anthem after the restoration of democracy in Athens, was thinking about entering politics and eventually standing for election to parliament as part of the new PASOK socialist alliance. Vangelis, however, had had more than enough of the socialists and had become a fervent supporter of Karamanlis' centre-right New Democracy party. Vasso had seconded her husband's opinion on this, as on all things great and small. Nick's Greek-American soul had been outraged by what he perceived as the outright anti-Americanism of the new Athens regime which blamed the United States for the rise of the colonels and the partition of Cyprus. Yannis had gotten dirty looks from everyone but Yorgos when he had pounded the table and shouted that what Greece needed was another strong military man at the helm of state. Even timid Eleni had volunteered her hesitant opinion that, despite last autumn's plebescite against the monarchy, she would feel better about everything if only the king would come back. Lena had shared Nikos' enthusiasm for PASOK, and Annoula had alarmed everyone by talking like an anarchist.

487

Marika, who had resumed writing her newspaper column as soon as the *junta* had fallen, had been mistrustful of all the politicians and adamant only that human rights must evermore be safeguarded. They had argued passionately, as Greeks do, with their hands and their eyes as well as their tongues. Only Christos, who still said he hadn't decided whether to make this homecoming permanent, and Yorgos, who couldn't talk at all, had remained silent about their points of view. But through it all, even when old Yannis had called for a return of the military dictatorship, Christos' face had been lit by a benign smile. How he had missed his fractious countrymen, and how he loved even their fickle natures and their insistence never to learn from their own and history's mistakes! They were ardent in this game of politics as in love. And his eyes had remained locked upon Marika.

It had been nearly midnight when they had put politics aside and madly scrambled off to church.

By the time they got there, each holding an unlit candle as they wended their way up the steep road with Nick panting in the lead like the Grand Marshal of a family parade, already the familiar service had moved outside and was nearing its climax. Resplendent in his white vestments, Father Petros was standing high on a platform illuminated only by the bright springtime stars and the three white candles which had been lit by the sacred fire carried here and to every Greek Orthodox church in the world from the Church of the Resurrection in Jerusalem. 'Come ye,' the *pappas* proclaimed, 'and take light from the unwaning light and glorify Christ who rose from the dead!'

From the priest to the faithful, the new light which symbolized life and resurrection went from wick to wick. Father Petros passed it to Nick, who gave it to Eleni, who distributed it to Yorgos and the grandchildren, who passed it to their parents. Nikos lit Marika's candle with his own, and then he gave it to Christos. Panagia mountain glowed with a thousand candles of light and belief.

At the stroke of midnight, Father Petros shouted the words that proclaimed the Resurrection. 'He whom you seek is not here; He is risen. *Christos Anesti*! Christ is Risen!'

Churchbells pealed. Fireworks exploded. Guns fired. Red roman candles sizzled and smoked as the congregation paired off for the traditional kiss of peace.

'*Christos anesti*,' Nick pronounced as he kissed Eleni on her cheeks.

'*Alithos anesti*,' she responded, 'truly He is risen.'

The ancient words were echoed from mother to son to cousin to grandchild. Christos kissed Nikos, Lena, Annoula, Vangelis, Vasso, Yannis, and then – with infinite tenderness – Marika.

After a second's hesitation, he closed the last steps between himself and his brother. The Kronos family caught their collective breath. Was this to be the final moment of reconciliation?

He bent over the wheelchair and kissed Yorgos on both cheeks. '*Christos anesti!*'

Yorgos looked into his brother's eyes, as close now as on that Peloponnese dawn when they had held knives instead of candles. His mouth worked mutely, but it was impossible to tell what he was trying to answer. His hands clutched for his notepad, but he had dropped it in the pell-mell rush up the mountain. Yorgos let out a great broken sigh.

As the congregation began descending home, each carrying his lighted candle which would bring a year's good luck if it passed over his doorway still afire, Marika drew Nikos and Christos aside. One thing more was unfinished tonight. She must share the secret she had withheld from this father and son. 'Come with me.'

'But mama!' Nikos was eager to be home for his grandmother's *mayeritsa* soup and the traditional cracking together of the scarlet hard-boiled eggs the women had dyed on Great Thursday. Always on Easter, he was the first one to make it home and therefore had the honour of burning a cross over the doorway to ensure the family's prosperity for the coming year. 'Can't it wait?'

'It's waited too long already,' she answered as she gave Christos a sidelong glance. Without waiting to see if he and Nikos were following, she began the descent to the sea and the Panagia chapel on the fringes of the village where she would finally break her twenty-five years of silence.

Yorgos watched in anguish as the three of them went their separate way.

From the same desperate impulse that had set him off behind Marika and Christos years ago on that Carnival night, he tried to turn his wheelchair to follow them. He had watched his wife and his brother making eyes at each other all afternoon and evening, but he couldn't let Christos win at this, too. She was his wife. *His*!

But stronger hands seized control of his chair.

'*Christos anesti*,' Kostas said.

Yorgos turned, and his eyes lit as he saw his *protégé*, not Captain Kostas any more, since he along with so many of the officer corps who had faithfully served the *junta* had been purged from the armed forces by the new democratically-elected civilian government. Yorgos hadn't seen the young man for weeks, and he hadn't realized he would be returning to the village for the holiday. Had he brought news from his cohorts in Athens? Yorgos looked from Kostas to the dark silhouettes of Marika, Christos, and Nikos whose candles still glowed as they coursed down the mountain. The two military guards closed ranks around him as Kostas began briskly wheeling him toward the Kronos household at the tip of the harbour.

Yorgos touched Kostas' hand in a final effort to make his former aide understand that he had to follow his wife. But as he plucked at Kostas, the candle in his hand sputtered and died in the spring wind. Yorgos flinched at the dire portent of the dead candle.

'Never mind,' Kostas said as inexorably he continued wheeling Yorgos toward the taverna. '*We* don't believe in those old superstitions, do we?'

Yorgos looked up, startled by the ugly undercurrent he thought he had heard in the voice of this young man who had served him so loyally for so many years. But although he was reassured when Kostas smiled down at him, still his eyes trailed longingly back to those three other candles whose faint light wavered in the night.

By the time Kostas and the guards had escorted Yorgos home, spry old Yannis had already inscribed the cross with his Pascha candle over the taverna door. But instead of taking Yorgos into the dining room where everyone else was already seated at the table – merrily butting their scarlet eggs together, laughing as they waited to see whose egg would emerge uncracked – Kostas left the military guard at the dining table and wheeled Yorgos into his bedroom at the far end of the house.

Yorgos' brow creased as Kostas locked the door and turned to face him.

'Now,' Kostas said, 'you and I have some unfinished business to conclude.'

Yorgos' face cleared. Since the fall of the *junta* last July, the dictatorship's supporters in the army had launched four unsuccessful efforts to stage another *coup d'état*. Apparently Kostas had come with news of a fifth conspiracy in the making. Eagerly Yorgos leaned forward. Surely the next coup would succeed. He and the others would be spared the disgrace of those vengeful trials. The government had announced its intention to try not only the colonels but those responsible for the torture of political prisoners and the sack of the polytechnic. He thanked God for Kostas and those other stalwart soldiers who were once again about to save Mother Greece from the politicians who always ruined her.

But when Kostas reached in his pocket and, instead of papers outlining the coup to come, he pulled out his service revolver, Yorgos looked in consternation at the former captain.

'For you,' Kostas said. He reached in another pocket and loaded the revolver with a single bullet. 'Finally I'm going to fulfil the promise I made to my father long ago. The night he died.'

Yorgos looked from the loaded pistol to Kostas' gleaming eyes. A generation ago he had laughed when he'd heard of the curse of vengeance

Kostas' father had pronounced on him for the death of his eldest son in that Greek Cross raid. But Yorgos brought his head up in the Greek negative. What he was thinking couldn't be true.

'Oh, yes,' Kostas answered. 'It's true, all right.'

When Yorgos gestured for paper and a pen, Kostas ignored him. 'No, tonight *I* will talk and *you* listen.'

He brandished the pistol. 'I promised my father I would avenge Andreas' death with yours. An eye for an eye, and a life for a life. For twenty-five years I've waited for this moment. I worked my way into your trust. I polished your shoes and made your coffee and did your dirty work for you. Not, as you believed, because I cared about you or your damned fascist cause. But so I could ruin you and your family like you ruined mine.'

Kostas' voice rasped with bitterness. 'You and your brother! The rich, important, know-it-all Kronos brothers! Both of you responsible for the death of my Andreas! You gave the order to kill him, but it was Christos who set up my brother and all those others who died that night in that camp. When you and those *malaka* militiamen murdered my brother, Christos was already halfway to Patras. You were in it together, you and him, that so-called Captain Prometheus!'

Yorgos' mouth gaped open, and then slowly again he reared up his head in denial.

'Still covering for him, after all these years!' Kostas shifted the gun in his hands. 'But he'll get *his*, too, just like I promised my father. Not tonight – like *you* – but some other night. When he, too, least expects it!'

Kostas preened as he began pacing back and forth before his captive audience of one. 'I thought I finished him off years ago when I sent that letter to the Boston newspaper.' He laughed as he rounded on Yorgos. 'Yes, that was *my* work, although everyone always blamed it on you. Neat, that was. It ruined Christos' political career and should have brought yours to a close, too. I thought Christos would put a gun to his head when it all came out – *like everyone will think you are going to do tonight*. But instead, here the bastard is back with us again.' Kostas smiled. 'I wonder, as we have our little chat, what he's doing with your wife at this very moment?'

Yorgos shut his eyes, and when he opened them again to his tormentor, they were filled with tears.

'Cry, yes, cry, like my mother did when we buried Andreas!'

But Kostas was not finished with his revelations. 'I was the one who tipped the military police off about Vangelis' subversive activities. I who kept Nikos under surveillance. And I who arranged for that "accident" that should have killed him along with his little foreign girlfriend. And it was I who turned over to the public prosecutor those papers I took from your safe years ago.

491

They would have convicted you for treason and corruption, you know. But you're not going on trial. I want the pleasure of seeing you dead and buried, not just rotting in a government jail.'

Yorgos' eyes still glittered with tears as he listened to the young man he had loved like a son chronicle his betrayals.

'One more thing.' Kostas' smile widened. 'Like all my family, I'm a Communist. Always was, always will be. For years I've supplied intelligence reports for Moscow. And you never guessed!'

Yorgos made a garbled sound and tried, but failed, to reach out and strike this snake he had nursed at his breast.

But now, in addition to the gun, Kostas was holding a pen and paper. 'For your suicide note.'

Yorgos squinted in disbelief at the mad captain. His eyes roamed the room, looking for a way out. But there was no escape. Yorgos sagged deeper into the wheelchair.

'Isn't there something,' Kostas prodded, 'that you would like to write to your family? Some final testament?' He put the pen and paper in Yorgos' shaky hands and then gave him a book on which to write.

For a moment Yorgos bit the end of the pen with his teeth. He hated to play the role Kostas had assigned him, but he couldn't resist the opportunity of having the last word. He glared at Kostas as he began to write to Marika. 'Everything is not as it appears to be in my life, your life, and this, too.' *There*, he thought, at least I'm giving them a clue about Kostas' role in all this. It wasn't enough, but it was the best he could do. He returned to his task. 'I have loved you for all my life and never more than now, when all is lost.' Christos, he thought, Christos! 'All I have done was for you, and the family, and the honour and glory of God and the motherland.' He hesitated. What final words, if any, did he have for his brother? For the last time, he fingered the scar cut deep in his cheek. '*Christos anesti*!'

Then he passed pen and paper back to Kostas, who scanned it and then put it on the top of Yorgos' desk.

'So,' Kostas said, wheeling Yorgos over to the window which looked out over Panagia island where so much had begun and ended. 'You might be interested in knowing that I'll say you begged me to loan you my gun since the soldiers took yours away when they put you under arrest. I'll say I couldn't refuse, that this was the only honourable way out for an officer and a gentleman.' His voice faltered. 'Both of which you are.'

When Yorgos merely nodded and waited with a sort of dignity for the end, again Kostas seemed to waver. He had not thought it would be so hard to finish this. He had supposed revenge would taste so sweet, not sour, like the vomit in his mouth. But he had said too much and gone too far to back out now.

Yorgos made the sign of the cross on his chest and stared at the island in the bay.

For twenty-five years Kostas had waited to throw these words back at his brother's killer. 'Died like a sheep.'

Kostas forced Yorgos' hand to hold the gun to his temple, and then he pulled the trigger.

On the dark path just outside the Panagia chapel, Christos started like a gun dog as he heard the single shot. 'What was that?'

'It's Easter, remember?' Nikos grinned fondly at the uncle who had been away from Greece so long he evidently had forgotten that the villagers would be firing their rifles all night long in drunken celebration of the most glorious holiday in the Orthodox calendar.

'Come inside.' Marika was opening the latch, stepping in the tiny whitewashed old church, and beckoning from the flickering darkness.

'Uncle?' Nikos, too, sounded impatient. He had humoured his mother long enough with this long walk away from home. He wanted some of his grandmother's *mayeritsa*.

Christos looked back again in the direction from which the shot had come, then shrugged off his strange premonition and joined Marika and Nikos inside the church.

Marika stood looking around the simple chapel where once, when she hadn't been certain she was pregnant, she had prayed with all her being to the Panagia. Except for the oil lamps burning in front of the altar and the silver-encased icon of the Virgin, the chapel was in darkness. She used her Pascha taper to light a candle in memory of her mother and then went to the icon, stooped to kiss the hem of the Virgin's robe, and crossed herself. 'Mother,' she prayed, 'help me.'

She waited as Nikos lit a candle for Liberty and Christos set one ablaze for his mother. So many losses, she thought. But here and now she intended to say the words that would bring not sorrow but joy to the two most important men in her life.

'Niko . . . Christo . . . I have something to tell you.'

They waited in silence for her to say why she had brought them here.

'It's about us, the three of us. And Yorgos, too.'

Nikos' face set in hard lines. He never had and never would forgive Yorgos for Liberty's death.

Again Christos looked out the open door of the church to where he had

493

heard that shot. He couldn't shake the feeling that something terrible had happened back at the house.

Marika went on. 'I used to come here to pray, Niko, the winter before you were born. Especially before I was sure I was pregnant.' She looked at her fine young son and remembered that sometimes in those anxious weeks she had prayed for an empty womb. But without Nikos her life would have been shorn of so much richness and joy. When her son returned her smile, she drew the strength to continue. 'Since then, all these years I've been living a lie. Ever since you left, Christo.'

His guilty eyes fell from her burning gaze. 'I never told you about all that. About why I left. I wanted to write. I should have. But then you married Yorgos. And – '

She raised her hand to hush him. 'Let me finish. Later we can talk about *that*. About everything. But that's not why I brought you both here.' She moistened her dry lips with her tongue. How could she find the words to tell them what had to be said? 'Maybe I should have told you years ago. Both of you. God and the Virgin know I wanted to . . .' She stared from one to the other, and then she focused on Christos. 'I should have written this long ago.' Her voice broke. 'Maybe everything would have turned out differently, then. For all of us.'

Nikos was staring at the tears in his mother's eyes. 'What are you trying to say?' But he knew. From that first evening with Christos in London, he had guessed. 'Tell us, mama. Now!'

Marika took a deep breath and blurted out the truth. 'Niko, Yorgos is not your father. When I married him, I was already pregnant. By Christos.'

'Mama!' Even in the uncertain light of the shadowy chapel, Nikos' eyes blazed with joy as he looked from his mother to the man whom already, in those six months they had spent together in Boston, he had learned to love like a father. They had played music together, laughed in the plastic Parthenon together, dissected socialism together. So it was true! What he had dreamed of was really true! He spoke the sweet word. '*Patera?*'

But Christos was taken utterly by surprise. He opened his mouth as if to say something, but no sound came out. He reeled and might have fallen if Nikos had not stepped forward to take him in his arms. The son's arms supported the father, and Christos held on as though his life depended on never letting go. 'My boy, my son!' The father and son wept not only for all they had lost but for all they had found.

So it's done, Marika thought, watching the two of them finally together. She was about to slip away so they could be alone to begin to make up for all those years apart, when Christos turned and – still holding Nikos tight –

his green eyes glittered not just with tears as he gave her a sidelong thunderbolt glance and beckoned to her with his crooked finger.

'No,' she said weakly. And yet, without even being conscious of moving, suddenly she found herself in Christos' arms.

Nikos grinned and stepped aside. Discreetly he left his mother and father alone. He all but flew home, running down the beach, shouting his news to the sea and the wind and the stars. 'My father! He's my father!'

Back in the chapel, Christos kept murmuring her name as he held her in his arms. 'But why didn't you tell me? Why did you wait so long?'

'I didn't know . . . I wasn't sure . . . You left me in that cave.'

'Yes.' He looked down into her icon eyes. 'We have to talk about that.'

She waited for the twenty-five-year-old explanation.

'*Now?*'

'I don't want to rush you, Christo. But yes, *right now.*'

He laughed. She *had* changed in their years apart. This humour was new, and so was the confidence. Middle-aged, Marika was far more of a challenge than the desperately romantic young woman he had left behind. To his fond eye, the woman she had become – with that rounded figure and that face whose defining lines and fine wrinkles bespoke a character fired by suffering – was even more beautiful than the girl he remembered. He recalled her astutely talking politics this afternoon. She had sounded like a bit of a reactionary, but apparently she had become as passionate about her politics as once she had been about . . . about *me*, Christos thought. Was she still? Had those looks she had been giving him since he arrived been only a prelude to her revelation about Nikos, or did the two of them have a future together as well as a past? He supposed everything depended on what he said now.

As he felt in his pocket for his cigarettes, suddenly she was out of his arms.

'Not in the chapel.' She was already outside, standing on the cliff looking out at the sea.

By the time he joined her, she was smoking. 'So.'

'Right.' He lit his cigarette, collected his thoughts, and looked out at Panagia island. 'I hardly know where to begin.'

'At the beginning.' Her tone was sharper now. 'When you left me in the middle of the night.' She waved her cigarette toward the island. 'Out *there.*'

'You knew I was leaving with the *andartes* at dawn.' Even to his own ears, the excuse sounded lame. He would have to do better.

'Not for a quarter-century.' This time she wasn't joking.

'I thought I'd be back the next week.' He committed himself. 'And that we'd be married after Easter.' He tore his eyes off the island, dark now, dark as the years of their separation. He was certain. He wanted Marika back. He *had* to have her back. 'You must believe me.'

'So what happened?'

'Yorgos happened.' Christos' gaze shifted to the taverna, and again – oddly – he remembered that gunshot. 'My brother came after me on that Greek Cross raid of his. But surely you heard of *that*?'

'That's about the only news I *did* hear. But that still doesn't explain your leaving for America and never so much as sending me a message.'

'But I did. With one of my comrades. Andreas.'

'Andreas died in the Greek Cross raid.'

'No!' Christos urgently touched her shoulder. 'But he shouldn't have been there. I sent him back to Panagia before I left for a cadre meeting in Tripolis.' Steadily he looked into her eyes. 'You must believe that I sent Andreas with a message for you to wait. That I'd be back as soon as I could. That I had to deal with political problems first.'

'You used to say that a lot, Christo. Too much.' She ground out her cigarette. 'That was no excuse then. And it isn't now.'

'But Marika! Do you remember those times? The fighting, not just the *andartes* against the government forces, but the leftists against each other. The Communist Party had me on a death list. *That's* what I discovered in Tripolis while Yorgos was killing all my men in that raid. But I never thought he'd gotten Andreas, too. I thought you'd have my message.'

He *sounded* sincere. But Christos had always been glib. And he still hadn't explained away everything. 'So then what happened. After Tripolis?'

'Yorgos must have told you.'

'Told me what?'

'He tried to kill me. In an ambush. It came down to him and me. With our father's knives.' Christos shook his head, remembering that Peloponnese dawn.

When he said no more, she prompted him. 'And?'

'I wouldn't kill him. And he wouldn't – or couldn't – kill me. But I remember cutting him on the cheek with my knife. He still has the scar. I saw it today.'

'You did *that*?' It was her turn to be silent as she recalled her husband's habit of stroking that scar as though it were the source of his greatest pride . . . or was it shame?

'I told Yorgos, too, where I was going and why. I hoped he would pass that on to you. But, considering how everything turned out, I suppose you never got that word, either.'

'No. Never, in all these years, has he ever mentioned that fight with you, much less even a veiled message you sent for me.'

'So you thought I'd just gone off and left you.'

'In fact, that was what you did. All the way to America!'

496

'But you must understand – '

'Would you stop saying that? I will understand if I decide to understand. *If* I believe you.'

He lit another cigarette and continued his defence. 'I left for America because there was no other choice. If the government forces caught me, they would have shot me on sight. Or sent me off to prison camp forever and a day. If the Communist Party got me, they would have slit my throat. I had no choice but to go.'

'And *me*? Did you ever think about how your leaving would affect *me*?'

'Every day. I planned to bring you to America as soon as I could. But remember, I thought Andreas had delivered my message. And I had no idea you were pregnant. It took me months, after waiting in a camp in Italy, to get to America. By the time I did, my father said you'd married Yorgos. I thought *you'd* betrayed *me*.'

'Did you have so little trust in me, Christo?'

'I could ask you the same question. You could have written me, you know. If I'd known you were pregnant, I would have moved heaven and earth to get you there so we could get married.'

It was her turn to plead. 'But Christo, think back to how it was, then, in this village. I was pregnant. You were gone – dead, for all I knew. I could have aborted the baby, but I didn't want to. Not *your* child.'

He took heart from the tremor in her voice. Until now, her interrogation had made him doubt if she had any feelings for him other than resentment. He let out his breath in a sigh. 'Nikos!' His voice rang with the wonder of the discovery that he was his son. 'He's a wonderful young man. You did quite a job, raising him on your own.'

'But I wasn't on my own.' Now, as before, Yorgos stood between them. If she and Christos were to try again, first they would have to lay that ghost to rest. 'I had a husband. Just as you had a wife.'

Christos was not about to be sidetracked with an explanation of Penelope. He had married her years after Nikos had been born, and whatever had been between himself and his wife had been finished for a long while. In the divorce, he had gotten custody of Christina and visiting rights two weekends a month with Sofia and Helen. Since then, Penelope had become a best-selling author, she was still with that Liz, and despite her lesbianism there were rumours that she was still to run for her uncle's old Congressional seat. Doggedly he returned to the questions *he* had for *her*. 'Of all the men in the world, how could you marry *him*?'

'It's very simple. I couldn't marry *any* man in the world. I wasn't a virgin any more, remember? And I didn't have any *prika*. Don't forget, too, that the war had killed so many. I needed a husband – fast – and Yorgos was willing.'

'More than willing, if I know – or knew – my brother.'

She couldn't help being pleased at the naked jealousy in his voice. So he still did care! But she surprised herself by defending the man she had never wanted. 'In his own way, he tried to be a good husband. And father. Not just to the girls but to Nikos. Even though I think he always knew you were the father.'

'You're talking about him as though he's dead.'

'You saw him today. He is, really. And that trial next month will finish him off.'

'So you love him.' Christos' eyes were hooded. In the end, his brother had won.

'I never loved your brother. Mostly I've hated him. Though I suppose now what I feel for Yorgos is pity.'

'So,' he said. He looked back out at the island, and the sight of it emboldened him. It was now or never. He slipped his arm around her shoulder. When she let it stay there, he turned and looked into her eyes. 'So what now?' He would go or stay, whichever she wanted. 'I'm here now, Marika. I'm back. Late. *Very late*, even by Greek standards. But this time I won't be going away. *If* you want.'

She had wasted the last twenty-five years, but she didn't intend to squander the rest of her life. As soon as she had caught sight of Christos, she had wanted to throw herself in his arms. But, men being men, he wouldn't have valued her much if he had won her back that easily. But now she followed her impulse, raised her head, and kissed him. 'I want.'

They clung together on the cliff.

And yet, just as she thought she would spend forever here in his embrace, he was off again, striding the path cut in the cliffs, down to the sea.

This time, fleetingly wondering how she had so suddenly lost her advantage, she ran after him. She had liked him being so contrite. She had even thought she would make him grovel before she *really* took him back. And yet a little sexual thrill coursed through her as she followed his lead. She was in love with a man, not a pet dog. 'Christo, where are you going now?'

'Back to the beginning.' And again, over his shoulder, he shot that thunderbolt glance at her.

She laughed like a girl as she raced after him, down the length of the beach toward the village. When she caught up with him, already he was trying to turn over a rowboat. 'Help me. I can't do it all myself.'

She caught her breath. 'The island? The cave?'

'Of course.' He would show her – and himself – that love wasn't only a young man's game.

'But Christo, it's the middle of the night. It's Easter.' She shivered. They had been young when they had last rowed out there on that bleak February night. But now, even though it was April, they were too old to repeat that romantic odyssey. 'I'm cold.'

He grinned. 'I'll keep you warm.'

Again she laughed as together they pushed and heaved until they righted the boat. They kicked off their shoes, hauled the boat into the shallows, and waded until they were knee-deep in the frigid water. She hopped in first and took one oar. He followed and fit the second one into the lock. Together they strained back and forth, toward the island of their youths.

'It's further away than I remember it,' Christos said in a gasp. 'But we've come this far. If we pull together, we'll get there.' As they rowed over the wine-dark sea, the wind was in their hair and the salt spray was on their skin. They both felt as though they had just drunk from the fountain of youth.

Finally, however, as they neared the island, jumped in the shallows, and beached the boat, the laughter died on their lips. Their eyes met in a smouldering gaze. Without a word, Christos began climbing the path to the cavern cut eons ago in the cliffs. After a moment's hesitation, she followed.

But Marika balked as Christos beckoned her into the Cave of the Great Goddess. 'No,' she said. 'I'm forty-four years old, and you must be fifty-three. We're too old for this.'

Christos laughed. 'But I feel the same. No, *better*. Love, like good Greek brandy, can sometimes mellow and grow richer over time.'

She laughed into those green eyes, and then hand-in-hand they disappeared into the darkness of the cave.